Chaz Brenchley has ma[...]
eighteen. He is the auth[...] [...]vels for adults, and
one book of short stories; he has also published three books
for children and some poetry. He lives in Newcastle upon
Tyne, with two cats and a famous teddy bear.

Find out more about Chaz Brenchley and other Orbit
authors by registering for the free monthly newsletter at
www.orbitbooks.co.uk

Hand of the King's Evil

THE THIRD BOOK OF OUTREMER

Chaz Brenchley

www.orbitbooks.co.uk

An *Orbit* Book

First published in Great Britain by Orbit 2002
Reprinted 2003

Copyright © 2002 by Chaz Brenchley

The moral right of the author has been asserted.

Visit the series website at
www.outremer.co.uk

A CIP catalogue record for this book
is available from the British Library.

ISBN 1 84149 035 0

Typeset in Garamond by M Rules
Printed and bound in Great Britain by
Mackays of Chatham plc

Orbit
An imprint of
Time Warner Books UK
Brettenham House
Lancaster Place
London WC2E 7EN

This one's for Jean and Roger,
who liked the books so much
they built the website.

Empire of
Marasson

Roq
de
Rancon

Elessi
Elessi

Tallis
Tallis

Less
Arvon

Less
Arvon

Sharai
Lands

Surayon
Surayon

The
Dead
Waters

Ascariel
Ascariel

The

Great

Waste

Phaba

Empire of
Ekhed

Map of
OUTREMER
after the original by El Adei

βλεπομεν γαρ αρτι δι εσοπτρου εν αινιγματι
τοτε δε προσωπον προς προσωπον αρτι
γινωσκω εκ μερους τοτε δε
επιγνωσομαι καθως και επεγνωσθην

– The First Epistle of Paul the Apostle
to the Corinthians, 13, 12

The chapel had been altered since he was first here, last here, since he'd belonged. Fifteen years ago, that was, and hard years they'd been for him: years of exile, for all that he'd been back in his own country and serving his own liege lord. They had stripped him naked and sent him away from this place, had turned their faces from him and closed the gate behind him as he stumbled out. The taste of that shame was fresh and bitter still in his mouth, fresher even than the ever-fresh memory of cold rain against his skin as he'd run weeping down through the dark, down and down, heedless of the height and danger of the road. He'd cut his feet on sharp stones, bruised his shoulder against the wall of rock and felt neither cuts nor bruises, only the wind and the rain and the immeasurable shame. A young man then, he'd thought his life was over, he couldn't live with this. He had been judged and condemned, and rightly so. If he'd missed a turn, blinded by the night and the rain and his tears, if he'd fallen from the road it would have been the God's sterner judgement on him; no one would have cared, none in the castle and himself least of all.

Fifteen years. When he was driven out they'd still been building, raising new walls higher than the old; this chapel, like everything in the original fortress, had been left all but untouched for lack of time or men to work on it. He remembered the rough raw plaster where heretical mosaics, Catari blasphemies had been chiselled out by the pious men who first won the Roq and claimed it. The word then was that it did honour to the God, when the very walls of His chapel showed how they had been wrenched free of black religion and consecrated to His service.

The word must be different now. It was called the Knights' Chapel these days; he supposed the knights had paid, or their families or sponsors. They must have paid handsomely. He knew little of such matters – in Elessi they kept their chapels simple, white walls and dark wood, only the candles' flames to stand in the eye and remind a man of his God – but the lamps and vessels on the altar here were silver where they were not gold, and he knew the value of that. The walls had been plastered and the plaster painted; everywhere he looked he saw images of the saints and their deaths, or else images of the God's victory here and through-out the Sanctuary Land. The glory of Ascariel glimmered gold behind the altar. Even the candle-stands were silver, and all the silver was chased.

It was all alien to him and he liked none of it, but he came here none the less. The great hall was too public and too familiar, it held too many memories. Every day since his arrival at the castle he had come, leaving at first his men to their ale and his lady to whatever entertainment she could find or make; he had spent hours on his knees in the darkest corner he could find, relying on cap and shadows to obscure his face from all but the God. There were few to see, in any case. They might call it the Knights' Chapel, but the knights used it seldom. Brothers came in sometimes, alone or in pairs, for private prayer and meditation or else for confession; their murmuring voices offered little distraction and no one gave him more than a sidelong glance, no one challenged his right to be here.

Only the once had he been singled out, had he been spoken to directly. That had been a challenge, perhaps, though not to his presence in the chapel: to his faith, rather, and to his betraying soul. His reply had been a confession, but nothing that could soothe or cleanse.

Still, the encounter had gifted him with hope. So he still came to the chapel daily, he still locked himself in private prayer like a man who walked a wilderness alone. In many ways he was alone, more so than he had been these fifteen years; his lady charge was gone, and his troop after her. She'd slipped his guard and run with strange companions, heretics and worse. Her lord husband had led the search for her, with Marshal Fulke of the Ransomers hot at his side; different spurs drive different men with equal fire.

No trace had been found, no tracks, no rumours of their passing. At last the baron had gone back to Elessi, and taken all his men with him; only Blaise he'd left at the Roq, 'in case she should return, sergeant, in case she should be found. A familiar face to greet her, and sharp eyes to watch her welfare . . .'

Sharp eyes to watch her straying feet he'd meant, and Blaise had understood him perfectly. Twice now she'd slipped her guards and fled, shaming her husband in the eyes of all; she shouldn't be allowed a third adventure, but gossip said that the preceptor of the castle had an eye for her beauty, and would make an unreliable custodian. It was wisdom to leave a man of Elessi, to be sure that she could be kept until she was collected.

It was cruelty to name Blaise as that man, to leave him so alone beneath the burning-glass of his own disgrace. The young baron couldn't know that, though; if his uncle the elder baron knew, he kept his counsel.

Blaise had been offered a private chance of redemption, right here in the chapel; that was all he had to cling to. The conversation was burned into his brain. His faltering confession, the history of his time within the Order, and then:

'*I was stripped naked and sent into exile, Magister. Forbidden the habit, and the service of the God. And I, I have lived with that all this time, but I do not think I can bear it any longer.*'

'*You must. When you endanger a brother, you betray the Order. There can be no remission.*'

'*No, Magister. I know. But . . .*'

'*But that is not to say that you cannot serve the God, or the Order. Many men do, who do not wear the habit.*'

'*I am no knight, Magister.*'

'*No, but we have other servants yet. The time is coming, when we will need more fighting men than are sworn to us; I dislike to accept mercenaries, but when I must I will. Will you fight with us, brother, when that time comes?*'

'*Not for money, Magister!*'

'*Well, you may do what you will with the pay. I cannot put* you in a habit, but I can put a sword in your hand and give you a place in the line, if you will take it.'

'Yes, Magister. I will take it. And thank you.'

'I am not finished yet. That time will come, but it is not here yet. Will you serve me and the God in the meantime? Without a habit and without pay, without honour or recognition, in secrecy and obedience even when you hate what it is that I ask you to do?'

'What will that be, Magister?'

'It may be this, it may be that. I cannot say. I do not explain myself; but I want private servants, sworn to me in silence. Will you be one among them?'

'Magister, I will.'

'Good. Listen for my voice, then, and obey when you hear it. The time will come. Serve the Lady Julianne, and serve her well, until I call you; then serve me better . . .'

And so he had waited out his time, enduring day by day, hour by hour, moment by terrible moment. He had exercised his body and his horse in order to be ready whenever that call should come, regardless of the pain it cost him to ride or sweat among the brothers, where he was no brother now. Otherwise he had held himself apart, as a guest ought. He attended the noon service whenever he could bear to, praying in the gallery with other strangers; he fetched his meals from the kitchen and ate in solitude, in his own rough quarters; and every day he came back to this small chapel, to spend hours on his knees before the God and to hope, almost to pray for another visit, another conversation with the one man who could save him.

*

Almost, he had given up hoping. Almost he thought he had been forgotten or dismissed, that the chance once offered had been withdrawn again. But he did devoutly believe in second chances, his faith required it; the God's sign glowed before his eyes, a path that turned and turned and came back always to the centre.

And so he did come back always to the chapel, even on his darkest days, at his most despairing; and so at last he was rewarded.

On his knees in the shadows and the silence, his belly clamped around its perennial hunger – he lived like a guest but ate like a brother penitent, bread and porridge and no meat, no midday meal, no satisfaction – and his mind clamped around its perennial sense of loss, he heard the whisper of a robe that brushed the floor. He tried piously, hopelessly to pretend that this was not what he had been listening for, that his thoughts had been entirely on the God and not at all on his surroundings; failing in that, he only waited for the bitter disappointment that must surely follow, that he had grown quite accustomed to over the weeks of his waiting, when the newcomer proved to be of interest surely to the God but none to him.

The soft sounds came closer, till he could hear the footsteps beneath the robe, till he could hear even the man's quiet breathing. He held his own breath, still not quite daring to hope; the man knelt beside him, and murmured a brief prayer in the old tongue.

Then, at last, Blaise lifted his eyes to look. And saw in the lamps' glow what he had dreaded not to see, even now: the robes of a master, the balding head above defiantly uncovered before the altar of the God, the thin pale face turned towards him.

'Magister . . .'

'Sergeant. Are you still willing to do as you said, to serve me?'

'Yes, Magister. Of course.'

'Good. I have a mission for you.'

'Magister, I have been ordered to remain in the castle here, against the Lady Julianne's recovery . . .'

'She will not be recovered now; or not to this place. She is long gone from here. You are right, though, you must defy your lord's command to obey me. Will you do that?'

It required barely a moment's thought. 'I will.'

'Listen, then. There is disease abroad in the Kingdom, a plague that no medicine will cure; I believe that it is a curse from Surayon, the Folded Land. There is also a man who follows this plague from town to town. He heals, he says by the touch of a saint's hand; he says he is no saint himself. He also preaches, and he is gathering an army of the poor and dispossessed about him.'

'To what end, Magister?'

'I do not know; but he preaches against Surayon, as all true believers must. I want my man among his people, Blaise. I want to hear everything he says, to see everything he does. His army is nothing, a peasant rabble, a joke; but he may be a weapon I can use . . .'

PART ONE

The Road to Revanchard

1

A Shadow Behind the Eyes

The flood had not reached so high; neither had the men of the house come up here since, to tramp wet mud from dirty feet across the gritty floor. The only signs to be read had been left, must have been left by those she hunted: her enemy, her friend.

'Look,' she said to Sherett, who held a lamp above and behind her, where she crouched low on stone. 'A bare footmark here, the touch of a robe against the opposite wall there; neither one has had the time to dry. He brought her this way, and not so long ago.'

'We are all of us barefoot,' the older woman said mildly enough, 'our feet and robes are wet. A restless man, a thinking man – a hungry man perhaps, looking to see what food might have been stored here and forgotten?'

'There is none – and after that feast, who could be hungry? Besides, this is not mud.' She had it on her finger now, a little of the dark damp stain she'd found and followed from mark to scattered mark. She sniffed it, nodded, held her hand high. 'Taste.'

Sherett did that, touching tongue to finger's tip. 'Blood,' she said. 'Julianne's?'

Elisande managed a smile, slightly, as perhaps she had been meant to. 'Even I don't know the girl that well. She can't be dead,' *she can't be*, 'or why would he carry her body away? He left the guards he killed. This is their blood, I think, he must be marked with it.' *And you can taste their bodies if you want to, to compare. Not I . . .*

'He might have left her somewhere else, there is no sign that she is with him . . .'

'He carries her, across one shoulder. Why else would the one side of his robe brush the floor, the other not? Her weight drags at him.' She was a big girl, Julianne. By Elisande's standards, at least, she was big: little shorter, little lighter than Morakh who had taken her. He was all desert, that one, all bone and leather and no water in him: bone and leather and black spite to match his black robe. Elisande would like to find a black thread to prove it, but he must be the abductor. The men who'd watched at Julianne's door had second mouths for throats; their bodies had been wrapped before Elisande had seen them, but she'd heard the talk and seen the broad stains on the passage floor. Morakh had killed others that way, swift and silent. Besides, who but a Dancer could face two alert companions and surprise them both, get behind each in turn?

She'd been with Sherett when the news reached the women's quarters, a message sent from Hasan, *come quickly*, no more than that. No more had been needed. They'd left goblets of *jereth* heretically unfinished, had gathered up their skirts and run through the crusting mud on the valley floor to the house of the Beni Rus. There they'd found a mill of men in the hallway, furious and aimless, weapons drawn and voices raised. In the Sands, Elisande had thought as she squeezed her way through in the larger woman's wake, in the Sands they'd have been more cautious; they would not have wasted their anger so. All that water, and a hopeless fight survived: relief and wet feet had made them slippery of discipline. She'd have thought them wedding-night drunk, except that the Sharai did not drink alcohol.

There had been more order on the upper floor, but still no direction. Even Hasan had been pacing, to and fro across his carpets. Julianne's bride-gifts had been scattered from their tray; of Julianne herself, no trace remained.

Sherett had been quick, sensible, controlled. Only her eyes had given her away, and those briefly, before she fixed them on her husband and called him sharply to himself.

'Hasan. What has happened here – a thief?'

'She has not run away. Not this time. Two men are dead, the Dancer's work . . .'

'I saw. If you don't calm those headhot fools below, they'll forget the Dancer and blame the Saren or the Kauram, anyone they can see. Then there'll be war here in Rhabat, and that will consume us all. You go down, go now. Organise the men, search the valley, look for camel-tracks beyond. Pointless, I think, but do it, put them to work. Send messages abroad, if any mount of ours survived the flood: your wife is stolen from you, no Dancer should be trusted. Anything, but keep them from fighting the tribes . . .'

He'd looked as though he wanted to fight the tribes himself, all of them at once and by himself; but even this outrage, even the loss of Julianne hadn't been able to take his eye for long from his greater goal. A tribal war would destroy any hope of the war he sought, perhaps for another generation or longer, his chance lost. He'd nodded, turned, stridden away.

Sherett had fingered the scattered jewellery, stooped to retrieve a piece or two, said, 'These must be counted and checked, to see if Morakh has stolen aught else but our sister. Not now, though. Let the men search below; they will make a lot of noise, and find nothing. You and I, Elisande, we will search above . . .'

Elisande had been thinking that there was nothing but solid rock overhead, that Hasan's chamber stood at the height of the house. She'd been mistaken, forgetful: there were corridors that climbed higher yet, leading to store-rooms that were little used, ultimately to a great cistern where rainwater from the occasional storms could be collected against a future need. A complex web of channels had been cut through the rock, to draw it down from the plateau above; she knew that, she should have remembered. Only yesterday she'd fetched water herself from the cistern in the women's quarters. Why was she, why was everybody being so *slow*?

All of those drains were wide and high enough to accommodate a man, if barely. They must be, necessarily, or how else were they cut? Elisande had squirmed through a few in her time, following giggling friends. And Morakh was a small man, no spare flesh on his body. He could likely contrive to make his way through to the air. How he would do so cumbered with an unconscious girl, Elisande couldn't guess, but there was certainly no other escape up here, no other point in the climb.

Morakh had left few marks, but marks there were, enough to make a trail. It did lead past the store-rooms to the far end of the passage, to the cistern. The air was cool and damp; Sherett's lamplight showed her a low roof above a dark, still pool. The water looked deep, and chilly. She suppressed a shiver as she gazed about. The cistern was encompassed by a narrow walkway; to left and right, it was overhung by spouts carved from the rock of the walls. Above each spout was black emptiness, where the light could not penetrate. An agile man could haul himself up, a strong man no doubt could boost a girl so high; a thin man could insinuate himself into either of those channels. Could he drag a girl behind him? Well, perhaps . . .

Where a thin man and a tall girl could go, so could a skinny short girl. She thought about that, and shivered again. Looked lower, to see if she could find that trail again, and found her eye caught by the water.

And laughed, a little shrilly perhaps, and said, 'Esren.'

A shimmer in the lamplight, an intricate coil of air as fine as her friend's hair plaited; the djinni was there at her word. 'Lisan.'

'I think you will know where Julianne has been taken.' It was a quick-learned habit, almost second nature now not to ask questions.

'You are right.'

'Go after her, and fetch her back. If you had to slay the Sand Dancer to achieve it, I would not much mind that.'

'Neither would I; but I may not do it.'

That was a surprise, but *don't ask why not!* 'Well, so long as you restore my friend to me, that one can die later.' At her dagger's point, for preference.

'I meant that I may not do what you require. The daughter of the King's Shadow must seek help from otherwhere.'

Elisande gaped. Her mouth moved soundlessly for a moment; no need for Sherett's urgent hand on her arm, she had no questions to ask. Then, slowly finding words, finding an almost-anger to drive them, she said, 'Spirit, you swore to obey me . . .'

'I swore to come when you called me and to act at your command. That is not necessarily to say that I would obey your commands.'

Was it not? Well, perhaps not; but the difference was as fine as a single one of Julianne's hairs, and should have been as easy to snap except that Elisande had a question now, *why will you not obey me in this, as you have whatever I asked before?* and it burned so brightly in her head, so hotly on her tongue that she could think of no way not to ask it.

And then had no need to ask, because the djinni offered her an answer regardless. 'Lisan, close your eyes.'

Startled, she did so; and heard its thin voice again, 'Tell me what you see.'

'Nothing. A darkness . . .'

'Show it to me.'

'I cannot!' Her eyes snapped open again, glaring.

'No. It is neither day nor night, it has no existence outside your own mind; and yet you see it, it is there. Similarly, I cannot walk in the place where the Sand Dancer has taken the Shadow's daughter. He took her from here to the plateau above; but now they are not quite in this world, nor yet in the land of the djinn.'

'I don't understand.'

'You have seen how the Sand Dancers can move when they choose, unseen from one place to another.'

'Yes.' They flicked in and out of view, they were here and then they were there without seeming to cross the ground between; but, 'Only short distances, though, only moments of time,' only just long enough to pass from one man to another and be behind each of them in turn, convenient to cut their throats.

'Yes. The effort costs them, and they grow uncertain of finding their way back to the world, if they linger. This one is half-mad, though, and knows he will be hunted. He has risked much to seize the Shadow's daughter; he is risking more to keep her.'

It was the risk to Julianne that concerned Elisande. She said, 'I still don't understand where they are, that you cannot reach them.'

'You know of four directions in your world, north and south, west and east. Conceive of a fifth that has no name, that stands an equal distance from each . . .'

That made sense to her, suddenly. 'I know of this; it is how we have Folded my land, out of the reach of our neighbours. But the djinn can visit us in Surayon, when they choose to.'

'Indeed. Surayon exists where it always has, within its borders, and we can find it there. The border, though, where the shift is active – neither human nor spirit can find that. The Dancer Folds the land as he goes, and he walks within the crease. As long as he does so, he is beyond me.'

Elisande still found it hard to credit, she'd grown so used to djinni omniscience. Djinni honesty, though, was an article of faith; Esren would not, could not lie. So she gave one more glance to the darkness of the narrow rain-channels, and felt a shudder of relief that she need not claw her way through those in pursuit of her friend. Then she thought suddenly of Julianne's being trapped within a worse darkness, sucked helpless into the space behind her eyes. Dizzy and confused perhaps, terrified certainly . . .

'Esren, wherever they are now, they must be heading somewhere, Morakh must have an ambition in this world. However mad he is, he must come back to what is solid,' *he must bring Julianne back*, 'and you can surely see where he will touch ground again.'

'Perhaps; though I have been long detached from the spirit-weft, and my vision is uncertain.'

'If we get closer, you may see more clearly. They went to the plateau, you said. Take me there, Esren. Quickly, before the men get so far.'

She felt herself swept up and almost closed her eyes again, against the expected swirl of dark as Esren opened some strange pathway to the stars. Except that she was afraid of that particular darkness now behind her lids, and so she held them wide; and so she saw the rush of Sherett's lamp and the racing shadows of the passage beyond as she was carried back, all the way back to Hasan's chamber. She saw a blur of startled, bearded faces, his men, the man himself.

No time to speak to him, to any. She was carried out of the open window, into the night and up, high above the narrow valley. Briefly she did have time to think how Julianne would have hated this hellride, and yet to yearn hopelessly to have that girl beside her, and to wonder what use a djinni was if it could not bring her the miracle she sought. Then the broad stretch of the plateau lay below her, blacklit by a blaze of stars.

Before the men get so far, she'd said, because this was her hunt, she'd thought, and hers alone; even Hasan had less claim than her. She'd been too slow, though, despite her urgency. One man stood alone, a shadow on the bare rock; her mind caught hold of the word, *a Shadow indeed,* and she whispered, 'Esren, set me down. With him.'

It was strange, how she seemed constantly to forget about Julianne's father, constantly to discount one of the most powerful men in Outremer and so constantly to be surprised by him. Or else it was not so strange, because he was such a self-effacing man in many ways, he seemed almost to discount himself until he was needed or felt an urge to intervene; and then again it was perhaps not strange at all, because a girl could get into the habit of discounting fathers altogether. It was a hard thing to remember that some mattered, and to their daughters too.

She set bare foot to chilling rock and stood beside the King's Shadow with her djinni at her shoulder, a golden glitter in the dark. At least she knew how he had come here ahead of her, long ahead of all the rumpus; with his title came his power, or some of it. Like the Dancers, he could cover distances in a single step; unlike the Dancers – or so it seemed, or why else would Morakh have wriggled his way through narrow channels to reach this height? – he could step through air or rock or whatever stood in his way. Sometimes, she thought, he stepped through his daughter; in him, she could not quite contrive to resent it.

Sometimes, as now, he seemed to step out of his title and

power and all to be a man again; usually, she thought, to be a father.

'Coren? Can you tell which way they are going? Esren can't.'

'Can it not?' A question, but aimed at her even in his distraction; he was not a man to be careless, at such a time or anywhen. Even so there was a note of surprise, almost disbelief in his voice, and his eyes did seek the djinni for a moment.

'It says not. It says they walk in the crease where the world Folds, which is like the dark behind your eyes, nowhere at all, it says it cannot find them . . .'

'Well. I wasn't aware that the djinn had such poetic tongues.'

'The djinn do not have tongues at all,' Esren said, 'unless they choose to do so. Like human poets, though, they sometimes seek to describe what is, in words that their listeners can understand.'

Elisande felt that she hadn't understood one word in three, but that wasn't important now, though Coren seemed to feel that it was. She called him back to what truly mattered, repeating her question impatiently. 'Do you know where they have gone?'

'West,' he said certainly, turning to face towards the Dead Waters. 'That much I can feel, though Djinni Tachur is right, they have touched this land only fleetingly.'

'Can you follow them? And take me with you, if Esren cannot?'

'I can follow, but not I think as fast as they are moving. Definitely not, if I have to carry you. It's been a long night, Elisande, and I will not risk your life.' *As Morakh is risking*

Julianne's were the words he did not add, because he did not need to.

'Well, you go, then,' enough of this standing around, 'and Esren and I will follow you, as best we can. Or,' another thought, suddenly, 'Julianne said that the King could place you anywhere,' *like a chess-piece,* she had said. 'Can you not ask him . . . ?'

'The King could lift me up and put me exactly where they will next touch to earth,' Coren confirmed wearily. 'But this is not his Kingdom; and no, I cannot ask him. He acts as he pleases. My daughter's health and welfare are perhaps not his priority. Let us see what there is to be seen, from the rim of the plateau . . .'

The King's Shadow stepped into a hazy golden light, and was gone. Elisande half-moved to go after him, but checked herself as the light dwindled; instead she called to Esren, and rode the wind to the high escarpment where she and Julianne had stood the previous day to watch how the djinni sucked up the waters of the sea.

Quickly though they'd come, Julianne's father was once again there before them, standing on the extreme edge of the cliff.

Perhaps he'd heard the rush of their coming, perhaps it was the sound of her tight breathing that alerted him; whichever, he spoke without turning his head, without shifting his gaze from the dark glimmer of the still-restless water far below.

'Djinni Tachur, I cannot be certain, but it is my impression that they came to this place, that they stood exactly here. I would be interested to know whether you can divine the truth of that, more clearly than I.'

'It is so. If I have lost the ability to foretell what may be to come, I can yet see what has been. The man and the girl were here, and they climbed down.'

'No,' Elisande blurted instantly, 'she could not, she is terrified of heights . . .'

Even as she said it, though, she remembered Julianne's glazed wonder at herself just hours earlier, her stunned murmur, *Elisande, I climbed a mountain,* and how the proof of that had been embedded in her hands: cracked and broken nails, skinned palms . . .

'What she could do once, she can do again,' her father said, as though he could read Elisande's thoughts without even looking at her face. Perhaps he could. 'If the djinni says she climbed, I think we must believe it. They are in any case not here, and he could not have carried her. Shall we go down?'

He went, without waiting for a reply. Again the night shone with the light of his leaving, again Elisande followed by her djinni's grace, gliding down almost within arm's-reach of the cliff. She found some measure of consolation in the thought that Julianne would have had to climb only some of the way; from perhaps halfway there were steps that had been carved into the rock centuries before, to give access to the caves that pitted its face.

But still, the image of her tall friend stumbling down at Morakh's heels, bent one way or another to his will – no, there was small consolation in that.

Less still when she thought where they must have been headed, where they must have gone after they reached the long-redundant quayside where she stood now, where Julianne's father had once again arrived before her.

Again he was looking out over the water, seemed almost to be listening to the surge and the swell of it. How long would it take, she wondered, to calm a sea after it had been ripped from its bed and let run back? Less time, she thought, than it would take to calm Coren de Rance, who had had his daughter ripped from him and did not yet have her back.

This time he did at least turn his head to acknowledge her, seeming entirely calm as he said, 'There are no boats on the Dead Waters.'

'No.' For how much longer, she couldn't say. The djinni Esren had destroyed all traffic on the waters, all fish within; but the djinni Esren was with her now. Perhaps if Hasan and the other tribal leaders fetched living fish, fetched wood for hulls, perhaps some new life could come to what was dead. But the waters were foul still, she doubted anything except a malignant djinni could survive them long. And the Sharai were not made for boats, would stay she thought a long time frightened by so much water; and Rhabat was ruined, almost, and its people would be leaving with the tribes . . .

'There is no trail from here that I can sense, only that call to westward; but I do not believe that even a Sand Dancer can dance across water, any more than he could dance down a cliff.'

You had no trouble, coming down that cliff without climbing. Could you not have passed something on to your daughter, more than stubbornness and guile . . . ? 'They must have gone the other way, up the tunnel.'

Julianne's father was the soul of patience, or so Elisande had thought him. Tonight, it seemed he lacked the patience to pace even the shortish distance past the gully's mouth to the further end of the quay. He walked in light and took only a moment or two to do it, to be not here now but there, she could see the fading glimmer of his arrival.

Elisande balked at turning to Esren for so little service. She ran instead; and if she seemed lighter on her feet than she expected, if each leaping step seemed to lift her higher and carry her further – well, no doubt anxiety and strangeness and urgency could explain that.

It was only the rank and salt-soaked air that made her gasp a little, when she reached his side. She thought he'd already opened the hidden door to the climbing tunnel, but he denied it: 'No, I found it so. Proof positive, I think, that they came this way, even if they didn't climb with mortal feet. Sand Dancers trace their steps in strange country, but they still need an earthly path to follow.'

Which you do not, so why can you not hunt them quicker than they can flee? No point in posing the question, he was as elusive as the djinn, and as dangerous to hold a debt. Besides, it didn't matter why. It was the case, nothing else counted. If it had not been the case, he would have been hot in his daughter's pursuit by now; his every move betrayed him, as did his stillness between one movement and the next.

She gazed blindly into the absolute black of the tunnel's opening, and spoke hesitantly. 'There was an 'ifrit, Marron said, guarding the further end . . .'

'I do not think it will have kept its watch.'

'And if you are wrong? Esren cannot kill it, face to face.' That was the wrong way to say it, the djinni had no face, but the words were true regardless. Spirit could not touch spirit and survive; it had needed the water's force to wreak its fierce will in the valley.

'If I am wrong, then I will meet it. Face to face. I have slain an 'ifrit before this. But if I am wrong, if it lingered past the flood, then it seems likely to me that it stayed to meet Morakh and my daughter. By arrangement, or otherwise. Like the djinn, the 'ifrit have some sense of what will come.'

Like most of the djinn, perhaps. Not like Esren, or not much. That one was stunted still, after its long imprisonment; stunted again, perhaps, by its sworn service to Elisande. She turned her head to find it, meaning to discover whether it knew if the 'ifrit waited for them or not; before she could sort the words out in her head, though, the King's Shadow had made them redundant.

His misty light, his brisk step into it, his sudden absence, gone before the light was gone: she pictured its hurrying to catch him as he strode doggedly in the space between worlds, hurrying to slip ahead, to be ready to receive him, to light his path when he stepped back onto the height above.

No easy walk through light for her, to rise from sea to peak. Rather a blind and sickening rush, turning and turning until her stomach rebelled. It was a long slow ride down this tunnel that had brought them into Rhabat, their way lit by guttering, failing torches. Now Esren dragged her in the opposite direction at terrible speed. Her desperate eyes sought something, anything to fix on in the utter dark, and found only the thin golden rod that was the djinni at her shoulder. But that too was spinning, spinning against the twist of the tunnel in a way that jerked her eyes out of rhythm with her belly, and she thought she might vomit indeed. So she closed her eyes, swallowing a thin and sour saliva as it trickled into her mouth. It was like being drunk, she thought, when the walls of the chamber would spin around her; she could survive that without disgracing herself.

Usually, she could survive that . . .

Just in time, something solid kicked cruelly at her bare feet, and kicked again. Her startled eyes sprung open and she saw rock, solid rock plunging beneath her. No, it was she who was plunging, staggering, falling towards it – except that she felt the djinni's strength grip her body and hold her upright until she could catch hold of a tentative balance.

At least she didn't feel sick any longer, only giddy and furious. She drew herself up cautiously, tried to outglare the djinni and said hissingly, 'Esren, when I asked you to take me up, I meant straight up through the air, as you had brought me down . . .'

'Indeed. I wanted to try the tunnel.'

Was this what it had meant, that it would act at her command but not necessarily in obedience? She foresaw a lifetime of such journeys, its will set against hers; and gritted her teeth, and said, 'We will discuss later the terms of your oath to me. In the meantime, enough of folly. Tell me where Coren is.'

'The King's Shadow is yonder, at the cliff's edge beyond the temple. You should go carefully, you are not yet steady on your feet.'

That was humiliatingly true. She stepped forward with exaggerated care, past the simple temple that guarded the tunnel's mouth, past a crumpled heap of clothing that she thought might hide the body of the imam who had served as watchman before the 'ifrit came – and no, there was no 'ifrit now, unless Coren had killed it or driven it off – and so came

to where Julianne's father was an unshifting statue, a silhouette against the glory of the stars.

Keeping a sensible, almost a Julianne-distance back from
the drop, she asked softly, 'What do you see?'

'Pestilence, and war,' he said gravely. 'I do not see my
daughter.'

'No.' Even those brilliant stars couldn't hope to give light
enough for mortal eyes to find her, even from so high a vantage-point. 'We need Marron,' she went on, giving voice to
a hopeless yearning, 'his sight might find some mark of
her . . . ?'

'Not even his, I fear. And Marron is in the land of the
djinn, with Jemel. Leave them there, Elisande.'

Oh, she would, she would. Desperate for something, anything to justify their coming here, to wash the bitterness of
utter defeat from her mouth, she said, 'Esren, you may be
able to see more clearly from this height, to find some echo
in the spirit-weft . . .'

'The weft does not echo, Elisande,' any more than its
voice could echo, so cold and unbreathed as it was, 'and I am
still untuned to its touch. There is perhaps something,
though. There is perhaps a castle, and an army. To the west.'

Oh, not the Roq, she thought in desolation, *let us not have
to return to the Roq again.* But Roq de Rançon lay a long way
further north than west. 'There are no castles in the Sands,
and no armies.' None bar Hasan's army of the tribes, at least,
that he meant to lead against her own land, unless Julianne
could stop him. 'She cannot be in a castle.'

'No. But she may be, in time to come. I can see no more
clearly than that.'

'To the west lies Outremer, beyond the Sands,' Coren

said heavily. 'There are many castles there, and more armies than a man could count. Come, this is pointless. We will not find her by staring into the dark, nor by chasing vainly through the desert. We should go back. I need my bed, and you yours, Elisande. For what little is left of the night, at least.'

He didn't move, though, not yet; which gave her time enough to say, 'Take me with you, Coren,' and to say it as though he were her only concern, as though she thought he should not go alone. She doubted if she had fooled either one of them, the man or the djinni, but he nodded graciously and took her arm and led her into his golden gleam of light. It afforded her a safe and easy passage back to the valley, and there were times when a girl simply didn't need the challenge of an unruly servant, the threat of another wild ride.

2

A World, a Man Unransomed

Anton d'Escrivey stood on the height of the wall at Roq de Rançon, and knew himself possessed; and could not truly have said which of two spirits it was that possessed him, nor which of those two was good, which evil. He knew what his Church would say, he believed that he knew what his God would say, and in this at least they would speak with one voice. Put him to confession, though, or put him to the question, dig for the deepest truth in himself and he could not be certain what his own voice would answer.

He stood in the last of the daylight, when it was dark already on the plain below. He saw the glimmer of torches on the road, a late patrol riding in; he had some interest in their report and might have gone down to meet them if there had been time. He could hear the news later, though. For now, his eye reached further out, looking perhaps for some other light, some hint of life among the distant hills.

He saw nothing, only purpling shadows on their peaks and unbroken black beneath. Every day for weeks he had stood here, and seen the same. It was wasted labour to climb so high, wasted time to wait for what would not be there; all of this he knew. The preceptor had opened the King's Eye more than once at his urging, and each time to no avail. No, there was no sign of the escaped heretic, nor of the baron's runaway wife, nor of his own treacherous squire. They had vanished in the chaos of that dreadful night: vanished by magical means for sure, long before they could have ridden beyond the reach of the King's Eye. That gift of sight could show little beyond the borders of the Kingdom, but it should not have failed so soon; some evil working must have blinded it, something of Surayon. If that wicked land could hide itself so utterly that none could find it, though its borders were known and had been charted, then no doubt its sorcerers could cast a blanket of darkness over such a party of small souls, so dark that even the King's pure light could not find it out . . .

So they said, at least, in the halls and the guardhouses; and so Anton believed, because he must. As he believed because he must believe that all in that small party were long gone from this land, seeking the safety of hidden Surayon or some greater safety further off.

And yet still he came up here high, each evening; and still he watched for some touch of light that might perhaps be a fire, might just possibly be a sign of one soul returning. Returning part way at least, too frightened to come closer but loath to leave entirely, held as Anton himself was held, to the betrayal of all vows true or false, betraying new companions just as he had betrayed the old . . .

Hopeless watch, but the knight kept it none the less; and did not turn until the great bell called the garrison to prayer, just as the sun fell from sight and that sea of shadow below swept up to engulf him.

He might have said his prayers there on the castle wall, with Marron's whisper in his head for company. To silence that distracting voice, he might have moved a little along the wall to join the guards who must watch and pray together. He might have gone back to his own chamber and prayed alone, as he used to do.

But times change, and men must change with them; old habits must be cast off, when men dress for war.

Anton took the stairs rapidly and then strode through the wards and passages of the Roq until he met the tail of his confrères, a slow procession winding into the great hall, torchbearers before and behind.

He joined that procession, as he seldom had before this month but now did every night. He paced in steady step with his brethren and left his head uncovered, as some half of them did routinely now, a badge of extra oaths that they had sworn.

Briefly, he remembered the occasion of those oaths. After he himself had caught and confronted the runaways in the stable yard, after they had laid him low with some numbing, bewildering spell on his mind – *after Marron had refused to leave them and come to him, but never mind that now; this was sanctified ground, or that was* – and after he had recovered himself and run to the broken gate and seen them riding out, even after so much he had gone back to the stables and discovered worse.

He had discovered the stalls where a squad of men had been waiting as guards and grooms, where they waited now in an eternal stillness and a bath of blood, their ruined bodies not to be distinguished each from each. Some evil curse had torn them, flesh and bone; and the few bound and terror-stricken survivors had accused Marron himself of doing this thing.

Marshal Fulke had come then and declared that the source of the work was Surayonnaise, whatever the instrument. There in the stables, among a breathless crowd of men, he had called not vengeance but justice on that wicked state; he had declared a holy war, and asked who would ride with him against this evil.

Used to orders, unused to invitations, the Brothers Ransomers had hesitated; it had taken the knights, the nobles' sons to push forward first, to make a path that the brothers could follow.

First among the knights – necessarily first, for his own squire's sake who had been first cause of all this horror – had been Sieur Anton d'Escrivey.

Soon now, any day now, the long ride would begin. Until then, Anton lived as he had not before, side by side and sharing with his confrères. First among equals, his superiors said, though he was not aware of that; he thought himself only a hypocrite and weak, drawing needful strength from others.

They would ride, and they would find Surayon; and they would destroy it utterly, and that was good.

He did not expect to find Marron within its borders, and that was good.

He did expect to find Marron, somehow, somewhere,

sometime; and that too, the God forgive him for he himself could not but that too was good, and hungered for.

In the great hall, on the dais that stood below the sign of the God, Marshal Fulke stepped forward to preach to all the Ransomers, brothers and knights together on their knees. *It must look as though we all of us kneel to him.* The thought passed suddenly, shockingly through Anton's head, and would not be dismissed. It was a nonsense, of course; there was no arrogance in the man, only great confidence and certainty of purpose that were both of them founded on faith unquestioning, unquestioned. Fulke might stand with his back to that tremendous, overhanging sign, the double loop that spoke of a twinned eternity, but it might as well have been branded on his high forehead, below his receding hairline; it might as well have been contained within his eyes, so that he saw the world in ever-doubled vision. For sure he carried it liquid on his tongue, whether he spoke to one man privately or to an army gathered.

And yet he was a man and must have all men's faults, however deeply buried beneath the discipline of his belief. How could he face a sight such as this, so many heads bared and faces lifted, so much breathless silence, and feel no possession of the moment? He had been sent by the Church Fathers to be provincial commander of the military arm, no more than that; he was subordinate to the preceptor here at the Roq, and to many men else; and yet this was his army, they were his men, they would rise at his word and he must know it. There was a leashed eagerness in them, they strained to hear that word and to follow him, and he must know that also.

'My brothers,' he said, his voice soft but carrying, like the whisper of a whip in the air before it cracked, 'all these weeks I have been telling you of the evil nestled like a worm in the heart of Outremer, that nestles also in the heart of each one of you, eating at your virtue. All these weeks you have waited to hear me cry you forth, like hounds upon a hunt. A month back you saw that I was right, when those you had welcomed here turned to sorcerous wickedness, and many brothers died. Since then, you have ached to wreak the God's vengeance on the vile, to ride against the heresy that is Surayon.

'You need wait no longer. The time is now, and you are the hand that shall strike, hard and clean into the heart of sin, a light to drive out darkness.

'How can I know this so certainly, you want to ask, only that obedience and awe must hold you silent in this holy place? I will tell you. I have been granted a vision; I have seen our enemy, as clearly as I see your thoughts, your hopes, your doubts.

'This last night I rose from my pallet and walked abroad while you slept, or else I dreamed that I rose and walked; I cannot tell whether my body in truth left my cell, or whether it was only my spirit that was called forth by the God. No man saw me or spoke to me, no hand touched mine unless it was the God's own hand that gripped me.

'However that may be, I felt myself drawn to climb high, to a place on the walls where I might overlook that ancient tower which has no doors or windows, to which the King himself gave a name when he was here, the Tower of the King's Daughter.

'As I stood and gazed upon it, it seemed to me that I saw a misty light shine out through the very stones of the tower.

They turned to mist and faded, to leave a doorway where there is no door.

'Out from that doorway, I saw a flood of creatures come: demons I would call them, from the pits of hell. They were black and many-legged like spiders, and they glistened in an unearthly light.

'I saw them swarm up the wall behind the tower, where there is no walkway and so we set no guards. They were so many and so fast, they seemed to flow like water, like a foul and shining river over the wall and so out of my sight.

'When they were gone, the tower's stones were restored, and the glow died back to darkness.

'I have thought all day on what I saw, I have prayed and fasted, and this is my reading of it. There can be no doubt.

'Whyever it was built and whoever built it, that tower now stands in our eyes for the Folded Land, for Surayon. Think, my brothers! Only think, and you will see that it must be so. No doors, no windows – it exists and yet it is sealed to us, we can gain no access to it. Only sorcery could lead us through its walls. Is this not also true of Surayon, has that land not been closed to us by magical means?

'And yet, we know, the evildoers of that forsaken country pass its borders to mingle all unrecognised with us. We had one of their kind in our own captivity, under our guard some few weeks since, until he was released by powers beyond our reckoning. You all know what price we paid in that escape; I promise you, the price that Surayon must pay when it falls to us will be the heavier for it.

'What I saw, though, what the God showed me in His kindness was more than a few wicked men stealing out to work mischief among us. It was what we have long feared, what the Surayonnaise have long been preparing for behind their hidden borders. It was an invasion, an army issuing forth to wreak havoc in the Kingdom, to challenge the rule of the King himself.

'By the God's grace, we have been warned; by your strength and faith, we can forestall it. More, and better: we can use this knowledge, this chance to strike at last against that canker that lurks at the heart of our land.

'One man may slip silently, unseen through a curtain; an army cannot. The sorcerers of Surayon must open their borders, to send forth their strength. If we are there and ready when they do, we can pass inside; and then the God's vengeance will be ours to enforce.

'I have spoken with the preceptor, and this is our plan. Already birds are flying, messages have been sent; the lords of Outremer will rally at this news, we will build an army of our own to meet the men of Surayon. Even magic-workers are mortal, and may be slain. But we, the Order of Ransom, knights and brothers both will hold ourselves apart from that battle; we will ride into Surayon as soon as the way is clear, and there we will work the God's will against that heretic people, and so bring the King's most wayward daughter back into the heart of her family, from where she has been too long lost. Prepare yourselves, my brothers, cleanse bodies and minds, confess if that is needful; you must come pure to your trial, and we march in the morning.'

There was more, the marshal was a master at setting fires to burn in men's hearts; but Anton's attention drifted. He remembered how he had seen Marron and the others, the night they fled – how they had been grouped in the court below his window, at the foot of that same Tower of the King's Daughter, all lit by a glowing ball of fire. That had been a sharp blue witchlight, not at all what Fulke described – but still, it was all of a piece. They had looked like travellers balked, or warriors defeated. That had been his thought then, and was still his thought now. He had wondered ever since, why there? It was the furthest part of the castle from the gate, not guarded perhaps but overlooked by all the knights' windows, a nonsensical place to meet. Unless they'd had some other objective, another way to leave perhaps, some mystical door that the prisoner from Surayon could open, except that they had found it closed against them . . .

He thought that what Marshal Fulke had seen was no sleeping vision; he wondered if perhaps it was not either a visitation from the God, but rather simple truth. This was after all a land of miracles and magic, and not all beneficent. There had been ample proof of that, when Marron had slaughtered his troop in the stables. With a blood-demon by all reports, a monster of terrible strength – something that he had perhaps come by within the tower? For sure the boy had owned no supernatural powers earlier, Anton himself could testify to that; only the native charms of shyness and beauty, a pair of eyes that could snare a man's heart . . .

It might be blasphemy, he thought, to question a divine vision. It was certainly disobedience to his vows, to question the affirmation of his superior. Well, let it be so. One further sin on his conscience, what did that matter, one among so many? And no, he would not be confessing it before they marched.

Having no squire now, he made what use he could of his confrères', what little time he could beg their servants from them – he who had been so independent for so long, forced to plead for service; he had been spoiled in more than the one way, he thought, by a few short weeks of Marron – and was still kept unaccustomedly busy on his own account, packing and preparing for what must be a lengthy absence, what could be months of campaigning in the field.

And so it wasn't until the following morning, when the castle and all the chaos of a dawn march lay hours at his back, when he had at last the peace of a steady horse below him and the silence of his brethren all around him, that he found the time and the space to think a little. Even that silence had been slow in coming, for all the rigour of the Order's rules. Young men who ride to battle will be talkative, and his fellow knights spoke to Anton now as though he were one of their own: only a little older than most and a finer swordsman than any, a favourite of Marshal Fulke's too and so very much worth their time. He was still not used to that. A sudden popularity was hard to deal with, harder to set aside.

Eventually, though, the weight of cloak and armour under a fierce sun beat down the most insistent tongue. With his hood drawn up and its rim hanging low to shade his eyes from the glare, Anton could feel himself alone amid a crowd, as he had been for so long before this. *Before Marron* . . . For some few years he'd all but hidden at the Roq, given implicit licence to hide by virtue of his name and fame. Or infame, rather, the truth and rumours that attached to any whisper of that name. He'd rarely left the castle walls, except to patrol the borderlands where there were none to whisper, only wild tribes who fled at sight, the occasional Sharai raiding-party to be tracked or attacked.

His recent venture east as part of Julianne's honour-guard had been curtailed, but had still reaped a taste of trouble among the Elessi.

Now, though – now he was headed directly into the heart of Outremer, and could not hope to escape the public eye. All down this long road there would be petty grandees offering food and wine and hospitality, offering their sons to the adventure, perhaps throwing their marriageable daughters into this lordly company. Blustering barons, hopeful boys and giggling girls alike would seek to learn his name.

Above all there would be constant fresh arrivals, recruits come to join this building army. The Order might make the hammerhead, but every hammer needs a solid shaft. There were swords, bows, axes in their hundreds aboard the wagons at the column's tail. Any man who offered would be armed and welcomed to the march; every lordling who answered the preceptor's summons would be given his place of honour, and would mingle as of right among the knights. Anton could no more lie about his history than he could hope to hide his face. Anton d'Escrivey rode out into the world again, after so long silence; let the world make what it would of the fact, of him. He would be interested to see the results.

And might see them sooner even than he'd budgeted for; a group of men was waiting at a crossroads up ahead, two of them mounted and the rest afoot. Some minor noble and his eldest son, this ought to be, with a dozen retainers, all that their estate could spare. First to join, and they would carry that like a banner, Anton thought: *before the horde, before our liege lord even, there were the Ransomers and there was us, they treated us like brothers . . .*

So much so that Fulke himself rode on ahead to greet them, to offer honour where it was so manifestly due, so manifestly expected. He could be a diplomat, then, as well as an inspired preacher; whether he was or could learn to be a soldier, that was yet to be seen.

There was – of course! – a shrine at the crossroads; there was also, *mirabile dictu*, a spring that still gave water in this height of summer. Or not such a miracle, perhaps: he'd grown so used to the drouth of the Roq and its lands of dust, he'd forgotten how fertile the Kingdom was in its long lie between the mountains and the sea. Even one morning's ride south into Tallis, a rising purple shadow to the east gave better protection from the desert wind and the drifting sand. There was more roll than jut to the hills, more soil than rock, more green than grey. The spring was a slow bubbling pool rather than an overrunning freshet and they daren't let the animals near for fear of their hooves churning it into an undrinkable mire, but if the column rested for an hour – and if the brothers and squires worked all that hour, fetching and filling with their knees in the mud – every horse and ox could be refreshed. *Never lose a chance to water your mount* was an order ingrained into every man of the Order, after a few months' service at the Roq. Of course, they would pause.

And of course the knights would not scurry about with their boys and their black-robed comrades, after they had all knelt before the shrine to say the midday service with Marshal Fulke. Of course they would gather in a separate and superior group, to eat and talk quietly among themselves. And of course Anton would linger with them, sooner than make a target of himself, one man apart from all. And of course the noble's son would drift away from his father, towards the young men whose dress and armour bespoke their rank, whose bearing and demeanour must seem so attractive.

He was an open-faced, cheery lad no older than the squires who were busy tending their masters' horses, sixteen or seventeen at most, and he was possessed of a tongue that wouldn't stop wagging. Anton was more accustomed to shyness and quiet obedience among the young, after his years in the Order; this boy was almost a revelation, certainly a reminder that he was riding into a different world.

'. . . This isn't my place, not really, it ought to be my brother's, to ride with Father; but he's been sick for weeks, he's had the fever, and our mother wouldn't let him come. He swears he's well enough now, but he's thin yet and he can't stop coughing. So Father said I could come in his stead. Mother was against that too, she thinks I'm too young, but he said he wouldn't ride alone while he had two sons and one strong enough to bear arms for the King and the God. It's what I've always wanted anyway, always. Not Roben, that's my brother, he has a farmer's soul, Father says, he loves our land and never wants to leave it; it's a blessing, *I* think, that he's been so ill. Now that he's getting better, I mean. He can stay, as he really wants to, and I can go to the war.

'Roben would never make a soldier anyway, but I think I will. I mean, I hope so. I've never been afraid to fight. Not that Roben's afraid, I don't mean to say that; nor a weakling either, it's just that his heart's in the land, do you see what I mean . . . ?'

'Emphatically,' Raffel murmured. 'Halben, a soldier's first duty is service – which is generally taken to include standing quiet among his betters, as a good servant does. Do you think you could manage that?'

'Oh. Forgive me, sieur. My mother always says I was born with a brook running out of my mouth, but . . .'

'I'm sure she does. It's all right, lad, I was teasing. It is true, though, that a young warrior should look first to serve; have you ever thought of offering your service to the God? As we do, I mean, as knights of the Order?'

'All my life,' the boy said simply. 'Father wouldn't countenance it, though, he says it's too expensive. If I had been the elder, then perhaps; I think he would have liked to see my brother take the white for a year, and earn his badge. But Roben doesn't want it, and Father won't pay for me to stand in my brother's place.'

'He may change his mind, if he sees you do well with us.' Even from where he stood on the edge of the circle, Anton could see the look on the boy's face, and guessed that that idea had already occurred. He hid his smile better than some of his confrères, but then lost it completely as Raffel went on, 'If you cannot make your vows to the Order, you can at least offer us your service before we come to battle. One among us has need of a squire, if you would be willing . . . ?'

Of course Halben was willing, his speaking face said so even before his thrilled voice could confirm it. Anton felt his own face darken in response, with that clouding scowl he'd seen so often mirrored in others' wide and frightened eyes. For once he took the necessary moment to dispel it, before he pushed his way through the mill to where he had least intended to find himself, the centre of the circle and the focus of each man's gaze. Raffel wouldn't frighten, after all, and the boy was an innocent in this, he didn't deserve even the margin of Anton's anger.

He didn't deserve even as much as Anton must give him, here and now.

'A soldier's duty is to serve, perhaps; a soldier's wisdom is never to volunteer, at least until he knows to what he has promised himself. To whom. I am the one my brother speaks of so casually. When you have heard my name, you may not be so eager to stand as my servant.'

'Sieur, I will gladly attend any Knight Ransomer who thinks me worthy . . .'

Perhaps there was some trace left after all of Anton's scowl; the boy stuttered into an unaccustomed silence, as their eyes met.

'It is not your worthiness that is in question, Halben.' Anton tried a smile, but even he could feel the bitterness of it as he went on, 'I am called Anton d'Escrivey. If you have not heard that name, you should ask your father's advice before you commit yourself to it.'

No need for that, transparently. The boy had heard the name, and some at least of the stories attached to it. He went first pale, and then scarlet beneath his farmer's tan; his feet carried him backwards seemingly against his intent while his arms flailed to shape excuses in the air, while his tongue ran loose and desperate. He should not give himself against his father's express desire, his father would in any case require a squire's service of him, his mother had always cursed him for a clumsy oaf who couldn't serve a cup of wine without spilling it, and usually on whichever poor man it was whom he was serving . . .

By the time the lad had squirmed his way through the

press of men at his back and scurried off to join his parent, still apparently crying alibis to the wind, Anton had a better hold of his temper.

'Raffel,' he said, and felt pleased with himself for the moderate tone in which he said it, 'that was not fair.'

'Was it not? Then I apologise. But you could not have hoped to keep the secret longer than a day or two, Anton. There will be many more who join us, and there must be some to know you, you have not changed so much . . .'

'I have no intention of keeping secrets. I meant that it was unfair to the boy, to offer me as the fulfilment of his dreams. He was all on fire with delight, with this chance and this company; likely now some part of him at least wants to creep home to his mother. *He* will know that he can never be quite comfortable with us again, even if you do not.'

And never a word about his own discomfort, or his own distress. To have been offered a lively younger son as squire and companion, a boy who couldn't stop talking about his brother – no, that had been neither fair nor kind, at a time when Anton must needs confront ghosts with every mile of the ride, and it was the ghost of his own brother who overshadowed all. Almost, Anton could find himself longing to be back at the Roq again, and only yearning for Marron's impossible return. Almost . . .

All afternoon, small groups of men joined the column, petty nobles and landowners with their retinues. There were enough youngsters among them that Halben found his courage, left his father's side and spread his whispers widely: *you see that man, that one there, the dark head and the haughty glare? That's Anton d'Escrivey. Yes, that's right, the fratricide who*

*fled his brother's body and his father's wrath to hide in the arms
of the Order. They say he's a boy-lover too, that his brother caught
him at it and so died; and he asked me to be his squire, me . . .*

That much Anton could live with, as he must do. There
would be weeks more of it to come. He urged his mount and
a few chosen companions forward, to ride in the column's
vanguard and so escape the sidelong glances, put some little
distance between himself and the muttering boys; but that
only provided the chance that broke him for this day. They
met a priest on the road and gathered about him for his
blessing, threw back their hoods to show the strength of
their vows – and Anton saw an accusing finger rise to point
him out, heard his own infamy declaimed.

'You! I know your face and style, however you try to mask
yourself in holy robes. I had heard that you ran to the
Ransomers for sanctuary, that you sought to flee the King's
justice by buying a place among their ranks; I had not
thought to see you ride out so brazenly, in defiance of all
honour. You are a marked man, Anton d'Escrivey. Your dress
and vows may shield you from your desserts, though it is
shame to the Order that it granted you so much favour;
they will not shield you from your disgrace.'

'My disgrace is my own,' as was his sudden fury, though
that at least he did try to mask behind the chill of a long-
practised voice, 'for me to carry as I may. My soul and
honour are given, not sold, to the God. As are yours, if your
own dress speak you true. My sins have been confessed,' or
some of them, those that the world twisted in whispers, 'and
I have served penance for them all. Do you not believe in
redemption, that the Church says may be granted to all who
repent?'

'I believe in the King's law, that says murderers shall answer for their crime, and suffer death when it is proved against them.'

'So do I, but the God's law takes precedence even over the King's. Besides, I am sorry to disappoint you, but I have never yet been a murderer. Now stand aside, or I may have a better case to answer.' He could keep the anger out of his voice, but his body rebelled against control; his hand touched the hilt of his sword Josette.

'Would you threaten a priest, sworn to the God's service?'

'No, but I see no priest here. Only a man whose words deny his robes, who sets public gossip before the teachings of the Church, whose blessing would taint our venture. Stand aside, or I will ride you down.'

He urged Alembert forward; the man scurried to the side of the road in a swirl of skirts and dust, as Anton's companions closed around him. At their backs, they heard a shrill curse sent against them. Some made the sign of the God superstitiously against brow or breast; Anton kept both hands on the reins, and his eyes firmly on the horizon.

'Anton, was that well done?'

'No, probably not. But it has been done, and may need to be done again and yet again before we come to Surayon. You need not ride beside me, if you fear the curses of the stupid.'

It was a sign of how things had so recently changed for him, that his confrères laughed at that and promised to stay close. It was a sign of how he was not so immune as he had thought himself, that he led them deliberately slowly until others could catch up, Marshal Fulke among them.

'Magister,' he said then, 'the sun will be setting in an hour; it might be good if some few of us rode a little ahead, to find a place where the army may camp for the night. Unless you know this land . . . ?'

'Not I. All Outremer is new to me. But I had thought to press on until we reached Allansford. We will be late, but we can say the service as we ride, the Order has dispensation to do that on campaign; and the preceptor's messengers told men to gather there . . .'

'All the more reason to avoid it until the morning. If we arrive tonight, in the dark, it will be chaos and we'll get no rest. Come the light they'll be looking for us, and we can arrange the column as we wish.'

Fulke nodded slowly. 'Ride on, then, see what comfort you can find. The knights will want ground to pitch their tents, no doubt, and the animals will want water. You know what is needful, Sieur Anton. Go and seek it, with my blessing.'

Was there perhaps an extra meaning to that, as though the marshal had met a raving, cursing priest beside the road? Anton wasn't certain, but he said his thanks more gracefully than he might otherwise have done, before he spurred forward to rejoin his companions.

Anton knew this country little better than Fulke did. He had travelled all the length of Outremer, which few of his generation could claim, but only the once and only to reach Roq de Rançon, to be as far as the land could take him from any word of home. His mind had not been on the landscape then, his eyes had been focused on matter less solid and more real than the trees and fields he had passed by. He had almost no memory of those weeks, only that he had ridden his horse and himself to exhaustion every day. He must have bought or begged food on the journey, but could not remember a meal; he must have slept, but only when he was too weary to sit the saddle any longer. He thought he did remember toppling to the ground more than once, and waking next morning where he had fallen.

Now he gazed about him as he rode, and saw fields of corn and millet on either side. Alembert's hooves splashed through streams in the valley bottoms; where the land rose too high and dry to support crops, ancient fig and olive trees spread their twisted branches above twisting roots. He began to wonder whether they would find any stretch of ground clear enough to make an encampment for even this small force, these few hundreds of men; whether they might not after all have to ride on in the dark till they came to the township at Allansford.

After another valley with an infant river in its cleft, though, there came another ridge; and the road climbed higher than ever yet, through olive-groves to a rocky summit too bare to nourish any tree. There was no water, but the beasts could be picketed along the river-bank below while the men made camp on the height. If the baggage-wagons must come up with his confrères' tents and kettles, no doubt the brothers could haul them.

'This will do,' he said, turning his eyes southerly and seeing nothing better in the long, late shadows that cloaked the road. 'Torres, will you ride back and tell the marshal what we have found? Quickly, before the sun sets? Say your prayers with him; and tell him that we will make a beacon here, to catch the eyes of the Order and promise rest after a long day's ride.'

He had no right of command, but the knights listened to him now, where they had only laughed before. Torres nodded, turned his mount and went swiftly back down the ridge.

'Come, then! Hewers of wood and drawers of water we must be, while the sun lingers. Raffel, will you take the horses down to drink, while we gather windfall branches for a blaze?'

'Gladly, if Tomas will assist. Give me your reins here. A knight may care for his mount and his companions' at need, but gleaning wood is brothers' labour. Brothers or peasants, and I am neither.'

'There's no disgrace in labour. Brother.' A hard word for Anton to say, and he meant it hardly. 'And would you deny our confrères a light to fix their eyes on, a sign of journey's end? They'll welcome it, I swear to you . . .'

He spoke lightly, teasingly against Raffel's pride, but Anton meant it deeply. It was what he had looked for every night from the castle walls and been denied, what he had truly never hoped to see, a glimmer of hope in the darkness. He could offer to others what no one offered to him, and that was another change in him, he thought.

Sherard carried an axe at his saddle-bow, but would not use it. 'No sense in angering the master of these lands. They are not our trees to fell. And if they were, still I would not touch them. Older than us, older than the Kingdom: some of these olives are older than your family, d'Escrivey, or mine. Some might have been rooted here before the God walked this country. Would you cut that thread of history, would you kill a tree that the God Himself might have seen and touched and eaten from, for the sake of a fire on a hot night?'

'Not I,' Anton murmured, smiling. 'Olives as old as these will drop their branches under the sun's weight as a boy with cracked knuckles drops his sword. Let's gather what they've let fall, and be thankful.'

Collecting wood meant unaccustomed labour, scrambling over steep slopes with uncertain footing, dragging awkward branches. Anton was not the first to strip off his heavy cloak and mail, nor the last to envy Raffel and Tomas their easier task with the horses.

Eventually, though, Anton could strike a light from flint and tinder, to coax a fire into life. As the boughs began to catch, he straightened and turned his back to the rising flames, in time to see the last red touch of the sun flare across the distant line of the sea.

Back at the Roq, a day's travel behind them, Frater Susurrus would be tolling the hour, calling the castle's complement to service, brothers and guests alike. On the road, Marshal Fulke would lead his army's voice in prayer as he led its body towards war. Here there was only Anton to do that work, and only his few companions to hear. That would not matter to them, nor to the God; he wished that it did not matter to him. He remembered praying in his own quarters, with Marron's soft voice joined to his; he remembered one morning when they had prayed together as they lay together in his bed. The Church would call that heresy. At the time he'd thought, he'd even said that the God would not. Now he wasn't so sure, he wasn't so proud in himself; all that he was sure of, he would hear Marron's whisper answer him every time he led anyone in prayer again.

It had to be done, though, none of these would steal the

lead from him. And so it was done, although his soul could have taken little profit from it. He had turned his eyes to the altar more and more in the days since Marron had been lost, since evil work and demon-possession had stolen the boy away; he had believed that worship could outrank love, military and spiritual ardour between them could burn out physical desire and enchantment. He did still believe it, perhaps. Adoration of the God was both simpler and more noble than any human love; it ought surely to have a fire's power over flesh, to sear and destroy. If so, he felt little heat from it tonight. He could thrust his arm into these leaping flames beside him and watch it blacken and wither, feel its slow death; he tried to thrust his haunting affection for Marron into the furnace that tempered souls, but felt nothing beyond a queasy wrongness, as though they inhabited two separate worlds and could not be brought together. *As though Marron has no place in the God's eye, for sin or for salvation* – but that again must be heresy, for the God's eye watched over all. The fault was his own, then, and easily found: an offering snatched back from the altar, a gift withheld. Whatever his private protestations, however deep his loathing for the Surayonnaise and their witchery, he still didn't want or perhaps couldn't bear to let Marron go.

And still wouldn't confess it, even now; and so his prayers were tainted and his burden unrelieved.

'Go down,' he said to his confrères after the last words of the appointed ritual had died into the night, after they had stood respectfully silent in the firelight for a minute longer, after he had sought and failed to find any sense of solace or release within himself. 'Go down and meet the men in the valley, when they come. I will tend our beacon.'

They went, with smiles and warm words but also a prompt obedience, all three of which Anton still found hard to fathom. Had he really changed so much, to force such a change towards him? He didn't believe so. Perhaps it was that the world had changed around them all, demanding new dispensations . . .

New, but not so new. He still found himself alone on a height, and by his own arrangement. The fire blazed, the wood crackled and spat, he felt his skin tighten in a rush of heat; in a rush of memory he heard young boys screaming as they died and almost saw Marron's face this night as he had seen it then, across a distance and through the flames, frozen ice-hard and close to shattering.

Turned hastily around and saw shadows instead: soft and liquid shadows flowing all around him as the flames weaved among the boughs they burned, like the shadows beneath a tree in leaf as the leaves dance in a wind; and striking solid through that shifting tapestry of light and dark like the trunk of a tree lay one single shadow that blurred only at its edges, which was his own.

Through the snapping and shifting sounds of burning wood he heard noises rising distant but clear from the valley below, voices and the jingle of harness, the creak of wheels; and thought how this must look to the arriving men, how he must look, a figure silhouetted against a flaring light. He had said that he would set a beacon, to draw their eyes like a promise; he had not intended that it should be himself.

Then he heard the tread of booted feet climbing the road, one man alone. He'd thought that his confrères would come up together in a laughing, grumbling mass, twisting and stretching and rubbing their sores after a full day in the saddle; or else that they'd send their squires scrambling ahead with kettles and packs.

Anton moved back into the shadows. His eyes were so seared by the blaze, he could see nothing but the faintest moving outline to distinguish black from black, but he needed no more, not so much. One man coming up alone and no one following, that had to be by order. Only one man could give such orders in this army, and would do it only on his own behalf.

The road drew him up into the light; Anton bowed – just slightly, a touch more than a nod, as though he were on horseback still and saluting from the saddle – and said, 'Magister. I hope that you find this satisfactory. It's a hard bed, but every man has a blanket, and we can spread as far as we need along the ridge. I thought it best to leave the horses below; if we watch from up here, we can see any danger that threatens long before it reaches them.'

'What danger do you imagine, Sieur Anton, in the heart of Tallis? We are far from Surayon.'

'That is not our only enemy, Magister. We are just one day's ride from the border, and we left a much-reduced garrison behind us.'

'Do you think the Sharai will know that, and raid at our tail?'

The question forced a reluctant smile. 'No, Magister. But I am a soldier, and I have watched from a high place for years now; perhaps it is become a habit.'

'No bad habit, for a soldier. I do not criticise your choice, Sieur Anton. Tell me, have you ever fought in a war?'

'No. Skirmishes only, and that one night at the castle . . .'

There was an obvious question leading on, but only imper-tinence could ask it.

'Nor I,' Fulke said, gifting him the answer regardless. 'We are soldiers by training only, I know the frustration of that; but the God will use us in His time, and I believe that time is now. Come, I have something to show you. Do not be afraid.'

He produced a candle from his sleeve, a candle of white and black tapers intricately plaited into one; stooping, he snatched a brand from the fire and lit its several wicks.

'Forgive me, Magister, but I have seen the King's Eye opened before, and found nothing in it to be afraid of.'

'I think you will not have seen how I intend to use it.' And then, a seemingly irrelevant question, 'Why do you call me Magister, as the brothers do? The Rule does not require it of knights.'

'They are not life-sworn to the Order, as I am.'

'No. A curious creature you've made of yourself, Sieur Anton – neither true brother nor truly knight, despite your dress. Well, let it stand. The God will dispose all, when He brings us to the test. In the meantime, watch and learn.'

Fulke murmured a few words, and passed his hand across the candle. Its feeble yellow light grew incandescent in a moment, as its flickering flames stilled and rose like white-hot rods of steel.

This was nothing new to Anton, familiarity had almost – almost! – worn the wonder out of it. He couldn't understand the marshal's words, nor see how those words could cause these things to happen, but he was no superstitious peasant, to fear what he could not understand. The Sharai practised forbidden magic, the Surayonnaise were sorcerers, and a sen-sible man would fear both even as he fought them; Fulke was the God's man, a priest as much as a warrior, and what he wove here was miraculous and blessed.

What he wove was light, bending those columns of rigid flame with word and touch and gesture until they spread out and down like fingers, until they broke apart into a thousand threads that glowed like golden wire. The threads made a tapestry, an intricate image in the air; Anton saw the whole of the Sanctuary Land, all of Outremer spread out before him like a map.

'See,' Fulke said, and the map moved and swelled, fraying into invisibility at its edges as the centre spread wider and more detailed, 'here is Surayon where we are bound, where we hope to come. Nothing can be Folded in the King's Eye.'

There it was indeed, couched between its mountain walls: smallest of the five states that made the Kingdom, little more than a single broad valley. Despite himself, Anton bent low to peer at it. Any more detail, and he might be looking to see the arch-sorcerer, the Princip in his palace, working at his spells . . .

'That is not what I mean to show you, though,' Fulke said. Surayon swirled away; for a moment Anton felt like a hawk, swept from his soaring by a wind too strong to beat against. A wind driven by another man's will, and that will strong enough to break him, feather and bone, if he tried to resist its forcing . . .

Almost he managed a smile then; he didn't often think himself bird-delicate or vulnerable to storms. But he didn't often have a companion like Fulke, so focused, so determined, so certain of his course. It occurred to him that they could both perhaps benefit from a little self-doubt, a passing touch of humanity; except that the last time he'd let himself be touched by human feeling he'd been betrayed, he might have been destroyed, he carried the damage of that touching yet . . .

And then there was no more time for thought, as he stooped – yes, very like a hawk – and was dragged down once more towards this strange and glowing landscape, this map of wonder. A moment's disorientation, where he had to remember that he still had a body and that it was under his command, that he could draw back from the King's Eye; he did so, and a frowning effort helped him to identify the land laid out before him. That had been Less Arvon that had just rushed past him, swifter than any hawk could fly; this was Tallis now, and not so far from where he actually stood on solid rock and earth. A day's journey to the east, perhaps, a day closer to the rising mountain-range.

It rose, or he fell; or neither of those, but it appeared so. He saw hills and valleys etched in light, and it was more and more like falling as his field of view narrowed to one particular valley that seemed to open and engulf him; detail massed before his eyes and the surrounding hills loomed high on either hand. He lost sight of the horizon, and couldn't properly see even the ridge he stood on, for this dazzling tapestry thrown over.

What he could see was a river that ran like living, livid gold, not yet at its natural size but soon, surely, if it and he drew any closer. He could see no sign of man's work in the valley, no trees or planted fields, though the true land was fertile and farmed; when he squinted, he thought he could make out a roughness on the hillsides, as though the King's Eye were sharp enough to delineate individual rocks. Nothing moved among them, there was no sign of anything that lived.

He had thought himself familiar with the King's Eye, he'd boasted so, but he'd never encountered it like this: only as a map, a chart scrolled with lines of light for ink upon an unseen parchment, or else as a model showing all the shapes of hills and cities. This was something entirely other, where a man might find his map burn like a fiery landscape all about him. *You will not have seen how I intend to use it*, Fulke had said, and Anton would not argue with him now.

'What is this,' he murmured to the man at his side, 'what have you brought me to?'

'The heart of a miracle,' Fulke replied. 'Here, take my hand, and follow close.'

Anton couldn't turn his eyes from the glittering marvel that had swallowed him. Like a hawk come to ground, he stood now on the river's bank or so it seemed, although he could not hear the water's movement. If it were water. He had heard stories in his childhood of a land where rivers ran with molten gold; he'd never thought to see it, never truly believed it till this moment.

He felt Fulke's fingers close around his, and grip tightly. He could almost find comfort in that, though not enough; when the marshal tugged at him he resisted, or his body did, lacking his consent to move. It was only Fulke's soft laugh that impelled him to take one step forward, and then another.

It was as though he had crossed a border he could neither see nor sense. He was wreathed in steam suddenly, that seemed to be rising from the river which was hissing now beside and below him, though it had appeared quite silent before. Even the hot, swirling steam had a golden gleam to it, dazzling and stinging his eyes. He blinked, rubbed at them and found his skin damp to the touch. Cautiously, he touched his tongue to his finger; the acrid, burning taste of it made him spit.

Again, Fulke laughed. 'Do not try to drink the water, Sieur Anton. It would be fatal to you.'

'Where are we?'

'In Tallis, as you saw – and yet not in Tallis, as you might find it by riding. By the God's grace and the power of the King, we are granted a passage into the Eye at need, into any place that the Eye can show us.'

'Even into Surayon?'

'Aye, even there,' bitterly. 'But there is like this, a golden desert country in the God's eye, not the land given to us for our habitation; and we have found no way to step from this to that. Even the God does not grant us wings, Sieur Anton,' for all the world as though he knew how that hawk's image lingered. 'If I blew out this candle, you would find yourself back on the ridge, beside your blazing beacon. I shall do so shortly, and you will. One may walk beneath the lid of the King's Eye, and so come safely to the place one seeks; one may use it as the preceptor does, to overview any part of the Kingdom and what moves there; or one may use it as I have tonight, to come to this half-land that resembles our own, and is not.'

Anton nodded, striving hard to appear calm in the grip of wonder. 'What point, then, in the journey? Why have you brought us here?'

'For a meeting. We should find a man here, to whom I have taught a little of this skill. He is no priest, but if his faith is as strong as he proclaims it, if he serves the Kingdom and the God, he should have managed to cross from our world into this. It is a useful attribute, to have a place to meet that is hidden from enemies and doubtful friends alike; why else would the God and the King between them have given us this blessing?'

That didn't answer the greater half of Anton's question, *why have you brought me with you, why seek me out for this?* He held his peace, though, and simply followed Fulke a short distance away from the river, till they were free of the clouds of steam.

Then, 'Blaise!' Fulke's voice echoed strangely in the flat, lifeless air. 'Blaise, if you are here, show yourself!'

A shadow moved from behind a rock upslope of them – but no, it was not a shadow. A man, rather, in dark, drab clothing. With a start, Anton recognised the name, and then the man. Blaise had been the Lady Julianne's sergeant at the Roq; did he now serve Marshal Fulke? Seemingly so. The strangeness of that, though, was overborne by something stranger, as Anton's first thought caught up with him. The man cast no shadow as he stumbled down towards them, both hands wrapped protectively around a candle. A glance up at the sky confirmed what should have been impossible, that there was no sun to make shadows.

Anton had only ever seen Blaise dressed according to his rank and allegiance, as an Elessan soldier; it was plain from his greeting to Fulke, an awkward 'Magister', that he had once worn other garb. Easy to guess that Blaise had been a brother once, had lost the right to wear the habit and now clung to what little was left him. Less easy by far to divine what service he did Fulke and the Order now, dressed as he was in rough homespun such as any landsworn peasant might wear, gabbling as he was in what seemed to be terror barely and badly disguised.

'Magister, I have done as you bade me, but I don't know if it is an angel or a devil I follow, I cannot tell; and this place your power has brought me to, it is as hot and dead as hell itself, I cannot be easy in it . . .'

'None the less, you must learn to use it as I have shown you, as you have tonight. Not my power, Blaise, but the God's; or the King's, rather, given by the God's grace. Trust, and do not be afraid.'

As well tell a rock not to stand, Anton thought, or a river not to flow. Even here, those laws applied.

'We will be swift, though; we ought not to linger where we can come only on sufferance. Tell me briefly, then, whatever you have seen and done these last days.'

'Magister, I found the wandering preacher, and his band. I have not joined them, quite; they are saints all, I think, or else they are possessed. They do not speak to strangers, I have never seen them speak among themselves. But I am not the only one who follows at a distance.'

Fulke frowned at that. 'I want you close. Have you heard him preaching?'

'Oh yes, Magister. The plague runs ahead of him, and he follows it from village to village; at every halt he heals the sick – I have seen that, and it is terrible: one touch from the relic that he carries and even the dying, even the damned are whole again, our own people or Catari, no difference – and then he speaks. He speaks of war as you do, war against Surayon the cursed, the Folded Land. Then he moves on. Those he has healed, those he has touched join with his disciples; others follow. We are not an army to make war with,' at last a glimpse of the soldier through his fear, 'there are old men and children, women too among his disciples, and they carry no weapons; but the number grows every day. Even a rabble may be dangerous . . .'

'Even a rabble can win a war, if it is armed with faith,' Fulke responded. 'Have you learned his name yet, or whence he came?'

'No, Magister. He never says.'

'Get closer, then. Speak to him directly, ask him outright. Find a way. He has claimed a share of my war; it may be that he is a weapon of the God, to swing the fight to us.'

'Or an instrument of devils, Magister, to turn it against us. There is something cold in him, and in his people.'

'That too, it may be so. Find out, Blaise. However you need to.'

'Magister, I will try . . .'

'To try is to fail before you begin. Do it, Blaise. That is my command.'

And then Fulke leaned forward and blew out the sergeant's candle, whose flame he had shielded so nervously within his palms. Nothing changed, except that the man was no longer there. There was no noise in his leaving, no swirl of light or shade; only his absence, so sudden that Anton wondered for a moment if he had ever actually been there at all.

'We are all phantasms, walking in a dream of light,' Fulke said, with a thin smile that he threw at Anton like a challenge, the moment before he extinguished his own candle.

3

A Smudge of Light

Marron felt that he need be scared of nothing now.

With the Daughter in his blood and in his eyes, with Dard in his hand he could outfight any man, any number of men; with the Daughter in the air, in his sight, he could outrun man or spirit, slide between worlds as fast as sliding between one thought and another.

With Jemel at his side, he thought that he need neither run nor fight. He thought that the two of them together could simply walk away. They could go to the east, perhaps, where there was no Sieur Anton and no holy war; if they went far enough, beyond the wide stretch of the Sands, there would be no djinn and no 'ifrit either, and even the gods would be strangers to them both. They could become traders, perhaps, dealers in silks and horseflesh among the yellow men of myth; Jemel knew horses, like all his people, and Marron supposed that he could learn. They could both learn about silks. They might even trade with the Sharai, with Outremer, sending their baggage-trains west, sending messages to their abandoned friends but never coming back, no, making a new home and a new life for themselves alone in distant lands.

Or else they could be explorers, writing their names in legend as they traversed the land of the djinn and took back tales of wonder to transfix all who heard them; and those famous names could become a symbol perhaps of something greater than adventure, a sign that Patric and Sharai could live in peace together . . .

This Patric and this Sharai, at least. Others too, certainly others – but few, and far too few. He and Jemel were rare, each of their kind; or rather Jemel was rare and he was unique, and even they two had a ghost ever present at their feast, who might some time drive them apart if they spent too long in Outremer, if ever he stood physically between them.

Even now, even as they played adventurer at Marron's instigation, standing high above the wide and golden world with a hot marvel beneath their feet – even now, Jemel was agitating for what Marron wouldn't, couldn't allow, a swift return in pursuit of what he chose to call justice.

It had been Jemel who'd insisted that they come so far, once Marron had brought him here to the severed peak, where a whole mountain had been cut and polished like a jewel. Marron called it a mountain, at least. Marron came from a flat land, though. Jemel claimed to have seen higher in the Sands, and climbed them too. Perhaps it had been Marron's smile that had sent Jemel stalking so firmly across the shining, glittering surface, against his own good sense and Marron's warning, 'Careful! Keep to the edge, where it's only warm. It'll burn you, at the centre.'

'And you too, but you're too fool to notice. Better I show you how far you can safely go.'

Which had meant, of course, that he must needs lead all the way, must take Marron to the hot heart of what had been done here; and so he had, and so had danced from foot to foot like a scalded lizard on a skillet. It had been Marron who must move first, walking on towards the further rim.

Jemel had followed necessarily, that was as ironcast as Marron's leading. But now he was dancing again, here where the rock was cooler; and unless he'd blistered his feet badly with his earlier bravado, then there must be another reason.

'Jemel, Jazra is dead. Why are you so keen to follow him, so quickly?'

'Jazra is dead,' Jemel said, 'and I do not mean to follow him at all. I'll wait till you are dead, and follow both. But Anton d'Escrivey I will send after Jazra, as soon as may be. It is my promise.'

His voice was husky now, where it hadn't been before. Natural healing was taking over where Elisande had begun, Marron supposed, scar tissue forming where the throat had been so deeply slashed. His words must find their way around, and lost a little strength in doing so. Likely he would always sound so young, then, younger than he should.

At the moment he was acting also younger than he should, dancing his impatience on the hot rock.

'Morakh all but killed you, and Sieur Anton is a better swordsman than Morakh. I have fought them both, I know.'

'Morakh took me with a trick.'

'And what, do you suppose that Sieur Anton is any more honourable? In a duel with his own kind, then yes, perhaps, if he were observed or if his life were not at stake. But he will fight and kill an infidel any way that comes to hand. He has done so, you have seen. No, Jemel. He would overpower you, and you would die; and this time there would be no Elisande to save you. I think she would be angry to see all her work wasted.'

'I should be sorry to make her angry at me – but I have other concerns than her anger. I have sworn an oath, to seek my vengeance; if God slay me instead, that is His will and must be endured. I said I would see you to Rhabat, and I have done that much and more . . .'

'What, do you want me to quit you of my service?'

'I want you to come with me, Ghost Walker. As you know. I came with you, this far.'

'You did, and glad I am of it. More than glad. But I am the Ghost Walker, and I can't wander where I choose through Outremer in pursuit of my friend's folly.' *Though I will run with you, far and far from Outremer, if you will let me.*

'You wander where you choose here, in pursuit of some folly of your own.' Jemel's voice was sour, caustic enough to cut even the strings that had been twitching at him, so that at last he stood still and silent on the edge there. Halfway between the needle and the sea, between the construct and the inherent, the glamorous height and the unreachable depth. And actually where Jemel did stand, where they were – Marron could look north and say it was a peak, look south and say it was a plateau. He could say it was natural living rock that warmed their feet, because it was; he could say it was a thing utterly unnatural, because it was that also. He could say it was a nothing, a removal, an absence of form; he could say it was a mirror made to reflect the sky back to itself, dark rock that wasted its heart-heat in a sheen that showed nothing to nothing, to speak of the vast emptiness of this uninhabited world . . .

Except that the world was not uninhabited, and he should not think it so. Even as the thought did flit across his mind, dragging its own question after, he heard a susurration at his ear, the grate of wind on still air.

'Djinni,' he said, a warning to Jemel as much as a greeting to the spirit. That little was all the greeting that it would have of him; whichever djinni it were, Khaldor or Esren or some happenstance stranger, it was equally unwelcome. He could almost laugh at his own arrogance – as though any djinni could be anything other than strange to him, whether he knew its name or not; as though any djinni would care for the welcome he gave it, in its own land or elsewhere – but he could not smile at the interruption, however conveniently it came.

'Half-human.'

That turned him, as it must have known it would. It was a shimmer, a twist, an intangible string in the air but not of the air. In his own land it would perhaps have glittered as it spun, perhaps have gathered up some dust to make itself a visible body; here it did neither, and Jemel was probably not seeing it at all. Marron's enhanced eyes could find it, but barely.

'I have carried a few titles,' *brother, squire, heretic, abomination,* 'but half-human is new to me.'

'You have that within you that is not human. I do not know the proportions, whether you master that which you carry or whether it masters you; either is possible. I could dismember you, but that would teach me only that it survives what you cannot, and that I know already.'

'Djinni Tachur.' Easy to name it now. 'If Elisande sent you to me, then I am sure there will have been a reason.'

'There was. She required me to tell you that the daughter of the King's Shadow has been taken from Rhabat, by the Sand Dancer Morakh. I have not found them. Neither will you, but she would like to see you fail.'

No echo of Elisande's voice surviving in the djinni's, but something of the girl's desperation came through none the less. *Tell him that Julianne's gone, and how; tell him you can't help; tell him that I need him, urgently . . .*

'It will take us two days to come back to her, on foot.' Longer, perhaps. Time was hard to judge here, and they had not hurried. They could hurry now, but not defeat the miles. He was a doorkeeper, no more than that; he could not overleap time or distance, in his passage between worlds.

'I will take you, if you will permit it. She ordered me to fetch you whether you would or no; some orders I am prepared to disobey, though, and that is one.'

Too proud to be a slave, it would make a captious servant. That was for Elisande to confront; he'd watch when he could, and enjoy. In the meantime she had asked for him, sent for him, whichever. Marron said, 'I will permit it, djinni,' smiling a little at his own condescension even as he reached for Jemel's hand.

A whipping wind lifted his feet from the plateau, and he felt the sudden drag of Jemel's weight against his fingers. He tightened his grasp and hauled with easy, inhuman strength, yanking the other boy up to stand beside him on seemingly solid air, binding Jemel's body against his own with an arm wrapped around the narrow waist. Wide, startled eyes stared into his from an inch's distance; Marron smiled again for reassurance, *did you think I would let it abandon you?*

Jemel turned his head away. Marron gazed at tangled black hair and the tawny neck beneath, heard a broken whisper, half chuckle and half sob. 'Look down, Marron, we are flying . . .'

Obediently Marron looked, and saw that it was true. They were skimming like gulls over the flattened peak; for a moment he could see not a shadow but a dim reflection of his own body and Jemel's in the glittering gloss of its surface. Then they passed the southern edge and he saw the landscape fall away. Suddenly they were at eagle-height or higher, so high now that he lost that rushing sense of speed. They might have been soaring like an eagle indeed until the wide golden land beneath them began to fade, to lose itself behind a swirling darkness. Briefly he thought that he had Julianne's disease, an unexpected terror of great heights.

The darkness grew to encompass them all, to block out the shimmering light. The djinni shone within it, though, visible now like a shaving of that same light, like a twisting hair of gold. Not Marron's head that was spinning, then, and not his sight that had clouded. At last he understood, this was how the djinni would make the shift from this world to their own. Unlike the Daughter, which simply ripped an open way between, the spirit was taking them out of the one entirely before it brought them to the other.

Out of the one, and into what? Into a nothingness that had no light, no heat, nor need for either, Marron guessed, as surely nothing lived there. He was barely aware of Jemel's body pressed close against his, barely aware of his own; he wanted to feel himself pinched or punched or bitten, only to reassure himself that he could still feel something.

If the worlds he knew were rooms standing side by side, then the Daughter would have torn a hole through stone and mortar; the djinni had brought them rather into a passageway that must connect the two. Or if the worlds were tents pitched close together, the Daughter was a blade to slice through woven walls, where the djinni preferred – through good manners or lack of strength or sheer wilfulness, he couldn't say – to give its companions a glimpse of the desert as it led them out and in.

It was a dark and a chill and an inhospitable place, and Marron wanted no more of it. Would have preferred less, indeed, and a great deal less by the time he felt a bitter wind scour his skin, solid as a wall to lean against, stronger than Jemel though far less warm or welcoming. He turned his head upward and saw the stars like a glory, like a blaze of sparks strewn across the sky. This was his own world, they'd come back to it at night and but for the wind he'd not have felt the change from one cold darkness to another.

There was no sign of life below them. That was no surprise, though. The Sands were wide and the tribes were scattered, unless they were still grouped somewhere near Rhabat. The Sharai were as sparing of their fuel as they were of everything; Marron thought he could pass above an army and barely be aware of it.

He braced himself against the wind of their hurry, locked his arms around Jemel and kept his eyes fixed on the ground so far below. He could make out undulations in the sand that must be great dunes to those who had to cross them, that looked like mere ripples to him; he could see occasional breaks in the smooth still flow, that must mark an outcrop of rock; he thought he could see a glimmering mirror to the east, that ought to be the Dead Waters trapping the image of the stars above, as they had trapped this djinni that carried him now.

Rhabat was there, on the further side of that inland sea. Marron hadn't thought, hadn't had time to think where this chase might have taken Elisande already. The answer it seemed was a great distance, and westerly. Westerly, of course, lay Outremer; almost directly west of Rhabat lay Elisande's own home. Surayon, the Folded Land, the state that hid itself . . . Marron thought that perhaps Elisande would not be welcoming the direction of this hunt, if it led other eyes to look towards Surayon.

His own red eye was caught at last by the slightest gleam, a smudge of red light among the dunes. He was barely sure of it, so faint it was; the djinni, though, must have been certain because they were descending suddenly, fast and straight. As he blinked into the stinging wind, the glow resolved itself into a dying fire, with a single figure sitting huddled beside. Another lay on the ground at a little distance, sleeping as it seemed.

The djinni brought them down to the fire, and set them lightly on the sand. The figure lifted its head and was Elisande, a blanket around her shoulders and an exhausted tension in her face, in her voice too as she said, 'Thank you, Esren.'

'Indeed.' It said no more than that but stayed, a single golden thread in a gloomy tapestry. Its service done, it was only an observer now: curious, perhaps, if the djinn felt curiosity. This one might.

Elisande stood, and came slowly to him. He still had one arm around Jemel, but she rested her cheek briefly against his other shoulder and said, 'You, too. Thank you for coming. Both of you.'

'What else should we have done?' *We should have stayed and left you to your own concerns, we should have broken free —* but friendship was a snare, a cord that tightened against a struggle and would not break easily. Oaths he could break and had, but not this simpler binding.

She drew breath beside him, intending perhaps to answer what she hadn't really meant to be a question. Seeming not to find the words she needed, she just sighed and shook her head, touched his arm with chilly fingers and turned back to the fire.

'Tell us what happened, Elisande.' That was Jemel, making some little play to claim his own place here, both as Marron's companion and one among her certain friends.

Again she took a breath, again she tried to speak. This time there were words, but weariness and worry held her spirit in defeat; she could tell them little more than the djinni had already. Julianne had been taken, on the night of her wedding, three nights since. The djinni had been unable to track Morakh and his captive; she and the King's Shadow had tried, were trying yet, but were having little joy of the hunt.

'We've scoured the Sands, by Esren's grace,' she said, 'and all we've found is the remains of a fire here, some signs that were hard to read, and this.' She slipped something from her wrist and held it out to show him: a golden bangle studded with little gems. 'It might have been one of Julianne's wedding-gifts. Coren thinks so, at least. We believe that they are

with an 'ifrit; if it took a winged shape, it could have carried
them anywhere by now. We didn't find this place until this
evening, and the fire was cold by days. They must have
stopped to rest and eat, an 'ifrit can't fly at Esren's speed,
but . . .'

But they were long gone from here, so much was obvious.
The chase was futile; and yet Marron could understand the
need for it, the urge to be doing something. 'Would they
have crossed into Outremer?'

'Coren says not, he says that the King could find them if
they went within his borders. He may be right,' though her
tone suggested doubt, either of the Shadow or possibly of the
King himself. 'But there is endless country they could hide
in, this side of the border; and Coren's so tired, we both are.
Speak softly, don't wake him. He didn't want me to send for
you but I had to, I couldn't carry this alone . . .'

The King's Shadow might be tired, might be worn out
indeed from his own anxiety as Elisande was from hers, but
Marron was suspicious of his sleeping. He could hear the
man's soft, steady breathing, and thought he could sense a
wakeful, listening mind behind it.

'Why did Hasan leave the two of you,' a girl and an
ageing man, albeit a djinni's companion and a man of rare
abilities and rarer friends, 'to do his hunting for him?'

Elisande smiled slightly, where in a lighter mood she
would have laughed aloud. Marron missed the laughter, had
been consciously trying for it; he knew the answer before he
asked the question. 'Oh, he didn't. We left him, he couldn't
keep up. The camels died, all of them, in the flood. Horses,
too, though he couldn't have brought horses over this,' and
she sifted sand between her fingers while her other arm

waved at what must be dark to her despite the stars, to show him the windblown dunes that ran to every horizon. 'He went back to Rhabat, to try to keep the tribes together. He says that the theft of his bride from their own citadel is an insult to all the Sharai, not simply a matter for the Beni Rus. He says that if there are 'ifrit involved, it may need many warriors to retrieve her; he says that he will gather what camels he can from the local tribes, if he has to spend all the wealth in Rhabat to do it. Then he will follow, as quickly as may be. Esren carries messages between us, so he will know where to come. But we have to find Julianne first. If we fail, then Hasan will have his army at the gates of Outremer' – *at the gates of Surayon* she meant, or so Marron heard her – 'and he will not waste that opportunity, with his men hot for fighting. Even if we do find Julianne and rescue her, he will still be there, with his army at his back; I don't think even her pleading could hold his hand. There will be war, Marron, unless we can find her and rescue her ourselves before he come. That's why I wanted you, in case . . . But I think there will be war.'

So did Marron; so perhaps did the silent djinni, which would explain her hopelessness if it had been less silent earlier. A spirit with some sense of the future could spell doom to any prophet.

'Julianne's father is here,' Jemel said suddenly, pointedly. 'Where is yours?' His voice carried generations of tradition, of certainty in what was right and proper.

'He is with Hasan. For all I know he may be arguing still against bringing war to Outremer; if so, he wastes his breath.'

'He should be here, then. Why is he not here?'

'I have a knife. He has a throat.'

And that certainly was right, and wise in both of them. Elisande was as drawn as an overtight cable, and her father could make her snap at any time; at such a time as this, she might truly let fly with a blade where honed words would have contented her before. If not, his presence would still divide this little party into two, his and hers. Marron and Jemel would stand with Elisande, the King's Shadow with Rudel; youth would divorce experience, fire would fight with ice and they would travel more slowly and learn less.

Let him use his skills elsewhere, then, let him work yet on Hasan, *thus far and no further, pursue your wife but not your dreams, learn to live with Outremer* . . . It would do no good, Marron thought, one man's voice couldn't turn a tide; but let him try, at least.

It seemed that Jemel was thinking the same way, though Jemel would be hoping for what his friends most dreaded, Rudel's failure and Hasan's war. At any rate, he grunted his understanding and turned the conversation abruptly, urgently to a more compelling issue. 'Do you have any food?'

Elisande flashed him a sympathetic smile, her mood shifting in a moment to match his. She'd been in the land of the djinn, and for longer than Jemel; she knew, none better, how appetite was a stranger there but how it returned full force in this world. Even Marron felt hungry now, at the mere mention.

'Yes, of course. I'm sorry, I should have thought. There's plenty, Jemel – we've got bread, cold meat, cheese, fruit. Good bread too, not desert bake. Esren fetches it for us, with our fuel and water.'

'You use a djinni to fetch water?' This time, his tone was sheer incredulity, too startled even to be outraged.

'We have to; we've no camels, and we can't carry as much as we need.' She was busy as she spoke, passing over a water-skin and crouching above a pack, so that Marron had only her voice and the set of her shoulders to read. He knew her well enough, he thought, that he could do that. What she said made perfect sense, but there was more to it. Esren had let her down, through weakness or malice or for whatever reason; she was seeking any way she could to use it in humil-iation, ageless and potent spirit reduced to a handservant . . .

They said little more after that. For a while their mouths were too busy, Jemel's and his own, they couldn't chew nor swallow fast enough to meet the demands of their raging stomachs; Elisande sliced meat and cheese for them, tore bread, found cups for water.

Then the simple weight of food inside them made them sleepy, just as her own long day, her several weary days and sleep-short nights all too visibly caught up with her. The night was cold, and she offered them her blanket, but they wouldn't take it. Jemel had slept out colder nights than this, he said, and sat out colder still with only rags to huddle in, no robe such as he wore now. Besides, the warmth of the other world was with him still, crept deep into the marrow of his bones. With Marron at his one side and the fireglow at his other, he'd be content as any sheikh within his tent . . .

Marron, of course, was never cold at all. He had his own otherworldly warmth that went deeper than his marrow, went to his soul except that what it found there, it could never warm.

So they arranged themselves, he and Jemel this side of the fire and Elisande that, lying close to the King's Shadow who still hadn't moved and who still, Marron thought, was not asleep. Better that way, perhaps: a man of his age and cunning ought to be wakeful, thinking, conceiving and plotting. Ought not to be chasing hard across an empty desert in pursuit of a long-vanished phantom and a captured girl. Let his mind run free in the hunt, and perhaps his body would fail at last to follow; perhaps he'd be so weary come the morning, they could legitimately turn on him all together, prove he was unnecessary, send him back to Rhabat to rest . . .

Come the morning, Marron woke to find that old and exhausted man on his feet and active while their other companions still slept.

He had been active, rather; fresh young flames were licking at new-laid cakes of camel-dung among the ashes of last night's fire. Now he was standing atop a dune-crest at some little distance, standing like a monolith with its face set towards Outremer, when he should surely have been sitting close and taking in what heat he could to set against the ache in his bones and the morning's early chill.

Marron peeled himself carefully away from the huddled warmth of Jemel's back, with a silent apology for leaving it so exposed. He stood up and walked softly over the sand, feeling how the dawn wind whipped it against his ankles as he climbed the dune. Joining Julianne's father, he saw their two shadows strike a clear path due west, as though they laid a path that men should follow. Greyish dust swirled high on the gusting wind, while tawny sand skittered beneath in the slow, endless progress of the desert. *Give it a few thousand years more,* Marron thought, *and Hasan won't need his army, no need of all that fighting and dying that Jemel's so hungry for. The Sands will swallow Outremer, and none but the Sharai will have the heart or the wisdom to live there then . . .*

He watched the shadows' long run in the low light, and might almost have been talking to one of them, certainly didn't turn his head to face the man beside him as he said, 'Shadow? Tell me about the King.'

'My name is Coren.'

'I know, but—'

'But you have trouble calling men by their given names, when they carry titles. Respect is no bad sign in a young man; none the less, Marron, call me Coren if you can turn your tongue around the word. You are at least as important as any of us, and I would prefer it so. Jemel will follow your lead; Elisande is there already.'

'Elisande gives no respect to anyone. Not even to the djinni . . .'

'That is not entirely true, though she'd like to know you think it. Come, this is not so much to ask, where there are so few of us caught in such a turmoil.'

'Well, I will try. Must I call the King also by his name, to make you answer my question?'

That barb drew a quiet chuckle in response. 'No, I'll not ask that much of you. I don't ask it of myself, though I used to once. Long ago, when we were two adventurers together. I used to call him Marc, and quarrel with him for the sheer love of losing in a fight. These days, not – though one would still lose. Assuredly, one would lose.'

'Tell me about him.'

'What would you have me say?'

'Is he a man?'

'Oh, yes.' The question didn't draw a laugh, though, as it surely must have done if it were as stupid as it sounded. 'Trust me in this, Marron, he is most certainly a man. I've seen him bleed; I've *made* him bleed, more than once. I've seen him eat and sleep, defecate and fornicate, which are the four prime motivations of mankind. If that's been worrying you, rest easy. He may be King of Outremer, with all that that implies, but he's human yet.'

'I don't understand, then. All the stories I've heard, from you and others – how can he do what you say he does, if he's just a man like any other?'

'I didn't say that. He was never very much like other men. He's ten years older than I, so I never really knew him as a boy; even as a youth, though, he had talents that singled him out. His father was a powerful man, but he was the youngest son of five, so had no hope of inheriting land or title. He spent his early manhood in a monastery, but was, ah, persuaded out of it; then he discovered an interest in travel and soldiery, making war against pirates and bandit lords. He took me with him, me and others; we hung at his tail like daglocks from a sheep, we little boys, we worshipped him. But so did older men, all those who followed him.

'When the cry went up for an army to reclaim the Sanctuary Land for the God, he was the obvious man to lead it. He was created Duc de Charelles for that purpose, because the lords and churchmen who declared themselves for the venture would yield to no lesser rank. It's a courtesy title, Charelles is a lump of rock in the ocean which offers no better harvest than gull-droppings, but a duke is a duke regardless.

'So he went to war again, this time with thousands in his train, but I was closest. It was a hard journey, and a harder fight: many battles, many deaths, a great deal of evil on both sides. But he held the army together, lords and church, until we had won Outremer. The Ekhed had governed the land for centuries but they couldn't stand against us, they retreated to their kingdom in the south; the Sharai fought us tribe by tribe, and tribe by tribe we drove them back into the desert.

'Then there would have been trouble, as all those ambitious men fell to quarrelling over the spoils; but my lord and friend summoned the Conclave. He called the nobles and prelates into one building, the Dir'al Shahan that had been the greatest temple in Ascariel; he made them leave their weapons in the porch, he locked the doors with his own hands and pocketed the key, and he made his own divisions of the land. He told them who would govern where, he showed them on maps, he drew the boundaries himself. In the course of one day he created the five states that you know and gave them to the most powerful of the lords. To the Church he gave nothing. He knew what trouble that would bring, and so he allowed the Ransomers their castles, and he made his own son Duke of Ascariel; that boy was always the Church's man, more than his father's.

'Himself he declared King of Outremer and demanded oaths of allegiance and fealty from all, would let no one leave till they had sworn. Then he sent them out, and locked the doors again behind them. All that year, while the Kingdom settled into its new name, he was seen seldom outside the Dir'al Shahan; since then, never. For forty years he has ruled from isolation. I am his Shadow, I speak for him, but even I see him rarely and only when he summons me. I used to be his friend, but now? I am not sure.'

How does he eat and dress, Marron wanted to ask, *who serves him?* The question seemed trivial, though, against the sense of loss he heard in the other's voice; so he asked another, an easier question instead. 'You have named him a man, a warrior and a diplomat; how was he made a magician, then, where does he take his power from?'

'That I do not know. I've never had the temerity to ask,' *and neither should you, if I do not.* 'He has great power, but the source of it is as secret as his life. He summons me, or more commonly he sends me; I do as I am bid, no more than that.'

'And if he summon you today, this morning, now? Would you go, would you abandon your daughter to serve your King?' It was a question that turned and turned in Marron's mind, duty against love. He had answered it himself, he thought, both one way and the other; both had felt wrong, treacherous, bringing a deformity to the world. Both had broken what should have been most strong, had spilled what was most precious.

'Marron, when he summons me, he doesn't offer choices. I have abandoned my daughter before, remember? On the road to the Roq, and at other times too often to count. Not to such peril, I confess – but yes, I would go. I would have to.'

All the more reason to find Julianne quickly, then, and rescue her if they could. Marron had another thought, though, another question. He didn't believe that the King's Shadow had not had the same thought himself, but still he had to ask. 'Can you speak to him? From here, I mean, right now?'

'Not outside the Kingdom, no. He speaks to me, where and when he chooses. He has sent me from Marasson to Rhabat and further; I am only his Shadow, with a shadow's strength.'

'Well, if he speaks to you before we have her safe, could you not ask him to summon Julianne, the way he summons you?'

Coren smiled faintly. 'Oh, I could ask. I will ask, if the occasion arises. But will he answer me? I do not know. Years ago, yes – he would have risked his own life, perhaps his whole army for a child in danger. He has changed, though, since he came into his new title. Great strength and great responsibility will change any man; you know that, Marron, you have been changed yourself. Believe me, when I say that his alteration outweighs yours by all the distance of age and authority that lies between you.'

Forty years, and a Kingdom: Marron could believe that, without difficulty. He thought it ought to change a man beyond recognition; he thought that perhaps it had, by the touch of regret in Coren's voice. A friend lost, and perhaps a daughter too – they ought to command more than a touch, but the King's Shadow kept his humanity as hidden as his master, or tried to.

He was speaking again now, as his eyes remained fixed on the far horizon. 'It occurs to me, Marron, that I may perhaps be able to guess where Julianne has been taken. If they are wise, they will not cross the border; I do not know how the King would react to that, so certainly neither does Morakh, nor any 'ifrit. There is a place, though, that lies on this line, and a little outside the Kingdom. I don't understand why they would head there, but every bare sign we find suggests it. There is nowhere else, at least, and I don't believe that they are running aimlessly, although I cannot see their purpose. Wake Elisande; this day may bring us answers, of a sort.'

4

Spirit Snares

Julianne knew where she was, now, at last; she knew what she had to fear.

She'd been frightened before – or had she? – when her body had not been her own, neither her thoughts: when she had felt her bones and muscles pull and shift all out of her control while her mind kept barely a thread's connection to what was real in the world, while it swam and sank in sickening oils, a haze of colours and shapes that meant nothing and touched her nowhere and yet were sickening regardless. She'd had no use of eyes or feet or fingers, her own skin had been alien to her and there was nothing in her head that she could claim. She had known somehow that she was moving; had she known also that she was afraid?

She couldn't say. What had come later – after she had been allowed her body again, after she had been let slip back inside her skin, when she had fallen back on rough rock and shivered frantically for more than the cold bite of the night and sobbed at the taste of harsh dusty air against her tongue and throat – what came then had been terrifying too, or so she thought now, looking back. There had been a creature, hard to see it clearly because of the way its black body sheened in the starglow but certainly it had been an 'ifrit, an 'ifrit with wings, longer and broader she thought than those that had attacked at Rhabat. Morakh had spoken to it, though she hadn't heard it speak nor ever heard that such spirits could; and then it had spread those wings and leaped from the clifftop – which was when she'd realised that there was a clifftop, and they were too close to the edge of it. Staring around in starlight she recognised the place, high above Rhabat and the Dead Waters, close to the temple and the tunnel's mouth. Marron had mentioned an 'ifrit, she thought, and a dead imam – but that was days before, and the 'ifrit had been defeated. Hadn't they . . . ?

This one not, as it seemed. It had soared high, and swooped low; Morakh had hauled her to her feet, and she'd felt long claws bind themselves about her like a whip's coils as her body jerked like a whipped girl's, her neck snapped back, she was snatched abruptly into the air.

No comfort that Morakh was beside her, that they had this terror to share. She had dangled helplessly, eyes tightly shut, an unknown distance above a ground she could not bear to look upon; she had filled her mind with a constant repetition, a desperate litany, *I have climbed a mountain. Besides, they want me living or the 'ifrit would not have made one cause with the Dancer Morakh nor he with it, therefore it will not let me fall. Besides, it is dark down there and I could see nothing even if my eyes were open which they are not, therefore there is nothing to fear. My father taught me not to be afraid of the unknown, neither of anything I cannot change. Why fear a fall, where there is nothing I can do to prevent it? Besides – as my eyes are shut and the land is dark below – perhaps it is not so far below, perhaps this creature skims the dunes as a sea-bird skims the waves, and if I fall it'll be no further and no worse than falling from Merissa. I miss Merissa. She gave me a smoother ride than this, and faster too; I was never scared to fall from her. Besides, I climbed a mountain . . .*

But had she been truly afraid or simply falling back into old habits, hiding from what was new, being scared of heights because that was so much easier than being scared of an 'ifrit's claws around her belly, a dark and uncertain future? She couldn't say. All she knew was that the steady chant of her own voice inside her skull had lasted her from those first moments of flying until she was dropped on the sand, had kept her silent, had possibly kept her sane. If anything in this madness could have driven her mad, it was that first flight, and she'd survived it. Therefore – perhaps – she could survive whatever else might come, until her friends or her father or either of her husbands came to save her, as they must; for the only real certainty was that she couldn't save herself.

She had been dropped onto sand, and had opened her eyes at the shock of it to see the sun just rising over a rolling sea of dun and dusty dunes. Morakh was getting to his feet beside her; the 'ifrit was crouching a little distance off, fierce red eyes glowing in a body from a child's nightmare, glistening black and shaped for evil, too many legs and wings that wouldn't fold as they ought to in any creature of nature.

Morakh had slipped straps from his shoulders, dropping a faggot of fuel, a waterskin, a bag of flour. He'd lit a small fire and baked desert bread on a stone; he'd tossed a portion to her and she'd choked it down like an obedient prisoner, despite its rank taste and her utter lack of appetite. Food was important, strength mattered. Might matter, at least, if ever she had the chance to call upon it. Water too, and so she'd swallowed grimly from the skin when he passed it to her, although the skin had smelled rotten and the water's sliminess had almost closed her throat against it.

He'd lain down to sleep, and so had she. No question of his binding her arms or legs to keep her there, no need for it; the 'ifrit had been watching, and spirit never slept.

She had eaten, she had drunk; she'd tried to sleep as well, but her body wouldn't be forced despite its aching weariness, nor would her mind be still. She had seen small creatures frozen in terror before a stalking cat; she had heard of captives so numbed with shock that they slept and slept and could hardly be roused, and seemed to sleepwalk when they were. She had envied them, yearned to imitate, but could not; might as well have been 'ifrit herself for all the rest she had.

Not that she would have been let sleep very long, not long enough. Morakh had allowed himself only two or three hours before he stirred, grunted, rose. Julianne had kept her head down, watching in disbelief as he'd assembled his baggage and slung the straps about him, not moving herself, not rearing up in protest until he'd kicked her to it.

'You can't mean to move now. Under that,' with a sweeping gesture to where the sun had been climbing towards its highest and its hottest. Already the horizon had been blurring till she could barely see where sand faded into sky; already the air was drying and burning her throat as the light dried and burned her eyes. No one moved on the desert, while their shadows were this short.

'We will be followed,' Morakh had said abruptly, the first words he'd spoken to her since he took her from Hasan's chamber so long ago, last night. 'While they rest, we move. This will weary them.'

'Weary them, perhaps; it will kill us. Me, at least. Perhaps you can live on a mouthful of water in a killing heat, but I cannot.'

'It is cooler, in the air. We will fly high.'

Had that been meant to reassure her? Probably not. To discomfort her, perhaps; he might have noticed how shy she was of heights. But if he cared little for her reassurance, he likely cared no more for her discomfort. She was a duty to him – as she had been to Blaise on the road to Rhabat, and that really was a long time ago, half a lifetime it felt, two marriages – and he would shoulder her until she could be relinquished. Information only, she'd thought his conversation was, no hidden meanings either way.

She'd still had a bangle on her wrist, part of the bridal treasure that she'd been playing with when Morakh had seized her; she let that slip to the sand as a sign to whoever came in pursuit, and otherwise stood quiescent beside her captor and simply waited as he did for the 'ifrit's claws to snatch them again into the air.

And so it had gone, on and on: flights in sunlight and in the dark, with her body dangling and her eyes tight shut, her mind focused on simple breathing, on staying alive. They'd come to ground more often than she'd expected, though it could never be often enough for her. At every halt she had been given water; at sunset and sunrise the Dancer had made a fire, and baked bread. Her stomach had revolted, her throat had clamped, but she could be strong in this at least, she could force the vile stuff down. She'd tried to leave some token each time, though she had no more jewellery and the simple robe she wore had offered nothing that was clearly hers. A few threads picked from its hem and twisted together with hairs plucked from her scalp, the resultant string knotted into a crude double loop, the sign of the God in whom she had no faith at all: that had been the best that she could manage. Any woman of the tribes who travelled in the Sands would wear such a robe, of that deepest blue that filled the spaces between the stars; her people – Julianne's people now that she was married, married again, so newly married and how careless her husband was of her, to lose her so very quickly – the Sharai claimed it for their own colour, a gift from their own God. Any woman of the Sharai might have hair of such a length, and only a few shades darker than Julianne's; not for the first time in her life she could have wished to be a golden blonde, to leave a clearer message. But surely no woman else would leave the God's sign in this land, for any friendly eye that could find and read it . . .

So she had done what little she could and suffered all else that had come to her, bad food and bad water and the constant, dreadful stare of the 'ifrit, which had seemed to see no more of her leavings than Morakh did, though she'd held her breath in terror every time she dropped another tiny tangle of thread and hair. Every time its claws closed about her she had held her breath again, not to scream aloud as she was wrenched from the grip of solid ground. The effort of forcing air into her constricted lungs had been a blessing, almost, like the effort of keeping her eyes closed against any sight of the long long fall below.

By the time Morakh had used the last of his fuel, there had been scant water left in his skin and less she thought in hers; she'd felt parched and withered, wrinkled like a raisin. Either they must seek a well and a source of firewood, or else they were close to journey's end.

The weight of what was to come had hung over her; she'd felt almost as numb and quiescent as she pretended. She'd known that their direction was westward, ever westward, but not what that might mean. She'd had no vision of the land they travelled over, nor of what might lie ahead. Her inner sight had been as blinded as her eyes, and almost as deliberately.

It had been late and getting later in the day when she realised that they'd finally arrived. She'd learned by then to tell when they were climbing, when flying level and when falling – no, not falling, coming down to land. It hadn't all been chaos and terror in the air; now it could be terror understood, precisely calibrated.

So she'd known that the 'ifrit was descending, but what of that? It had done the same a dozen times already. She'd waited for the impact of crusted sand beneath her bare feet, the jolt that would knock her to her knees or send her sprawling. This time, though, they had plunged into a sudden, utterly unexpected shadow a moment or two before they hit; and what they hit had not been sand. Sandy, to be sure, but there had been level stone beneath the grit. The shock of it had made her yelp aloud; it had also jerked her eyes open against her will, as she'd fallen and rolled. She'd glimpsed walls, sky, more walls before she came to rest on her belly, aching and shaking all over.

Some kind of courtyard, long disused: they were stone flags that she had landed on, but they were cracked and broken under their coat of sand. Desert cold had been at them, since they were laid. Sitting up slowly, Julianne had seen rough-worked stones strewn around, where they had fallen from the height of the walls. Likely an earthquake had done that damage: it would take generations of frosts to do so much, cracking the mortar and shifting the stones fraction by fraction with every year that passed. She didn't think these walls had stood long enough. Even in the deep shadows of the courtyard there were tool-marks to be seen, the scars of axe and chisel surviving on the stones; they looked quite fresh, cruder work than the Ransomers had made of the Roq but surely no older . . .

Then she'd felt Morakh's deformed hand grip the back of her neck. She had shuddered, once for the simple chill of his touch and again for what must follow, what she had experienced once already, when once had proved too much for any girl to bear.

His four fingers had seemed to sink through her skin and flesh, altogether into the bone of her; she'd thought she could feel his mind whisper against the beat of her blood, an alien rhythm that overrode her own. She'd felt uprooted, disinherited, soul thrust from its native throne; she'd lost all possession of her body, as she had in the water-channels and on the cliffs of Rhabat.

The sickness had closed in on her in swirling pools of colour, colours that ought not to exist, that she could not have given a name to if she tried. Perhaps she ought to try, perhaps she should list all the colours that she knew, give a focus to her thoughts: *no, that is not violet, nor umber.* She couldn't do it, though, could only slip and fall through oily nothingness, fall endlessly where there was nothing solid to be clung to . . .

It had been a long time, the longest time imaginable before she realised that she had ceased to fall. The stillness that engulfed her after was so absolute and so welcome, it took her a while longer to understand it. Only a sudden, desperate need dragged her mind back from its drifting; she felt herself shaking, gasping, rearing up against a terrible weight, and only as she dropped back, only the lancing pain as her head cracked against stone told her that her body was her own again. That was the heaviness she felt, the weight of bone and muscle. She'd forgotten almost how to breathe; that had been the need that had seized her.

She lay quite still again, but consciously so now, deliberately taking all the time necessary to fit body and mind together, to make them one again, her own, herself. For a while she did nothing but breathe, forcing herself not to pant for it: to take in air and expel it slowly, steadily, to enjoy it as she never had before. It tasted dull, dusty, stale, but no matter. She could enjoy that too.

Then she reached out into the extremities of her skin, fingers and toes, stirring them lightly, checking that each twitched and danced to her own command and no one's else.

Satisfied, she opened her eyes at last; and thought herself blind, perhaps, thought Morakh had stolen her sight from her and kept it for himself. She needed yet more time to understand that it was dark in here, wherever here was; and that she was lying on her side and facing what might be a wall or a corner. She couldn't see it, but she reached out a cautious hand to check and was thrilled beyond measure when her fingers' tips touched stone just a hand's span from her face.

It took an effort, a tremendous effort to move more than that. She was scared of shaking herself loose from her body again, she felt so ill-attached. But she edged over onto her back and stared upward, and saw light.

Only a little light, a high horizontal bar of blurry grey; that was enough for now, that was dazzling glory. She thought that any more would have burned her.

She turned her head the other way and saw two glowing red coals looming high above her, set in uttermost black; and that was the opposite of glory, that was despair, to recognise that she shared her cell with the 'ifrit.

It didn't move, and neither did she. It didn't blink, although she had to; trying to outstare a monster was no game for a grown woman, but she played it regardless, if only to prove to herself that she wasn't scared. She'd never been alone with the creature before, but her sudden shortness of breath was just a brief slip of control, no more than that. She'd tried too much, too soon; she was still uncertain in her body, forgetful of what used to happen naturally. She could breathe like a normal girl, if she concentrated: in and out, in and out, there, like that. She wasn't afraid of the thing, why should she be? If it hadn't killed her in the days they'd spent en route, it wouldn't do so now. They were alone together, but nothing else had changed . . .

Were they alone? She wondered, briefly. There was no sign or sound of Morakh in the dim light and the dead air of this chamber, but he could be still when he chose, he could be sitting directly behind her . . .

She was proud of herself for not jerking round to see, for sitting up slowly and turning her head as though there were no hurry in the world. There was certainly no Morakh. Now that her eyes were adjusting, she could make out the low shape of a door in the wall at her back, but nothing else. She had been right, then, this was a cell and she was a prisoner; and her guard shared the cell with her, its glossy, ill-formed body cramped and awkward in this enclosed space. It had crouched as best it could into a corner but still took up half the floor, more. It made no sound, no creak of shifting chitin, no scrape of claw on stone, no stir of breath; its hot gaze never moved from Julianne.

She wasn't afraid of it, no. She was just slow, that was all, still disorientated, uncertain of her strength and its uses; no other reason why it seemed so hard to move herself, to stand and walk those few short paces to the door. Of course she didn't think the 'ifrit would pounce as soon as she twitched a muscle, of course she knew it wasn't going to eat her . . .

She'd seen a man, a known thief downed by a trained hound once in Marasson. She'd seen, felt, smelled his terror at the steady rumble of its growling, the bared fangs an inch from his throat and held back only by its obedience. Many times she'd seen the palace cats and the mice they played with, how often there'd been no pleasure in the game because the little things wouldn't scamper but only stood immobile, fixed with fear. But she was not a mouse, far from it; and this spirit-creature might desire her death – if spirit could know desire – but it would not kill her now. Orders or instinct or plotting restrained it. She was captive, bait perhaps, a ransom-prize but no worse than that. Not a victim, not a corpse.

Not yet a corpse, and moving would not make her so. And so at last she stood, deliberately with her back to the 'ifrit to show how very much she scorned it, how little she was afraid. Those messages might be too subtle for the thing to read, but not for her; right now she mattered more.

She stood – a little dizzy, a little off-balance, her body still seeming not to fit too well – and shuffled her way to the door. It was locked or barred, of course, she was a prisoner. The 'ifrit too, then: but the 'ifrit apparently had no reason to leave, so long as she was there.

Questing fingers and eyes that squinted in the gloom could find no handle and no hinge, only the heavy wooden planking and the iron studs that held it all together. Patiently she picked at each with her nails, hoping to find one loose enough to draw out, a spike to make a weapon that might dim those fierce eyes that watched her as she picked. They were an 'ifrit's only weakness unless you had a blade blessed by a priest, which she did not. Or unless you were a djinni with a sea at your command, which she was not. She wasn't sure that a door-nail would be enough to kill the creature, and was fairly sure that it would kill her first in any case; still, she thought she might like the chance to try. If things turned out that way, if there came no sign of friends, husbands, rescue . . .

No surprise, though, that none of the nails would come to the picking of her own. It was a well-made door: solid timber neither green nor ancient, no hint of worm or rot that her fingers could discover and no sign of any give when she leaned all her weight against it.

She didn't pound her fists or kick it, nothing so petulant; she'd found what she expected and felt almost satisfied by that, almost pleased that her enemies hadn't let her down. She liked a puzzle, a challenge, something worthy of her father's daughter. Which was why she wouldn't simply sit and wait for rescue after all; Elisande would not, and she couldn't bear to be thought more feeble than her friend. Besides, what better way to prove that she was not scared of the 'ifrit, than to kill it or evade its guard?

With the door so solidly closed against her and the light so high out of reach – and barred too, she saw, staring upward: it was a window the length of a man's arm, perhaps, and half that height, and barred with iron to prevent her leaving even if she stood on the 'ifrit's back to get there – she wondered why she was being quite so closely watched. No surprise that the 'ifrit were single-minded, she'd never thought of them as subtle creatures; but she could see no way out of here, so why did it waste its time? It might have all of time to play with, but even so . . .

She sat against the wall, as far as she could come from those eyes, and closed her own to shut them out, and thought about it. Not long, no need to strain, she hadn't turned stupid yet. Among her rescuers – if she waited for them, if they came – she could count three at least who could walk into a locked cell to claim her and then lead her out without chipping wood or stone or iron, without leaving a mark to show that they'd been. Her own father might step out of a golden nimbus at any moment, and she was a little surprised that he hadn't yet, she'd not thought him so slow.

Marron could cross back and forth between one world and another; she'd like to visit the land of the djinn, she thought, even with that boy for company. And then there was Elisande, whose temper might not break down doors of its own accord, but certainly could when it was allied to her djinni's. They could come like Marron from that other world, and spirit her away there; she thought it more likely that they would come through the wall, and leave more than a mark behind.

Except, of course, that the 'ifrit was here, and the djinni at least should know that if the others didn't. Elisande's Djinni Tachur liked to present itself as a poor stunted creature, cut off from the intangible current of spirit knowledge; Julianne wasn't at all convinced. She thought if that were true, then the djinni would have appeared long ago, riding the storm of her friend's fury to snatch her back to safety. That it hadn't come must surely mean that it knew an 'ifrit was keeping her company. A djinni and an 'ifrit couldn't meet in anger, without both being destroyed.

So no, as long as the 'ifrit was guarding her, she thought that the djinni would not come. Nor her father, nor Marron: the 'ifrit would be ready for either. It had changed its shape, she saw, as her eyes opened of their own accord to assess it better, to understand its threat. The cumbersome wings had gone, been resorbed into the body of the beast; it was armed now with giant claws like a lobster's, poised to grip and crush any man that ventured here in the moment of his appearance. She hoped that she was right about the djinni, that it would know and warn her friends; she'd rather be abandoned to her fate than see them come and try to save her, try and die . . .

She wouldn't abandon herself, though. If she couldn't be rescued, she'd simply have to escape. Despite the 'ifrit, despite Morakh's lurking presence somewhere beyond the door, despite whatever else might come.

The 'ifrit were said to share the djinn's foreknowledge; perhaps it knew in advance what she might try, and would forestall her. Perhaps it knew that its simple watchful presence would be enough. A never-sleeping monster should be adequate to guard an unarmed girl.

But no prescience was absolute, even the djinn could be mistaken or misunderstand. She would think and watch and plan, however fancifully. The 'ifrit might leave her alone eventually, Morakh might leave the door unlocked and unguarded, she might find a hidden tunnel beneath the flags she sat on where a slender girl could wriggle out and her dreadful guardian not. There might be another earthquake, to bring the walls down and crush her captors and let her walk away . . .

Or not; but anything might happen, and she swore to be ready if it did. In the meantime she rested, she closed her eyes once more against the glare of the 'ifrit, she forced her mind to think.

It would be useful, obviously, to know where she was. She could work that out even in the dark. She knew more than the history of the Sanctuary Land, thanks to her father's training, although she'd barely seen its northern borders. She'd gleaned clues enough, from the glimpses she'd had in the courtyard and her brief exploration of this cell; she thought now that she could touch a finger to a map and say with confidence, 'This is where I am.'

All that she'd seen – the high walls with their battlements, the blunt square design of the doorway here, the way the door itself was made – all of that was her own people's work, no question. The Catari did not build in such a fashion; the Sharai did not build at all. This was a Patric castle, then; and yet it was in the desert still, by all the blown sand in the court, not in Outremer proper. And it had been deserted, abandoned, some time since. She could think of only one place that answered such description; and that lay west of Rhabat and still east of the border, and perhaps she should have thought of it before.

When the Sanctuary Land was won again for the God, the Ekhed who had been rulers there were driven out entirely. The settled Catari by and large accepted their new Patric overlords, finding them little harsher and in some cases kinder than what had gone before, or so Julianne's father had told her; their wild nomadic cousins the Sharai could be held back in the deep desert, on the far side of the mountain ridge that made a natural eastern border for the Kingdom. Raiding-parties were commonplace, from both sides, but a fragile and unofficial truce developed quickly, supported by both trade links and diplomacy.

Except that there was one ancient settlement only a short distance to the east of the mountains, from where there was swift and easy access to the valley principality of Surayon, and from there to all of Outremer. The lords of the Kingdom were reluctant to leave it in the hands of the Sharai; they sent a force to seize it. The Sharai tribe that claimed that land tried to retake it time and again, was beaten back time and again. The Patrics built a castle; the sheikhs, united at last – the place had religious importance to them, as well as trading wealth – sent an army to lay siege. The Patrics were starved out and surrendered, returning to Outremer under safe conduct; the Sharai occupied the castle until the Duke of Ascariel led his own men back to retake it.

And so it had gone on, turn and turn about, until Surayon vanished within the mystery of its Folding. Now the castle was more isolated than before and men of the Kingdom more unhappy within its walls, seeing enemies on all sides and malign magic at their backs. Given the rumours of collusion between Surayon and the Sharai, the nobles were doubly reluctant to lose their outpost, but they found it ever harder to garrison. The King would say nothing about it; at length they sent their own emissaries to Rhabat, and made a formal truce with the sheikhs. The settlement should live as it had since time immemorial, a place of prayer and trade; the Sharai would not occupy it, and neither would the Patrics. The castle would stand empty, as a sign of good faith from both parties.

And so it had, so far as Julianne knew – until now, at least. This must be that castle; there was no other.

It was called Revanchard, a name that raised doubt and suspicion throughout the Kingdom: who knew, who could say what evil the sorcerers of Surayon might not be working there, or their cohorts the devilish Sharai?

Julianne knew, Julianne could say. Nothing, and nothing. There was only dust and rubble and emptiness, and now a girl, a fanatic and an 'ifrit.

It seemed to Imber as though he were losing time, growing younger, falling back through years almost as fast as the weeks passed around him. He felt himself fifteen again, passionate and helpless: mired in humiliation, caught constantly between tears and rage and able to indulge himself in neither.

Only his physical body had not changed, and even that was faithless. He craved to be sick, to have a killing fever that might legitimately keep him private in his grief and would make his family sorry to have lost him later. Instead he was robust, thriving, pale only in anger or sorrow; which meant that he was pale all the time except when he was blushing, which meant that he alternated all the time between white and scarlet, and even his skin was an accursed traitor.

His father, his uncle, his cousins: all had shown him a combination of sympathy and fury in their several different manners, and all had brought the blood rushing to his face every time their eyes met his, because he knew what they were thinking, what they were saying between themselves in their several different voices. *Imber the love-lorn, marries the girl and can't keep her, she ran away before the wedding and ran again after, straight after their wedding-night, and he pines over her posy because he cannot find her when he should be raging at the insult to himself, to all his family, to us . . .*

He blushed because it was cruel, and also because it was true. Sometimes he could be angry with Julianne for fleeing him, for making such a public mock of him; and yet he loved her, he wished her nothing but well, he wished that he could find her to offer whatever aid was in his power, to bring her out of what trouble she was in. Then he was angry with his family for their blindness, for their being concerned only with honour when his girl must be in need of help. And yet he had loved them all his life, collectively they were still his wisdom as they always had been, and when he was rational he saw that they were right in this, that it was wilfulness and nothing more that took her from him, and insult that she left behind . . .

He hadn't been so muddled in his thinking since the year of his manhood, the year of first blood on his sword and first girl in his bed; but that wasn't the only reason why he felt so displaced in time suddenly, why he could fling back the flap of his tent in the mornings and almost feel an urge to rub a hand through his beard, to check his height against the pole and be sure of the ring on his smallest finger, to reassure himself that the last four years of growth, maturity, marriage had not been merely a dream.

He was young yet, but he had been younger; and not since then had he woken to days like this, days of tension and confusion and embarrassment all blended together to keep him in a ferment, when he was glad of simple things to do to keep his mind from chasing phantoms far away.

Simple things like fetching his own breakfast from the fire, and eating on his feet with his confrères; like harnessing his own horse for the day's ride and grooming it at sunset, even cleaning his own tack under the stars. Troopers saw to the pitching of his tent, but he would gladly have done that too if he hadn't been so aware of his cousin Karel's eye on him in his shame.

Even the land they rode through was a reminder of his youth. At that age he'd been sent to ride the southern border of Elessi for a year with the regular patrol, wild lands and a rough apprenticeship for the future Count. Now he was back, watchful and anxious as he had been then, feeling the weight of another's critical gaze just as he had before. Then it had been the sergeant's, who commanded that patrol; now it was his cousin's, who commanded this.

Imber had spent days searching uselessly for Julianne, after her flight. Finding no certain sign of her, no trail that he could follow, he had at last returned to his father's house in Elessi to face the court's politeness, his uncle's rudeness, his own desperate puzzlement at how he had made Julianne so unhappy.

It had been pure relief when rumours reached the city about strange movements among the Sharai, all the sheikhs gathered at Rhabat and their tribesmen following. It must mean war, rumour and logic both agreed; and what more likely than a strike against Elessi, the hammerhead, the most vulnerable of all the states of Outremer? Let the Sharai but win Elessi, and they could ride into Tallis and so down all the length of the Kingdom, killing as they went . . .

Ambitious sheikhs had tried the same before, and had been rebuffed with many losses; Elessans were the finest soldiers the King had, everyone knew that. But they'd never had to face all the tribes united. It had been divisions among the Sharai, blood-feuds between tribe and tribe that had kept Outremer secure until now.

Every man who could be spared from other duty was ordered to the borders, north and east and south, especially south, where the desert rubbed its hot muzzle against unprotected farmland. No mountains here, to make a wall to guard.

Imber had leaped at the chance to ride with Karel and his troop: to leave squire and servants behind with the gossiping, fractious court, to leave fretful father and sour uncle to their maps and arguments, to spend the days staring into a searing dust-laden wind and half the nights sitting up with his cousin, twitching at every natural sound and trying never, never to think of Julianne. He almost hoped that the Sharai would come and find him; better to lose his life, he thought, than to lose the girl he loved. At least he could understand that, a bitter fight and bitter steel's touch at the end of it and so a sudden peace and no more blushing, if all his blood were let run out . . .

And that again was fifteen-year-old thinking, and he knew it; and thought it anyway, thought it deliberately, trapped in some strange mood between misery and defiance.

This day – riding miserably, defiantly a little distance ahead and to the south of Karel and the troop, courting danger and making a childish point of it, which his cousin was pointedly indulging – he scanned the smudged horizon as he had done times without number and saw nothing of what he hoped for, neither a moving shadow which might be a Sharai outrider nor a moving shadow which might be his Julianne unaccountably returning, as she had unaccountably left.

Closer to him, though, something was moving, and did snag his eye; anything that moved in this drear, dead landscape was unusual, and potentially a threat.

This was only a dust-devil, though, a slender twisting pillar; he'd seen a dozen such since he came south. One had struck their campsite in the night, and ripped Karel's tent from its moorings. He watched this one for lack of anything else to fix his eyes on, and registered slowly that it was heading directly towards him. He nudged his mount to the side, out of its path – and saw it veer, and realised that it was moving against the wind, which surely ought not to be possible. Unless it was some trick of the Sharai, some touch of sorcery, a wicked conjuration sent against him . . . ?

He turned his horse with a yell, saw how far he'd wandered from his companions and thought himself lost, even as he dug in his spurs. He had a moment to regret his bravado – this was not what he'd wanted even if he'd truly wanted that, there was neither honour nor satisfaction in being slain by a magical sending, without the chance to face an adversary blade to blade – and then the swirling cloud swept past him, steadied, and spoke.

It spoke his name, but he had no time yet to wonder at it; he was busy with his horse, which was rearing, screaming, terrified. It was all he could do to stay mounted; the beast backed away, entirely out of his control.

The dust-devil, apparition, whatever it might be hung motionless, except that its body was constantly in motion, a spiralling rope of dust and air. It stood between him and the troop. His horse was fighting the bit, straining to turn, to flee – but flight would take it and him south, where any evil might be waiting. Imber used spurs, reins, his mailed fist, everything he had to hold it still. When at last it subsided, quiescent and trembling, he lifted his head to face the devil, and heard it say his name again.

'Imber von und zu Karlheim, your wife has need of you.'

Imber blinked, stared; its voice was high and carrying, quite inhuman.

'I – I do not know what you are.' His own voice came out only as a whisper, it could surely not have covered the distance between them, except that the creature replied instantly.

'I am the djinni Esren Filash Tachur, and this is my message to you, that I am sent to carry: that your wife Julianne, who is daughter to the King's Shadow, is in need. If you would come to her aid, ride south to Selussin, to the castle called Revanchard. Ride swiftly; her peril is great, I am told to say. It may be true. The future is dark to me, but I at least cannot save her.'

'Wait . . . !' he cried, too late; there was a sudden soft fall of dust, and he could see nothing before him except Karel thundering forward on his giant destrier.

Imber pulled off his mailed gauntlet, ran his hand over the prickling cold sweat on his face, and wondered what in the world he should say to his cousin.

5

A Healing Possession

Blaise had thought that nothing could frighten him more than the company he kept these days, until he made his first journey into the King's Eye. When he was there, he thought that nothing would ever frighten him more than simply being in that place; now he thought that he'd been twice wrong. Soon he would have to go back there, to report his failure to the man who had sent him on this mission. He dreaded facing Magister Fulke, to confess that failure; he thought that the marshal's anger would be a more frightening thing than any that he'd yet seen.

He had called them a rabble, the people that he followed, but that wasn't strictly true. A rabble is disorganised, and loud. This was neither. The preacher led and his disciples marched behind – like an army, almost, except that it was an army of the poor, dressed in rags and lacking weapons. More like penitents in a procession, then, silent and involved, their thoughts turned to holy matters. Except that the preacher only ever spoke about Surayon, the need to crush heresy, to bring the God's light to unbelievers. Which made it an army indeed, intent on victory, though Blaise had no idea how that victory could ever be achieved. It was all a mystery to him, as much now as it had been on the first day; and that was his failure, that he was so frightened to admit.

He walked behind the procession like a camp-follower, he was so far reduced; and he was just one among the many, many who did the same. These really were a rabble. Some were relatives of those the preacher had healed. They had seen their husbands or wives or children called back from certain death, had seen them rise up and abandon family and village and all to follow the preacher, and had felt drawn to follow in their turn. Blaise had spoken to a few of them; he'd seen and heard and to some extent shared their confusion, their distress. Their loved ones shunned their company and would not speak. Those whom the preacher healed might as well have died, he thought, for all the good their resurrection did.

Others among his companions had heard the preacher speak, and answered more simply to the call. Men and boys largely, they had seized what few weapons they owned or could improvise and set off to do what the long generation of their fathers had failed to do. They would pit knives against nothing, mattocks against magic, and Surayon would open before them like a flower to a probing bee, because the preacher said it would.

And then there were those who would follow any band of men, for what gain or comfort they could find; and those who would follow any voice that cried to them to follow, wherever it might lead.

And among them all – the worried and the warriors, the

women and the weak – there was Blaise, who was one alone and quite unlike any whom he walked beside. Both worried and a warrior, neither woman nor weak and yet he felt so, he might as well be both for all the good he could accomplish here. Sent for a spy, he had foundered beyond rescue. The preacher spoke to no one when he was not preaching, and his disciples spoke to no one at all. What could a man uncover, in the face of such inhuman silence?

Nothing, nothing at all. Blaise had known and lived under the strictures of the Ransomers' Rule, with its penalties for idle or inappropriate talking; he knew how young men kept such rules, and how they broke them also. Since he left the Order he had served on the borders of Elessi, he had fought raiders and been a raider himself. He could hear a voice's whisper in a wind; as the sergeant of a young troop, he had learned to read the movement of a finger or the twitch of an eye, to know when lads were sending messages under the uttermost silence of his glare.

There was none of that here, nothing at all. The disciples, the healed ones walked at a steady pace all day, behind the preacher who led them; they spoke not a word, they passed not a sign between them. Nor a mouthful to eat, nor to drink. They would eat at dawn and at day's end if they were offered food – and they were, always, by villagers or family – but they showed no hint of need between. Even the hardest-trained army would sling waterskins along the line when the sun was high, and whatever dried meat or biscuit fell to hand, something to chew against the tedium of the road and the heat and the ache of wounds, perhaps, the bite of blisters. These, not. When they marched, they marched and did nothing other. As when they sat – in the evenings, in the villages, around a fire or a well while the preacher spoke – they sat and did nothing other, until they were fed or sent away to sleep. They did seem to listen to the preacher, but Blaise thought that it was only seeming. He thought that man's words fell as far short of them now as their wives' words did, or their brothers'. It wasn't to them or for their sake that he spoke, in any case; they were his already, as though he claimed their souls in payment for their lives.

Reluctantly, whipped into something fearful by his greater fear of Magister Fulke, Blaise limped ahead of the murmuring crowd. He'd had to change his good soldier's boots for a poor man's sandals when he put on this guise of a landless labourer; the straps had rubbed his heels raw, the thin rope soles were no protection against the sharp stones of the road and every step was a fresh reminder of futility.

He walked forward, to join the tail of the disciples' lines. For a while he made his way beside them, as silent as they were themselves; not a head lifted, not an eye turned aside to find him. He might have been invisible, a ghost in a parade of ghosts.

Eventually, he came up next to a boy whose name he knew, whom he'd had some conversation with just two nights earlier. It happened sometimes that the disease tracking ahead of them would turn suddenly to snap at their heels; that those who followed would wake in the morning to find one of their number weak and lethargic, unable to rise. Then the disciples would come to claim the victim, the preacher would work his abiding miracle in the dawnlight, and there would be one more disciple to trail dumb and obedient in his wake.

No one ever fell sick in the daytime, on the march. Blaise couldn't decide if that was sinister or meaningless. He'd like it to mean something; he'd like to believe that the preacher gave poison to his victims and then stole their souls while they were weak and failing. That would be a thing to say to Magister Fulke. He couldn't make any sense of it, though, no matter how he strained. If the preacher came slipping through the camp at night, it would be known, however light his tread; if he sent one of his disciples, it would be the talk of all the company. And if he did either one – or if he sent his poison by the birds, if an earthworm carried it, a zephyr – there was still no reason in his choices. Man or woman, young or old: whether in the villages ahead of him or among the followers behind, the sickness struck at random, as a sickness should. Perhaps the man was a monster, perhaps he fed on souls and cared not if they were virgin and innocent or raddled with age and sin; but why drag their emptied bodies behind?

Fess was a boy of fourteen, who reminded Blaise painfully of himself at that same turn of life. Born to be big but born without a father, without name or place in the world, he'd scavenged for bread and begged for work since he was a child; that showed on his skin, tight-stretched over raw bones and muscles like bowstrings, no flesh at all. Too many years of short commons and short sleep, it would take years longer to mend, to fill him out to the man he should have been. Blaise knew.

Like Blaise before him, Fess had been waiting till he was old enough to be sworn a military man: for the God or for his local lord, no matter. But then the preacher had come and Fess had seen a way to overleap his age, to be blooded young and so present himself a soldier ready-made.

He'd followed the march with the light of that ambition in his eyes, a burning hunger when Blaise had spoken to him, and thrilling at the chance to make it happen. Thrilling at the food, too, surrendering a lifelong hunger, eating with both hands at every halt. The villagers were generous, with their storehouses full of that year's second crop; or else they were afraid, such a rabble dogging such a strange parade and camping in their fields or their lord's pastures. Fear could make anyone open-handed, however little they had to spare. If Fess fancied that a soldier always ate like this – well, he would learn. And regard the lesson lightly, no doubt. Even barrack fare would seem like feasting, after a diet of cabbage-water and scorched grains gleaned from others' fields. Blaise knew.

Blaise had helped the boy to treat and dress a gash on his forehead, the result of a stone flung by a nervous goatherd; just a small cut, but it bled freely as scalp-wounds always do. After that they'd sat half the night over a glowing fire, while Fess talked and Blaise listened, sharing his memories in silence.

The following morning, the boy had lain stiff and still in his blanket, seemingly awake but unstirring, his eyes wide and blank as though his spirit were snared in horror. Blaise had struggled in vain to rouse him, finally had to be pulled away by others as the disciples gathered round. He'd been barely aware of the voices urgent in his ear, 'Let the preacher have him, let him be healed, there's nothing you or any of us can do for him now.' He'd wanted to fight with fists or knife, with whatever it took to keep Fess from a walking nightmare; better to let him die and bury him a stranger in a land where he'd never found a home.

It was only later, too late, that he'd thought he might have put his knife to another use, to help Fess to a speedy death. Instead he'd stood slackly, uselessly, while the boy was snatched up and hurried off to where the preacher waited. He hadn't watched the healing. He'd seen too many of those tainted miracles already; he'd busied himself with sifting through Fess's few belongings, keeping the short sword and rolling the rest into the boy's ragged blanket, which he would carry himself in impotent fury at the preacher, at the world, above all at himself. Once more he'd failed, the boy had needed saving and Blaise had let him slip.

So now he walked beside Fess, or the semblance of Fess. The boy looked as well as ever he had, and yet he looked utterly different, almost unrecognisable as he paced steadily along on stiff, inexhaustible legs. He used to walk with an ungainly slouch, awkward yet in his growing body; now he carried himself almost like the soldier he'd yearned to be, except that it seemed to Blaise as though something else carried him. There was nothing boyish, little that was even human in his gait; his face was blank of any feeling, and his eyes were strangely dark where they had been blue before.

'Fess? How is it with you?'

Nothing, no response.

'Fess, speak to me, lad. It's me, Blaise, I have your things . . .'

Again, nothing. The rough bandage was gone from the boy's head, and only a pale scar showed where the skin had been so badly torn only two days before; the preacher's healing touched more than the sickness. But Blaise had known that already. Cripples walked when they were blessed by the saint's dead hand, the blind moved about without guidance, lepers lost their sores. Whether the power lay in the preacher or in his blessed relic, even that much Blaise had not yet contrived to learn. The only certainty – at least to Blaise's eyes – was that no power passed to the one healed, there was no true strengthening in this medicine.

He believed in miracles, he had to, he had seen them in all their swift brutality; but he was losing his faith in miracle cures. There was nothing holy here. Seized back from death, these bodies had been seized by another's will, and marched to his desire. There was no healing in them, and only the illusion of health; they might as well be the animated dead of heathen tales. The preacher's cause might be sanctified, if he truly meant war against heretic Surayon, but what he had done to achieve it was pure wickedness and could not be forgiven.

Blaise tried again and yet again to speak to Fess, and won not the slightest reaction. In his frustration, he forgot to watch where he was treading; his foot came down on a sharp flint in the road. It cut through the ragged sole of his sandal and bit deeply into his instep. He cried out at the sharp stab of it, and still saw no reaction from Fess or any of the disciples. Hobbling, he lost his place, and was swept up in the following crowd. Someone there passed him a staff to lean on; even with that he could barely keep up, and was soon struggling in the dust at the rear of the march.

The road was roughly made, and it seemed that at every step his foot would come down on a stone, and hurt the more. At last he had to stop, to bind it up; he bound rags around the sandal too, and then around the other to forestall another accident. With both feet lame, he'd lose touch altogether with the preacher and his band. As it was, he had to hasten after with a cripple's gait, using the staff to cover great stretches of ground, hop and swing, before he could catch them up again. He'd been on forced marches that were faster, but not by much. The mountains were a constant high shadow to the east; they'd already passed the border between Tallis and Less Arvon, and another week or so should bring them to where the land was Folded, the impossible, impassable barrier that hid Surayon. What would happen there, Blaise couldn't conjecture. He was only sure that the preacher had an intent, a purpose that was equally hidden. There was something inexorable about their progress, something sinister and significant in the way that they could bypass settlements all day where the people were perfectly healthy; it was only in those villages where they stopped for the night that they found the sickness waiting.

As that night, when they came in the brief dusk to a small community of huts huddled in the foothills' lee, on the banks of a rushing stream. News of their coming had flown ahead of them, as it always did; they found a fire of welcome blazing in the open space between the huts, the village headman on his feet with an awkward speech prepared, and three quiet bodies laid out at his back.

The preacher stepped forward, pushing back his hood; his disciples made a ring around him, the headman, the sick and the fire, encompassing all within their silence. Blaise and his companions pressed close at their backs, and the villagers came shyly, hopefully out to stand in their own quiet knot a little distance off. They were Catari, but that was not unusual; this disease discriminated, it struck largely at the poor, and the poor of Outremer were most of them Catari. Fess had been an exception. Unless it was that the disease picked its places rather than its victims: never a castle or a town, always those convenient settlements a day's hard march ahead, always close to the rising hills but never so close as to slow the preacher's progress. Blaise's people kept mostly to the towns, even after forty years of occupation; out here the lords and their servants kept to their manors, where a rabble like this would be closely watched and questioned. If Blaise had wanted to move a congregation quickly through the country, he would have picked this route or one much like it.

'. . . Holy one, I have said enough. What more? There is only this: we are not of your faith, but our prayers have failed as our medicine has. Can you, will you save our children?'

'I can, and I will.' The preacher's face looked at its finest, its strongest and most noble in this light, all glare and guttering shadows. By day he seemed weaker, more gaunt, half mad; tonight, though, Blaise knew exactly what these hopeful, hungry peasants would be seeing. The high brow and the backswept hair that hung to his shoulders; the eyes that glittered from the blackness of their sunken hollows; the thin lips that snapped at words and were overhung by the great hooked nose that was its own monument. Nameless and potent, he made a striking figure, terrifying in the way that those who hold power and hidden knowledge are always terrifying to the weak and ignorant. Blaise counted himself with the villagers in this; at such a moment he could forget even that Magister Fulke frightened him the more.

'Bring them to me,' the preacher said, and the three still forms were carried forward, by men who flinched back from the touch of his shadow but were still prepared to lay their children at his feet.

These really were children, Blaise saw. Swathed in heavy blankets with only their faces showing, and those veiled by sickness and the uncertain light, they were indeterminate of gender, but children none the less. The smallest would stand only half the height of a man – even a short Catari man – if it could or would stand at all. Now, not; but it would do shortly. Nothing could be more certain.

The village folk must be less certain, they hadn't seen what Blaise had; but still they'd give their children over into alien hands, to an alien religion even, sooner than watch them die. Blaise thought he'd let any son or daughter of his go to death and paradise, before he'd let them go to a Catari priest for a dubious healing. But then, Blaise was not a father. Nor a husband, nor ever an acknowledged son; he knew that he didn't understand the kind of love that knotted families together. There were parents among the camp-followers who thought their healed children monsters, possessed, perverted, irredeemable. Blaise had heard them say so. And yet they followed where the preacher led, where the army marched, many miles from home towards a war that was nothing of theirs. It must be some tie of flesh that dragged them, a need that clung day after hopeless day, to keep gazing on a face they'd loved even when the spirit was long lost.

And every night they gathered around a fire such as this,

they watched this same scene played out time and time again with others' children, or grandmothers, or lovers. And they did nothing, said nothing, held their hands as still as their tongues when he thought they should have been screaming warnings, fighting to prevent another family from suffering as they did. He didn't believe that the pain could be easier, for being shared. There was an expression that Blaise had heard from the Catari, they spoke of white bones walking when they meant that a man was sure to die. Here it made a different, a terrible kind of sense. Himself, he'd willingly fling earth to cover the face of a dead friend sooner than see that face stare blindly into the sun as it hauled its shadow south. But he was a man alone, and most people were a mystery to him.

The preacher crouched above the children's silence. His long fingers reached to unpeel their coverings and the clothes they wore beneath, to show the dull grey slackness of their skin that even the fierce firelight couldn't enliven. Then he slipped a hand inside his own rough robes to pull forth the talisman that had brought them all this far, and would take them further yet.

A blessed relic, he said it was, the mummified hand of a long-dead saint that he had recovered from a cave in the wilderness. The instrument of his healing, he said it was, that also. Blaise had never seen it close; from this distance, from any distance it looked like a claw struck from some bird of myth and monstrosity. Black and twisted, glinting strangely, that dead thing caught the light and played with it as the living victims of the sickness could not. It had seemed bigger once, at the first healing that Blaise had witnessed; he remembered how everything had seemed bigger and more important when he was a child, and thought that he was ageing faster now.

There was nothing, almost nothing to the miracle itself. If this were true salvation — a life drawn back from the very mouth of hell, a soul's second chance gifted by the God's grace, the touch of a saint and the word and the prayer of a preacher — then there ought to be ritual, Blaise thought, there ought to be ceremony and more. A sight of the God Himself, perhaps, His voice in the thunder and His eyes' glare in the lightning of a storm. Something so momentous ought to rive rocks and send birds wheeling, screaming under a sky ripped like silk to let the stars fall down . . .

Instead of which, the preacher simply bent above the slack and heedless bodies, one by one. He muttered something that Blaise had never yet been able to hear, for all the nights of trying; he stretched down to touch the children's lips with the desiccated fingers of his saintly, shrivelled hand; he stepped away.

And one by one, in the order of their touching, the children stirred. One by one they sat up, ungainly in their all-but-abandoned bodies; one by one they rose slowly to their feet to stand naked in the firelight and silence.

That was all there was to see, figures and movement and stillness among the ever-shifting shadows. Blaise listened more than he watched, trying even yet to learn something, anything that he could offer to his master. He listened hardest in the moments of healing, but there wasn't so much as a tightening of breath from the children, a sudden catch on slippery life or a gasp at the snatching of their souls.

As they rose up, the quiet was absolute. They didn't speak, and neither did the preacher; nor the disciples, of course, nor the camp-followers who had seen it all before, so often seen it all, and had each of them their own reasons to hold their tongues; nor the gaping villagers, crushed mute by the casual impact of a wonder.

At last something snapped abruptly in the fire's heart, snapping also that endless moment that had caught them all like insects in amber. It broke the silence and the stillness both. The villagers surged forward, voices rising, crying in their own tongue that Blaise had never learned to understand; the preacher flung his arms out, his hands upraised to halt them, as he always did.

'Back, be still!'

They had come no nearer than the circle of disciples in any case, those dumb servants would let no rabble through; still, his voice and gesture quelled their rush. A few women were shrieking yet, mothers or aunts at a guess, but the rest were quiet if they could not be still, shifting restlessly on their feet, impatient to hear what he would say to them. They were his dogs for now, if he would use them so.

It seemed for a while as though he would not use them at all. He turned his back on the mass of villagers, and spoke to their children only.

'Dress yourselves,' he said, and they did, in the patched and tattered robes they'd worn beneath their shrouding blankets.

Then, 'What will you do?'

It took them a while, as it seemed, to find their voices. The words when they did come were slurred and tumbled across each other, though every child said the same and they were trying to speak together.

'We will follow you, preacher.'

'You hear them?' He turned around slowly, arms stretched wide. 'They came when I called, when I touched them with this holy relic; now they say they will follow me, although they do not know where I lead. That is faith, pure faith; they give themselves into my hands, from whom they have received blessing. That is as it should be. How many of you will do the same, when I tell you of the blessings that await you . . . ?'

There was protest, of course, there was the wailing of women, but Blaise had heard the same from what might as well have been the same women, night after night. He thought they wailed by rote, because it was expected of them. He gave it no more heed than the preacher did, or any who followed him, or the men of the village. The disciples sat down in their ordered circle and everyone else shadowed their movement, sitting behind in groups and clusters and huddles. Only the preacher remained on his feet. His voice cut easily through the women's noise, seeming to separate them from their distress as they were already separated from their menfolk, so that they fell quickly silent.

'Your children have been touched by evil,' the preacher said, 'and saved only by the touch of the God. They are not the first. Here with me are many others who have suffered the same, and have been equally blessed. More were not so fortunate; many have died before I could reach them, and their souls have been lost to eternity. This wickedness is spawned in Surayon, the cursed land of which you will have heard. It lies to the south, hidden by sorcerers. We are the God's weapon, which he will hurl against it like a spear from His own hand. Follow me, and I will lead you to a place from where we can strike deep into the heart of impiety, cleanse the poison from this our land, free all our children from the kiss of demon's breath . . .'

And more, much more, but Blaise had heard it all before. And much like it from Magister Fulke at the Roq. Once he'd been rapt, he was still persuaded; he simply didn't need to listen any longer.

He wished that once, just once someone would challenge the preacher, would ask the question that burned always in the back of his own mind: how a ragtag band of dreamers such as this could hope to do what a generation of lords and their armies had failed at, time and again. Surayon was small, to be sure, just a fingernail's width torn from every map he'd seen. Even so, these few could never overrun it if they'd been a well-armed military force. The preacher had a faith that blazed, and Blaise himself believed devoutly in the power of the God; but he was a soldier yet, and he believed also in the simple power of the sword, the weight of men in battle. There were fewer swords here than there were strong men, and those were few enough. Women and children outnumbered them; they added nothing, made only an extra burden, a weakness.

While he was sure that justice must eventually come to Surayon, and that it must come with the God's blessing, Blaise could not see that blessing here. He looked at the disciples and saw the soul-stolen, empty shells. Nor was he alone in that; and yet people followed regardless, and no one questioned the preacher.

When he came to unbind his foot that night, he ripped scabs away with the rags, wincing at the sudden sting of it and then again at the sight of fresh blood oozing from the cut. He'd been hurt before, and far worse, but a soldier needed his feet in good condition. So, self-evidently, did a spy.

Still, let it bleed. Let it wash out whatever dust and grit had worked its way inside during the day's march. He'd seen a man with his leg swollen up to the girth of a tree-trunk; when Blaise had cut into it to release the poison, he'd found a speck of black in the flood of yellow pus, a grain of dirt, the pearl in the oyster. Hard to believe that so much harm could come from such a small invader, but so it was, or so the doctors told him. And greater harm even than he'd seen: the man had died despite his rough surgery.

Perhaps that was what the preacher meant for Surayon, if the preacher meant anything at all, if he saw anything other than himself swathed in lightnings and striking heretics down with a glare. Perhaps he thought that his small force could poison somehow, ulcerate, keep the eyes and minds of the sorcerers turned inward so that they neglected to hide their borders. A greater army could come in to purge the valley princedom – and there was a greater army, that much Blaise knew. Marshal Fulke was marching with the Ransomers and many men else, more daily. That might have been the preacher's plan, it might have been joint strategy except that so far as he knew, the preacher had no inkling of that other force and certainly no contact with it.

No, there was no organisation in this. The man was mad, was all. Mad and gifted, and a holy fool withal; but a sanctified madman was still mad, and his disciples were the echo of himself, mindless and stumbling towards they knew not what.

No more did Blaise know; and Magister Fulke would ask him, ask him soon, and he would have no answer. That frightened him, more than any of the company he kept. He wrapped himself up in his blanket and in Fess's too, aware tonight of how cold it could be just the other side of the mountains. They held back the desert as a sea-wall holds the sea, but it seemed to him that desert air was slipping over, slopping over the brim, bringing the touch of desolation with it. He laid his head on good damp soil and smelled dry sand, and shivered. He closed his ears to the murmur of voices where he knew that mothers were speaking uselessly to their lost children, closed his mind to the future, tried to sleep.

And failed, as he had been certain that he would. His foot throbbed, his soul ached for sick children, deluded adults, himself. He lay on his back, on his side, on his belly; he gazed at the stars, at the dying fire, at nothing at all. Whichever way he lay, he could find no rest; whichever way he looked, he could see no path to glory, no hope for any one of his companions on this mad march. Only failure and death could lie ahead, just as death and failure were all that lay behind him, all his life.

Almost on the wings of that thought came a touch, a cold and clamping kiss on the sole of his foot. No natural cramp, no twinge of pain: he sat bolt upright, staring, and for a moment there seemed to be an eddy of mist around his blankets, that seemed to be sucked suddenly inward through the weave and through the rags he'd wrapped around his foot, as though the cut there had opened like a mouth to draw it in.

Demon's breath, he thought, as the chill of it surged up the bones of his leg, spreading in an instant through all his body. He opened his mouth to cry it aloud, to wake the sleepers all around him; and felt it reach his mind, clouding his sight and numbing his intelligence with a bitter lethargy.

Slowly, slowly he lay back down, as the strength ebbed from his muscles. His blankets had fallen away, when he sat up; he was so cold, he thought vaguely that he ought to reach out and pull them up to cover him again. His arm wouldn't respond, though, and he had no will to force it. He was aware yet, he knew who and what he was – *I am Blaise, I am a soldier and a spy* – but that was all, so little, he felt like a pale flame in a vast night, a spirit cut adrift from his body.

He lost all sense of time's passing. He could see the stars dimly, as though through a fog, and his eyes tracked their course as they wheeled above him. It signified nothing, he didn't understand that nor the gradual brightening in one quarter of the sky, the sudden swift uprising of the sun. He could find the word for it, he had its name but not its meaning now.

There were sounds all about him, as there always had been; they made no more sense than the moving lights did, stars and sun. Again he could identify, but find no pattern; what had been breathing, snores, the single bark of a fox became words, voices, talking. He heard the words, but they could not reach him.

He saw faces, bodies, people leaning above him. These did not talk. He felt himself lifted by many hands. The blueing sky turned over him, or else he turned beneath it, he did not know; the sun glared at him but could not burn through the mist that cloaked his eyes. After a hectic minute he was laid down again. The hands opened all his clothing, and then withdrew; a single figure loomed at his feet. His mind said *preacher*, but he did not understand it.

The figure stooped, reaching a thing towards him. It was black, it glistened like steel where the light struck; it was shaped like a claw, like a ravaged hand, fingers and thumb bent sharply. His mind said *relic*, though he did not know what that meant.

He felt one finger catch at his lip, tugging it downward; he felt something, a hint of nothing solid slide into his mouth. Not solid, but sharp regardless: it lay like a breath of ice against the coldness of his tongue, and was colder yet. His mind said *demon's breath*, and though it was only a name without significance, he still thought it was wrong.

It sank into his tongue and nested there, and seemed to draw everything that was chill in his body towards itself, and so grow still more chill. He felt the first warmth of the sun against his skin, but did not feel warmed by it, only that what hid in his tongue had stolen all the cold that was in him.

His eyes cleared; he could see precisely, the preacher's face with its sunken eyes and its beaked nose. *Beak and claw* he thought, and knew this time what he meant: how the preacher was a hawk, an eagle, fierce and predatory.

'Stand up,' the preacher said, 'and dress yourself.'

He understood the words, and felt his body stirring to obey, though not at his own command. He watched his own fingers fumble with cloth and ties, slow and awkward like a child's hands at an unaccustomed task. He wanted to show them how easy it was, but could find no way to do so.

He'd have liked to say his own name, if only to hear it spoken one more time, just the once; but found that he couldn't quite remember it, as though it were freshly lost. He might have liked to say anything at all, he thought, only that his tongue was cold and heavy, a stone in the mouth and not for talking. Something else was heavy, a weight inside his robe, a duty that had been fearful once. There was a man in a hot land, where there was no sun. The weight was candle; he must light the candle and speak to the man. But there were words to speak first above the candle, and he could not pin them down.

Besides, there was no need to speak where no one listened. His body knew what to do. There were others of its kind all around him, turning now, leading, and it followed, it carried him away.

All day they marched in line and he with them, the disciples, one of them. He left his bedroll behind, and the boy Fess's too, and the sword also. He felt no pain, no weariness; he felt nothing, not even fear. He could see, he could hear, but he was drifting, unconnected, unconcerned.

That evening there was no village, no sick ones to be healed, to be drawn in. Only the preacher, standing on a rock where all could see him in the last of the light. The disciples were clustered close around him, but he spoke over their heads, to the others who packed behind.

'The demon that is in Surayon holds its breath,' he said. 'There will be no more sickness now. Now is the time to run, to be ready to strike when we may. We few will be enough; the God has promised me. Those among you who can keep up, you are welcome; for the rest, follow if you will, do what you can. By the time you reach Surayon, it will lie open before you. Do not be afraid to kill; evil must be burned out, corrupted flesh cut away, or the demon will breathe again.'

He leaped down from the rock in a swirl of robes and began to run steadily into the gathering dark. His path no longer lay due south but south and east, towards the hills. The disciples followed, silent in their lines, their legs rising and falling, feet pounding all in time with the preacher's.

All through the dark they ran and on into the morning, while the land rose and rose beneath and around them. Sunlight showed them peaks and crags, bitter shadows. They ran on.

6

The First Meaning of Flight

If there were three sides to every question, Elisande had never been particularly interested in discovering the other two. She knew where she stood, sometimes she even knew why she stood there. That had always seemed enough to her, and so it ought to have been enough for others, for everyone else.

When it wasn't – well, that was when the fights started.

Where she stood just now, there were three sides to everything, and she hated that. The place even had three names. She thought it stupid, demeaning, and never mind that she had a few herself and had used others freely when she'd needed them; never mind that she had one – her father's daughter, of course she bore his name – that she'd not used in years, that she liked to think of as lying rotted in a grave or in a garden, all overtangled with thorns and rooted through and through, never to be raised up whole again.

People were one thing, places something else. Places, she

thought, should have just the one name, so that everyone knew where you meant and where you meant to go. This place was called Revanchard by the Patrics, for the castle they'd raised on the crag above; it was called Selussin by the Catari, for the ancient wisdom that it shared with all; its own people called it Torkha, and she had no idea what that meant.

Time was when the reputation of Selussin had brought princes across deserts, bearing gifts of gold in fee for the insights of the imam-scholars. Sometimes they brought their sons and left them here a year or two, to acquire religion and wisdom in equal measure. Religion and wisdom and diplomacy; everything here came in threes, and these people could rival Julianne's father in the celebration of manners without commitment. She thought them contemptible. Coren carried power behind his shifting veils, where they carried nothing at all. Empty hands and empty words: they were almost beneath contempt, living on past majesty, the dusty greedy ghosts of better men.

It was years, generations since they'd traded gold or wisdom. Once, convenience and curiosity had brought the caravan-masters here whatever their direction, north or south, west towards Ascariel or eastward to Rhabat. The Patrics' coming and the constant warfare since had broken all those silken ropes; either side might raid a merchant's train, and why risk goods and men and profit when there is always another way to travel, at a slower but safer distance from the sword?

The truce might be holding these days, but all truces break at last. The caravans had left Selussin and not returned; old trails blew themselves away across the sand,

and far-flung princes sent gold-emblazoned letters but kept their sons at home.

Daughters were not to be thought of, not considered. Elisande had passed this way once in her life already, when the world was bright and the future bountiful, except for the dark sucking well of bitterness that was her father. Her grandfather – who understood her waking or sleeping, whom she unconditionally adored – had sent her on the first great adventure of her life, to spend a year alone with the Sharai. *Away from Rudel* had been unspoken, implicit, a golden setting for the jewel. 'Go to Rhabat,' he'd told her, 'and run wild with the children there, while you still have licence to be a child. Let them teach you the city, while their fathers teach you the desert. I have small hope of their mothers teaching you anything a woman ought to know, but they may try. Go to Rhabat, and show them this for surety,' a ring too big for any finger that she owned, so she wore it on a thong around her neck. 'Your way will take you through Selussin; linger there if you like it, but I don't suppose you will. Nor will it like you, unless there's been more change than I can guess at . . .'

He'd been right, both ways. There were many Catari who'd sought shelter in Surayon, before it had been Folded; she'd grown up with their children, and was as comfortable with their ways as with those of her own people. There were Sharai too, who came slipping in and out through the Fold. Those had intrigued her, and she'd always stolen what time she could to spend it in their company. Little girls could claim what was forbidden to those who were older; she'd understood that, and had expected to find the same among any people who followed the same religion.

Not so, she'd discovered, in Selussin. There were schools and libraries and temples, more than she'd ever dreamed to find anywhere outside Ascariel; but they were as closed to girls as they were to women. The priests would not speak to her, seemed not to see or hear her when she spoke to them. The little boys told her to tend the fields as their sisters did, and threw stones at her when she refused to go. One day had been enough to learn that this was no place for her; the week she'd been forced to wait until her Sharai guides were ready to move on had been sheer torture to a curious girl denied any opportunity to explore. One day she'd climbed the hill and wandered through the empty castle, but it had held only dust and walls and darkness, no adventure.

These days it held more, they'd learned that much, though not from the wise ones here. Esren said that it held Julianne.

Julianne and Morakh, naturally, and the 'ifrit. Everything here came in threes.

At least there were no doubts, no questions now. This close, Esren could be certain, or so it said. It didn't need to pick its way hesitantly through a dance of future possibilities, out of step amid forgotten music; what was here was laid out like a map, it said, clear and incontrovertible. Julianne was there, in that looming structure that hung above the township like a thundercloud, like an anvil, storm-grey even when the sun lay full upon it. She was there, and so were the Sand Dancer and the 'ifrit; and so was Esren's destruction, the djinni said, if it should try a rescue. And so was Coren's, and Marron's too. Separately or together, it said, they could not bring her out. It was a baited trap, where death waited; death was sure.

A trap for which of them, and why, it would or could not say. Could not, she thought; its silence was resentful. In its own terms, in its own strange world it staggered about like a drunken beggar, half-blinded and befuddled. That was the impression it gave, at any rate: of a once-proud creature brought low, disabled and disgraced. Even the great djinn were not omniscient, of course – though the one great djinni that she'd met allowed some room for doubt of that, and none for doubt of its abilities – but Esren felt itself stunted, crippled by its long separation from what it called the spirit-weft.

Julianne was there and they were here and helpless, come so far to so little effect, blocked at every turn of the mind's eye, every leap of hope's imagination. It felt right, she thought, for Selussin: walls on all three sides, and an inaccessible darkness at the heart.

But she was not Selussid, and she refused to accept their count of what was possible, any more than she would accept Esren's. The 'ifrit could be no more certain than the djinn, of how any rescue attempt would turn out. She'd seen enough of those creatures die, to know that foreknowledge did not bring invulnerability. All they saw was possibilities, no more. If Esren saw three ways to try for Julianne, and each of them a failure – well, perhaps the 'ifrit could see no more. If she could find a fourth, she might surprise them both.

There was meant to be a fourth already on its way, what they were supposed to be waiting for, why they were wasting so much time and patience in this depressing town. Hasan was coming, with all the tribes of the Sharai. Necessarily he was slow, he lacked a djinni and had to carry water for so many men; it might take him another week to cross the

Sands. He was coming, though, and like the others she pretended that he brought their hopes with him.

Like the others, she had small faith in armies. To be sure, such a force could overrun a castle, slay a Sand Dancer and an 'ifrit; but however swift it was, it would be too slow to save Julianne. There needed only moments to slit a girl's soft throat, or pierce her belly with a claw.

Why Julianne had been taken was a question to which Elisande still had no answers. As bait, clearly – but bait for whom, and to what purpose? There was a fog in her mind, whenever she tried to think about it; even her curiosity didn't blaze bright enough to burn away the shadows. Answers could wait. The fire, the urgency lay in rescue. Rescue soon, rescue *now*, before Hasan came with his multitudes and his anger, to oversweep good sense and argument.

And so she was here in the dust and quiet of the morning, with half a plan in her head and small expectation. She'd left her companions in the little house they were renting by the southern gate; Coren had asked where she was going and she'd just said, 'Out, for a walk,' relying on her reputation for impatience and short temper to forestall any further questioning. He had smiled and waved a permissive hand, 'Try not to get into trouble.' Marron had still been chewing slowly on his breakfast bread; his red eyes had watched her leave, but he'd said nothing. Jemel, brewing coffee on the fire in the yard, hadn't bothered even to look up from his scented steam and his simmering, though she'd paused to call a farewell, determined that there should be nothing out of the ordinary for any of them to notice. A restless girl wasting energy while they simply wasted time in waiting, thinking, drifting – nothing unusual in that. It was the story of her life, she thought, and perhaps the story of life itself, that men would do what they wanted in defiance of what needed doing. Coren was more subtle than her father, more astute but no wiser when he should be, when she needed him to be, now. Marron was the opposite, more simple than her father, much wiser and more ignorant, hesitant to the point of immobility. Jemel simply followed Marron, who had no one to lead him; and her father – her blind, bull-stupid, blundering father, the epitome of all men, who could be absolutely relied upon to wait too long and then go roaring after shadows, as though noise and bluster could cover blood and waste – her father Rudel was not here yet but he was coming, with Hasan. He'd enjoy having an army to play with.

Which made it all the more urgent to forestall him, to snatch the bait but not to spring the trap; which was why she walked the streets of Selussin this morning, before the sun could rise so high that it would burn down even into the narrow, shadowed alleys of the township and drive all the inhabitants withindoors.

There was little enough traffic even at this time of day, and less chance of her finding any satisfaction from what few people were abroad. Once this place must have been open and outward-looking, welcoming to strangers, an oasis of the mind as much as of the body, a caravanserai to the world; now that it was isolated, cut off from the steady run of commerce and conversation, it had closed in on itself like a desert flower against the heat, preserving what it held. The houses and the people both were secretive, withdrawn: high walls and locked gates, shrouded faces.

By an hour after dawn, Elisande knew, all the boys of Selussin would have been already in their schools, chanting together as they memorised their holy books under a teacher's stinging rod. The women and the girls would have been out in the fields, tending crops and harvesting the wiry grey-green reeds that flourished in what was marshland in the spring, when the rains ran down from the hills. Like everyone here, Elisande had slept beneath the shelter of a reed-thatch roof last night, on a mat of woven reeds. The tough fibres of those same reeds could be beaten and twisted into cords and rope, plaited to make belts and sandals, knotted into nets or mixed with mud to give strength to bricks. They pervaded this dreary life more thoroughly even than the teachings of religion; the only surprise was that the Selussids didn't eat them too. Or perhaps – remembering the tasteless stringiness of last night's vegetable stew, the effort it demanded to chew and swallow – perhaps they did that too, and simply didn't say so.

The women and children were accounted for, then, in schools and fields till noon; that left only the men. It was a man that Elisande was in search of: a priest, rather, an imam. But every man here was an imam, or seemed so: dressed in heavy formality with swinging chains and amulets above dark and decorated robes, bearded and remote, scowling normally, hurrying between school and temple, between lessons and prayer. There must be others, she supposed, old men and idle men, butchers and herdsmen, dealers in reeds. None that she could see, though, none that found any business outside his house at this time of a morning; nor that she had seen since they came here. The man they'd rented their house from was a teacher and a priest, but he wouldn't speak to Elisande.

Neither, apparently, would any of his brethren under God. She'd had small hope of that, indeed, but still she had to try. And had to fail, and so to try again . . .

'Excuse me, sir—'

A glare, from beneath eyebrows like bushy crags; a quickened scurry of reed-soled feet in the dust.

'Pardon me, holy father—'

A hiss of indrawn breath, a tightening of the hood that hid the beard, a back as swiftly turned to the importunate indecency of girl, even girl as politely veiled and swathed as she was. It was girlness, femininity that offended, clearly, not a specificity of girl: not her in herself but in her body. Perhaps she should throw off the woman's dress and ape a boy again. Except that then no doubt she would be beaten for truancy, and dragged by the ear to her lessons . . .

Still, she would and did try again and yet again, she had to: waylaying every man that passed, chasing after every dim-glimpsed distant shadow that moved, being rebuffed and spat upon and never winning a coherent word but yet not giving up, haunted by the image of her friend so close in the castle above, so unattainable by magic means that her own strength was all she had to fall back on, her strength of will and body that lacked only the one thing that these men could give her, except that not one of them would.

Her hopeless pursuit led her from the tight twist of alleys to the wide and empty marketplace where there hardly seemed to be a market any more, and on into the shadow of the greatest temple of Selussin, a three-sided tower – of course, three-sided – built of mud reinforced by a framework of wooden beams, whose ends jutted irregularly from the heat-baked, crumbling walls. In this high hot season, every day left its debris; every winter, or so she'd heard, the people would slather fresh mud between the beams to repair the ravages of another summer's sun.

There were more men here, coming and going through the low dark doorway, but still they dodged her or ignored her, importunate as she was.

At last, falling back yet again from the stiff outrage of a male back and trembling on the edge of acceptance, of defeat, she heard a soft chuckle from behind her.

And wheeled around in a fury – did they laugh at her, these silent men? they'd be sorry if they did – and found herself face to face with Jemel.

'Have you been *following* me?'

His hands waved in a calming gesture that could not gentle her, not while he was grinning so broadly.

'Only for a little, Lisan. I came to find what you were at.'

'Well, you have seen.' And had found it funny, seen a joke in her desperation which amused her not in the least.

'Seen, but not understood. I cannot see your thoughts, that drive you to such an effort.'

She took a slow breath against her rage, decided that he could perhaps be forgiven, if not quite yet – and made a point of looking past him, for one that she knew already was not there.

'Where's Marron, what have you done with him?' *Why aren't you sitting at his feet as usual, or shadowing his steps if he's about?*

'I left him sleeping.'

There were two questions she might have asked to that, *why did you leave him?* and *why is he sleeping now, at this hour*

*of the day, when he's had all night for that and besides I thought
he never slept?* One answer she could guess at, though, and
didn't want to; the other she could perhaps discover without
asking. Days of dealing with Esren had taught her to be
wary of too many questions.

So she said nothing, only waited until he put a question
on his own account.

'What is it you seek, from these men who will not speak
to you? You know they will not speak.'

'Yes, I know. But it's such a small thing to them, so
important to me, and they make me so angry . . .' She hesitated a moment longer, then confessed. 'I want one of them
to bless my knives for me, that's all.'

'To bless your knives?'

'To make them effective, against 'ifrit.'

What else? She didn't need to say it. He knew she wasn't
a believer, in his God or any other.

She said it none the less, though, for his fee, payment in
kind and in advance; so that he could say, 'Are you expecting to meet 'ifrit, Elisande?' and she could say, 'Were you
expecting to meet 'ifrit at Rhabat, Jemel?' and he could
smile and say, 'Give me your blades, then, and I will ask.
And lay my scimitar beside them, in case I too should
unfortunately meet 'ifrit all unexpected. I wish you had
told me your thought before you came out,' he added,
frowning.

'Why, so that you could have saved me this humiliation,
begging in the street to no avail? So do I, then.' Perhaps.
Though she'd have come out anyway, she thought, dogging
his heels in another humiliation, sooner than stay and do
nothing at the house where Marron slept and Coren thought

his private thoughts about his daughter and would not share them with her.

'No, I enjoyed that,' with the flashing grin again, that came and went in moments. 'But I could have brought Dard also, for the blessing.'

'Marron doesn't need an enchantment on his sword, to slay an 'ifrit.' He was skilled enough – she thought, she hoped – to do it with a bare blade unblessed, a straight thrust to the hot red eye; or else he had the Daughter, he always had the Daughter. 'Besides, he doesn't like to kill.'

'I know,' Jemel said, his eyes briefly shadowed. 'Not even 'ifrit. He may have to, though, before all this is over. He might try not to kill, but if he did not know his blade was blessed, it might save him anyway.'

She could see what he imagined, Marron's deliberately not thrusting at an eye, expecting his sword to skitter off invulnerable chitin. But, 'He's stupid, Jemel,' – *of course he's stupid, he's a boy* – 'but not that stupid.' Not that cruel – she thought, she hoped again – to leave them both bereft. 'And the Daughter wouldn't let it happen anyway. The Ghost Walker is very hard to kill, remember? Trust its good sense, if you can't trust his. Anyway, he'd know, I think, if you had Dard blessed behind his back. He knows more than he ought to, more than he thinks he knows.' And more, far more than was good for him.

'Well. Give me your knives.'

It was the only choice she had, but still she hesitated. 'They're my blades. I want to see . . .'

He nodded. There was a bond between a weapon and its owner, of course there was, how not? Why else would so many give a name to steel? 'It will be done in the temple here, if I can find a man to do it. Unbelievers are forbidden to enter, but women are not, and the veil hides your race. Follow us inside. With luck, the imam will not know you.' The imam, she thought, would likely not even notice her. 'There will be a screen in the eastern quarter; watch through the lattice. You'll see as much as I do. It will be brief, in any case. These are busy men, these imams.'

There was a cynical note to his voice; she gazed at him curiously, remembering how many mornings she'd seen him leave even Marron and go off alone to say his prayers in the Sands. Mornings and evenings both, but it was the mornings she remembered: the pale light, the cool breeze and himself a silhouette against the new-made sun, all pride and purpose . . .

'Don't you mind?' she asked. 'That I'm there, I mean, if it's forbidden to me?'

'It is for God to mind, not me,' he said, oddly quiet. 'It may be that He will mind both of us, you and me. If so, no doubt He will make His displeasure known. If I can walk safely under His roof, then be assured, so can you.'

Boys, she thought. They always wanted to take the sins of the world onto their shoulders – and what were Jemel's sins, except perhaps that he had recently missed a prayer or two? His love for Marron was no sin in his own eyes, nor his tribe's, though he was tribeless now. Perhaps she'd ask him sometime; but not now.

Now she only slipped her knives from her belt and passed them to him, hilt-first. He took them respectfully, as though they had as proud a lineage as Dard that Marron carried; he stowed them in his own belt and stepped away from her, waiting a little distance off to show that they were unconnected, she and he. She turned her head the other way to emphasise the point, and watched him only through the heavy veil, from the corner of one eye.

A minute later, along came another of those ubiquitous imams, hustle hustle in his weighty robe. Like bees around a hive she thought they were, in and out of the temple in ones and twos and clusters, each intent on his own private mystery and little concerned with any other's.

Jemel tried to detain this one with a word, and failed as she had every time. Jemel was bolder than she'd dared to be, though, with the immunity of his sex; he gripped the man's arm and pulled him abruptly to a halt.

The priest was furious, all but muted with rage, spluttering incoherently; Jemel's voice cut easily across the gabble, loud enough for Elisande to hear even from her distance.

'Your pardon, holy brother, I do but ask a service of your wisdom. There is a fee . . .'

Whether it was the sight of silver coins in Jemel's left hand that stilled the imam's protest, Elisande couldn't say. It might have been what else that sight revealed, the missing little finger, coupled with what Jemel's clothes proclaimed, that he was Sharai but tribeless; no desert priest would offend a man who might be sworn to the Sand Dancers, even if he didn't wear their customary black. That confident 'brother' might have helped too, implying that they both served not only the same God, but the same cause also.

'What service? Brother?'

'Your blessing, on my blades.'

A moment's pause, just long enough for those coins to be passed from one hand to another; then, 'Come,' and the imam ducked in through the temple door, with Jemel on his heels.

Elisande waited for the space of a few steadying breaths, before she followed.

If Selussin's prime purpose was to teach, then its high temple was a lesson in itself, she thought, that the surface of a thing gave few clues to its innermost heart.

From the outside, the building was crudely made and eccentric, speaking more to the weakness of its people than the power of its priests. The difference inside was startling, all the more so because the materials remained the same.

The floor was pounded earth, and sandy near the door where the constant passage of feet dragged in the dirt of the town's streets. Further in, she saw a small boy with an aspergill sprinkling water where he walked: not enough to muddy the ground, just to dampen it and quell the dust. It kept the air cool too, and a little moist; she was reminded of the boys in the Sultan's gardens at Bar'ath Tazore, doing much the same out in the open to keep a jungle thriving under desert sun. The purpose here was subtly similar, she thought: to keep mysterious the place where power lived, to let no one pass from there to here without seeing, touching, breathing the change from that to this.

As Jemel had promised, there was a carved and pierced screen to her right, dividing the eastern angle from the body of the temple. She walked in that direction, obedient to his instructions, but with her eyes neither cast down in humility as they probably properly should have been, nor watching his back and the imam's where they stood and then knelt before the altar in the centre of the floor, the focus of all this space.

Instead, Elisande let her feet find their way unguided, while she stared upward: up and up, into twisted height and darkness.

There must, she supposed, be a roof; otherwise she'd see light and sky even through all the tangle in between, and this would be a burning-house at noon. If she climbed, no doubt she'd find it eventually, and even Julianne could make that climb; but from the ground that necessary roof was hidden by more than shadows.

She'd expected a ceiling, probably quite low, and stairs or a ladder climbing to an upper chamber, a succession of chambers one above another. So much height and space in the tower, in such a low-built town, she'd been sure they'd use it all.

And perhaps they did, but not for speech or sleep or storage. She thought of a candle's flame, the small hot glow at the heart of it where the wick burned, and then the rising column of light.

The temple-tower was a single vaulting chamber, undivided; and all that high-leaping space was criss-crossed by an intricate and eye-defeating maze of blackened wood. From outside she had seen the beam-ends and thought them strange enough, an irregular studding, a scaffold to give shape and strength to the friable mud of the walls. Here were the beams themselves. Tall trees they must have been to run as they did from wall to wall, clear across the temple at unpredictable angles, in no pattern or design that she could discern from the lights of many lamps and braziers. They made a baffling knotwork that drew the eye in and up, and wanted never to release it.

She stared, she frankly gawped; and was glad for once to

be a girl, and so ignored by all of the men who prayed or murmured heads together, or else had other business here.

She was meant, she remembered at last, to be watching two such men who had such business, and that concerned herself. Coming at last behind the women's screen, she dragged her gaze downward from the heights, found herself alone and so nudged her veil aside, hooked her fingers through the narrow piercings and set her eyes to the widest space that she could discover.

There were Jemel and the imam, kneeling before the simple altar, a rough block of black stone with a burning charcoal brazier set atop. For a wonder the stone had been hewn square, and the brazier was round; even the Selussids, it seemed, would not defy tradition so far as to give three corners to the focus of their faith.

There were the men, and laid on the floor before them were the weapons, hers and Jemel's, faintly gleaming in the smoky light.

The imam spread his hands above the blades and probably began a prayer, some well-used form of words. She couldn't hear, and had trouble believing that any blessing so lightly, so cheaply bought could truly prove effective. She'd seen sanctified weapons shear through where normal steel rebounded; that was more of a mystery to her than other, stronger magic that she'd met. She might not understand the Daughter but it was real, she couldn't dispute its existence and she knew what it did. A priest's blessing on a blade, though, when she gave his God no credence – it challenged her true faith, that the world was well-made whoever it was that made it. She might have believed that a priest's wisdom could invest some power in what he touched; but this distracted man with his wispy beard and his crass self-satisfaction? Jemel had more wisdom in his missing finger, and yet Jemel could not make a sword bite through 'ifrit armour.

Perhaps the imam could not do it either, and this was wasted time that would draw her into danger later. Perhaps she should not think of her blades as blessed after all . . .

'Lisan.' A voice spoke suddenly, shockingly in her ear; she choked on a gasp that might easily have come out as a scream, and twisted round.

And saw no one, though she wheeled in a circle to be sure. Good sense took a moment to catch up her racing heart and make her look again, more closely.

Esren was a spinning shadow among shadows, a finger's length of dust and gleaming darkness amid the confusion of light as it fell through the complications of the screen.

Second nature now to bite back the hot and perilous question, *what are you doing here?* Instead she took a slow breath and then another, as much time as she needed; when she was ready, in a hissing whisper, she said, 'Esren, I did not summon you.'

'Indeed not. I came. I was curious.'

About what, she wondered – the temple, the blessing, something else? No way to guess; if it wanted her to learn, then it would tell her. Obliquely, like as not.

'I don't suppose the djinn go often into church,' she said, trying to be oblique in her turn.

'I go where I choose.' *Now*, unspoken but ever there between them, that deep and ever-resented debt it owed to her, that it repaid with grudging and disputatious service. 'The same is true of all my kind.'

'But you don't worship this God, or any other; so . . .'

'Neither does this God or any other worship us. So far as we know. It may be a nonsense, a game of men to defeat the dark with lies and promises; but a blessed blade will still strike home, Lisan, as though it had the wrath of God behind it.'

'Tell me if those blades are truly blessed,' she said. She had visions in her head, knives hurled at iron-black body, hurled and bouncing back.

'They are. Any hedge-priest can do this work; his touch will be as potent as a saint's,' and the imam was touching the weapons now, she saw, one finger to each still blade. 'Have a care with those knives, Lisan. They may slay more than an 'ifrit.'

As ever, she looked for deeper meaning beneath its words; as ever, she ended up drowning in uncertainty. Would the knives be potent against other creatures of the spirit world – against the djinn themselves, maybe? Was it nervous for itself, could she cut the thread of its long long life and send it spinning into dissolution? It was not immortal, that she knew; a djinni could be slain. And yet it seemed to have no solid body to attack, being made of wind and whispers. Perhaps a blade charged with power could seek out some inner core, unravel what was wound so tight; perhaps it was afraid of her . . .

More likely of her ignorance, she thought, and set that thought aside. Grimly, for later consideration.

'I suppose it must be magic, then. Like laying a spell on the metal.' Or on a man's mind, such as she could do herself, laying a Fold in the pathway of his thoughts such that he could look directly at her and see her not at all. She couldn't keep the disappointment out of her voice. She might not believe in her people's God or any other, but still she'd always hoped that their earthly manifestations, all the little miracles of churchly life sprang from some source unknown, perhaps unknowable: a fount of mysterious power, to set against the slow-won understanding that defined her own kind of magic. She wanted to believe that faith could balance schooling, even where it was faith misplaced . . .

'You use words that have no meaning. That is magic; your hidden home is magic; I am a creature of magic,' said with a rich contempt, as it spun and sparkled in the air. 'It exists, Surayon exists, I exist; in that sense we are all alike, and so, yes, the imam's blessing is a kind of magic. But Lisan, so do you exist, and the mud floor that you stand on, and the flea that bites you.'

'I don't have – ow!' She slapped at her leg, decided not to lift up the skirt of her robe in pursuit: undignified under a holy roof, too likely to draw attention to her Patric skin – and Patric manners, she thought ruefully – and probably futile in any case. Sand fleas didn't linger. Their eggs did, though; she'd best get Julianne to check her over. Inch by inch, from scalp to toenails. In a day or two, of course, when Julianne was rescued. The eggs were easier to spot in any case, once they'd had a chance to harden and darken under the skin . . .

She flinched from the thought, and hissed, 'If that's all the use of your foreknowledge, to tell me I'm going to get bitten an eye-blink before it happens, then you might as well keep it to yourself.'

'Knowledge is always better than ignorance, Lisan. If you must be bitten, better to be aware and prepared. What I see is a flea-bite, to what I used to see: use it or not, as you choose. But that is the distinction, I think, between your magic and that priest's, perhaps all priests'. Yours is founded on knowledge; the people of Surayon understand more than most how the worlds are shaped, and so they can make a little difference to that shaping. The churches work in igno-rance, and never try to penetrate the cloak of it. Miracles happen, and they are content with that. If their prayers are spells, such that anyone could use them – well, they preserve them to the priesthood, and condemn a thief for heresy. Mystery and shadow suit them well.'

Wise and experienced as she was, Elisande found that she could still blush. The shadows of the temple suited her too just then, as the veil did, and the veiling screen, though she was sure the djinni could see through them all as easily as it saw through her. It was right to scorn mystery, of course it was – and yet she still craved a little mystery. There could be too much light in the world, an overweight of knowledge . . .

She'd never known Esren say so much, so very much to the purpose. Whatever its reasons – and if she treasured life's mysteries, Esren's motivations were surely enough for one girl's puzzled lifetime – it disappeared from her shoulder without warning, without another word. She was becoming used to that, but not used enough; she still wasted a moment in glancing around, to be sure.

And was still looking, still squinting into shifting shadows when all thoughts of the djinni were driven from her head by a sudden, bewildering noise. A high-pitched squealing, so high that it was almost painful; she couldn't place it except that it came from above, it seemed to come from every upper corner of the roofspace, every angle of beam and wall simultaneously.

And then it moved, it fell down towards her like a black blanket of unbearable sound. Towards her and towards everyone, all at once; she wrenched her gaze away for a moment and saw how all the men were staring up, transfixed and terrified. Some were crouching under the weight of it, grovelling almost on the floor, setting their voices against the noise in a rising prayer of desperation.

Her eyes were drawn inexorably back to the swirling darkness overhead. The living darkness – there were voices in that numbing scream, there was a pattern to the movement. She pushed her hood back to see better, then remembered the death-shriek of 'ifrit and abruptly moved herself, out from behind the sheltering screen, towards the poor protection of her knives where they lay before the altar. Jemel was stooping, she saw, to snatch up his own blade; *good,* she thought, *but you leave mine for me . . .*

For what little good they would do, against a strike by however many lurking monsters there were, enough to raise such a cry . . .

She turned her head upward again, looking for 'ifrit. Something hurtled at her, and she ducked instinctively; it skimmed above her hair, leaving a brief impression of gaping jaws, teeth, a red gullet – but small, so small, mouse-sized, no threat at all.

She gaped in her turn, stared after it, stared up; and turned to scuttle back behind the screen again, choking down a churn of painful laughter in her gut. All of them, she wanted to laugh at them all, herself and those cowering priests with their abandoned self-regard and Jemel who stood so proud and warrior-like among them, gazing about him now in bafflement that was only slowly turning to understanding, to catching up with her.

They deserved all the laughter that she had, all the mockery she could raise. So many of them and so pleased with themselves they'd been, until a shriek and a shadow had punctured their overweening pomposity.

Bats whirled and circled among them now in hundreds, thousands maybe, enough to fill the air and block the light as though the mass of their dark bodies cast its own darkness like a net about them.

Bats, and nothing worse. Bats that must sleep the day out among the beams and rafters overhead, clustering together like kittens for warmth and safety; bats that had been suddenly disturbed and so erupted in alarm, all of them together like a flight of birds, startled and stupid and beating round and round the narrow compass of the temple rather than brave the sun's glare outside . . .

Bats that had been suddenly disturbed – and here was Esren back as unexpectedly as it had disappeared, silent at her shoulder and somehow smug in its silence, she thought, exactly as a capricious creature might be that had made so much mischief in a moment.

'That was you,' she said, without a hint of a question in it.

'I did nothing.'

'Liar.'

'The djinn do not lie, Elisande.'

She ducked another flight, a skirmish-party that had found its way behind the screen – to its great regret, judging by the way it screamed and veered wildly as it passed close to

the djinni – and sighed extravagantly. 'Tell me whether you
went up into the roofspace.'

'I did.'

'Tell me why.'

'I was curious.'

'You knew that the bats were there.'

'Yes. I could sense them sleeping.'

'And you knew that your presence would wake them, and
that they would be terrified by your presence as any animal
is, and so you went up to see what would happen.'

'As I said, I was curious.'

'It is not amusing, Esren,' in her sternest voice, 'to use fear
to satisfy curiosity.'

'It is interesting, though. The bats are frightened by me,
which is perhaps appropriate, although I mean them no
harm; these men it seems are frightened by the bats, which
is absurd.'

'Not truly frightened,' she said, struggling to defend her
kind against the facts, 'only startled and alarmed.'

'I do not see the difference. They shrieked, they prayed
for protection; listen, they are praying yet, against whatever
evil spirit they believe has raised the bats.'

They were; and actually it was amusing, although she
refused to say so. They were right, after all, by their own
lights – except that no Catari priest would claim that the
djinn were evil. She wished briefly that she could take Esren's
experiment further, to find what would scare a spirit.

Instead she stepped out from behind the screen and gestured across the temple floor. Jemel seemed to be looking for
that exactly, her appearance, her impatience. He gave her a
cautious, distracted wave amid the confusion of men and

animals, shrieks and prayers. Even he wasn't immune to the
mood, though he had sheathed his scimitar by now. He
stooped to scoop up her knives from where they lay, blessed
now and she hoped more potent than they had been
before – and he stayed stooped, walking all but doubled
over as he came towards her. He might want her to think
that it was the pain of suppressed laughter that folded him
so, but she could see how his eyes were alert, how his head
jerked whenever he saw or thought he saw a stray bat or a
school of bats coming gape-jawed towards him. Their own
swerving always came late, at the last possible moment; so
many flying so fast, and yet not one had struck a beam or a
man, a hanging lantern-chain or even another bat, so far as
she could tell. The dense clouds whirled and circled, split
apart and melted together again as seamlessly as their individual voices knitted together to make that one endless,
penetrating scream.

Knowing was no substitute for instinct, though, and
never had been. It would take a brave man or a blind one –
blind and deaf – to walk through the maelstrom and not to
flinch. More than brave, perhaps: Jemel had courage to
spare, and was almost crawling under the intangible weight
of those packed and circling bodies above.

And what of a girl, could she be braver? Or more deliberately blind, perhaps? Elisande eyed the way to the door,
and thought about walking with her eyes closed. There were
too many obstacles, though, too many men scuttling to the
sun's shielding glare like crabs to the shelter of a rock. Or like
'ifrit, she thought, remembering the clawed black shapes
scurrying up out of the water. Then, inevitably, she remembered Julianne, trapped under an 'ifrit's red gaze; and strode

determinedly towards the bright summoning of the doorway, pulling her veil straight as she went and feeling glad almost for the first time in her life that she was so short. She could feel her headdress stirred by the wind from the bats' wings, she knew there was a living ceiling of them barely a hand's span above her; but if she kept her eyes down she couldn't see them, and if she just kept her feet moving she might not need to think how close they were, she didn't at all have to imagine how it would feel to get just one tangled in her clothing . . .

Then a small flight of them came swooping low, heading straight for her. She bit back a shriek, though it felt like swallowing a pebble, hard and painful in her throat; and that took all the will she had, she couldn't keep from ducking and twisting aside. Twisting into their own path, indeed, as they yawed, so that they had to turn swiftly, violently in mid-air to avoid her. The breeze they made in their passing pressed through her veil, bringing with it the rankness of their breath, the musty smell of their fur; one glimpse of yellow incisors and vivid throats and she did close her eyes after all, telling herself how small they were and how harmless to her, chanting it under her breath like a mantra against the way the image filled her mind.

She was still standing, still bent over like an old woman or an older tree, when she felt a hand grip her arm. Chanced a glance aside, and saw Jemel — of course Jemel, who else would touch her? Here?

He was standing tall now, despite the blurring darkness all about his head; she could see the effort he made to keep his eyes on her, and not let them go darting after the bats as they flashed in and out of his sight. She gave him a mirthless grin he wouldn't see — *be brave then, now, when you know that I'm watching: too late, but you needn't know that* — and let him urge her back into movement, towards the illusion of safety and away from the illusion of risk.

Head down and feet hurrying, her free arm coming up despite herself in a useless ward: at last they broke into sunshine and she could straighten up, draw a deep recovering breath — her first for a while, or so it seemed — and look up at the Sharai to see him blushing darkly, with an embarrassed grin.

Her own face would match his, she knew. The veil might hide that, if it didn't catch fire simply from the glow of her skin, which could outburn the sun; it couldn't hide the tremble in her arm where he was still holding it. She tossed her head defiantly against the world — or against her own malignant djinni, that could so humiliate her with a little casual curiosity — and said, 'Give me my knives, then.'

'Not here.' His own head moved more purposefully, to indicate the swarm of men who filled the square around them, who couldn't help but see the exchange however much their eyes might still be full of swarming bats. Men didn't yield weapons up to women; these men might not challenge it directly, but they would certainly remember, and likely talk. Elisande wasn't sure that secrecy mattered, but it was a good habit to fall back on.

So she followed Jemel meekly enough, away from the temple and its open square, into the tight tangle of alleyways that surrounded it. As soon as they were private, in a shadowy angle that was overlooked by no windows, he handed her knives across. She hoped to feel some tingle in the metal to say that they'd been changed, perhaps to see a new shimmer on the edge to show where power ran, and was disappointed; they seemed the same as before, sharp and finely balanced, nothing more. She knew that they were dangerous to mortal flesh, but whether they could hack or skewer the chitin of an 'ifrit – to learn that, she'd have to get closer than she liked, closer than she'd been yet.

Which must mean doing without Jemel's company or the djinni's, going alone against the world, the way she'd always liked to. She sheathed the knives invisibly within her robe, and gave him a respectful bow that was less mocking than it might have looked, than he might have thought it. 'Thank you, Jemel. Will you go back now, to seek Marron?'

She was out of practice at asking questions, which was curious in one who had always been more curious than was good for her. Even to her own ears, that sounded more like a command, the rising inflection at the end only a meaningless courtesy.

He might have been angry, indignant, resentful, and was none of those. He couldn't have failed to recognise the dismissal, but neither did he go. He stood before her, smiling as he said, 'Will you go to seek Coren?'

'I – no. Not, not yet. I thought I might wander the town a little, learn its ways . . .'

'As you did yesterday and the day before, as we have all done since we came here? Or did you think that today perhaps you might go a little further, outside the walls – up to the castle, say, a nice distance for a day's exploring . . . ?'

She was blushing again, and sure that he knew it again. She was becoming distressingly easy to read, or else simply too dangerously close to these few friends, who were stealing all her secrets from her one by one.

'Well then, yes,' she said. 'Yes, up to the castle, why not? The gate is open, we know that; the 'ifrit watches Julianne, we know that. There's only Morakh left, then, and he can't watch everywhere at once . . .'

'The gate is open, and the trap is baited; will you walk inside?'

'The trap is baited for Coren, surely, not for me.'

'We don't know that, it's a guess. Besides, a rat-trap may catch a mouse as easily. Morakh can't watch everywhere, but he can watch the gate; there's only one.'

'So I'll climb the wall.'

'And if you climb the wall and meet another Dancer, what then? Morakh may not be alone in there any longer.'

'Esren says that he is, and the djinn do not lie.'

'No, but they can be mistaken. They are dangerous creatures to put your faith in, Elisande.'

'True; but I am a dangerous creature too. More so, now,' touching the hafts of her daggers. 'I am going, Jemel. Esren will not, nor will Coren, nor Marron; they are all afraid of the 'ifrit. With reason, perhaps, but their reasons don't apply to me. Julianne can't help herself, so one of us must help her.'

'Two of us,' he said flatly. 'If you go, I am coming with you.'

'Marron will be angry with you.'

'He would be more angry, if I let you go alone.'

That might be true. What was certain was that she was afraid, even without her companions' reasons. Her knives might be blessed, but they were still pitifully small weapons to set against a Sand Dancer and a spirit-monster. She hadn't looked for support from Jemel, hadn't dared to hope for it; to have it offered unexpectedly was a gift, a blessing in itself.

Perhaps, if she really tried, she could see it even as an omen of success.

'Let's go, then,' she said firmly. 'Quickly, before Marron comes looking for you, or Coren for me.' It would be that way round, it would have to be, but almost – almost! – she didn't care.

There were three sides to Selussin. The wall that gripped the town was shaped like an arrowhead, and the point of it faced the desert. Raiding Sharai would break like a wave around it; raiding Patrics would meet the opposing wall head-on, like a hammer. For both cultures, that seemed appropriate to Elisande.

Each wall had a curve to it, an inward bowing that would allow defenders to target any attacker along its length; each wall also had its gate at the centre, which must have allowed easy access for the traders who used to come in such numbers but would place any attacking force at the heart of the field of fire. For what good that would do. It looked well, she thought as she trailed Jemel out through the westerly gate – dogging his heels like the very picture of an obedient Catari girl, as Selussin was the very picture of a well-defended settlement – but she couldn't picture those priests and boys up on the walls and making any kind of fight to protect their schools and temples.

There had been no need in recent history, or at any rate no attempt. Sharai and Patric armies both had been intent on the castle; they'd simply absorbed the town into their temporary possession, riding like conquerors through wisely-opened gates in search of food but largely ignoring it else. Neither side had stationed a garrison there. The priests could count themselves lucky, perhaps, to have faced no Ransomer fanatics; the Duke of Ascariel was said to be a religious man, but not a foolish one. He'd let the temples stand and the schools survive, for the sake of peace.

Abandoned as the landscape, empty as the Sands before it and the hills behind – abandoned long since save for birds and spiders, adventurous children, presumably now one girl, one zealot, one evil clad in chitin – the castle loured none the less above the town, a thundercloud of threat, and all the more so once they'd passed outside the shielding walls. It seemed almost to stoop from its height like a vulture on a crag, not so much guarding as inspecting what lay open and vulnerable below, picking over what might be worth the scavenging.

A vulture with battered and dusty feathers it might be, and yet it stood out before the broken hills that made its backdrop, thrust itself forward indeed, made its declaration. *Mine! What you see from where you stand, all of this is mine,* and Selussin was only a morsel, it seemed to suggest, and might not abide there long.

And yet the town was ancient and the castle was new-made by any standards that were not Patric and so new-made themselves; the town thrived, where the castle stood forlorn; the town's walls were high and whole while the castle's were crumbling. Even from this distance, Elisande could see gaps in the parapet where stones had fallen in. More than single stones, surely, for her to make out their absence this far away; great mounds of rubble there should be, she hoped there would be in the inner courts. Jemel must be right, that Morakh would watch the gate; she'd like to be proved right in her turn, that they could climb in over the wall and behind his back, now that her djinni had proved unreliable. The more damage the better, as far as she was concerned. Going up or coming down, she'd sooner clamber than climb.

There were patches of cultivated ground all around the walls, where the women and children grew what food they could while their men studied and prayed the days away. Beyond the parched green of those fields lay another harvest, though it looked like nothing better than coils of grey-green wire, running in tangled, matted blankets to the first slope of the hills. Halfa-reeds: even the word seemed strange, to a mind grown accustomed to desert drought. But there were marshes here after the spring rains, where the mountain run-off pooled; the reeds grew tall, then wilted under the summer sun. Tough and fibrous but shallow-rooted, they could be pulled by the smallest child, then worked in a dozen different ways or else bound into bales and traded with what caravans still came this way.

Between the fields and the halfa-beds a road ran, danger-ously below the castle's overlooking eye: Morakh's eye, if he were on the watch. Perhaps Elisande should have asked the djinni to carry them into the hills unseen; but Esren was so wary of the 'ifrit, it might have refused even so much help.

Well, too late now. If Morakh were watching, he would have seen them already. And could have seen nothing, after all, bar a man in local dress with a woman submissive at his heels. Not so unusual, surely. Except that no one else was moving or even visible, they were alone in the landscape; with the sun rising to its height, the fields had been aban-doned. None who lived here was fool enough to carry water to the crops or sweat to pull halfa in the heat and glare of noon, why would they?

'I'm sorry, Jemel, I should have thought – we must stand out like ants on white linen down here, in our robes against this road . . .'

'Do you want to go back?'

'No.'

'No, of course you don't. Well then, shall we go up and walk in at the open gates after all? We might as well.'

And fight their way past a Dancer – at least one Dancer – only to be confronted by an 'ifrit that would know they were coming, that would be ready and waiting as the Dancer was? But then the 'ifrit would know anyway, however careful or clever they were. It was too much to wind her head around the complexities. Enemies that sensed the future were beyond all reason. Friends that did the same were as bad or worse; she thought evil things of Esren, and said, 'Jemel, beat me.'

'Do what?'

'Beat me,' with a nod towards the stick that he carried in his belt like all true Sharai among settled folk, to show that they were camel-riders and no pastoralists, 'as if I were a lazy girl who hadn't done her morning's work. Then stand over me, while I gather reeds; we'll make our way across the bed there and into that cleft, where we'll be out of sight of the castle. Then we can climb, and find our way across the hill and around. If he is watching, it'll be the road that he watches.'

'With good reason,' Jemel murmured, surveying the rough crag. 'It'll be a hard climb, and worse going after. And you'll be sore. Are you sure?'

'You don't have to beat me hard,' she growled. 'Just make it look good, from a distance. And yes, I'm sure.' It was that or go back, there were no other options; and to go back meant failure, today and tomorrow. Jemel would tell Marron; Marron would tell Coren, those two were suddenly close as cousins; and Coren would look anxious and forbid her to try again, and never give her the chance anyway.

Jemel shrugged, and made great play of drawing his riding-stick as though it were his scimitar. She thought he made rather too much of it, indeed, flailing it through the air a few times before he gripped her shoulder and brought it whipping down across her back. She flinched as she heard its whistle, fearing that he'd entered altogether too willingly into his role; but the rod only stung when it struck her, and that lightly. She'd been beaten enough in her life, in various guises, to know the true cut of a cane; he must be holding his stroke at the last moment, doing all for effect.

Even so, half a dozen such strokes left her smarting, aching, having to bite down on her tongue to stop herself yelping; wishing almost for observers within earshot so that she could let go those yelps, sob and plead and play the beaten girl as vigorously as he played her husband, brother, whichever he'd decided in his arrogant male head . . .

'Enough,' she muttered, glaring up at him over her shoulder as he raised the stick again. 'Hit me again and you'll feel my blessed knife in your ribs, I swear it.'

He grinned, and let her go. 'I said you'd be sore. Go on, then,' with another great flourish of the stick, this time using it to point towards the reed-beds. 'Go and gather, girl. I'll stroll behind, I need the rest. It's hard labour, disciplining a recalcitrant sister . . .'

Sister, was it? That would make better sense than wife, she supposed. To him at least, and maybe also to her. Well, she could play his browbeaten, back-beaten sister, for any eyes that watched their comedy.

And did: hunched over to emphasise her pain, cowering from his shadow, she scuttled to the edge of the reeds. Bent lower to claw her fingers into the dry, knotted mat, and tugged. Ripped up a poor handful, and felt a stinging in her palm; gaped down at it and saw blood, saw how the skin was sliced.

Cursed the superstition that forbade the reeds to be cut by any blade, blessed or otherwise, and showed her hand surreptitiously to Jemel.

'It's tough as wire, and as sharp. How do they ever make cloth out of this?'

'By dint of much soaking and beating. But have you tried wearing it? As well wear woven wire. That's why they trade for wool, this makes better rope than robes. Just pretend,' he urged her, 'make a show of it, that's all we need. And you'll want your hands whole, for climbing.'

She would; she did. She made her bent way crabwise towards the crag and the cleft that would hide them, never quite facing the direction her feet were taking her; facing her feet, indeed, stooped over like a crone and swinging one arm like a monkey, down and up in great looping movements like a fool's imitation of a harvest. With luck, no one would see from any distance that her hand came up as empty as it fell, that the arm she held crooked in her body's shadow held no gathered crop.

Jemel paced slowly behind her, occasionally tapping shoulder or thigh with his stick like a man who drove a donkey; she thought she might turn and bite him soon, like a donkey driven too far.

'How do little children ever pull this stuff?' she murmured out loud, if for no other reason than to remind him that she had a voice, and a mind behind it. 'The women here have hands like hide, as women everywhere; but children . . .'

'There'll be a trick to it, a twist of the wrist; but their grandfathers stitch them palm-guards out of camel-leather, haven't you seen? It's holy work, if it keeps the women busy and the little girls at their heels.'

She had seen old men on their doorsteps plying needle and thread, and had thought it more practical than praying, and the first useful work she'd seen any man do in Selussin. She'd just assumed they'd be making a piece of harness or mending a shoe, though, as men did in other towns.

Foolish assumption, in this town; she should have known. Too bad that she couldn't blame Jemel for knowing about the palm-guards and not fetching one along, but some levels of unfairness were beyond her. *Beyond even her*, her father would have said. She thought her father would like it here when he came; she was glad he couldn't see her now, he'd love this, and wish more strength to Jemel's arm . . .

'If we disappear into that cleft and don't come out again, Morakh's going to wonder what we're up to. Isn't he?'

'Not necessarily.' There was a pause in the steady pace of Jemel's footfalls, the sudden pop of a cork; she glanced back to see him drink from a water-flask, making a great pantomime of being hot and weary. Then his stick urged her on again, as he said, 'With luck, he'll think we're just resting in the shade. It'll be an hour or two before he starts to worry, if he doesn't forget about us altogether. By then we should be safely up and out of sight of the castle gate.'

Somewhere round the back of the castle, indeed, and looking for a way in or over; it was an odd definition of safety, she thought. But Julianne's need was pressing against her thoughts again, urgent and imperative. She moved on until the walls of the cleft grew high around her, until cool black shadow cut off any chance of their being overlooked. Then she straightened slowly, easing her sore shoulders and stiff back while she gazed upward at the climb that awaited them.

Height held no fears for her, she'd climbed often in the quiet valleys of her home and again in the Sands, with the Sharai. Here on the desert's rim, though, in the shelter of the cleft, neither rains nor sandstorms had softened the sharp edges of the rock. She chewed her lip for a moment, looking at the holds, and said, 'I wish you'd bought two pairs of those palm-guards, Jemel.'

'I didn't know we'd need them.'

She knew that, she'd only been talking for its own sake, to postpone the moment. Her one hand was cut already; the other would be leaving its own trail of blood before they'd hauled themselves out of the cleft and onto the broken ridge above.

She led the way, knowing that Jemel would follow; she stayed determinedly ahead of him all the way, although it was like climbing on knives. She tried not to think about her fingers, nor about how Esren could have lifted them both up in a moment. Instead she forced her mind to focus on Julianne, thinking how her friend would have hated and feared this climb but how her courage would have driven her to it despite that, if it had been Elisande who needed rescue; wondering how that courage was holding up after days of captivity, whether she still clung to hope or felt herself abandoned. Whether she might hope for abandonment, indeed, knowing herself to be bait in a trap . . .

Too bad, if so. The others might abandon her, but Elisande not. She climbed until she could drag herself over the crag's edge, and into the shelter of a massive boulder. She waited until Jemel had joined her there, then spent a little time and a little strength that she could ill afford to take his hands in hers and still the bleeding, knit torn flesh together. She heard him gasp softly, at the warmth of her healing touch; all he said, though, was, 'What of your own? They're worse than mine.'

'Alas,' she said with a thin smile, 'that I can't do anything about. We may be witches, we Surayonnaise, but we cannot spell ourselves.' Healing was a journey into another's body; if anyone had learned the art of journeying within themselves, she'd never heard it. Now that the strain of the climb was behind her, she could feel every gash in her throbbing, blood-slick hands. Nothing she could do, though, except allow Jemel to tear strips from his robe to wrap them crudely.

Above them lay a slope of loose boulder-strewn shale. Scrambling over that tested her again as stones turned and slid away beneath her feet, forcing her to grab for insecure holds with stinging palms, eventually to crawl like a spider. Resisting the impulse to look behind and see how Jemel was coping took her mind from her own gracelessness until she'd reached the top; once there, she fell gasping on her back and called it generosity to stay so until he joined her.

From this new vantage-point they could look down on the path that came up from Selussin, look up to see the castle, with its gate standing open as they'd been told. They kept flat to avoid being seen in their turn, watched for any sign of Morakh on the walls and saw none. Had it been wasted effort, then, that savage climb? She couldn't be sure, there was any number of places where a man could stand concealed behind an embrasure or an arrow-slit and still have a view of the town and the way up.

She was busy mapping the landscape in her mind, plotting a route that would lead them around in secrecy to the rear of the castle, when Jemel nudged her suddenly.

'Look . . .'

She followed the direction of his nod and saw movement on the road that came down from the mountains, from Outremer. Movement that resolved itself quickly into a line of people, dark against the dust. Briefly she thought it was an army, men on the march in defiance of the abiding truce.

Another minute's watching, though, and she was only confused. The people were organised like an army, running steadily in two long files behind a single man; but they were all afoot and there was no glitter of armour among them, barely the glint of a sword's blade where they ran in sunshine. And she could see women and children among their number . . .

'Who are they?'

'Your people,' Jemel murmured, 'not mine. You tell me.'

That she couldn't do, but she wasn't sure that he was right in any case. Some, many looked to be Catari, even if none was dressed like the Sharai. The only certainty was that they were bound for the castle; she huddled low in the shade of a rock and watched as they turned in at the gate. Perhaps half of them were inside before she thought to count. There were more than a hundred, though, she was sure of that. And still no sign of Morakh. Could he have been expecting them, not an invasion but a reinforcement? These were not Sand Dancers, but still . . .

'This changes things,' she said positively. 'Coren needs to be told.'

'Yes. We'll go back.'

'No, not both of us. You go, Jemel. Julianne still needs our help; it may even be easier for me to sneak around in there, with so many others to confuse Morakh and the 'ifrit.'

'I said before, I won't let you go in there alone.'

'There isn't any choice now. If we go in together, how long will it be before Marron comes blundering in after us, looking for you? He'll be anxious already, you know that. And there's no telling who he might meet, or what might happen after. Or Coren might come, and stumble straight into trouble. They've got to be warned, Jemel; and I've got to go in. Remember, I've always got Esren to whisk me away if I get caught. You don't have that protection, you're not safe in the way that I am . . .'

That was a direct lie, but she thought, she hoped he wouldn't recognise it.

Nor did he; he only grunted unhappily, and said, 'Be careful, then. Don't do anything stupid, don't fight Morakh and the 'ifrit by yourself. Just learn what you can, find out who these people are and what they want, and then come back.'

She promised, lying again; and waited while he slid away on his belly, watched while he slid back down the slope, raising a cloud of dust and a small landslide as he went. Then she turned her eyes and mind back to the castle, to her quietest way in. It meant another climb with her hurting hands, but she was prepared for that. She tried to prepare herself too for what she might find inside, what further surprise awaited — and was none too surprised, not really surprised at all when she saw the gate swing shut against her, against the world.

7

Out of the Sands

Marron stared at Jemel – blood on his hands and on his robe where he had heedlessly wiped them, sweat in his hair who almost never sweated, news that sounded like betrayal on his tongue – and felt his anger rise to meet the Daughter who had risen already. Controlling that was nearly too much for him; controlling his temper too was altogether too much.

'Elisande went into the castle – and you left her, you let her do that? Alone?'

'Yes,' said quietly, sullenly, aware of its moment. 'Would you have done otherwise, could you have stopped her? I could not.'

'You could have tried.'

'I did try.'

'You could have tried harder.'

'Marron, peace.' That was Coren, pushing his way physically between them, and only just in time. Rage made him stupid, rage was a danger to his friends but he would rage despite that, despite them. 'You cannot think rationally while Jemel is bleeding, the Daughter prevents you. This is disturbing, of course, but good may yet come of it. Jemel, change your robe and wash the blood from your hands. I don't have Elisande's gift of healing, but I have an ointment that will stem the flow, enough to quiet what burns inside Marron. Then we will talk, and decide what's best to do.'

Marron knew already what was best to do, the only thing that he could do. Jemel had abandoned Elisande; Coren would find some reason to do the same. That meant it lay with him to go after her and try to bring her back. With or without Julianne. There had been altogether too much talking. Words had left Julianne too long in her captivity; they wouldn't do the same for Elisande.

Jemel unlaced his robe with awkward fingers, let it slip from his shoulders; Marron turned his back on that well-known and well-loved body and stormed out into the yard, first steps on a far longer journey—

—and was stopped, was startled to find a djinni spinning strongly in the gateway, barring his access to the street.

Don't ask it questions, but he might have done that anyway, his fury burned so hot. *Who are you?* perhaps, or *what do you want?* Or he might simply have given it orders, *out of my way, spirit,* and if it didn't react he might simply have leaped the wall and run towards the hills, towards a pair of needy girls who could hope for no one other.

But the djinni spoke before he could; it said, 'Ghost Walker, do not walk into foolishness. Think. I know where you mean to go, and what you mean to do there. If I can see this, who can see so little' – it was Elisande's djinni, then, the only one that would so brag of weakness – 'of a certainty the 'ifrit can see it too. If you went to the castle, you would meet nothing there but a waiting death.'

'Then so will Elisande.'

'Then you would be too late to save her; she is within its walls already. But Lisan moves more quietly through the world than you, Ghost Walker. She slides between the threads of the weft and leaves them barely singing, while you tear wherever you touch. She is within the castle, and not dead yet. Believe me, I would know. The weight of my oath is a burden; her death would free me, and I am not free.'

'So obey the terms of your oath, and help her!'

'What is true for you is equally true for me. We have spoken of this before. If I go to the castle, I will be destroyed there. Lisan would not be helped by that. Be patient, and take counsel; there are wiser men than you among your party, and others coming.'

They would come too late, he thought, and wanted to disregard the djinni and go after Elisande whatever the consequences, as Elisande had gone after Julianne. But then Jemel would come after him, surely, despite angry words; and Coren would certainly come after them all, and one by one they would be easy prey. The djinni had shown him that, as it had meant to.

He sighed, and heard it say, 'Now you are thinking clearly,' high and clear as ever above the sound of his breath but somehow moving further off, although it was not moving. He saw it not fade but reduce to a shimmer, a whisper of wind, and wanted to call it back. But he was not Elisande, to order its comings and goings. He had enough trouble already with the supernatural.

He stood silent until it had disappeared entirely, until a

cautious step forward confirmed that the way lay open to the street, although he would not take it now. He lingered a while in the yard, telling himself that he was only waiting until all traces of blood had been washed away within; it was nothing to do with what harsh words had passed between him and Jemel. And yet, when he did go back inside, his feet lagged heavily against his will. He felt as though he waded through turbulent water all the way to his friend's side, as though the weight of a boy's dark gaze was enough almost to hold him still. His hand reached out nervously to touch cool clean robe and cooler skin beneath, still damp from a hard scrubbing; his fingers hesitated, tremulously uncertain, before they dared to circle Jemel's elbow, the most casual of touches.

'I'm sorry,' he said; and was rewarded with a smile as anxious as his own, more than sufficient.

'I should have followed her, perhaps. I thought I should; but she forbade me, and she is hard to ignore . . .'

That brought stronger, safer smiles to each of them, and a chuckle from Coren where he was wiping his hands in a corner.

'Hard? Impossible, I should have said. And no, you should not have followed. Sometimes the gallant thing, the thing of honour is the most foolish. To lose Elisande would be bad for us, worse for her father; to lose both of you and not know how would have been worse for us all.'

'The djinni says we have not lost her yet,' Marron murmured, shifting his arm round Jemel's waist and feeling the jolt of that news, that double news snatch his friend breathless.

It was Coren, always apparent master of his emotions, who said, 'Djinni? What djinni?'

'Hers, Esren Tachur. It came, it wouldn't let me go to her . . .' That was a confession that won him another hard stare from Jemel, but it was followed by the weight of the boy's head falling against his shoulder, warm breath on his neck and an awkward hug, hands held apart. Marron rested his cheek on wiry hair, gazed down at those hands – one maimed, a finger short for his sake, as Jemel insisted – and saw how both were deeply scored and glistening where they caught the light, coated with a sweet-smelling ointment.

'Did it, indeed? That's . . . interesting. Has it ever come to you before?'

'No, never. Why would it?' *Why would I want it?* Even when it kept him from an impulsive stupidity, even when it led to reconciliation he didn't want it. Marron had grave doubts about the djinni, and all the djinn. They had surprised Rudel, and now they were surprising Coren; they must surely have some purpose of their own, to be so interfering in the lives of mortal men. He didn't even trust Esren's oath; it seemed to keep its word or not as it chose, and find some plausible-sounding reason whenever it chose not. To be sure, the djinn did not lie; but even so . . .

Even so he felt like a piece in a game of stones, moved according to another's will, and all of it a mystery to him. Again he wanted to step out into another world and leave all of this behind; and again he could not, this time he couldn't even take that first step and fool himself for a while.

There was something frightening and frustrating both, in being the tool of a creature that could see even a small way into the future, that knew what he would do before he did it. He nudged Jemel – who might try, who might yearn to know what he was thinking, but could come only as close as nature and knowledge would bring him, which was still outside Marron's skin, if barely so – and said, 'Let's walk in the sun a little.'

'Patric madness. The wise man avoids the sun.'

'The wise man sits in shadows all his life, for fear of being burned. And light would be good on your hands, come. I want you.' *Not Elisande, not her djinni, you I want.*

In honesty, the worst of the sun had passed. Even Jemel could be drawn to confess that at this time its warmth was almost pleasant, though he had to add that only in the true Sands did you meet the true sun, God's hammer against the infidel and the tool with which He tempered the steel of the one true people, the Sharai.

Marron didn't argue. Born and raised under gentler skies, he was sure there was some touch of truth in Jemel's vision, beyond the pride of a demanding people. He might have lost his own faith, he might give no more credence to priests of his faith or any, but he'd been wrong before; and if there were a God – any kind of God, Patric or Catari or otherwise – then surely this land of fierce light and heat must be His country, as the priests of every people seemed to claim. And if not, Marron still believed that there must be a power in sunlight that reached beyond the known things of the world. Even as a child, butter-brown in summer and roaming his uncle's lands amid the heady scents of the herb-strewn hills, bird-cries and insect-cries the only noises, not a whisper of a thought in his drowsy mind, only the ease of warmth and long contentment – even then, he'd known that there was a magic to the sun that lay outside the miracles of the Church, perhaps even outside the miracles of the

God, although they thanked Him for it. It wasn't an idea to mention to the priest, nor to his uncle; he tried to tell his friend Aldo once, and failed, and stepped quickly back onto safer ground as soon as he saw and understood the failure. Good boys didn't wonder about such things, certainly didn't ask such questions; and Marron could be good in those days, if Aldo was.

They set their backs against the sun; squinting into its brightness would mean also squinting up at the castle. That way lay the girls in their danger, the risk of blame rising again. Better to go the other way, to go nowhere: to walk without purpose as the town came to slow and sullen life around them, to skirt the marketplace, to press through the throngs of boys released from lessons – ignoring how they stared at a Patric face, how those stares were redoubled at their first sight of his eyes – and so to come at last to that high angle of the walls that faced due east, back to the Sands and Rhabat. Nothing was neutral in that direction either, but at least those memories were a story told.

There was a flight of steps leading up to the wall's height, and a man standing watch at the top; truce or no truce, Selussin had learned to be wary. He glanced down as they climbed, but if his face held any expression Marron could not read it. He said nothing, and his body showed no tension; his hand stayed far from his scimitar's hilt.

After murmuring a greeting which brought no response, Jemel led Marron to stand at a little distance.

'He thinks I am mad, no doubt, keeping company with a Patric who dresses like a Sharai and has the eyes of a devil. Mad or heretical, or both. Perhaps he is right, perhaps I am.'

'Mad, or heretical?'

'Both. You have made me both, Marron. You have turned me from my good sense, so that I stand bareheaded in the sun; and you have turned me from my God also, so that I cannot remember when last I prayed and meant it.'

'Do you regret either?'

'No.' He might have said that with a laugh, or with a gesture that would speak of love that overrode both sense and God, but he did not. 'I have one purpose left that you cannot turn me from, one oath yet that you will not make me break; so long as I have that, I am still Jemel. All else that I am is yours, and I do not regret it nor ever will in this body. If God condemns me for it when I am dead, then perhaps will be the time for regrets; but I can always plead madness,' and he still wasn't smiling though he should have been, surely. 'Duty would be a better plea, I think. So long as I follow you and love you, I betray no one and can still hope to fulfil my oath.'

His oath, of course, was to kill Sieur Anton d'Escrivey. Marron harboured his own secret oath, to prevent that by any means in his power. So long as Jemel was mad enough to follow him, he thought he could achieve it; his dream of travelling came back to him, the call of the far lands to the east. That way, perhaps, lay safety among strangers – but not yet. Sieur Anton was still a small world away, in Outremer beyond the mountains; Julianne and Elisande were closer and in peril, in need. Even if he could find no rescue for them, he could not leave them yet.

He gazed outward, feeling the lure regardless, trying to see past all the country he'd walked thus far, into the haze beyond – and was distracted suddenly by something closer, significantly close, a stirring twist of dust that hid dark figures at its heart.

'Look,' he said softly. 'There, do you see?'

'No, nothing. What is it?'

No dispute, no suggestion that perhaps there was nothing to be seen: Jemel had desert eyes, but knew that Marron had the Daughter's.

'They are coming.'

At last, they were coming. Marron hadn't realised until this moment came just how much he'd been waiting for it, for them. Waiting more in hope than expectation, perhaps, but waiting none the less. At least he could be sure of something's happening now, something's being forced to happen. A handful of people could sit quiet within a township's walls, perhaps; an army not, and this should be an army. Coren could be patient, Coren could outsit a mountain; Hasan not, and this must be Hasan.

'Who, and how many?'

Marron smiled; even his eyes couldn't make out banners or numbers at this distance. 'You could guess, better than I can see. These are your people. A group of men, though, it's not a column, the dust is settling at their backs; and they're riding swiftly. Outriders, come to scout the land?'

'Of a sort. There will be two dozen men, and I could put a name to each of them. Will you wager?'

'Would I lose?'

'Oh, yes.'

'Name your terms.'

Jemel chuckled, and brushed the back of his hand lightly against Marron's arm as he shook his head. 'Gambling is a sin, forbidden. But I will tell you, and you will see how well I know the tribes, and be impressed.'

'Isn't vanity a sin too?'

A purse of the lips, a rocking motion of the head: 'It is preached against. Does it offend God, or simply courtesy? I am not sure. Ask an imam; I am a warrior. And this I am sure of, that Hasan leads those riders himself, and at his back you will find the sheikhs of every tribe that rides with him. Where else would they be but at the head, how else could they bring the tribes to follow? Besides, this country is known, their coming cannot be hidden; what need of scouts? If any, they would scout themselves, and trust their own eyes before another man's.'

Marron nodded. Hasan, the sheikhs – and one other, sure to be riding in that party.

'One of us,' he said neutrally, 'is going to have to tell Rudel that his daughter has gone into the castle.' When Jemel didn't answer, he went on, 'We could leave it to Coren, perhaps?' Let the diplomat break the news . . .

But Jemel was shaking his head, as Marron had been sure that he would. 'No. If there was a fault, it was mine; if there is a storm to come, it is mine to endure.'

Not alone; Marron would stand beside him. But, 'If there was a fault, it was Elisande's, in choosing to go.'

'You did not think so when I told you. Perhaps her father will not think so either.'

'I was wrong, Jemel, and I am sorry for it. And Rudel knows her better than any of us, he will not make the same mistake.' *He knows her better and loves her less,* he might have added for his friend's comfort, except that he didn't believe that it was true.

'You think so? You may be right – but he is still her father. We should go and meet them.'

'They'll be a while yet.' Indeed, Jemel was still straining to see what was so clear to Marron, the distant figures and the dust-cloud of their passage; the watchman close by hadn't sighted them at all. 'No point walking so far out that we have to run back at their stirrups.' Marron could run all day, with the Daughter's strength allied to his own; Jemel only thought that he could. 'Wait a little, and watch.'

'If we wait much longer, he' – the watchman, indicated with a contemptuous jerk of the head – 'will see them at last,' for all the world as though Jemel saw them clearly himself, 'and strike his alarm,' an iron ring suspended from a tripod at his side.

'And then?'

'And then they will close the gates, and we will be prevented from leaving the city.'

Only Jemel could call this little township a city; surely only Jemel could imagine that it would have fire enough in its belly to defy an army of the Sharai. Marron smiled, and said, 'Wait. If they will not let us out, then we will wait until they let Hasan in. I do not think it will be long.'

It was long enough before the watchman spotted the approaching riders – so long, indeed, that Marron was tempted to go to him and point them out.

At last the man stiffened and stared, muttering nervously into his beard; then he snatched up a bar and belaboured his alarm-ring, crying out above its clatter to reinforce its warning.

Marron turned to watch the streets below, and saw the

panic that he'd been expecting: people spewing from every house amid a rising babble of voices, men and boys milling uncertainly, looking for leadership and finding none while the women came running in from the fields, herding their daughters before them and trying vainly to gather in their sons. Some of the men carried arms, and some of those came to the walls, but more were hurrying to the temples where their greater confidence lay, their better chance of another survival.

'We should go to the gate,' Jemel said urgently.

'If you think so.'

It was easier to make their way along the wall than through the streets, there was far less press of people. The men who had climbed up stood for the most part numbly clutching a useless scimitar or spear, or else gripping the parapet two-handed, gazing at the plume of dust that foretold their greatest fear. Some were silent, some spoke of the supposed truce, of the faithlessness of the Sharai; more than once Marron had to drag Jemel on, where he would have stopped to dispute that.

When they reached the gates in this south-easterly wall, they found them still standing wide, abandoned even by their guards. Jemel exclaimed aloud; Marron grinned, and led his friend down the steps to ground level.

'Why slam a door, only to have it broken down and needing repair after? These people cannot stand against the Sharai, Jemel, they know that as well as you do. They will welcome Hasan as they have welcomed my people before this, and yours again before them; they will starve themselves to feed his army, and pray only that he leaves or is driven back into the Sands before they starve indeed.'

Even as he said it, here came the welcoming-party: a group of flustered elderly men in ornate robes, clutching talismans or plucking at their beards with fretful fingers. They arrayed themselves in the road below the gateway, jostling for precedence or seeking to deny it, some of them, pushing others forward in their stead. Jemel hissed in irritation; Marron swallowed a chuckle, and pulled him into the shadow of the high gate.

The harsh, doleful tolling of the alarm stopped abruptly. The whole township seemed to be holding itself in stillness, all the clamour of the last minutes fallen to nothing. Marron gazed up at the baked mud of the arch above the gate and thought he could feel how ancient this place was, and how weary as it faced yet another force of men, yet another invasion. Weary but strong, strong in patience and in faith: and that faith would be rewarded, that patience would win in the end. This army would leave in the end, as every army before it. Selussin would remain.

Strength to endure, simple survival – it was a quality that Marron admired, envied, hungered for. Every living man is a survivor, of course; every man endures everything he meets until he fails, until he dies. Marron had endured more than many and survived it, he expected to endure more yet and to survive that too; but it wasn't his own strength that had brought him this far or would take him further. *The Ghost Walker is traditionally very hard to kill.*

The boy in him – what was left of the boy in him, when he could find it – yearned for another kind of life, but could not speak of it even to Jemel, especially to Jemel. He was ashamed of his own dreams, because even if there could be a life for him without the Daughter, it still wasn't his own strength that he dreamed of. He still wanted to live in strength's shadow, sooner than be strong himself.

He'd seen many kinds of strength since he came to the Sanctuary Land. Here about Selussin was the simplest form, high walls that were undefended, that could do nothing but stand; and here came a couple of strong men who were anything but simple, who rode veiled against the dust they raised, whose hearts were as obscure as their deeds were daring.

Hasan and Rudel, side by side: and even that could be significant, where the two dozen men who followed were indeed tribal chieftains and could each have claimed the place of honour at Hasan's elbow. Perhaps Rudel only rode there to save the others fighting for it; that was not impossible. Or perhaps Sharai had come to an accommodation with Surayon, *thus far and no further*, that was possible too. That could be hoped for, at least for a little longer . . .

Any man arriving so, out of the Sands with a band of seasoned warriors at his back and first signs now of a greater force behind, any such must have caused the priests great anxiety. When such a man threw back hood and veil, gazed down and said with quiet authority, 'I am Hasan,' pure terror showed for a moment on their faces. All the world knew that Hasan was hungry for war with Outremer. If he'd chosen this time and this place to fight it, they could see the final end to Selussin's long history played out in blood and destruction, their libraries burned and their temples ransacked, their people's lives and their own consumed in blood and pain.

The eldest among them, gaunt and white-bearded, recovered himself quickly. He took a slow pace forward, leaning on what might have been a staff of office or else simply a support for unsteady legs; he bowed his head lightly, a gesture of respect from priest to warrior but nothing more, no hint of a surrender; he said, 'Hasan, our gates are open to you as they are to all who follow the true faith, if you come in peace.'

The gates were open in any case, however he came. Hasan bowed in his turn, though, and said, 'Always in peace to you, most holy.'

'Your numbers do not suggest a mission of peace,' which was a challenge more direct than Marron or possibly Hasan had expected.

'True. I come to reclaim one who is most precious to me, and has been stolen away; but she lies in the castle yonder,' a gesture towards the high dark shadow that the Patrics called Revanchard, 'not within your walls. The tribes will not disturb your teachings. I shall see to that.'

The old priest nodded his gratitude, seeming to accept the promise at face value. Marron wondered if he could truly be so naïve. Having come so far with an army at his back, Hasan was unlikely to settle for Julianne's recovery, whatever his agreement with Rudel. Outremer was too close, too tempting – who could say if he would ever gather such a mass of men again?

Selussin's best hope must be to see the Sharai overrun the castle and then march on across the mountains, to fight their war within the borders of the Patric kingdom; their greatest fear would be a defeat for Hasan, a swift retreat with his enemies harrying hard. His men would flood into castle and township both, lacking time to lose themselves in the Sands; the decisive battle of this generation would be fought out against Selussin's walls, and that spelled doom, dust and ashes for the generations following.

For the moment, though, all parties were prepared to pretend otherwise. After further exchanges of courtesy, the priests stepped back and Hasan rode in through the gates with the sheikhs following in a crush, crowding for position, not to be seen ceding place to any other.

Rudel ceded place to them all, then came on only as far as the arch. A jerk of his head for beckoning, and both boys ran forward. Jemel went to his stirrup while Marron hung back, still close enough to unsettle the camel but not to drive it frantic.

'Someone must go back and speak to the tribes,' Rudel said, 'which means me, since these are all too grand to act as messenger, even to their own. Wait for me here, and be patient; it may take a deal of shouting before they'll listen.'

'What will you tell them?' Marron called.

'Much the same – wait, and be patient. Otherwise the hotheads will ride up to investigate the castle and either trigger a disaster or more likely fall to quarrelling among themselves when they find the gates slammed against them, while the old campaigners head for the town and make a liar of Hasan. I presume nothing's changed at the castle, Morakh is still there with Julianne?'

'And the 'ifrit, yes. But things have changed, Rudel, they're not alone any more . . .'

'How so?'

'Be quiet, Marron. It is mine to tell,' Jemel insisted. 'Rudel, we were watching the castle, Lisan and I, looking for a way in when people came, on foot, from across the mountains. About a hundred, not well armed, not warriors, women and children among them. They went in, and the gates were closed behind them. I came back, to tell Marron and Coren.'

'And my daughter?'

'She climbed the walls and went inside, we think. That was her intent.'

Rudel sighed slowly. 'Of course it was. And nothing you could say would stop her. Don't look so guilt-ridden, Jemel; there's only one person I know of who could conceivably shift Elisande when her mind's made up, and I gather he wasn't there.'

No, I was talking with Coren, doing nothing while my friends took it on themselves to make something happen, and walked into danger without me. Rudel hadn't moved his eyes by so much as a fraction, but Marron understood him perfectly. So, he thought, did Jemel. Swiftly he said, 'Djinni Tachur told me that she was well,' which wasn't quite true but true enough.

'Did it?' Like Coren, Rudel was instantly interested. 'What exactly did it say to you?'

'That she was inside the castle, and unhurt.' Exactly, it had said *not dead yet*, but he wouldn't pass that on to her father. 'It was seeking to stop me following her.'

'Which it did, clearly. We must hope that it was right to do so. Unhurt does not necessarily mean uncaptured; she may be as much a prisoner as Julianne. If the djinni speaks to you again, Marron, you might ask it – or no, not ask, but try to find out. I must go to the tribes,' with a glance over his shoulder that drew the boys' eyes after, and showed them all the dust of the army's approach. 'Wait here.'

He turned his camel almost savagely, beat it into a run; Jemel watched him go, and said, 'He is upset.'

'Of course he's upset, she's his daughter. Never mind how bitter it is between them, she's still his daughter.'

'Yes. Patrics are a strange people; they spit at each other in public, and where they love they conceal it.'

'Not all of us,' Marron said softly.

'No? Sometimes I think your heart is veiled, and no more honest than your eyes: not the true Marron that speaks to me or rides with me or lies beside me in the night, that one holds himself elsewhere.'

'Jemel . . .'

'Then I remember that it would have to be so, or you would not be Marron, nor the Ghost Walker.' A brilliant smile, entirely unexpected; a sudden kiss, all the more so; a nudging elbow to drive him back into the shade of the wall, no more Patric madness in the sun. They sat down and settled their spines against mud that was as hard as rock, as hot as a rock in the land of the djinn after a morning's baking. Jemel squirmed for a minute, then said, 'This will cook us before he comes back, we might as well sit in an oven. Let's go up and watch the tribes disperse. Gambling is forbidden – but I would lay money on which will squabble over camping-grounds, and which squabbles will lead to blood. Hasan has led a war-party before, but never an army; and that was holy for us all, and this is a matter of honour and insult, or he says so, which is less than a matter of God. There will be some who do not want to ride for the sake of a Patric woman, and many who do not see why Hasan should need so many men and all the tribes together; true that she was taken from Rhabat, but from the house of the

Beni Rus. It should be a Beni Rus affair at most. So they will be hot and angry after a long day at the end of many long and hard days before this; and now Rudel will tell them that they cannot come into the town nor go up to the castle by their own sheikhs' orders – that is not true, but he will say so, because he is not foolish, that one – and they will fight each other instead. Not much, perhaps, and not for long, but there will be fighting. It won't matter, though; nobody will die. They would not risk a blood-feud here.'

Marron followed Jemel back up the steps and onto the wall, more Patric madness after all and perhaps it was infectious, like the tempers of the tribes. They stood shoulder to shoulder and watched the far dark mass of men in its slow dispersal.

'You see?'

Marron did indeed see, better than Jemel if more strangely. Through the red cast of the Daughter's eyes he saw a dozen sudden flurries, stabs of sunfire as the light caught a thrusting blade; he saw dark figures stumble and crouch wounded on the sandy ground, he could almost smell their blood from here; he saw himself as a raptor, or a vulture rather, drawn from great distances towards any hope of carrion, called to launch himself out off the wall on the strong wings of the Daughter.

None of the injured died, though, as Jemel had predicted. Spilled blood was nothing, a scar of honour that laid no burden of debt or vengeance; and each time Rudel was there at speed, wheeling on his mount and gesturing widely, speaking too soft to hear or else crying out loud enough to stir the dead in their cemeteries in the dusty hills, doing whatever was needful to see knives sheathed and quarrels cooled. Each time he couched his camel and stepped into the brittle peace, to spend some little time talking as it seemed to those who had been wounded.

'They will meet again to argue later, by the wells,' Jemel prophesied, 'but there will be no more weapons drawn. We will fight for water rights but never by the water, for fear that blood should taint it. It is a desert law, but it will hold here. It would hold anywhere. That is why your people pushed us back into the Sands, because there is so much water beyond the mountains there and they would poison it all to win the land, where we would not. I have heard that they *drowned* all their Sharai prisoners, sewed them into sacks and threw them into the water until they died . . .'

That was an awesome death, clearly, terrible and shocking and profound. Marron had heard that all prisoners had been treated with honour and ransomed back to their tribes; he was inclined now to believe neither version. There were men of virtue and there were men of cruelty, and they could be found on either side. Some men could be both at once, but he didn't want to think about Sieur Anton.

'Morakh attacked you by the well, before we reached Rhabat – when I brought Elisande back from the land of the djinn, when I ran to fetch Hasan, remember?'

'I do not forget. Morakh fights by his own laws; he is no longer of the Sharai, and so no longer of the desert.'

'You are a Sand Dancer yourself, or so you keep proclaiming. Doubly outcast, you, tribeless one. Does that mean you are no longer of the Sharai, or of the desert?'

On some subjects, Jemel would not be teased; he gazed levelly back and said, 'You know what I am.'

Not really, no. Servant, lover, follower, friend, all of those;

and Sharai, and of the desert, and so the sworn enemy of
Marron's people; and Sieur Anton's sworn enemy too, which
only made him more complicated than ever – but Marron
knew where he was, here at his side, and that was good
enough. He would have kept the thought close, but remembered what Jemel had said about his veiled heart and tried to
prove it untrue. 'You are with me,' he said, 'the Ghost
Walker's companion.'

'Indeed.' Jemel didn't seem satisfied, and in honesty
Marron couldn't blame him. His tongue was tied, though;
another figure stood always between them, forbidding any
deeper confession. His heart was as infected as his blood; he
was tainted by two worlds, two lives, yearned for both and
could trust himself with neither.

Jemel pulled his hood up then, *enough of this Patric madness*, and they stood in silence while the tribes slowly
dispersed; stood until they saw a single rider come wearily
back towards the town.

They went down to meet Rudel where they had before,
below the arch of the wall. This time he dismounted, and
went to pass the reins to Jemel with a sigh of exhaustion; but
he checked himself, this time seeing the state of those torn
hands.

'In the name of mercy, what have you been doing to
yourself, lad? Losing one finger wasn't enough for you, but
you had to try to take the rest off too?'

'Climbing rocks that were edged like knives. Lisan healed
them once, but I had to come back without her,' that last
added like a deliberate reminder.

'Yes, so you said. And I said you are to take no blame to
yourself for that. Well, give them here. I have followed my

daughter across Outremer; tired as I am, I can follow her in this also.'

Marron wondered briefly why Rudel should be suddenly so tired, when he had seemed fresh enough an hour earlier; then he remembered the wounded among the Sharai, those stupid squabbles that had led inevitably to knifework. Of course, he would have healed there also. Indeed Marron had seen him do it, and not realised.

Jemel's hands were not so serious a hurt, despite the pain they'd cost him. Coren's unguent had been enough to stem the bleeding; Rudel needed only a moment's magic to knit ripped flesh and skin together and leave them whole and quite unmarked. Jemel rubbed his thumbs across the pads of his fingers, where the deepest cuts had been, and said, 'Lisan took longer, and her touch was not so hot . . .'

'There are some ways yet that I can best my daughter. Not in wilfulness: she had that from her mother, though her stubbornness is my own. It's an unhappy combination. Tell me more about these other people who came to the castle, Jemel; them I confess I don't understand.'

'No more do I. It is as I told you, they were not an army, not all men; they looked like peasants, Patrics and Catari mixed, but they followed one man, and they ran like wolves.' Then, with a glance back over his shoulder, 'They ran as Marron runs, as if they could run all day and all night too. Perhaps they had done so, all through the mountains, but there was no sign of weariness on them. Not even on the children. And they went in as though they were expected, and closed the gates behind them, as I said. I cannot think what they would do with Morakh, nor he with them.'

'No. It is strange, but all of this is strange. We had guessed that Morakh waited there for something; this may be it, although it is hard to understand. I'd been looking for Sand Dancers, perhaps, or more 'ifrit, an army of ghûls. Assumptions are dangerous; we must remember that, and be careful. I could wish that Elisande had been more careful, but that is the story of her life, and mine. At least she has a gift for being overlooked, when she chooses to use it. Now, where are we going? I remember the shape of this place, but little more; it is a long time since I last brought books to Selussin, or good wine to Revanchard.'

'You've been inside the castle?' Marron demanded, a beat ahead of Jemel.

'Yes, but years ago, and not so deep as my daughter. Not so deep by a distance now. Whether she's free or taken, she'll be down into the dungeons and looking for her friend, as she was at the Roq. I was never let in past the bailey. It was garrisoned by the duke's men in those days and they were a suspicious breed, wouldn't trust anyone who traded with the town. Wouldn't trust anyone at all, if they hadn't grown up as neighbours. You never came far enough incountry to see it, Marron, but Outremer can be like that; and the closer you come to Ascariel, the worse it gets. It's not like being a stranger in the Sands, Jemel – the Sharai will either kill you or kill a goat to welcome you, but the Patrics will do neither. They will watch and guard, and never welcome.'

Jemel frowned, opened his mouth to question – then closed it again and shook his head. Marron guessed that he didn't, wouldn't, couldn't understand.

'My wine, though – that was welcome enough, after the beer they brewed below. They loved me for my wine and took me in, but never beyond the first court. Little use that knowledge is; we must rely on my errant Elisande, I fear, to find the way to Julianne. And then come back to tell us. Now,' again, clapping his hands as Jemel did this time take the camel's reins from him, 'where are you taking me?'

'Uh, I'm not sure where Hasan has gone, with the chiefs . . .'

'Are you not? I am. Haven't you found the priests' house yet? I remember that, at least. The next building behind the great temple; every house hides its secrets here, but some at least reveal that they have great secrets to hide. This one has gates of bronze, etched with the words of the prophets. All the elders of all the temples live there in its safety, cut off from the sight of alluring women and the noise of those vexatious boys. That's where they'll take Hasan and his entourage, there's room enough. As an unbeliever – even a Surayonnaise unbeliever, and they've had some dealings with me and mine, a great many dealings over the years – I'd be no more let in there than you would, Marron, with your eyes on show. No, take me to Coren, wherever you've left him, and let us mourn together over our missing daughters.'

Jemel led both camel and guest towards their rented quarters, while Marron trailed some distance behind. The camel must needs be bedded down in the small yard outside the house, where every family in Selussin kept what livestock it might possess: a mule, a few chickens, perhaps a goat or two. That would make it difficult for Marron to pass in and out without raising panic in the beast, which was foul-tempered enough already, groaning and tossing its head, balking at every tug. No help for it, though: there wasn't even a window that opened to the street. These Selussids kept their secrets locked behind high blank walls – but then so did Marron, or so Jemel claimed. That boy was good at learning secrets, though, and hearing names not spoken. He had reason enough to leave a veil over Marron's heart, when he knew what lay behind it.

When they came to the house it took both Jemel and Rudel to force the camel through the narrow gateway and into the yard. Marron watched uselessly until Rudel went inside, leaving Jemel still struggling to settle the unruly animal.

'I'll go to the market,' he called out, 'buy her some feed.'

A wave of the hand was all the response he won, assuming that the curses that came with it were not also directed at him. He grinned and turned and walked away, accompanied for some distance by Jemel's opinions on the camel's birth and breeding. Without those, so loud and fluent as they were, he might have been able to eavesdrop on the older men's conversation inside the house, but no matter. He knew some part of what they'd say, the stories they had to tell each other. What more they might say or decide or discover, he could learn later from them or from Jemel.

At one time, the marketplace at Selussin must have been a sight to rival any in the Ekhed empire, when the town was a trading station as well as a centre for learning. The great open area below the temple would have been like a confluence of many waters, where caravans came together from all over the known world; big as it was, it could barely have been big enough. It must have seethed with crowds, with colour, with merchants crying the value of their silks and jewels, their spices, their camels and slaves. Now the people traded only with themselves, and only what little they could spare. One family had killed a goat, perhaps, and couldn't eat all the meat before it turned, couldn't spare the salt to keep it good; another had a precious harvest of apricots from a pair of trees nurtured in the yard, but needed oil.

So the women would gather as the sun came down, setting out their stock on a blanket in one shaded corner of the wide and wasted space and haggling almost desperately with their neighbours, trying to eke any benefit they could from their meagre goods.

No one traded halfa-reeds, of course, when they were free to gather; besides, Marron wasn't sure that even a camel would eat that wiry stuff. But here was a woman with a sack of withered greens, the outer peelings of her morning's harvest. Elsewhere they might have been thrown on a dung-heap to rot; on his uncle's land they might have been fed to the pigs, but never sent to market. Here they had value, they could be traded. No pigs to eat them in this town, of course; there were donkeys, though, as well as goats. Now, there was a camel.

She was an elderly woman, or looked it from what little Marron could see of her body, eyes and hands. One of the eyes had a cast in it and both were rheumy, crusted with dry yellow matter; the hands were twisted and their skin was loose and wrinkled, heavily ridged with scars across the palms. The hunch of her back as she sat suggested that there'd be no straightness in her when she stood. Perhaps it wasn't age that had bent and shrivelled her, perhaps it was only hard years of work and hunger under the hot sun, children and disease and all the ill chances that come of being poor, for no god has ever loved a starveling; but Marron could deal with the world only as he saw it. Peering beneath the skin of things was a trick for subtle men, for Coren and Rudel and others. One other in particular, but this was no place nor time to be thinking of him. Marron wanted no sharp mind probing beneath his own skin; enough that they saw his one ghost burning behind his eyes. Who else haunted him was a private matter, emphatically not for sharing.

And the world was what it was, what he saw, no subtlety or deception; he crouched politely and said, 'Old woman, I think I may have what you are seeking.'

She snorted, showing him a mouthful of good hard teeth as she said, 'Not so many years ago, boy, I might have had what you are seeking.' *Not so old as all that,* she was saying; the world never was what he saw or thought it ought to be, however hard he tried to treat it so. 'All I seek now is dung to make my fire, and I do not think you have so much of that.'

He couldn't begin to guess what she was seeing, with her gaze so twisted and her infected eyes; not the blaze of his, though, that seemed certain. There was no trace of fear or question in her voice, only a dismissive contempt.

He found that familiar, reassuring; and besides, he felt a sudden flood of joy at the simple economy of her bargain. She would provide fuel, feed for an animal; she would take fuel, what came out at the other end, what her greens were converted to.

'Actually,' he said around his grin, 'we have a camel, and you are welcome to the dung if you will feed the beast for us, as long as we are here.' Which he hoped, he prayed would not be long at all now. 'I hadn't thought your needs would be so simple, or so simply met; I'd meant to offer silver . . .'

He trailed that expectantly, and watched her gape: silver, for a mess of sun-shrivelled greens? She might not have touched a coin in months, in years; this was not a money mart. In truth he'd handled little enough himself, lifelong. The coins in his pouch had come from Coren, and still seemed like an alien gift.

The woman recovered tongue and wits sooner than he'd expected. 'Silver? And so you shall offer silver, boy. One camel's daily dung won't keep my fire, nor earn its food. Show me your silver . . .'

He fingered out a few small coins, wondering if they were too few or too many, willing to give her the whole pouch if she asked for it. As he leaned forward to offer them to her, he heard slow footfalls at his back. Three people stepping uncomfortably close, standing silent above him; his blood fizzed with the sense of danger, the Daughter waking to it, just a moment before the woman went entirely still before him. Briefly he thought he saw a faint shadow of smoke touch her sick eyes. Then she toppled over, to lie sprawled across her sack of greens.

Marron stood, and turned. Two men and a woman, one Patric and two Catari and none of them a warrior, each of them simply dressed with that same lean look and weathered skin that spoke of a lifetime's labour for small reward. There was a blankness to their faces, though, that had nothing to say of their lives at all. Their bodies were present, and a very real threat; their souls he thought were somewhere else altogether.

That emptiness seemed to suck at him, almost to sing to him, a greater danger than the blades they drew. None of them was a warrior, perhaps, but each of them had a knife.

Well, so did he; and his vow not to kill was no hindrance here. With the strength and speed he borrowed from the Daughter, evading these slow strange creatures shouldn't be a problem. He was more worried about the woman unconscious at his back. He'd brought this trouble on her; if he ran, she'd be abandoned. She'd get no aid from her fellow Selussids. All about him, he could hear the cries and panic of the other women at the market as they snatched up their goods and fled. Even if their menfolk came, they'd surely come too late for her. And there had been too much abandonment already.

Besides, Marron had another, a better weapon than his knife, and he shouldn't need to use it. The threat should be enough to drive these hollow people back to whatever hole they'd crept from. He could guard himself and the woman both, if he just released the Daughter.

His blade was in his hand. A touch of the point to the ever-unhealing wound in his arm, blood and red smoke issued forth while pain coursed inward, through his bones. He had a momentary memory of another smoke, a black smoke insinuating itself into the woman's eyes; and then the Daughter shaped itself in the air between him and his three opponents.

They made no move, and neither did he. It felt to him like a long, long time that they stood there, gazing at each other through the scarlet haze of the Daughter's almost-body.

He thought that he might have to escape with the woman into the other world, as they seemed to lack the intelligence or the will to flee what was far more potent than themselves. But there was a chill biting suddenly at his bleeding arm, different from the pain that he was used to; it sapped his strength, and his own will also. He felt it strike deep into his body, numbing and draining where it passed; he dropped onto his knees, too heavy to stand any longer, and a grey fog clouded his sight. It clouded his thoughts, too. He was vaguely aware that the Daughter was losing its coherence, shifting into smoke and flowing back through his wound, into his blood again; it was hard to focus on how strange that was when he had not summoned it, harder to remember why it mattered.

And then it was within him, and the Daughter's heat met his cold invader; and had he thought that he knew pain before? He rolled on the ground, dimly aware that he was screaming; that hands were seizing him, lifting him, gripping with a strength that defied even his bucking struggles; that rags were stuffed into his mouth to silence him to the world as he was carried away.

8

An Exchange of Knives

It was children who came running to carry the news to Jemel. He was waiting at the open gateway, watching for Marron's return and keeping a careful distance from the grumbling camel; he'd finally got her couched and tied, but any close approach brought her head whipping round and her teeth snapping. His robe was liberally spattered with her saliva, and he'd barely missed losing another finger in a careless moment. He had hopes that food might pacify her, but those hopes were not strong. Mostly he only wanted to have Marron safely back at his side. There was – or should be – little danger to the Ghost Walker within the walls of Selussin, but that didn't stop him worrying.

He looked for the familiar silhouette of his friend turning into the lane, burdened with any luck by a bale of fodder; instead he saw three small figures racing pell-mell around the corner. Just boys at a game after lessons, he thought at first. But they slowed as they came closer, and he saw how their eyes were wide and their skins were flushed with more than exercise.

They came to a staggering, hesitant halt just a few paces from him; their leader, a scant finger taller than his fellows, forced a few words out around his panting.

'You are his man.'

'Yes.' No need for Jemel to pretend, *whose man?* or *I am no one's man*; no need for the boy to name him, *Ghost Walker* or *red-eyed whiteskin*. Of course the boys would know, where and how this foreign party lived; of course Jemel would understand them. 'What has happened, did he send you to me?' Fishing for hope now, for something short of disaster; pretending after all, perhaps, because their faces denied him before he'd even shaped the question.

'Strangers came to the market,' the boy said, 'and a woman fainted. He called a demon, a creature of smoke, we saw it; but then it turned on him, he was hurt by it, and the strangers took him away.'

Jemel understood the demon, but nothing more: not why Marron would release it, nor how it could have hurt him. 'What strangers were these?' he demanded.

'Two men, and a woman; we had not seen them before,' and that was strange too, and disturbing. They couldn't mean the Sharai chiefs who came into the town with Hasan, nor anyone from the tribes camped outside, if one had been a woman; if there were other strangers in Selussin, the children surely would know.

There was one other group at hand, though. He said, 'From the castle?'

The boy glanced at his companions, and shrugged. 'Perhaps.' There was no surprise at the suggestion. Children were natural spies; growing up among the Saren, he and his fellows had prided themselves on knowing the movements of every family and every solitary rider for miles around. Boys got everywhere, and sharp eyes saw it all. 'They carried him off towards the western gate,' the youngster added, confirmation enough. That way lay the castle, and nothing else but the road to Outremer.

'How long ago?'

'Not long, but they were swift. Will you come?'

'Show me.' He ought to take a minute first, to tell Coren and Rudel what was amiss; but a minute's delay might be one minute too long. And the old men would insist on coming too, not to weaken their party by dividing it further. He satisfied his conscience with a wordless bellow back into the yard, that started the camel roaring; that would alert them to trouble. They'd come out to find him gone, but perhaps they could follow his trail in the dust, or his scent in the air. If not, there would doubtless be other boys to guide them.

These boys, his boys were already on the move, throwing little summoning glances back at him. He ran after, working his scimitar in its sheath as he went. No need to draw it yet, but he wanted it loose. He wanted swordplay, he realised suddenly, he wanted the heat and fury of battle to quell the chill of his fear; he wanted to spill the blood of those who had frightened him so, who were trying to steal Marron from him. He pressed on faster, dragging the boys in his wake as he charged through the winding, narrow ways, turning always towards the setting sun. They might have known a quicker way – *show me*, he had said, and gave them no chance to do so – but his legs were longer and his urgency burned his soul; he couldn't wait for them, for anything.

Even so, he came too late. He'd hoped that the guards might have challenged unknowns with such a burden, might have closed the gates against them, but this was Selussin. His first sight of the walls showed him the wide and open archway, a few men standing, staring out. As he came closer, he could make out a distant moving shadow in the sudden dusk, running figures on the road.

They'd gone too far, with too good a start. He could chase them all the way to the castle, and not catch up with them. He let himself stagger to a halt, gulped down a cry of promise and despair; his voice would never carry to Marron, and he wouldn't so disgrace them both in front of strangers.

The boys had gathered in a hard-breathing pack at his back. He fumbled in the pouch at his belt, drew out a few coins and let them fall from nerveless fingers; then he started running again. Retracing his steps, heading back to the old men, the wise ones, those who would tell him what to do.

Whether he'd listen was another matter; it would depend entirely on what they said. He'd listened and listened since they came to Selussin, first to Coren and then to Lisan; Julianne was still a prisoner and now Marron had joined her, and Jemel felt that there had been altogether too much of talking and of listening. Lisan had taken action, on her own. So would he, if he had to. He'd let her go alone into the castle largely to stop Marron coming after; now Marron had gone the same way, against his will and in pain. Nothing would stop Jemel following, with company or without it.

He came pounding down the lane and into the yard, startling the camel out of what was doubtless a hungry doze. Ignoring her, he plunged into the house – and found it abandoned, both men missing and no message, no hint left behind to say where they were gone.

For a moment he stood irresolute, before he turned and ran once more. Driving against aching legs and a pounding heart, whipped on by fear and determination in equal measure, he went up to the marketplace. That wide space was deserted now except for a few abandoned blankets and some scattered, trampled produce. Men were gathering in the long shadow of the temple tower, agitation showing in their jabbing hands and their raised voices, but they held no interest for Jemel.

Instead he trotted past the temple, to find where the imams' house stood behind its high wall. The bronze gates were shut; he stifled a momentary yearning that the town's watchmen might have been as careful of what they were sworn to protect. If they'd closed all the gates they guarded when Hasan and his army had appeared, the strangers from the castle could never have come within the walls, and Marron would be safe now, the camel would be fed and quiet, all would be as it ought to have been with only the girls to rescue . . .

Pointless to dream; this town welcomed its enemies as eagerly as its friends. Rudel would call that good sense, Coren politics; to Jemel it was cowardice, no more. Better to fight and die than to be overrun. Here they had been overrun so often they had slave souls, it seemed to him, always looking for a master.

The council of imams made different rules for themselves, apparently, but he would no more sit and wait to be noticed outside these gates than he would outside the castle. He tested them to be sure that they were locked, which they were; he hammered his fists against the heavy patterns of their decoration to be sure that the booming summons would go unanswered, which it did. Then – conscious that he was being watched from the temple doorway, but confident that the men there would do no more than watch, would not come to interfere – he took a dozen paces back, steadied his breathing and his body, and threw himself forward.

As he reached the gates he leaped up, arms stretching as high as he could reach above his head. He just managed to curl the fingers of one hand over the sharp edge of bronze; briefly he hung there, feeling his grip start to slip as he cut himself once more and blood welled out. He swung his other hand up, for a doubled hold; his bare toes scrabbled for purchase and found it in the deep indentations of the design; he scrambled up and hauled his body over, dropped down into the half-dark of the courtyard beyond.

Dark where he stood, crouched against the gates and breathing hard; light elsewhere, light spilling from the doors and windows of the house, more lights moving in his direction as men came with lamps to see who dared disturb their holy masters' peace.

Jemel straightened slowly, tugged his robe into the best state he could manage – not good, stained as it was with camel-spit and now again with blood – and walked boldly out to meet them.

They came with weapons drawn, of course; he kept his hand a careful distance from his scimitar, far enough to say *I mean no violence to you or yours* yet near enough to say also *I am not afraid of you*, ready to close and draw in a moment if he needed to.

'I am called Jemel,' he said, his voice carrying clear and grim throughout the courtyard. 'I have an urgent message for Hasan. Take me to him.'

One man stepped forward, confident in the weight and authority of his office. 'Hasan is in conference, with his council and ours; they may not be disturbed. This house is closed. Give up your weapon, and await judgement for your intrusion.'

'I said my news is urgent. Hasan will not thank you for delaying me; it touches on his friends.'

'Hasan will not hear of this. It is our laws that you offend, and all the laws of hospitality besides. The deliberations of the councils are more important than gossip overheard by a camel-boy; I would not pass you through if you bore letters of state.'

'No? I bear something sharper than a letter,' and now he did draw his scimitar, 'and will use it if I must. One way or another, I will see Hasan. Go to him, tell him Jemel is here; he will come.'

'There are six of us, boy, and none will carry your message. Do not add stupidity to your offences.'

'Six indeed, and I am alone; but I am no camel-boy despite my youth and dress. I am Sharai, of the deep desert. And I am a Sand Dancer, see my hand?' as he held it up palm out against the house's lights. 'And more than all of these, I am the chosen companion of the Ghost Walker, of whom you may have heard. I have killed men, Sand Dancers like myself; I have killed ghûls; I have killed 'ifrit. I would not willingly harm one of you, but I will kill all six if I must. My news concerns the Ghost Walker, who is my friend and Hasan's; it is not I who is being stupid here. Will you go, or must we fight?'

At last there was some doubt among the men he faced, some uneasy shuffling and sidelong glances. It was like such men, he thought, to be afraid of words where they hadn't the sense to be afraid of a blade.

Their leader said, 'Those are not words or names to bandy with at a time like this. We will take you before the council, and let them judge; Hasan may speak for you, if he will. But if you are playing with us, your punishment will be severe.'

'Trust me,' Jemel said, trying to sound grateful, 'this is no game.'

He went to sheathe his blade, but the man checked him. 'You must give up your weapon. I will not take you armed before my council or your own, if you are as dangerous as you say.'

And there, of course, lay the penalty of boasting, and being taken at one's word. Jemel had lost too much time already, in argument; he laughed and reversed the scimitar in his hand, presenting its haft as he walked forward. The man took it warily, his own blade still upraised.

He didn't know much about the Sharai, if he thought Jemel disarmed or rendered harmless. There was a knife in plain view hanging from his belt-rope, which was neither ceremonial nor used solely for eating. Jemel stepped closer to the man, to distract his eyes from dropping so low, and said, 'If you hold my blade, you should hold my name alongside. That you have, but I do not know yours. How am I to find you, after I leave the chiefs?'

'Ask for Limen, if you still have a tongue to ask with. I cannot speak for the Sharai, but the elders of Selussin will silence a man who speaks against their wisdom. Nor would

I count on your own lords to protect you. They may ride over our lands, but they will make a show at least of respect towards our laws.'

'No doubt they will, and I have no lords in any case, among the Sharai; I am outcast, tribeless,' which Limen should have known, Jemel wore his condition so loudly. Any Catari should be able to read it from his dress. 'Some of the chiefs would sooner kill me than hear me,' he went on cheerfully. 'There is only Hasan to speak for me, and him I once swore a blood-oath against, which is why we are so dear to each other now.'

Limen could find nothing to say to that. He only beckoned with a jerk of his head, and led the way into the house.

At least, they called it a house as Rudel had; to Jemel it was a palace. This was the first glimpse he'd had, perhaps the only surviving memory of Selussin's fabled wealth. His bare feet walked on cool and coloured tiles, while the walls were richly hung to hide their simple brickwork; jewels sparkled in tapestries that were faded with age, but still vivid within their folds. One room they passed was lined from floor to ceiling with more books than he had ever seen in his life before, more than he had imagined to be within the world. Reading was a slow and a difficult art to him, but he did understand its power; he gave a snort that was pure Sharai and pure deception also – *of what use or conceivable interest is so much dry and dusty paper, to a man whose life is given to the Sands?* – and went on without a glance back, trying to hurry the men around him where they would not be hurried.

At last they brought him to a pair of high, massive doors,

closed doors. They were bronze as the gate had been, made and decorated he thought by the same craftsmen. No one stood on guard here; they were guard enough, Jemel supposed, for the privacies beyond. Limen paused before them, seeming to summon his courage before he pushed them open.

The doors swung apart slowly and silently, at the first pressure from Limen's hands. Their interwoven patterns glimmered and shifted in the changing light, speaking of mutability in permanence – like the Sands, Jemel thought, that changed daily and were never changed – while their imperious movement spoke of weight, of balance, perhaps of God. And, of course, of expense beyond measure, beyond any man's needs for a lifetime. Jemel – who liked to count wealth only in camels and had none at the moment, had never had more than he needed for bare survival, which was not wealth at all – felt himself staring and could do nothing about it, caught up as he was in their vast and dull indifference. He gazed in fascination at the steady sweep of their lower edges over priceless rugs, the brazen lustre of their exposed hinges, the perfect moment of their halting.

Only when they were still again could he pull eyes and wits together, as he needed. Show him something he could neither eat nor carry, something that in the desert could have only cost and no value, and he gaped and drooled like a baby. Too much time spent with Patrics had infected him, perhaps, with their own watery vision of the world . . .

No matter. He turned his eyes into the chamber that lay beyond those wonderful doors; he straightened his back and lifted his head and walked in alone, ahead of the hesitant

Limen. It was as though the ponderous opening of those doors had crushed all talking; he walked into a silence as heavy, as intractable as stone, and about as welcoming.

He walked boldly to the centre of the room, which was the centre of a circle of seated men. With each step he felt the silky softness of ancient carpets beneath his soles, the lulling smokiness of perfumed air against his throat, the height of the ceiling above him and the vanishing distance of the walls on every side. Over all, though, he felt the weight of the eyes that watched him come, the pent breath of those who waited to hear him.

Only that one would not wait or did not care. Not Hasan who rose, and no words of welcome or enquiry: rather a hiss of fury, a dagger drawn and flung so that it bit deep into the piled carpets and stood erect, barely a hand's span before his feet.

And this was so like it had been before, when he had been brought before the council in Rhabat and had been met by a dagger tossed to greet him; and it was the same knife, he thought, and certainly the same man who threw it, who faced him now before a wider band of witnesses and with a hint of triumph underlying his contempt.

'You are a fool to break in upon us, boy.'

'Maybe so, but I am a fool with news. Hasan—'

'Hasan cannot help you here.' And indeed Hasan stayed where he sat, cross-legged on the rugs, and made only a small gesture of regret to confirm his helplessness. War-leader he might be, but this was a council of chiefs and imams, and he was neither. 'Nor will the King's Shadow come wandering in this time to save your worthless skin. You have affronted our hosts, and for that alone you stand condemned; but you were condemned already, your very existence is an affront to me. I have waited, and I see no reason to wait longer. You gift me my excuse.'

It was true, Jemel supposed. The man was sheikh of the Saren, who had once been Jemel's own tribe. If any man wanted his death this was the one, in payment for oaths of fealty broken. He could pick up the knife and throw it back, and so accept the challenge; he could ignore it, and so be shamed before all the chiefs and the imams of Selussin also. This was no time to be fighting, but . . .

'It would seem a shame,' he said softly, 'to stain this beauty with blood, yours or mine.'

'Yours, renegade, it would all be yours.' Likely it would, too. The Saren was younger than most tribal chiefs, barely in his middle years, and broader than most Sharai, heavier and stronger far than Jemel. 'I will kill you in the courtyard if you prefer it, as a courtesy to our hosts. Unless you have your fellow creature in wait for me outside, that abomination you call the Ghost Walker, that should have been killed in Rhabat along with you. I will not walk into a trap.'

'Neither would I lay one. Marron is sick, in pain and captured; he has been taken to the castle. I don't know why.' There, at least he had said what he came to say; he saw Hasan receive the news, puzzled and concerned.

'All the better. We can hope that he will die there.'

'If he die in the castle,' Jemel said, 'Morakh the Sand Dancer will be the new Ghost Walker. Is that what you want?'

'Better a Sand Dancer than a Patric heretic.' *Better war than a corrupted peace,* he meant, and none here would dispute that. Not even Hasan; especially not Hasan, who had led the tribes at last towards his war. If Marron's death was the price of it, Jemel thought their friend would pay it.

His own death was still the price of the message. He fingered the livid scar on his neck, where Morakh had so nearly claimed that death already, and said, 'The Sand Dancer sides with the 'ifrit, who killed so many of your people – all your peoples, sheikhs – at Rhabat. Will you join with him, with them now? Any of you? Will the Saren ride with demons, and do their bidding?'

'They will not – and you are damned again, for saying so.'

'I am damned in any case, if I return your knife. If I slew you, the Saren would not rest until they had my blood for it.'

'If you do not return my knife, I will kill you anyway, for the coward that you are. Choose, tribeless – but swiftly. You rub my patience thin.'

'Oh, I will fight you, sheikh – but not here, and not yet. I have other battles first, that I deem more important.' And he stooped, pulled the sheikh's dagger from the carpets and thrust it into his belt, drawing his own knife instead and tossing that to the sheikh's feet. 'Do you keep my blade, and I yours. We'll exchange them later, once Hasan's wife is free and the insult to all Sharai has been redeemed. Then let our blades decide.'

Trying to sound as casual as his words and trying to look entirely uninterested after, striving to remember how to breathe as he waited. At length – and it seemed a long, long wait – the man who had once been his sheikh and would now be his executioner stooped to pick up the knife. He examined it scornfully, then slipped it inside his robe.

'Very well, I will let you live a little longer – but do not try to run, or I will hunt you like a hare and drag your naked body on a rope at my saddle's bow.'

'I will not run from you, or any man,' Jemel said flatly. He turned his back on the sheikh – *another insult, another cause to fight me, let him add it to the list; he can only kill me once* – and found Hasan at last rising to his feet.

'Jemel, where did you take Rudel?'

'To speak with Coren.'

'And where is Coren?'

'I don't know. Not in the house now, either of them. They didn't come here, they didn't follow me to the gate, to the castle road . . .'

'There is another way for those men, to the castle or any-where. Coren can walk his friends through shadow-paths.'

Not so shadowy, more golden and alight; besides, 'If he wouldn't do so to bring his own daughter out, nor Rudel's, why would he go for Marron?'

'Perhaps if he thought the Ghost Walker more important than my wife, or her friend? It's possible.'

It was possible. Jemel held the other's gaze with a surging hope – then crushed it, with a slow and deliberate shake of his head. 'No. The 'ifrit would know and be ready for them, whoever they went for. That's why they've left the girls, because they cannot help them. The same must be true for Marron. It's something else they're doing . . .'

'Then go and find them, Jemel. Don't bring them here; we'll rally by the western gate. I hadn't meant to move tonight, but I'll let Morakh know we're here at the least, that he can't bring any further of his friends inside, nor steal any more of us. Before you go, though, tell me how it was with Marron. I don't understand how he can be hurt, he's the Ghost Walker . . .'

'He can still be hurt,' Jemel said, who had seen the truth of that too often. 'But I don't understand this either. Not hurt, sick, the children said. I didn't see what happened, but they said that what he carries – his demon, they called it – turned on him . . .'

Jemel wasn't sure where to look, even where to start looking for the old men. As he left the imams' house, though – through the gate this time rather than over it, with a silent Limen swinging one leaf open for him, handing back his blade – he found the boys who'd brought him news of Marron lingering outside. He hadn't realised that they'd followed him this far, but of course they would have done; he'd probably given them the most excitement they'd known thus far in their young lives, and certainly the most money.

Well, he still had coins, and they were welcome to those also. He touched a suggestive hand to the pouch, all the hint they'd need, and said, 'The old man, the father of my house, and the guest who came today – where can I find them, do you know? Or can you learn?'

'Wait here,' was all they said before they scampered off in three different directions, sending strange high calls to each other as they vanished into the dark. Jemel recognised the tone, if not the meaning: he and his cohorts had had a similar language when they were small, designed to carry across the cliff-face of his home and further.

He waited long enough for the gates to swing wide at his back, and all the chiefs to come riding out. Even Hasan passed without a word; he rode straight towards the western wall, while the others turned south, heading no doubt to find the camps of their own tribes and stir their men to unexpected action.

He watched the gates close behind them, conscious of Limen's hard stare through the narrowing gap. There was no boom as the two leaves met, no grate of lock or bolt; they were as well made and as well hung as the doors within, preserved through generations of conquest by the simple expedient of never being closed against the conquerors.

Only against him, he thought, as so many ways were being closed to him. His old life was lost now, sacrificed in a moment's determination at Bar'ath Tazore; his new life had been given to Marron, and might be lost in its turn if that boy died. He didn't know where he'd go then. No tribeless man could live long in the Sands. He had friends from Outremer, but Hasan meant to destroy that country and reclaim the land for the Catari and their God, under the governance of the Sharai. Perhaps it would be as well if the Saren sheikh did kill him, so long as he could contrive Sieur Anton's death first, to redeem at least one of his oaths . . .

He waited, immersed in gloomy imaginings and barely aware of the occasional eerie cry rising from the darkness of the town around him. Soon though they were louder, shriller, coming closer; he peered into the night, and saw first one and then the other boys come racing back.

'The men you seek are in the woman Holet's house,' the eldest said triumphantly.

'Will you take me there?'

'We will.'

They didn't move, though. Jemel grinned, and worked his pouch open with sore fingers.

He couldn't see and wouldn't really have known the value of the coins he handed across. The boys knew, though, and were more than content, to judge by the flashing white of their smiles.

'Come, this way. It is not far. The widow Holet is sick, and your fathers are tending to her.'

It seemed a curious priority, at such a time. Jemel asked no questions, though. He only followed the small figures through a bewildering network of lanes until they brought him to a ramshackle house, little more than a hut crammed in among its neighbours. A low door opened directly onto the filthy alley. A dim light burned within, oddly blue; as he ducked beneath the lintel he saw a globe of witchlight hanging below the ceiling.

Coren and Rudel were both there, as he had been promised. The man from Surayon was crouched over a bed of rags; Jemel had to look twice before he saw the dark shadow of a woman lying on the bed. Coren was crushing herbs into a bowl of warm water, scenting the air with a sweet savour. He glanced up and said, 'Jemel. What's afoot in the town?'

'More to the point, where's Marron?' Rudel grunted, without looking round.

'You don't know?'

'We heard stories. I'd sooner hear them from you, they'll be less garbled.'

Not much so, if at all; he could tell them only what he'd been told himself by the children, and then what bare glimpse he'd had of figures hurrying away up the road to the castle. He added that he'd been to the imams' house, and told Hasan; he didn't mention what had passed between him and the sheikh.

Coren asked what Hasan meant to do.

'He will lead some men up to invest the castle tonight. He asks that you two meet him by the west gate.'

'Well, we will go,' Rudel said, his voice as grim as Jemel had ever heard it, 'but not before I have tried once more here.'

'What are you doing?'

'Failing to save this woman's life, I think. I cannot find the beat of her mind, the paths of her body nor the cause of her sickness. She confounds me; and I confess, that terrifies me every time I lay hands against her skin. But I must try. Once more, I will try once more before we abandon her.'

Jemel leaned forward to peer over Rudel's broad shoulder, and saw that it wasn't only the pallid blue of the light that had made the woman seem so shadowy. All her skin was grey, true grey between her wrinkles, and the shape of her bones showed beneath it as though her muscles had lost any lingering touch of life. He watched, and couldn't see her breathing.

'Is she not dead already?'

'She might as well be, for all the good I can do her.'

'Who is she?'

'A woman, from the marketplace. When you cried out and left us, we went there, not knowing which way you had gone; and found the market deserted and her lying there, while her neighbours watched from a distance. They gabbled of a demon, as your children did. We assumed that Marron had been there, and that her sickness was in some measure due to him. There was nothing we could do to his benefit, and we couldn't simply leave her to her death. I persuaded some of those watching to bring her home' – whether with coin or a sword, he didn't say and Jemel didn't ask – 'and have been trying to cure her since, but she has defeated me. Or rather, what has possessed her is defeating me. Be quiet now.'

He drew a slow breath, and Jemel wondered at the trembling in his hands as he reached to lay them on the woman's scrawny chest.

Jemel had seen Rudel's daughter heal him of a wound that should have killed him: he had heard her confess, however reluctantly, that her father's gift was stronger than her own. Despite Rudel's protestations and Coren's silence, he waited to see the woman stir and rise.

Waited and waited, and saw only the sweat that gleamed on Rudel's brow, the vacant stare of his eyes that was worse somehow than the vacant stare of the woman's. It was a moment out of time, a moment that stretched almost beyond his bearing. Coren sat over his aromatic water and did nothing but stir it lightly with a finger; Jemel stood and did nothing at all; Rudel hunched above the woman and seemed also to be doing nothing, at least in his own body.

The witchfire light faded slowly, but that was all one with the woman's slow and irredeemable dying, Rudel's failing struggle to save her. Coren's finger fell still in the water.

Eventually, Rudel blinked.

Blinked and sighed, unless he was only breathing and it was because no one had done that for so long that it sounded so loud; and lifted his hands from the woman with a soft gasp, as though it hurt like tearing a clotted bandage from a wound, and pressed them to his sweat-slick face and seemed not to be able to stop himself from shaking.

The other two went on waiting, for entirely different

reasons now. Even Jemel's urgency seemed to fall back from him a little, in the face of Rudel's extreme distress.

At length the Surayonnaise dropped his hands into his lap, or let them fall rather, as though he lacked the strength to hold them up longer. His head he could lift and turn, seemingly, into the perfumed air, and appeared to take some relief from it; the witchlight flared brighter suddenly. All he said, though, was, 'I don't think your taranth-water will do her any good, Coren, where my touch does nothing.'

'This is for you, Rudel,' was the answer, in a voice as quiet as his own had been. 'Bend over the bowl here and breathe the steam, while I find a cloth that's not so rancid as to destroy all its virtue.'

In the end it was Coren's own sleeve that provided the cloth, although Jemel offered his own; perhaps that was too rancid with camel-spit, he thought when Coren rejected it, and surprised himself with an inward smile before he went back to waiting.

He waited while Coren wiped Rudel's face and hands, while he talked too soft to hear; waited until the one man was sure that the other was sufficiently restored to make a move. By then Jemel was at the door, fidgeting and fretful, conscious of the boys still lingering outside in hopes of yet more bounty but far more conscious of the stars' turning overhead, of Hasan's summons going unanswered, above all of Marron's imprisonment, his sickness and pain that were worse far than Rudel's weakness.

Through all of that he was conscious yet of the old woman on the bed in the corner, not dead yet but snared within her dying, beyond all help that any of them could offer except perhaps the swift kiss of a knife to send her on her way; and none of them could offer that bar Rudel who had tried so hard to save her, and he would not. Even now his head kept turning back, and there was a mute despair on his face.

'I was like a man abroad in a blizzard,' he murmured, 'searching for another where I knew there was no hope, and only my own death promised if I stayed. Almost I lost the way back, I went so far . . .'

'That I had been afraid of,' Coren said. 'If she's gone or going, then let her go. Death is not so terrible. You know that, better than most.'

'Hers might be. It was terrible to come even as close as I did, and that not close enough to find her. I've never known a feeling like it . . .' And he shuddered again, and needed to grip both hands tightly together to still their trembling.

'We should go,' Jemel whispered, half-hoping that they would not hear; he felt like a child on the fringes of an adult world, mystified and demanding. Of course death was terrible, how not? And Marron might be dying even now, and still they only talked over the dying of a woman they couldn't even put a name to . . .

Coren nodded, and reached to help Rudel to his feet, swaying a little under the other man's weight before he found balance for them both.

'We should go back to your house, Jemel, so that Rudel may ride. Can you find the way from here?'

No need for that, his loyal servants attended him still and he had coins left to buy their services. He thought that Rudel might be better walking than fighting his camel's wilfulness, but kept that private. He wanted to be moving, that was all: moving towards Hasan and ultimately Marron, however slowly they must go.

They went at last, although they had almost to pull Rudel through the doorway and he would not leave until the woman had been covered over, though she was so cold to the touch that her rags were useless to her; and they did indeed go slowly, behind their persistent guides. Rudel recovered a little in the night air, but not enough to quiet Coren's anxiety. Neither Jemel's, though his had a different source: childlike again, he burst out, 'If Marron's sickness is like the widow's—'

'Widow, was she?' Rudel interrupted in a broken mutter. 'I didn't know. What was her name, boy?'

'Holet, the boys said. But *listen*, if Marron is sick as she was, and you could not help her . . .'

'If so, then you are right, I cannot help him either. Failure has taught me nothing except how to fail. And how the thing is done, of course, what it looks like, how to recognise it. I expect I shall fail faster, next time.'

Try less hard and less often, he meant; try hardly at all, perhaps, for Marron. Rudel would still far sooner see him dead than flying loose, so long as he could control the Daughter after.

Jemel wanted to seize the man, to shake him, to drive his own intense spirit into that flagging body and that bitter mind. No point in it, though, he was no magician to possess another with even a fragment of himself; besides, Coren was ahead of him, and wiser far in his approach.

'You are too tired to see clearly, Rudel. You have found the path to failure, yes, and it has exhausted you; rest and reconsideration may show you the path to success. A night's sleep will restore you.'

Rudel snorted. 'You think I or any of us will sleep tonight?'

'You will, yes. I will insist on it – and make it happen, if I must. Do you know where we are now, Jemel?'

'What? Oh, yes. Yes, I do. But . . .'

'Pay off these boys, then, and send them home. Otherwise they will follow us to the gate, and maybe further. Let's see them safe, at least.'

It was a wise precaution; at their age, Jemel would certainly have sneaked out at the tail of the army to see what passed on the heights. To crush any hope of further gain, he loosed purse from belt and tossed it unopened to the eldest boy. With luck, they'd be too busy arguing over the division of the spoils to think of dogging him further.

Another few minutes brought them to the house. They found the camel sleeping; as he'd guessed, she was vicious when she woke, and he doubted any man's ability to stay on her back.

Coren soothed her, though, with a hand on her muzzle and a few words spoken into her ear. Magic again, Jemel thought; all the Sharai fancied themselves to be camel-masters, and he'd known a few who seemed to have a genuine charm in touch and voice, but none that worked so swiftly or so well.

He fetched saddle and harness and riding-stick, and saw Rudel mounted before he unhitched the hobble to let the beast stand. Still suspicious of her sudden docility and wary of her rider's weakness, he offered to lead her to the gate, but received a contemptuous snort for his pains.

'I may be weary, Jemel, but I'm not helpless. Besides, you can see, she's dozier than I am, thanks to Coren whispering her into a maze. She'll sleep on her feet all the way. You walk behind, and poke her if she starts to snore . . .'

'More likely it'll be you that snores first,' Coren said, falsely cheerful. 'We'd be better off walking one either side, to catch you when you fall. Now come, we've wasted too much time already.'

In fact it was he who led the way, with Rudel urging the camel on behind him. Jemel did walk a little while watchfully beside the beast, till he was sure Coren had been joking; then as an antidote to his own impatience, to keep his feet from racing ahead of his companions he forced himself to lag behind, glancing back a time or two to be sure that those curious and acquisitive boys weren't still following him.

The western gate should have been closed since nightfall, and was not; in the open ground beyond there was a mill of men and camels, bright torches blazing. He let out a huff of relief, and now could and did run on past Rudel, past Coren to seek Hasan.

He found him where he'd expected, out on the road and furthest from the gate, with only a few trusted men about him. Hasan would give precedence to the chiefs in council, but not on the field of battle, not where it was his own presence that had brought the tribes this far.

Besides, this was his own battle, for his own wife and friends. Of course he would lead; of course they would follow, if only because Hasan could not be allowed to ride alone or die alone for his own private reasons when he had all his people to die for . . .

Jemel surprised himself with that touch of cynicism, and

then again with a touch of pity for the man. That felt like heresy, Hasan had seemed so godlike to him just a few months ago; but heretical or not, the thought wouldn't be denied. Better to have no destiny, to carry nothing in your hands: better to be like Jemel himself, free to come and go without shaking worlds as you pass, free to live as you chose and to die if you wanted to, to ride over a cliff in the dark or drink bad water or have a foolish, fatal quarrel with a friend . . .

Except that Jemel's friend whom he had chosen to live with and would share any of those deaths with quite happily once one or two other small matters had been attended to, Marron was sick and hurt and quite possibly dying, alone and apart; and Marron was one of those world-shakers whom God noticed, and Jemel mattered to him and so perhaps to God also, and was in any case not free after all. Pity anyone, he might as well pity himself, and that was pointless.

And yet he did still feel pity for Hasan, who would have a long lifetime of this, who would always be too important to let go. Marron could always leave by virtue of what he was, and wanted to, and would, or Jemel thought so. Had tried it once already, perhaps, those days they'd had just wandering in the land of the djinn. And he'd taken Jemel with him, and come back of his own will when Lisan had asked it, and that was important too. If he could run away from Sieur Anton – and he had – then no one could hold him against his will. Except when he was sick as he was now, and they must be very sure he'd not recover, they'd never dare to touch him else . . .

'Where are they, Jemel?' The question snapped at him like a lash and he could pity no one but himself for a moment

under the full force of Hasan's glare, and marvel at his own
insolence in pitying such a man.

'They are here,' with the jerk of a thumb back over his
shoulder.

Hasan peered into the darkness, shielding his eyes from
the glare of torchlight, but even from camelback could
apparently not make out the men he sought in the throng.
Still, he accepted Jemel's word and said only, 'We ride, then.
There are spare mounts among the men; seek them out, and
bring Coren and Rudel to join me as soon as you may.'

Then he wheeled and cried out, loud and strong, drawing
all men's eyes to him; he raised his riding-stick and gestured
forward, up the road; he kicked his camel into a run and
rode away without a backward glance. Jemel stood and
watched for a minute, caught up in the thrill of it as the
gathered chiefs swept past him with their retinues. So far
from pitying Hasan now, he envied him: not the power but
the confidence, the certainty that all these quarrelsome and
divided men would follow him, here and wherever he might
lead them.

He saw the Saren sheikh pass by with never a glance
down, snared like so many by Hasan's personality or else
obedient to an idea that drove them both, a vision of a world
restored. Then he remembered his own obedience, and dived
back into the churning multitude in search of riderless
camels and the old men who were his own particular charge.

When both were found and brought together, he tried at
first to lead them up the narrow road at a camel-canter.
Rudel's beast was still half-stupefied, though, and couldn't
match his mount's pace nor Coren's.

'Can't you rouse her now?' he yelled at the King's Shadow, more agitated than politic. 'Hasan said—'

'Hasan has not seen. Rudel would fall, and only slow us further. I thought patience was a virtue of the Sharai?'

So it was, ordinarily, but Hasan had shown little sign of it tonight. And the thought of Marron burned in Jemel's blood, so that he had none to call on; and then there were the girls, and he didn't, couldn't believe that Coren was truly so calm, or Rudel so weak.

Nothing he could do, though, but rein back. Lisan's father swayed in the saddle as their way steepened, and did look now in genuine danger of falling. Jemel thought he might have left him or sent him back to sleep the night in Selussin: *if* he had been Hasan, *if* he had seen, *if* Rudel was the kind of man who'd listen and obey any such command . . .

None of those applied, and so they came last and laggardly to the plateau where the castle stood, its great rough walls looming high against the stars and its gates closed hard against them.

The Sharai had spread themselves already, the men from each tribe watching a portion of the walls and raising tents, building fires while they watched. Hasan had been wise to bring only a small part of his army, Jemel thought; they'd circled the entire castle and still there was barely space enough for these, with their camps set uncomfortably close. He might have been wiser to have brought only his own tribe, the Beni Rus – except that then he might have lost the others, all the tribes else. Why should they wait down by the town, while the Beni Rus stole the fun of battle and the

chance of loot? What were they here for, to dance atten-
dance and applaud? They might, might well, almost
certainly would have packed and mounted and departed to
the Sands, and most likely Hasan would never have been
able to bring them together again. This way they would all
stay, though this way there was the constant risk of arguments and bloodshed before ever they faced what lay behind
the gates. Where the sheikhs went, there went the tribes: into
battle for Hasan or with each other, or possibly over the
mountains and on into Outremer. Possibly, probably – certainly it was what the men left below tonight would be
urging tomorrow, the only real argument for their having
come this far. Hasan had never needed such an army to win
back his wife, they'd all of them always known that. Whether
Julianne lived or died – and Elisande and Marron and himself, whether any of them lived or died – that issue would be
decided by these comparative few who coiled like a serpent
around the castle walls.

And would be decided soon, Jemel thought. If there'd
been a Patric army mewed up in there, the Sharai would
have been willing to stay for a long siege and months of
bloody fighting, as they had before to deny the infidel a
foothold on the margins of the Sands, a firm grasp of the
holy schools at Selussin. As it was only a stolen wife and a
renegade Sand Dancer who held her, they'd expect Hasan to
settle the matter swiftly, by parley or by force.

The Sand Dancer was the one who counted, in Jemel's
mind and so he was sure in the minds of all the Sharai. It was
the Sand Dancer who had stolen Julianne, he was known
and named. The other people in there were Patrics or Catari
out of Outremer, farmers and peasants, not worth dwelling

on. Though they had stolen Marron, or so it seemed, and done so with a power that could silence or turn his Daughter: it wasn't, it couldn't be their own power to do such a thing, no mortal magic, and so he could still dismiss them. And then there was the 'ifrit, and that was curiously hard to think about at all; it shifted shape in his mind, fluid as a cat and insubstantial as its shadow, he could get no kind of grip on it. How could you think about a creature that might know what you were thinking, and so change . . . ?

So when he thought about what might happen beyond those concealing gates, he thought about killing Morakh, all the many ways he wanted to kill Morakh. Let older heads and wiser minds consider the 'ifrit and how to defeat it when it knew your plans and all your moves already, let them consider the strangeness of the band from Outremer. He would kill Morakh, then kill anyone else who came between him and Marron; he would kill everyone in the castle if he had to, if that was the only way to break the spell that gripped his friend.

Or see them dead, at least. He couldn't kill them all alone, which was why he needed Hasan and his troops. Hasan, it seemed, needed old wise heads; Hasan had snapped at him already for being slow of delivery, and now was turning and twisting his camel before the gates, heedless of the chance of arrows from above as he called to Jemel's companions in a fret, almost a frenzy of impatience.

'Where have you *been*? I sent for you to meet me at the gates of Selussin—'

'—And so we did, but there was all your army between us—'

'—And then to join me at the head, did the boy not say?'

'There would have been no point in his saying; we could not have reached you with Rudel. Better to travel carefully, and to arrive.'

'What is the matter with Rudel?' The warlord seemed suddenly to register how quietly the older man sat his quiet camel, and how unusual that was. 'Is he sick too?'

'Sick of a great sickness,' Rudel said himself, surprising Jemel as much as Hasan; they were the first words he'd uttered in a while, and the voice at least was stronger than it had been in the town. 'I have met a darkness tonight, and all but lost myself in it. I need to think . . .'

'He needs to sleep,' Coren said flatly. 'Let him seek a bed among your men, and take your counsel with me tonight, Hasan, for what good it will do either one of us. I am tired myself, and devoid of ideas.'

Hasan grunted, and turned his back to the castle. 'Come, then. Rudel shall rest, and think until he sleeps; you and I, Coren, we will eat and speak together. I do not believe that the King's Shadow is helpless, here on the borders of the King's country . . .'

Jemel sat still on his camel and watched them go, thinking that the King's Shadow was not helpless, no, only outplayed and defeated, his powers blocked by a greater. Hasan would learn tonight, Coren would teach him; an army was no more use than a magician, if you did not dare to use it. So long as the 'ifrit watched her, Julianne's life was forfeit however they approached the castle. And Elisande was somewhere, doing something, he had no way to find out where or what; and Marron . . .

Wondering how he should pass the night, sure that there was no point in his trying to sleep, he turned to gaze at the prohibiting gates again; and would do so unrelentingly while other watchers came and went around him, while they ate and talked and slept perhaps a little, and so would be the first to see them open.

9

Out of All Shelter

No sunlight ever broke into the cell through that single slit of a window, high though it was; high only to her, Julianne thought, high only in here. Out in the yard, she fancied, it would lie at ground level, and the height of the castle's walls must keep it in perpetual shadow. All her days were grey and her nights were black dark, punctuated only by the ceaseless glare of the 'ifrit's eyes which cast no light but seemed rather to suck it in, to make both day and night darker.

Terror had abated long since, under the dragging weariness of unmeasurable time. She knew herself to be bait and nothing more; neither Morakh nor the monster had any interest in her, except to keep her here and well guarded. Once in every day the door would be opened and she would be brought food, hard bread and dull flat-tasting water in a wooden beaker. Until now it had always been the Dancer himself who brought it; today, though . . .

Today she'd been playing games in her head, dreaming rescue, not with any hope of its happening but only to pass another weary hour, to find some way to break the endless monotony. She didn't need to close her eyes any more, in order to dream; it was better not, indeed, because sometimes in the private darkness of her mind she thought that the 'ifrit was looming over her, its patience at last exhausted, its hot gaze searching for her soul and its jaws already reaching for her throat. Then her eyes would snap open again and she would be shaken and scared again, little comforted by the sight of the creature still crouched where it always was crouched, quite unmoving and unmoved, only watching and watching.

So she dreamed awake when she could, she dreamed alert; and today she had dreamed of the door swinging wide and a hero striding in to slay the monster and whisk her off to freedom. Not the first time for such dreams, not the hundredth; the chill numbing shadow of these days was bearing heavily on her spirit, grinding the blaze of her imagination down to its last fitful glow, where the only thought that survived was the thought that somehow she might escape this place. She couldn't do it by herself, she needed rescue, and so she dreamed of heroes.

Hero-fathers, hero-husbands, hero-friends: she didn't care, she wasn't choosy. Any or all of them would be welcome. She was past worrying about them now, long past praying that they not come after all. The nobility of self-sacrifice was something else that she'd lost, had let dwindle slowly far beyond recovery. All she yearned for now was a miracle, a breath of hope that could rekindle the fading spark that was herself, that was so drained by the 'ifrit's relentless stare and the unremitting ache, the slow slow grind of time against her bones.

She had gazed at the door and seen it shatter, seen the twisting fury of Elisande's djinni in its frame and the small solid figure of Elisande herself in the passage beyond, her hand cocked ready to cast a knife that would transfix the 'ifrit's eye and kill its glow, drive deep into its skull to kill the creature entirely.

She had gazed at the door and seen it shine with gold, bright enough to dim even the fierce red of the 'ifrit's glare; she had seen the spectral figure of her father walking through it, holding out his hand and drawing her into his mystery, leading her away before monster or Morakh could find any answer to him.

She had gazed at the door and seen it outlined with dim red fire, Marron opening a gateway that she could dive through into the land of the djinn, fast and easy and the way closed instantly behind her so that she would be safe with him in that strange and sunless country.

She had gazed at the door and heard its bolts drawn back, had seen it open to her friend Jemel, his scimitar bloody in his hand and his eyes alight with battle; or else to Rudel, his clever fingers signing her to silence, to be swift; or else to her husband Hasan with his warriors at his back, or else wonderfully to her husband Imber in all his panoply of war, his laughing cousin at his side . . .

At last, she had gazed at the door and truly heard its bolts drawn back, had seen it swing open for real; and then she had gaped, gasped, reached to rub at her eyes to assure herself that this time she actually wasn't dreaming.

There was light out in the passage, that must be falling through an open doorway or a wide embrasure; by contrast with the murk in the cell where darkness seemed to be woven into the very air, it was bright enough to dazzle. She needed a moment to blink her eyes clear, and a moment more to realise that the man who stood out there was neither Morakh nor any of her imagined rescuers.

Realising that she knew him regardless, recognising his silhouette even before she saw his face – that was an act stolen utterly out of time. How long he waited, how long she stared – that was beyond counting, as the fact of it was beyond wonder.

Then, slowly, forcing her mouth to shape his name and her voice to utter it, she said, '*Blaise . . . ?*'

He stepped into the cell, she took an equal pace back; shadow engulfed him.

'Blaise, what are you doing here?' He wasn't dressed as an Elessan sergeant now, rather as a peasant: a disguise, surely, and she kept her voice soft in response, but why Morakh should have let any peasant into the castle she couldn't understand. Nor why it should be Blaise who came to rescue her, when she'd thought him long since fallen out of her story, left behind at Roq de Rançon several adventures since . . .

Both his hands were full; he held them out, and she took bread and water uncertainly. She was close enough to read his face in the dimness, and it might as well have been carved from wood. No wink or smile, not the slightest hint of a message, no recognition at all.

Neither did he speak. His duty done, he turned and walked away. Julianne reached out to stay him, then drew her hand back to abort the gesture. She'd seen the shift of a shadow out in the passage: Morakh, perhaps, watching his new and bewildering servant, ready to snare her if she tried to slip away? That might explain his silence, his care not to reveal himself. He might think it enough that she knew he was here.

And so it had been enough, at least for a while. Now she need not dream of rescue, now it was here – somehow, bizarrely – and she had all the strangeness of its source to marvel at, to feed her starved mind as she chewed mechanically to feed her uninterested body.

She didn't give much thought to practicalities, how Blaise meant to steal her from the cell under the unending watch of the 'ifrit. If he were here – and he was, no fever-dream; she'd smelled his breath, she'd almost touched his fingers taking this goblet from him, she could still feel the warmth of his grip in the wood – then she had her miracle already, and the rest was mere detail. Any god who could conjure someone so unlikely into such a place could conjure the pair of them out as easily; no god would go this far and then betray her when she'd been so helpless. She felt safe already, and only cast into astonishment by the means of her salvation.

So she had sat and dreamed again, but this time dreamed of herself outside the cell, her hand clasped securely in Blaise's as he guided her to the wall where a rope lay coiled and ready, or else to the gate that he'd left unbarred and standing ajar. She had dreamed of stars and wind, of freedom, and not at all of Morakh rising from the shadows to challenge their escape.

And later, after the cell had darkened, when she'd heard again the sounds of the door being unbolted she'd been certain that this was Blaise come back to claim her and to lead her out. She'd risen to her feet, heedless of the motionless 'ifrit, and his name had been half on her lips already when the door had opened and not he but two other men had come in, with a body slung unconscious between them.

This time there was no light, in the cell or outside, but she was alert in darkness now, finding messages even in the movement of air. The bulk of their bodies crowding through the doorway and the sounds they made counted their number for her, and had her scuttling back against the wall just before she could betray herself with an eager whisper of Blaise's name.

Her mind reeled under a crushing disappointment, all dreams forsworn. These men were as silent as Blaise had been, and they paid her as little attention, less. He at least had handed her a meal; they simply laid their burden on the floor and departed.

Confused, distressed, she heard the bolts slammed shut and still stood where she was, hands and back pressed against cold stone, shuddering against the loss of hope. It took a while before she could move at all, a while longer before she was certain that the 'ifrit would not. At last, though, a rising curiosity overcame both fear and despair. A few short, stumbling paces took her to where the newcomer lay sprawled on the floor, unconscious or even dead, perhaps. She dropped to her knees beside him and reached out nervously to let her fingers discover what her eyes could not.

It was a man, a young man to judge by his slimness, the smoothness of his face; not Blaise, then, at least there was that to cling to. She might have thought him a Patric, except that he wore the robe of a Sharai . . .

Those two thoughts joined together, to suggest a name. She gasped in shock, fumbled for his left arm and found there what she had suddenly dreaded to find, twisting ridges of half-healed flesh.

It was Marron, then. *One more to rescue, one fewer to rescue her* – but that was a fleeting thought, swiftly dismissed. This was Marron as she'd never thought to know him, Marron in a desperate condition. Not dead, no, she could feel the faint stir of his breath and a fluttering pulse in the depth of his unhealing wound; close to death, though, that she was sure of, and she'd never thought the Daughter would let him go so far.

His hair was matted with a stinking sweat, his robe was soaked with it, and yet his skin was dry where she touched it, as though there were no more water left in him to be sweated out. It felt both cold and hot alternately beneath her palm, and stretched drum-tight across his bones. He'd always been brutally thin, but this was different. She thought his body was a battleground, with sickness surging through his blood, fever and chill at war; she wondered which one was the enemy. Unless they both were, and he was doubly infected . . . ?

That made a sudden sense to her, thinking of the Daughter and how it lived its strange half-life inside him. It was like a fever, like an infection, a burning that did not belong; and if he fell sick otherwise, of course it would fight that new invasion. If the sickness fought back – well, here was the consequence, and she thought Marron could not survive it unless help came soon. Small chance of that. He needed more than an ordinary healer, he needed wisdom and magic both, Rudel or Elisande, and she was far past hoping for miracles now. She did what little she could, moistening the hem of her robe in what remained of her water and wiping his face with it, but when she touched his brow a moment later she found it baking hot and dry again.

She might have cried then from frustration at her helplessness, from the dread of having him die under her hands and the fear of what might follow with the Daughter; but a sound intruded from the passage, the soft scrape of bolts being carefully drawn back.

She lifted her head, almost daring to hope once more, thinking that Blaise could carry Marron if he could only find a way out of this suddenly populated castle. For the second time that night she was certain of the sergeant's coming; for the second time she was deceived.

The door opened barely a shadow's width and a figure slipped through, drawing it quickly closed again. Not Blaise, that much was clear even in the dark; this was someone slender, light-footed, a young lad or a girl. But who, and why . . . ?

'Julianne?'

The voice was her answer, and her second miracle of the day.

'Elisande!' It came out in a breathless hiss, almost on a sob. A moment later her friend had found her; strong arms wrapped themselves around her and dragged her unexpectedly back into a corner. She grunted in puzzlement, then understood as she heard the whisper of steel drawn, as she felt Elisande set herself between her and the 'ifrit.

'Don't, don't worry. It doesn't do anything, it just sits there, waiting . . .'

'Maybe it's been waiting for me.'

Maybe so; if it could see anything of the future as the djinn could, it should have known that she was coming. There was no movement from the creature, though, only the steady burning of its eyes.

'I thought it was waiting for your djinni,' Julianne said weakly, and was astonished again to hear Elisande chuckle tightly.

'So did Esren. That's why it didn't come to pull you out of here, sweetheart; nor Marron, nor your father. They were all scared of that accursed thing. That's why I had to come myself.'

And for a moment, for one blessed moment Julianne fancied that her coming was enough, that the two of them could slip out as cautiously as Elisande had slipped in, and still the 'ifrit would do nothing. An hour ago, they might have tried it. But, 'Marron did come, he's here.'

'Oh, *what*?'

'On the floor there. Elisande, he's dreadfully ill, he needs healing . . .'

A cold instant later she was squinting and covering her eyes against a flare of blue light, bright enough to scorch the inside of her skull, or so she felt.

Elisande swore, and the blaze faded to a glimmer; when Julianne risked a glance, she saw a globe of witchlight hanging in the air above Marron's body, bright enough still to dazzle her dark-adjusted sight. Elisande had dropped her knife and was huddled down beside Marron, touching with gentle, questing fingers.

Nothing Julianne could do there; she stooped to pick up the discarded blade, eyeing the 'ifrit warily. It might respond to magic, where it cared not at all for the girls. She didn't think it had moved, though, and certainly it wasn't moving now. It might even have retreated a little, from that sudden eruption of light; she thought its eyes seemed duller against the pale blue glow.

Soon, too soon Elisande sighed, and turned her head to find her. Julianne knew what was coming, before her friend could find the words.

'I can do nothing for him like this. I never could, when he had the Daughter in him. It resists, it won't let me in . . .'

Julianne nodded. 'I think that's what's happening now, something has got in and the Daughter's fighting it. But it's killing him, Elisande.'

'I know.' Two short syllables should not be able to contain so much grief.

'What can we do? Blaise is here, I saw him, but he may not be able to come tonight . . .'

'Blaise will not come at all. He's with them, Julianne, I've seen him too and his spirit is snared somehow. We have to get Marron out ourselves, somewhere safe where we can release the Daughter and work on him. We should take him to Rudel, he's stronger than I am. We can carry him between us, he weighs nothing.'

'Call the djinni, and it could carry us all.'

'It would not come. I said, it's afraid of the 'ifrit . . .'

'So am I. Do you think it will let us leave? It's watched me so long, I'm the bait in its trap, and the trap's not yet sprung. It wasn't set for you, at least.' She waited, had no response, at last said, 'Elisande?'

'My blades have been blessed,' her friend replied at last, 'but two short knives would never be enough, against that monster. And no, I don't think it would let us leave. But listen. I was wondering earlier, what would frighten a djinni.'

'The 'ifrit, you said.'

'Yes – but there's something more. You know how Esren was trapped in the Dead Waters, by a stone brought over from the other world. I think it would be terrified of being caught again. The 'ifrit use the same trick to control their ghûls, so we know it works on other spirit creatures; and the djinn and the 'ifrit are close kin, even if the djinn deny it . . .'

'I don't understand.'

'No, but trust me. In a minute, I'll ask you to do a thing; do it boldly, sweetheart. If you get the chance. It may be the only chance that Marron has.'

And then she drew her other knife and touched it lightly to Marron's wounded arm, letting out a drop of blood, letting out the Daughter.

'Elisande, what are you *doing* . . . ?'

'I can't work on him while that's inside him; if it's loose, I can perhaps rouse him just a little. Besides, I need it free. Stand ready, Julianne – and watch the 'ifrit . . .'

She was doing that already. It had stirred, in the moment of that first wisp's smoking up from Marron's arm; it was stirring yet, shifting claws and pincer-feet and the plates of its distorted body in countless, constant motions that still kept it exactly where it was, crowded into its corner. She'd have said it looked scared already; hoping to scare it further, she tightened her grip on Elisande's knife.

She was scared enough herself: scared for herself, and for Elisande, and especially for Marron. With the Daughter free – and more than that, free of his control – they might all be in danger. If she was right, though, his sickness would be free too to rampage through his body. Whatever sickness it was, that could fight back against the Daughter's strength and possession . . .

It had Elisande to face now, a different kind of daughter. The light dimmed further, as she focused; she had her hands clamped on either side of Marron's head, and a terrible determination on her face.

A determination which seemed to falter suddenly, seemed almost to fail altogether; Julianne saw her forehead suddenly slick with sweat, heard a groan escape her lips. But she set her jaw, closed her eyes, rallied to try again; and Marron's eyelids fluttered open, he gazed about him vaguely, tried to speak.

'Marron.' That was Elisande's voice as Julianne had never heard it before, high and tight and demanding. 'Take control of the Daughter, make it open a gateway to the land of the djinn.'

He mumbled something that Julianne couldn't catch. Elisande heard it, though, and replied.

'You can, and you must. For your life, and ours. Only for a little while; Julianne will go through, and bring back a stone. With that, we can win our freedom and take you out of here. Do it, Marron, do it now . . .'

And astonishingly, almost miraculously – because perhaps there was not yet an end to miracles after all, when a boy so racked could even understand what she was saying, let alone find the will and the strength to obey her – Marron did it.

It was a poor, weak job that he made of it, reminding Julianne forcefully of his early efforts to control the Daughter, under Morakh's tutelage: a twisted, shifting frame and the smoky red of it a sullen crimson glare, as though it were remembering rebellion and had only the outward habit of obedience to hold it still.

Julianne gazed at the narrow gleam of gold that struck through the centre of the Daughter's frame, the portal to the other world. Elisande wanted her to go through there; and she would, of course she would, because her one friend asked her to and her other friend needed her to, and either one of those would have been enough. The two together were imperative.

And yet she couldn't help remembering those early trials, when desert creatures had died and died again, as Marron failed and failed again to hold the gateway open against the wild nature of the Daughter. Even if he managed to stretch it wide enough to let her through – and it was far from that as yet, barely wide enough to pass her hand and still her hips' height from the ground, far too high to jump when just to touch the rim of it was deadly – could she trust him to hold it so while she went and returned, not to lose control and let it close while she was yet in the land of the djinn, or – worse – when she was halfway through the gate and would die as those desert rats had died, in screaming terror?

No: one glance at his face confirmed that she couldn't trust him so far, she couldn't trust him at all. Elisande was struggling against whatever had infected him; Marron seemed to have given up already. Even his blood was sluggish as it dribbled from his arm. Perhaps Elisande should have cut him deeper, let him bleed some more . . .

Elisande had her head down beside Marron's now, her mouth at his ear, whispering, whispering. His eyes opened, his gaze seemed to focus – and abruptly there it was, gateway and frame, solid-seeming and all Julianne need do was walk across the cell and step through into that golden summoning light . . .

Except that the 'ifrit moved first and moved fast, before she could force her unwilling feet to do it. It half scuttled and half flowed, losing its insect shape even before it reached the Daughter, pouring through the portal like a long thick sinuous ribbon of smoke.

Julianne stared in wonder, in amazement, once more astonished beyond words; distantly she heard Elisande's voice, exhausted and triumphant and still demanding more.

'Close the gateway, Marron. Quickly, let it go, it wants to anyway. Good,' as the frame dissolved and the Daughter assumed its more natural shape, a veiled monstrosity not so very different from the 'ifrit, only so much harder to see or understand. 'Good boy, you've been wonderful, you've saved us all. Now, one thing more. I can't keep you awake much longer, and I don't think you should sleep while that thing's free, it needs you keeping an eye on it. Besides, you've bled too much already, you need all your strength if you're going to get well again. Will you take it back for me, Marron?'

'It hurts,' he said, clear enough this time, his voice sharp with dread.

'I know it does, love – but it keeps you alive, I think. It stops you sinking. You have to do it, Marron, you have to take it back. Just for a while now, till we can get you to Rudel. He'll be able to help, better than I can. I promise . . .'

Slowly, with what seemed to be reluctance on both sides – as if the Daughter relished a return to battle no more than Marron did – the half-seen monster shifted to smoke as if in echo of the 'ifrit, and slipped back into Marron's blood. He writhed, and his mouth gaped open in a soundless scream; Elisande bent low above his head, and Julianne thought she was weeping even as she struggled to soothe him.

At last he lay still and she looked up again, dragging her sleeve across her face. 'He's gone again,' she said. 'It was all I could do, to help him into unconsciousness. We have to get him to Rudel.'

'What if the 'ifrit comes back?'

Elisande laughed harshly. 'It won't. I don't think it can, they can't move between the worlds the way the djinn do, they need a gateway. That's why I did this, to give it an opportunity to flee.'

'I don't understand, I thought you wanted me to go, you said so . . .'

'I was lying, sweet. I hoped it would be scared by the threat of a stone, scared enough to run. Just as well that it was, I wouldn't have known what to do with the stone if you'd brought one. You had to be ready, though, it had to sense a real danger.'

'It didn't happen, though, I didn't go . . .'

'Because the 'ifrit fled, it didn't happen. They don't see the future exactly, only possible courses. It saw what I wanted it to see, a future where it would be at risk; that was enough. Now come on, let's get out of here.'

'How? We can carry Marron between us, but there's still Morakh, and all those other people. And Blaise, shouldn't we look for him?'

'No. I told you, Julianne, Blaise is one of them. But leaving isn't a problem, now the 'ifrit has gone. Esren!'

She called out and the djinni was instantly there, shimmering brightly in the haze of blue.

'Esren, take us to Rudel. Through the gate or over the wall, I don't care. Whichever's faster. You'll be all right, won't you, Julianne? If we meet Morakh on the way, we've each got a knife for him.'

Julianne was less troubled by Morakh than by the ride, but she'd endured worse these last weeks, with friends and enemies both. She swallowed, nodded, said, 'I'll cope. Let's hurry.'

He had forgotten his name and any sense of purpose, until the prisoner gave them back to him. He had forgotten almost everything, including how to think or why he should. He still understood the meanings of words and he knew how to obey, he could follow orders, but he had no other use for language and so he'd ceased to use it, even inside his head.

Until he had been told to take bread and water to the cell, and give it to the girl there. That he'd done; but as he did it she had said a word, *Blaise*, and he'd remembered it to be his name.

I am Blaise, he'd thought; and that thought had stayed with him even after he'd bolted the cell door and come away.

Before it had had time to fade and lose itself in silence, he'd caught a glimpse of his face reflected in a barrel of water as he stooped to drink as he'd been told to.

I am Blaise, and I am a man.

There were others behind him, waiting their turn at the water; he looked at them and saw that they were not Blaise, not him. Some were men, like him but not the same; others were women and others children, boys and girls. He didn't know their names, only that they were not Blaise, not him. Nor did they know that he was Blaise; neither did he tell them.

The prisoner in the cell had been a girl. He remembered that, though it was past now. She had gifted him his name, she had known and remembered it. Perhaps he might remember hers if he tried, if he had reason to try. He thought that he might remember her face, as she had remembered his.

He was sent to climb steps, to stand upon a height and watch. As he climbed, he saw walls and towers all around and knew that he was in a castle. He had been in other castles before this. He remembered one in particular, a greater castle than this was, and he thought the girl had been there also, though she was not a prisoner then. She had been in his charge, though; because he was Blaise, and she had called him *sergeant* then, and he had called her *my lady*, although her name was Julianne.

I am Blaise, and I am a man; I was a sergeant, and I had charge of the lady Julianne . . .

He stood on the wall above the gate, and watched the road below as he had been ordered. For a while nothing moved below, while thoughts and memories wandered almost randomly through his mind. Then as the sun set he saw distant figures coming up from the town, a small cluster, three people carrying a fourth. They came to the gate and no one followed them.

I am Blaise, and I am on guard here, as I have been elsewhere; though I do not serve now those that I served before. I do not serve the lady Julianne. She is a prisoner here, and I serve those who have imprisoned her.

They had imprisoned her with a demon. He had seen it in the cell, but at the time he could not recall what manner of thing it was. Now he knew. It was black and shaped of cruelty, with eyes of fire.

There were two men he served in this castle. One he had followed here, but the other gave the orders now: feed the prisoner, watch the road. He remembered the words and he remembered the meaning, but they were different memories. That one gave his orders in a language that Blaise did not understand, and yet he knew what to do each time. The words had a shape in his ears, and another shape in his mind.

He remembered fear, but not how it felt; he could not feel it.

In the dark, he saw many points of light that glittered and moved together outside the town. He had seen such things before. They would be torches, carried by men. When they began to stream along the road, he knew that an army rode against the castle.

He watched as he had been told to, and saw the army come; he saw its fires leap to life around the walls, he saw shadows of men at every fire and tents set up beyond. He remembered the word for this; it was called a siege.

When he was called down, he went in obedience, because he could remember no other way to act.

There were many people in the yard behind the gates. The lady Julianne was not among them. She was in her cell, he remembered, with the demon. He remembered pity but not how it felt, he could not feel it.

These were all the people who had followed the man to

the castle. Blaise had been one among them then; now he thought he was not, because he was remembering so much.

The man who had led them here – they had called him the Preacher, he remembered, when they had had voices they could use and words to fill them – that man stood close to the gates, facing the gathered people.

The other, the one who gave his orders in a tongue that Blaise could not speak, that man was not here. This one did not speak at all, any more; he had no need to. His will was their will. It might as well have been the will of the world, and perhaps it was.

It made no difference how much Blaise was remembering; he couldn't remember how not to follow the Preacher's will.

I am Blaise, I was a sergeant, I served the lady Julianne because it was my duty; now I am Blaise and it doesn't matter, I serve the Preacher because . . . because I serve the Preacher, because I do.

He walked to the first of the people where they stood together, because it was the Preacher's will that he should do so. He was vaguely aware of another man on the other side of the group doing the same as he did, pressing his lips against the lips of the person he faced.

This one was a woman. He remembered kissing in homage, as a sign of fealty; he remembered kissing in desire, in passion, though he could not remember how that felt. This was neither the one thing nor the other, not a kiss at all. Their open mouths met, and he felt not warm breath but the touch of something cold, a chill pass from her to him.

The woman screamed.

Blaise remembered pain, though not how it felt; he

thought the woman was remembering now, and feeling too. He watched her subside, he watched her roll and thresh on the ground and remembered another word, remembered agony.

Then he moved on, to the next in line. This was a man, an old man; after Blaise had done that thing that was not kissing, after the slip of cold had passed between them, the man stared, choked, collapsed in silence.

Blaise moved on.

Men and women, and children: for those Blaise had to bend low to touch his mouth to theirs. From each he claimed a chilly breath, and each one fell when that was done. Some screamed, some bled; most did neither.

Fess did neither, when Blaise came to him and knew his face, and remembered his name but could not speak it.

He remembered another word, which was death. He left Fess among the dead, and moved on.

The sense of coldness grew beneath his tongue like a swelling, chilling tumour – unless it was within his tongue, he wasn't sure. He was conscious of the weight, the strength of it in his mouth as though it were solid, hard-shelled, and each sliver that he took wrapped another skin around it.

He thought it was good that there were two of them reaping this harvest, claiming souls for the Preacher. One man might never bear so many. He had been sick, he had been drunk, he had been overburdened and exhausted; once he had smoked a herb that had kept him erect and urgent throughout the night, for all that two separate women could do about it. He remembered all of those, and none had been like this. The chill was in his mouth, but the power of it filled his body from skin to skin, throughout. Filled and almost overfilled: one more, two more and he thought he might burst entirely, like a blood pudding badly cooked and erupted from its casing. He thought he was a vessel, a jug top-full and fit to spill.

He walked, and could barely believe that he was doing that. Like a storm that must break, he thought that he should pour and thunder across the land, not step with these impossible legs, one pace and then another and balance in between.

He took another soul, and there was only one left and the other man took that one.

All the yard was crowded with dead and dying, or so he thought them, all those people who had been ferries, carriers to their small fragment of what was in him now. And what he held was only half of what they'd brought between them; and he thought it could rive the world if it were let loose, and he had no way to contain it.

He remembered dread, but not how it felt; he could not feel it.

He and the other went to the gates, where the Preacher wished them to be. They slid the beam aside and drew them open – high heavy gates, he could have moved them with a finger, he did move his leaf with a single, casual wrench that hauled it almost off its hinges – and then fell in behind the Preacher as he walked forward, out of the castle's dark shelter and into the gaze, the glare, the bristling suspicion of the enemy.

He remembered fear but not how it felt, he couldn't feel it. Magister Fulke had frightened him, he remembered suddenly, both in his person and in his demands; he thought that this should frighten him too, at least as much. If he'd ever been closer to death, he hadn't remembered it yet.

There were men all about him, men of the desert, those he had fought all his life. They were hostile and watchful, and more than their suspicion bristled; scimitar-points and arrow-points tracked from every side, following the Preacher, the other man, himself every step of their way from the castle gates to the tent of their enemy.

I am Blaise, I was a sergeant and I served the lady Julianne. This I remember. Now I serve the Preacher, and I cannot remember why . . .

Neither did he understand how, exactly: only that he carried something in his mouth that was not himself, nor any part of the Preacher. It lived, he thought, in its own cold way; it had lived in all those people and now it lived in himself and in another, and soon perhaps it would be whole and free.

He did think of it as one thing, however many fragments it had made; not like a nest of bees or a school of fish that swarm or swim together but are still separate creatures, rather something mythical and monstrous that could shatter at will and reform, like ice-shards melting and running into a single pool of water.

All the people he had drawn it from were dead now. It would be drawn out of him soon, he thought, and then supposed that he would die also. That was something else that ought to frighten him, and did not. He couldn't find the place where fear lived inside him, though he had been a fearful man, he was sure.

He remembered how frightened he had been in that strange land that Magister Fulke had sent him to. He thought of it as the heart of the sun: everything had been hot and golden, even the water, and there was no other sun in the sky, so where else could it be?

He remembered how he had got there, by means of a lighted candle and a few muttered words that he thought were a demon-spell, that the Magister said were a prayer. Now that he was remembering so much, the words burned in his mind, in the Magister's voice repeating them over and over until he was amazed that he had forgotten them at all, or remembered anything else first.

He still had the candle, too. He'd carried that beneath his robe for safety, against his skin in case he lost his pack, as he had done somewhere in the time that he'd forgotten, the great gap when even his name had been left behind until the lady Julianne gave it back to him.

He could feel the candle now, pressing against his belly like a reminder of the terror that he'd felt when he had lighted it and said the words and found himself in that dreadful sun-country. The taste of terror was gone, but he could still remember the fact of it. It had overwhelmed him then, and he thought it ought to be doing the same now as he followed the Preacher into the enemy's camp with death in his tongue, death threatened on all sides and treachery to come. He was sure of very little, but he was sure of that. He remembered truce, he remembered parley, but this was something entirely other.

He might have cried a warning even to his enemies, *do not trust the Preacher* – but his mouth was full of evil and he could not speak.

They were taken to a tent behind the ring of fires. The tent was large and bright with lamps, warmed by a brazier. It was furnished simply, rugs and a wood-framed cot, no more.

Half a dozen men stood to greet them as they entered, as their guard dispersed around the tent walls, still with arrows nocked and scimitars drawn.

He stood shoulder to shoulder with the other man, the two of them a little behind the Preacher. They faced the men whom they had come to see, and Blaise looked at their faces and knew two of them as he had known himself and the lady Julianne, and Fess.

There was the King's Shadow, father to the lady Julianne, who had left them by magic on a road long ago, and so all Blaise's troubles had begun; and there at his side was Rudel, who had claimed to be a jongleur at the great castle but was not, though he sang very prettily.

Both men were gazing at him. Their faces were very still, but he thought that their minds were not.

He knew Rudel, he knew the King's Shadow as they knew him, which was distantly. The other men in the tent were strangers all, and all of the desert. He remembered their own name for themselves, which was Sharai: Elessans used it, Ransomers used it, he'd known it and used it all his life. It was their blood-kin the Catari who worked the land in Outremer, defeated and tamed and seldom even defiant. *The Sharai are Catari*, he remembered, *but to be Catari is not to be Sharai*. Many of those dead in the courtyard had been Catari, by their dress and skin; he thought not one of them would have been Sharai.

'I am Hasan,' one of the Sharai said then, and Blaise remembered more: the night raid on the castle when he was not allowed to fight, the bodies in the morning sun. Hasan had led that raid, and failed, and been driven back into the badlands. He remembered the sourness of triumph, though not how it had tasted.

'I am Hasan, and I do not know whether I welcome a friend or an enemy to my tent; but you are welcome to it none the less. You need have no fear for your safety. Guests are sacred to us; the guards are . . . precautionary, because there is an 'ifrit in the castle, and they are devious beasts. Should it come to meet us, we are ready. Allow me to name my companions to you: here are the lords of several tribes, and princes also from Outremer . . .'

Blaise remembered the word 'ifrit from childhood stories, from the warnings of his elder brethren when he had been a Ransomer, from campfire tales when he had been a sergeant of Elessi. There had been other words, other creatures spoken of; he remembered that he had never truly believed in any of them, until he saw a djinni on the road to Roq de Rançon. Today he had seen a demon, in the lady Julianne's cell; he supposed that was the 'ifrit, though he would still use his own name for it. There was another demon in his tongue, for which he had no name at all.

The Sharai Hasan named the men who stood with him, one by one; then he waited, to hear the Preacher name himself and the two who stood behind him. He waited in vain; the Preacher said nothing.

After a time, Hasan took a breath and asked directly. 'Will you tell us your name? It is the custom, at a parley.'

'My name is unimportant; I have not come to parley.'

'Have you not? To what end, then? My wife is captive in that castle, and if those who hold her will not parley, they will die. Do you speak for Morakh the Sand Dancer, or for the 'ifrit, or for all those who came later, or for whom?'

'I speak for the God I serve, and for none other.'

Blaise didn't understand or believe either man, though it didn't matter. Unless there was another woman prisoner in the castle, Hasan must be speaking of the lady Julianne; but she was married to the Baron Imber, Blaise had seen that marriage made himself. And the Preacher surely did not serve the God that he proclaimed, a hundred corpses demon-slain could testify to that.

Unless their deaths were necessary, for a greater good? Innocents died in war, that was universal; but Blaise felt the chill inside his mouth and did not believe there was any good in it, nor in the Preacher who had caused it.

'How does your presence in the castle serve your God? And why have you come to us? If you want free passage out of the castle for you and your followers, you may have it, so long as you have done no harm to my woman.'

'I have done no harm to anyone,' which was a lie direct at last, though Blaise could not speak to denounce it. 'I am a healer, blessed by the God and by the relic of a saint. See, I will show you.' He reached inside his robe; Hasan moved not a muscle but the guards tensed, alert for any weapon despite all promises of safety.

The Preacher produced the black and twisted hand, and held it out in plain view. The guards relaxed slowly, as fascinated as every man there by the way light glistened on its glossy skin. Rudel took half a pace forward, only to be stayed by the King's Shadow with a touch on his sleeve and a murmured word.

'There is a sickness abroad in the Sanctuary Land,' the

Preacher went on, 'which I have named the King's Evil. It is sent by the God as a reprimand, because the King has allowed heresy and false teachings to thrive within that holy land. Only my prayers and the touch of this relic will cure it. Those that I have healed follow me; I led them here that we may strike together against the greater sickness, which is Surayon.'

'Surayon is hidden,' Hasan said mildly, 'and you are not many, to make war against a state.'

'It will be opened to us, and the God's strength is in our arm. Nor will we be alone. I have seen this, and it is sure.'

'What would you have me do? I have my own quarrel with Outremer, but I am here for my wife, who has been taken by one of our people. I have said that I will let you pass, if you can bring your followers out of the castle; though I am curious to know why the Sand Dancer let you in.'

'The gates were open, and he welcomed us as you have welcomed me. Perhaps he is not the enemy you think. Or there may be a greater reason than his own, why he has drawn you here. He too is a servant of the God, though he may not know it. And you are an army, poised above Surayon and sworn against the Kingdom; if the Folded Land should open . . .'

If the Folded Land should open, Blaise thought, not Hasan himself could hold his army back, even should he want to; and the glint in his eye said that he would not. He might consort with a Surayonnaise sorcerer, but he would still lay waste to Rudel's land on his way to Ascariel.

He said nothing, though, and neither did Rudel. It was the King's Shadow who spoke, who said, 'However that may be, you and your people are free within the castle. Would it be possible for you to bring my daughter out, among your number?'

'There is no need,' the Preacher said. 'Look, where she comes . . .'

And indeed she did come, the lady Julianne blundering in through the doorway of the tent, and talking already as she came: calling, but not to her husband, nor yet to her father.

'Rudel! Rudel, are you here? Oh, Rudel, come quickly! Esren would bring us no closer, I don't know why, but we need you, Marron is dreadfully sick, Elisande is with him but she cannot help, she says she needs your strength . . .'

Not Rudel, but Hasan who reacted first: Hasan who strode forward to claim the girl he spoke of as his wife, while the rest were simply staring. Hasan who had been so careful with his doubtful guest, who forgot all that care in a moment: who passed within a hand's span of the Preacher in his urgency.

And as he passed, the Preacher struck. Not with a blade, not with a fist: with the distorted black claw that he called a relic.

He used it like a weapon, not an instrument of healing. He slashed it across Hasan's face and the hooked fingers dug deep, leaving long red weals where the blood rose.

Briefly, everything was very still within the tent. Even the lady Julianne's pleading voice fell into silence.

Then three bows sang, and the Preacher wheeled once before he dropped.

Hasan raised a puzzled hand to his cheek, touched the blood there, made a choking sound and collapsed.

The lady Julianne cried out incoherently, hurtled forward and dropped to her knees above the fallen Sharai.

Her father's voice was louder as he called, 'No!' and ran to seize her shoulders, to drag her away.

She resisted; he said, '*Look*, Julianne! Use your eyes, use your mind . . . !'

Her gaze followed his pointing finger; so did every man's in the tent. So did Blaise's.

The relic, the saint's hand lay where it had fallen on the rug, where the pierced Preacher had dropped it as he died.

It lay there, and it moved.

As though the life had passed from man to thing, it flexed and squirmed, began to stretch upward. It never had looked much like a hand, so bent the fingers were, so withered the palm; now it seemed more like a blackened plant in hasty growth, reaching for the sun.

At the same time, a wispy smoke stole from the Preacher's mouth and twined itself around that sprouting darkness, and was absorbed. The thing swelled outward and grew more vigorous.

The lady Julianne gasped sharply, and flung herself full-length across Hasan's stillness. 'It has eyes!'

'Indeed.' The King's Shadow confirmed calmly what Blaise too had seen already, red points glowing against the black. No doubt the eyes had always been there even in its shrunken state, though they must have been hidden behind a fold of chitin. 'It's an 'ifrit, daughter – and as far as I'm aware, you're lying on top of the only blessed weapon in the tent.'

Blaise watched all this dispassionately, as he must; but then his own mouth opened as the dead Preacher's had, and he felt the ice in his tongue uncurl.

He saw it issue from his mouth, not ice but smoke, black

smoke rushing to feed the demon, the 'ifrit. The same was happening to and from the other man at his side, nameless and doomed.

Blaise remembered terror, agony, despair, he remembered how they felt; he felt them all.

The pain started in his feet and crept upward, a rotting, consuming fire. He fell quickly, wanting to roll and thresh against the searing; but despair was a lethargy that engulfed him entirely and far more quickly. Screaming was waste of precious air, struggling was purposeless; better to lie still and suffer, and so die . . .

Except that he was lying on his belly in an enemy's tent, with treachery all around him. Here was neither honour nor justice, and he did not want these people to have the disposal of his body.

He had no care for any of the chaos above and about his head. He could feel the candle that he carried, pressed against his stomach; despite his pain – or because of his pain, perhaps, a whip to use against black melancholy that might have overcome him else – he could work his hand in to draw it out.

And when he held it, he could drag himself on his elbows the little distance that he needed, he could hold the wick of it in a puddle of burning oil from a lamp that had tumbled from its tripod and would burn all the rugs and the tent besides if it were not attended to; he could cup his hands around the flame and whisper the words that Magister Fulke had branded into his brain. No matter that his breath came in shudders and his voice too. The soft hiss of it was meant not for mortal ears, but for the God.

And the God heard: there was a glimmer of gold in the eye-dazzling light, a taste of gold in the air, a touch of gold in the warmth soaking up into his pain-racked body, and he was quite alone and could die so, and would be glad to do so even here where he had been so scared before.

Elisande was so in dread for Marron's life, she couldn't understand why the djinni had left them here, outside the circle of besieging fires but still a distance short of Hasan's tent. Surely it had understood her urgency, her order . . .

Stranded close and yet not close enough, she'd sent Julianne to run into the tent rather than call Esren back and argue with it. There was little profit anyway, she'd learned, in arguing with a djinni; it would do what it would do, and it always had an answer.

Instead she waited as patiently as she could, cradling Marron's head in her arms and glaring at the Sharai who gathered uselessly around her, muttering to each other but saying nothing to the point and nothing at all to her. Peering between their pressing bodies, she watched the door of the tent, waiting to see Julianne come racing out with Rudel on her heels – and waited longer than she'd wanted, longer than she'd expected, far longer than she thought Marron could afford. His skin was shifting constantly beneath her touch, ice-cold one minute and burning hot the next, as the Daughter struggled against his strange invader without seeming to care what damage that battle did to its host body.

Distantly she heard noises coming from the tent above the babble of the men who surrounded her: sudden shouts, she thought the hiss of arrows. Before she could cry out in warning, she saw something emerge at last – but it was not, it was far from the human figures she'd been watching for.

Something black and long, so long: its body was snake-like, she thought, except that it seemed to move on twig-thin legs. It moved fast, whatever it was, gone into the dark before she could raise an arm to point it out; and it left her in terror for what might have happened in the tent, what new tragedy they would come to tell her of while she knelt help-less, nursing a boy she could not heal.

Too late there was a yell from the castle gates and a figure racing out, sprinting after the creature. That was Jemel, inevitably – cocksure in his own courage, determined to be first and foremost in the battle. At least he had the weapon for it if battle there proved to be, he'd had his scimitar blessed alongside her smaller blades; but unless the creature waited for him, he simply wouldn't have the speed. Young and agile as he was, he couldn't hope to match that insect scuttling.

Nor did he. For a minute, Elisande was torn desperately between desires. She wanted to watch for him and also watch the tent with its sudden crush of frantic men outside it, shouting and gesticulating and almost coming to knives, and she still didn't know why, what the monster had wrought inside; she wanted to run to discover, to find her friends – and, yes, even her father – to be sure that they were safe, at the same time as she wanted to run after Jemel in case he did have his battle after all and one scimitar proved not to be enough, blessed or otherwise. Julianne had one of her blades but Elisande still kept the other, she could help. And she wanted also to stay just exactly where she was, Marron's head in her lap; she couldn't leave him, not possibly, so she wanted everyone to come to her with news and comfort and succour for the grievously ill, all at once and now . . .

Her eyes flitted from side to side, seeking friends, seeking reassurance, finding none. She thought seriously about screaming, loud as she could, simply to silence the babble briefly so that she could drop her questions and demands into that space she made. Almost, she took a breath to do it; but then there was movement where she'd been looking for it, beyond the firelight, and there stood Jemel. He looked briefly defeated, before he saw all the fuss and excitement around Hasan's tent. He started to walk, had a word with a standing guard, started to run.

Soon he was close enough to hear Elisande, without her having to scream.

'Jemel! Over here, I have Marron . . .'

That was safe to fetch him, and it did. He stood staring down at his unconscious friend, and even with his back to the firelight she could see how his complexion changed; even through the hard panting of a young man who had run too far and too fast, she could hear his sudden breathlessness.

'Sit down, Jemel,' she ordered roughly.

Somewhat to her surprise, the tough young Sharai obeyed her: of necessity, she thought, his legs giving way entirely beneath the weight of his distress.

'I have been searching for him, in the castle.'

'I thought you must have been. Esren brought us out,' and she could almost have smiled at the absurdity of it – Jemel running in at one door, no doubt, while they flew out of another – if Marron hadn't been so ill and both of them so anxious, if the memory of that swift flight to freedom hadn't been overlaid by the sight of heaped bodies in the castle forecourt.

'Will he live?' The voice was gruff, the question brusque, the truth of his feelings entirely betrayed by the way one hand reached out and lay hesitantly in the air above Marron's face, just a fingertip short of touching.

'I don't know,' she answered honestly. 'He's lived this long,' rather against her expectations, though nothing could make her say it, not to him, 'so there must be hope. I can't help him; I sent Julianne to fetch Rudel, but something's happened in that tent. You saw the 'ifrit come out,' and she couldn't think how that had come about, as she was sure no 'ifrit had been seen to go in, 'and there's been no sign of anyone since.' Not that anyone else had had a chance, with that great scrum of men around the doorway, but her heart was full of misgiving. That at least she wasn't afraid to admit to. 'I'm scared, Jemel. I want to know what went on in there, but I couldn't leave Marron . . .'

'Go now,' he said. 'I will stay. But send Rudel, as swiftly as you can.'

'I will,' she promised. *If he still lives . . .*

She pushed herself to her feet, a harder effort than she'd imagined; her own legs were none too steady.

She turned an ungainly stagger into a gentle trot, and soon reached the pack of excited Sharai who had made such a wedge at the tent's mouth. Being small was useful for once as she squeezed between them; so was having sharp elbows and a woman's voice. The guards at the doorway had clearly been in no mind to let anyone through, but here recognition helped, as perhaps did the memory that she had a djinni at her beck and call. They made no move to stop her, as she slipped beneath their drawn blades and stepped into the tent.

She'd been dreading what she might find here, how many dead. There was a moment's sheer relief as she saw only one man down and Coren, Rudel, Julianne all unharmed; she thought she ought to feel relief too for her country's sake when she realised that the figure slumped on the carpet was Hasan.

For her friend's sake, though, she couldn't do it. Julianne held her husband's head nestled in her lap, much as Elisande had held Marron's a short minute earlier; her own face was bowed and hidden, but Elisande could see black gashes on Hasan's cheek. Even clotted blood should never look so dark, she thought. Nor should such disfiguring but trivial wounds leave a man looking as Hasan looked now, sick unto death, again much like Marron; nor should they have left a powerful healer like Rudel looking so defeated.

He acknowledged her first, with a glance and a few quick words that stole her breath away.

'Elisande. I'm glad you're here, we need you.'

She gaped, she couldn't help it; then, recovering her voice, she demanded, 'What happened here, where did that 'ifrit come from, what has it done to Hasan?'

'Hasn't that djinni of yours taught you not to ask questions yet?' He sounded exhausted and troubled in equal measure. 'I'll tell it all, but not now. Hasan is beyond me; he would be beyond you too, or the both of us together, so don't suggest it. Call up your djinni. The only hope that I can see is to take him to your grandfather, as fast as that spirit can carry us, if it will.'

'Oh, it will.' Her grandfather could work miracles, she'd

always been confident of that. And seeking her grandfather meant Surayon, and home; for a moment her soul rejoiced, despite the circumstances. Then, 'There's Marron too, he has something of the same sickness, I'd guess . . .'

'Can the djinni carry them both, and us too?'

'Esren carried all the Dead Waters at once, don't you remember?'

'Then we will take them both. Why not? The two greatest threats our homeland faces, and we will carry them to the heart of it to save them if we can. Never tell me that the gods have no sense of humour. Swiftly now, Elisande. Minutes matter.'

Not as much as he thought, perhaps; but just then Julianne lifted her head like a blind creature seeking the sun. One glance at her face, tear-stained and racked with grief, and Elisande dropped to her friend's side, put both arms around her and said, 'Don't mourn the living, sweet. Save your tears for where they're needed.'

Julianne gave her a wry glance – *and you've shed none for Marron?* – but her voice was sour barrens as she said, 'He's as dead as need be, if Rudel cannot wake him. The 'ifrit might have killed him utterly, just as easily; it left him this way, I think, to make me suffer the more.'

'Then it made a mistake. Two mistakes. One, to think you so weak; and again, to think Hasan as good as dead. Whatever it's done to him, my grandfer will undo it. Trust him, if you don't trust me. And hold tight, we're going to hurry.'

Julianne clenched her hands tight in Hasan's robe, but then straightened suddenly, as if she'd only just realised what was meant. 'Your grandfather – but he's in Surayon, isn't he? And Surayon is . . . gone. Closed, Folded . . .'

'There's always a way in, love, for those who know it. We'll be with him by daybreak. Esren!'

The djinni was there at her call, silent for once; she said, 'Take us along the road, to the border with Surayon. Me, Hasan, Julianne, Rudel. Marron too, we must collect him. And probably Jemel with him. Coren?'

'Yes. I will go with my daughter.'

'All of us, then.' And with an idea of making the ride a little easier for Julianne this time, that she not have to ride on empty air, 'Esren, take us on the carpet.'

'As you command.'

The rug beneath them rippled and rose, began to move towards the tent's doorway. The other men not named, all those haughty and useless sheikhs crowded hastily back to give it room; the crowd outside fell over itself to make way. There would be more quarrels shortly, Elisande thought, as an essential balm to wounded pride, unless the wonder of a flying carpet were balm enough to soothe the humiliation of crawling in the dust. Somehow, she doubted that it would be.

Marron and Jemel: and of course they couldn't have one without the other, and she wasn't even resentful any more. She could even yield up what had been her place at Marron's head to the Sharai boy, and do it with a good grace yet, though it meant her sitting instead beside her father.

As she had nothing to accuse him of, they both sat in their customary silence. She poked experimentally at the rug she sat on, feeling how it was not stiff in itself like a boat's boards, nor was it laid over solidity like a rug laid over boards; it gave just a little beneath her finger as it did beneath her weight, as though it floated on something more sustaining than water. As it did: it wasn't the rug that flew, Esren simply carried that as it carried them, on a soft firm cushion of nothing at all. It would help Julianne, that was all, not to see the ground rushing by below them. That girl had her head bent low above Hasan's again, she wouldn't be seeing anything just now bar his ruined face, but she'd look up sometime, look around. Better, Elisande thought, if she couldn't also look down.

Darkness would help also, and it was entirely dark now except for the stars and the horizon's hint of a moon to rise shortly. She glanced back, and saw the fires of the Sharai dwindling behind them.

'What will they do?'

'The tribes? Come after us, of course. We have Hasan; they followed him this far, they'll follow him a little further. Besides, there's no point their watching an empty castle.'

'Morakh,' she objected, remembering him for the first time in a while, though he'd been the cause and motivator of so much. 'It's not empty, Morakh's there . . .'

'You think so? Still? Use your mind, Elisande.'

That stung, as it was meant to. She thought briefly, bitterly, and said, 'No. He would not linger. Either he has what he wanted' – Hasan not dead but sick unto death, and Marron the same, perhaps – 'or he has abandoned his plans. Either way, the tribes will not find him in the castle.'

'They won't even look. Hasan hunted Morakh for Julianne's sake; they followed Hasan for his sake, and their own, and perhaps for Outremer. The sheikhs will follow immediately, with their retinues. The army will come after, as quickly as it may. All the way to the Surayon border they will come, more than have ever been massed against us before.'

'They can't get in,' she said, trying to sound certain, to believe herself.

'No, probably not. But they will see all the rest of Outremer spread before them, and no army there to hold them back. And no Hasan. What do you think they will do, Elisande? When we fought them tribe by tribe forty years ago, we barely defeated them; they know that. They are together now, if not exactly united. Even without Hasan, they can hold together a few days longer. Long enough to march on Ascariel, at least.'

She told herself firmly that she ought not to care, that Ascariel was her enemy also; but that was impossible to sustain. 'Should we have left him, then, and let him die? Let Julianne be a widow, for Outremer?'

'Julianne can still be a wife if she chooses, to the Baron Imber. And many would say that we should have done exactly that.' He sighed, and went on, 'I might say it myself, I'm afraid we will all have cause to say it in the days ahead. I couldn't have done it, though, any more than you.'

'There must be some hope,' she said stubbornly, 'some way to stop them.'

'Must there? Well, then, maybe there is. There's Coren.'

'Coren? But—'

Her eyes shifted, she couldn't help it, across the carpet to where that venerable old man sat beyond Marron, beyond Hasan but still not far away, not far enough. Of course he had heard; his eyes twinkled at her, though he didn't speak.

'When fathers follow their daughters into some mad or

foolish adventure,' Rudel went on blandly, 'it's not always or entirely for the girl's benefit.' He might have been watching her closely, to see if she blushed; she determinedly didn't look at him, for fear that catching his eye might make her do so. 'Coren could have stayed with the sheikhs, and tried to argue against their riding after us; he would have lost that argument, and been nullified thereafter. On the other hand, if they have a long and tiring ride on a difficult road, and round the final corner to find him there waiting for them, perhaps with news of Hasan, they may be more inclined to listen to him. He is the King's Shadow, and that commands respect among the Sharai, especially on the border of the King's country. That's so, is it not, Coren?'

'I have hopes,' he agreed quietly.

And what of Julianne, then, who has hopes of her father's support as she takes her ailing husband into a strange land, and gives him over to strangers? There was no point even putting the question into words, she knew the answer already. No doubt Coren would be sorry not to be with his daughter at such a time; no doubt at all that he would do his duty or his King's bidding regardless. Julianne showed no signs of having heard the conversation, but if it were put to her directly she would know what to expect. She'd been trained in a far harder school than Elisande; she understood her father's priorities, and so far as Elisande knew had only rebelled against them the once. That once had brought them to Jemel, to Rhabat, to Hasan and so to here. That was far from nothing, but still Julianne was wedded to Imber first, as her father had decreed . . .

Well, she might yet be glad of that, she might need Imber

in the future; but he would be no use to her now. If Coren
too was absent, then she would be dependent on her friends,
which meant chiefly on Elisande. At least with Jemel on
hand to watch over Marron, the two girls could stay close
and worry with each other, each about her separate man.
And Julianne should not be the only one to worry over
Hasan; Elisande was struck with a brilliant notion, bright
enough to touch her face with a brief smile.

Rudel noticed it, of course. 'What was that thought,
then?'

'An idea, that's all. Something to do, after we're home.
Nothing mad or foolish,' and she could almost have smiled
again, if it hadn't been him she would have smiled at. 'I
won't even leave Grandfer's house.'

'You've made me that promise before. And broken it.'

'I made *him* that promise,' and broke it, yes. How else
had they all come here? She was no Julianne, to sit obedient
beneath her father's commandments. 'Under compulsion,' if
that made any difference. Between the two of them she
thought not, where everything was under compulsion. 'This
time it isn't a promise. I'm simply saying it. I wouldn't want
to go anywhere, anyway. I wouldn't leave Julianne.' Nor
Marron; she'd let Jemel claim the nursing of him, but she
wouldn't wander far from call.

'No,' Rudel said, 'I don't believe you would.'

And then she did blush, fearful that he might have added
mind-reading to his many talents; and quickly said, 'Tell
me what happened in the tent. I don't understand where that
'ifrit came from, nor what it did, why it didn't kill you
all . . .'

'No more do I. We'll trade stories, Elisande; you tell me

how you escaped your own 'ifrit, and I'll tell you what I saw. You may make better sense of it than I can.'

That she couldn't do, though she puzzled over it even while she told her own tale, and so took less pleasure than she felt she owed herself from her description of how she'd tricked the 'ifrit into flight, faking a future it could fear. Rudel was complimentary, but there was little pleasure in that either. After half a lifetime of setting herself against him at every opportunity, she wasn't about to warm to his congratulations now. Absolutely not.

Instead she stared out and away, looking perhaps as though she were deep in thought; she hoped so. The truth was that she was simply staring, and seeing less even than the dark and their speed could show her.

She had made this journey twice before, going and coming home, and the first of those had been the better. Much as she loved her grandfather and the land he governed, she had loved her freedom more; being away from Rudel had been her definition of freedom even then, and coming back had inevitably revoked it.

She'd never ridden this way at night, though. Even by daylight it had been shadowed and dangerous, barely more than a goat-track at times for all that they called it a road, little used and not at all maintained. The surface had crumbled constantly, she remembered, beneath her pony's hooves; occasional overhangs of visibly loose rock had had her wishing that the beast could tiptoe, for fear that a noise might bring them down.

She was glad to be flying now, for the safety and silence of their passage as much as for the speed. On horses or camels or on foot, she thought, this would be a terrifying path at night, worst for Julianne but bad enough for her; she didn't envy the sheikhs who would follow. Good sense should tell them to wait till the morning, though she doubted that they'd listen.

The djinni was a little pillar of flickering light at her shoulder. She'd told it to take them along the road and it obeyed literally, deliberately hurling them around every twist and turn in the winding way. The wind grew bitterly cold as they climbed high into the mountains; she drew her hood up and almost, almost huddled against the strong solidity of her father, did hunch into the lee of his stocky body for what slight protection it offered.

Julianne moved too, for the first time, when she felt the wind's bite; but she lifted her head into it and shook her hair free, so that she sat erect and silent and utterly still, her hands folded on Hasan's chest and her eyes wide and wild. She had always been promised Outremer, and had seen only the fringes of it in all her life thus far. She could never have thought to come to the living heart of the land – to hidden Surayon, no less, anathematised and cast out – like this: twice married and never widowed yet, wed now to the country's greatest enemy and on a desperate mission to save his life, riding a carpet carried by a spirit-creature out of myth and stories. Given her history, it seemed unlikely that she was seeing anything of what her eyes were looking at, the great crags and crevasses of the high mountains, the way the road clung to sheer cliffs as it snaked between unclimbable peaks. Elisande wondered what her friend might be thinking, and decided it was better not to know. Marron snagged as ever at her own mind, Marron and Jemel together snagged at the corner of her sight, and all she had as shield was Rudel who had never, never been a figure of comfort; her own thoughts were bleak enough for anyone.

For a short time, at the road's height, it seemed as though the mountains had been ripped fresh from the earth beneath, stark black shadows of what she remembered as stark black rock, like a wall erected between Outremer and the Sands. Too weak a wall, she thought, for all its massive strength: no wall could be stronger than the doors set within it. This was perhaps the hardest of the passes and they could cross it in an hour by the djinni's grace; the sheikhs who followed would need the night, no longer, and their army would catch them in the morning. No one would be expecting this, there would be no responding army to meet it. If Coren could not stop them at the border, the Sharai would have an easy ride down to Ascariel, and there would be blood enough to drown the city before the war was done. There had been one great slaughter there already, when her people took it in the last terrible battle for the Sanctuary Land. She felt a touch of inner cold as she realised that two of the men on this mad flight had been there at the time: her father, and Coren himself. At least he'd know the horror of it, then, if he failed. That might spur him to try the harder, if being the King's Shadow were not spur enough.

The King – there had been no King in Ascariel the last time. She wondered whether that might make a difference, whether he could act to stop a war. But why should he? As the simple Duc de Charelles he'd started the last one, after all . . .

Perhaps it was the darkness and the chill that drove her thoughts so blackly, coldly deep; if so, perhaps it was the first hint of warmth in the wind that drew them up again and her with them, back into the immediacy of the world.

They had come over the mountains, faster she thought than any human ever had before them. Now as they descended there were other, lesser peaks to north and south, a spur of the great range that declined into gentler hills as it ran westward almost to the sea. Ahead and below them lay her own home, hidden but present none the less and compounded in her mind of bitterness and joy together, the uncountable memories that had made her what she was.

The air smelled rich and damp, to senses long used to the desert's dryness; summer's heat lingered here even at night, cupped as it was within mountain walls. Those walls might be fallible, might be breached by the storm approaching, but still they gave an illusion of protection, as they always had. Elisande felt her anxieties stilled by hope. Surayon would stay safe within its Folding, her grandfather would work his reliable magic on Marron and Hasan both, Coren would hold the Sharai army back until its commander returned. And surely then simple gratitude would demand that Hasan led it back to the Sands, and Outremer too would survive at least a while longer, whether or not it deserved to . . .

She breathed deeply, hungry for the smells of home. The road was wider here as they came to the valley's mouth, if in no better repair; soon it forked, one branch running away southward towards Ascariel. Esren needed no telling; the carpet with its riders swept on along the other branch.

Soon it slowed, though, soon it settled to lie flat and inanimate on the stony road. Elisande stirred at the sudden unfamiliarity of hard ground beneath her; she got to her feet a little awkwardly, stretched and stamped like a sailor come to land, testing the solidity of earth.

Others rose around her, Coren and Rudel. Jemel and Julianne stayed predictably where they were, with the two sick men. Julianne turned her head, though, with that same unseeing gaze.

'Why have we stopped?'

'We've reached the border, sweet. We have to stop, to open a way through the Folding.'

Directly ahead of them was a strange discontinuity, like a rippling veil drawn across the road, transparent but disguising. There seemed to be more starlight than there ought to be on the other side of that invisible curtain, less shadow: soft rolling hills to north and south rather than the height of mountains, and an open aspect ahead. Elisande almost fancied that she could hear the sea, almost expected to scent it on the warmth of the breeze.

Between where she stood and what she saw lay a whole country, wrapped in magic and concealed from view. If she tried to walk forward through the barrier, she knew that she would feel dizziness and very probably sickness for a few moments, she'd lose all sense of balance or direction before suddenly she found herself in that scene she could so impossibly see from here, some thirty miles from where she stood and a bare mile from the sea. If she tried to ride through it, whether on horse or camel, her mount would panic and she'd likely be thrown off.

Far more than a simple illusion, the Folding was a powerful defence: a necessary defence for Surayon against the forces on either side, the Patric dukedoms that denied all brotherhood and would crush her country if they could.

Still, it was a wall with doorways for those who knew how they could be opened. Elisande knew, and had used that knowledge when she'd felt it needful, though it had been a difficult and draining exercise for a girl working alone. No need for her to face that strain again. This time she had her father with her.

Rudel had already walked forward, to stand within touching distance of the boundary. He glanced at her, all the summoning she needed. She told Esren to be ready, to whisk the carpet through as soon as the way was opened; then she went to join him.

It felt strange, so strange to be doing this with him, father and daughter working as one as though there were no ghost unlaid between them. It was an old ghost, though, and seemed to be retreating; sometimes she had to struggle to remember the taste of what had poisoned her love and tainted everything so many years before.

Just now, it was almost meaningless under the urgency and importance of the moment. She shrugged thoughts of it aside, surprised to find how easy that could be, and focused her attention on Rudel.

Even with two, this would be no simple task. Surayon had been Folded, slipped aside from mortal eyes or understanding, but it was still fixed as it must be, still rooted in the everyday world. Her grandfather and his fellow savants who had achieved the Folding had laid bonds of power all across it, from one border to the other in every direction, tethering north to south and east to west like a needlewoman stitching and gathering a fold into a sheet to isolate a stretch of the material. Their task now, hers and Rudel's, was to cut some few of those stitches, to make a breach large enough to pass all their companions through. The difficulty lay in remaking the stitches afterwards, to seal the boundary again; the greater danger was that if they lost control of their cutting, the whole intricate network of the bond might unravel, to leave Surayon utterly exposed.

Another glance between them, and both Surayonnaise reached out their hands to touch the insubstantial curtain. It was like healing, Elisande thought, looking below the skin of the world to see the reality beneath. Here were threads and cords of power like woven music, chords rather than ropes; she could hear their throb and pulse, if she closed her eyes she could see them like lines of light against the darkness of her lids, wrapping around her fingers as she probed the mesh. She could feel the suck of them as they sought to pull her far, far away; it took concentration to deny them.

Rudel, she thought, would not have closed his eyes. Older and stronger and far more experienced, he would stand foursquare and demand that they yield, that they part to his touch. She heard his voice now, through the subtle insistence of the web: 'I have begun, Elisande. Do likewise, but remember to keep hold of the threads, we must knot them after.'

She knew that, of course she knew that; for a moment the age-old resentment rose like bile in her throat. She swallowed it down hastily, fighting to keep her mind on what her fingers did. This was no time to play the sullen child . . .

The beat of the music was the beat of her blood. She had the right and the power to do this; besides, she had done it before, and alone. Not so great a tear, nor holding it for so long a time, only the moment that it took a slender and agile body to slither through the smallest gap she could create; but she had done it then, and mended it after.

Her fingers unpicked the strings, like a musician plucking her instrument and snapping where she plucked; but she sang her own song in silence as she worked, and so held the mesh together. It was like having other hands, hands of the mind that seized the threads as they broke and wouldn't let them fly. She could grip this many and more, this one and that, more yet; she felt them strain against her control but would not let go, simply refused to allow it. And her father was at her side, he could lend his strength to hers if she should need it, though she would not ask for it yet . . .

But then suddenly there was another body between herself and her father, she felt it loom beside her and she didn't understand it at all. Only Coren was up and about, not settled still on the carpet; and he wouldn't come so close to disturb them, he if anyone must know the delicacy and danger of their work. Besides, the smell was wrong: the mustiness of unwashed wool with the dry spicy smell of a man from the Sands underlying all, that was certainly not Coren . . .

Her eyes opened despite herself, so that she struggled to keep her mental grip on all the threads she held; and she saw Morakh close enough to touch except that her hands were vitally busy already, and he was facing her father and had his scimitar drawn.

Rudel was staring at him, his own hands caught in the barrier's weave, helpless to defend himself. There was the touch of a smile on Morakh's face as he raised his curved scimitar and brought it down.

One swift stroke, it seemed almost too casual, too small a

thing to end any man's life, let alone such a man, such a life.

Coren was shouting something, but he sounded a long way off and Elisande wasn't listening in any case. Elisande was screaming, wrenching her hands free of the intangible web that held them, forgetful of everything except the knife in her belt and the sight that filled her eyes, her father fallen in a gout of blood with his head half severed from his neck.

Morakh seemed slow somehow, so slow to turn. Her fumbling fingers had time to find the knife and draw it, time to thrust it deep into the Dancer's belly before his sword came up again. She was screaming still, she could hear herself, as though she'd forgotten how to stop; he made no sound at all, only sagged heavily against her so that she staggered backwards and almost fell herself beneath his weight.

He took her knife with him as he slumped to the ground. She didn't care, she was transfixed, seeing a strange smoke rise from Morakh's slack mouth; but then there was the 'ifrit scurrying out of the moonshadow, still shaped long and stick-like on slender legs except that it had claws now, and the smoke twined around its body and was absorbed even as those claws reached towards her.

She had just time to remember that her knife was blessed, and then to remember that it was out of her reach now, lost beneath Morakh's body, and so she was as dead as her father or would be in another moment.

The 'ifrit seemed to lose sight of her, though, even as it poised to strike. Its head turned, blindly questing; its claws flailed at the air. She stood frozen yet, lacking the wit to run, the sense to do anything at all. Someone else was running, she heard his steps and couldn't so much as look around to find him; and then Coren was there at her side with Hasan's great curved scimitar in his hand. He hewed and the blade cut, he thrust and the point drove through the 'ifrit's gleaming chitin and deep into its body, and it died and dissipated like dust on the wind.

And still she stood there, staring at her father's brutal corpse; and it was only when he said her name, 'Elisande,' with a terrible sadness that she remembered what was worse, what was the greatest horror of this dreadful, suddenly more than dreadful night.

Now she could move, although she didn't want to. She moved only her head, and that only a little: just far enough to see what no one had seen for thirty years, Surayon her homeland unFolded and unsafe, open and exposed, where all her grandfather's careful protective magic had frayed to nothing and was gone because she and Rudel had let the web unravel.

PART TWO

The Road to Revelation

10

Into the UnFolded Land

Anton wouldn't say that he lit the candle in all innocence, no, he couldn't conceivably claim that. None the less, he declined absolutely to accept any guilt in the matter. If pressed to it – if there were any who would dare to press him, which there were not – he could quite legitimately deny that any guilt existed, in him or any man else. Guilt for what offence? Marshal Fulke was sought, and could not be discovered anywhere within the bounds of his army's camp; there was one in the company – one Sieur Anton d'Escrivey, whose name might be known for other matters and whose deeds might be spoken of in whispers, scorn and nervousness together, but no matter for that, it wasn't relevant here – who knew where the marshal might be found, and how to reach him there. There could surely be no objection if that same Sieur Anton went to seek his master commander, wherever he might have wandered. Marshal Fulke was a man of virtue, obedience, rigid discipline; who would dare suggest that he of all this number would tread forbidden or unholy ground . . . ?

That at least was the argument that Anton was quite careful not to rehearse, as he never expected to need it. He could argue against it with an equal facility, how all men knew that there was ground permitted to their seniors that was utterly forbidden to them, and that it must have been clear to the meanest pack-boy that this was such a case. To the military and the religious both – and Anton was both, as was the man he followed – his coming here without order or sanction was contrary to all law and duty, and stepped perilously close to heresy.

And yet there had been no hesitation in him when the moment came and the temptation – no, say the opportunity arose. He'd been on watch half the night, and making his way towards his bed when he was overtaken by a runner with a message for Marshal Fulke. They'd gone together to the marshal's tent, where a soft light glowed through the walls; Anton's call had produced no answer, though, and they'd gone in to find the tent deserted. On a simple camp table had been an oil-lamp burning, and a linen roll unfolded to show a number of candles, black and white tapers intricately plaited together. For Anton, that had been better than a clue to his commander's whereabouts. He'd questioned the runner, whose message was an urgent summons; the lad claimed to have tried everywhere in the camp before he'd dared come to disturb the marshal's sleep, and Anton had found little difficulty in believing him. Marshal Fulke could be charming when he chose, but he had a chilly reputation among the men.

Anton had a reputation himself, of course, which had been made evident in the runner's blushing awkwardness. It could have been an act of simple kindness to dismiss the boy to find food and rest among his own friends in the encampment, and he might have done it for no reason else. In fact, though, he'd had another motive, a sudden curiosity that he'd made no great effort to suppress.

Left alone, he'd scooped up one of the candles and abandoned the tent, to take his search elsewhere. Not towards the mysterious, intangible border where Surayon ought to be and was not; Marshal Fulke was known to spend a lot of his time on that front, watching and praying, but the lad had come from there.

Instead Anton had turned the other way, towards the rear of the camp. He'd walked through the lines of horse-pickets and the groups of sleeping men, further than he thought a nervous and hurried boy would have ventured in the dark; he'd found the men on watch around their fires there and questioned them, and yes, the marshal had come through the lines alone and only a few minutes ahead of him.

Leaving the scattered line of fires behind him, Anton had walked on until his eyes had adjusted to the moonlight. Then he'd stood still, scanning the slopes of the hills that closed in around the road there. He might not have spotted a black-clad figure moving through the darkness, but he hadn't been watching for that. After a minute, he'd seen a momentary spark, another, and then a flickering point of light to his left and above him.

Not so far; he'd stepped softly over the stony ground, slipping between thorns and scrub while he slipped the candle from his robe and his own flint and tinder from a pouch at his belt.

Soon he'd been close enough to see Marshal Fulke's silhouette, stark against a guttering light; close enough also to hear the marshal's voice, chanting quietly. He'd heard the words before, and this single repetition was enough; he'd always prided himself on a sharp memory.

Shielding the candle with his body against both wind and the marshal's eyes, he struck sparks until the tinder caught, then lit all four of the candle's wicks. Straightening slowly and already murmuring the chant, he turned to see the marshal weaving cords of light, stepping into a golden nimbus. For a moment it hurt to watch, but the glow faded quickly, and the man was gone.

Anton followed swiftly but not hastily, guarding the candle's light with a cupped hand and speaking the words clearly now, trying to be confident both of his actions and of his intent.

In the one at least, he was successful; the flames of the candle were suddenly white and still as glass, brilliantly flaring. Anton touched them, bent them with his fingers as the other had before him; they seemed to cut a doorway in the dark, and he felt only a moment's lack of courage before his determination took him through.

This was not like the last time: no vision of the country spread out below him, no sense of flight or falling. Instead he was snatched instantly, urgently from one place to another, though so far as his eyes could tell he had simply stepped into a new landscape, other hills, these bathed in light without source so that they cast no shadow.

He had come – as he had hoped, intended, expected, almost prayed – to the golden country where he had stood before with Marshal Fulke. The ground was dry beneath his feet, walls of rock were dry around him, even the air felt dry and strangely lifeless in his lungs; nothing grew, nothing could grow here. There was no sun in the pearly sky, and all the land gleamed dully gold; he wondered if night could ever come to such a place, and felt briefly glad not to see it.

The marshal was standing a little distance ahead of him, just where the gully opened out onto a plateau. Beyond that still figure Anton could see another, a man lying fallen on the ground; his clothes, his bulk and the unlikelihood of chance made that man Sergeant Blaise.

Anton thought that he could maybe see something more, a slight disturbance of the air above Blaise, some twist of wind and light that seemed to sparkle faintly. In his own world he would have dismissed that as a mirage; here he was less sure.

Fulke walked forward less briskly, less confidently than was normal. He was still a few paces short of the body when a voice spoke, thin and silvery and seemingly out of the dead air – but it came, Anton thought, from that air that seemed not dead at all, that had a little spin to it, a touch of shine.

'Stay back, human. He is not dead, and I can prevent his dying, though he will be dead to you. It would be as well if you did not touch him.'

'He is my man,' Fulke said, quite calmly.

'He was, perhaps. No longer, and not for a while now. He has been a man of the 'ifrit; soon he will be nothing at all, unless I make him mine. Which I will do.'

'If he is injured, we have medicine of our own.'

'He is not injured.'

'Well then, what ails him?'

It seemed to Anton that there was an extra hum to the

voice suddenly, as though the creature – whatever it was – had been pleased by the question.

'You have asked, and I will tell you – though you will owe me a debt for the answer, and I will claim it later. The 'ifrit do not breathe and this is not a poison, but you might say that the man has been first poisoned by the breath of an 'ifrit, and then possessed by a fragment of its body. When it abandoned him, the poison remained. Or you might say that the 'ifrit cast a shadow in your world as a snake casts its skin, and that shadow has fallen over him and he has breathed within it, breathed it in. It is a cold thing, and eats at the will of creatures such as yourself. This one is strong, he did well to make the journey here, though it has drained him now; most would not succeed so far. The djinn do not breathe either, but my own breath, if you would call it that – or else my own shadow, even here in my own world – will rouse him, if only to my service. He is lost to you. Accept that, and go back.'

'I will stay, and see if he recover as you say. And hear what he says, after. The deceits of demons are legion, and he is a servant of the God.'

'I am a djinni; we do not lie. Perhaps he will serve your God, in serving me. That I do not know. You would be wise not to speak to him; if you ask him questions when he is mine, you will only increase your debt to me. But stay if you will, both of you. I do not forbid it.'

Now Anton could stand back no longer; he walked out onto the plateau, and saw Fulke's brief surprise.

'You, Sieur Anton? You followed me?'

'There was a message,' though the excuse sounded ridiculously thin, here and now. 'Besides,' more honestly, 'I was curious . . .'

'Well. Curiosity can work to the good; we are both in a new world tonight, where we face new revelations. Though I did not know that the King's Eye would shield creatures of the underworld.'

'Creatures of spirit,' the voice, the djinni corrected. 'The King's Eye sees far, and it sees deeper than you can, human. Do not rush to judgement in your ignorance; you stand in my world now, and it is not less than yours.'

'If you would save Blaise,' Anton said neutrally, thinking that that was an argument that could run for ever, and Marshall Fulke might well be in the mood to argue it, 'it would be as well to do it soon.'

'Patience. Mortal flesh is not as weak as you suppose, though a simple scratch opened his body to the 'ifrit. He might live here for days before he died. I do not plan to linger so long, however.'

The djinni fell silent then and seemed to contract a fraction, insubstantial though it was. Anton thought that the coil of its spinning had grown tighter, like a spring compressed; he thought that perhaps there was a difference to the quality of the air immediately between the djinni and the man, a stronger dust of gold; he saw a stir in Blaise's hood, as though a bellows had blown that hot and glittering air down upon him, directly into his face. He supposed that you could call that breathing, if you were a djinni.

Then there was other movement, this time in the man himself, a little shift of muscle that became an inch-slow squirm, a cautious stretch – like a snake flowing back into its skin, Anton thought, or a man rediscovering the limits of his own body – and then at last Blaise gathered himself together and stood up.

His hood fell back, and they saw his face for the first time. It was Blaise, and yet not quite. All the features were right – the bull brow and the once-broken nose, the jaw that could outstubborn an ass – but they had once all been animated by a spirit both men could recognise, and they saw no hint of it here. Blaise's face, yes, but occupied by a stranger: that was as close as Anton could come.

'Blaise!' the marshal said, apparently disregarding all the djinni's advice, though it had sounded good to Anton.

The man turned, slowly, from where he had been regarding the floating column of the djinni's intangible body.

'If you would call me so.'

'It is your name, Blaise. You have been far from it, perhaps, but you own it yet. As you do your rank of sergeant. Come back, and all your life awaits you, as it was; serve this creature and you imperil all, as well as your immortal soul.'

'It has touched me, it has claimed me; there is no life that can compare with that. I will go with it—'

'—And betray your masters once again, and betray the God. Blaise, you once asked, no, you *begged* to call me Magister. I granted that as a sign of your redemption, your returning to the wider brotherhood of faith. If you denied me now, I should be sorry.'

'I cannot help your sorrow.'

Anton almost had to choke down a laugh at that, so apt a reply from a man who had never been quick-witted till now. The humour lasted only a moment, though, as the implications of the thought sunk in. This was not Blaise – not quite? not at all, more like, another spirit entirely, just clothed in Blaise's body – and he was afraid that Marshal Fulke would forget that.

The marshal surprised him, though, and not for the first time. He showed no sign of temper; there was only reason in his voice as he said, 'You could dismiss it entirely, if you chose to come with me. Back to your own world, Blaise, even if your old life holds no attractions. You cannot live here; this place was never made for mortal man.'

'I can live in a djinni's shadow, until it choose to let me die.'

'That is no life for a man – and I think this is no man's true voice that I am hearing, djinni. His mouth, your words, I fancy.'

'That is not as true as you think. The choice is his, to stay or to leave; he would live in either case, but he will choose to stay. Just as those who are touched by the 'ifrit will choose to die. Perhaps you would have had me let him be.'

'Perhaps I would. Better to die, than to trade this half-life for his immortal soul. That is a deadly bargain.'

'I do not see how serving me will cost the man his soul, if he should have one. But I will not argue theology with a Marshal Commander of the Order of Ransom; that is a fruitless occupation.'

'Begone then, demon – but leave my man, I conjure you, by the power of the God!'

That was bluster only, Anton thought; and the djinni thought so too, he guessed. At least it surprised him, it surprised them both by laughing, a sound like a high-tuned peal of bells.

'Oh, I will leave you your man, Marshal Fulke. But I will take my own.'

'We will meet again, Marshal Fulke,' Blaise said unexpectedly; and to Anton's ears it was much like hearing the djinni speak through the sergeant's voice, with just the same cadence to it.

Before Fulke could draw breath to reply, the man was moving away across the plateau – moving but not walking, not running, seeming to glide rather as though the djinni were sweeping him away on an invisible cushion of air.

The two Ransomers, marshal and knight stood and watched, fascinated and helpless as the spirit-creature and its captive – or its convert, perhaps? – dwindled into the distance. It was hard to be sure, but Anton thought that they reached the edge of the plateau and simply carried on, not falling but truly flying now.

When they were utterly gone from sight, when he could no longer make out even a dot against the horizon, he stirred and rubbed his strained eyes, and looked about him. There was a sign left behind, he saw, to show that this had not all been some fantastic illusion; Anton was almost grateful for it, as he stepped forward and stooped to pick up the broken candle.

'Blaise must have fallen on it, in his sickness.'

'Indeed.' Fulke's voice was cold and distant; his eyes had still not left the far horizon, and it seemed that neither had his thoughts. 'I had heard tales, of course, before I came to this country, but I never thought to meet any of the demon-kind. I was never sure till now that the tales were even true.'

'Sergeant Blaise reported meeting a djinni, on his way to the Roq.'

'Yes. I thought it merely a heat-dream, no more than that. Blaise was the type to insist, against all logic . . . But no matter. We know the truth now, or some little of it, and

Blaise is enslaved to that creature. Remember, Sieur Anton, that all demon-spawn are the children of lies.'

'The djinn do not lie, according to all the stories I ever heard. It said so itself . . .'

'Precisely so. It said so; it was lying. That is axiomatic.'

Well, maybe so. Anton wouldn't argue the point with his commander. He was both wonderstruck and exhausted; he wanted nothing but to get back to the encampment, and to bed.

Fulke had another matter on his mind, though, that he wanted to settle immediately. 'Explain to me how it was, Sieur Anton, that you followed me to this place.'

Anton sighed and offered his prepared excuse again, the undeniable summons; and then confessed his curiosity again, as a good and obedient Ransomer should.

Fulke made an impatient sound. 'I did not mean your motives; those I understand and even applaud, although I do not condone your stealing the candle from my tent. I mean how you contrived to follow me through the King's Eye to this spot. I looked into the Eye and saw where Blaise would be, and came to him; but you lack that skill. If you'd simply lit the candle and said the prayer, you should have stayed on the site of the encampment.'

'That I cannot explain, Magister. I lit the candle and recited the words, much as Blaise did, I expect, knowing nothing of their meaning; and the way opened, and I stepped through here. Perhaps I was so close behind you that the wind of your passage carried me in your wake?'

'Perhaps,' though the marshal sounded quite unsatisfied. 'Or perhaps we should not enquire too deeply into mystery. It is not named the King's Eye for nothing; he watches all of us within his Kingdom, and he may have had his reasons to send you after me. This message, for example. It may be important . . .'

Important, surely, to have the commander of the guard send for the marshal in the deepest hour of the night, when even Fulke might have been sleeping. But important enough to have the King in his far palace twist the nature of the world to send a discredited knight across a magical realm in pursuit of his superior officer, simply to ensure its prompt delivery? Anton said nothing, but his mind balked.

'Blow out your candle, Sieur Anton, and we will go to investigate.'

Startled, Anton glanced down at his hands, to confirm that he was indeed still holding the candle. Its flame burned quite normally now, pale in the opalescent light of this place. He drew a breath in obedience, but then hesitated, struck by a wandering thought.

'Why didn't Blaise go back to the world we know, when he fell on his candle and extinguished it?'

'That I cannot say either. Perhaps the King required his presence too, for what reasons we cannot guess; or perhaps that – creature – worked some casting of its own, to hold him here in its snare. You must let go of Blaise, Sieur Anton, as I have already. A man lost is a man mourned, but no more than that. Blow out your candle.'

Anton hesitated no longer, but did as he was bidden; and found himself abruptly back on the hillside above the road, and blinking against the dark.

A moment later, there was a transitory gleam of gold and Marshal Fulke stood once again at his side.

*

They walked back to the encampment in silence, through the sleeping soldiery and the horse-lines, past the officers' tents and on, till they came at last to the guard-fires that marked the border.

It was the attitude of the guards that first alerted Anton to some great change. They stood in unaccustomed huddles, speaking in nervous murmurs; as the two men passed they fell silent, and some abandoned their posts to drift along behind. Anton waited to hear their sergeants call them back, and heard nothing; he waited then for Fulke to snap an order, and again waited in vain.

The man in command of this watch came running, as soon as he saw the marshal's familiar figure in the fires' light.

'Magister, I am so glad that you have come . . .'

'You sent for me?'

'Yes, but that was before . . . There was a voice, a creature, spirit or demon I know not, I could see nothing but a flickering light, like a marsh-phantom; but it spoke to me and said to send for you, and so I did. But—'

'But what?'

'Look, Magister. See what has happened since, just in the last few minutes . . .'

Fulke looked where the desperate man was pointing, across the border; and so did Anton.

Even in the dark, with only the faintest line of light in the east to promise a new dawn rising, he could see now what it was that had changed.

The border had been a terrible thing but a constant, immaterial and yet dreadfully real, a line torn across the natural world. By daylight or at night, it had been equally clear:

a rift in the hills' march, a shift in the fall of sunlight, a break even in the unending pattern of the stars.

Now there was nothing, it was gone. Now they stood on the road and saw that road follow its proper course, running onward along the bank of a stream that they had not dared to drink from, because it flowed from an invisible and accursed source. Now they could see its path glinting beneath the restored sky, they could see where it met the road and how before that it came plunging down a high hill that had simply not been there when Anton left his place of duty a bare hour since.

They could see how the road wound on around the base of the hill, and vanished into shadow – and they knew what lay beyond that shadow, and that even so much shadow could not linger now, would be burned away with the rising of the sun.

In short, they could see the way to Surayon, that they had waited for and prayed for all this time.

'Rouse the men,' Fulke said, after a swift murmur of blessing, gratitude to the God which should also be proof against any lingering, leaking corruption from the cesspool that was Surayon. 'See them fed, and then break camp. We ride at sun-up.'

Not knowing what they rode into, except that it was accursed; none in their ranks could remember – or would admit to – passing through Surayon in the years before it was Folded. Not knowing what would result either, except that there would be a cleansing, a great scouring of the poison that oozed from Surayon to infect all of Outremer.

Poisoned flesh must be cut out, the doctors taught; Anton had seen the truth of that, time and again. Trying to save a rotten limb could kill a man. Better to seem harsh than kind; better to strike, swift and sure in certainty, than to meddle and hope with doubt.

The land lay before them, the breeze was fresh and the night was paling; there would be blood and death before this new day was over, and that only the first of many days. It would be a hard and a cruel time that people would still speak of generations hence, as they spoke yet of the winning of Ascariel, where bodies had floated on the pools and lakes of their own bleeding.

Anton couldn't wait.

Coren had been here before, of course. He was the King's Shadow, and the King bestrode this land from northern march to southern sand, from western sea to eastern height where Coren was standing now. The King sat in Ascariel and never left his palace, but his Shadow fell wherever his will might glance; in forty years that will had pried into every secret corner of this country, and much that lay outside its borders too.

But Coren had known this pass even before he was the King's Shadow, even before there was a King. At that time it had been a killing-ground, where they had hounded the Sharai through the mountains and back into the desert.

Ten years later it had been a way of trade, a constant passage between Surayon and the Sands. By then, though, Surayon was already anathema to its neighbour states, and its dealings with the Sharai only further evidence of its debasement. All of Outremer traded across its borders, it had to in order to survive; but the other states traded only goods, what could be bought and sold from camel trains. Surayon traded in knowledge, the arcane wisdom of its Princip and his court for the witchcraft and indecent practices of the Sharai. That was heresy and should have been forbidden, only that the King was silent on the subject. There had been worse rumours too, even that the lords of Surayon traded in people also: not the slavery that was common throughout the country, but their own children sold to sorcerers deep in the desert, apprenticed to the blackest of the arts.

And then Surayon had Folded itself away before the other states could bring the God's clean justice down upon it, and like every path across the border, this road had passed into nothingness and out the other side of Surayon.

And so Coren had seen it for the past thirty years, like every traveller who came this way. As the King's Shadow he could come and go throughout this land, no work of man could bar him, but his eyes still saw what other mortals saw.

He'd always hoped to see it again as the God had made it, the high pass running down into the broad, deep cleft of the valley principality. He'd never truly expected it, though; he was too wise in the ways of his people. Mistrust and bigotry fed off each other and could thrive for generations, building higher and stronger walls even than these mountains. He hadn't dared to hope that Surayon would unFold itself in his lifetime, and he'd been sure that no outside force could break in through the Folding.

He'd been sure, and he'd been wrong.

For all the King's insight and his own, for all their knowledge and their great anticipation, he could never have imagined that he'd find himself here like this, in the road with the Folding dissolved and gone, an army from the Sands marching towards him and the body of his friend laid out in the dust at his side.

He'd insisted on that, against Julianne's tearful pleading and Elisande's tight silence. 'I'll bring him home,' he'd said, 'as soon as I may. That I promise. But the Sharai respected Rudel while he lived, and they respect the dead who died bravely. If I cannot persuade them to turn back, it may be that Rudel can. Without Hasan's determination to drive them on, they might choose not to pass his body; it could win us a few days' grace, if nothing more.'

Privately he thought that the opposite was more likely, that finding the road open and having pursued Hasan this far, the Sharai would pursue him further, all the way to Surayon town and the Princip's palace. This was a desperate cast of a die that was weighted against him, against them all; but he'd still seize any slight chance that he could. The sheikhs might at least honour Rudel's memory far enough to turn back to the fork in the road and ride for Ascariel instead. That would be a small, if a bitter victory; the King held a special fondness for Surayon, as did Coren also. And Ascariel at least mounted an army, which Surayon did not. Perhaps the tribes' love of battle would draw them that way; perhaps in Hasan's absence, the sheikhs would yearn to show that he was not needed, that they could achieve what he had not. Sharai ambition had won many a fight for the Patrics, before this.

But they were coming now, and he was dreaming. This was a situation that might more properly call for prayer, though he made none: neither to the God he had long since ceased to worship – though not to believe in; he had seen too much to allow of any doubt, but too much also to allow of any praise – nor to the King whose hearing he was more sure of, whose help he might have hoped for. He had learned long since that such hopes were commonly vain. The King ruled, but left his country for his Shadow to administer.

Coren stood foursquare in the road beside the body of his friend and waited while the long shadow that was only the outriders of the Sharai army came slowly down the defile from the mountains. It would be past dawn on the Sands, he knew, but not yet in Surayon; there were still stars to be seen above him, though they were fading now. Light was creeping into the sky, but matters here would still be decided in the dark. However they fell out, the sun would look down on a new-made world by the time it had climbed above the mountain wall; he doubted if that world would be better made.

It was as ever the sheikhs themselves who led the line of march with their immediate retinues, young men of their close families. He knew them all by more than name and reputation. He knew their tempers and their temperaments, their pride and ambition, their quarrelsome natures and every quarrel that lay between them. Under other circumstances, he would have been confident in playing one against another until their unity was shattered and the best that they could hope for was a chaotic withdrawal, the worst a pitched battle between their tribes. Here, though, on the very borders of the country that was as holy to them as to his own people, he felt himself weak and helpless. His own reputation would protect him personally, not one among them would raise a blade against the King's Shadow, but he thought that nothing could protect the land or the people at his back.

Nothing unless it was the King himself: now would be a good time for him to guard his realm with an earthquake or a vision of fire, something to terrify or tear apart these long files of desert men, rip the courage from their hearts or the ground from beneath their camels' feet.

But the King did not and would not work that way. Sometimes even Coren did not understand the King, although he'd known him longest and best. Except for the Princip of Surayon, of course, always excepting him. Maybe even the King would make an exception for the Princip . . .

But he did not, and Coren had still not expected him to. The leading sheikhs rode up and reined in, three abreast, as many as could be accommodated without crowding on the road.

Coren read their mood on their faces – exhaustion, anticipation, exaltation – and almost stepped aside without a word, almost bowed and waved them on their way. The smoothest voice in Outremer, which was his, would do him no good here. He held his ground, though, scrabbling after every little minute he could buy for Surayon; he folded his arms passively, impassively, and awaited their questions.

'What has happened here?'

'Rudel has been murdered, by Morakh the Sand Dancer, while he was working us a passage into Surayon. As you see, that has undone the Folding. Also, we were attacked by an 'ifrit. We slew them both, spirit and Dancer; Morakh's body is over yonder,' a casual wave of his arm towards the rocks beyond the road's limit, 'if you wish to bury your man before you continue on your way.'

A general hissing, hands touched to scimitar-hilts, and, 'Morakh was not our man!' from several throats at once.

'No? Strange, then, that he was so eager to ease your path for you. Honourable men would refuse to accept this gift he has left you,' a bare movement of his eyes to show what gift he meant, the death of a man they knew well. 'Honourable men would turn back and wait word from Hasan, whom we are seeking to heal.'

This was the crux, confrontation the only tool he had where diplomacy was bound to fail; he did not think that it would be enough.

Nor was it. There was mocking laughter at his words, and, 'Hasan must take his chance. If he recover, he may join us or not, as he sees best. The Dancers serve God, and so do we; if Morakh won us this opportunity, he is among the blessed in Paradise.'

'Will you serve the 'ifrit, as he did? They tried to destroy you at Rhabat; now they will use you to destroy the Patrics. Is this wisdom?'

'It is as God wills it. Do not stand between us and our own lands, Shadow, unless you desire to follow Rudel sooner than you might.'

That was it, that was all he could do; he had lost, as he had been sure that he would. He stepped off the road and stood watching in silence as the Sharai began their slow ride across the border into Surayon at last, going quietly in single file past Rudel's body, each man offering a salute or a blessing before lifting his eyes towards the country so long hidden, so long desired.

Imber was a deserter, he supposed. For sure that would be

how his uncle treated him, when – if ever – he went back: as a milk-sop and a coward both, a weakling who ran away from family and duty at a time when danger threatened, who went in search of a fled woman without even the poor excuse of dragging her back. He was reconciled, never to live with Julianne; she'd slipped away from him twice, and he wouldn't be so cruel as to force a third time on her. He'd find out why, though, he was determined on that. She had seemed – well, not unagreeable to the wedding. Not distressed, as some girls were when they were forced to the altar. Sometimes – brief times, they'd only had brief times together – he'd thought she might return his own affection; something surely had burned the air between them when their eyes locked . . .

First he had to find her, though, before he could understand her. Find her and rescue her. *Great danger,* the djinni had said, and so he had come at great speed; and the major, the overriding surprise to him was that his cousin Karel had come with him, and half their men beside.

'They're more or less the names I would have chosen,' Karel had said the first night as they walked the bounds of the camp together, supposedly choosing picket-sites, 'if I'd had my pick of the squad. They would have come for me, if I'd ordered them; and I'd have done that, you know, if you'd tried to sneak off alone.'

'I know,' which was one reason why he'd asked for more than Karel's blessing. Better to ride in company than to be hunted. 'But you didn't need to order anyone.'

'No. They volunteered. They'd have obeyed me, because I'm a soldier,' which was the other reason Imber had wanted him along, 'but they follow you because of who you are.'

'Because of what I am, you mean.' The Baron-heir, the Count's son, too valuable to be let wander unprotected in the Kingdom or outside it.

'That's not what I mean at all. You're too young yet to see it, but the men know. They fear your uncle, and so they obey him; they respect me, and so they obey me; you they simply love, as they have loved your father. You give them cause for it, without realising what you do. Can you imagine your uncle riding patrol as you have these last weeks, living with the men and sharing their work, their food, their discomforts . . . ?'

Imber smiled briefly. 'No, perhaps not – but it was only because of Julianne. I couldn't find her, and I couldn't sit in the palace and do nothing. Besides, there was need, we have to watch our borders . . .'

'Exactly, that's my point. The men understand all of that. They'd have known, if you were doing it to win their favour; they're hardy souls, and hard to fool. But you came because your girl had driven you to shame and anguish, and they've all been burned by women in their time. And you came because it was your duty, and that's something else they're glad to share with you. And then a will o' the wisp from the desert sends you on a mad ride south, the wrong side of the mountains in a time of war; of course they follow you, how could they not? They're glad to have me here, but they'd have come without me if I'd stayed. If I'd ordered them to stay, I'd have faced a mutiny. And that's the difference between us, Imber, and by the time you hold the County you'll have learned how to use it as your father does now, and then it'll be all the difference in the world.'

Imber wasn't accustomed to having his character so

dissected – except perhaps by his uncle the elder Baron Imber, who held a far less flattering view of it – nor to hearing such plain speech from his merry cousin. Startled and embarrassed, he could say only, 'They didn't all come.'

'Of course not. Some had to stay, to watch the border and to report back on the fanciful and foolish doings of the young Baron-heir.' That was better, the teasing was back in words and voice together. 'Those who chose that course were largely the ones I'd have left in any case. The ones who really do think you're foolish to go chasing off after a woman, unless you intended to see her publicly whipped for the offence she's given to you and your family, which they know you don't. Though I think whoever carries the message to the palace may be surprised by his reception. You're loved there too, and not only by your father. Your uncle will condemn your wilfulness, and his friends will support him, but even he will say that our duty lay in protecting the County's heir-apparent. I tell you, Imber, there's only one man who'll come out of this adventure with his reputation entirely gilded, and that's my own virtuous self. Which is, of course, entirely why I came with you.'

'Of course it is . . .'

That had been days ago: days of hard riding in a hard and dry country, with the mountains an impassable wall to bar them from the safety of the Kingdom – riding wrong-handed, Karel called that, and grumbled about the impetuosity of boys who wouldn't take an extra day to put that same wall between themselves and trouble – and the open desert on their left ever a threat. They bypassed all settlements with caution; the few people that they met at wells

or watching flocks were Catari, vassal clans to the Sharai.
Those were reluctant – reluctant with reason, Imber
thought – even to speak to an armed troop from Elessi, but
at least there was no sign of their masters. This was too small
a party to risk a quarrel with the Sharai, its mission too
urgent to tolerate distractions.

At least the ground was seldom difficult for horses here in
this half-world, between the wide sand and the high rock.
Often it was easy, hard-packed shale with a smoothing of
sand, and there they rode long hours and at speed, resting
only once in the heat of the day and again through the deep
chill of the night; their big destriers had the stamina to take
that pace, and Imber refused to slack it until they must. The
only real trouble came to Karel, whose mount found the
only pit in miles for its hoof to trip in. Their fall was spec-
tacular. Karel was bruised and shaken, no worse than that;
the horse's leg had snapped, which was the worst possible
news. Imber slit its throat himself, and then insisted on putting Karel up on his own beloved stallion while he rode a
spare horse from the string. The commander needs to draw
the eye of the men, and this was still Karel's command. His
Mutassar was a pure shimmering white, unmistakable, the
obvious and only choice; only later did he think that this was
another gesture that the men would love in him.

In himself he felt wild, driven. He'd been given the
chance to redeem his lady, and that was all his focus. Surely
this time she would not run from him. He rode in daylight
or in the dark with his eyes fixed always on an unseen goal,
a castle he didn't know and circumstances that were impossible to predict. His mind invented a hundred desperate
situations, and in each of them he emerged triumphant,

with Julianne clinging to his arm. It was only there that his imagination failed. She was an unfathomable mystery to him, and he didn't dare put words into her mouth or feelings into her heart. He barely slept, even when Karel forced a halt and ordered him to his blankets; he had a burning energy that banished weariness. It would prove fickle later, it must fail at last – but not yet, not till Julianne was safe and what lay between them was finally resolved, whichever way that fell. Then he could afford exhaustion, then he might welcome it. Until then, he would use himself and his companions, drain them all and their horses too . . .

Short or long, serene or panicked, every journey has its looked-for end, though that may not be the end of the journey.

Some few of Karel's men had been this way, this far before, on a mission for the Count; there came a night when they promised him Selussin in the morning, and the castle before noon.

Sunlight woke something in him that he thought had been awake and afire already, but had only been smouldering after all. *Today I shall see her, somehow, though all of the men and spirits of the desert defy me.* The thought was like sundazzle on bright water, fierce enough to draw tears from his eyes. The slender height of her and the long dark fall of hair, skin soft as rose-petals and coloured like the roses of his mother's treasured garden, all the pure image of a tender girl who had made him love her from the moment of their meeting; and then the gaze that pierced, the tongue that was as sharp as the mind behind it, the joy in him to have found a girl with whom a lifetime of days and nights would never be enough to explore every complicated corner of her . . .

More than anything he wanted only to meet Julianne again, to sit and speak with her and learn his future from her lips: whether they could be married in body as they were in law, whether they could ever be married in love. This time there could be no demands, no question of forcing her to anything. He would ask, as plain and simple as his nature, and trust to her subtlety to see that he could make her happy.

Soon, now. Soon . . .

Not soon enough for Imber, but eventually they did see the tawny outline of mud walls and towers rising to the east of their path, and the cold grey shadow of a castle on a height to the west, seeming to smother even the glare of the sunlight that fell directly upon it. Imber's thoughts had been so fixed on what would happen after, he'd all but forgotten the greater imperative of this journey, the need first to save Julianne from whatever threatened her: *great danger,* the djinni had said. They were half a company, and that castle could withstand an army's siege for months if it were garrisoned. For the thousandth time, he wished that the djinni had been explicit about his lady's danger; for the first time, he began to doubt his ability to rescue her.

Even so, he turned his horse towards the rise, and the road he could see climbing up from town to castle. After a minute, Karel drew up level and gestured for him to rein in. He did so reluctantly, and his cousin said, 'We should go into Selussin and speak with the people there, Imber, learn what we can before we approach Revanchard.'

That was right, of course, common sense and good military practice both at once; but he shook his head despite a lifetime's training. 'No. Send a man, send all the troop, go yourself if you want to. I'm going up.'

'Imber, your safety is my responsibility.'

'As Julianne's is mine. Karel, I will be careful; I don't intend to ride straight to the castle gates and beat on them with my sword-hilt. But we've been a full week on the march; we may be too late already, and I won't waste another half a day in seeking out some braggart who claims to know more than eyes and wits can show me. Julianne is my wife and needs my help; it may be wisdom or stupidity, but I will go.'

Karel gazed at him levelly, thoughtfully for a moment. 'What would be wisdom,' he said, 'for an ambitious captain and a cousin to the Count, would be to knock you from the saddle and have my men bind you until I was certain how the land lay, before us and behind. However,' grinning suddenly, 'I too have been in love, and mad with it. Besides, life has been too dull lately, and overcaution has lost as many battles as foolhardiness. Very well, my lord Baron-heir, I am with you – but cautiously. I'll send two Catari-speakers into the town, to learn whatever they can; the rest of us go up together. And you ride in the centre of the troop, and if we find an ambush waiting, then the men around you take you down again, whether you will or no. I do not want to be the one who confesses to the Count – or to your lady mother the Countess, which would be worse – that I have lost their infant son and the hope of all the County.'

A well-laid ambush would deny them any retreat, willing or forced, but Karel knew that as well as he did. He disregarded the teasing and nodded his acceptance of terms that he certainly couldn't change. Karel made his dispositions swiftly; two men peeled away while the rest reformed and began a more steady advance, scouts ahead and a rearguard behind and Imber safely nested at the heart of all. He resented both the pace and the protection, he yearned to be racing on like a hero from a ballad, leaving all his companions in his wake – but heroes from ballads often expired in their ladies' arms, mortally wounded in the course of their bold rescues. He would be little use to Julianne with an arrow in his throat, dying without ever knowing whether or not she could have loved him.

They skirted fields and reed-beds, and made better speed once they reached the road; Karel trusted his scouts, and was not seriously expecting an ambush in any case. Imber knew his cousin. This would have been good country for it, steep rock walls crowding their way – but whoever they faced at the castle called Revanchard could not have been expecting them, and would have had no time to lay a trap. Nor, Imber was sure, would the djinni have sent them into one without a warning.

He wasn't sure whether Karel would trust to the same uncertain oracle, but Karel trusted himself and his own judgement, in a way that Imber thought he never would. *The God preserve that man, for when I must be Count* – which was the first time he had thought that or anything like it, and he couldn't decide if this was a strange or a likely time to be having such a thought, nor how comfortable he was to find himself thinking it.

But it was there in his head and it seemed to make sense,

to fit a pattern. There was Imber, Count Imber; and there was Karel, holding whatever title he might choose that Imber was free to give him so long as he held his place at Imber's right hand, as – thinking back – he always had done, as Imber's uncle had stood always at his father's side; and there on Imber's left, holding his left hand literally was Julianne, Countess Julianne, and it was all so clear and right that it felt like a sending.

The God grant that it was no false vision. Imber felt that he was looking at Karel with new eyes suddenly, measuring him against men a generation older, and finding him in no sense wanting. He almost opened his mouth to speak, to say something of what he saw; but just at that moment the road turned around a jut of rock and ran out onto a plateau, and there was the castle in all its grim menace, directly ahead of them.

There were the castle gates, and they stood wide open; and all around were the ashes of many fires, and there was movement both within the gates and on the plateau, and none of it was at all what Imber had expected even in his wildest imaginings.

They were peasants, or so they seemed by both dress and manner, who were so busy here: Catari and his own people mixed, so they couldn't all have come from the town below. They were men largely, with a few young women among them; and they were all in grief, silent and distressed, a grief that was greater than seemed justified even by the work that they were at.

There must have been a battle here, or a slaughter rather. The people were carrying bodies out from the castle, a terrible number of bodies that they laid out in line on the ground; from his saddle's height Imber could see old men and women among the dead, and children too. Most seemed to have no mark of death upon them; so perhaps it was not a slaughter after all, perhaps it was poison or sickness that had carried them off. After a moment, it didn't seem to matter. He scanned the line feverishly, and didn't see her face; he turned his eyes to the gates and spurred forward, crying, 'Julianne . . . !'

'Imber, wait! Come back—'

There was, there could be no going back. He rode into the castle forecourt and found more corpses, in a jumbled pile. The people there fell back and gazed up at him mutely, accusingly, *you came too late*.

That he knew already. One hasty glance assured him that Julianne did not lie among the bodies here, but there was small comfort in that. The djinni had said that she was here, and he had all the castle yet to search. *In great danger*, the djinni had said, and he had been too slow, too careful on the road . . .

He was neither slow nor careful now. He flung himself from his horse, heedless of the sound of hooves behind him and Karel's voice yelling; he raced madly in through the nearest open doorway yelling himself now, crying Julianne's name and hearing nothing but echoes returned to him.

He ran through darkness and through sudden beams of light, as though his own despair and occasional flickers of hope – *not here, not yet, I have not found her yet so perhaps she is not here* – had been turned physical in the air around him by the strength and depth of his emotion. He plunged up stairs and down, turning corners where they came and taking passages at random, never stopping for thought or balance, so that he was swiftly lost within the castle's defensive maze. He stumbled over risen flags and fallen corbels, once he fell sprawling over an unexpected step; but he touched nothing but stone and old wood, he discovered no one living and no one dead, his hoarsening voice raised no answer but the dust.

The second time he fell, it was in the deepest dungeon and the deepest dark that he had found thus far. This time he had tripped over a simple bucket; he heard its hollow rolling and sobbed suddenly for more than breath, sobbed for the loss of all that was most precious, light and faith and dreams and Julianne.

He was still lying there, still sobbing when there was a light brought into the darkness by the sound of boots, and then a voice; and that was Karel, of course, come to find him in his torment, and he said, 'Oh, get up. How dirty do you want to be, for the men to see you?'

'She, she isn't here, Karel . . .'

'No, she isn't. At least, if she is, we haven't found her yet, though we're more likely to do it than you were, running and screaming like a child playing lost. Torches are good, in dark places; so is the patience to search in corners. So is it good that we haven't found her, Imber. There are no bodies in the castle; all the dead are out in the yard.'

'You don't know that. Perhaps those are only the ones that they've found so far, and carried out. The djinni said that she was here . . .'

'I think they died out there – but perhaps you're right, or perhaps the djinni was wrong, or deceptive. Let's go and find out, shall we? Those people seem used to men of

Outremer, unless they're just too distressed to be frightened. We'll ask them. You may want to clean yourself up first.'

There was a scullery above, with a well that drew clean water. Imber washed hastily, rubbed a little at the stains on his surcoat, then shrugged and walked out into the stabbing brightness. No matter what the men saw: they knew already, and he would not, he would *not* be ashamed of his feelings, his lady or himself.

Karel was right about the people outside. Frightened peasants confronted by an unknown soldiery would stop working, gather in knots, flinch even from an undrawn sword; these might have been briefly disorganised but now they were back at their labours, carrying the bodies one by out out of the hot suntrap of the yard and laying them neatly, reverently in the hill's shade.

One man – bearded, middle-aged, lean and sinewy – seemed to have taken charge, if anyone had. Karel approached him, somehow letting authority slip from his own shoulders in favour of a respectful solemnity; he said, 'Who are these dead, fellow, are they yours?'

'Ours, aye, every one. Our mothers, our children, my wife.'

'My friend here, he is looking for his own wife . . .'

A swift assessing glance, a shake of the head. 'Not here, not among these. We know all of these, between us.'

Not his face, but something in the man's look was very familiar, if utterly out of place; his accent confirmed it. Imber spoke haltingly, reacting without thinking: 'You're Elessan.'

'I am, and my wife – was. I know you too, my lord

Baron. You came to our village once, we saw you, I lifted my boy up to give him a better view of you . . .'

He nearly broke then, as Imber had broken already; he would have done for sure, his mouth was twisting out of his control when Karel interrupted with the questions that Imber couldn't be troubled to ask. The facts were enough for him, but not for his cousin.

'I am sorry for your loss, but tell me, I must know: what is a man from Elessi doing here, in this company? How is it that you left your land, your family, your little boy? And what caused all these deaths?'

'Truly, sir, we don't know. We found them so, after we had followed them for so long. They should have died before, but they were saved, we thought; and there were promises made, to those of us who followed . . .' Promises that were all dust now, that much was clear even to Imber, who had come here in pursuit of a promise also and knew the bitter taste of betrayal too well himself.

'I don't understand,' Karel said.

'No more do I, sir. I will try to try to tell the tale, but it is hard . . . There was a sickness came to the village, a cold kind of death. And then a healer, blessed by the God's favour, he claimed, and with a holy relic of great power. He gave life to the dying, and not only to those who were sick; my wife hurt herself working in the fields and should have died of the bleeding, but he touched her with his saint's hand and she was whole again, except that she would not speak to me or anyone, not even to our child. Those he had healed before had followed him thus far, and so did ours when he moved on; and so did we. I left the boy with my brother and went after my wife, though she was strange to me now. I hoped to

bring her back, but the healer preached a great war against
the Folded Land, and said that we were the God's army to
strike against heresy. We were no soldiers – there were old
men and children he had healed, and we had few weapons
between us – but we had seen the power of the God in him,
and so we believed. He said we should strike from here; but
he led the healed ones on at a great pace, and we fell behind.
When we arrived this morning, we found this as you see it,
all our kindred dead and the healer too, we found his body
outside the castle. He had been killed with arrows, but not
these. We don't know how they died, except that my wife
had bled terribly from her old injury. Perhaps when the
healer died, all his healing was undone; but that cannot have
been the God's work, sir, he would not treat us so . . .'

'No. There is a devil in this, man.'

'Yes, sir. What can we do?' He had been strong too long;
now suddenly he was lost, too far from home and from the
life he understood, bewildered by finding tragedy where he
had looked for hope. Imber understood him perfectly.

'Do what you have been doing, it's all there is for now:
take out your people and find a place to bury them decently.
My men will help with the digging, once we have thoroughly searched the castle. And I can say the funeral service
over those you have lost, if you would like it, in the absence
of a priest. I have done that before.'

'Yes, sir. Please, if you would . . .'

Imber went all through Revanchard again in the hours that
followed, this time with a torch and a companion. He found
nothing, not even the scant evidence of occupation that others
turned up, indications of a small party staying recently.

The men Karel had sent to Selussin came back with news of more moment. Julianne's father, the King's Shadow had been in the town this last week, along with three companions whose descriptions tallied with the jongleur, the renegade Ransomer boy and the girl Elisande from the Roq, all of whom had accompanied Julianne in her flight.

'That's proof positive,' Imber said, feeling his spirits lift for the first time since they had come to Revanchard. 'The djinni did not lie to me; she was here, and she was taken away before this happened,' with a gesture towards the great burial pit that was being dug close by. 'But taken where, where is she now?'

'Wait, there's more. Yesterday an army came out of the desert, the Sharai on the march behind that war-leader Hasan who attacked the Roq before our arrival. The town is full of rumours, some even claimed that he had married Julianne, which must be nonsense; but what is certain is that they brought siege to the castle last night, and went on into Outremer this morning. They sent messengers back, who said that the Folded Land lies open now. I don't know if that's true, Imber, but if it is, I think we must look there for Julianne. In any case, that way lies our duty. The Sharai are in Outremer, and we must follow; every man will be needed. These, too,' with a glance of his own at the people laying their dead in their last home. 'They were promised a holy war, and they shall have one, if they are still willing. We can arm and equip them, from the town and our own supplies; they may not be soldiers trained, but dispersed among our own men, they'll be fit to fight. Half of them are Catari born, but even the Catari fear the Sharai. I'll take any who swear loyal to the King.'

   Imber nodded distractedly, impatient only to be mounted
and on the move again, in pursuit of Julianne though all the
Sharai of the desert, all the wizards of Surayon, all the oper-
ations of malign destiny lay between him and her.

11

The Healing Heart

One of the hidden, the unexpected things about growing up, Elisande thought, was the way simple words changed their meaning. Concepts that were once fixed and clear and sat easily in the head became murky, slithery, impossible to keep a grip on.

Take her, here, now. She was home, visibly and incontrovertibly; and yet she was not, quite, and she thought that perhaps she never would be again, quite. Whether she stayed and waited or went in search, wherever she stood in the world, she thought that home would always hereafter be a step ahead, a glance aside, somewhere just a little elsewhere than where she was.

When she was very small, home had been her mother: more specifically her mother's lap, her mother's hug and the curtain of hair falling all around her.

Her mother had died, and then home had meant her father: a cold place, dark and grim, where she lived in storm and ice and ran away whenever she was able.

When she was older, when she was away she thought that perhaps home was not a house at all. Home was her country, home was Surayon and everything that was contained within those borders: hope and fear, strength and loss, beauty and brutality. Her grandfather, her mother's soul, her father – all were a part of the whole, and she encompassed it all within her head, within her heart, within her home. Substance casts shadow, bitter redeems the sweet; danger gave a spice to life, and death gave it a meaning. She sought out danger, more than once she challenged death, and all the time held her vision of home like a banner in her thoughts. Her feet marched to the unsung songs of Surayon; her toes all but touched rich Surayonnaise tilth whether they walked on rock or sand or marble. She would work even with her father for her country's survival.

Now she had seen her father die for that same cause, die and so fail; and she had seen him die and so failed herself. She was back to the land that she had held for so long as treasure, a substitute for mother and father both, but she couldn't – quite – say that she was home. Not without qualifications.

She was home, but it was not the home that she had left, that she had always hugged to herself as an immutable talisman, sealed behind its impregnable borders. This Surayon was a shelled nut, and there were scavengers on every side.

She was home, but she was not the girl she used to be: neither the sunshine child nor the adolescent ridden by the dark. She almost couldn't recognise herself in these familiar surroundings; she wasn't sure what she had become, nor where or whether there was any place for her.

She was home, but not to the welcome that she'd looked

for, her grandfather's healing wisdom. She'd brought too much else with her, disaster for all; that had overridden all her private disasters, so that she'd had barely time enough to tell her tale before he'd left her.

She was home, but her father was dead. That above all, that was a clamour in her head that struck echoes from ten years before, that made her want to rage now as she had raged then, when her mother died; except that this time, there was no one to rage against. Morakh was dead too, she had killed him herself, and she had no other target. Which was what left her feeling so stranded: she was very afraid all the time and if she only thought for a minute she could make herself terrified, but she had no one to hate any more, which to her was no definition of home.

She stood on the terrace of her grandfather's palace, which was absolutely her grandfather's home and had once been hers and was still the one place that she would always come back to, whether she belonged here or not.

She'd been standing there a long time, unless it had been only a single moment indefinitely prolonged: she couldn't say, couldn't begin to guess. It felt like time enough for her bare toes to have dug down through the cracks between the rough-laid stones underfoot, to have taken root in the hidden dark of the soil beneath; but two steps on Surayon ground had always been enough to make her feel sunk soul-deep in the land. Two steps, one breath of that air that she'd found nowhere else in the Kingdom or outside it and she'd always felt immediately enfolded, possessed, encompassed. That was not a feeling of unadulterated good – in some senses, in some moods it was like being hugged by her father, he was so associated with this country, dug in deeper even than she was herself – but it was what she had always thought of as coming home.

Today the air had a stranger taste, there was a sourness to the moist earth's scent, even the sunlight seemed a little dark; she felt as though she had arrived somewhere that was almost Surayon, but only almost. Not quite home.

She had come and done terrible, lethal damage to what she loved; and her father was dead already as her land was likely going to die, and that also was her own fault, his death lay across her conscience as his blood had stained her clothes.

And more even than that, there was a hollowness at the heart of her, an empty place where something had been ripped from her body. Her blood's beat echoed there, hammer-hard and hurting, *he is dead, he is dead.* Never mind blame, never mind consequences: only the fact of it pounded through her brain, burned behind her eyes like thoughts turned to flame, *he is dead . . .*

He was dead and it really shouldn't matter, but it did.

From where she stood, on the terrace of the Princip's palace above Surayon-town, she had the best sight of what she swore was the finest aspect in all the Sanctuary Land and all the world. When she'd been very little, she had thought that it was all the world; even after she'd grown bigger and hence wiser, she'd still insisted that it was all the world that mattered.

She had never seen Ascariel, and those who had would laugh at her, would call her foolish, ignorant; would talk of the Dir'al Shahan that the King had taken for his own and the walled and golden city that surrounded it on its great mount, and say that they should not speak of daylight who had never seen a sunrise. She'd not been troubled by their mockery, not even when she was small. Grown-ups understood so little; they thought that every travelled mile added to their knowledge, when really all it did was dilute what they'd known as children, thinning the rich stew of wonder to a tasteless broth.

It was always possible to go higher, of course, and so to see further. The palace itself was built into the slope of a hill so massive that she used to call it a mountain; they took her to the top of it and showed her the real mountains, but those were distant shadows and she couldn't understand how they were bigger than this, or how what was far away could matter more than what she stood upon. More importantly, she could see all of the valley of Surayon and its tributary vales, and how the principality was cupped like water in the hands, within the twisted belt of the mountain range. She nodded wisely when they told her that if they opened the borders, it would be like opening her fingers and letting all the water drain away. But she still felt that she could see the country better from her grandfer's terrace below.

She'd felt so then, and she felt so still. The air couldn't actually be clearer down here, but it seemed so; and when she stared at any particular distant thing, it seemed to come nearer and more sharply into sight. A faint smudge of movement on a track so far away that it seemed hair-thin and half imagined, only visible because she knew that it was there: a moment's concentration and she would see the bullock-cart and the dust-trail rising behind it, she could count the woman who rode and the boy who led the bullocks, she could almost say what was in the sacks that piled the cart so high. If he were with her, her grandfather would say, and she never doubted him.

At the time, she'd believed him also when he called her eagle-eyes, desert-eyes; looking back, she thought there was some magic he'd invested in the site. He'd spent long hours here all her life, gazing out across his penned princedom, watching literally over his people, guarding them she'd always thought against monsters that he could sear with a glare. He must have woven some touch of his power into the stones of the terrace or the balustrade or perhaps into the air itself, so that what lay far-off could be brought closer to the eye. It had worked for her then, before she knew it; it worked for her now, and she truly wished that it would not.

She stood on her grandfather's terrace and gazed out across his country, her best hope of home; and she saw fire and death, the imprint of war all over.

She stood and saw her land in flames, her people slaughtered; and that should matter more than anything, more even than Marron still sick, still unhealed, still dying in the room at her back; so why, *why* was it her father who so possessed her thoughts, when he was only one man and dead already, a cold waste of passion?

She stood for hours, seeing almost nothing, her true gaze turned deep inward; or else she stood only for minutes and saw too much. One or the other, she wasn't sure. Had the sun been so high, when she came out here? She couldn't say; she hadn't been aware of it one way or the other, she hadn't been thinking about time at all until she'd found herself trapped within its mazes.

Long or short, that standing had to end; and it did, she

ripped herself away from it like a tree tearing itself from its deep-buried roots. She felt herself very like a tree, silent and suffering; she thought she might carry that eloquent silence a long time, years, a lifetime. *He is dead*, and the thought had nowhere else to go from there, and no more did she.

Her body could move on, that at least. She walked slowly towards the high arch of the open door, pausing to touch the rough-worked stone of the wall for luck before she passed within. She'd done that all her life, picking at lichen-flakes and loving the contrast with the smooth plaster of the inner walls. No ice-slick marble fascia here, no age-worn sandstone or brute blunt defensive rampart; like the town below, the palace was built of a creamy-pale stone shot through with veins of blue that glittered where they were cut. She'd always thought that the stone reflected the land where it was quarried, and the spirit that her grandfather had fostered here: cool and restful, but permeated with a cloaked power which could flare into life when it was needed. That fiery blue reminded her of witchlight, and of all the secret resources of Surayon. Besides which, the walls of the palace had been left deliberately rough, an open invitation for a light and nimble-fingered, nimble-toed girl to climb, all the way up to her mother's garden on the roof. How could she not love it, a private access to a private place that was entirely barred to her father?

There were several rooms that opened onto the long terrace. At the further end was the Princip's private library, where even she never dared to venture without invitation. Next came the wide audience-chamber, a space of pillars and light with many windows; then there was this, the solarium they'd always called it, a quiet bright room where

Elisande's mother had loved to sit with her ladies over her needlework and talk until the sun failed.

Now, today it was a hospital. All the furniture had been cleared to one side; soft pallets had been laid on the floor, and there lay Marron and Hasan, their drawn faces cruelly exposed by the fall of light through the casements. The one was fighting still, she thought, or being fought over, while the other simply faded. The battle raging within Marron was clear to be seen on his skin, fire and shadow surging against each other; Hasan was grey, chill, quite unwarmed by anything that man or sun could offer. The gouges on his face showed like black bars, like a fresh brand.

Julianne sat on the floor by his head, as still as her husband and fading just as fast. Elisande thought that she should be similarly sitting beside Marron, grieving as deeply and as silently; except that Jemel had claimed that place, and had a far better claim to it than she could muster. It had been his aching distress that had driven her out onto the terrace, as much as her own unacknowledged pain; she envied him his honesty, and its legitimacy.

In the Princip's absence, other men had come to tend the patients: old men, wise men, helpless men. They had touched and probed, had laid hands on Marron and Hasan individually and then by twos together, then all at once. And had shaken their heads, spoken in soft voices, advised patience until their lord's return.

Patience was a slow, grinding torment to them all. A table in the far corner had been laid with refreshments, quite untouched; Elisande went over there to pour a beaker of well-watered wine, and carry that to Julianne.

'Here, sweet. You won't eat, I know, and I won't press you

to it; but you could drink, at least, you still remember how to swallow.'

'You're not eating either.'

'No. But I'll share your drink.'

Julianne sipped without interest, then looked a little surprised at what she tasted. 'I thought it would be *jereth*, to tempt my appetite?'

'No. Not for this. We'll drink *jereth* later, when they're well. And I won't share a drop of mine with you.'

The badinage was unthinking, meaningless except to say *we have a friendship that goes deep, deeper than pain, and we will recover it. Later. When they're well . . .*

Julianne shook her head. 'When they're well,' she said slowly, borrowing Elisande's determination only to show how weak it was, 'we still won't want to celebrate. Only to weep together, for how much we've lost.' But her eyes moved to the view of the far horizon, the far side of the valley, and suddenly she sounded weak herself, weak as a child's arguments, as though she had completely misunderstood herself. 'He will come, won't he?'

'Of course he'll come, sweet. He lives here, this is his home.' She wrapped her arms around her friend, chin on shoulder for a tight hug and said, 'He will come, Julianne, I promise. *He* promised. As soon as he can. But he doesn't have the King's Eye,' *though he has the next best thing out on the terrace there, whatever spells he's woven on the wind to bring far-sightedness,* 'and all his country is under attack, he had to go out to see . . .'

'Of course he did,' on a sigh, reaching a faltering hand out to stroke the bitter cold of Hasan's brow and then snatching it back, as though to touch him hurt as much as

not to touch him. 'And perhaps he also had to go out to be
alone an hour, after the other news you brought him. Rudel
was his son, as well as being your father. You can't mourn
him properly, you're so tied up inside. I can't, because —
because of Hasan, I can't feel anything clearly. Someone has
to.'

Men should not outlive their children, she was saying,
though old men did it as a matter of course in time of war or
famine or disease, which meant in Outremer and in the
Sands. Not in Surayon. Julianne was right, of course, or
partly right, and Grandfer might indeed prefer to shed his
tears ahorseback, hidden behind a riding-veil or a visor. But
Elisande could be mulish, even now.

'He was a soldier before he was — well, what he is now.
Princip, sorcerer, philosopher, what you like. As your own
father was, Julianne. Coren kept his tears back and would
use Rudel's body if he could; my grandfer would have done
the same. Of course they will mourn, but not yet. Not when
there's fighting today and a battle tomorrow, and all this
country lies beneath the sword.'

If Julianne thought her cold or hard, so be it; at least it
would give the girl something fresh to think about. Elisande
might crave such a heart-whole pain as Julianne was feeling,
but she knew too the exhausting weight of it.

By the same token, she supposed she ought to welcome
her own distractedness, her fear for Marron offset by her fear
for Surayon, and both of them outmatched by the unexpected ache of grieving for Rudel. She couldn't do it, though,
she could find no sense of balance. Any one of them would
have been enough, too much to carry; the three together she
thought would crush her. She yearned to be like Julianne,

like Jemel, utterly absorbed in their distress; and was not, and couldn't fake it even to herself.

Restless anxiety dragged her to her feet again, away from her friend. She barely glanced towards Marron and his attendant Sharai, she couldn't take a step in that direction. Instead she went back to the doorway and on to the terrace again, desperate and driven. *He will come,* but she needed him, they all needed him to come soon; and yet he had the defence of all this land to organise, against forces too powerful for a peaceful people to resist. Their troubles were small and individual, his were vast and overmastering. They shouldn't be so selfish as to look for him; and yet they were, she most of all. He might be Princip of a state that stood on the very edge of destruction, but he was still her grandfather, her beloved Grandfer who had been her secret treasure, her sustaining family all these years. And now when she wanted him most, she couldn't have him; and that knowledge detracted not one grain's weight from her wanting.

She gripped the parapet with both hands, glad of roughness against her skin, something to rub against, something to feel. She stared out across the valley, scanning, searching. There were fires on the flanks of the northern hills, and when she squinted she thought she could see terror beneath the smoke, running men being ridden down. When she stretched all her senses, she thought she could smell burned flesh and hear screaming that was not the screams of men.

She drew back suddenly, letting that extended awareness slip rather than bear witness to the unbearable. It must have been imagination, surely; she was fantasising, turning nightmare tales into truth in her foolish, stupefied head. Or else

that had been the screaming of horses, perhaps, trapped in a
burning barn. Not women, no, surely not children . . .

The preceptor had burned children at the Roq, she
remembered bleakly, chillingly. But these were her own
people here, and their own people too, they were all Patrics.
Even the most devout Ransomers would not burn their own.
Would they . . . ?

She remembered Marshal Fulke's preaching against
Surayon, and couldn't doubt it longer. And turned, shuddering, to look eastward for her grandfather; and saw
instead – or thought she saw – the tribes of the Sharai spread
out from wall to mountain wall, doing wicked work with
scimitars for the greater glory of their God.

And didn't want to look any more, westward or anywhere; didn't want to go back inside either, to face the other
tragedy of the day and try to persuade herself again that it
was lesser, when it hurt as fiercely and as deeply. So she
stayed, she stood where she was and closed her eyes against
the terrors before her, and found no rest and no hope of eva-
sion there either, only her father's dreadful death played out
freshly behind her lids, a tragedy too many.

When an arm laid itself across her shoulders, when iron fingers gripped her tightly through the sleeve of her robe, she
could have screamed from sheer startlement if she hadn't
been so fathoms-deep in weeping. Instead she choked
painfully on a sob that was hard as a pebble and filled her
throat as thoroughly; she twisted vainly against the strength
that pulled her close against soft fabric cloaking a man's
body. A small, lean body – that was the second surprise,
that had her blinking upward to find his face and know

him, when she'd been just about to topple into the security of his hug except that suddenly he was not the man she'd thought him.

'*Coren?*' Well, Coren was good enough, a splendid second-best; she'd let him hug her as much as he chose and dry her tears willingly against his shoulder, so long as he promised to mention them to no one else.

'Aye, lass. I've brought your father home.'

Which made her choke again, because it could never be home again without him and without her loathing of him, a necessary counterbalance to her love for house and country, grandfather and folk.

But choking made her turn her face away from his, and turning made her see. Another man had come out onto the terrace from the cluttered, chaotic library where no one went without the Princip's direct authority, and was standing gazing at her. Built like a woodcutter, short and broad, with a barrel chest and legs like firkins; crowned with thick white curls beneath his hood and bearded like a hedge in snow; scratching at that beard now with thick, spatulate fingers that looked so much better suited to gripping an axe than a pen or even the sword that he wore half-hidden under his cloak . . .

'Grandfer!'

Elisande wrenched free of Coren, who laughed softly as he let her go. She flew into her grandfather's arms, and no matter that he was wearing chain mail too beneath his surcoat. Even if he couldn't mend what was irrevocably broken, he was still a solidity that she could cling to, where all else had proved so frail. She did cling, and might have cried again now that she'd found access to such a well of tears, except that through her mindless mutterings and his gentle soothing she heard something else, Julianne's voice say, 'Elisande . . . ?'

She turned against her grandfather's rough hand where it was stroking her hair in animal comfort. Her friend was standing in the solarium doorway, leaning against the stonework as though that were all that was keeping her upright. Coren moved swiftly to his daughter's side, to take that duty on himself; for a moment, gazing at their matched elegance, Elisande was sharply aware of the contrast. She had always secretly enjoyed her grandfather's peasant appearance, been glad of his rude strength. She'd inherited his lack of height, but her mother's elfin bones; that had been one more thing to welcome, to thrust like a banner in her father's face.

All the bitter triumph of those memories was ashen now, though – as ashen as her friend, who hung on to her own father's arm much as Elisande herself was hanging on to her grandfather: two girls who had come too far under too great a burden, and needed now to have it lifted from them. Despite everything that was happening in Surayon, the Princip had made time to return to them; Elisande tried to find some hope in that as she lifted her eyes to her grandfather and said, 'Please, you can help them, can't you, Marron and Hasan? Say that you can . . .'

'I can try,' he said, which was far short of the promise that she was looking for. She'd tried herself, others had tried and failed; Rudel had declined even to try. But the Princip was stronger, wiser, more practised than any. She'd believed in him all her life, when faith was such a hard thing for her to achieve; surely he couldn't let her down now.

'Take me to them,' he said, for all the world as though he were the guest here rather than the host. Elisande unwound herself from him, except for keeping tight grip on one arm; she led him past Julianne and Coren and into the bright solarium, thinking that desolation ought never to be so well lit.

For a minute, her grandfather only stood and looked down on the two sick men, where they lay on their pallets in the sunshine.

When he spoke, his voice was quiet and conversational. 'A wise man would do nothing,' he said, 'for either of these, except perhaps to help them into their deaths. The boy is a danger to himself and all around him, a greater danger to the King whom I still serve; the man is the leader of that army, one of those armies that are laying my own land waste. If he is restored, he will seek to destroy Outremer itself, and he is likely the only man who could do that. Without him the tribes will splinter, loot and scatter. Why should I save his life, even assuming that I can?'

'Because he saved mine, and all ours,' Elisande said quickly, desperately. 'We were attacked by ghûls at the Dead Waters, but Marron fetched Hasan' – she couldn't resist slipping in a small word for her own boy, in hopes of its having weight later – 'and he slew them, he and his men . . .'

'Well. That is a reason, certainly, if not a good one. It may not be enough. Honour is a tentative idea, in times of war.'

'He is my husband,' Julianne said, her voice as faint as her colour. 'Perhaps, if I speak to him, he will lead the Sharai out of your land for my sake.'

'Perhaps, though I doubt it. That is a better reason. His sense of honour may be greater than mine. Now if you had said, "He is my husband and I love him," that would have been sufficient without the other.'

Julianne's eyes widened. 'Do you want me to say that?'

'No need, little one,' though she overtopped him by a hand's breadth or more. 'It is written all through you; he has left you as marked as the 'ifrit has left him. I hope you will find a way to be glad of it, though I think that journey will be a hard one. Keep back, now. There is danger in this. Hope too, you may certainly hope if you wish to; without that, you wouldn't have brought him to me, and the 'ifrit's work would have been wasted. But that creature has left something of itself inside him, and it may be fit for mischief yet.'

There was something in that which Elisande simply didn't understand, and no more did Julianne by the look on her face; but they'd been fogged in confusion for a long time now, it was beginning to feel like the natural order of the world. Besides, the Princip had a serious aversion to answering questions.

Conversely, when he volunteered information, it was wise to pay attention. He had said this would be unsafe; she took Julianne's arm and hauled her bodily backwards.

Not too far: she wanted still to be able to see, and she wanted Julianne to see also. Success or failure, life or death, it seemed important that they both stand witness. If Hasan did not survive, it would be too easy for trouble-minded tongues to spread lies about the manner of his death under Patric hands.

Easier than she'd imagined, even: she blinked, when she saw what her grandfather did. Kneeling down beside Hasan's pallet, he touched the Sharai's grey face, and sighed. Elisande knew how cold and lifeless that skin felt; she shivered a little in sympathy for him, for his having to send even his strong spirit into that chilly body.

Except that he didn't, or not immediately. First, he drew a dagger from his belt and a gasp from his granddaughter as he laid it against Hasan's unresponsive wrist and cut swiftly.

The blood followed the blade, but sluggishly. It seemed unnaturally dark in the vivid sunlight, just as it had seemed dead black in the lamplight and shadows of the tent outside Revanchard; it was certainly slower to run than it ought to be, as though it were thickening inside Hasan's body, almost starting to clot.

Julianne made one soft, unstructured sound that was none the less perfectly articulate. Elisande scowled ferociously, reached up to snatch the hand that Julianne was now biting on to save her giving herself away further, held it tightly in both her own and hissed, 'Show some faith, girl – that's my grandfather over there! I've been telling you for months how he's not a man at all, he's a demigod . . .'

'You have. Wiser than the djinn, was it, and tougher than the mountains at their roots? He still wants to let Hasan die.'

'No, he doesn't – that's the one thing he wants not to do. He was desperate for you to feed him an excuse. If you hadn't, he'd have done it anyway, just out of curiosity to meet the great Hasan; I know my grandfer. Though he might have locked him somewhere very safe afterwards, for all the rest of his life. He might do that yet, unless you plead for him.' *Whether you plead for him or not* was what she actually meant – she knew her grandfer – but this wasn't the time for Julianne to learn that particular lesson.

'Well, whatever he wants or doesn't want, Hasan's going

to die in any case. See how he bleeds? That's not human harm, that's sorcery . . .'

'Of course it is, it came from an 'ifrit. That's why we brought him to the greatest sorcerer in the Kingdom for his healing. Grandfer may look like an old braggart soldier your cooks wouldn't welcome in your kitchen; that's because he is an old braggart soldier your cooks wouldn't welcome in your kitchen, but he could still chew up an 'ifrit and spit the shells out. He'd pick his teeth after, mind, he's really uncouth that way. Hush now, hush and watch.'

Now the Princip did what she'd expected him to do first thing. He spread his hands across Hasan's chest, every fingertip on a separate rib; he took a slow, careful breath and closed his eyes and sent his thoughts, his will, his spirit questing for the source of so much damage.

Elisande knew that journey well. She knew how hard it could be to seek out the subtleties of invasion, how easy it was to become lost. She felt her muscles tense and her thoughts try to follow her grandfather. Hopeless at this distance, not even touching, but still she was dizzy at the spiralling down and down, still she was sick at the cloying, engulfing surge of corrupted blood.

You are not there, you are not him . . .

It was the phrase all her teachers had used as they showed her how to begin this healing, as she first tasted the exhilarating terror-slide into the beat of another's life; it was an anchor and a chain for an over-anxious, over-eager girl who might otherwise have plunged so deep she forgot herself entirely. Today it had a special piquancy, because she really wasn't there; she was neither the Princip seeking nor the helpless Hasan, and she would do well to remember it.

Julianne had taken a bear's grip on her, crushing. Nothing to do but stand, then, support her friend and trust her grandfather. So she did, she did both and felt herself rewarded, or at least relieved beyond measure, to see at last a hint of smoke rise from the coagulating blood on Hasan's wrist.

The Princip grunted, clamped his hands tight around the Sharai's chest, twisted his face into a dreadful grimace; the wisp of smoke thickened and tightened, drawing itself together even as it was forced out of its stolen body.

Except that it was black, it looked almost like the thread of a djinni's assumed body, hanging in the air above Hasan. Some fragment of an 'ifrit, with at least some vestige of life left in it: and yes, she believed her grandfather entirely when he said that this was still dangerous. It was still dangerously close to him, and he looked exhausted suddenly, slumping where he sat.

She couldn't bear, she couldn't abide his loss on such a day, when so much had been lost already. She had a knife that was blessed, and now she might have pushed Julianne on to her father and hurtled forward to defend the Princip – but what use was a blade, however strengthened, against a creature that was virtually bodiless, an emanation of evil, nothing but smoke?

No need to find out today, no opportunity. She was encumbered, Coren was not; he stepped forward and she saw him make the smallest of gestures, heard him murmur the quietest of words.

Sharper than any dagger, his slender and courtly fingers; more deadly than any imam's blessing, his gentle voice. She saw that corporeal shadow dissipate into shreds and nothing, she heard her own slow sigh of tension released, she felt that she could have copied her grandfather in his boneless collapse if Julianne hadn't been so wrapped around her, still taut as a strung wire. It took all her will to force her head to turn, and her voice was little more than a whisper as she said, 'I didn't know you could do that.'

Coren smiled faintly. 'Against such as that, yes. It was only a fragment; malign, but struggling simply to hold itself together in a world not its own. It had no true life, no spirit. It might have sought to infect another body; Marron is always vulnerable, with that open wound on his arm. Even the Daughter could have lost its fight then, and who can say how much we might have regretted that?'

Marron, yes. There was still Marron, and the Princip was exhausted. She stole a glance towards Jemel and saw him sitting beside the young Patric, his eyes fixed on her grandfather, his gaze burning. *Give him time, let him recover, he's an old man* – but she couldn't say it aloud, to make a hypocrite of herself. The same urgency was scorching her. Marron might have no time, the Daughter could fail at any moment or his body be laid waste by the battle raging within it. She wanted to run to the Princip herself, as Jemel apparently would not; she wanted to disregard age and weariness and all, haul him over to the other pallet, demand another miracle.

Jemel would not do it because he was proud, because he was Sharai in a Patric house, because he had the hard patience of the desert and his own strong sense of honour. She could not do it, because she still had Julianne.

Finally, though, she could at least pass that burden on. She looked into her friend's eyes and smiled.

'Is it, is it over now, is it done?'

'It's done, sweet. Come . . .'

She led her friend forward on stumbling feet, to the pallet where Hasan lay. Julianne gave another of those wordless little cries and dropped to her knees beside him. Elisande saw that the dreadful grey cast was gone from his skin, and the blood ran bright and fresh now from the gaping cut on his wrist. That at least she could attend to; she crouched beside him, reached to touch and felt the warm tingle in her fingertips as her own healing ability was awoken.

She knitted flesh to flesh and skin to skin. It was easy, it had always been easy here at the heart of her life. She could see the trembling in Julianne's fingers as they touched Hasan's face, as they confirmed the new-risen warmth in him; she wished it was as easy to mend what was damaged in her friend. There was a hesitation in Julianne's breathing too, which turned to a gasp of disgust and wonder as she touched the three ripped wounds on his cheek and the scabs there crumbled and fell away to show healthy tissue beneath, if dark seamed scars were ever healthy.

'Those he'll keep,' Coren said behind her, 'as a memento. I'm afraid he's spoiled for looks, though he won't think so and neither will his women. His other women. If you'd wanted pretty, you should have stayed with Imber.'

She all but ignored that, as was only right that she should; she had one fear left, and addressed it to Elisande. 'Why doesn't he wake?'

'He will, sweetheart. That was a deep working; they ought both sleep a while now, your Hasan and my grandfer. He is only sleeping, though. We could wake him if you want.'

'No. No, leave him be. But – Elisande, could you send your djinni to fetch someone for me?'

'Yes, of course. Anyone, from anywhere. Who do you want?' Actually she knew already, she'd only been waiting for Julianne to realise who she wanted. Let the girl think it was her own idea, she'd benefit the more.

'Bring Sherett here from wherever she has gone, if it can find her. He, he would like to see her, when he wakes.'

He would like to see her, truly; but Julianne had said 'fetch someone for me', and that was true too, Elisande thought.

'Esren will find her, and she will come. She won't even argue.' Much. Probably . . .

In the brief time that it took her to summon the djinni, send it on its errand and elect to ignore Coren's quiet amusement, the Princip had roused himself, at least a little. He called a page into the room, and sent the boy running for a towel and a ewer of water – 'Just too late,' Elisande murmured to a suddenly gigglish Julianne, 'I could've sent Esren, I'd have enjoyed that' – then pushed himself slowly to his feet, ran both hands through his mane of hair and stood looking sombrely down at Marron.

Also, inevitably, at Jemel: who stared back, silent and demanding.

'Patience, lad. I will attend to your friend; but that will be a delicate matter, and I need to think a little first. There are other matters than his health to be considered.'

Not for Jemel, plainly; and not for Elisande either, though she did understand her grandfather's hesitation. He was like Rudel in that, seeing the boy only as a vessel for what he carried, and a weak vessel too. A dozen times or more, she'd heard her father as good as say that Surayon and the whole Kingdom would be better off with Marron dead. What they should do with the Daughter once that happy end had been accomplished, she'd never troubled herself to enquire. In her time of hating him – and it was hard, so hard, too hard sometimes to remember that that time was cruelly over, it had occupied her so intensely for so long – she had always assumed and sometimes said that he no doubt wanted it for himself, that he could imagine no man better suited to carry such a burden.

Now that she couldn't hate any longer, now that she had been surprised by mourning, she thought that perhaps he had been right. Thinking of all the men she knew, if anyone had to carry the thing, none would have made a safer guardian than Rudel. Force seldom wielded, strength under strong control, the skills of war overmastered by a furious demand for peace: these would all have been virtues in the man who held the Daughter. Marron was learning, but painfully and at cost to others. Rudel had been better equipped at birth, and had added a lifetime's experience since.

If Rudel had been carrying the Daughter, likely he would not be dead now. But Marron likely would be, his gift for finding trouble was in no way dependent on his stumbling attempts to be the Ghost Walker . . .

She wasn't going to play that game, setting one death against another and trying to weigh which mattered more. She was not. What mattered was that the Daughter had been brought to Surayon, which was what she'd set out to do in the first place. Her prime reason for that was gone, now that the land was unFolded; but there were perhaps better reasons now to guard it as though it were a treasure of the state. If Morakh had been Ghost Walker as he'd wished, she thought that nothing would have stopped the march of the Sharai.

Or if Hasan were? He had shown no desire for that, he'd offered Marron his blade's protection rather than its edge; but that was in Rhabat and this was Outremer, where all his dreams were physical desires, within reach of his hand.

She thought that she knew what her grandfather would do, now that she'd brought Marron to him; she thought it might be the most dangerous choice, but she thought he would do it anyway. Grandfathers were like that, like their sons, so little inclined to listen that there was seldom any point in talking at all. Which was no doubt why she was so natively quiet, so restrained, why she kept always such a curb on her tongue . . .

The Princip splashed cold water liberally over his head, till his hair and beard were dripping with it. He gave them a brisk rub, then tossed the towel over his page's shoulder and dismissed him with a stern warning not to linger in the corridor outside. To judge by the boy's face, Elisande thought that a waste of breath; curiosity would outweigh obedience, as it always had.

She fetched her grandfather his preferred drink of fruit juice laced with wine, doing a page's service herself and hoping at the same time to hurry him just a little, to give him a gentle nudge towards the inevitable. As ever she wanted to be doing, or at least to see things done; delay was an animal that gnawed at her bones. She could pretend to the Sharai's desert patience, but only in the desert, where it was more necessity than virtue. Here, even Jemel's distancing shell showed signs of cracking; her own was in shards already.

The Princip took the beaker she brought him, with a glance that spoke. He would do what he must to Marron when he was refreshed and ready, and not a moment sooner; would she have him botch the work, because he was still weak and ill-prepared?

She scowled up at him and his lips twitched in a transient, knowing smile. He did drain the beaker in a single draught, though, before handing it back with a word of thanks; and then he did make a gesture with his arms that was sure to draw everyone's attention, as if he didn't have it all already.

'I said that last exercise was risky, and it was, despite Coren's talent at waving away trouble. This is worse, this could be lethal. I have to free the Daughter, before I can treat Marron's sickness; we dare not hope that he can control it, which means that I must. I should ask you all to leave, except that I know you would not go; if my own page won't obey me,' said loudly, with a theatrical glower towards the door, 'I have little hope of it from those of you who love the lad. Nor would I venture to give commands to the King's Shadow, when we stand once again unequivocally in the King's realm. However, I will do nothing until I am satisfied that you are at least as safe as you can be. Hasan is no longer bleeding; if any others among you have a cut, a scratch on your skin, say so now. Be sure.'

None of them spoke. The Princip nodded heavily.

'Very well, then. Even so, I want you all at a distance. You must forsake your place at his side, Jemel; not for long, if all goes as it should, but I cannot have you close. Help to carry Hasan out onto the terrace, then watch from there. Coren, be ready to come in if I call you, but not otherwise. Even you are not immune to this thing, and I don't wish to find myself explaining to the King how it came about that his Shadow is now the Ghost Walker, or else spread messily all across the walls of my solarium.'

The words might be lightly said, but their meaning was entirely serious. Coren nodded his acceptance while Elisande and her friends dragged Hasan's pallet out into the sunshine. Then they grouped themselves together in the doorway, Julianne dividing her attention awkwardly between the unconscious figures of Marron within the chamber and Hasan without. Jemel stood stiff and detached, until Elisande tucked her arm firmly through his; then all his muscles seemed to lose their rigidity at once, so that he slumped against her side.

The Princip started with Marron much as he had started with Hasan: the little touch to the face, a first tentative contact, less assessment than acknowledgement.

And then the knife, though less than the cut that he'd made on Hasan's wrist, because so much less was needed. Just a nick to the enduring wound on Marron's arm, much as she'd done herself in the cell at Revanchard.

Now as then, the Daughter came seething out with the first drop of blood. This time, though, Marron was that much further sunk into his fatal lethargy. Her grandfather could have had small hope of rousing him to control the thing; indeed, he didn't even try.

Instead he stood up to face the shifting cloud of red as it shaped itself into the blurred echo of a creature, hinting at a body as monstrous as any 'ifrit ever chose. Elisande held her breath. This was the moment of greatest danger, when it was free and subject to no man's will. She'd taken a terrible risk herself when she'd loosed it in the cell, gambling on her ability to draw Marron back to consciousness. Her grandfather was gambling only on himself and his knowledge of its ancient and mysterious nature, and she wasn't sure how deep that knowledge ran.

Deep enough, it seemed, at least for now. He raised both his hands palm-out, as if they defined a wall; he spoke a few soft words and pushed his hands slowly forward. The smoke-drawn creature seemed to eddy for a moment, then drifted away from him as though it were caught in a draught. Watching it go, Elisande thought it had lost a little of its definition; she found herself straining to make out the sketchy lines of its implicit body. She glanced at Jemel beside her, and saw a wet sheen on his face who almost never sweated; when she looked back towards the Daughter, it took her a moment to find it at all. She wondered if it had slid entirely out of the room; her momentary panic – Marron hurt, she knew, when he sent it too far from his body – was only slightly assuaged by her finally catching sight of a faint red haziness in the air.

'Grandfer . . . ?' The appeal slipped out before she was aware of its forming on her lips, long before she could bite it back. This was no 'ifrit-shadow, the half-aware remnant of a dead spirit, to be dispersed into nothingness by a touch of Coren's power. It was something far stronger, and far stranger; and it was intimately linked to Marron. She couldn't imagine what would happen to him if it were scattered or destroyed.

'Don't be alarmed. I have simply confused it – much as you would confuse the mind of a man you wanted to slip by unseen. This was more chancy, as it has no true mind to be played with; but I have left it only the slightest awareness of itself, and none at all of us. That frees me to work unfettered with your friend. There is still danger here, though. I must do something that I think has never been done before, and the less you hinder me with questions, Elisande, the better my hopes of success.'

She nodded silently, uselessly; he wasn't looking at her. He had crouched down beside Marron once more, and laid his hands on the boy's pale ribs.

It was Jemel who spoke, if thinly; Jemel who turned his head, so close that she felt his curls brush her cheek, and whispered, 'What does he mean to do to Marron?'

'Heal him,' she murmured. 'Heal him completely, I mean. He's trying to break the link between Marron and the Daughter. Hush now, and watch. Pray if you can. I can't, I've been trying but I've forgotten how . . .'

That wasn't true, she hadn't been trying; but Jemel had been observant all his life until recently, and it could do no harm if he rediscovered the old habit now.

Whether Jemel did pray, she couldn't tell. But he did fall quiet again, and he did remember or rediscover his pride with his resilience, withdrawing a little way from her and standing alone, standing straight as he watched and waited.

Elisande was sorry for him, glad for herself, tired of being leaned on.

*

The Princip didn't labour so hard over Marron's body as he had over Hasan's. A worm of doubt turned in her gut, for all that she tried to dismiss it as unworthy. She loved him, she understood him, she distrusted him mightily; she thought that he wasn't seriously trying to drive the darkness from Marron's blood and bone. Even when she saw the faintest possible mist of grey rise like a vapour from the pinprick cut in his arm, even then she thought it was only a gesture, she didn't believe it would be enough. Hasan had carried a half-living thing inside himself, that had taken strong magic to disperse; this was less than a warm breath on a cold morning, the waft of a moth's wings would scatter it . . .

Certainly Coren made no move to trouble it; neither did it appear to trouble him. It wavered in the room's tugs and shifts of air, that she thought would be too light to disturb a falling feather. When her grandfather shifted his position, she took her eyes from it for a moment; when she looked again, she couldn't find it. *Like the Daughter,* she thought, and scanned more closely. But this had been only a haze to begin with, and so far as she could see it was nothing now. It had in truth been nothing all along, she thought grimly, trying to be angry: a charade, a lie, a distraction . . .

'Grandfer, that can't be all.' *At least tell me straight if you're going to let him die, I don't want your kindness.* And Jemel was Sharai, desert-made, as soft as camel-hide and just as tough. He'd seen one lover go down into death, and had sworn an oath of vengeance that she thought still lingered behind his silences; she feared that he might swear another, if he ever felt he'd been deceived.

'Truly, child, there's nothing in him now that is not his. He was infected by a breath, not a blow as Hasan was. The

Daughter had kept it weak and denied it any nesting in his body; now it is driven out and gone. The question is whether I can deny the Daughter its desire to return – and how it will react, if I do so. Keep you back, girl, the danger is not over yet.'

No, that she knew. She tried to look in two directions at once, at her grandfather where he held Marron's arm across his lap and at the Daughter where it was nothing but a hot and heavy cast to the air, as though a forge were venting into that corner of the chamber. The Princip's thumbs were working all along the brutal ridges of Marron's scar, and she desperately wanted to see what he did there; but there was suddenly a turbulence to that dim and smoky redness in the corner opposite, and she thought that someone ought surely to watch that and be ready to cry a warning.

There would be little even her grandfather could do about that scarring on Marron's forearm. He'd left Hasan's claw-scars quite untouched. Torn flesh and broken bones could be encouraged to mend themselves, sickness attacked, even a tumour could be shrivelled in time; but what was already healed solid and knitted-in could no more be shifted than a face could be reshaped. More likely he was trying to feel out what bonds there were connecting Marron and the Daughter, seeing if he could sense some intangible affinity between the wound and the – creature? No, it wasn't quite a creature, though the more she thought about it, the more resemblance she could see between it and what had come out of Hasan's blood, that fragment that had seemed to cling to the memory of being an 'ifrit . . .

Elisande thought that the affinity was with Marron's blood; she was sure that her grandfather would feel nothing, because there was nothing there that human fingers were capable of feeling. Certainly the Daughter was sensing something, though. More than a stir, there was a violent agitation now throughout the thin cloud of its apparent body. Not enough to draw it back into a full understanding of itself, nor to make it a threat even in its ignorance; it seemed more deranged than dangerous, like an injured insect battering senselessly at door and shutter, so pulled by instinct that it was barely aware that it was hurt or trapped.

Trapped it was for sure, unable to bypass whatever hidden barrier the Princip had created to hold it. It seemed to seethe against a wall of wind, although there was none. Elisande had never been truly frightened of the thing before – more through idiocy than courage: she'd even meant to carry it from the Roq to Surayon, and had given barely a thought to bringing it unclaimed, unstolen through all those miles, all those men between there and here – but she was frightened now. Since it had been – what, hatched? – it had always been Marron's, almost a part of Marron, his will woven in blood and smoke; and she had always somehow trusted Marron, even where he was stupid, even where he was blind.

Her grandfather's fingers were moving inward now, into the rawness of the open wound, the flesh that would never skin or scar.

Grandfer, be careful . . .

She knew just what he was doing: how his mind was reaching into the beat of Marron's blood, how it followed that tide and coursed through his body till it found the damage in his arm, how it interfered. She had done the same herself or tried to, but only when the Daughter was in him, and so she had failed again and again. She'd never dared to risk this. She was frightened for all of them, terrified for Marron; she could almost hate her grandfather for taking such a chance, if she hadn't understood him so well.

His fingers moved inside Marron's gaping wound, to mirror how his awareness moved, so much deeper within. Slowly, carefully, thoroughly he would be mending what was ripped, sealing what lay open to the world; slowly, carefully, thoroughly he would be closing off the Daughter's gateway to its human host.

Elisande felt the sun's heat against the back of her neck, and hugged herself hard against a terrible chill.

Sometimes she remembered to breathe, or her body did: great wracking gasps that shook her like sobs, as though she were weeping after all when she was so determined not to do that.

Occasionally she remembered her friends and where they were, around her; she thought she might look about to find them, but she never did. There was a separation between thought and action, between mind and muscle. She was as harshly cut off as the Daughter, lacked the power to move at all.

It was the Princip who released her at last, by moving himself: by sighing, stretching, rising from his place at Marron's side. Even then, though, it was a frustrated freedom that he granted her. She'd barely taken the smallest pace forward before he was glancing at her, glaring at her, gesturing her back beyond the doorway.

'Grandfer . . .'

'No, Elisande. There is nothing that you can do in here but harm. The boy is well enough, for now; whether he stays so is not in your hands to determine. Neither yours, Jemel,' sharing his glare around. 'Coren, again I may need you, but wait my call.'

When the King's Shadow bowed in acceptance of the command, she could do nothing more than fidget and fret, chew on a fingernail, watch as she had been watching. Her eyes followed the Princip across the chamber, towards where the Daughter billowed against its constraints. Had she thought that there was danger before? She had deceived herself, too scared to see ahead. Now it was truly unfettered, it had no home, no master, and her grandfather was setting himself against it. He couldn't tame it, no man could. It was a wild thing, a spirit, beyond mortal managing. She had no idea what it would do when he released it from its current cage. Perhaps it would flee to Marron's body, find that shelter closed against it and so destroy him in its fury. Or perhaps destroy her grandfather; perhaps it would destroy them all . . .

Her breath came in whispers now, and she resented even so much noise. It was louder than the soft grating of the Princip's boots on the grit on the flagstone floor, and that was too loud already. For his sake she wanted utter silence in the world, she wanted the birds on the hillside to stop singing, the wind not to blow.

It had been an anxious time recently; she could find no nails left to chew. Instead she reached her hand out and snatched at Julianne's – *Hasan's asleep, Sherett is coming, you can share my worries for the next long minute or two, and if you resist me it'll be your nails that I'm chewing, girl* – just as the Princip reached his own hands out towards the Daughter.

In the same moment, his mind must have unpicked the

bonds that had held it pinned and confused. It drew together sharply, no longer a diffuse and harmless-seeming cloud but suddenly that familiar insect-shape, sharp and deadly.

She thought it would attack him, mindless and desperate; she felt mindless and desperate herself, knowing that even he could have no defence against it. Instead, it only hung in the air, potent but undriven, apparently adrift.

Her grandfather held his hands high, on either side of the thing, perilously close to touching where the wisps of its blurred edges frayed into the air. At the same time, he startled her by starting to sing.

Even before her ears had caught the words, the cadence and rhythm of his voice had sent her mind hurtling back to childhood, to those nights when she was too hot or too excited to sleep. Sometimes her mother had come to her, and that was always good; sometimes her father, and in those days that was better. Sometimes, though, occasionally it had been her grandfather who came, and that was best of all. He'd talk to her a little, cuddle and kiss her out of tearfulness, then he'd lie her down on her tummy and his strong peasant hands would caress her head and back, rough skin but a gentle and tender touch, while his voice sang this same song in a whisper that seemed to gather up her soul and carry it swiftly away into restful dreaming.

At the time, she didn't even understand the words. It wasn't until she'd made the trip to Rhabat and learned much from the women there that she'd finally recognised it as a form of the Sharai *sodar*. Her mother sang her lullabies to help her into sleeping; Rudel used the same strange song as her grandfer with the same soothing touch, and her child's mind had thought it just another kind of lullaby.

Which it was, she supposed, in a way. That it was also tribal magic had been a revelation; that she could find no tribe familiar with that particular song had been a curiosity, a question she'd have liked to put to her grandfather if she'd had any hope of winning an answer from him. By then, she'd been long past questioning her father.

To hear it used now, and to such a purpose, was bewildering. The *sodar* was a way to quiet fretful minds and bodies, to sway them into sleep; surely he didn't think that he could lull the Daughter as he'd lulled a restless girl?

He could, though, and he did. While she watched, aghast, while she listened and still felt the seductive tug of it despite all her apprehension and all the years since she'd last succumbed to its insistent magic, her grandfather sang his song.

To her continuing astonishment, the Daughter felt it too, or appeared to. It contracted slowly, its colour deepening and the lines of its body becoming clearer, more solid-seeming. The Princip's hands closed in around it as it curled into itself, much like an insect withdrawing into its shell; it looked almost as though he were guiding it, even pressing against it as its red skin turned hard and textured . . .

Touch was always an important, even the crucial element in the *sodar*. Even so, she couldn't hold back a gasp when she saw that he was touching the Daughter for true, holding it firmly in both hands as his song died in his throat. The lightest touch was lethal, when it was blood-bound and alive. Never mind that she'd seen it handled before in this passive state, never mind that Julianne had carried it all through the Roq, never mind the logic that said her grandfather must be safe or else he would be dead already;

she gasped regardless, and then she did the other thing that she'd been aching to do against all wisdom and instruction. If he wouldn't be wise, then neither need she.

She plunged forward through the doorway; she hurtled across the chamber to her grandfather's side and tried to wrest the thing – the globe, the sphere, the red ochre ball, the Daughter – from his hands.

He held on to it, as though he'd been expecting just such an assault.

'Elisande, stop it. You're being foolish.'

It was the unexpected mildness of the rebuke that stalled her, that quelled the ferocity of her tongue, that left her with nothing to do but stutter feebly, 'If, if you'd been bleeding, anywhere at all; or if you'd touched it at all before it was ready, before you'd made it safe—'

'—Then I'd have died, or else it would have conjoined with me instead of Marron. Yes, I know. But neither of those things happened, and therefore I have made it safe, and therefore I can hold it perfectly well without your help.'

She let go then, realising only as she did so that her fingers had been quietly exploring the ridges and runnels, the glossy segments and the abrasive hollows of the Daughter's enclosing shell. She'd only seen before, she'd never touched. She remembered how it had been before, how Marron had woken it all unknowing; from that memory she found the resilience to scowl at her grandfather and say, 'You still shouldn't hold it like that, you don't know what might happen. You could tread on a nail, bite your tongue, stumble and fall and graze your knee . . . It isn't safe, it's never safe when a man is near it; and you especially, you shouldn't take such risks, your people need you . . .'

Especially now, she meant; and *I need you, especially now,* she meant that too.

'It's precisely because I'm fit to take such risks that my people need me as much as they do.'

Its being true, that was hard to argue with. Instead she turned the discussion, chanced one straight question.

'Did you, did you know that the *sodar* would make it sleep?'

'No, I didn't know. I knew that it had been left this way in the Roq, therefore I knew that the thing could be done; I guessed a while ago that the *sodar* – that particular *sodar* – might be an influence on it. The words are very old and hard to understand, but they clearly amount to more than a convenient way to hush a noisy child. I thought it worth the experiment.'

'Not worth your life! Marron has carried it a long way—'

'—And should carry it no further. This kept him alive, to be sure, but he must have been a living ghost. Look at him, Elisande . . .'

She shook her head. Jemel would do that, was probably doing it already. She'd seen Marron before in fatigue, in weakness and in pain; she didn't need to see him now, she'd rather look at her grandfather. Who looked suddenly weak, exhausted, deeply hurt – worse than he'd been after driving the 'ifrit-fragment out of Hasan, worse by a distance, if only because this time he had not collapsed. She could see the determination in him, the absolute certainty that he could not allow himself that luxury, and therefore would not; and she could see how even that determination was draining him further, costing him more.

More than he could afford, she thought. *This man lost a son today, his only child, and very possibly his country too . . .*

And slowly, respectfully, she reached out and took the Daughter gently from his grasp, so that he could at least afford to fall if he must.

This time, he let her take it; she'd been sure that he would. She saw herself reflected in his eyes, and thought that she'd grown since last they'd stood together.

It was surprisingly light in her hands, but he seemed to be stronger for being relieved of it, if only marginally.

'You should sleep,' she told him, 'recover your strength.' That was how she needed him, how they all needed him: bull-strong, the spirit of his land.

'I should; but when will I get the chance?' The glimmer of a smile accompanied the words. That was reassuring, but not enough.

'Right now, while I find somewhere secure to stow this.'

He shook his head; even so little movement had him rocking on his feet, but thankfully Coren was abruptly there to steady him with a grip on his elbow.

'No, child. I have one duty more, before I can think of resting. And so do you. The King's Shadow has kindly brought my son, your father home to me; it is for us to see to his resting now.'

And so she found herself going down, down many stairs to the crypt below the palace, with the Daughter still clutched like a talisman in her arms. Although she didn't like to use the slightest magic so close to something so old, so powerful, so little understood, she made a witchlight shine to show their way where no lamps burned. Her grandfather was past raising a glow — too old, too tired, too distressed: any one of those would have been excuse enough, and he could have offered all three if she'd asked him, which she didn't – and Coren didn't have a hand free to hold a torch, too busy using both to help and guard the Princip on the stairs.

Down and down, into the chill, still air that the hills hoarded in hidden caves. The crypt had been just such a cave once, that had been found by digging; quite how the Princip had known just where to dig, Elisande had never bothered to ask.

Now it was a place prepared, though never yet occupied. The walls were smoothly plastered white and set with sconces, with niches for lamps, with shelves for coffins or shrouded bodies. There were biers of white stone on the floor; on one of those lay Rudel, still in his travelling clothes, still in his blood.

On another were set bowls of steaming, scented water, cloths and oils, cerements of linen. Elisande thought this was a test, at Coren's instigation; she glowered at him, and he gazed neutrally back. Then she was certain.

Well, she could do this. With her grandfather at her side, she had to do this.

She set the Daughter to one side, lit the lamps in their niches and let the witchfire die. If she had to do it, she'd do it properly and with no distractions, nowhere to hide. Let these men see how grown she was, how ready.

She and her grandfather stripped Rudel's body, slowly and ceremonially. They washed blood and dirt from his skin, bound up the dreadful gaping hole that should have been his throat, anointed him and dressed him for his long sleep. At some point, one or the other of them had started to hum the *sodar*; now they were both doing it, though it was no part of any ritual that Elisande knew, Sharai or otherwise.

When they were done, the Princip said, 'It should have been his task, to lay me here. I never thought to do the work for him. I built this place for me and mine, but they should follow me . . .'

'Grandfer?'

'Yes, child?'

'Don't leave him here. It's cold. Too quiet for him, too far from, from Cireille.' Largely at Elisande's own sobbing insistence, her mother had been carried home to her family's estate on the other side of the valley, where she lay in warm earth in a grove of olives. 'Let him lie with her. Please? He'd have liked that so much more.'

'I built this place for me and mine,' again. 'Am I to be lonely here, when I come?'

'No, Grandfer. I'll follow you,' *if I don't come ahead.* 'Keep a place for me.'

'Would you not choose to be buried with your husband, little one, wherever he may lie? It is the custom. I miss my own wife's company, more even than I'll miss my son.'

Her grandmother was long dead, long buried in another land than this; she had never seen Surayon.

'I'll not marry,' she said softly, almost thankful for it as she gazed at the empty niches, that might otherwise have waited for her own children. 'I'll live and die as I am, and when I'm dead I'll come to you, Grandfer, and our ghosts can guard Surayon above till the stars fall.'

'If it's there yet, if we can guard it now,' was the dry response. 'Coren, I'm too weary for all those stairs again . . .'

Coren smiled, and they all stepped into light; and she thought, remembered, realised that they could have done this coming down, he could have brought them here in a moment. Which meant he'd had a reason not to do it, which her grandfather had understood. Old men, they were hateful sometimes; it sometimes seemed to her that they had planned her every word and action. After the long toil of the descent and the hard reality of her father's body waiting at the bottom, of course she would rebel against leaving him here in the cold alone. They must have known that, they had known it. And so he would lie where he had wanted, where they wanted, where she had spent half her life insisting that he should not be, at his dead wife's side. They'd made her ask it; she felt used, manipulated, nothing new.

It was a small gesture towards a petty independence, but she needed something and she needed it now; so without asking consent, without even saying what she'd done, she left the Daughter where it was, in a vacant niche in the wall of her family crypt. It was, she thought, as safe as anywhere, now that Surayon was no longer safe at all. They would realise or remember soon enough, if they didn't know already; but just for this little while she could pretend, she could convince herself that she had made her own choice and acted on it. She could even make believe that her father was not entirely lost from her story, that she left him on watch over the Daughter, though she'd never let him watch over her.

12

A Blade for a Boy

Servants came, with an offer to carry Hasan and his pallet back inside the chamber; Julianne said no, persuaded them rather to help Jemel bring Marron out to join him. They would wake sooner, she thought, man and boy, with the sun on their faces and the whisper of a breeze across their skins. The breeze whispered 'war', even she could smell the taint of smoke though it came from miles off; she would have spared them that if she could, but thought grimly, bitterly that they were men and warriors both. They should rouse to that, if nothing else.

She had more trouble with the servants when they brought her food, and she refused to eat it.

'I'll eat when my husband eats,' she said softly, stubbornly, wiping the vivid scars on his cheek with a cool cloth and willing him to wake soon, now, at any rate before Sherett arrived. She had no idea how fast the djinni might fetch her sister-wife; it might have been an eyeblink, it might yet be hours, but Sherett was coming and should not come to find him still asleep.

He should wake, and he should do it soon if Julianne's wishing had any power; but what he should not do was wake to see her face-full and chewing, callous and careless of his needs. She explained this hotly to the Princip's servants, when they pressed.

'What would he think, that I was here by duty and heedless of him, just taking my pleasure in the sun?'

'No, he'd think he had married a girl with sense enough to eat when she was hungry.' This from a blunt, solid woman in her middle years, simply dressed and simply spoken. 'No better way for him to wake, child, it'll have him thinking about his own belly and its emptiness. I like a hungry patient.'

'I can't . . .'

'Oh, don't be so foolish. If you're too delicate to eat alone and that Sharai boy won't join you, then I will. There's plenty here for all.' She set her tray on the parapet and plumped herself down beside it, picked something from a platter and passed it to Julianne.

Golden-brown pastry, sticky and flaking between her fingers; the sweet savour of ground meat and spices flooding her senses, flooding her mouth. She had bitten before she knew it, had swallowed without chewing and bitten again; the meat-cake was gone in moments and she was licking her fingers and looking for more.

'That's better, isn't it? *I* knew,' the woman said smugly, as her fat, nimble fingers filled a plate. 'You've a starved look about you, girl. I don't believe you've eaten well for days. Take this and set about it while I put some water in the wine, it'll go to your head else and make you foolish.'

Days? Weeks, more like: the last good food she'd seen

had been at her wedding-feast, and she hadn't eaten that. The last of any food she'd seen had been in her cell, and yesterday: far away, a different world — bleaker, more frightening but less doomed, she thought, sitting in the sunshine and smelling smoke — and suddenly very, very long ago.

She ate like a starveling indeed, ravenously, with both hands and no manners. Shadow's daughter, Hasan's wife — *and Imber's wife too, just as much, just as little* — she shrugged off a lifetime of courtly graces and barely contrived to keep one eye on her sleeping man; she kept no hold at all on the guilt she'd thought would consume her. Let him wake now — please? — and she'd greet him with delight, with her mouth full and her hands greasy, her lips coated in crumbs . . .

When she could talk again, when there was space and breath for words, she asked, 'What's your name? I'm Julianne.'

'I know you are, pet. The Lady Julianne, and all your titles too, but I can't be troubled with that. They call me Gerla, when they remember who I am.' That might have, perhaps should have sounded bitter, but did not; Julianne thought that actually most people who mattered to her would remember Gerla.

She saw the woman casting thoughtful, determined glances at the heedless Jemel, who had resumed his position stone-still at Marron's head. Working out some way to make him eat in his turn, no doubt . . .

'Leave Jemel to me,' she said, 'I'll see that he finishes what's left on that tray. You don't need to wait on us, Gerla. I may be the lady Julianne with enough titles to trip over,

but I've grown used to looking after myself. And others.'
Stubborn boys a speciality . . .

'Oh, yes. Grown used to going hungry because you lack
the sense to eat, I suppose. But it's a girlish trick, and feeding boys is another. Aye, I'll leave him to you, if I have your
promise for it. There's plenty else for me to be doing.'

'Gerla, tell me something, before you go?'

'Aye, lass. Anything.'

'Why are you still here? In the palace, I mean. Fetching
trays of food to awkward children, when . . .'

When a wave of her arm was all that she needed, and all
that she had to express what she was burning to say: that
Surayon was burning, and she didn't understand why the
most loyal servant would stay.

'What, should I run away?'

'Not run, no – not unless you chose to.' Though hiding
from the Sharai was no bad idea, in Julianne's estimation,
and hiding from the Ransomers was a better. 'But there
must be people you're worried about, people you could help,
something you'd rather be doing than this, somewhere else
you'd rather be . . .' In Marasson, she thought, a similar disaster would have emptied the palace; and she thought that
was right, it was proper. Even slaves should find freedom in
catastrophe.

'By all the saints and martyrs, girl – do you think we're
saints or martyrs ourselves, to stay to serve our lord when
we're crying to be gone? Or bonded here, and frightened of
our master?' She seemed genuinely incredulous; Julianne
found herself blushing. 'Listen, then, and mark it: you were
raised to another understanding, maybe, but you're in
Surayon now. All the men fit to bear arms – yes, and some of

the women, too – are long gone, to fight or find their families. The rest of us, from Pym the page-boy to old Shalira in the laundry, we're here because we want to be. You couldn't chase Pym from the Princip's side, not if you carried a battle-axe and had a hundred 'ifrit howling at your back. And me, well, I've no family that I care a button for, and I can be useful here. Not just to feed foolish children, either. The hurt will be brought here, as swiftly as may be. I'm not the Princip but I have some skills in healing, and there'll be too many for him to tend them all, even when he's in the palace. This is my place, Julianne; I wouldn't be anywhere else, a time like this.'

Briefly her gaze moved beyond the parapet to where the ravages of war were closing on her country. Even after seeing the expression on the woman's face, Julianne still couldn't regret her question. She felt better than reassured, somehow, she felt as though a promise had been fulfilled. She'd never expected to find Surayon a haven for all that was good in the world, despite Elisande's portrait of it. What she had wanted, what she had needed to find was a country that was simply different from what she'd known thus far: the cruel sub-tleties of Marasson, the chill dedication of the Ransomers, the hot but fickle fires of the Sharai. She'd ached to see a land where generosity governed ambition, where trust displaced fear, where above all hatred could not dominate.

There was loyalty everywhere, of course, from the Roq to Rhabat, even in the Emperor's court; but elsewhere it was shaded by desire or duty or tribal allegiance. Here it seemed to be freely given, won by love. To Julianne, today, that was a plashing fountain in a dry, dry garden.

She stood up, and stooped over Gerla to give her a gentle

kiss on the cheek. 'Actually,' she murmured, 'I think, neither would I.'

Then she picked up the tray – that still felt heavy enough to feed a small army, despite her own and Gerla's depredations – and carried it over to where Jemel sat next to the unconscious Marron.

'He won't be stirring for a while yet, love. Look at Hasan, he was healed first, and he shows no sign of waking. So take your eyes off Marron for a moment, and look at this instead. You're desert-bred, you don't believe in waste; the Sharai feast in time of plenty, and there's plenty here. Besides, if you eat your fill now, you'll be ready for when he does wake, you'll be able to tend to him without feeling faint from hunger . . .'

That won her a look, a sort of startled glare at the suggestion that a Sharai should ever feel faint, for whatever feeble reason. She simply grinned, and kissed his cheek too.

'Jemel, you'd feed a camel before you took it into the Sands, wouldn't you? Well, feed yourself, then. I don't know what kind of mood that boy's going to wake into, but it's going to be something different from anything you've seen before. He's going to be a different person, all himself instead of half the Daughter, only that I don't know if he'll remember what self that is. It could be a long journey to find out, and you've got to stay with him. So eat, you'll need your strength.'

That was the argument that swung him. He fell to among the meats and pastries; purely for companionship – unless it was perhaps also a little for teasing, because a Sharai warrior would not ordinarily eat with a woman, and she liked to remind him sometimes just how far he'd fallen from the figure of his own ideals – she squatted down beside him, picked up a soft almond biscuit and nibbled on it. She was wondering if perhaps she should try to make him talk, or if that might be a step too far, when he glanced up and then a little further up, above her head. His eyes widened momentarily, before he could control them; she could feel the effort that he put into his voice, to sound quite matter-of-fact as he said, 'Elisande's djinni is returning, with your husband's wife.'

It sounded so odd, when he said it like that. Perhaps it was supposed to – except that it wouldn't seem odd to him, that Hasan was much-married. Harder for Jemel to understand was her own uncertain status, with two husbands living. To be sure, it was quite hard for her also. By Sharai custom her marriage to Imber was annulled, because it had not been consummated – but then, neither had her second marriage to Hasan. *Not yet . . .*

She was confident that no church court in Outremer would recognise that annulment, if only because they had been Sharai who decreed it. So in the Kingdom she was married yet to Imber, in the Sands she was married to Hasan; that seemed to be the easiest way to think of her legal condition. Privately, personally, it was more complicated. In her body, she was married to neither; in her heart, she thought, to both. Here in Surayon, where Sands and Kingdom met, she would have spun like a dizzy dancer between the two and never guessed or hoped which man's arms would seize her first; except that Imber was not here, and Hasan was in need. That made things easy, for today and perhaps for tomorrow. She didn't dare look any further forward.

*

She got to her feet again, turned around and understood Jemel's brief reaction, the equivalent in him of goggling surprise. Never mind that they'd both seen miracles, these last months; never mind that she'd travelled this way herself, and so had he. They'd neither of them seen it from the ground before, and for all that she'd been waiting to see it, it was still an astonishing thing to see. Perhaps his eyes had caught the figure in the sky when it was simply a dot far distant, perhaps he'd tried to think of it as a bird at first, until it became impossibly large and unlikely.

For herself, looking too late to be deceived, it was a wonder that came with a cold shudder of sympathy, her own terror transferred. She watched Sherett glide down towards the terrace, seeming utterly unsupported in the air; she wondered how the woman could look so calm, how she could bear to keep her eyes open as she hung so high with nothing for her hands to grip to.

That was Julianne's own nightmare, though, and others she knew did not share it. Elisande positively relished flying by her djinni's grace. Perhaps Sherett was another of that kind. Or else she simply had that same Sharai pride that could make a posing idiot of Jemel, and would sooner die than shame herself by showing fear, even when she'd been snatched into a hurtling horror-ride that must have outraced the wind to bring her here so soon . . .

Julianne walked a few steps away from Jemel, away from the sleeping on their pallets. Her sister-wife was so much lower now that she could see the djinni as a spinning thread of distortion in the air, behind her shoulder. She could see also that Sherett's veil was demurely in place below her hood. That brought a soft, unexpected snort of laughter, affectionate admiration rather than mockery. That insistence on the decencies was a part of what she loved about the woman, along with her fierce independence of thought and her open delight in her husband, their shared husband. Those should all have been contradictions, Julianne thought, but somehow were not in Sherett.

Bare feet touched to ground, as lightly as a falling feather; curse her, she didn't even stumble as she turned graceful, impossible flight into graceful, stalking walk along the terrace.

It was Julianne who stumbled a little, suddenly running: hurling her arms around Sherett's neck when she'd meant to be so cool and dignified, brutally disarranging that modest veil as she kissed a greeting, almost sobbing as she mumbled, 'Oh, Sherett, thank you for coming . . .'

Dark eyes flashed in the sunlight, hard hands hugged her too briefly, a caustic voice said, 'I wasn't offered a choice. Snatched from our tent, under the eyes of all our family – they'll be talking about it still, and blaming me. Or you, perhaps.'

Julianne's family too, although she didn't know them; there were still two senior wives she hadn't met, and children also. To her shame, she realised suddenly, she'd never even asked their names . . .

Well, there would be time enough. A lifetime, possibly, if the luck fell that way. For now, 'They can blame me, if they choose. I asked for you. Do you, did the djinni tell you why?'

'It said Hasan was sick, no more than that. I didn't ask further.'

No, of course she hadn't asked. For swift mercy's sake,

Julianne forced a smile. 'He should be well now, only he hasn't woken yet. I'm sorry, I should have thought to tell the djinni to say he had been healed. He was very ill, though, an 'ifrit wounded him and he might have died; I thought you'd want to be here, I thought he'd want to see you . . .'

'You were twice right, then – but what you mean is, you wanted me.' A hand gripped hers, greatly reassuring, and, 'Take me to our husband, then; and while I watch him, shameless, you can find yourself a veil.'

'Oh, Sherett, you don't need to wear it here!'

'In a stranger's house, for my husband to see me exposed before princes and slaves? Indeed I do, and so do you.'

Julianne groaned inwardly, but found a sudden determined stubbornness. 'I will not leave him,' she muttered forcefully, 'to go bothering servants in a house at war to fetch me a useless length of cloth. Sherett, I will not!'

'You are married now, we are married together – and you will dress and behave as a wife ought, and you will do as I say. I will teach you that, if I teach you nothing else. However,' relenting abruptly, surprisingly, 'there is perhaps no point in chasing a veil until someone brings you a decent robe to replace that filthy rag you're wearing. This is too fine a house for such neglect – but as you say, they are at war. I have seen that, though I barely know where I am. Here . . .'

Hands tugged at her clothing, and she remembered with a sinking heart just how filthy it was indeed, and how filthy she was herself beneath it. Just at the word she could feel all the grime and the greasiness on skin and fabric both, the lank mats of her hair; no doubt she smelled quite rancid to one newly come from the dry clean air of the Sands. Probably she ought to go and seek out a change of dress, at least a jug of water if not a bath. Even if it meant missing Hasan as he woke, she oughtn't to let him see her in this state . . .

But Sherett pulled the hood up over her head, found a way to twist the robe so that there was an extra fold that could be pulled across nose and mouth and held there, so long as she remembered to hold it.

'For now, that's sufficient. Till he wakes, till he's seen you and spoken to you. He's been hunting you so long, he won't want to wait. He has no more patience than a puppy, that one.'

That was so untrue that she might have protested it, if she hadn't been so grateful not to be sent away.

She guided Sherett – pointlessly, the woman could see perfectly well for herself, but she did it anyway – over towards where their man lay quiet on his pallet. First there was Jemel, with his own quiet man; the two Sharai greeted each other, exchanged compliments and hopes, for all the world as though they had met by chance on neutral ground in the heart of the *mul'abarta*.

Hasan still hadn't stirred. Only his blood stirred within him, and it was hard to be sure even of that. Every now and then Julianne was shaken by memories of the black sludge creeping from his veins, so that she had to snatch at the pulse of his neck or wrist to count the slow, healthy beating of his heart for reassurance.

No such fretful fancies for Sherett. She squatted beside his pallet, laid one hand firmly on his brow and spoke in a normal, everyday voice, as though halfway through a conversation with him.

'Well, you my man, you've been sleeping long enough.

The tribes are riding, and it's time to wake. What, will you let them ride without you? Their head is yours if you will take it, man . . .'

For a moment, he seemed to shift beneath her touch. Sherett merely tutted, and went on talking. 'Very well then, laze. If you will sleep deeper than my *sodar* could have sent you, I'll rouse you ruder than your mother ever did . . .'

And she set her two hands, one on either temple of his head, and began to sing: soft and slow and gentle, so that Julianne became deeply confused. She knew the *sodar* that sent strong men to sleep and restless girls with them, that had even lulled the Daughter into stasis. This sounded like enough to that, but simply overhearing it – in sunshine after a long night and a heavy meal, when she could and should have been drifting, drowsing, even solidly asleep despite every duty and summons of the day – her blood was stirring and her skin alive, crawling beneath the strata of her dirt. What it must be like for Hasan with that call focused on him, beating into his head and heart as he lay fathoms-deep in dreaming, she couldn't imagine and thought she never wanted to learn.

The effects of it were clear to be seen, however it felt inside. Hasan frowned, and his whole body shifted on the pallet; he opened his eyes and blinked up at his wife, while her hands shielded him from the sunlight and incidentally from any glimpse of Julianne. Well, perhaps it was incidental. 'What, still no rest?' he murmured, sounding more amused than querulous, more awake and aware than he had any right to be.

'Too much, already. Besides, God and the tribe and all the tribes together have claimed all the common hours that you have; and yet you are a husband too, though you are inclined to forget that. Is it any blame to us poor abandoned wives, if we seize any stray minute that we may?'

He must have heard that deliberate plural as clearly as Julianne did. He lifted his hand slowly to touch Sherett's brow in a gesture that was simple, private, modest and somehow heartshakingly erotic all at once; then he said, 'Where is she?'

'Here, Hasan.'

He tried to turn his head, against the strict constraint of his wife's strong and determined fingers; and grunted as he felt it, and said, 'May I not look on what is my own, Sherett? Has she become ugly, since I saw her beauty last? Or is she marked,' seriously now, a tug of anger in his voice as though a sluice had opened, 'has that demon Morakh done her damage?'

'Oh, you may look all you like, so long as you lie still to do it. You are the one who has been marked, Hasan,' and a thumb stroked lightly over the triple scar on his cheek. 'You have been walking with death, and are barely back from the journey. What you may not do is move about, until the Princip has seen and spoken with you.'

'The Princip, is it? Am I in Surayon?'

'You are.'

And so is your army, Julianne thought, though she said nothing. Hasan gave a short, soft sigh that might have meant anything. All he said was, 'That family seems to be dogging me. The son, the granddaughter, now the old man himself . . .'

Now she had to speak, and did. 'We brought you here to save your life, Hasan. Rudel lost his, in fetching you through the Folding.'

'Is Rudel dead? I am sorry, though my people may not be. These are stories that need to be told; later will do, if it be not too late. For now, immediately, show me my recovered jewel, Sherett. I promise, I will lie as still as— well, I had meant to say death, but not that. As still as an ailing man in the presence of his newest lady, not wishing to make a flailing, whimpering idiot of himself . . .'

Sherett took her hands away and Julianne slid forward, to where he could see her easily without either turning his head or squinting into the sun's glare. She remembered to hold the cloth across her face as a substitute veil; he reached up and touched his fingers to her brow, much as he had saluted her sister-wife.

'Julianne. Wife. I looked for you . . .'

'I know you did. And found me,' *in a manner of speaking, and too late.*

'Did I? I remember finding a madman . . .' He frowned, and she could almost see the memory slip from his tenuous grasp. 'Well. Later. Show me, I said . . .'

His hand had no stronger grip than his mind, but it served to nip the veil from her unresisting fingers and ease it aside.

'Don't worry,' he said, 'I won't be scolded. There's only Sherett to see, and it'll be you that she blames.'

Now he smiled, and it had been worth long waiting for. Now he stroked her cheek, and pushed back her hood to draw her long hair free. She knelt patient while he played, not daring to risk a glance at Sherett. It was all she could do not to kiss at the inside of his wrist, where the skin might smell sourly of his recent illness but was still his, was a part of him and so near, so tempting, so easily reached for kissing after so long; and who cared if that made her no better than some tavern slut in Marasson, kissing every man who came in reach? There had been only the two come that close to her, and thus far they'd both escaped her kisses.

Thus far, and just a little further: she did resist the yearning, not to shock Sherett beyond bearing. Then she did take her husband's hand and lay it firmly back on the blanket that covered him; and she did tuck her hair back inside her robe, and draw the hood up over, and pull her makeshift veil across her face again.

'You're too thin,' he said, reaching out again in defiance of her discipline, folding his hand loosely around her wrist. 'A girl should be slender, but not hollow. Were you much mistreated?'

She shook her head, but not in denial of anything he'd said. They were all of them too thin, she and all her friends; each of them had their reasons. 'Later,' she said, throwing his own word, his own decision back at him. 'Time enough for all our stories then. I'm being fattened up again, in any case. For now, if we can't talk about little things, things that don't matter' – and they couldn't, how could they, when something that mattered so much was going on all about them, and they were the cause of it all? – 'then let's not talk at all. You may feel like you've slept an age, but most of that was with an 'ifrit inside you,' and even that was more than she should have said, judging by the bemused interest on his face. Hastily, trying to cover up, 'You still need rest—'

'—And food,' he interrupted, with a grin: thinner and less piratic than his standard, but convincing enough. Bathed in malice, she thought it.

'Yes, and food. Fit food,' with a little gentle malice of her own. 'No meat, no sweets, no feasting. Not till you're recovered.'

He groaned superbly. 'How shall I ever recover, if you starve me on slops?'

'Slowly,' Sherett said, reinforcing Julianne. 'In your sleep, largely. We're going to leave you for an hour now; will you lie still and rest, or shall I call up my *sodar* to enforce you to it? I'll fetch the Princip after, and then if he allows it you can sit up, take a drink and a little to eat.'

'Where is the Princip?'

'With his granddaughter,' Julianne said. 'With Rudel.'

'Then go, by all means, wherever it is that you are going. I have Jemel for company – and will you wake Marron, as you did me? What's wrong with him?'

'Let him sleep,' Julianne said shortly. That was another story she didn't want to tell. 'The longer the better, for Marron. And you're not to plague Jemel with questions. Jemel, if he tries, you have your own *sodar*—'

'—And will use it. I promise.' She believed him. He ached visibly for silence, for solitude, so long as he could share them both with Marron. This all-but-empty palace was too populous for him, as Rhabat had been before. He wanted his friend fit and the open Sands, a spare camel and his wits and skills to live on, nothing more.

Perhaps he could have that now, she thought, with an unexpected flare of hope. Marron was harmless without the Daughter, meaningless in the machinations of the wise. They had no reason to keep him, and he surely had no reason to stay. So he would go, and Jemel would go beside him; and they would find no welcome anywhere in Outremer, so they would be bound for the desert in the end. For the desert and perhaps for happiness, in some scale . . .

As was she, perhaps, in some scale. Hasan could make her happy, she thought, if he didn't bring too great a burden of grief and guilt dragging in his shadow – if he didn't seek to instal her in Ascariel, junior wife to its tyrant overlord of her conquered people. If he did that she would be needed, yes, useful beyond the uses of a junior wife, but not she thought happy.

Sherett could make her happy also, in other ways. Sometimes quite unexpectedly, as now, plucking her up by the elbow and wrenching her away without a word, without time to say another word to Hasan. For a moment she felt as though she'd been ripped from all the good that was left in her life. Then, as she was towed through the solarium, she found breath enough to ask, 'Where are we going?'

'In search of a bath, and fresh clothing. I have been caught in a sandstorm and felt cleaner afterwards than that djinni has left me, with all the wind's dust in my hair; you stink worse than a midden. Patrics may not care about such matters, but you will learn that we Sharai are a fastidious people.'

It might not, surely it could not last; but for the moment at least, Julianne felt blindingly, blisteringly happy.

If she'd come this far into the palace earlier, she wouldn't have asked Gerla that foolish question about her staying. It was all too clear that the building was half abandoned. They bustled through corridor after empty corridor, and Julianne was just beginning to think they'd have to stand in the great hall and shout for attention when at last they found their way into the kitchens.

Here at least there was life, and activity. In her experience there always was, in kitchens. No Gerla, alas: but a steward with a limp, a staff and a compensating scowl, a couple of women chopping vegetables at one end of a long table, a sullen boy up to his elbows in water, scrubbing pots.

Here was proof positive, Julianne thought as she faced their range of bemused and curious stares, that Gerla had been wrong in one aspect at least. Not everyone still in the palace wanted to be here. The steward, she guessed, would sooner be out in the field, but that his twisted leg prevented him; the boy she was sure of. By the hunched look of him, the steward must have been working out his own temper on the boy's back when the appeals grew too insistent or too impertinent.

'Ladies? May I assist you at all?'

The steward's staff clicked on the tiled floor as he made his slow way towards them. Julianne wanted to gesture, to tell him to be still, not to trouble himself on their account; Sherett said nor did anything, though, and so neither could she.

Just before he reached them, Sherett showed her own pride, in a swift murmur. 'I don't speak your tongue with any ease, Julianne. Ask him for the bathing-chamber, and a change of dress. Say that we don't need hot water, cold will do . . .'

Julianne shivered, at the thought of a hard scrubbing in icy water. Before she could speak, though, the steward smiled thinly, and changed languages with a quiet fluency. 'I understand Catari, my lady. My name is Baris, and I am steward of this house. I do apologise, that you have had to come and seek me out; we are short-handed and distracted today, but that's a poor excuse for neglecting guests. Of course the baths are ready, and the fires hot. Roald will show you where.'

A snap of his fingers and the boy scuttled forward, abandoning his pots and apparently his sulks both at once. Julianne was glad to have the improvised veil to hide her smile as she saw how carefully he kept out of reach of the steward's staff.

His bruises couldn't be that bad, though; they hadn't marked his curiosity, nor his confidence. He shifted his shoulders beneath his loose, grimy shirt of damp linen, found a slouching way to walk that didn't hurt too badly as he led them back up the stairs and demanded boldly, 'Ladies, is it true that you flew in here this morning on a magic carpet?'

Julianne choked on a sudden, startled giggle. When she'd recovered, she said, 'I don't know. Is it? I suppose it could be. Didn't you see?' He was the sort of boy who should surely have been watching, staring, pointing, yelling – there had been enough of those, a dozen or more hanging out of the palace windows and streaming onto the terrace to make a circus of their coming, when she'd been so fraught with grief and hope together.

'I was in the stables,' he said disgustedly, 'and everyone else ran off, but I had my hands full with the Princip's brute of a stallion, and I couldn't just leave him loose, could I? By the time I had him stabled, I was the last left, and the master wouldn't let me go.'

'No, I don't suppose he would.'

'And then the Princip wouldn't let me ride out with the other men, even as a messenger. He *needs* messengers . . .'

'I'm sure he does. He probably also needs to feel that those in his charge are as safe as they can be. The time will come when he'll have to answer to your family, Roald, for his care of you.'

'I haven't got a family, that's why I'm here. The Princip takes us into the palace, until he can find us another home; some of us he keeps. I've been here five years,' which was obviously a source of pride rather than humiliation, except that his voice turned suddenly as he went on. 'I'm not a *child*, though! He sent the little ones away this morning, up into the hills, and he tried to send me with them, only I wouldn't go.'

'So what did you do?' Julianne asked, knowing the answer already, feeling guilty already for dragging it out of him.

'I hid,' and surely he couldn't get any redder. 'Until they'd given up on me and gone. Then I came out, I was sure they'd let me ride messenger now – but Baris caught me before I got to the Princip, and he took me to the kitchens.'

And beat him into the bargain, but Roald was clearly not going to mention that.

'And then we came.'

'And then you came, and the baths are just here, and I'll build up the fires for you, lady, because the other lady's Sharai and you both came from the desert and I expect you like it really hot – but tell me about the magic carpet? Please?'

Julianne laughed. 'It's not really magic. A djinni brought us here, and there were so many of us, it was just easier' – *easier for me, and Elisande thought of that, even while everything else was happening* – 'if it carried us in on a carpet, like half a dozen glasses on a tray. It fetched Sherett for me later, and she flew in with nothing to stand on at all.'

'Oh.' That was obviously something of a disappointment. A djinni was one thing, a magic carpet something else entirely. A boy might dream, she supposed, of finding or buying or possessing a magic carpet, but not a djinni. Emphatically, not a djinni. 'Why was the djinni doing that? They're not usually so . . .'

Helpful? Cooperative? Exciting? Involved? A gesture filled the space of the missing word, and she sympathised deeply.

'Never mind why,' Sherett said sharply, as they came into the first cool chamber of a simple hammam. There was a shelf of oils and unguents there; she inspected it while the boy ran off to tend to his fires.

He came back sweating under the weight and hammer-heat of an iron basket full of scorching rocks, which he carried through to the inner chamber. When he came out, following billows of scented steam, Sherett ambushed him with a grip on his elbow, a push towards a long bench and a brisk command: 'Take off your shirt, and lie down.'

'What? Lady, no . . .'

'You might as well,' Julianne said, amused. 'She'll do it for you, else. And give you more bruises on the way.'

Sherett snorted. 'I wouldn't beat a boy useless, on a day like this.'

'I'm not useless!' A furious protest from Roald, even as he clung desperately to his dignity and his shirt, wrapping his arms tight around his body in an effort to keep them both together.

'You will be when you start to stiffen up, unless you let me at your muscles now. I found a salve here that'll help to soothe the burning, and don't tell me it isn't burning now. I know all the stages of a beating, me.'

Of course she did, and from both sides, most likely. The boy was mulish, though, eyeing the door in hopes of a get-away, determined to keep his clothes on and his privacy secure; it was Julianne who found the weapon to break down his resistance.

'If you won't be medicined, you'll need to be healed; there's no room here for a boy who can't work. Can Gerla do it, do you think, or must I ask the Princip?'

The horror of such an idea struck Roald mute, as it seemed; he made no answer. Slowly, though, very slowly he unlaced the neck of his shirt and pulled it off over his head.

Julianne deliberately turned her head aside, not to increase his mortification, and didn't look back until Sherett was done with him, until he was easing his shirt on again and flinching as the worn linen fell against his skin. She thought the salve might be doing some good, watching as he straightened his shoulders cautiously, as he looked a little surprised that it felt no worse than it did; she thought she had a salve for his soul, which might do even better.

'Roald, come here.'

He came, bristling with suspicion, wary of some further degradation. She smiled and said, 'I have a task for you. A secret task, can I trust you not to shout it?'

'Of course, lady!'

'Good. Who guards the Princip, with all the men gone to the war?'

'The Princip never has a guard, lady. He is . . .' Again a gesture, in lieu of the word he didn't have; the gesture seemed to mean all-powerful, invulnerable, perhaps simply 'Princip'.

'Well, he may need one now. There is more than one

army in Surayon, and creatures more subtle and more evil than men; even the Princip may have his mind distracted, and his eyes not watching his back. I want you to do that for him, as much as you may. The older boys have gone, his little page is too young for this, and who else is there? Baris would be too slow, even if he had no other duties, and it is no task for a woman. Here, take this.'

Roald eyed the blade that she offered him, with something close to yearning on his face. All he said, though, was a stout, 'Lady, I have my own knife.'

'I'm sure you do.' She was sure she knew its type, too: a nocked blade handed down through generations of lads, hollow from too many years' rough sharpening on any convenient stone, its handle split and bound with fraying string. No doubt he cut his meat with it, and his nails too when he thought to cut them; she doubted strongly whether it was good for much besides. 'This knife is special, though, for more reasons than you can see,' and he should be able to see plenty in the chased steel blade, the wicked double edge, the haft inlaid with mother-of-pearl that must be vanishingly rare in this country, must have been more rare still in Rhabat where Elisande had found and claimed it and its sister. 'It has been blessed by priests, to be proof against 'ifrit and other spirit-creatures. This blade will protect the Princip, where perhaps nothing else can do it. Will you take it? For him, and because I ask you to?'

She pressed it into his hands before he could answer, to let him feel the cold smoothness of the hilt, the vicious edge. Even so, he hesitated.

'Lady, this is too good for a kitchen-boy . . .'

'Yes, it is. But it's not too good for the Princip's ward; and it's essential for the Princip's chief bodyguard, his *secret* body-guard . . .'

And to overcome his last wavering doubts, she unknotted the ties of her robe and began to slip it down off her shoulders.

The boy fled, taking the knife with him.

A minute later she was pouring a dipper of water over stones so hot that they cracked in their iron cradle, she was breathing deeply and sighing luxuriously as steam engulfed her and she felt the sweat start to break through her ingrained crust of dirt. She could sit here and lose more than the stink of her prison cell; she could lose all the distress of the last weeks, all the darkness that had gathered in the corners of her mind, wash it all away and be pure, clean, her father's proper daughter . . .

Sherett cut across her thoughts with a question. 'Why did you give that boy your knife?'

'Because he needed it. Everyone in Surayon needs something today,' and she wished that everyone's need could be so easily satisfied, or satisfied at all.

'You'd best warn the Princip, or he'll wonder why he's being shadowed everywhere by a kitchen-boy with a dagger in his hand.'

'I will. If we see him. He may ride out again, when he and Elisande are finished . . .' And then, because that reminded her of what he and Elisande were doing, which reminded her in turn that she couldn't after all wash or sweat the world away no matter how hot the bath or how dense the steam, she said, 'Sherett, what's it like out there? The djinni brought you over in daylight, you must have seen . . .'

'Aye, and been seen in my turn,' the woman said, with half a smile that was clearly for something that might have been half funny, on another day. 'But yes, Julianne, I saw. I saw what my people are doing, bringing the dry desert to this wet country, covering the green with ash and smoke. They are burning crops and villages, and slaying where they ride: my greedy people, destroying what they cannot take away. And doing all in the name of God, Julianne, to recover the holy places. We say that God chose us from all the people in the world, and set us in the Sands to test us, to keep us pure. If that is true, then perhaps God is using us now to test the people here, fetching in the fire and death that we live with daily to see if they are soft or strong.'

'Or perhaps that's a thin excuse,' Julianne said bitterly, 'to justify theft and cruelty and murder, because it was these people who took these lands from your possessing, and you want your revenge.'

She expected a sharp rebuttal from her sister-wife, and didn't get it. Sherett only nodded slowly, and said, 'Perhaps so. But it is not only the Sharai who are making war in Surayon.'

'No, I know. I heard that. There is an army led by Ransomers, come in from the north.'

'And more, a party from the east too, following the tribes. A small party, but I saw them. They saw me, too,' and that difficult smile was there again, more heard than seen. 'They are led by the man you were married to, before.'

Julianne stared, trying to make her face out through the veiling steam. 'I don't understand. How do you know that?'

'The djinni told me. The Baron Imber, is that right?'

That was right, it was absolutely right; but, 'There are two Barons Imber.'

'This is the man you married. Your husband, the djinni said. That is not correct, of course, the djinn can be mistaken; but they do not lie, Julianne. It is he.'

She sat with the steam and the sweat coursing off her in runnels, with the warmth and the heat of all her Imber memories coursing through her veins, and still she shivered in the chill of this news, still she couldn't believe that she had ever felt so cold before.

13

A Hollow Heart, An Empty Hand

It didn't feel like waking, but then what came before had never felt like sleep; his awareness of it had been nothing like a dream.

He'd felt rather as though he were caught, trapped in a grim despair – as though he could have opened his eyes at any moment, but that he could see no point in it. Just as a prisoner in a dungeon knows the crushing weight of the castle rock above his head, just as an exhausted traveller shoulders all the night's sky and drags its burden of stars along in his wake, so Marron had felt a world's insupportable heaviness bear down upon him, cold and merciless and all-suffusing.

He'd also felt a lashing fire, a fierce vortex that surged and burned. He'd been slowly, dimly aware that there was a battle that raged between the two, and that he was not a simple spectator here, but a victim also; they fought each other, but their fighting injured him.

He'd been aware of that but only vaguely, distantly. He

was crushed and burned, and he could care about neither. There was a pointlessness to their passionate warring, as there was a pointlessness to his life. He didn't know where he was, and lacked the curiosity to open his eyes. Or try to. He didn't know if he had eyes, if he was still in his or any body. Perhaps heaven hurt, very likely there was pain in hell.

Certainly there was pain here, which didn't seem right, it was so very much not what he was used to; but there was that distancing also, as though he felt it acutely but a long way off. It didn't seem to matter.

And then the pain had gone, the fire had gone and there had been nothing to hold him any longer, nothing for him to do but fall. Which he had done, subsiding under the chill grey weight of the world and struggling not at all, having no sense that he could struggle. Where everything was distant, nothing could be further off than anything else; he'd remembered a boy from his childhood who had fallen through ice on a frozen winter river, who had been carried like a pale shadow beneath his own feet where he had stood terrified on the glassy, cracking surface. Or perhaps he was that boy, perhaps he always had been.

Except that that boy was dead, and he was not. He felt the heaviness disperse before it could entirely entomb him, he felt the cold recede. It seemed to him that there were currents of warmth that seeped slowly through his body and carried him with them, so that at last he reached all the way to his skin and all of it was his own again, more so than it had been for a long, long time.

It might have been soon after that or it might not, he had no way of telling, but a time came when he could reach out even beyond his skin and take note of the world around. He heard voices, though he felt still too far away to listen. He was aware of softness underneath him and warmth above, warmth that lay across him like a blanket. Not desert heat, which he regretted; this was something gentler, that felt to him like something hollow, a mockery-thing, far less than it ought to have been.

He felt much the same way about himself, though he had hopes of altering that. If he lay still long enough, he thought he might remember all his story, and its proper order; he might know where he was, and what had happened to him. He thought he'd have the patience to do that, he thought that patience might be his greatest gift. There seemed to be no urgency anywhere, in his body or his mind. There was a question that he thought he ought to ask, but he wasn't sure what it was, nor whether it really mattered in the least; it could wait.

So he lay and waited also, feeling as light and hollow as the sunlight, an egg sucked dry; or better would be a shell remade and ready to be filled with meat or matter. He had come through the fire and the chill, he had taken all the weight of the world on his shoulders, on his soul. Perhaps he was a saint, cast back into his martyred body for a miracle that should punish the unbelieving heathen. Something was missing, though, more than the story of his days: perhaps he had been a saint and made miracles, and now for his reward he was made again to be a normal man, to live without the holy fire in his blood and die at last and never live again.

He knew his name but little more except a lack of wholeness, something lacked, like the answer to a question not yet voiced. He waited, perhaps for the hand or spirit of the God to touch his mind with understanding as it had touched his body with warmth; but the only hand he felt was outside him, on his skin.

Perhaps that should be miracle enough, that he could feel, that he could be touched. Perhaps he should be content, live hollow and contented . . .

He opened his eyes, because he thought he ought to.

There was a sky of pure pale blue, which was all wrong. There was a sun to dazzle, to make him blink and squint; it had burned the sky white all around the fierce beaten gold of its own face, and all of that was wrong.

Then there was a shadow, a silhouette between him and the light. It eased his eyes but left them seeing only darkness, so he let them close again. He had other senses, all his body was his own to use: he could feel the dry, warm touch of fingers on his brow, a palm against his cheek; he could smell the spicy desert tang of unwashed robes and a dust-washed body beneath . . .

'Jemel,' he said, recognising the shape of it in his mouth as he said the word, recognising the meaning of it in his head.

His own, 'Marron,' was given back to him in answer, in a cracked and broken whisper; and that might be the difference, the only difference, that he said the one name and was answered by the other. To anyone else they might be indistinguishable, might as well be one.

He opened his eyes again and this time saw a face in the shadow as it hung above him, now that he knew what to look for. A sharp nose, dark sunken eyes, black curls, skin the colour of an ageing bruise: it was the details he found rather than the face complete, just the proud curve of the nose or the gleam of light reflected in the intensity of an eye. They were enough to jolt him into memory of Jemel and therefore of himself, his recent self; that rush of memories was enough to teach him all the differences that lay between them, how easily they could be told apart.

Above all, the one great difference: *he is Sand Dancer, of a sort; I am Ghost Walker, of a kind—*

—And there, just there it all broke down, as he realised what it was that he had lost, what had been stripped from him, blood and brain. Eyes too, the red cast of it was gone from his eyes, so that his sight was both clearer and more blurred, both at once.

'Where is it?' he asked, and yes, that was the question.

'I do not know. The Princip took it from you, and healed your arm after he had healed your sickness, so that it could not go back. He sang a *sodar* to make it sleep, and then Lisan carried it when they went away. I do not know where they have gone. Do you want it back, Marron?'

He wasn't sure. *What am I, what are we when I am not the Ghost Walker?* Was Jemel a Sand Dancer still, did his oaths count for anything? And what lay behind the oaths, what mattered so much more – would that endure, or would it be fractured or broken or abandoned altogether, another measurement of loss?

'Do you want me to take it back?' *Do you need me to? Or do I . . . ?* Jemel had only ever known him as the Walker, marked out by more than red eyes and an unhealing wound. If he was to be his simple self again, the boy he used to be – well, that boy had been Sieur Anton's entirely, and not Jemel's at all . . .

Jemel only shrugged in echo of Marron's own confusion

and shifted his head a little, as if to break the contact of their eyes. The sun's glare was a sudden, unbearable dazzle; Marron turned his head to escape it, turned away from Jemel and couldn't bear that either.

He sat up with an effort that left him dizzy and weak, a stranger in his own body now that his strong companion was gone. He reached out for his friend's support – and checked the movement abruptly, drawing back his arm. His left arm . . .

There were all the scarred ridges of his wounding, nothing could heal those now; but the heart of it, where it had lain open all this time, was sealed over with fresh pink skin. He prodded at it experimentally. It was soft and smooth, untouched by sun or dirt, and the flesh was firm beneath. There was no pain, no matter how he worked it.

Black stars sparkled behind his eyes; his mind whirled. His arms were wooden suddenly, too heavy to hold or move. He felt himself sway, begin to fall, could do nothing to prevent it. Other hands gripped his shoulders, held him upright while a strained voice murmured urgently, 'You should lie down, you have been very sick . . .'

Healed or not, he felt sick still; even his tongue tingled strangely, and it was hard to speak. There were more questions now, though, and these might win an answer, could at least do no more damage.

He did lie down, though not quite on the pallet. He wriggled sideways – against little resistance – until his head lay nested in Jemel's lap. Then he said, 'How did I get sick, Jemel – how could I, with the Daughter to protect me? And where are we now, why did you move me? We were in Selussin, I remember that . . .'

And that name, that memory brought others again, so that he could almost have answered one of his own questions. He remembered faces in a market, a silent threat; he remembered releasing the Daughter himself, and then a cold invasion.

'There was an 'ifrit,' Jemel said, 'or something of an 'ifrit, some little poison of itself. It found entrance through your hurt, and what you carry – what you *carried* then fought with it, until we brought you here. This is Surayon, the Princip's house. He has freed you from the 'ifrit's shadow, and from the other too; but Rudel is dead, and Hasan has been gravely hurt, and there is war all around us, you can smell it on the wind.'

Whether he meant that literally or not, Marron sniffed for the scent of it, for the direction and the distance; then closed his eyes for a moment, shook his head on the Sharai boy's knees and said, 'No, I can't. Not any more. I could have done, before.'

'You can now. I can. There is smoke in the air.'

'You have a desert nose, Jemel, to match your desert eyes.'

'Perhaps. The air is dry in the Sands, and scents carry; we learn to read the wind. But these fires are close, even this wet breeze will say so. You could smell them if you tried. Wet your nose with your finger, and stretch to catch the upper air where it moves . . .'

'I need not try, so long as I have you to do it for me. Besides, you told me to lie here and be still. If I sit up again, I will likely faint and you will be angry with me.' And then, losing his smile in a moment, before he could even see whether it was returned, 'Tell me, Jemel. How is Rudel dead, and Hasan hurt? How long have I been ill, for so much to happen? And how have we come to the Folded Land, and war followed us?'

He had to wait, while Jemel fetched a beaker of cool fruit-juice and propped his head up just far enough to enable him to drink; and then again for the time it took to persuade his friend that no, he was not hungry, the juice was enough for now, he couldn't possibly eat.

At last, though, with his head cushioned once more in the warm lap and Jemel's fingers playing lightly with his hair, all his questions were answered – or all except the one that he couldn't bring himself to ask again, for fear of hearing in his voice what his words would not say, *I want it back.*

Jemel's husky voice spelled out the situation, all of it – or as much as he could tell – in a quiet, neutral tone, much like a messenger reporting to his lord. Like the King's Shadow reporting to the King, perhaps: if ever he did it so, if the King didn't simply pluck the information from his Shadow's mind. Marron almost smiled at the picture his mind made, of the elegant silver-haired Coren standing or kneeling beside a throne like a page-boy waiting to serve – but no, there was nothing funny about it. Coren had the pride of his station, to be sure, but that was all reflected, he had none of his own. He wouldn't balk at a page's duties, running errands and pouring wine; he would do that service or any other if he thought it right or needful.

Not funny, and not important now. Marron knew why his mind was drifting, why he was letting it drift. He still had half his mind on Jemel's voice, he was still listening, but he didn't want the images that came with it, neither the hushed and desperate flight of his friends nor the brutality of war that trailed them.

'—And that is all the news I have,' Jemel finished, having said too much already but nowhere near enough.

'Then we must find more. Is Hasan here still?'

The softest, briefest of chuckles, and, 'Marron, he is asleep on the pallet next to yours. Fling an arm out too far, and you would hit him on the nose.'

'Oh.' He didn't turn, didn't look, didn't move except to say, 'How long has he been sleeping, can we wake him yet?'

'We could, perhaps,' Jemel said doubtfully, 'but for what? He knows less than you. The women did not talk with him long, and told him nothing that mattered.'

'Women? What women?'

'His wives. Sherett and Julianne. Lisan sent the djinni for Sherett – I said that already, weren't you listening? But then they both left him, and he fell asleep. You should sleep too.'

No doubt he should, but it wasn't going to happen. He said, 'Well, if Hasan cannot give us the news we need, let's go and find someone who can. Julianne is with Sherett; very well. Where are Elisande and the Princip?'

'I don't know. I said—'

'—And you don't think I was listening. I remember, Jemel. They took my Daughter – no, the King's Daughter – away from me, and you don't know where they went. So we'll have to hunt them out. It shouldn't be too hard. I don't know the Princip, but his granddaughter makes enough noise for two. We'll just ask anyone we meet, *where's the little loud one?* They'll know.'

'Marron, you must not move. They said it of Hasan, he was not even to turn his head . . .'

'Well, I've done that and more, I sat up straight, remember?'

'And fainted, when you did.'

'Nearly fainted. You held me up. We can do the same again. Slowly, this time. I promise, Jemel, if I feel giddy, I will say. If not, we can go exploring. You won't go alone, I know that.'

'No.'

'So we have to go together. Unless you're prepared to sit here quietly and watch me sleep while the world burns all around us? Even the women are off doing something, Jemel. Do you want to be left behind?'

'No,' again, a fierce whisper.

'So help me up, and we'll see who we can find, and what we can learn.'

Standing took time and care, so much of each that he ached for the Daughter's fire in his thin blood and its strength in his weary bones. He felt as though something of himself, all his value had been stolen from him while he slept. He ought to be glad to have it gone, but without it, what was he? Just a boy, an insignificant blade unsure who to fight for and unwilling to kill, sworn to both sides and trusting neither.

Standing now, leaning heavily on Jemel, he looked down on the sleeping Hasan and then out, over the parapet for his first sight of Surayon.

He saw a valley like a garden on a grand scale, green and growing – or rather it had been, and should have been yet. Whichever way he turned, though, west and north and east the air was smudged with smoke. He forgot almost that he had lost the Daughter's eyes; he seemed to see sharply at great distances despite that all-encompassing haze, and what he saw was death and fury.

This was what Hasan had yearned for, he thought bleakly, and Sieur Anton too – a bolt shot at the heart of the Kingdom, a purifying fire, a holy war for each of them although they followed different gods. Try as he might, stare though he did, he could see nothing holy: only men in armour, men in black, men in midnight blue, all blood-swathed and screaming. Three armies, he thought: one was Ransomer-led, one was Sharai and not led by anyone, its only hope for a leader here at his feet. The other must be from Ascariel.

Between them all the Surayonnaise, fighting like farmers for their lands and lives. Better if the armies fought each other; that must come, surely, as soon as Sharai tribes met knights of Outremer. However soon, though, it would be too late for Surayon. The land had been blighted already, in a morning's work; another day or two, and it would be destroyed.

Jemel was gazing at Hasan. 'I cannot believe that he sleeps in Outremer, while the tribes are fighting.'

'You haven't been where he was, Jemel. I can believe that he would sleep and sleep; I wish I could. Besides, better that for Hasan than to rise up and make a killing choice. This is Outremer, yes – but it is also Surayon. The Sharai have had an understanding with these people for many years. Elisande lived a year in Rhabat, do you remember? And was not the first to do so. The Princip saved Hasan's life this morning; should Hasan demand a mount and a weapon, to fight him this afternoon? Or should he betray the tribes who trust him, who followed him this far?'

'Hasan should do what he believes is right, what he has always taught and argued for.' Jemel's voice was as tight and unforgiving as his face. 'It is a coward's way, to escape into dreams when the road is hard. He knew that Surayon was part of Outremer, he has always known that. It was Catari land before, and holy to us.'

'And what would you do, if he made that choice and went to lead the tribes? Would you join their slaughter, as you wanted to before? It is a slaughter, Jemel, just lift your eyes and look. Or listen, can't you hear the screaming? There are children's voices in the screaming.'

'There always are. Children, women, the old and the sick – they die, whosoever hand directs the blade. That is war, Marron. You know this, you have done this too. You say you will not kill again; I say wait, the time will come. Hasan might control the tribes a little; the slaughter will be worse without him. But no, I would not follow if he left. I followed him once, and Jazra died. I swore then that I would never follow him again, but kill him rather. I was hot then, blaming him for saving me; that oath was foolish, and I broke it. But now he is sleeping in the sun while men die – yes, and children too – and I will not follow him again. A man should not be weak when he is needed. Besides, I am sworn to stay with you, and that oath I will keep, foolish or not.'

Marron might have wished the last answer to have come first, but he was glad enough to hear it at all. He nodded his acceptance, although privately he wondered if his changeable friend might not turn once more, when Hasan was awake and in his strength again. That man had a drawing power in his voice and manner, that Jemel had been helpless to resist before.

For now, he just nodded his head towards the open doorway that led off the terrace and into the palace beyond.

*

Standing had been hard enough; walking was worse, even with Jemel's shoulder as a crutch beneath his arm. He felt absurdly weak, utterly drained and more. He shuffled along like a man old and spent, as though all his youth and vitality had been ripped from him. His body had not forgotten the steely inexhaustibility it had borrowed from the Daughter. With every step he expected to recover it, and with every step he was betrayed into a trembling helplessness.

Probably any man so cruelly reduced would hunger for what he had lost. He couldn't blame himself for yearning to have the Daughter back in his blood again; his soul's freedom didn't seem worth the price today.

They passed through a wide and empty room, and came to a corridor that led straight and far, too far, seemingly into the hillside the house was built against. There was still no one in sight, no sound of movement from any of the many doors that opened to left and right. Marron wondered foolishly if the entire household had abandoned them and ridden off to the war. More seriously, he wondered if he could possibly walk as far as the corridor's end, even with Jemel's support. If he did, and if they found nothing but empty rooms all the way, he was utterly certain that he would not be able to walk back.

Jemel knew; he said, 'This was stupid from the start. We should sit on the terrace and wait. The Princip will come soon, Sherett said so.'

Perhaps Hasan is not so cowardly and weak, then, eh? The words hovered treacherously on Marron's tongue, and were not – quite – said; instead he only sighed, close to yielding already, only wanting not to make waste so quickly of the great effort that had brought him this far.

He hadn't felt like this those times when Elisande had healed him, neither her father Rudel. Perhaps the legendary Princip was cruder in his work, coming to it late as he had, lacking the subtlety of the native-born miracle worker . . .

Even as the thought occurred, he heard voices, down at the further end of the corridor. He waited a beat, to know who they were and what they were saying; then remembered that it was the Daughter's trick and not his, to hear such details across such a distance.

So he waited in an ordinary way, as Jemel waited beside him, two young men adrift in a strange house, not at all where they were thought or meant to be. He could have been nervous, he thought, at being found – or caught, he might have said – like this. The boy he'd been, Sieur Anton's squire would likely have ducked through any convenient doorway to avoid it. Now he didn't care, except that he hoped not to startle whoever was coming.

Two of them, figures coming up through an archway, arm in arm and arguing hotly. Marron didn't need the Daughter's eyes, nor its ears to identify them now. The one he'd lived and travelled with for many weeks, while the other was actually easier for him to name from some little way off. The squat figure, the barrel chest, the beard – he might almost have thought that Jemel had lied to him, if the beard hadn't been white and Elisande hadn't been so closely in the stranger's company.

'Grandfer!' Her voice rose, easy to hear every word suddenly. 'I thought you'd healed him?'

'So did I.' It was a fit voice to come from such a chest, from such a man, deep and carrying. 'And so I did. He's not

bleeding, not possessed, not grey and fading into death —
what more do you want?'

'You know what more!'

'And you know what little I had left me, or could afford
to give . . .'

But he was talking to empty air; Elisande had disengaged
her arm from his and was running the length of the corridor,
skirts flapping awkwardly about her legs as she came.

She hurtled into Marron, clutching at him, all but knocking him over with the force of her arrival. It was Jemel's wiry
strength that held them all upright; that earned no thanks,
though, only a glare and, 'What were you thinking of, to let
him leave his bed?'

'Have you ever tried to keep him there?'

Elisande blushed furiously; Marron felt a little tremor in
his friend's arm and thought the Sharai was laughing, deep
inside.

Then the girl took his hands in a tight grip, muttering,
'Just hold him for a minute, let me work.'

She closed her eyes, perhaps to see the better. Marron
felt warmth flood into his fingers, into his wrists, wherever
her skin touched his. It chased through him, blood and
bone, the course the Daughter always used to take; he felt a
pang of near-recognition. But this was something far less
harsh, sunlight and not fire; what it left in its wake was not
the limitless energy nor the seeming immunity that he could
have borrowed from the Daughter. Rather it was an awak-
ening, his own strength stirring as his muscles fed, as they
drew from Elisande something of what they had lost in his
draining.

Not all: she couldn't give him what had not been his.

Nor could she restore to him the full power even of the boy he'd been before, the brother Ransomer who would sweat and endure and achieve through sheer stubbornness. What he had now, though, what she gifted to him felt like another miracle, a pulsing wonder in the deep hollows of his body, a secret flame whose light could not be hidden, whose source would never show.

'Enough.' That was the Princip, who knew that source too well. Elisande nodded and released his hands, looking pale and shivering herself now, apparently glad to step back into the shield of her grandfather's arm.

Jemel frowned as Marron did the opposite, straightening and stretching and peeling away from the Sharai's supporting hold.

'It's all right, Jemel. Look, I can do this now,' standing by himself and smiling at his friend, secure on his own feet. He could do a lot more; he felt as though he could run the length of Outremer, race Jemel on a camel, on a horse, whatever. It wasn't true, of course, he'd fail sooner than he ought to; it was only with the Daughter's strength that he could run all day, the granddaughter's wouldn't sustain him long at all if he were wasteful of it.

'You can, yes,' the Princip said, with an edge to his voice that was patently saying, *and see now, she cannot*. 'Forgive my sounding churlish, Marron, you are very welcome to Surayon, and to my house; but she should not have spent so much of her energy where it was not needed.'

'Oh, what, not needed?' Elisande roused herself into instant outrage, squirming against the arm that held her pinned to his side. 'He was falling down, you saw him—'

'—And could have been picked up by Jemel there and

carried back to his bed and kept in it, tied down if necessary, until he had eaten and drunk and slept his way to health again. It would have come, in time.'

'He might not have had time,' she argued, with that sullen look that said she knew she had lost the point already.

'No, that is true – but if Marron lacked the time to recover naturally, then so will everyone else who comes here in search of healing. And they will come, Elisande, they are coming now. And what will you say to them, to the men with their wounds and the women with their burns and the children with their terrors and their broken bones, when they turn to you and you are too spent to help them?'

'There are other healers,' she muttered, twisting again against his grip, this time trying to avoid his level gaze and his steady voice.

'Yes, there are. Some are stronger than you, and some are less strong, and all will be needed – but none among them is granddaughter to the Princip. It makes a difference, Elisande.'

'I know,' she said, sighing, subsiding. 'I'm sorry, Grandfer. But Marron can make a difference too,' added determinedly, a new justification. 'He's no good to us lying on a pallet in the sunshine.'

'Forgive me, lad – but what good to us is he on his feet and twitching with your borrowed strength? As Ghost Walker, he was dangerous to both sides equally; as a boy, he's all bone and nothing.'

'He can fight. He's a demon with a sword, I saw him outfence four Sand Dancers at once . . .'

That was the demon with the sword, not me, though it was true that he had his own skills. But he didn't say so, he said neither of those things; he had something else to say that was more important. 'Elisande – I will not kill.'

'What, *still*?'

'Still.'

She glared, with an exasperated affection; he made a helpless gesture, *sorry, but your grandfather's right, I'm no use to anyone* . . .

Surprisingly, it was Jemel who offered a way forward. Jemel the fierce warrior, always ready to kill anything that did not kill him, Jemel said, 'The wounded will be brought to this house?'

'Yes, any who are seriously hurt. They'll be looking for me, but I can't be here – no, Elisande, I *cannot*! I must go out to the field again, I've delayed too long already.'

'Which field? There are three armies on your land now.'

'Each of them in turn. Naturally.'

'And do what? Fight and die an old man's death, too foolish to remember that your body is not the force it used to be?'

'Experience is like armour in a battle, Elisande—'

'—Yes, it slows you down—'

'—And I don't plan to fight much in any case, only to organise the defence of my country.'

'Oh, that needs you, does it? It's not as if everyone in Surayon hasn't known for thirty years what they should do when this day comes . . .'

'Knowing and doing are different things, when there is fire and death at your heels. I simply have to be there, the Princip has to be seen. And no, you may not ride with me. You have to be here, you're as much a symbol as I am. Rudel is dead, and you are more than ever the continuity of the state. I've indulged you before, but no longer. You stay here, and you help my people, your people – which does not mean wasting what energy you have to make your friends feel better!'

Jemel spoke again, quickly across the seething silence, before the storm could break. 'It will not have been wasted. We will ride out, Marron and I, if there are any horses left in your stables; we'll help to bring your wounded in. Armed men defend the weak simply with their presence. And if we meet a war-party, well, I am Sharai and he is Patric; between us we may turn them without need to fight. Both our peoples have honour enough, not to attack the injured or their escorts. They may need only to be reminded of it, in the heat of the day.'

More likely, Marron thought, he and Jemel would simply incite extra fury in those they faced, regardless of any codes of honour. Sharai and Patric riding together, in this cursed and desecrated land? That was reason enough for more slaughter.

Still, it was a good idea. Even the Princip couldn't deny that. He nodded briefly, and even managed a glimmer of a smile as he said, 'There are horses remaining, though they may not meet your standards, Jemel. I've mounted the Sharai before, and even my finest would barely satisfy. Now my finest are dead, or ridden half to death already.'

Jemel shook his head. 'I wouldn't waste a warhorse, nor a racing horse. If we fight, we fail, and we will not flee. Give us sumpters if you have them, they can carry two at need; give us dray horses if you must. Perhaps we should take a dray . . .'

'Perhaps we should,' Marron said quietly. 'Jemel, I can't

ride— Oh. Oh, yes. I suppose I can, at that.' A breath, which didn't help at all, and then, 'With your permission, sir? We'll do what we can.'

Another nod from the Princip. 'Go. Tell them in the stables – if you can find anyone to tell – that I will come shortly, and I need my Boucheron saddled and prepared. No doubt there will be others riding with me. *Not* you, Elisande,' before she could utter the first syllable of the argument they could all see rising to her lips. 'You stay, and play princess for me as your mother would have done. Marron, you feel well just now, but you are not. Do what you can for my people, and by the God's grace I will thank you for it later, but don't drive yourself into exhaustion. There's no more either one of us can do for you today.'

'Except one thing,' Elisande said swiftly, determined apparently to have some kind of final say, if not the one she'd wanted. 'An armed man needs a weapon, Marron sweet, or he may be very scary but he isn't very armed. Esren!'

The djinni appeared at her word in its common form and place, a darkling rope above and behind her shoulder.

Hanging seemingly unsupported in the air below was a sword in a belted scabbard of white leather with silver edging.

Marron would have thought it lost, if he'd had the time to think it missing. His rush of joy at its recovery told him how much he would have mourned that loss.

He spoke his joy in a wordless cry, in a sudden movement that pulled him free of Jemel's restraining arm. He reached past Elisande and snatched for the sword; there was a moment's resistance, and then Dard's familiar weight fell into his hand.

'For a young man who doesn't want to kill,' the Princip observed mildly, 'you seem uncommonly pleased to have your weapon back, Marron.'

'Uh, yes, sir . . .' He was too busy buckling the belt around his waist to worry about the old man's unabashed interest, Elisande's smug self-content, even Jemel's stony silence. They all had their meanings, and any one of them might mean trouble to come, but he could puzzle them out later. He shifted the belt until the sword hung perfectly, put his hand to the hilt and drew the blade a hand's span from its sheath. He wanted to go further, to examine its edge and run his fingers along its chasings, to come that little closer to Sieur Anton. This was not the time, though; he released the hilt and let the sword slide down into its sheath again. In that moment of separation, he remembered again his other, his genuine loss. And looked at Elisande and said, 'Where have you put the Daughter?'

'Where it will be safe,' the Princip replied brusquely, when she hesitated. 'The fewer who know, the safer it will be.'

Safest of all if you don't know, that seemed to be what he was truly saying. If safety meant separation, if keeping them apart was its true measure, then even Marron thought that he was right. Already something in him looked at the Princip and thought *thief,* thought *give me back what you have taken from me . . .*

If safety meant separation, though, then Marron had been safe before, behind the Daughter's distance. Sometimes a veil, sometimes a shield, always a breach, it had lain between himself and the world, numbing pain and weariness but numbing sympathy also, holding him that little way apart from the concerns even of his friends.

Now that distance had been snatched away, and he stood entirely within mortal touch again, and was not ready for it. Not the Princip, but the world stood by to give him back everything that the Daughter had taken from him.

14

A Bridge to Fall

This was not like watching from the terrace, even with the spells of farsight that seemed to bring close what was truly distant. That was only seeming, like a tale told of a battle fought; there was skill and wonder in it, but it was a long, long call from being there, from the taste and the touch, the glory and the terror of it, the chill of steel and the hot run of blood.

The terrace, the palace lay above and behind them, not so very far in ridden road but all that other, greater distance between the tale and the truth. Up there they had watched and listened, seen and heard; down here they were in the landscape, part of the picture, actors in the play. They were what they had been watching.

Down here and a long ride yet from any fighting, drifts of smoke on the wind were occasionally heavy enough to sting at their eyes, and they had to veil nose and mouth against a fall of dust-fine ash. The sun seemed hazy, high and cool in a thickening, shadowy sky; that was a portent, surely. With the air so bad to breathe and the light failing far too soon, it was an easy message to read. Death had come to Surayon, and spread its hands wide across the valley.

Himself, he rode towards it. His teeth were gritty with the sour taste of burning, his nostrils were stretched for the first scent of blood; the horse beneath him was as jittery as a boy on his first raiding-party, and he was little calmer himself; and yet, and yet . . .

Jemel couldn't help, couldn't keep himself from laughing.

He was riding deliberately in front now, but still kept twisting round despite himself, despite every effort at proper discipline. They rode to war, if not to fight in it; this was no time for foolishness, for giggling.

And yet what better time, for a Sharai who should treat his life as lighter than his honour? The tribes were never solemn before battle, honour demanded a coarse joke, an arrant boast and a grin flashing brighter than a scimitar in the sun; today – as he was supposed not to get involved in any battle that they came across – honour demanded, honour absolutely required that he laugh.

Since the night Jemel had seen him first, running tirelessly with his eyes a smoky red, Marron had always been the Ghost Walker. The name had come from legend, from a thousand firelight stories; the truth of it had been a thing to learn over weeks and months, was still a shadow largely unexplored, known only by its borders. The one fundamental, though, the self-evident truth had always been that the Ghost Walker walked or ran, and never rode. No animal would allow him anywhere near. Horses reared and kicked, camels roared and bit whoever was most handy, and usually Jemel.

So it followed that Jemel had never seen Marron in a saddle, until now. And now – seeing the gawky gracelessness, the shambolic slouch of it, hearing the excuses punctuated by yelps as boy met saddle, bouncing – well, how could he help but laugh?

'You be quiet, you. I haven't ridden a horse in months and I never could handle a charger, we only ever had ponies at home and I didn't like those. Fra' Piet mocked me for my riding and so did— so did everyone else, I don't need your teasing too.'

'This is not a charger, Marron.'

'No, it's a raw-boned nag with no manners and nobody could ride it with any hint of style, so stop that giggling and keep your eyes on the road, we could meet trouble any moment.'

True, it was a raw-boned nag that Marron rode, but Jemel's mount was worse and he rejoiced in handling the creature with deliberate, ostentatious style.

But it was also true that they were riding into trouble, and he should be watching for it. A Sharai earned his laughter on enemy ground by being always ready to meet that enemy, which meant reading the land, the sky, the wind; and meant also trusting the man at his back to guard his back when he was first man in the file, while his eyes and attention were all turned ahead.

Enough of teasing, then. He turned to face forward, to scan the country as he rode, as he chuckled; and it wasn't long before the chuckle died, before he was calling on the furthest stretch of every sense to help him and still felt that he blundered blindly in the dark.

This was hard, hard land to read. In the desert, the

slightest sough of a breeze might tell him how far he was from water, or how long it would be before a dust-storm hit. The glimpse of a bird could show where camels might find grazing, or where a man crouched in cover. Every mark on sand or rock was a sign that spoke loud and clear, ink on a page and all the better for the wind's action on it; this was writing that said just when it was written, and often who else had read it since.

Here, though, all was confusion. Surayon seemed as empty as the Sands, and he did not believe it but he couldn't read the signs that would tell him otherwise. This was wet country, there were open streams to cross, there was a wide and shining road in the valley bottom that they told him was a river. Look at a footprint in the muddy ooze before a ford, see how water pooled in the bottom, and who could say how long since that print was made? Not he . . .

They had skirted the turmoil that was also Surayon, Surayon-city. War hadn't reached it yet, might not for another day or two, and there were men enough to meet it when it came. One glimpse through the open gates, and Jemel had felt infinitely grateful not to be going inside; walls and roofs made him uncomfortable, people in number made him nervous. What use would he be, who could use a Sharai boy in a city? Better far if he and Marron rode the open country and offered help where it was needed, where he had it in him to offer . . .

Or so he'd thought. So far they'd found the road deserted, except for the one time when a rising thunder of hooves at their back had forced them back into the verge, to allow the Princip and a party of his men to pass at speed. They wore half-armour, mail shirts and helms, and were mounted on good Sharai stallions, fast and fierce, not the giant destriers commonly favoured by the Patrics. Jemel had seen these horses in the stable yard, and his raider's soul had yearned to steal a couple. It would have been easy, with so few hands to saddle and harness such a number; it would have been gloriously funny, a shocking abuse of hospitality at which his hosts couldn't conceivably complain; above all it would have been utterly and magnificently Sharai, a tale to be told around desert fires till the end of his days.

But he had said _I wouldn't waste a warhorse_, and had meant it too. He'd take them for a joke, and then what? Have nothing to do but lead Marron into a war which they should neither of them fight, or else shame himself and that same raider's soul by bringing the horses back.

So no, he had scoured the Princip's stables and found two ageing saddle-horses kept for sentiment, he guessed. They seemed to have half-forgotten that they were ever ridden; his was remembering its manners swiftly under his insistence, while Marron's would be ruined entirely if it should survive the day.

The war-party had chased its own shadow into the distance, lost itself in the acrid haze; Jemel and Marron had ridden on slowly, and thought the land as empty as the road. Perhaps everyone had run to the city, who had not run to the war.

Or perhaps these farming folk had clung to their farms, their dirt and weeds, their treasured peasantry; perhaps even now a dozen pairs of eyes were watching the two ride past, perhaps a dozen arrows were aiming at their breasts, _two in Sharai dress, both armed, so casual on stolen horses, they'll pay back the lives they've taken . . ._

He didn't know, he couldn't tell; he couldn't read the country. Even the sky confounded him, shrunk as it was between mountain walls, limited, contained. There was no true horizon here. He didn't understand how people could choose to live in a bowl like this, locked in, with only a dream of distance. In the desert, there was little that mattered more than that smudged line where sky and sand should meet: it warned of strangers and of storms, of oasis and of bare rock's rise, of any change approaching. These Surayonnaise squatted in the bottom of a well, and their enemies could drop on them like vultures and never be seen coming.

The wind was as mute as the sky; its back broken on mountain rock, it was warm and damp, weak and shifting, telling him nothing except what he knew already, that he was all but helpless here. He could fight if they came to fighting, but he'd have no warning of it; he felt all but blinded and deafened too, swathed in a bewildering dampness that washed the world away.

Then he thought about Marron and what had been done to him this morning. Himself, he was only far from home and out of sympathy with the land, baffled by its strangeness; his friend was carrying a loss far greater, all the stretch and strength of what he'd borne so long ripped away without his consent, without his even knowing until the thing had been done. If Jemel felt disturbingly adrift in this country, then how must Marron be feeling?

He glanced back one more time, not the hint of a smile on his face or in his mind. His eyes met Marron's – with that momentary jolt that he still couldn't prepare for, when he saw once more that they were deep brown and utterly human, no trace of alien red – and it was his friend who smiled this time, and briefly they might have been two boys riding anywhere for any purpose or for none at all.

They had ridden for some time, some distance past the city before they met any traffic coming the other way. Still going down but less steeply, the road was also far less straight even than it had been, and to Jemel – who was used to desert trails that ran as directly as possible from water to shade, from rock shelter to oasis – it had not seemed straight at all before. Now it snapped back and forth like a whipsnake's trail as it ran between high banks topped with hedges of thorn, that broke only occasionally to allow access to fields and orchards, groves of olive trees, long runs of vine. At another time, to another man, Jemel could grant – albeit reluctantly – that there might be a pleasant aspect to riding this road, turning and turning slowly amid the green and brown of the crops, the bright and varied colours of the fruits, the heady scents rising from them, the constant batter of birdsong and the sudden gurgling rush that spoke of another stream to ford just around the next corner.

To Jemel, though, here and now, it was a frustration that amounted almost to a torture. He was desperately out of tune with this landscape, all the sounds and scents of unaccustomed farmland threatened to overwhelm his senses altogether, used as he was to the bare and singular experience of the Sands – and now the road, the only path they had to follow was so contrived as to deny them any glimpse of what might be climbing up from the valley bottom.

To those who knew and could read the country, of course – those who could hear an invader's footfall in the sudden shriek or silence of a bird, who could smell a horse's sweat behind the perfume of a vineyard in the sun – there was an advantage in such a road, that could baffle and confuse an enemy as it had baffled and confused him. He was wise enough to admit that. No doubt the whole length of it could be spied out from the Princip's clever terrace high above, and those gateways into the fields made perfect ambush-spots, while the sheer height of the banks and hedges would prevent any invader breaking away from the road.

What Jemel couldn't be was wise enough to endure the frustrations calmly, nor to be sensibly careful. The gentle, steady fall of the slope encouraged his horse, where it would have slowed a camel; he did nothing to hold the animal back. Nor did he check behind again, to see if Marron were keeping up as his pace increased from an ungainly trot to a comfortable canter.

So he found himself alone as he came around yet one more corner, alone and abruptly facing half a dozen Patrics who blocked the road from ditch to trickling ditch. In his own land he'd have seen them, heard them, very likely smelled them long before this; here he was all but under their swords already. *Three fighting men, a woman, two children. Her own, by the way they cling – don't discount her as a fighter. One horse, its rider wounded. Blood and pain-sweat, I can smell them now, too late. The youngest man is frightened, dangerous; his father – if that is his father, leading the horse, I think this is a family – his father is disquiet but no worse. Weaponless, though, and his hands busy, in no case to stop the boy if he chooses to be stupid . . .*

And the boy might indeed have made such a choice, he

looked as though he wanted to. He was carrying a billhook – *too heavy to throw and if he charges me he dies, despite this nag beneath me and our mission here, I'm not sitting still to be hacked at like a wild vine* – which he lifted threateningly, poising himself to charge indeed as he hissed, 'Sharai! Father, beware . . .'

If the boy had carried a bow instead, Jemel thought he might have been dead already, with an arrow in his breast. As it was, he had that moment's grace, while the boy made up his mind; just time enough for the father to say, 'Hold your hand, Thom. You've seen Sharai before, and not sought to kill them.'

'This morning changes that.'

'It need not. Use your eyes, boy. Those we fled, that slew our friends and wounded Soren – they came from the east, and rode in their tribes. If this lad has a tribe, his robe denies it. Besides, they were mounted on camels, not the dregs of some public stable. Hold, I say – unless you want to find yourself spitted,' added shrewdly, with a wary eye on Jemel's ready stillness. 'But this is not a good day for a Sharai to ride out alone. Where from, lad – Surayon-town?'

'The Princip's palace,' Jemel said softly. 'And not quite alone,' as Marron finally came trotting round the corner at his back, all out of time with his mount and grunting with the effort of it.

'No, so I see. What's this? Another boy, another cast-off nag, Sharai dress again but not Sharai blood, I think. What *are* you?'

'Guests of the Princip,' Jemel replied, seeing that Marron had neither breath nor words. 'He sent us to help those on the road, if they should need it – those like yourselves, with wounded in your party. They are ready for you at the palace.'

'We saw the Princip a while back, riding north . . .' For the first time, suspicion shaded his exhausted voice.

'He has his country to protect. His granddaughter is waiting in his stead.'

'Is she so? I thought she was off wandering, she's not been seen all summer.'

'She returned with us today.' *And broke the borders, or the borders were broken through her*, but there was no need to say so much.

'Good enough, then. I'll trust that girl to heal an arrow-wound, and hope her grand-da can do more. We'll need no help to get there, thank you kindly, even without the horses we gave up at the bridge. There are others behind in greater need – though I doubt how much aid you two are worth between you. Those beasts won't double up with wounded men, not more than once or twice for that climb to the palace, and there are dozens that we passed too weak to walk it. And you're hardly dressed to inspire confidence as escorts, on such a morning . . .'

Jemel felt a bright cruel bubble of laughter rise in his chest to say that he knew it, he knew all of it. But he was struck by an idea at the same moment and swallowed the laughter down, glancing aside towards his friend. 'Marron, we could ask Lisan to send her djinni for the injured . . . ?'

'Yes – or they could, to save us going back.' To the family's bewildered stares, Marron elucidated, though not much. 'When you reach the palace, tell Elisande that she could send her djinni to fetch in the badly wounded. Say you met Marron and Jemel, and they suggested it.'

'Elisande's *djinni*?'

'Yes. Its name is the Djinni Tachur, but she calls it Esren.'

'I don't understand. How could she, how could anyone – any mortal – tame or possess a djinni?'

'Did I say it was tame? Go now, go; your man there—'

'—My son, Soren—'

'—Your son is bleeding yet, and needs attention.' Marron had edged his horse close, to check on the wounded man's condition; Jemel could see how he flinched still from an internal absence, coming so near to the stink and flow of blood and feeling nothing, no responsive surge, perhaps a hollowness at his heart. 'Tell Elisande what we have said and other men's sons may be saved also, though they lack horses and the time to reach her.'

'Tell her to have it use the carpet,' Jemel added, 'to carry them; they'll find that easier. She'll understand.'

'Better for you to ride ahead, if that's how these Patrics react to seeing me. They won't all be farmers' boys with pruning-hooks for weapons.' *Besides, if you go first, you won't lead me into the fighting,* where his own blood would certainly take him. Though he still didn't know which side he'd fight on, or for what cause.

'There are Patrics too have crossed the border,' Marron murmured. 'And I'm a stranger and dressed strangely, I don't look Surayonnaise at all and I carry a nobleman's sword.'

'You are still of their own blood.'

'You think that makes a difference? Marshal Fulke is of their own blood. They're more scared of Outremer than they are of the Sharai, or they ought to be. They've traded with the Sharai for a generation – they've traded their children, remember, Elisande lived a year in Rhabat – while they've hidden their whole country from the Kingdom. They should kill me as readily as they would you, or sooner.'

'If you ride first, then I can watch your back.'

'Jemel, we'll ride together and face them down together, whoever challenges us. If you can remember that I slow down on hills, going up or coming down.'

In the Sands, it was bad practice to ride side by side: twice the dustcloud to warn an enemy that you were coming, twice the target for his arrow, and your own friend an obstruction to your sword-arm or your camel's turning. They were not in the Sands now, though. Let them ride peaceably together, then; his good arguments didn't matter in any case. The two of them must have ended up like this, riding side by side, because that was how Marron wanted to ride.

He had sworn – or thought he had sworn – his life and service to the Ghost Walker. Manifestly, Marron was no longer that; and yet he still held sway, Jemel would follow his will regardless of good sense or good tactics.

He wondered when and how that had happened, or why he had been so slow to realise it; and thought it was a question that might interest him for a long time to come, if he were granted life long enough to consider it.

The road wound on and they rode their winding way, meeting more refugees around every turn now. First they sat above an endless line, and then pushed through a crush of weary, filthy faces; only the badly hurt were mounted, and those on a donkey or an ox more often than a horse.

Fairly soon they gave up crying encouragement to the weak, or directions to anyone. These people knew their way.

They must have been expecting this day for a generation. The wounded were making for the palace, as quickly as they might, riding or walking or carried on stretchers; their families would go with them, or else into the city below. Its walls would protect them, they could help to protect its walls. Good. But they needed no one to shout them where to go, any more than they needed swords to watch them. On this road, they were in no danger except from the sky, and that was narrow between the hedges; besides, Jemel had never heard that the Patrics could fly, and he knew that the Sharai could not.

'Ifrit could fly, if they took that shape upon themselves. Jemel had a bow slung across his saddle-horn, but no blessed arrows. Better not to look for 'ifrit, then, for fear of calling them with his questing. There was trouble enough in Surayon; the tribes were in the east, Patrics in the north and the west, and it was a small, small country. What need 'ifrit in the air, or anywhere? A small doomed country, bleeding already; when the various armies met, it would be drowned in blood. Not all its own, but enough, oh God, enough. This land would be rank for a lifetime. The other Patrics called it cursed already; they would learn better, or their children's children would. There were places of great slaughter in the Sands, where dry bones still rolled in the wind. Here they would rot and stink, and poison all the water that this greedy country claimed.

There was water everywhere: he saw it, heard it, smelled it, breathed it. His horse waded in it, and there was mud in the ruts on the road and mud in the ditches. There must have been more mud, the road must have been mud entirely for the wagons to make those ruts; but even now at summer's end, the earth was wet enough to ooze a little, openly under the sun.

That and the noise perhaps should have warned him, even before the walls fell away to open grassland and a road that ran straight at last. He should perhaps have been prepared, though nothing, he thought, could have prepared him truly; only enough that perhaps he could have pretended, he needn't have sat staring like a slack-jawed lackwit.

Jemel had seen the Dead Waters, but they were poison and just another wonder of the Sands. Besides, they didn't move, except when the djinni moved them. They only lay like a salt plain, vast and glimmering and useless, harbouring nothing good. Or had done, till Elisande came to interfere. They might grow sweet again now, he supposed; then they would be a wonder indeed, so very much water and all of it to drink. Then let the Beni Rus and other near tribes look to their borders; so much water must spell a great quantity of war.

There was less water here, immeasurably less if it were or could be measured by the moment, but even so he had to sit and stare, no, gape in a way that he had not – he thought, he hoped – at that other shore, before those other waters.

Jemel had seen an inland sea, but he had never seen a river. Neither had he ever seen a bridge. He knew the words from stories, and from talking with his friends; he had seen aqueducts and castles, and thought he knew both how water would flow within a course – slowly, quietly – and how men would build a crossing-way above it, strong and straight and practical.

But this was Surayon, and he was wrong and twice

wrong, as a young man often is when he imagines that
things will be as he has drawn them in his mind.

For all the seeming gentleness, the roundness of the valley's
bowl, the slopes were steep above. This much he knew; the
palace was set at the road's height and he and Marron had
ridden down from the heights today. The headwaters that
fed the river were set far higher, up where only goat-paths
and foolish children climbed, and there were many of them
in the mountain ranges to north and east and south.
Snowmelt and spring rains would bring a torrent in their
season; even here in summer's lee, Surayon never ran dry and
neither did its river. There was always rain, blowing in from
the sea and caught by the mountain wall; the Sands were dry
because Outremer was not, and this was the wettest of all of
Outremer. If the rains should fail, there were still springs and
hidden lakes high above, lakes that froze in winter and glared
back at sunlight so that they could feed frosty streams with
their meltwaters all summer long. Such streams plunged
toward the valley, young and hectic; met each other, and
became a rabble; heard others like themselves, and raced to
meet them too.

   And so soon, very soon, all come together, they made
this river that Jemel sat staring at: this riotous roaring body
that flexed ice-green muscles and spat a bitter, glittering
froth, that even at this dead end of its season was still a fury
contained but not caged within its channel of rock, that
threatened to reach out and snatch him in.

   If he'd not been mounted, if he'd been standing on his
own weak legs and closer to the bank, he thought it wouldn't
need to make so much effort. He thought he'd have been

sucked in simply by the noise and the rush and the irresistibility of it. Even seated with hands gripping saddle-horn and heels clamped into horse's sides, he still felt dizzy, unrooted, plucked at, dismayed.

He didn't think to wonder what men might call the river. It was a wild thing and far beyond the impertinence of naming. As well name the lion that kills your flock at night, the eagle that takes a lamb, the sun that drops you dead after it has soothed its own thirst by drinking all your water from your skin . . .

And then there was the bridge.

Something broad and solid and built entirely of stone Jemel would have looked for, knowing how the Patric mind turned always to weight instead of speed, how they felt that a castle conquered a land: a very fixed point with squat heavy legs driven deep to deny the force and chaos of the river, armoured perhaps at either end with turrets and embrasures, perhaps even gates against a more deliberate enemy. Serviceable and ugly he would have expected it to be, and defensible in Patric terms, which meant standing and stand-ing and never giving way.

Instead he saw a bow bent against the sky, a challenge against all reason. When he saw people and horses use it as a bridge, he thought that was brave and impertinent, another kind of challenge. Even when he was close enough to see that it actually was a bridge, innocent as he was he did not for one moment believe that all bridges were like this, nor even – or especially not – all the bridges that the Patrics built.

Before and some way before the road ever reached the river, it met a stone embankment, a ramp, a pier that lifted it into a smooth, steep climb to echo the fall of the hillside behind. Leaping from the pier's end came the bridge itself, a tracery of beams interlocked to form a single graceful, high and unsupported arch that bent too steeply and stretched too far surely to be any unaided work of man.

It spanned not only the river, but a wide margin of land on either bank. Jemel couldn't see any reason for that, unless it were the simple reason that they could do it, they could build so high and so strikingly and therefore they had done it, for their own triumphant pleasure and no more. Which perhaps was more djinn than human – he remembered the levelled mountain, the soaring pillar – and certainly not at all Patric.

Roads followed the line of the river on either bank, but again at a distance from it, so that the footings of the bridge served as crossroads. The margin beyond was thickly grassed, right to the river's edge; land here in the valley might be fertile, but there was little enough of it and none to spare. The Sharai did not farm, but even to Jemel's inexperienced eye that grass looked rich and long, ready to be cut and dried in the sun to make hay for the winter.

Today at least, though, another use had been found for those broad margins. Thin but constant streams of people were trailing in from west and east, some on foot and some on horseback, none of them on the roads. Those would be sacrosanct, Jemel guessed, not to have warriors or urgent messengers delayed by refugees. Where the people met at the bridge armed men were taking their horses from them, except for those who were fit enough to ride but too hurt to walk. The impounded beasts were tethered in lines beneath the bridge's arch. Close beside them Jemel could see a few figures lying in the grass, men and women too exhausted or too badly wounded even to ride any further, defeated perhaps by the prospect of the long climb up to the Princip's palace. Children could be carried in a man's arms or a woman's at need, they'd met a few such on the way, but these would need stretchers if the djinni didn't come for them.

He and Marron rode slowly on towards the bridge, shifting their own mounts onto the grass to leave this road free for the refugees. Some were burned and smoke-stained, some were bleeding or had bled; all looked numb, defeated, too worn to show the fear that must be eating at them. Scanning the sky and the far horizons, Jemel saw firesign everywhere but no hint of any enemy.

Two men from the bridge's guard came walking towards them, hands on sword-hilts, not quite threatening but visibly wary of strangers in Sharai dress. With an effort, Jemel kept his own sword-hand in plain sight on the horse's reins.

'Who are you, and where are you bound?'

'Guests of the Princip,' Jemel replied economically. 'Where bound? I think perhaps here. He sent us to watch the road, and to help the wounded; but they need no help that we can give' – *unless the djinni come, that's better help than any, and they'll never know that we gave it* – 'and that road watches itself.'

The one man smiled thinly, while the other went on watching. 'Aye, we've had thirty years to build for this day. The croplands are labyrinths, both sides of the valley. They'll slow down any army.'

Slow, yes, but no more than that. Not halt, and not defeat. The Sharai liked to fight in the open, on the move, on horse or camelback; they would hate that maze of walls and shadows as much as they hated sieges and castle warfare. He thought perhaps that was why Rhabat had always been a place of truce, because no tribe would want to battle for it. But hate it or not, the tribes would enter the labyrinth and take it, field by field if they needed to. It wasn't a castle or anything like, it couldn't be seriously defended.

No more could the Princip's palace; and the town of Surayon had walls, but no other fortifications that Jemel had seen. No keep, certainly no castle, nowhere to make a stand. And yet they'd had thirty years, and knew that this day must come . . .

'Are all your defences meant only for delay?' he asked, as soon as the question occurred to him. It won him a suspicious scowl, but after a moment he got his answer too.

'Well, if the Princip mounts you, he must vouch for you – though I'll dismount you myself, in a moment. Yes, lad, they are. We couldn't ever fight and hope to win, there aren't enough of us and never will be. We could build a castle stronger than the Roq de Rançon, and it would still fall in the end. So we delay and delay, and pull our people back into the high vales, where the roads don't run. There are stronger defences there, walls from cliff to chasm, and no space for siege-engines to reduce them; those we can hold for a while.'

'And when they fall? Or when there is no food, when your stores are gone?'

'Then we're gone too. Princip's guests or not, I'll still keep some of our secrets in the folds of my own mind. But they won't have the massacre they've come for, neither your people nor his,' with a nod at Marron.

It is the Patrics who seek your deaths, Patric – my people want only the land, and the holy places . . .

But at that moment a woman came shambling towards them, her head swathed in a crude blood-soaked linen bandage that came down to cover one eye and half her cheek, but still couldn't cover the whole of her hurt: he could see the clotted tail of a curving slash reach out from below the bandage, almost to the corner of her mouth.

He didn't need to see the way she shied away in a touch of pure terror, that moment when she lifted her gaze from the road to see who sat the horses. Even on so little evidence, a thumb's-length showing of a wound, Jemel could name the weapon and the blow that did that to her, and neither was Patric.

Head-cut from a scimitar, from a mounted Sharai, and he could have been ashamed of his people, except that shame would be no use to her, nor him, nor anyone. He sat quite still, watching as she edged past on the further side of the road, as she lowered her head and trudged on to face the hard climb up to the palace and some measure of healing, though she would carry the scar for life and had probably lost the eye already. Then he turned back to the guard and said, 'You might have given her a horse. Or I could go after her and offer mine . . .'

'No,' the man said, as Jemel had known that he would. 'She's fit to walk, if barely. Horses are reserved for fighting men, that's why we're here. We'll take yours too, if you've no pressing need for them.'

Neither he nor Marron could argue any pressing need, now that they'd seen the situation on the road. He thought perhaps that was another reason why the Princip had sent them here; it might have been the best use he could make of them, to deliver two more mounts from his stable.

The guard was already reaching for his bridle. Jemel would have nodded, dismounted, handed over the reins with no argument, except that just then there was a shout from across the river.

He looked, Marron looked, the guard turned to look – and no question now of handing the horse over, bow-backed nag though it was. It was still a horse. The guard's hand fell away and he ran for his own mount or any mount, shouting to his confrères while he ran; Jemel slammed his heels in hard to kick forward past his suddenly pale, motionless friend and ride to the bridge.

On the further bank, the slow line of refugees had become a turmoil, a hectic race to cross the river. The guards on that side were at the horse-lines, fumbling with saddle and harness, their desperation clear to be seen. *Tension breeds clumsiness; grace and speed come from confidence.* That was a Sharai law, and confidence was a Sharai characteristic; boys were taught to trust themselves.

Even where they couldn't trust their mounts, or their companions. Jemel had no faith at all in the beast he rode, it was only that he'd sooner be on horseback than afoot; he had little enough faith in Marron's following him. Quite apart from that oath the boy had sworn and clung to so determinedly, not to kill again, there was something else to hold him back from this.

It was riders that had made the people flee, that had sent the guards to horse and kept Jemel in the saddle: riders breaking out onto the grassland, with swords in their hands that gleamed not at all in the sunshine, that were dull and stained with hours of use already.

There were not many of the riders, a dozen or so. Still, they were enough to sow panic just with their appearance; and it was that same appearance that had seized Marron in the moment of his first seeing them. They were Patric, of course, mounted on heavy Patric horses. No surprise in that. But the officer who led them wore white dress with a black cloak thrown over, though the black was ripped and the white was darkly marked; the men who followed him wore black entirely, in sign of their brotherhood.

Jemel could name the brotherhood, just from that first sight of them. Marron had belonged to it, had been a brother among brothers and was still not properly free, although they had cast him out. They would burn him as a witch, Jemel knew, if ever they could catch him. Jemel was his only shield, and would have felt more comfortable in that role if he'd been sure of his ward. Marron was still troubled by his slaughter at the Roq; he might see some dark justice in his being given over to the flames. Worse, he might almost welcome his capture, if it could lead to his meeting with the knight Sieur Anton d'Escrivey.

Worse yet, Jemel had sworn an oath to meet with Sieur Anton d'Escrivey on his own account, and could not be ungrateful to see those black-clad fighting men appear on their horses. His only other chance to keep the oath had been for Marron somehow to lead him to that meeting, all unwitting; this way it could happen more naturally, by God's mocking will or his own steel determination. If those ravens were abroad in Surayon, Jemel might contrive to find his man, if they were not simply tossed together. That might even be Sieur Anton on the destrier there, a gift already given, if Jemel could believe it hard enough.

Oath clashed with oath, ringingly in Jemel's exhausted head. If he rode on, if he crossed the bridge that spanned the river Marron would follow, with one reason or another but truly only because Jemel had gone before; if he held back he would make a coward and a traitor of himself.

In truth, there had never been any question about it. He rode on, to the stone footings of the bridge and so up.

At first there were ridges of stone in the cobbles to allow shod hooves a grip in whatever weather. Soon, though, the surface changed. Daunted by the steepness of the wooden arch, his horse defied his heels for a moment, standing stock-still, tense and shivering. He needed hands and voice both to urge it forward again; it needed to find where fillets of wood lay like ribs across the planking to give it purchase. They were there and it did find them, and slowly learned to trust as its shoes bit and did not slip.

Slowly was the only way to make the climb in any case, against the flow of terrified foot-traffic. The bridge was no narrower than the road had been, its breadth surprised Jemel as much as its height and grace, but here the press was urgent; his horse might have balked in the crush or even been driven back by the sheer weight of it, except that he drew his scimitar and held it high. The people squeezed themselves ever tighter together in response, to let him pass. Some screamed when they saw him and cowered back, looked half inclined to fling themselves into the roar of the torrent sooner than face him. More seemed too numbed to care, hurrying only because their companions hurried them.

The bridge rose and rose, the people surged past; at last he reached the crown of the arch and checked the horse. There must be an end to this flow. Let it dwindle and die, let the animal see the cross-pieces where it could safely set its feet for the descent, let the riders see that the bridge was defended.

Let Marron come up to join him, if Marron came. It would be a choice, perhaps a statement: *I ride with you who are my brother* or *I ride to face those who were my brothers* or *I ride to seek him who was my master,* any of those or all, they might all be one in the muddled mind of a boy who had lost and lost and lost again, seeing everything he'd ever come to value taken from him.

Already there were fewer refugees fleeing over the bridge, past Jemel where he sat watching, waiting on the height. More figures milled on the grass below; some ran east or west along the river, while others clearly meant to stay and fight. Only those had taken horses; Jemel was impressed.

The riders were still some distance off, but coming straight down the road towards the bridge. Hoping to take it, no doubt, and to hold it until the main body of their troops came up to reinforce them; looking upstream and down, Jemel could see no other way to cross the river. This would be pivotal, then, its defence crucial to Surayon. He sighed softly, thinking that this was not why he had come to Outremer, nor why he had brought Marron out of the palace today. Perhaps there was after all a god directing events, setting the two of them at the heart of the day's most vital battle from a spirit of sheer mischief.

At his back, he heard the slow sounds of a climbing horse. It might be Marron, urging his mount up with difficulty and determination; it might not. He thought the guards would be coming too, though he thought that they would make an easier, swifter job of it.

He sat without turning his head, watching the riders close towards the bridge, watching the last of the refugees scatter right and left before them, ignored for now but hardly safe so long as these men or others like them rode free in Surayon.

'Ransomers.' A voice at his back and it was Marron, of course it was; he had been sure that it would be.

'Yes.'

'What will you do?'

Jemel laughed, he couldn't help it. 'I will fight, of course. I have fought Ransomers before.' *And lost Jazra to them, and found you.* The debts were complex and confused, running both ways; it was simpler far to fight.

'For Hasan, you fought before. For his visions, his grand dream. Will you fight for the Princip now?'

'The Princip has Hasan. That makes it easy,' which was not true, but easy at least to say. The Princip had visions also and his own grand dream, but they were Patric and had no place in a Sharai imagination, just as a Sharai had no place in a Patric army. 'What will you do?'

'I don't know. I always thought that when the day came, when the time came – if it did, if it ever did, it didn't have to – then I would know, I'd know how I felt and how to deal with it. But—'

But a shrug was the best that he could manage, seemingly, a confession of helplessness.

'They are killing these people, Lisan's people, who have given us sanctuary.'

'Yes.' And he still couldn't kill them, or any more of them, even now and even so; that was inherent in his voice, in his stillness, in his sheathed sword.

'If they find you, if they capture you, they will kill you. With fire, I think. You said you have seen them do that.'

'Yes.' And he still couldn't or wouldn't ride away, go back to the palace, keep his distance, run and hide.

A Sharai would do both, or ought to: kill quickly and draw back, raid and run and live to raid again. But this was a Patric war, on Patric lands; even the tribes were not raiding but invading today. Jemel thought that he was likely to fight an alien battle himself, and so die. He would make a stand with what few Patrics here could swing a sword, warriors or farmers. They would struggle to hold the bridge, because that was such a Patric thing to do; he could almost think like them now if he tried hard, and to their minds it must make sense, it must seem imperative. So they would struggle, and they would die. They would lose this bridge, and die trying to save it; and he would die beside them, because he had no better sense.

Or because that might be Sieur Anton in the black cloak with the bloodstained white beneath, and if not the knight might still be somewhere there, north of the river, out of reach if the bridge were lost and they to the south of it. That thought alone might be enough to hold Marron; it might be enough to hold Jemel.

Something held them both, or they held each other; they held the crown of the bridge until they heard more horses coming up behind them, the men who had had guard of the southern foot.

'What are you waiting for?' one of them growled, suspicion resurgent in his voice. 'There's but half a dozen of our men out there against twice that number, and none of ours is a soldier trained . . .'

'All the more reason for them to take the first shock,' Jemel said softly. 'If you must lose men, better to lose the weakest. They will break the force of the Ransomers' charge; we will meet those who come through, and perhaps we will only have to face one each, or one at a time. But we are not helpless even here, or I am not.'

He lifted the bow from his saddle, ready-strung. It was heavier and clumsier than he was used to, not designed for shooting from the saddle; but he was used to shooting on the gallop, and this horse might move like two gawky boys in a mareskin but when it stood it did stand remarkably still.

The quiver hung beside his leg, Sharai-style. Patrics might carry theirs on their backs, but his people planned always to fight from their horses or camels. A Sharai dismounted was a Sharai crippled, and probably abandoned. Not among the Saren, which was why, one reason why it had been so hard to leave Jazra, even dead Jazra, at the Roq; but the Saren were special, had been special to him. Which was why, one reason why his mind felt so cold and clear, his hand so steady as he took an arrow and nocked it. Those were Ransomers down there, and they were in range now; and they had killed Jazra and not him, and so he had met Marron, and so taken the vows that he had and so been cast out. And so he had lost and won and lost again, and those losses must be paid for before he could even begin to understand the victory.

The knight, the officer might yet be Sieur Anton, and should not die by an arrow, not even Jemel's own. Blade to blade they must be, when they met. He had sworn it. Jazra's shade would be watching him from Paradise; he could be forgiven many things, anything – Marron was not even a case for forgiveness, the question didn't arise – but not that oath. There must be a meeting and there must be a death, blood to pay for blood and loss for loss. That it would be Marron's loss was a strange by-blow, fate's malignancy, a bitter thing for both of them; they did not speak of it. If they had, Jemel would have said that Marron had lost his Sieur Anton already and long ago, that night he fled his brother-hood, his people and his oaths. It was true, it was inarguable – and yet it made no difference. Just as Jemel carried lost Jazra in his heart, so Marron carried the knight.

And when the knight is dead, when I have killed him, Marron – will you swear an oath against me in your turn?

That was why they did not speak of it, there were too many questions they dared not ask. That might even be the true reason why Marron refused to kill, to make it possible for him not to kill Jemel, but Jemel could never ask it.

What he could do, he could kill Marron's former broth-ers: as many as presented themselves before his blade, or now before his arrows.

He sighted, drew – to the chin with the long bow at an angle like the horseman he was, not straight and to the ear like some mudfoot Patric – and shot, watching the arrow carefully in its flight. Like the bow, it was longer and heav-ier than he was used to; no great surprise to see it fly a little shorter and drop a little sooner than he'd intended.

Only a little, though, on both counts. It didn't reach the rider whose heart had been its aim; it took his horse instead, full in the chest and sinking deep.

The horse plunged to its knees, to the ground, dead in a moment. Its rider was flung forward and to the side, directly under the hooves of his confrères who charged beside him. Another rider fell, as his horse stumbled; only one of the two men came to his feet again, and he seemed dazed and hardly dangerous.

'A good shot.'

'A good weapon,' Jemel grunted, already drawing again.

Two men down had not checked the charge; neither would the unsteady line drawn up to challenge it. Warhorses against hacks and nags, it was a battle lost before the men were measured. When the lines met, that would mean an end to archery and a time to ride, a time for swordwork and sweat, to set one more nag against a destrier and test Sharai swiftness against Ransomer weight.

Time yet for one more shaft, though. The range had shortened, there was still no wind; he picked his man and shot, and this time urged his horse into motion while the arrow was still in flight, barely keeping enough attention on it to note that it took his target sweetly in the throat.

The horse was nervous on the downslope, wedging the toe of each hoof firmly against a cross-piece before stepping forward with the next. It would be more nervous in a minute, Jemel thought.

Onto the stone footings at last, and now he could sling his bow across the saddle-horn, kick his beast into a reluctant gallop, draw his scimitar and scream exulting as he rode to war. It would not last, but there was a glee in slipping his restraints at last, abandoning friends and anxieties and all, plunging headlong into the simplicities of battle. The men in black were to kill; the man in black over white was most liable for killing, because he was an officer and never mind whatever other reasons might apply; the blade in his hand was for killing with, so long as the horse between his knees could hold him up.

*

As he'd expected, the charge of the Ransomers had carried them through the first thin line of Surayonnaise defenders, without harm except that their formation was broken short of the bridge that was their target. Now they wheeled and slashed like hunting dogs at the kill, brutal and merciless. Panicked horses broke riderless from the mêlée, and were let run; the men who had backed them were of less interest even than the horses, lying as they were on road or crushed grass, crippled or dead.

It pleased Jemel's sense of the proper order of things, that warriors should defeat farming folk. It would be a great offence if Patric defeated Sharai; at these odds – just the one of him – it seemed not unlikely. He'd send one or two more of them on ahead, though, he was determined on that, before their weight of numbers killed him . . .

The glitter of steel in sunlight and the grate of edge on edge, a blade to meet his and the shock of that meeting jarring his body all through, all but lifting him out of the saddle; and his horse was stumbling and fighting the bridle and had to be hauled around, and the Ransomer's mount was swifter to obey its rider but slower in its movement because it was so much heavier, so that neither sword could strike again before the other; and so they traded blows, hack and thrust and parry while the warhorse bit and kicked and Jemel's nag struggled against his control until he was almost praying for the Ransomer to slash its throat for him, save him the trouble.

It sank abruptly onto its haunches, screaming its pain as an iron-shod hoof connected. Jemel saw the great sword lift above his head, and knew that nothing could stop or block its fall. But he was so slow, this Ransomer, as slow and heavy as his sword, his horse, his thinking . . .

Jemel dropped the reins, put his hand on the saddle-horn and vaulted as the nag surged up again beneath him, that bare moment that he had before the sword could crush body and bone in its fall.

His own strength and the horse's rising threw him high, or high enough. He swung one leg across the hindquarters of the warhorse, just as his shoulder struck the Ransomer in the chest, below his upraised sword-arm. The force of it knocked the man loose from his stirrups, almost knocked him from the saddle altogether. Briefly both were fighting for balance, rather than fighting each other; the Ransomer even dropped the sword that was threatening to overtopple him, letting it swing loose on its lanyard while he clutched at mane and reins to haul himself upright again.

Breathless with effort, Jemel could suddenly have been breathless with laughter instead, though not kindly so. His legs gripped hard on the horse's flanks; his left arm took a grip around the Ransomer's ribs and pulled with a will; he almost expected the man to turn and thank him.

Instead the man died, as Jemel's scimitar moved feather-light across his exposed throat.

It took only a moment to fling the body down, another to slip into the saddle. The Ransomer had been a taller man than Jemel, his stirrups hung too low and all this Patric harness was too heavy, too clumsy to be comfortable in use. But the nag had turned tail and fled, driven off by the pain and bloodstink of the battle. Better a strong and daring horse beneath him, anyway, however awkward its handling. At least it wasn't trying to buck him off; probably too stupid to be loyal, he thought, content to obey whoever sat its saddle and drew on its reins.

He must hope so. The man he wanted, the black-cloaked officer was riding him down already, his darkened sword extended like a lance as the massive destrier hurtled across the ground. No hope of countering such a charge; Jemel's blade would snap if he tried it, just an eye-blink before that great sword skewered him.

At the last moment, then, Jemel flung himself down, wrapping both arms around the horse's neck and sliding half out of the saddle to keep its body between him and the flailing blade.

As soon as he'd felt the wind of its passing, he slithered upright again. One vain slash back at the destrier's crupper, which only demonstrated the deceptive speed of those vast horses; then he was dragging his new mount's head around to follow, not to be a standing target a second time. This wasn't a good moment to play Sharai riding-games, on an unfamiliar horse using unfamiliar tack. The destrier would be slow to halt, slow to turn; when it did, the officer should have neither time nor space to build up to another dangerous charge. Jemel would be right there, eye to eye and blade to blade. He'd been too busy evading his lethal sword to look at the man's face during that first brief passage of arms; this time he'd be ready, and he'd know in a moment. Not likely that it would be Sieur Anton, there were many knights in the Order; but if that one knight were among the invading army, then where else would he want to be but here, riding this dangerous, glorious mission to seize the bridge ahead of all his troops?

Jemel could see the man sawing on his reins to force the

destrier to a halt, and surprised himself by hoping that this was not after all Sieur Anton. It would make little difference whether he was or not, the man was dead either way, white bones riding – but Jemel would be disappointed if Marron's idol turned out to ride so ugly.

This man yanked his horse's head around, but he must have heard Jemel's riding behind him, he must have been ready; he did it one-handed, dropping his shoulder to put all his weight on the haul. That meant there was no good target for Jemel's opening slash as the destrier twisted almost on the spot, only the long sword rising to meet it.

The two blades clashed and rang with the force of the impact, deadening Jemel's fingers but doing no damage else.

Sword and scimitar locked hilt to hilt for a moment; time for one quick glance at the officer's face, and no, it was not Sieur Anton. No matter. This man could die now, and the other later.

Or, of course, Jemel could die now and the other not at all, or not at his hand. Steel battered against steel; he felt his arm start to tire and his horse shy back from the weight and aggression of the destrier. On a Patric warhorse he was trapped into fighting Patric-style, the beast knew nothing else, but he wasn't made or trained for this. His opponent was stronger and wily with it, experienced and fast. In the end, though, the simple strength would be enough. Jemel had blocked a storm of blows, but he couldn't block for ever. Those rare chances he had to cut or thrust, his blade was fended off with a twist of the wrist, a sweet timing that seemed almost contemptuous. He had killed Sand Dancers, but it seemed he could not kill even this one Ransomer, who was not the one he wanted; and he had been so urgent once to kill them all. He bared his teeth in a savage grin, reminded himself that the stars did not in fact turn around his head however often he'd felt certain that they did, and hacked two-handed at the Ransomer's unbreakable guard. His arm was too heavy now for any grace, for any speed or elegance. This was survival or else it was the other thing, and he thought he knew which. It was a matter for regret, and Jazra would be angry, but—

But the Ransomer was backing his horse where he should have been pressing forward, to lean that tremendous weight against Jemel's mount. That was why they bred their destriers so big, not just for the shock of the charge but to overbear their enemies; so why was this man relenting, retreating? Why was he staring past Jemel, over Jemel's shoulder and up, with such an appalled look on his face?

A trick, a trap of some kind, surely, but it could prove lethal to the Ransomer captain before ever he sprung it on Jemel. He'd left himself open to a classic head-cut once already, in the moment of his pulling back, except that Jemel had been too slow to see it in time, too tired to take the chance. There would be other chances, though, as long as the man was so distracted; all it needed was for Jemel to go forward, to grant no respite, to ignore whatever might or might not be happening at his back and claim another life against the immeasurable debt that was Jazra's loss.

What it most needed was for Jemel not to pause, not to hesitate even for a moment, above all not to be tempted into giving even the briefest glance behind him, to see if the Ransomer were faking or truly distrait . . .

Jemel glanced behind him and was entirely still for a

moment, forgetful of Ransomers and war, of friends lost and left behind, forgetful of everything that he knew for certain about the strength and reliability of the world.

While he fought, the river had been rising from its bed. It thrust into the air like a dreadful snake, the waters woven together into a long and sinuous body of black that rippled and sheened with all the dark strength that he had sensed in it before, when it had run noisy but obedient in its channel. Now it was striking out, rebelling, uprising with a will and a wickedness that reminded him forcefully of the Dead Waters when the djinni had been trapped within them . . .

Except that he could still hear that same noisiness that it had in its obedience. And that noise was the rush of water on rock, the grinding of rock on rock within the water, just as it had been before; so no, this was not and could not be the river risen. Which made it a creature risen from the river, not snake-seeming but truly snake; and its snake-head stood as high as the arch of the bridge, and there was a figure on the bridge, a boy on a horse, not moving . . .

Just where Jemel had left him, Marron sat trapped between impossibilities, the shards of broken oaths waiting to pierce him on either bank. He could go neither forward nor back, and so he had gone nowhere; but if he stayed where he was, then that snake was going to eat him. And there would be another oath broken, Jemel abandoned by another oath-breaking boy; Jazra had left him that way, dying when he had promised not to.

He would have turned to slay the Ransomer, strictly in order not to see Marron dying on the bridge; but at that moment the great snake turned its shapeless head – more worm than snake, perhaps, some water-worm compounded of its own element by the way its body seemed to shimmer, to ripple and run – and he saw the dim glitter of red eyes buried deep.

'Ifrit, he thought, he wanted to shriek, *'ifrit!* Not snake or water-worm at all, no creature of the river but spirit-demon on its own malevolent course. These monsters had pursued his companions since the day he'd met the first of them, the girls; they had pursued singly and in battalions and they were pursuing still, and still Jemel had heard no one offer a convincing reason why.

Reasons didn't matter, though, right now. What mattered was Marron, stranded on the bridge without Jemel, without the Daughter, without defence.

Move, ride, run . . . ! He ached to cry out, but he had no breath to do it; and he was too far from the bridge in any case, and Marron would never hear above the roaring of the water and perhaps the pounding of his own desperate blood, or else the screaming of his horse. Marron's blood was a great uncertainty, even without its former passenger; the horse Jemel thought he could rely on.

It did scream, he could see that and hear it too, thin and high enough to sound even above the tumult of the river, as the fighting failed all around him. Whether the 'ifrit heard, he couldn't tell. They seemed to live in silence, only death dragging any kind of noise from them; perhaps they had no sense of sound.

Eyes were enough. Those smoky, sunken lights glowed like irons in a fire, as hot and dry as the creature's native land. Whatever kind of view they gave it – and he couldn't believe that it saw the world as he did, in bright and varied colour; more like Marron's Daughter-tainted sight, perhaps, sharp-drawn but all in red, all hues of blood – that view still showed it everything that stood around, and what there was to kill.

Bent at the neck like a swan, like a hook, like a column of water forever falling and forever failing to fall, it turned its head towards the bridge and couldn't fail to see Marron sitting there like a victim, like a sacrifice, like a boy rapt by the prospect of his own death coming.

Marron wouldn't scream, any more than he would fight. Jemel would do both on his behalf – and had the blade to do the fighting with, ready blessed for the occasion, more use than Marron's precious Dard – but lacked the time to get there. And the mount: his stolen warhorse stood fixed beneath him, all four legs braced and trembling now that it had seen what stirred in the river.

The horses picketed beneath the bridge were in worse case, lathered with terror, rearing and plunging in their lines until they wrenched pegs from the ground or snapped the ropes that held them and went galloping blindly off into the haze.

The one horse above them, on the bridge was the only one that Jemel cared about. He saw it scream again, its ears flattened to its skull, its head flung high and lips drawn back as though it were half stripped of flesh already, displaying all the bones beneath the skin.

Then, blessedly, its terror restored its wits. It bucked once, while Marron clung frantically to mane and saddle-horn and barely kept his seat; the sharp whipcrack sound of its own hind hooves striking the planking acted as a spur, to send it plummeting pell-mell down the bridge.

As the horse skidded headlong from wooden arch onto stone footing, the 'ifrit struck, above and behind.

It coiled back the immense length of this body it had made, and then hurtled forward: like a wilful hammer, like a snake balanced on its tail and using its head to batter at its chosen prey.

It didn't swoop on Marron nor his horse, nor any of the caught or fleeing horses; neither did it bring the crushing weight of its glistening water-made-flesh down upon the men who had been fighting, who fought nothing now but their own horses' need to run, Ransomers and Surayonnaise and a single rapt Sharai.

Instead it rammed its dull and jawless head against the timbers of the bridge, just at the height of the arch, and just the once.

Nothing made by man could have withstood the force of such a blow. The walls of the Roq were perhaps the strongest thing built, certainly the strongest that he had ever seen, and he thought the walls of the Roq would have cracked and crumbled under that assault. Not all at once, though, and not flying apart as though the stones had been just crudely stacked and never sealed together. To be sure, this was – no, this had been – a wooden bridge, almost a thing of paper next to the Roq; but none the less, he thought it should have offered more resistance. He thought the beams should have held until they splintered, not simply scattered themselves like blades of dry grass lifted on the first breath of an encroaching wind.

The 'ifrit drew back, reared up, for a moment was terribly still; Jemel saw how its hot eyes surveyed the river's banks, and he drove his heels so hard into his mount's ribs that the startled warhorse had leaped into a gallop before it truly knew that it was moving.

Back towards the stone footing, a smooth rise that stopped abruptly in a sudden fall now that the bridge was fallen: like a man-made miniature cliff, it was a road's end and nothing more, except that it had been the saving of Marron and was still his refuge. He had, of course, fallen from his horse; the only surprise was that he had clung so long, long enough to fall on cobbles rather than planks, and so save himself the long and lethal fall from the bridge's height.

He stood on the bridge's remnant like a man abandoned, alone on an island of rock in a grassy sea; but that was only seeming. Like every man there – every man but Jemel – he was staring up at the 'ifrit as it stared down.

'Marron! Here, to me . . .'

Blooded scimitar into his left hand, the hand that held the reins; his right stretched out and down, reaching to seize Marron's wrist as the horse thundered past, drag him up without pausing. Boys among the Saren played these games for fun, only realised later that they were battlefield training.

Patric boys, perhaps, never played these games at all. This boy never had, for sure; he was late in holding his hand out for the grip, slow to jump, a dead weight that almost over-toppled them both before Jemel could haul him up and leave him belly-down and kicking across the horse's crupper.

A slow, steady draw on the near rein to bring the horse wheeling around, not to let it run away with them both into the mists and smoke of the river and the day, as it so clearly yearned to do. As soon as he was sure of it, Jemel swivelled in the saddle to help Marron, to hold him as he swung one leg across the barrel width of the horse's hindquarters and pushed himself upright, pale and distraught but somehow almost laughing.

'I forgot,' he gasped, working his way over the cantle so that both boys were squashed into the big Patric saddle, wrapping his arms tight around Jemel's waist for more support than he should strictly need, 'the Daughter would have made the jump easy, but . . .'

'But you don't have that any more. Besides, the horse would never have come near you, if you had still carried it.'

'That's what I forgot. One of those, both maybe,' and he really was laughing, sinking his face into Jemel's neck and his teeth into Jemel's robe to silence it. His own robe was sodden, Jemel realised as the damp began to soak through where their bodies were pressed close together; even his hair was wet and chill, saturated with the water thrown off by the rearing 'ifrit, so close he had been to it. 'I almost forgot it was a horse I was sitting on, until it threw me off. Then I forgot everything except – well, that, there – and then I saw you coming and I was going to leap up swift and easy, just as I could have done any day since we met, and the God's truth, Jemel, I miss it so . . .'

Jemel shook his head. *Later, we can discuss your idiocies later. If we have the chance, we may all be missing it soon. And dying for the lack of it, and one more reason to curse these meddlesome Patrics . . .*

Some men had died already in their own brute squabble; others would die soon, that much was clear, for lack of any way to fight an 'ifrit of any size, let alone this one that stood higher than any tree Jemel had ever seen or imagined, almost as high as the highest tower he knew of in this world, which was the Pillar of Lives that the Dancers had built, and he had climbed that.

This unclimbable, unkillable thing stood high and then fell, dropping its head like a rock driven by a terrible weight of water, all the weight of its neck and body, and that only as much of the body as they had seen so far, rising from the riverbed.

The head dropped, not to savage nor to consume, simply to crush. Like a rock with eyes and with intent, it picked out a still-tethered horse and came down upon it with force enough to drive its own broad snout an arm's length into the ground. Jemel didn't look, didn't want to see what remained of the horse in the bottom of the pit left by the 'ifrit as it withdrew, as it reared up and cast about. Its skin had the slickness of water, nothing clung for long; it scattered earth and grass with the slow swing of its head, a great worm seeking fodder.

It reared up and cast about, and this time found a man unhorsed, afoot. Jemel would have given much to have had his bow and a few arrows to hand still, even unblessed; he would at least have had the vulnerable eyes to aim at, small hope perhaps but hope enough to justify standing off and shooting. Distance spelled safety, of a sort. He could crave safety, when Marron sat at his back and would not be unseated.

His bow was gone, though, and his arrows with it, slung on the saddle of the horse that bolted. He might almost have wished to be Patric in that instant, to be the kind of man who carried bow and quiver at his back; but he was Jemel, he was Sharai. He carried Marron at his back and a scimitar in his hand, and that scimitar at least was blessed.

The man on the ground was running, but his legs were far too short for the work, or else the serpent-spirit was too long in its body, far too long. It stretched, it seem to hang a little in the air and then it struck the man just as it had the horse, so violently that a ripple flowed back all along its length. It couldn't really be made of water, surely, but it did seem so.

Then its head arose, and there was no man now, other than whatever mess lay compacted in the hollow that marked what had been his dying-place.

One of his confrères, though, one of the Ransomers was charging the beast. He might have started his ride as Jemel had, riding to rescue; he must have seen his companion on foot, dazed perhaps and straying too close to the killing-ground.

Unlike Jemel he'd been too slow, come too late. The man had caught the monster's eye, and it needed no more. Now all the Ransomer could do was die bravely or try to flee before he caught the monster's eye himself; but these big horses were slow to halt and slow to turn and slow to speed again.

He had made his choice in any case, determined or despairing. He rode forward at the gallop, driving his horse so hard that it had no chance to bolt or break. It looked half mad already, eyes rolling white and its skin shining sickly, stretched tight to show muscle and tendon wherever it wasn't coated with foam; but it ran obedient to rein and spur, directly towards the 'ifrit.

Jemel spared a glance to find the other Ransomers, and saw one riding frantically back up the road to the north while the others massed uncertainly around their officer. He thought they would charge all together, once they saw another man down. With a messenger sent already to their commander, none of them had any excuse to run. They must rescue or revenge, if they had any honour. Or die trying, of course, which they would do.

Not his land and not his people, this was emphatically not his fight. He was just looking about for the Surayonnaise when he felt one of Marron's arms uncurl from around his waist, and heard the sound of steel scraping from scabbard.

He twisted in the saddle to stare in bewilderment at the glittering purity of Dard drawn and deadly, except that nothing in Marron's hands was deadly now, and nothing on this river-bank could ever be deadly to that monster. Jemel could hurt it, if he were close enough, but surely not to death; and if he were close enough to hurt it, then he would be close enough to die.

'Marron, what—?'

'Will you sit here and watch them be slaughtered?'

'I was slaying them myself, five minutes since. And you were watching.'

'Jemel, that's an 'ifrit, and they don't know how to fight it. And they are men, brothers. Ride, damn you!'

'Whose brothers? Not mine, I am Sharai. And you are renegade, they'd burn us both.'

'They would, aye. And if they were Saren, Jemel, would you still not ride?'

He opened his mouth to say so, and could not. If they were Saren or Beni Rus or any of the tribes – yes, he'd ride.

Even so, 'Not you, Marron. You won't kill it; you can't kill it, with that sword. You can't even hurt it. What are you thinking?'

'I can batter at it,' grimly smiling. 'Poke and prod.'

'Poke and prod? *That?* Marron, *look* at it . . . !'

Plenty to look at suddenly, as the charging Ransomer closed with the 'ifrit. He stood in his stirrups, his straight arm extending his sword-point beyond his manic horse's head. For a moment, as the 'ifrit seemed simply to lie waiting for his strike, Jemel wondered if the man might not carry the luck of the ignorant with him. One good strike to the eye would kill this or any 'ifrit, regardless of size. The Ransomer might not know that, but any warrior charging such a beast must surely aim for the eye . . .

The 'ifrit lay like a snake along the ground, with its unseen tail still in the river if its tail weren't all of the river as it ran all the way to the sea; and just when it seemed as though it was unaccountably dead already, it proved itself viciously, lethally alive. It lashed its body like a whip across the grass, knocking the sword-point aside as though it were a blade of straw and striking the heavy warhorse hard enough to smash every bone in its legs, so hard that the impact hurled it high into the air. Its rider flew from the saddle, fell as it fell, and must have broken bones himself in his falling. Perhaps too many bones, perhaps a fatal number; he lay still after, while the 'ifrit rose up to loom large above his body. It swayed its massive head from side to side, very like a serpent watchfully possessive of its prey.

'Well?' Marron hissed, in Jemel's ear. 'Now will you ride?'

'For what? He is dead.'

'Not yet, not necessarily.'

'White bones, not even walking.'

'Then ride for a glorious death of your own. Why not? When were you ever so shy of it?'

When I found you at my back, but it was hopeless to say so. Jemel sighed and kicked the horse forward, thinking that this was not after all such a terrible place to die, nor such terrible company. He could go to Paradise hand in hand with Marron, leaving their bodies under the shadow of the 'ifrit; Jazra would be forgiving.

The 'ifrit's skin glistened and ran. Its head had stopped its swaying, and the gaze of both unblinking eyes was focused directly on Jemel or else on Marron behind him, on this horse that carried both in under its shadow. Literally so: that towering head blocked the sunlight now, and Jemel was holding his breath, he realised, waiting for it to fall.

In the moment before it did – in the delicacy of that point where the world is toppling beyond fate's measure, where destiny can be fixed by a breath this way or that, where what will be irrevocable, irrecoverable, irreconcilable is still waiting to occur – he ducked and twisted in the saddle, slipped free of Marron's one arm and under the other, gave him a hard shove and watched him fall to ground.

Flinched as he hit; dragged on the horse's rein to check its speed and bring it circling back into that deadly shadow, fighting against its sudden shuddering terror; realised that the monster had not struck after all despite the tempting, dancing target that he made; and still looked first to find Marron, to see him getting slowly to his feet.

'Watch over the Ransomer!' Jemel shouted. That man was lying still, hadn't moved, needed little watching. Jemel's abruptness had simply freed him to tackle the 'ifrit in his own way, without argument and without that draining, distracting urge to keep Marron safe at all costs.

He wasn't safe now, of course, there was nothing safe

about being on foot beneath the brute power of an 'ifrit in its strength, but Jemel was hoping to keep its attention diverted towards himself and his scimitar's edge. He looked up at last to find that poised and perilous head—

—And found it turned away from him, saw the savage eye fixed on Marron as he ran towards the sprawled black body of the Ransomer.

Didn't have time or breath enough to curse. He wheeled the horse with a brutal wrench and forced it forward to the river's edge, where the vast mass of the 'ifrit's body emerged from the water and rested its weight on the bank.

Perhaps one day he would learn to leave the thinking to others, leave his wild ideas to blow away on the wind. For now the wind of his own wild speed was in his hair and he feared that it was not enough even as he crouched low beside the horse's neck and screamed encouragement into its ear, as he beat it on with the flat of his scimitar, as the dank darkness that was the 'ifrit's shadow above and below them gave into the damp darkness of the living wall that was its body directly ahead.

Now, at last, Jemel let the reins slacken in his hand, he gave the horse its head just in time. Its body veered heavily, its hooves bit deep into the turf, it managed – just – to keep its balance and its speed; it swerved past the rising column of the 'ifrit's body, close enough that Jemel could have kicked the thing without taking his foot from the stirrup.

Instead he swung his scimitar, putting all his strength into a single backhand slash as he passed. This close, he could see that the 'ifrit was clad in scales, rather than the inflexible chitinous casing he was used to: a myriad scales, small as his fingernail and overlapping, each one seeming to gleam wetly even in the shadow, each one doubtless as impervious as chitin to any common blade.

His blade was nothing extraordinary, though it was well-made and he kept it wickedly sharp. It was, however, uncommon in the one thing, the blessing that overlaid its edge. So Jemel hewed at the 'ifrit, and there was nothing more extraordinary in the stroke than there was in the weapon, only a young man's determined and desperate strength, his last hope to save his friend. He hewed and felt the blade cut something, cut into something as though through hide and into belly-fat, resistance followed by soft sucking matter that tried to seize the blade. The mad speed of the horse beneath him tugged it free with a jerk that almost snatched the hilt from his hand, that wrenched his weary arm from wrist to shoulder.

It took him just a moment to recover, while the horse tried to outrace the eager river; it took a little longer to steel himself to what must come next. Then he was hauling on the reins again, hauling its head around, turning his own head to see.

A slim straight figure standing above the fallen, the glitter of a sword raised high to poke and prod, the dark swaying shadow over all: relief blurred his vision, so that he had to dash the back of his hand across his eyes and look again.

Marron stood like a symbol of defiance, and should not have lived so long; should not be living now except that the 'ifrit was ignoring him suddenly. Its head wasn't swaying, it was turning: turning to gaze down at its own body where Jemel had slashed it and then turning further, turning to find whatever small thing had committed this outrage.

Jemel could be defiant too, standing in the stirrups and

waving his scimitar; but that was gesture only, his eyes and thoughts were furiously busy at other work. Marron had held off the 'ifrit somehow, for too long to be easily explained. He himself had hurt it but not badly, enough to distract if not enough to harm; when he glanced back he saw water gushing from the darkness of the creature's body, like a spring discharging from a basalt pillar.

It had been smoke before, he'd never seen them bleed anything but smoke and decay had followed, disintegration. This one had come from the river, true — but they'd done that before, he'd seen them erupt from the Dead Waters like a plague of crabs. And those that had eaten rock in the siq, they hadn't bled rock or rock-dust when they died, only that same black smoke, so how was this one holding so much water in its gut?

No matter how. No matter how it sealed the wound either, how the gush slowed to a trickle, to a halt. What did matter was that head, those eyes that pinned him with their hot stare, the long and flexible body twisting back on itself to bring the head down atop him. Mouthless, featureless but for the eyes it would crush, batter, pulp him into this wet earth and leave nothing worth saving, nothing worth the journey back into the Sands.

But he stood as best he could in the low stirrups and yelled, whirled his scimitar, pointed it at the thing's dull snout. If he could only hold firm as the 'ifrit drove down, it would impale itself before ever it reached him. He had no illusions, that would help him not at all, the vast weight of the thing would still fall entire on his head; but if the 'ifrit had any seat of reason, it should be there between its eyes, and his blade might find it out . . .

If the 'ifrit had any physical seat of reason, it shouldn't be able to exist in its own country as a twist of darkness, less palpable even than smoke. In this world, though, it had to form itself a body. Perhaps it had to form itself a mind also. He didn't know, and he thought he never would. He thought he would be dead in moments; he thought it was probably a dream that said perhaps the 'ifrit would be dead also, or hurt enough to die.

He had time for so much thought, and more yet. Puzzled, he stared up at the 'ifrit where it bulked huge in the sky above him: huge but not expanding, not filling his sight, not falling. Huge but growing smaller, receding, drawing back . . .

He must have been right, then, there would be deadly damage done if it skewered itself on his scimitar in trying to reach him. It knew that, it saw that in some shadowed future path, and so it turned away, and so once more Jemel did not die when he was ready to.

But it had done the same with Marron, pulling back from his raised sword; and that was only Dard, a weapon of fine work and lethal edge but it might as well have been a muddy stick, raised against an 'ifrit . . .

No matter. Jemel was alive, and that mattered; Marron was alive, and that mattered more.

And Marron was standing guard above a fallen Ransomer, and there were half a dozen mounted men riding towards him now and going to reach him before Jemel could get there; and they were all Ransomers, and that mattered most of all just now, because Jemel couldn't imagine what he would say to them, except that it was likely to be something stupid, dangerous, disastrous. His name, perhaps, and his history . . . ?

If he had the time to do it. The 'ifrit hadn't gone away; it still loomed above the gathering men, the weight of its body imprinting grass and ground between the road and the river, breaking the bank where it trailed down into the water. And even if it were shy of Jemel's blade and shy of Marron's too, it had shown no such shyness with regard to the Ransomers. A body of men riding in under its shadow now, they must surely attract more than its attention.

Marron and their own man were both boosted up onto others' horses. The Ransomer cried out as they lifted him, sharp enough for Jemel to hear it above the muted thunder of his own mount's hooves and the gusty wind of its breathing; he couldn't be too badly broken, then, if he could hurt so much and still have air to scream it.

Riding behind a black-clad brother, Marron kept his sword aloft. Jemel wondered briefly if any of the Ransomers would recognise the blade, but that was a small concern if it could keep the 'ifrit at bay, by whatever miracle the boy had manufactured now.

It did that. Somehow Dard was giving the monster pause, holding it back from its strike. He was riding one-handed himself with his scimitar held high in the other, more a reminder than a real threat as his eyes moved constantly between the black above and the black ahead, the creature that could kill in a moment if his attention wandered and the group of men on horseback who were bearing his friend away.

They cantered beyond reach of the 'ifrit, beyond its furthest conceivable stretch, and drew rein on the road. They stood their horses so close together, Jemel could not see Marron among them now that Dard was no longer waving above their heads like a banner, like a needle of light to stitch the eye. He didn't know whether his friend still sat another man's horse, whether he'd slid gratefully to ground the first chance he'd been given, whether he was crouched above the wounded man to offer what small help he could or whether he was lying hurt or dead himself already, victim to a swift and cruel justice.

All he did know was that there was a body of men, a wall of men between himself and Marron: men he'd been fighting with only minutes previously, brothers to men that he'd killed in their full view. And he was Sharai, and he was in Surayon. They ought, he thought, to be merciless.

He pulled gently on the rein, easing the lathered, exhausted horse down through its paces to a steady walk; at a safe distance from the 'ifrit he wiped his scimitar on the saddle-cloth and sheathed it at his side. Sitting straight in the saddle, proud and calm, he rode towards whatever doom they held for him.

Weapons drawn but not raised against him, simply held in hand, and that was nothing but good sense at such a time; he'd have kept his drawn if his position had been less vulnerable or his confidence greater. Faces watchful, wary but not he hoped judgemental, not condemning, in so far as he could read Patric faces, which was not so far at all.

First a silence, and then a voice:

'Sieur Parrish, Fra' Colcan, brothers, this is Jemel of the Sharai, and you have seen what a warrior he is, and what a foe even to that devil . . .'

And that was Marron's voice, and the relief in hearing it might have had him tearful in a moment, if so many hard-eyed men had not been watching him. He tried to peer through the shifting hedge of their bodies to spy his friend, but was distracted by another voice, bitter and resentful.

'A fine warrior, aye – he killed Sim, and Breck too if those were his arrows come from the bridge . . .'

'Leave be, for now.' The officer, the knight came shouldering through his men, his authority as heavy, as forceful as his destrier. 'We killed our share.'

'Not of his people. And what's he doing, fighting with the heretics? He'll not be alone, make no doubt of that. If we take him back and put him to the question—'

'Leave be, I said! You, Jacquel – I'll have silence from you, or we'll all hear you after service tomorrow night. Unless you'd rather follow the Sharai, and ride alone against that – thing?'

'I'll do that, sieur,' sullen but determined, from a broad, scarred man in his middle years who pushed his hood back suddenly to show Jemel his face, and his contemptuous scowl. 'I'm not afraid . . .'

'Then you should be,' Jemel said softly. 'Has Ma— my friend not told you what that is?'

'An 'ifrit, he said. And so? Demons die before the true faith, as heretics die in the God's fire and unbelievers at the sword's edge.' He hefted his own sword significantly; Jemel moved not a muscle, answering the challenge only with his stillness. 'I say I'm as fit to face it down as any hell-damned Sharai boy – that's if the devil-dealing boy didn't summon the thing himself. Would you trust him, sieur? Or this dog of his, this cur who came to feed on our wounded?'

Now Jemel's hand did move, despite all resolution; it gripped his weapon's hilt and would have drawn it, but that the knight forestalled him with a gesture, *patience, leave my men to me . . .*

'Who came to stand over our wounded, Jacquel, and protect him from the 'ifrit. See the world as it is, man; there is honour even here, however tainted. Yes, I will trust these men, both of them, though I think you might be wrong about who dogs whom between them. It would honour you to do as the Sharai has done, it would honour any man. I will not order you to it, but—'

'You should forbid it, rather,' Jemel interrupted. 'Not you nor any man can ride against that and live.'

'What, only you, Sharai?'

'Yes, though I intend no insult by it.'

'What else is this, but insult? Our horses are as fast or faster; that's Sim's stolen mount beneath you now. Your horsemanship is superior, perhaps, but not by much, and our beasts know and trust us. Our arms are as strong as yours, boy—'

'Stronger,' Jacquel growled, 'he's a mocking puppy, nothing more.'

'Stronger, sure,' Jemel admitted, 'and yet the 'ifrit would kill you, where it holds off from me who hurt it once and from my companion, who has not hurt it at all. The virtue lies in our weapons, and those we cannot share with you.'

'Our swords are as sharp as yours, and better made.'

'Doubtless so, and yet they will not bite that hide. No normal edge, no point will mark it unless the weapon's been blessed by an imam. Mine is, yours are not and cannot be. You saw how it scorned your own man's weapon,' with just a flick of his eyes to find that man, laid on the grass now, pale and unmoving, 'and you saw how it feared my blade, how it withdrew. It's too big, though, a scimitar alone can't hope to slay it . . .'

'Nor scimitar and sword together,' Marron said suddenly, pushing through the mass of men with some excitement. 'But, Jemel, you saw how it held back from me, and Dard has never been touched by one of your imams. I said a prayer over it myself, just now, as I was standing there; and the 'ifrit had been coming for me, and it stopped at that moment, as I blessed the blade . . .'

Jemel shook his head, bewildered. 'You are no priest. Not even of your own religion.'

'No – but I was a brother once, of this Order of Ransom,' said proudly, defiantly, staring about. *Doom,* Jemel thought grimly, seeing how the faces changed. 'We are all – I mean, I was consecrated to the service of the God, as all the brothers are. That's as good as being a priest; we can lead the services at need, say a prayer over the dying on a battlefield to haste them into heaven – and bless a weapon too.'

The men were muttering; Jemel heard 'heresy', and thought that a congregation of imams would say the same.

'How did you know the blessing would hold?' A man might trust to such a thing and find too late that it was no more than empty words, spoken over unheeding steel.

'I didn't, but the 'ifrit thought it would. If I was wrong, we both were.'

Could an 'ifrit be wrong, about such a matter? Jemel wasn't sure. They could be deceived by someone sly enough to work the trick, Lisan had done that in Julianne's cell; but Marron was so afflicted with honesty, he couldn't deceive the most gullible of innocents. Surely the only sense here was that this 'ifrit had heard him bless his blade, had felt the edge of that against its future and so backed away. In which case . . .

'You say any brother of the Order can act as priest?'

'If I can, then surely any. I was cast out, I must have been anathematised after I left the Roq, and I no longer follow the teachings of the priests – and yet the virtue holds. I think the virtue holds . . .'

Jemel turned to the knight again. 'You heard. He speaks as true as he knows; if he's right, it may not be any of us who dies this day. Say a prayer over your weapons, bless each separate blade, dedicate it to your own God's good and maybe, maybe we can fight that creature, if we fight it all together.'

The knight smiled thinly, and shook his head.

'Not me, lad. I'm no brother, sworn to the Order and the God. We knights take different vows, and mean them less, sometimes. Fra' Colcan!'

'Sieur?'

'You are the men's confessor; that is as good as a priest. Come, bless my blade, then all the rest.' Then, as the other man hesitated, 'Where's the harm? A Sharai's idea, true, from a recusant's suggestion; but no matter for that, it would still be a prayer to the God. If it means no more, there is still no hurt in it. We can flee that demon, or we can fight it; and I for one do not mean to flee, so long as we have any hope of fighting. Nor do I mean to see any man under my command ahead of me. I have heard stories all my life about the invulnerability of spirits; I have also heard that the God can conquer all. You have given your life to that belief. What holds you now, if you are true to your own calling?'

'Sieur, I don't know what to say.'

'You heard the preceptor bless us all, before we rode. You have heard prayers and blessings every day of your life, man, and repeated them to the priest. Is it so hard to find a few words now, when you need them more? Here is my sword; come, put the God's light into its steel, to set against the blackness of that soulless thing. Or would you see a Sharai boy better armed for the fight, and the only one still living when it's done?'

'No, sieur . . .'

The older man laid an ungloved hand on his officer's blade, ran the tip of his tongue across his lips and began to whisper.

'Louder, Fra' Colcan. I want all the men to hear it, to know that the God rides with them and their steel cannot fail.'

Men could still fail, where steel was strongest. Jemel said nothing, though. Nor did he listen, as the Ransomer's voice rose in a strong petition to his God. He was wondering what 'recusant' might mean, and how to extricate Marron and himself from among these men when – if ever – the 'ifrit was killed or driven off, now that the bridge was down and they were all trapped together on this side of the river.

First, though, there was the 'ifrit to face, and no certainty as to how that would fall out. There could be no certainty in the world any more, he thought, where a Sharai who hated Ransomers could ride with Ransomers in Patric country against a spirit that threatened nothing that was Sharai.

Only a bridge, he thought, *it only came to kill a bridge* – except that Marron had been on the bridge, and perhaps it had come to kill him? If so it had failed twice already, once on the bridge and once on the bank, when it had seemed almost to use the injured Ransomer as a lure. Even without his blood-companion, Marron was proving extremely hard to kill; Jemel intended to keep him so.

'Look,' one of the Ransomers muttered, pointing back past Jemel's shoulder. 'It's coming out of the water.'

The 'ifrit looked more than ever like a giant worm, creeping up out of the river and shimmering darkly in the sunlight as it dragged itself across the grass. It was vast, massive like a living wall, flexing like a whip; slow, though, slow to move under all that rippling weight of water. Swift to strike, they'd all seen that, but not made for progress on dry ground. A man on foot could outrace it, if he were not rigid with fear; on their horses they could ride in circles and torment it like hunting dogs around a bull antelope. If their weapons were potent after a Patric blessing, if their horses would obey . . .

'Excellent,' he said. 'It made itself for the water; it's too stupid to know how weak it is on land.'

He drew his scimitar to show these Patrics once more how speed and skill and determination could override both the brute strength of the 'ifrit and the terror of the horse, at least in the hands of a Sharai. The Ransomer knight was ahead of him, though, snatching a newly blessed lance, tucking it firmly beneath his arm and urging his horse into motion.

Draw its attention one way, strike from another, strike and run, wheel back and strike again – a Sharai party wouldn't need to be told. He hoped the same was true of these men; if they didn't know already, it was too late now to teach them how to fight desert-style. And this was a desert spirit despite its watery body, made for desert men to kill.

He cried out and kicked his horse forward without a backward glance, permitting himself just the slightest huff of relief when he heard voices raised, the pursuit of hooves at his back.

They rode to the other flank of the 'ifrit, yelling and waving their weapons. Once they had closed almost to within its striking distance, though, their captain called out to them, a few words that brought them swiftly into battle order. If three or four attacked at once, the 'ifrit could not kill them all, and they would see then what kind of damage they might do. Always remembering that Jemel had slashed the black hide open once already, only to see it repair itself . . .

The 'ifrit moved, snake-swift suddenly where it had been worm-slow before. Its head struck out towards the knight, while its body coiled for strength and balance. Before blunt black vastness could reach slender steel-tipped lance, though, the creature reversed itself shockingly, making a brutal lash of itself as it had before, whipping around like a flail aimed at the small group of horsemen opposite.

They lifted steel against it, all they could do, flimsy pinprick weapons against unconquerable bulk; and just before it reached them, the 'ifrit reared, snatching its head into the air so that it skimmed just above their points' reach.

It does, it fears those weapons now . . . Jemel yelled exultantly, to encourage the same understanding in the Ransomers; then he kicked hard, to urge his reluctant horse in closer.

The Ransomer knight was charging in earnest now, sods flying from his destrier's hooves as man and horse thundered towards the knotted body of the beast, the lance before them like a thorn thrust towards a waterskin.

The 'ifrit turned its head to watch the approach, seemed poised to strike down, ruthless and unanswerable – and then did not, tried rather to slither away. Too late: the knight drove his lance home with a cry, with all the strength of his arm backed by his horse's weight and speed.

Which was the moment that Jemel realised he'd been holding his breath, because it fled from him all at once in an explosive sigh as the lance's point sunk deep, half a shaft's depth into the great barrel thickness of the 'ifrit's body.

Water spurted from the wound it made, such a forceful jet that it soaked the knight in a moment and all but knocked him from his saddle. The next moment, his horse finally succumbed to terror. It reared up screaming, forelegs threshing the air; half-fallen already, the Ransomer clung desperately to the arched neck, barely contriving to keep his seat, losing stirrups and reins in the process, surely losing any sight of what went on around him.

That was the time for the 'ifrit to strike back, before the knight could recover and draw sword against it. Jemel caught his breath again, watching for the monstrous head to fall even as he lashed his own mount with the slack of his reins, trying to reach the man in time to save his life.

Trying his utmost, and doomed to fail: he'd been too slow to start and there was too much ground to cover. Courage could be repaid with honour, as it deserved to be, but not alas with rescue.

Except that he was not the only other man in the field. While he rode to the aid of their commander, the other Ransomers drove in like a spear's head – except for one who couldn't force his horse to do it, who abandoned the beast and ran in afoot – to slash and hew at the 'ifrit's flank. Its writhing scattered them in a moment, but where it writhed it sprayed water from half a dozen fresh wounds. Its head twisted about, abandoning the knight in search of this new threat but not striking down at it, fended off by the harm promised by a hedge of glittering steel raised against it.

By the time it turned back to find the knight again, he had recovered seat, reins and stirrups, steadied his frantic mount and drawn his great sword.

The 'ifrit seemed to squirm for a moment, caught between implacable and dangerous foes on either side. It was still losing water from where the lance-shaft was sunk into its side; if it healed its every other wound, Jemel thought, it could not heal that so long as the weapon stayed caught in its hide.

It had the same thought, perhaps; or else it had achieved what it had come to do, or else it had failed and lost its chance. Whichever, it sought to turn, to retreat into the river. Jemel had reached it now, though, and knew his own best way to hurt it. He galloped past it as he had before, closing so swiftly that his horse barely had time to register its fear before they were away; and as he passed, he swung his scimitar, just as he had before except that this time he passed on the near side and cut forward from the shoulder, hacking down.

A man, any animal of flesh would have been laid open to the bone by such a stroke. The 'ifrit had no flesh, no bone; there was only the water that came gushing from a great rent ripped in its shimmering skin. The weight of water fell on them both, Jemel and the horse, like a buffet to shove them further off; cruelly cold and drenching, it was too much for one of them at least. Staggering from the hammer-blow of the flood against its ribs, the horse ignored good sense and Jemel's instructions from rein and heel. It tried to swivel sharply away from the looming, lashing body of the 'ifrit; its hooves slipped on wet grass when it was unbalanced already, and it came crashing to earth.

All his life, Jemel had had ponies and horses fall beneath him. Usually it was his own fault, and often deliberate; it was a battle move that had brought many an enemy down to his death and every Sharai boy practised it, every Sharai mount was trained to make it and to recover after.

Jemel was slipping his feet free of the stirrups as soon as he felt the horse's shoulder go; before the animal hit ground, he was out of the saddle and rolling, one arm flung out to keep his scimitar from slashing him.

He rolled twice and came to his feet on the third roll, muddy and soaked but barely bruised, blade at the ready. The horse was still struggling up; Jemel let it go, less use than his own feet now. The twisting coil of the 'ifrit's body loomed above him, spewing water; a little distance off was the Ransomer knight, also dismounted, standing close by the monster and simply chopping at it two-handed.

The skin still rippled, but it was flaccid now, hanging in wrinkles where it had been firm and full. Jemel thrust his scimitar in and sawed like the crudest of farmers, seeing it bulge and split, seeing how there were almost two layers to the hide before the water spilled out to spoil his sight of it.

The monster's tail came flicking around, in a desperate attempt at them. With its former strength and speed, that blow might have killed them both at once, would certainly have broken bones and left them helpless; but they met it each with his sword's point and felt the shudder that racked the creature, heard for the first time a shrill whistling scream even though it lacked a mouth to make such a noise or any.

It was hard to stand in sodden clothes on the slipperiness of mud and force tired muscles into another stroke and yet another, when every stroke was followed by another bitter rush of ice-cold water. They endured, though, watching each other now as much as they watched the 'ifrit, or more than that. Jemel felt a smile rising even through the filth and the sweat of the work as he recognised that the Ransomer knight was not so much older than himself, and that neither one of them was ready to slack off before the other did.

It was butchers' work before long, the 'ifrit lying slack and leaking from a hundred punctures, like a water-skin pricked by a swarm of sandflies. It was enough, Jemel thought. He waded through the muddy run-off to the creature's head, gazed for a moment into the abiding glitter of its hot eye, and thrust his scimitar in to follow his gaze.

The whistle shrilled for a moment, and was cut off. The fire dimmed and died around Jemel's blade as he withdrew it; curious, he touched his hand lightly to the steel and found it hot beneath his fingers. Clean and dry also, as though he'd sunk it into the Sands at noon, or into the sands of the djinn's country at any hour; and yet the 'ifrit was full of water, and that was so cold . . .

Yet more opportunities to prove that, as the glimmering black body clouded over, turned to mist and faded with its death. All its remaining water was left behind as though it had been always a separate thing, the 'ifrit simply the living skin that contained it. Jemel touched his chest uncertainly, thinking of heart and belly and guts as something alien, other than himself; and then he was deluged by the water's collapse, knocked from his feet with the force of it, spluttering beneath it for one terrible moment before it could spread out across the wide grassland and let him come slowly to his feet. He had been sodden before, wetter than he could remember; now, smeared all over with liquid mud, he felt as though the wetness had soaked all the way through to the dry desert soul of him.

That must have been why he was laughing.

He squelched over to where the knight was lying spread-eagled and struggling to rise under the weight of chainmail and mud on all his many garments, under the exhaustion of a day's fighting and this hackwork to follow, under the paralysing grip of his own all-consuming laughter.

Jemel reached his left hand down, gripped a gauntlet and hauled mightily. Felt his feet start to slip, just as the knight came up; for a moment they hung in balance, each dependent on the other for a desperate support. Then their legs scrambled for purchase and found it, they saved themselves with an ungainly lurch together, and still managed not to let go of each other's hands, neither of their weapons.

Briefly they stood eye to eye and grinning broadly; then the knight took a pace backwards, released his grip and bowed formally.

'My thanks, for your sword and your wisdom too, for knowing how to meet it.'

'That was my friend's wisdom, more than mine,' and he was already looking around to find Marron, to be sure of him, left alone with enemies all over. He seemed well, but more than that, he seemed distant; too much so. Like the creature that Marron used to carry in his blood, Jemel could go only so far from him and be comfortable.

So he turned and began to trudge through the mire. There were other Ransomers, too many of them and not all like this; Jemel meant to be at Marron's side before any started to ask questions about what he'd said before. None had reacted violently to Marron's face and he still might not have given his name, but that didn't mean that he was safe among them.

The knight was at Jemel's elbow in a moment, and beckoning to his men where they stood a little distance off, on the other margin of this temporary swamp the 'ifrit had made in its fighting, in its death, first ploughing up the grassland with its writhings and then saturating it with all that water.

Jemel was still astonished by the water, and still confused. He had stood often beside the Dead Waters and been overwhelmed by so immeasurable a quantity, when a man's remaining days of life in the Sands could be counted out in waterskins; he had seen those waters rise up and flood Rhabat, and what had happened here was a puddle, the rushing roaring river was a trickle next to that. But yet the Dead Waters were a poison, and a man's life could only be measured by what he might drink. What this 'ifrit had drunk first a man might drink after, Jemel had tasted it on his lips and not died, been sharply refreshed; and he had rarely been all wet with water, had never been half-drowned in so very much. He was shaken by the simple solid fact of it, by the mud that sucked at his legs and the unaccustomed weight of what he wore, and he was baffled by the sweetness and purity of what had come from the belly of an 'ifrit.

He had grit on his lips now, and spat rather than swallow. Almost he wanted to run back and jump into the river just as he was, to have its fierce currents suck all the filth from his skin and clothing. There might be a rock he could cling to, to save being washed away and battered to nothing, to a brutal end on other rocks between here and the true sea that he had not seen, that he could not quite imagine. If there were, if he did, he wondered if he might lie in the water and open his mouth and have the river scour him inside as well as out, if it might flow swift and harsh through gullet and belly and gut to leave him cleaner than marble, cleaner than the high dunes after a sandstorm, cleaner than starlight on a dreamless, sleepless night . . .

That picture in his mind showed him another unexpectedly, almost same, and he wondered if he knew now why the 'ifrit had been so full of water, and how it had grown so big; but there was dry grass under his feet now and Marron was not so far ahead, and there were other questions that mattered more. Questions that he dared not ask, despite that laughing moment that he'd shared with the knight.

No more laughter in Jemel, then, and none that he could see or hear in the knight. Marron was laughing, though; possibly laughing at them both, though his eyes were fixed on Jemel. He was on his knees beside the broken man he'd saved, they'd saved together. There really shouldn't have been anything funny in that, but he was definitely laughing, though he did it as quietly and privately as he did everything.

'Mud-babies,' he said, in response to Jemel's stare. 'We had a story when I was growing up, where a barren woman makes herself a family of babies from the river's mud. She loves them dearly, until her carping neighbour tells her that they're dirty. So she fetches a bowl of water and she washes them, and they all dissolve to mud again. You look just like a mud-baby, I'd be afraid to wash you . . .'

The Sharai told the same story only drier, with a single baby made from sand and spittle. Perhaps all the stories would be wetter in a country like this, where they could let so much water run to waste.

'The 'ifrit nearly washed me into the river,' he grunted, scowling at Marron for his mood. If ever there was a time to be serious, to be vigilant, to watch every word, this must be it.

'You pricked it like a waterskin, it dribbled itself to death.'

'I think it was a waterskin,' he said, 'I think it made itself that way, just a skin and filled itself with water, to be long enough to reach the bridge. Those we fought at Rhabat must have eaten a lot of rock to make the size they did. This one lacked the time to feed itself, perhaps.'

'It might have been smaller and done its work as easily,' the Ransomer said at his side. 'That bridge was built to fall; I was sent ahead to capture it before they could knock out the pins that held it from collapsing. My commander will be displeased with me, but even he didn't foresee a demon rising from the river.'

I think the demon foresaw Marron, standing on the bridge; and so it made itself so long, to strike so high and have a chance at him. Though why it would, when he is harmless now . . .

'Tell your commander of this,' Marron said, perhaps not so harmless after all; he did after all know the ways of these people, as Jemel did not. 'Tell him that these demons, these 'ifrit are the true enemy. We can know that, without knowing why they are so active against us. Against us *all*, as you have seen. Tell him to bless his weapons, and to hunt 'ifrit. Tell him there is more virtue in cleansing this or any land of such monstrosities than there is in hunting men who say their prayers another way than he, more honour in this fight than in burning women and children, tell him that. And say that Marron said so.'

Jemel flinched at the name; the Ransomer seemed not to react to it at all. 'I do not think that I will tell the marshal what you say, but I might tell Sieur Anton.'

There was a stillness that had no connection with the wind, a chill that was nothing to do with ice-water still dripping from their clothes. Jemel felt it in Marron, and in himself; each of them was suddenly very watchful of the other, though their eyes they kept fixed on the Ransomer.

'Your man here,' Marron said, speaking just as carefully as the knight had before him, 'he could live, but he needs urgent care. He would die before he reached your camp, if you tried to carry him. He needs healing, and we can fetch him to it; but you must trust us, and those whose land this is.'

'Trust him to Surayonnaise sorcery, you mean.'

'Yes. If you want him to live.'

'Sieur, no!' That from one of his men behind. 'We should kill them both, the Sharai killed ours . . .'

'And would you see Tryss die, after what's been done to save him? By these men, as much as ourselves?'

'We've only his word for that. Tryss is tough . . .'

'Not too tough to break. You helped bear him back from the demon's shadow, you know his hurts. The boy's right, we have no infirmarer fit to heal those. Give me your word that he'll be returned to us unharmed, lad, and you can have him.'

'Returned and healed, I swear it.'

'Marron,' Jemel said, 'how can we take him? How can we go? The bridge is gone, and we cannot cross that water.'

Which was good news for Surayon, perhaps, that neither could the Patrics, or this army of Patrics, these Ransomers. There was another army to the south, of course, come from Ascariel; and then there were the Sharai to the east, who might be on either bank or both. When all those armies met, Jemel thought, there would be a killing great enough to dam even this river, if it were not blocked already with the dead of Surayon.

But Marron only smiled, and said, 'Esren.'

It sounded like a summons, though spoken quietly, as Lisan spoke it. Jemel looked instinctively for a distortion of light in the smoky air, and could not see one. But he saw the Ransomers look wary, and back off up the road; he heard Marron say, 'Yes, keep your distance – and put up your weapons, you could do great damage here. You too, Jemel.'

He slipped the point of his scimitar into the sheath on his belt, and slid it home. Then, only then did he turn, to see a carpet waft its way towards them, hovering at knee-height above the torn and trampled grass. He could have laughed again, perhaps, at the absurdity of it, except that he was not given the time.

'Esren, take up Jemel and this wounded man. Take them to Lisan, at the palace.'

'I will, Ghost Walker.'

That was wrong, he was not Ghost Walker now; but there was more wrong than words could cover. Jemel twisted back,

met Marron's steady and expectant gaze, and was startled
again by the soft unexpected brown of the eyes; startled into
stammering as he said, 'What, what about you . . . ?'

'I am not coming.'

'Marron . . .'

'I have to speak to him, Jemel.'

'About what? Peace, no more killing? He will not hear
you.'

'No. About war, and slaughter. He will hear me, I think.
Tell the others, Jemel; there are other armies on the march,
other commanders who need to hear. Esren, take him now.'

'No!'

But there was a band of solid air about his chest, a weave
of wind that he could neither find nor fight. The djinni
lifted him onto the carpet as a man might lift a struggling
babe, and set him down beside the broken Ransomer, and
carried him away so swiftly that he barely had the time to
watch his friend dwindle out of sight, out of all staring.

15

Little Lights

Tired of cautious counsels, Imber had struck out wild and chancy, and taken his little army with him.

Had struck out wild and chancy and wrong, and was paying for it now, finding it priced in equal parts shame and frustration.

Had overruled Karel to do it, in front of his cousin's own men, and so shown himself to be callow and foolish and unfit for any command, all those accusations that Karel conspicuously did not level against him. He felt them all the more keenly because he had to make them all himself.

It had all been so clear to him at the time, at the noon to which this was the sunset. They had trailed the Sharai army all day, like carrion crows drawn to the stink of smoke and blood. Even though the dead were Surayonnaise or occasionally Sharai and so cursed either way, he had still been sickened by the slaughter, farms and villages surprised and brutally destroyed. The Sharai had been swift about their work; the Elessans could have followed from the mountains to the sea and found nothing but leavings, gleaned not a life, not a thread of life from the ruins.

And so, when he had ridden to the top of a sudden knoll and stood in his stirrups and seen how the river turned in a long loop ahead of them before coiling back so far that almost it met its younger self, Imber had made a decision. The Sharai forces were keeping to the north bank, and so had been forced into a wide detour; he and those he led would cross by the arching stone bridge he could see just ahead, and cut across the narrow span to meet the river returning. That way they might hope to get ahead of the Sharai, if they pressed hard now. At the least, the shortcut would bring them in touch with those they chased.

He had been deeply pleased with the plan and with himself, and correspondingly furious when Karel rejected it. No point in getting ahead, Karel had said; why add their little strength to the Surayonnaise and so be overwhelmed beside them, fighting with outcasts and heretics? Better to sneak up behind, though it took days to do; the Sharai knew they had left a desolation behind them, so wouldn't be watching their backs too closely. That was the chance for a small force to do significant damage, in the dark and by surprise. Besides, it was stupid to take a chance on unmapped country. How did he know there would be a bridge downstream, to bring them back to the north bank and the enemy?

Of course there would be a bridge, Imber had snarled, this was farming country and the river was unfordable. He would stake his life and honour on there being a bridge; and Karel might be older and more experienced but Imber was the Baron-heir and would be obeyed in this, the men would follow him . . .

And so they did, and Karel too, wary and unhappy. Even the peasants they led were troubled, though at least they weren't tested by any more scenes of slaughter. They were better armed than they had been, as the Sharai hadn't stopped to scavenge weapons from the fallen, but their eyes were wide with this first taint of war, and Imber had been glad to offer them at least a little relief from it.

He had led them across the ridge that had forced the river aside, and so down to meet it returning – and, of course, there had not been a bridge.

From there to here there had still not been a bridge. He had been disbelieving at first, sure that they must find something, bridge or ford around the next bend, or the next after that; how could people live, with their land so impassably divided?

'Carefully,' Karel had answered, with a light touch to his voice that only emphasised his abiding anger. 'If you lived in Surayon, would you not be careful? The people may have their own secret ways to cross – tunnels, perhaps, or sorcerous devices – but they have ensured that an army does not.'

Certainly, they had done that. The Sharai army was on the other bank, and he had no way to come at it; only a handful of bowmen, as little use as a thorn-twig against an armoured knight, and Karel had told them to save their arrows. The Sharai had arrows to spare, it seemed, and sent a flight over at intervals, with mocking calls for seasoning. Karel kept the march out of range and sent men running to glean those shafts, against a future need; he told Imber to be grateful for his enemies' generosity.

That was when they had the time to be generous, when they weren't concerned with real fighting, rather than teasing his mockery of an army. They were facing true resistance now, as the Surayonnaise organised; watching from his distance, Imber saw squads of mounted men meet and part and meet again, leaving some of their number fallen at every meeting. He saw men afoot ambush camel-riders, and die largely. He also saw what was no honourable warfare, what had to be the sorcery he'd heard of all his life: gouts of fire flung from the hand to sear and burn whatever flesh it touched, man or camel. Instinctively he made the sign of the God to ward off evil, though none had been flung towards him or his men. They had been ignored, indeed, apart from the Sharai mockery; they had met no one on this side of the river, finding only homesteads recently abandoned, barns and stables deserted, flocks of sheep and goats wandering untended.

Above all, though, what Imber saw on the other side of the river was the steady advance of the Sharai. Opposition delayed them, magic disturbed them but nothing lasted, nothing was for long. They slew or drove off whoever confronted them; they burned whatever crops or buildings they discovered; they rode on.

All Imber could do was to match them, to keep pace. Through all that was left of the day he had done that, and now as the sun set he could still only shadow, only watch from across the water and copy what they did. They made camp in the last of the light, not to venture into unknown territory in darkness; so did he. They scavenged food and firewood from an abandoned farm but camped on open ground, not to be surprised in the night and trapped within walls that could burn; so did he. It was the Sharai way in any case to scorn buildings and sleep beneath the stars, but here there was good sense to it; Imber understood that, after Karel explained it to him.

In truth, it was Karel who chose the site, set the perimeter guard, made all the decisions for his own men and the ragtag brigade that followed them. Publicly he deferred to Imber, and that was salt on the wound, making it oh-so-clear whose fault it was that they were so divided from the enemy, so useless and alone; privately he made suggestions, and Imber was far too sick with himself to argue. Besides, Karel was doubtless right, right again. They'd lost their chance at the Sharai, he had squandered it with his naïvety and pride. The most they could hope for would be to do the God's work, bring the God's justice on the heretic Surayonnaise. He supposed he should be ordering the fields and the buildings burned as they passed through, but he refused to imitate the Sharai that far. He wouldn't even have the livestock slaughtered, beyond the men's need to eat. Fire and death lay heavy on this land already, the air was thick with it; he was here in pursuit of Julianne and to fight the Kingdom's enemies, not to pillage and despoil. This was good fertile farmland, a jewel to the eye after the dust and drought of the road he'd ridden to come here. Nor had any sorcery made it so: only water and work, he knew enough to see that. So let it lie, leave it be. He thought new hands would glean this season's crop, what survived of it; Surayon could not live through this. No need to harm it further.

He hoped, prayed that Julianne could live through this, but didn't know how to help her. There had been no sign of her on the trail, no hint even that they were right to seek her in Surayon. Ever since they'd crossed the border he'd looked constantly for the djinni to come again and tell him where she'd gone, where she'd been taken to; all he'd seen was the devastation that marked where the Sharai had come before him.

Even the sunset was a vivid desolation, fierce reds and oranges, colours of burning. He was glad to see the last of its light leave the sky, though the stars that followed could offer him small comfort, glimmering through a murky haze.

There was a fire at hand, the men's company, and roasting meat; there was another fire, strangers' faces, the peasant army he had enlisted at Revanchard. He could sit among them and learn their stories, as a good commander should. There was a tent where he could be alone, to sulk or scowl or sleep; there was always Karel, who would always talk or listen as he chose.

But there were also fires like distant flecks of gold, and that was the Sharai beyond the river, and he thought their lights were mocking him, *here we are*; there were other, duller glares behind, which were the blazes the Sharai had set in corn and cabin, barn and barley-field. Those accused him, *they are here, and this is what they did, and where were you?*

He could settle neither at one cookfire, nor at the other; he couldn't play either the popular young lord or the determined captain, not tonight. No more could he retire to his tent and lock himself away behind canvas walls. They were too restrictive and too thin, both at once; they would keep him in but not keep the world at bay.

Restless and angry with himself even for being restless, for giving so much away, he paced away from the firelight with a muttered word to Karel about making a round of the pickets.

They'd been set at all points of the compass on this hostile ground, two experienced men to each and no lights permitted; but it was easy enough to find them when he knew where to look, when he'd had a voice in placing them. He had no trouble in slipping by.

He wanted only to walk, to calm his restless spirit and confront his failings away from the silence and the stares of other men. If he walked on the open grassland, though, the pickets were sure to spot him. A figure moving in the night, when all their own men were known to be within the circle of their camp – he'd be lucky to live long enough to reveal his stupidity. All the archers in the troop practised night-shooting. The Sharai might have scouted ahead and found a bridge at last, which Karel had refused to look for; the Surayonnaise might appear at last on this side of the river, to fight any and all invaders; one thing must be certain in the pickets' minds, that no one beyond their perimeter could be a friend.

Still, he needn't make a target of himself. Forced by Sharai arrows to ride at the southern margin of this meadowland, he'd seen how the cultivated ground beyond had been divided by dry stone walls into a myriad of small fields. In the last few miles, those walls had risen higher and higher, so that now they would stand even above the head of a mounted man.

He didn't understand the walls – what sense was it, to build so high and make more shade for crops that loved the sun? – but he could use them now. Karel had distrusted them deeply, seeing their rare entranceways as snares or sally-ports. Imber didn't believe in hidden hordes. If Surayon had an army, they must surely have met it by now; it wouldn't be lurking while its country burned.

He walked westerly along the wall with his left hand brushing the rough dry stonework, his eyes growing sharper as he left the lights of the camp ever further behind him. He could still see the glimmer of Sharai fires in the corner of his eye and the smouldering glow they'd left in the countryside behind them, but didn't turn his head to look that way, to dwell upon his failure. Nor to look the other in some hapless search for redemption, for justification, for a bridge.

He gazed due north all the way to a dense ragged rising curtain, the mountain wall that ought to be a guard to this valley principality and was not. It made a flat and sharp-edged shadow against the dull glitter of the sky, like a piece of parchment ripped across; its near flanks were lit well enough to give it shape, and Imber could see dim lights in the deeps, high in the vales. Signs of habitation they must be, some kind of defensive fastnesses; the land was not so empty as it appeared, though he still thought he was right not to look for an army. At least the people had had somewhere to run to. There must be others too on this side of the river . . .

Below the first low spurs of the mountains he could see terraced farmland that descended into an irregular patchwork, a pattern of darkness that was clearly the mirror of what he had here, small fields separated by high walls. And then the meadows running down to the river, mirror again.

The river itself ran too deep or was banked too high, he couldn't see the rush of the water, only hear it distantly like a constant whisper against his thoughts, as the smoke in the air was a constant whisper in his throat to say that war was here and he was a part of it.

Not far ahead now was the next opening in the wall,

giving access to the fields beyond. It would be darker in
there, with no view of the valley, but the darker the better to
suit his mood; he wasn't going in for his eyes' sake. He
wanted to pace, and the constriction of walls was preferable
to this endless run of grass; out here there was nothing to
make him turn, he might walk all the way to the far marshes
and be thought to have abandoned his men.

Distress always had him on his feet and moving, or yearning to move. His wedding-night had been a torment to him,
lying cramped in a cot in the preceptor's study, awake all the
night and painfully, brutally aware of Julianne being equally
wakeful in the next room, afraid even to shift his weight for
fear of the bed's creak alerting her to his own discomfort.
Worse than the ache in his muscles had been the ache in his
heart, and both had been urging him up onto his feet to out-
pace the dark, the one thing that he would not do, could not
do to her.

He couldn't have done it tonight either, anywhere in
camp. Bad enough to make a fine fool of himself; worse far
to underscore it with a display of petulant weakness. Out
here and unobserved, he could pace till dawn if he was
driven to it.

He paused in the entranceway for one last look across the
wide empty pastureland, and saw that it was no longer
empty.

Saw something moving, something so dark and low that
any distant sentry might easily mistake it for a drift of
smoke, a flock of ground-running birds, even an eddy in the
wind stirring the grasses in some mockery of pattern or
intent.

Standing closer as he was, alert as he was to every nuance

of light and shade, he could name it for what it was, which was unnameable: a creature but nothing natural, nothing he had ever seen or heard about. Something come out of the river, he thought; something heading certainly, directly for him.

It was black as an insect, as a beetle is black; its body shimmered in the starlight. It was swift, too, as an insect is swift to scurry. He couldn't see how many legs it had, but many, he thought. Too many, he was sure.

He gripped the hilt of his sword where it was hanging at his belt and gave thanks for that much good sense, at least. Only a fool would have slipped away from his company on hostile ground without a weapon; but then, only a fool would have slipped away at all. Surely only a fool would not now shout to draw friends to him, rather than face something unknown and sinister in this confusing light . . .

None the less, Imber did not shout. He stepped cautiously through the gap in the wall and took shelter behind it, never taking his eyes from that rapid shadow. As it drew closer he could make better guesses at its size and shape. Because it was low like a beetle, because it moved and glinted like a beetle, he'd half prepared himself to meet and do battle with a beetle: cruelly overgrown, perhaps, malign certainly, but a beetle none the less.

Assumptions were foolish, assumptions in the dark were dangerous, ignorance was always deadly. The creature's body was segmented like a millipede's, and it scuttled on as many legs. It stood as high as a man's waist, perhaps; looking at it now, seeing it close, Imber felt no inclination to stand his ground and discover its measurements by his sword's length. It had eyes that glowed red in the dark, and mouth-parts that

champed together as it ran. Whatever kind of monster this
might be – and he'd never heard that even the apostates
of the Folded Land bred anything so vile as this – Imber
couldn't imagine himself fending it off with a longsword.

He could see no more of the creatures crawling up from
the river's bed, who might have assaulted the camp. Just the
one, and coming straight for him: he didn't believe in coincidence, nor in ill chance. He did believe in spirits, since he
had met his first. He remembered how the djinni had sought
him out and found him, simply by an act of will; there were
other spirits in this Sanctuary Land, no doubt some that
had the same authority over aspects of the world not know-
able to mortals. Magic, the peasants called it, and priests
and children also. He thought he could smell its working
here and now, unless what he was smelling was his own
terror of it, that he'd thought he'd long outgrown.

Nothing but wisdom, to be afraid of what was coming:
what he could see under starlight, what he must meet alone
and ill-prepared, armed but unarmoured, understanding
nothing of what he saw. In his wisdom he stepped backward
into the seeming shelter of the high-walled fields; once out
of the creature's sight, he turned and stared about him, praying not to have stepped into a trap.

Relief: there was another opening in another wall, a way
out of this stone box. He ploughed heedlessly through a
flourishing crop of waist-high millet, till he came to the
darker shadow of the gap in the wall.

Looked through – and of course it was not a way out,
only a way into the next field. But this one too offered an
onward path, a further opening; and the alternative was to
go back and fight the creature, which was what he'd already

considered and rejected. A man might choose rightly or wrongly, but once he'd chosen he should stand by that choice. In woman, or in war: which was after all why he was here, how he'd found a war while he was looking for his woman. He'd be as steadfast in the one as in the other, which for now meant steadfast in flight. If the monstrous thing caught him before he found safety – if there were any safety from that thing, any safety at all in this cursed country – then he'd fight, because he must. Until then, he would run.

And did run, through crop to opening; and paused there to look back, and saw no sign of creature following. Went through thinking that perhaps he did have a chance, perhaps it would grow confused within this maze of walls, and lose his trail. Tried not to think about the djinni, how impossible it was to imagine that spirit confused by any mortal choice.

Glanced up at the sky, within its sudden square horizons – and was suddenly confused himself, reeling almost, as though the ground beneath his feet had shifted sharply out of true. Turned itself around entirely, in fact, because all the stars lay backwards overhead, as mind-twistingly wrong as a river that ran uphill . . .

No. Absurd. It only took a moment to recover. Not the ground, not the stars: it was himself all turned around. He couldn't think how in so short a space, but high walls and speed and fear together must have confounded his sense of direction. That way lay north as it always had, the stars proclaimed it so; which meant he was facing south, which was a puzzle but none the less a place to start from. And the way out of this field lay to the east, and he should take it quickly, before the scuttling demon caught him up.

And did, and found himself facing three blank walls, and

thought he had run himself into a trap after all; except that as he twisted around in desperation, he saw another way out in the wall that he'd just come through, barely three paces from the way that he had come.

That shouldn't have been possible, or else the other way out should lead back into the field that he had come from, no advantage. But he hadn't seen it from the other side, and thought it hadn't been there; and when he ran through it he was in a field of sunflowers, where he certainly hadn't been before. And he looked up, and again the stars were lying wrongly strewn across the sky, and there was that shuddering sense of dislocation before he could pull his own understanding into line with them.

He was beginning to comprehend. There was a spell bound up in these walls and fields, different from but like to the greater spell that had hidden Surayon away for a generation. That had lost a country; this would lose a man within a labyrinth and likely keep him lost, turning him more dizzy at every doorway, having him step unseeing from world to world. If he tried to retrace his steps, he thought he'd never find them.

If not for that, he might have felt quite grateful; for neither, surely, would anyone find him by following his steps. It was his body being shifted and shuffled around here, not his thoughts. Even the demonseed that tracked him should have trouble chasing his shadow through this unpredictable dance. He could have accepted even the staggering uncertainty that seized him every time he glanced up to what was fixed and immovable, the patterned stars, if he hadn't felt these walls as a man-trap closed about him. A spell like this must be built to keep what it captured, another protection for the land.

Then he saw the creature he was fleeing; he saw its silhouette blank out the stars as it rose above the wall ahead, flowed over and ran lightly down. Still on a direct bearing, entirely unperturbed by magic, still heading straight for him.

The spell lay in the gates, then, and it knew to avoid them. And had the legs, the build to do that, to run like a millipede up and down the walls. Perhaps it had always known that he would seek shelter in this maze; perhaps it had waited deliberately to catch him here, though its reasons were obscure.

Imber could climb walls, and hope to see a way out from the top; but he couldn't climb as the monster did, as easily as running. It was coming through the sunflowers, the blooms were high enough to hide it but it must be close, it must catch him in a moment.

Imber turned and ran, back the way he'd come.

As he'd anticipated, it led him not out into the open but further into confusion, into fields he had not seen: more crops, more doorways, more moments of jolting shock as the stars realigned themselves at every turn. His head spun, his muscles ached, his breathing laboured as he drove himself on and on, faster, harder – and often, often he saw the creature that he fled, ahead or to one side or the other, always coming over a wall with that smooth scuttling run that spoke of infinite stamina, infinite knowingness – *I will always find you, little mortal* – and infinite patience, *you cannot always run.*

Soon he found himself stumbling over his own tracks in the soft earth, but they were no use to him, going this way or that, no kind of guide. The earth was soft and watered, the crops were tended, weeded, must be harvested – men must come and go within this maze. Magicians, no doubt, immune to any spell: though it was hard to think of such men grubbing their fingers in the earth to grow millet for their morning porridge.

It was hard to think at all, as the sweat ran and the air stung his throat, his legs trembled beneath his weight and he all but fell as he plunged through one more doorway.

Plunged from near-darkness into soft and simple light, and all but fell again from the simple shock of it; and did fall to his knees – more in wonder than in worship, though how much more he was glad not to be challenged on – when he saw who stood there among the broadleaf greens.

There were two figures in the light. One was a boy who held a lamp, a page in service to his mistress; the other was Julianne.

They made a strange and troubling tableau, standing with their feet in leaves that were green where the pool of lamp-light fell, that turned silver under the stars and black beneath the walls; they looked as though they stood on the stillness of the ocean, as though they were statues cast in light against the darkness that only they could hold back, and only for a time, what time they lingered here. He did not think they would linger long. Not for a moment did he think that Julianne was here to be rescued, by him or anyone.

She smiled at him, and gestured: *stand up, come closer.*

He did both, slowly and reverently, which might equally have been said *slowly and fearfully*, because that too was true. He felt as though he were approaching some sudden manifestation of the God, a revelation to be both feared and revered.

When he was near enough she reached out a hand, though, in a way that was all wife and nothing saintly: as though she needed the reassurance of his physical touch as urgently as he did hers.

Their fingers met, and gripped: fumblingly at first, and then with a solid certainty. He might have crushed her hand between both of his; he might have dragged her to him, crushed her slenderness against his weight; he might have crushed any resistance in her, to claim her as his again. He thought there was permission, implicit in her touch.

He did none of those. He let her choose how tightly she held him, tighter than a social favour but not tight enough for passion, never tight enough for him. He felt a tremble in her fingers and thought that she was fighting her own instincts, holding back.

He stood and gazed at her. His lips shaped her name without breath, without sound. He marvelled at her as he always had, at her height and beauty and the straight gaze of her measuring eyes. He wondered how he stood in her assessment, and only then why and how she stood here, waiting to assess; and only then – when the boy shifted at her side and all the shadows danced in time with him to remind Imber of what had driven him here to find her – only then, too late for any dream of safety, did he realise how very far he'd failed her.

Still breathless from the running, breathless from the startlement of her, breathless as ever in her presence, he gasped what little air he could and croaked, ''Ware, run, there's a demon, I'll face it while you flee . . .'

It came out strangled, all but incomprehensible; it was in any case too late. His arm had pointed back, behind him, through the opening, but the monster came over the wall as it always did. This was like a child's dream – a dream of his own, as he'd found that becoming adult was no defence against the nightmares that had always dogged his sleeping: a dream of being hunted by an unchanging, relentless evil that would always, always reach him in the end. Except that he had never for one moment imagined that he was dreaming tonight, despite the unearthly horror and uncanny knowingness of what he fled, the impossibility of what and who he'd found. That thing was real and really here, and so was he, and so appallingly was Julianne.

He gestured her back with his arm, and the boy with her, so that they at least had the gateway to flee through, and he had the creature before him. It had followed him this far, perhaps he was all it wanted; if not he could buy them some time at any rate, though not he feared a very great deal of time. He could see the thing more clearly and more closely now that he was no longer running, now that it was coming to him across a ground-crop, now there was a true and steady light. If he'd ever felt a moment's shame at how he'd fled at first sight of it, he could have abandoned that at a glance. Some creatures were not made for men to fight. This wicked beast had horns and claws and antennae like whips, such as no millipede that ever walked the world; its glowing eyes were shielded within plates of black and gleaming armour. Its innumerable feet marched forward like tattooing-needles, swift and sharp and deadly. It would overrun him, he thought, and never pause, never need to glance behind. Every step would puncture and pierce deep; never mind a man, a hundred such steps would shred a bull to rags and threads of flesh, and it could take a hundred steps to cover the length of a man, the length of him . . .

'Run,' he said, making the effort now to find his voice, too late. 'Julianne, run – and you, boy, go with her. This thing is mine.'

'If yours, why should we run?' she countered stubbornly. 'Imber, has that blade been blessed?'

'What?'

'By a priest, a man of faith sworn to the God . . .'

'No.' What was she talking about, why was she talking at all, why was she not in flight? Because she had some care for him, and would not leave him? That was madness, they would all die together, to no point. He drew breath to say so: to scream it, indeed, to throw her from him by the sheer power of his desperation and all of it located in his voice. If he were a djinni he would have made a great wind to carry her far, far from here, far from wherever she had come from, out of this cursed country and safe home to his own hearth which ought also to be hers . . .

No djinni he, and not fast enough even to shout; she cut across him, and was as sharp and piercing as any one of the monster's needle legs that had carried it so close now, almost the length of the field and she was still talking.

'Then put it up, it'll do you no good. That's an 'ifrit, and no mortal sword can cut it. The knife I carried is blessed, but . . .'

'But I have that, my lady.' The boy, his first words of the night, and Imber was almost too distrait to hear them, far too concerned, confused to care.

Until all the shadows shrank and turned and stretched at once, as the lamp was lobbed high over his shoulder and flared as it fell, splashed like a coughing ball of fire onto the monster's head.

The creature – 'ifrit, she had said, and perhaps he should have named it himself, he surely should have known – reared up till half its length stood tall, higher than a man, legs and antennae waving wildly and ineffectually while the oil blazed between its eyes.

A small body hurtled past Imber, chased by a voice, Julianne's, shrieking as he had meant to shriek himself:

'Roald, no! It's too short, you can't—!'

But he could, or he thought he could, or he thought he had to try. And he was a boy, with a lady to defend and a knight to watch him do it; she had no hope of calling him back. Imber recognised the impulse even as he started forward himself, too slow, too late again.

The boy Roald had a knife in his hand: a knife that lacked perhaps a little elegance to be appropriate as a lady's blade, but lacked much more to be a weapon fit to face a monster such as this. Imber had run from doing that with his own long sword.

Now he had to, unwilling as he was. He advanced against the beast, but not fast enough to catch the boy ahead. He was vaguely aware that Julianne was shouting something at his back; it might have been a name – *Esren, Esren, damn you!* – but it meant nothing to him.

What he saw meant little more. There was light, but not enough; the flaring oil had burned bright enough to blind him to the more delicate web of starlight, and now that flare had subsided he was squinting, struggling with shadows.

Worse, though, was the insanity of what he watched, like a tapestry of myth brought into life. The monster was compounded of demonseed and horror, all the terrors of all the stories of the dark; the boy was just a boy, a rough-clad serving lad with a poniard in his fist. He'd likely never used a knife in his life except to cut himself a trencher from the loaf, and the thing he fought was vastly bigger than himself and vastly malign. There was a smell this close, a dry and dusty odour, the spice-smell of the desert, nothing at all unpleasant except that Imber's soul abhorred it. It was the stink of evil embodied, all that he most loathed, that he'd been trained to fear and to resist; and so he should not be surprised to meet it here in Surayon, and yet he was. A faint sense-memory said it had the same core-smell as the djinni, and that was a surprise too, but the greatest was to see the boy Roald not overwhelmed by anything about the creature, the 'ifrit: not its size, not its appearance, not its emanation of wickedness.

Roald simply ran at it while it was still erect, in pain or shock from its burning; he held his blade high and two-handed – his tiny blade, it seemed, against the looming black of the monster's belly and the waving menace of its legs – and plunged it home.

And it sank home where it truly looked as though it shouldn't, as though that shimmering black armour ought to shrug it off without a scratch; sank haft-deep through the belly-plates of the beast as easily as though it slid through the mirror surface of a pool. Roald screamed in triumph and dragged it down like a slaughterer's man opening an ox, and Imber looked for the slipperiness of guts to come tumbling out of the rent he made.

Nothing did, unless there was a little smoke or steam, a mistiness suddenly around them. Well, the creature had fire in its eyes; perhaps its guts were smoking hot. Perhaps its guts were smoke. Whatever, it was wounded; and Roald was at it again already, slashing at its threshing legs. They were blows without force, driven by pure fury – and fury was enough, because wherever blade met limb it was the limb that failed. The boy might have been cutting taut strings with a razor, or lopping branches with his father's billhook.

The creature was peering down at him, though, from its reared height; and it had legs enough and to spare, and seemed not to be too deeply hurt. As Julianne had said, the knife was simply too short to do much damage. The boy was doing brave work, but it needed a man with a man's strength and steel to finish the task.

Conscious of Julianne at his back – Julianne in danger, yes, but also and very much Julianne watching him – Imber called out, 'Back, lad, you get back, you can do no more here,' as he closed with the creature.

Distracted as it was, he had an executioner's time to set himself, time to swing. Brought his long sword scything round with all the power and timing of a lifetime's training, backed by his long hunt and his bad day and his own determined fury, not to disgrace himself before this girl, this stranger his wife. There was a sweet edge on his blade, that he knew, and it should have sheared the monster's body half through, given how easily the boy's small knife had cut it.

Instead the edge met the armour and didn't cut, didn't mark, didn't even skid off at an angle; it simply stopped. Stopped dead, as though he'd been trying to hew granite. The jar of its stopping snagged every bone in his body, numbed his arms up to his shoulders and snatched the air from his lungs again; the blade rang falsely and dropped from his helpless fingers.

Stunned, bewildered, he was as checked as his blade: standing useless, only peripherally aware of Julianne's bellow from behind, hearing without understanding as she roared, 'I *told* you, your sword's no good! Back, both, the knife's as bad . . .'

But Roald wasn't listening to her any more than he had to Imber. He was still there, a close arm's reach from the 'ifrit, still hacking and slashing, still carving his way into the monstrous body. Every stroke cut through the carapace that had halted Imber's heavy sword; it was slow work, though, and the 'ifrit was aware, poised like a snake on its tail, and it seemed to Imber as though the whole world were equally poised and still, waiting for the strike. Only the boy seemed oblivious, grunting and cursing under his breath as he chopped. Julianne was shrieking at him again, but he was as deaf to her as he was to the moment.

Imber might have tried to seize him, to snatch him back, but that would only have meant both of them falling under the monster's horns, and no defence for Julianne thereafter. Instead he fumbled on the ground for his fallen sword, scrabbling to pluck it up with deadened hands. He lifted the point again against the 'ifrit, thinking perhaps to thrust it into a wound that the boy had made before him, if he couldn't cut through that impervious shell, see what damage a length of good Outremer steel could wreak in a demon's innards, if once it could get in there . . .

Still slow and shaken, though, he couldn't come at it soon enough. Something had got through to the boy, Julianne's sudden silence perhaps where her voice had never reached him. He glanced up from his butchery, and must have seen two baleful eyes of fire, with a blinded one between: eyes that must have swelled against the glitterdust of the sky behind, as the creature's head drove down.

Perhaps he did not, could not see the horns that impaled him, throat and belly; perhaps the double blow came so swiftly that he felt nothing, neither cold nor heat nor terror before he died.

The creature's head flung sideways, flung the broken body off; and then it turned, seeking its next enemy.

Imber was there, and he could hear it hiss as it found him. It had lost all its speed, though, it was floundering almost on its belly from the loss of legs and substance where Roald had hewn at it; and Julianne was calling again, and this time Imber would listen.

'Its eye, Imber, strike at its eye, that's all the hope you have . . .'

And her hope also, for she lacked even a knife to meet it with, she'd said so. She used to flee from him, now she depended on him; somehow that firmed his double-handed grip, steadied his nerve and his trembling muscles both, gave him safe footing and a clear gaze.

He tracked the turn of the creature's head, watched his target and trusted his lady's word; waited his moment, which was just that moment before it thrust itself forward to destroy him.

He plunged towards it, all his weight behind the blow. The creature seemed to rise to meet the blade, so perfect was his timing or so gracious the hand of the God at his back to hurl him at it.

His point found the sunken socket of the 'ifrit's red eye,

and all the length of his blade followed it down. Down and down, while his body twisted to avoid the reaching horns; he felt the quillons grate against its shell, and then a terrible wrench on his shoulder as the creature hurtled abruptly upwards, hissing like water on a fire now, like water falling over broken stones.

He let go of the sword's haft, or felt it slide from his grip rather as he fell hard on his back. Lay gazing up at the black shadow of the 'ifrit's bulk as it eclipsed half the sky, half the stars that he could see; it was a shadow that swayed, that was going to topple at any moment, and when it did it would topple towards him, land atop him, crush him entirely out of life and there was nothing he could do, he was more than winded this time and could move his body no more than dead Roald could move his own . . .

A moment before the 'ifrit fell, Imber remembered what the djinni had said to him on that strange summoning day that had begun this journey, if in truth it had not begun before, the day Julianne had snared his heart and kept it. *Great peril,* the djinni had said, and he'd thought it meant at Revanchard, he'd thought himself come too late to save her, failed in adventure as he had failed in love. But she'd been in peril here, terrible peril. He and the boy between them had met the need of the moment; neither one of them could have done the work alone. He was sorry for the boy's death, but glad also, as he was glad of his own that was coming; he felt that a price had been paid tonight, innocence and honour, and it was a small price for her life and less than she was worth . . .

And then the 'ifrit began to fall; and as it fell it faded, so that he could see the stars through its body like jewels through a thickness of veils. Brighter and brighter they shone while the dark came down like a curtain falling too slowly, losing all its rush: a curtain of finer and finer fabric as it seemed, more and more sheer, until when at last it touched him it was only smoke drifting coldly in the windlessness, drifting and dying and gone, and his sword fell down heavily beside him as though a cloud had held it for a time and dropped it now, weary of its weight and pointlessness.

He lay still for a while, wondering how long he had been dreaming, just when he had parted company with the reality of the night. Then he tried to sit up, and the sharp ache in his shoulder, the soreness down his ribs and spine, the slow exhaustion in his legs all said that there was no dreaming here: that he had fled a monster, he had met Julianne, he had seen evil dissipate in death.

Unsure whether to feel shame or comfort that he had needed that assurance, the physical proof of wonders, he sat up despite the pain of it, and looked around. He was looking of course for her, for proof positive, and finding her of course where she should be, where she had to be because she was Julianne: not with him but with Roald, kneeling above the boy's body over by the wall where the demonseed had tossed him, cradling his head in her lap while her hair fell down to hide his face and her own.

If Imber could sit, Imber could stand, or so he told himself. And so did; and if he could stand, he could walk, and so did. Slowly, totteringly almost, but thinking to stoop on the way to retrieve his sword and the dagger also that the boy had used, that was lying amid the crushed leaves of the ruined crop, that had seemed to own some special virtue.

Blessed, Julianne had called it; and so it had proved. She had also said that it was hers before the boy had it; he would give it back to her, she deserved the protection of the blessed, but not yet. First she must endure his own protection, for as long as she would take it. Weakened and bruised he might be, broken he was not. With his sword in the one hand, with her magic dagger in the other, he'd still place his body between her and any peril that came at them, whether it was another 'ifrit tonight or a Sharai warrior tomorrow, a conjuror from Surayon in this strange valley or his raging uncle in his own home in Elessi . . .

He could do that, he could stand against any danger and live or die on the hazard, because he knew what to do and why he did it. He didn't know what to say to a weeping girl – this weeping girl, his wife – where she crouched over the body of a boy who'd died for her sake.

Imber knew Roald's name, but nothing more. He could say what would surely be said later by some officious fool, what they would have said in the court at home, that the boy had died bravely and with honour and so had won his place in heaven; he thought it would sound facile and empty here. He could say how glad he was, how grateful that Roald would give his life to save Julianne's; but she might be neither glad nor grateful, she might despise a man who felt that way or who expected her to feel it.

He could say nothing, and so did, and despised himself for the weakness of it even while he tried to comfort himself with excuses: that she'd prefer a patient silence to fatuous words, that she needed that silence to say goodbye to the boy, or to recover herself from grief and be ready to face him.

In the end, though – soon, though – she would have to

lift her head and look at him. Because she was Julianne, because he was Imber. Because they were married, in every way except what the law allowed to married love.

Because she had to do it, so she did; and it was soon, too soon perhaps for her, dragged unwilling from her mourning by what must have seemed his quiet patience.

'I met him today,' she said, her voice hoarse with shouting, thick with unshed tears. 'Only today. He insisted that he come with me. I said, I said it was only to escape the kitchens for an hour; he was so angry . . .'

He died with honour; *I am glad he came*; both were still impossible. Nor could he reach to touch; the gap between them was small, but unbridgeable. He must speak now, though, her eyes demanded it.

'Julianne,' and it was something even to speak her name against that gaze, something else to speak it in her hearing, the first time in how long? Too long, week after unbearable week of trying not to speak it at all for fear of debasing it by misuse or hearing it debased by others. 'Julianne, how are you here?'

'How?' A dead note to the repetition, to match the corpse-light in her eyes. 'We were brought.'

By whom? Who had fetched her from the castle, where was her allegiance now? He would not ask, not yet. 'Why, then?' A girl and a boy, unwatched in the heart of a war – it would have been unwise with any girl, with her it was unthinkable. *Great peril*, the djinni had said, but that needed little foresight here. Even without the 'ifrit, her peril must have been great.

'Why? To talk to you, I thought. I'm not sure now . . .' And her eyes strayed back to the body she was nursing.

'To talk to me? But – you couldn't know, how could anyone have known . . . ?'

'The djinn know the future, Imber,' as her hands stroked the hair back from the dead boy's brow. 'Some, at least. Not everything, not enough; but enough at least to put us in your path.'

And in the 'ifrit's path also, so that Roald died. That was so clear, neither of them needed to say it.

But, 'What have the djinn to do with this?'

He thought she might be weary of so many questions, but if so, she made no protest. 'It was a djinni brought us here.'

He'd have liked to close his eyes to think the better, as he had done all his life; but that was a child's trick, and he was a man grown. A man grown and married, desperately parted from his wife and bewilderingly reunited, and he could not close his eyes to her face. But a djinni had brought her here, and a djinni had sent him in pursuit of her with a warning of her peril; and that djinni, his djinni had named itself as Esren Filash Tachur, the strange words were branded in his memory, and he had heard her crying 'Esren!' as he fought . . .

He thought, he *thought* that his thinking was telling him that the djinni had placed her in the peril from which it had sent him to rescue her; he thought that Julianne was telling him that it must have known what it was doing. If it had known the outcome too, it would have known that Roald the boy would die; if not, it had risked his life and hers, and Imber's also, and for what . . . ?

'What could you tell me, Julianne, that a djinni could not? Why do this,' *risk a girl and kill a boy,* 'why fetch you here?' Where she could not have met him if he had not been chased by the 'ifrit, proof positive that the djinni had known exactly what it was doing, if it knew anything at all.

'I was to tell you – oh, that there was a greater danger than the Sharai, greater evil than the Surayonnaise abroad in this land. Well, that you have seen. Which I expect is why it fetched me here, to be sure that you would see. And survive, to say what you have seen.' Her voice had passed beyond bitter, into some depth of cold savagery that he had never thought to hear from any woman, never mind his gentle, politic Julianne. 'I was to tell you also that there is an army come up from Ascariel, hastily gathered but more potent than this raggle-taggle that you lead. They are to be found to the west, along the line of the river. There is no way to cross it now, I was to tell you that. They lack a commander of rank, and will listen to a lord of Elessi. And if there's a priest with them, have him bless their weapons. Have him bless yours, twice over; it works, you saw . . .'

'I did – and this is yours, my lady.' He handed her the knife, and saw her shudder in the stars' dimness before she took it, the haft still warm from Roald's tight and clumsy grip. Warmer than his hand, perhaps, by now. 'But I will not go any further west, now that I have found you. I have what I came for. We'll leave this cursed land, I'll take you home . . .'

'No,' she said, soft and determined. 'I am not free to leave – and nor are you, Imber. We've all of us been fetched. Besides, you could not cross the river now. The way you came is barred, and there's no path through the mountains south, only holds that shelter frightened people who have seen their lands in flame.'

'What, shall I go west, then, and take command of an

army? This is a bad night to ask it, but I will if you are with me, Julianne. You're free to go where I go, nowhere else. You are my wife.'

'And another man's,' she said, confirming the impossible with a sad little smile, 'and can follow neither of my husbands now. No, don't touch me, Imber. There never was any force between us, and will not be. Esren . . .'

This time it came, the djinni, a suck of darkness and a glitter string, starlight caught on a thread and spun around velvet.

'Esren, take us back, Roald and me.'

'Julianne, wait!'

'For what?' It seemed to him that she was half gone already, more than half, although she hadn't stirred from where she knelt; she'd moved no more than the boy had. 'I can't take you with me. Find your own role, Imber – go back to your people, warn them, lead them, be aware. And don't slay any more innocents.'

'I have not—' he began, and then thought that perhaps she meant Roald, and wondered if perhaps she was right. And choked down denials and confessions both, and said instead, 'Julianne, I'm lost in here. There is a curse on these fields, they lead me all awry . . .'

'Call it a blessing, for those who live here. But there's a trick, they have to tend their crops.' And she smiled, just a little, as she said, 'When you pass through a gap turn left, keep your left hand on the wall and follow it around to the other opening. Even if that's directly opposite, even if it's only three paces to your right: always turn left, and always follow the wall. That's all, that will see you out.' The smile vanished all too soon, as she added, 'Roald told me that, while we were waiting. Now, please, Esren.'

And he thought she rose up and flew like a witch, with the boy's body in her arms; except that he would not believe that of her, and it was hard to see with the sudden swirling lights and the suck of the dark that seemed to close around her, so perhaps it was all an illusion of the djinni's.

One thing was no illusion, though, that she was gone. If it weren't for the aches in his body and her words bright in his head, he might have thought her an illusion altogether, just a fever dream.

But she had been his Julianne, and she had been there. The crops were flattened where she'd sat; there was the stickiness of blood on the leaves where Roald had fallen. She was his certainty, his rock. If she held true, then so did all about her. There was the 'ifrit, the boy, the news, the message; the urgency of the message confirmed by his own experience, brutally driven home by the boy's death. Even Julianne could never have persuaded him, he thought, if he hadn't seen for himself. How was he to persuade his cousin Karel?

Well, he would confront that when he came to it. He had to get there first. He put his left hand to the wall and leaned against it for a moment, dizzied by memory or anticipation, both; then he straightened, took a glance upward to see how the stars were set, and started walking.

Bhisrat was young to be full sheikh of his tribe or any, but the Saren were an exceptional people and he was an exceptional man.

Also he was a proud man, although there was nothing exceptional in that for a Sharai, among his tribe or any.

Tonight he was an angry man: cheated of his proper authority, he felt, betrayed by something he could not understand and so humiliated in front of his peers, the sheikhs of other tribes. They mocked him with their silence, and he could do nothing. If he spoke, if he gave a moment's notice to the issue, they would mock him with words instead. Then he would be forced to fight, and would die eventually although he would kill a few of those sneering elders first; and so his name would be written in infamy, as the man who lost his tribe in war and then in fury turned on other sheikhs – *as a child in temper turns on his playmates,* they would say – and so lost the war for all the tribes.

It could happen, it was there to be done. Already half the men had forgotten why they were here, whether that be to recover Hasan or to recover the land, drive the Patrics into the sea. They were content to raid and burn, to fight when they could find a fight; not finding fights enough, they were close already to fighting each other over a word, a gesture, a bolt of looted cloth.

Without Hasan they made a poor army, an ill-disciplined mob; and the sheikhs who led them were little better. The council could not meet without arguing, nor keep its arguments a secret, with firelight and wind its only walls. Let one of those arguments come to steel and there would be no Sharai army, only a dozen tribes more at war with each other than they were with the Patrics, though they fought on Patric land.

So Bhisrat held his peace against the silence, which was almost but not quite worse than spoken taunts; and he sat with his face to the fire, keeping his back ostentatiously turned to the high walls of the field-maze, where the dirt-grubbing Patrics laid their deceiving traps for honest warriors.

He had men watching the walls, of course, watching for any sign of his missing riders; it was not true that he had lost the tribe, though they were saying so at every fire but this. He had only lost the best of his tribe, the finest, the pride of his blood. And it should not have happened, it bewildered him, and so he was raging inside and ready to rage at a moment's carelessness, water or words spilled accidentally around him. So long as the silence held, so long could he hold his fury leashed, but no longer.

In Hasan's absence, no sheikh would risk giving orders to another, *scout that way* or *search there*. Instead they vied for the place of greatest danger, sent their men to outrace others to the fight, made promises of blood now and loot to follow.

There had been disappointingly little of either, this whole day's march. A Patric troop tracked them on the wrong side of the river, and could not be closed with; this morning they'd met farmers and peasants largely, as easy killing as their flocks and as poor as the land they tilled: 'rich in earth and wisdom' was a Surayon boast, contemptible to the Sharai. Meat and a few plough-horses were small recompense to a host promised conquest. Why fight, why ride at all for so little profit?

They fought, of course, because they loved to fight; but there was better fighting, better raiding in the Sands. Much better raiding, now that all the fighting men were here. It couldn't be long before one tribe or another would think of that, speak of that around its fires, slip away before the dawn to enrich its tents at the cost of its elders' honour.

Determined that it should not be the Saren that turned back first, Bhisrat had led them in a furious race to find the fighting men of Surayon. They did exist, he knew that; he himself had seen them, talked with them, fenced and wrestled with them. There had been truce and trade between Surayon and the Sharai for many years, more true a truce than ever with the rest of Outremer. He had fostered Surayonnaise children in his tents, had sent his own sons to learn what they could of the arts of the Patrics, and never once thought to call them hostage.

But that was in the past, all truces had to break and this was shattered, as it must have been when God and honour called together. And so he had led that charge in search of men to fight, ahead of those tribes that searched for gold amid the stores of barley; and had found only skirmishes and traps, tricks and sorceries that stole his tribesmen's courage and his own pleasure in the chase.

When the walls rose up around the fields, the only good running was squeezed down towards the river, but there was no one to run after. The cursed grubbers laid ambushes, appearing suddenly from behind the walls, shooting arrows or riding down stragglers and then vanishing into shelter again.

So of course he'd sent men in after, to flush them out. Not a sheikh in all the tribes would have acted differently; he clung to that thought now, too late. He had held the bulk of the tribe outside on the grassland, used all his influence and command to make them wait while he sent in small bands of men afoot to chase the lurking Patrics out, like dogs who put up finches for the hawks.

At least these were real fighting men, he'd thought, there'd be some honour in this hunt and a tale to tell after, more than other tribes could claim.

He'd waited, and the men he'd sent in had not returned. Surprised, impressed, suspicious, he'd listened to the clamour of his people and let larger groups go in search of their brother tribesmen and the foe to follow. He'd warned them to beware of lurking magic, but still he'd let them go.

And had waited then, with what remained of his warriors, while the other tribes caught up; it had been their passing taunts that sent a number more into the maze of fields intemperately, in ones and twos into the unyielding silence.

And none of them, not one had yet come back. He'd have taken all that remained of his men and led them in himself if he hadn't recognised that there was strong magic at work here, and if he hadn't been exceptional. It was patently clear that no spell could be outfaced even by a sheikh in his wrath; it was patently clear also – at least to Bhisrat – that throwing himself into its clutches regardless would be an act of heroic but monumental vanity.

So he had chosen to endure the unspoken contempt of his peers, rather than immolate himself to a foolish badge of courage that could lose himself his life and his people his leadership when they needed it most.

So he sat at the elders' fire where all the sheikhs held council, with his back to the wall behind which he had lost the pride of his tribe; he kept his own pride in check, not to be known as the man who wrecked the hope of all Sharai; he pretended to listen to the older men's talking while he waited for news, any news from what Saren he had left to watch the wall.

There was news, other news from other tribes, where they watched other borders of the camp. Things moved in the dark, they said, that were not men. They had shot arrows without result, or with no result that they could see. None was willing to venture far, to check. Bhisrat thought that the fate of the vanished Saren was perhaps weighing on their minds, turning common cowardice into good sense; it was good sense not to say so, though, so he said nothing and kept his face immobile.

For as long as he could, he kept so. Despite all temptations, all the hostages that fortune laid before him, his control was only broken when there was a stir in the half-light beyond the fire, between this fire and the next; when there were voices raised in startlement, crying out in disbelief; when two figures came stumbling awkwardly out of a deeper dark than the starlit night and the firelit camp could own between them.

They were awkward because they leaned on each other – no, because one leaned and the other had to support him, and could do that only lopsidedly because he carried something heavy in the opposite hand. Their sudden appearance was shock enough; it was their recognition, though, that made men cry aloud for gladness and for fear, and for rage.

One of the figures was Hasan, and the sight of him raised joy that spread like a fire through the camp, that was as quickly followed by fear because he needed his companion's strength to walk, he was pale and scarred and terribly weak who had always been so strong and masterful, master of himself before he mastered any other man. And then there was another kind of fear, as news spread of what the burden was that swung on that companion's other side: some grisly trophy, a thing that had never been human, and the tribes had not come here to fight the obscene get of the spirit world . . .

The rage was Bhisrat's and his alone, and it made him add his voice to the tumult in a bellow. That companion, with his one hand gripping Hasan and his other raising high the vile thing it carried – that was the tribeless boy, the oath-breaker who offended all the tribes but the Saren specially, he who followed the bastard Patric Ghost Walker and should have died twice by now, twice at least. And he had given a finger to join the Sand Dancers and still he was let live, he was let walk into camp as into Selussin and Rhabat and this folly had to end, how long must Bhisrat endure it . . . ?

The boy walked into the firelight, into the heart of the elders' council, and didn't even pretend to be there simply as a prop to the sick Hasan. He settled his master carefully in the heat, to be sure – but then he straightened himself and turned a full circle, showing what he held to every man that watched.

It was a ghûl's head, female and monstrous at the same time. Hewn from its owner after death, it must have been; it had needed more than one stroke to separate that from the neck it had inhabited before. Bhisrat guessed furiously at what blade had been used to do the work, and saw his guess confirmed as the nameless, shameless boy dropped the head and then knelt beside it, with Bhisrat's own good knife in his hand.

There would be no honour in slaying the boy, it was only a necessary duty owed to the dignity of the tribe, a restora-tion. He would do it in the Sands, on Saren land and under Saren eyes. Even so, this blatant parading called for some response. Half the men around him were waiting for it, he thought, even while they babbled questions at Hasan and were entirely ignored.

'Enough!' he cried, into the general clamour of rising voices; and sure enough, those voices fell silent too quickly to be trusted. Urgent as they were with their own demands, the sheikhs all wanted to hear from him, to see what he would do. Perhaps they thought, very likely some of them hoped that he would heap shame upon shame, take out his temper on the boy's flesh in utter disregard of Hasan, of the situation, of his own oaths and promises.

He did not. He impressed himself with his own forbearance; he spoke to Hasan and said, 'There are many questions, and we will ask them all; but first, tell me how it is that you allow that outcast to strut at your side, even here at the heart of our camp? This is the third time he has forced himself into our councils. His arrogance will earn him brief reward, when the time is right, but I do not understand why you give him your support.'

'It was rather the other way about,' Hasan said softly, drily. 'And is that your chief concern, this night? Well, let it be. He is here because he has something to show you, that I think you ought to see.'

'A ghûl's head? I have seen one before.'

'Not the head alone, something more.'

'You could have shown us yourself, why let the boy bring it?'

'He slew it,' mildly.

'Better it had slain him, saved me the work.'

'See him as a prop to my weakness, if that is easier for you, and a bearer of burdens. I could not have carried that head tonight, and you needed to see it. All of you need to see it. Show them, Jemel.'

The boy wrenched open the dead thing's mouth – too long for a human jaw and too pointed, but still disturbingly female, as though in deliberate mockery – and slipped the blade inside. His hands worked, one gripping while the other sawed; they emerged with the tongue of the ghûl hanging like a miscarried foetus, dark and dripping.

'So the boy is an incompetent butcher. And what?'

'Look . . .'

The boy himself had still said nothing, and he said nothing still. He probed the point of the blade into the heavy wet meat of the tongue, found something, grunted his satisfaction.

And cut it out, and held it up for all to see: not a growth, nothing that could be natural even to so unnatural a thing as a ghûl. A small stone, a large seed: something like an olive-pit, except that it was itself the size of an olive.

'What is that?'

'A spell, an enchantment; a whip, perhaps. Break it, Jemel, or Esren leaves you stranded here.'

The boy placed it on a broad, flat stone near the fire, that had been used an hour before for baking bread. He still held the dagger, Bhisrat's own blade in his other hand; now he reversed it, and brought the pommel slamming down. Bhisrat cried out in protest at seeing his knife so abused, but this time he was ignored.

The little thing had been a stone indeed, and had broken open under the blow. Stained dark on the outside by the body or the blood of the creature it had inhabited, it showed its golden heart in the firelight. Now half a dozen voices asked the same question again while the boy went on silently, heedlessly ruining the dagger's fine hilt, using the weight of it to crush the stone to powder.

'What *is* that?' the voices asked, and answered themselves in a ragged and rising chorus. 'It's a stone, that's all, just a piece of rock, what was it doing in that thing's tongue, what's this about?'

'It was fetched over from the land of the djinn,' Hasan said; and quiet, tired as he was, his voice cut through the sheikhs' uproar as they all sought to outshout each other.

They gaped at him, so many fools with their beards hanging loose. Bhisrat wore no beard, but still he could feel his own startlement writ large on his face in the firelight. No way to recover that, only a brief opportunity to seize leadership again, before another man stepped into the silence.

'Hasan, I – we – do not understand.'

'It is, it was a pebble from the land of the djinn,' he said again, more clearly, 'fetched over by the 'ifrit to be a tool, to make the ghûl a tool to their will. There is some virtue if you would call it that, some glamour in the rock of that place, that gives it power here. The 'ifrit have used it to bind a djinn, the same that brought us here – but you know that, you were in Rhabat and saw what came of it. They use it also to bind ghûls. Those are ghûls that haunt the borders of your camp tonight, but they are ghûls with a stronger mind behind them. They are being driven against you, and it's the 'ifrit that drive them. I do not know why, but the 'ifrit have attacked us before; they have attacked others along this river this day.'

'It is obvious why,' Bhisrat growled. 'The 'ifrit are bound or in allegiance to these Patrics of Surayon, and are sent against their enemies.'

'It was the Patrics of Surayon that saved my life today,' Hasan returned mildly, 'and an 'ifrit that threatened it.'

'Seeming so. And as a result you come to us, you are returned to us – to say what? I do not think to lead us to Ascariel, or to plunder. Have they turned your head, Hasan?'

'Have they? No, I don't believe they have. You are right, though, Bhisrat of the Saren. This much I am convinced of, that the 'ifrit are the greater enemy and the greater cause tonight. We must fight and defeat them before we think to fight further for our land, that the Patrics stole from us. Not to forget that, but to put it aside for now; and if that means we must fight alongside the Patrics for a short time, then let it be. When men ride out against the spirit world, they do well to ride in numbers. And I do not think it will be for long.'

Bhisrat snorted, was ready to say that he did not think it would be at all, that the Sharai were too wise to be so trapped. He was forestalled, though, by the oathbreaker.

'Bhisrat of the Saren,' the boy murmured, loud enough to carry. 'Yes, indeed. And where are your Saren tonight, Bhisrat? I remember all their faces, and I don't see any of them hereabouts . . .'

He could not have seen in the dark, in the crush of bodies packing in around the firelit circle. He must have known before; and of course he did, because he had come with Hasan, which meant he had come from those Patrics who had snared the Saren in their cursed labyrinth. True warriors of the tribe, of the Sharai, and they were being sneered at by this boy of shifting allegiance, who had long since forgotten how to spell his loyalty or what oaths he'd broken and to whom.

Bhisrat's roar of fury was building in him like sand blown in a storm against the tent of his resistance. He must break his own oaths now, at any moment, he must draw his scimitar and smite that reckless, feckless boy's head from his dishonest shoulders, let it fall down beside the ghûl's and lie there, kind by kind . . .

But again Hasan cut in, just a moment before Bhisrat must have lost control; again the breathy fragility of his voice was somehow a quality that must be listened to.

'Jemel, enough. Don't be petty. Go and fetch them now.'

'Very well, Hasan.'

With half a smile and a mysterious glance that was meant surely to infuriate further, as it surely did, the boy rose easily to his feet and began to walk towards the wall that hid the ensnaring maze. That route took him directly towards Bhisrat, who had chosen that place explicitly so that he could be seen not to give even a glance at the wall.

They came face to face and Jemel said nothing, only waited politely for Bhisrat to move aside.

Instead, he stood four-square in the boy's path and – almost choking on the effort to speak, grinding the words out – he said, 'You know where they are.'

'Oh, yes.' For a moment, he held that same mocking smile; and then, relenting, 'They are not dead, Bhisrat, only lost and wandering; and they have been my brothers all my life, till now. I will fetch them out.'

'They are my tribe, outcast. I will fetch them.'

'Oh? Go, then,' with a courteous gesture. 'I will wait with Hasan; he needs me, if the Saren do not.'

'You know I cannot fetch them without your help.'

'And you should know that I will not help you to fetch

them. What, shall I lead you through your confusion, while you dog obediently at my heels?'

That was another reason to kill the boy, that insult flung so casually, so contemptuously at him, and in public hearing too. But the tribe's safety lay between them, in this strange and unknowable land; he swallowed his fury and said, 'You need not watch your back, so long as I walk behind you. When I kill you, trust that it will be face to face and blade to blade, as I promised before.'

'That was not my concern; I had not thought to fear my own knife at my back.' *Even from you* was not spoken, it did not need to be; only Bhisrat among all the Sharai, his voice suggested, could be so dishonourable as to conceive of the idea. A murmur among his audience seemed to confirm it, although half these thieves and liars would slit their own brothers' throats for a camel and a press of dates. 'What I fear rather,' the boy went on, raising his voice and looking around, playing to his listeners now, 'is seeing you restored to the trust of your tribe, as you come from the dark to lead them free. A sheikh should be wise and temperate, and you are neither. I care yet for the Saren, and I would not see them endangered at your hands. You have lost them once on this adventure; where will you lead them next? Or send them, rather?'

There was laughter all around. Some surely must be at the very idea of a Sharai sheikh being wise or temperate, that was a known joke, but most of it was purely aimed at Bhisrat.

'Stay, Bhisrat,' Hasan said mildly from the fire. 'Let the boy fetch your people; he has your blade for his authority, they will follow him out of the trap they're in. Stay, and aid our councils here; we need wisdom, we must talk about the threats we face and how we're best to meet them.'

He had no choice; he stepped aside and let the boy slip smiling into the dark. But his voice would be wasted now, as his searching would have been before: every time Hasan mentioned wisdom, he knew, everyone who heard would remember the oathbreaker's jibe and discount Bhisrat as foolish and intemperate. If they had plotted that whole scene between them, they could not have played it better. Already Hasan was talking defensively about meeting threat, not about advance or assault, and already the sheikhs were listening.

And the boy was right, Bhisrat would lose more than the respect of other sheikhs by this night's work. The Saren too would be eyeing him askance, and less inclined to listen or to follow. Tribes had risen against their sheikhs before now, on lesser provocation; and that boy would provoke them mightily as he led them out of the labyrinth, he had the tongue and the knowledge to do it and to do it well.

Oh, they were clever – but there would still come that moment, a circle of bodies and a stretch of sand, where the boy met Bhisrat's steel and choked on it. That would make much worthwhile.

In the meantime, Hasan was tipping the baking-stone towards the fire, brushing the golden dust of crushed stone into the flames like so much wasted flour. It was not such heavy work, but the strain of it showed; another man asked him why he did it.

'The djinni would not come, while even that dust lingered in the air.'

'Djinni? What djinni?' A hundred voices now, hushed by his gesture as they always had been.

'This,' he said; and, 'Esren . . .'

The djinni came like a break in the darkness, like a fault in a rockface that showed the glitter of hidden wealth, unattainable wealth beneath. Bhisrat heard the rushing whisper on all sides, *where has he been, that he comes back with command over the djinn?*

They were fools to be impressed, twice fools to trust him now. He had been with sorcerers, and there were too many spirits in this story; Bhisrat smelled the stink of betrayal in the air, and dared not say it against so many true believers.

'Esren, when Jemel comes out of the fields with the Saren lost, I want you to take him back to the palace.'

'He will not want to go.'

'I know that. Marron went with the Ransomers; this is his stubbornness, that he means to go with the Sharai. I mean him to go back, he causes nothing but division here. Tell him Marron will return shortly.'

'The djinn do not lie, Hasan.'

'I hope that it will not be a lie.'

'Neither do the djinn hope. I cannot see what Marron means to do.'

'Well, tell him nothing, then – but take him anyway. Regardless of his protests. Lisan told you to obey me, not him. Take him away from here, and back to her.'

Hasan was speaking to the sheikhs now, speaking of 'ifrit, but Bhisrat would not listen. He had his own thoughts, his own suspicions; he would make his own plans, if he could only find some men to follow him.

Ronan de Montclair had expected miracles and wonders

ever since he came to the Sanctuary Land, and had been sadly disappointed for more than twenty years already.

He'd learned to live with older men laughing at his fancies, and boys too, boys born in Outremer and wise within their world; before long, he'd learned to keep his dreams private even from his friends. He'd never learned to stop looking. The priests' teachings and the old legends both were burned into the bone of him. He knew that the God had walked this country and blessed it in His passing, and he believed also that there were spirits and demons here that his homeland had never seen. He watched trees and rocks and rivers, he prayed with his eyes on the stars, and – like his homeland – he had never yet seen a shadow not cast by the sun, a shimmer not made by wind on water or a fire not struck from a flint. He had sat on his horse on a hilltop and seen what he thought was the gleam of sunlight on the domes of Ascariel, the God's own city; but he had never come closer than that far view, and even he couldn't read a distant glitter as even the promise of a charm. That had been when he was a youngster still, a squire in his lord's retinue. Now he held his own land in his own name, directly from the Duke. It was what he had come for, but it had made a farmer of him, where he could have been a knight; he had earth under his fingernails and his feet had sprouted invisible roots, which his father might have called a miracle indeed but he would not. Married with children, twice tethered to his holding, he still prayed at all the proper hours and at other times too, when he was abroad in his fields; he still watched for strangeness, for any sign that creatures not mortal had visited his land; he still saw nothing but what he had always seen: the actions of light and weather, the flights of birds, no angels.

It was good land he was granted, fertile and well-watered. It should have gone to a man of better blood than his, but that it lay close to the road north and the northern border of the dukedom, that strange dislocation where lay the Folded Land.

He had never gone that far, either, not though the ride would promise a touch of magic at its end. Some wonders were accursed, and he would not willingly seek them out.

He could face them, though, if the need arose. When messengers rode wildly south from the border's guards, when a small and hasty army came marching north in response – *the way is open, Surayon lies where it always lay; to arms, to arms and march!* – he didn't hesitate to join it. All of Outremer might be vulnerable to the Princip's spellcasting; his own land was vulnerable to any evil that might have been breeding in darkness this thirty years, that might issue forth this night or any. The Church might call him, his liege lord might send him, but he rode for himself and his family, the land he held for his sons and their sons to come.

From the moment they crossed the border, he had expected to see sorceries levied against them, fiends and ghasts and foulness; all day and half the night, he had again been disappointed. He had seen houses, herds and crops, and he had seen them all laid waste. He had seen groves and orchards that reminded him of his childhood home, so much softer the climate seemed in this closed valley; he had seen men at the trees with axes and with fire. There were many years of wrath banked up behind those blades and torches, but he thought that wrath belonged to their masters, their lords and bishops; he thought that wrath unleashed them, but that it was fear that carried the men themselves in their hectic rush to hack and burn. Wrath licensed a destruction that fear compelled.

Nor was it only trees that suffered, or only crops and cattle. Those same axes had hewn at men; those same flames had burned women in their cottages, women and children too. Ronan had no wrath, but his own touch of fear survived; he had watched every death warily, only waiting to see the first strike of evil in response from the dead or dying. After so many years of watching the border road in anticipation of some demon-led invasion, he couldn't believe that these heretics and sorcerers would simply die as they did die, like farmers and families or any mortal folk, as though they had no spells to protect themselves any longer, no magic in the world.

And yet they had done that, they had died and died, and fought with little more than swords and courage first. There had been a few balls of fire flung, that had burned hotter and longer than an oil-flame ought; but he had been a soldier before he became a farmer, and he had seen such things before. If there were magic in these fireballs he couldn't distinguish it from the science of the artificers he'd served with, who could compound pitch, naphtha, sulphur and charcoal into a murderous firepot.

He told himself that he should feel no disappointment in that at least, that this quick-mustered army wasn't having to fight spells and demons on its way. It was hard to rejoice, though, as the priests demanded, where he felt little better than a bandit falling on ill-defended farms. He was a farmer himself now, and recognised the land-love that could set a man with a billhook against a troop of horse; he was married now with children, and recognised the protective terror that could throw man and then wife against a hedge of blades even where there was no hope of turning those blades from the babes they sought to shelter. A part of Ronan was disappointed that his captains had led him to this slaughter, and that he had followed. A smaller part of him, little more than a whisper in the uttermost privacy of his skull, was disappointed that the Surayonnaise showed no vestige of their much-vaunted powers even in defence. Never mind his lifelong yearning to see signs and wonders, he would have welcomed the sight of women and children vanishing into a veil of mystic smoke, if only to save his having to see them trapped behind a curtain of fire, nothing but their voices rising free.

They'd made camp at sunset, on a low knoll that they could encircle with thorn and brush for a crude palisade. Ronan had tried to eat with the others, but had found fresh-killed meat too hard to swallow. And the fires too hot, too bright with faces and the crackling, snapping voices of the day's dead calling to him, asking questions for which he no longer had an answer.

So he had walked away: had made his way past the guards at the cut-thorn hedge and out through the narrow wynd they'd left in case of need. With his back turned to fire and company, he'd walked far enough for folly, and further yet.

And stood now amid the tough grasses of the river's bank, gaping at what he'd been waiting twenty years to see, what he'd been ready for all day until this moment, what he had feared and dreaded and yearned for all at once.

He saw magic, he saw what was impossible, what he'd previously found only in tales that he'd barely more than half believed. It didn't seem so much really moment by moment, it wasn't half as portentous as he thought it ought to be; and yet the whole of it, the thing itself left him shaking, gasping, reduced to a child too stupid to feel terror in the face of what was wonderful and dreadful both together.

It started with a light against the dark, a warm bright glow he should have welcomed, except that it came from no source that he could guess at and burned nothing that he could see. It was just a light, a line of light like a rip in the fabric of the night, that spread wider like a door opening and spilling glory.

It was right in front of him, not ten running paces ahead; it lit all the grass between them, though none beyond, as though there truly were a door in a wall of dark and the light it spilled could fall only towards him.

There was, of course, a figure outlined in the light. There had to be.

A figure of dark it was: a shadow that grew sharper, that loomed larger, that came towards him like a demon rising from the depths, quite unhurried.

Ronan should perhaps have run, but he'd been told all his life that flight was no defence from evil, that wickedness had wings to outspeed a racing horse. This figure had no wings that he could see, and he had never run from men in any guise; courage or ignorance or both held him where he was. He might have cried out for help, he should certainly have prayed to the God to shield him from hellspawned creatures, but there was a weight on his tongue that might have been terror or might have been doubt, though it felt more like simple wonder, untouched by the world and its worries. Whatever made it, it was heavy enough to hold him silent. His thoughts trembled on a hair, on a razor's edge, toppling between amazement and his long-familiar disappointment. Here was what he'd looked for all his life and what he most dreaded, both together and somehow quieter than he'd ever imagined, a man walking through a door and how could he kneel to that, how could he scream at it, only because the door to his eyes was not there? He'd always thought that magic would be huge and fiery, not cool and small and simple . . .

The figure moved forward and was a man, no question, neither a demon come to curse him nor an angel come to bless. There was relief in that, but – of course – a hint of disappointment too, a sense of something missed. Ronan found it hard to remember even that he ought to draw his sword. It was a second figure that reminded him, following the first out of the light: this one more obviously a man, a young man fumbling a little for his footing, turning his head as though he found it hard to see or to understand quite where he was, or how he had come there, or why. And he over-topped the first man by a head, and had twice the breadth of shoulder . . .

A warrior, following a sorcerer? The first of a line, of an army of warriors? The Surayonnaise had hidden their land for so long, this was much their kind of magic, dark and silent; no doubt this would be much their kind of war, to attack at night and without warning.

Ronan did draw his sword, and he drew his breath also to shout that warning, the great alarm that should rouse all the camp behind him; but the first man – the little man, the sorcerer – lifted his hand, and Ronan felt that weight pressing on his tongue again, except that this time he felt it truly, like a pebble in his mouth. It gagged him, like a pebble in his mouth. Gagging, he lifted a finger to pluck it out, but there was nothing there: only his silence, the emptiness of his voice.

'Easy there,' the man said softly when Ronan might have turned to flee, except that he had never run from any man; when he might have lunged forward, except that the sorcerer was small and unarmed and old, he could see that now, and there had been too many such at the sword-point today who had felt that sword thrust home. Besides, if one hand could weave air into a stone of silencing, what might both hands do? And he had that young man at his back, and the young man had a sword and looked ready and fit to use it. Ronan thought he would never reach the sorcerer. He would die twice on the way, and farmers were practical men where young warriors were hotheads . . .

He must in the end have lunged or run, and would have done one or the other if the sorcerer had so much as moved another finger of his spell; but the man stood entirely still, and went on talking.

'You've nothing to fear of me, nor of my companion. We too serve the King. This young lord is Elessan, and his family name is Karlheim; that should be enough. He is not meant to be in this war, so we will not declare him further. My own is Coren de Rance, and I am the King's Shadow in Outremer.'

The walls of night were dark and high to north and south, but there was starlight and there was riverlight, and Ronan thought that together they were enough. An honest man himself, he believed in honesty writ plain to see in others, on others' faces: in the way their eyes held his gaze, the way their jaws were set, the lineaments of their mouths.

Ronan did not, could not doubt them for a moment. He sheathed his sword, bowed to the lord, might have knelt to the Shadow but that the man's swift gesture refused him leave to do so.

It seemed also to melt that absence from his tongue; he could have spoken, except that he could find no words to say in the face of mystery gifted by the King, and so – presumably – sanctioned by the God. The Church had its own mysteries, the King was a mystery in himself and a mystery altogether to his people; the King's Shadow fell somewhere between the two, a servant with a sovereign's command in his tongue's tricks, a prelate's power at his fingers' ends.

As Ronan had seen. But there was to be no more magic, it seemed, unless there were spells in words alone. The King's Shadow said, 'Come: if you have no duties of watch or guard, will you take the two of us to meet with your commanders? There will be hard work in the morning, and the news of that should be broken now, to give all possible time to prepare. And be easy, man – the work may be hard, but at least it should be cleaner than the work you've done today. Enough of burning, I say, and enough of slaying the innocent.'

Something turned in the river, something rose like a rock so that the star-blanket broke and flowed like shards of shimmer falling, fleeing the great dark that divided them. Ronan touched a useless hand – cold, sweating, proclaiming its own mortality in the face of something entirely other – to a useless sword, and said, 'Of course, my lords – but come quickly, if you will. I cannot protect you here.'

'Nor we you,' the young lord said softly, his eyes on the same massive disruption in the river, watching as it sank and was gone, as the waters settled again above where it had been. 'Perhaps all the men in your army cannot protect you, or us, or each other; but that we will learn in the morning. For now, let us go and surprise some few of those men, before something comes to surprise us altogether.'

Ronan led the way, as was proper, but he couldn't keep from glancing back as he went, both at the wonder of the two men who followed him – who had come from nowhere with legends at their backs, one of them his very name a legend and yet both seemed so unsorcerous, so physical – and at the river, where something vast had moved against its current. He'd seen nothing but a darkness, an implication of body, perhaps a glimmer of starlight on black but no more; such a brief glimpse and so little to tell from it, and yet that too was a moment of magic, a demon-touch, what he had sought so long. A vision of light and a vision of its absence, in the space of two breaths or so it seemed; the first had brought perhaps the help of men and the second perhaps a monster, and the one was warm and the other chill, and both he thought were equally threatening.

'They always said this place was cursed.' He said it aloud, if quietly, only for the comfort of hearing his own voice which could cast no spells and presage no disasters; and of course he was answered, by the King's Shadow himself.

'They did say so, and they were wrong. Surayon is endangered, as it always has been. That same danger threatens us, all of us, from the Kingdom to the Sands and further, to Marasson and the lands beyond. Not a curse, though, and not attached to this small land. Surayon is only a focus, it draws the attention of the world and worse, the powers beyond the world.'

And where was the God, where was His shielding hand? Not here, Ronan thought, not poised to shield him.

Even before he turned, Anton knew – or told himself so, at least, in his later solitude.

There was something in the stillness, in the silence, in the utter sense of a world in wait. He couldn't mistake that for a moment, he who had lived with his own waiting moment by moment through month after month of moments.

And so he had turned, and so he had seen Marron, and there had been no surprise in it at all. Or so he told himself later, when such a thought might have seemed a comfort, if he had needed comforting.

For now, tonight, he felt the impact, the weight of the moment before he knew what it meant – like the stillness that presages a tremor in the earth, like the sudden suck of air before a conflagration – but only by an instant. Understanding broke over him like a wave of water, brutal and destructive; and so he turned, and so he saw Marron.

Unless in honesty it had happened the other way around, that he had turned and seen Marron and so met that swamping comprehension, so understood the dangerous silence of the men about him, his men with their eyes and focus not entirely on him. Perhaps in honesty it was that way and not the other; but it did not feel so, and he thought the God would not betray him so extremely. He thought he would be allowed a moment's warning, time to take a breath and perhaps a stance in a tipping world, he thought he had earned that much with all his years of service.

So no, he chose to believe that it was as it seemed to be, that he did know what he would see before he turned.

It was no help to him.

He turned and saw Marron, and was barely conscious that the boy was not alone, that he and the boy were not alone together. His tongue reached for words, for what words were right and necessary, and for the moment could not find them; which proved to be a blessing, because the man who stood with Marron spoke first, and what he said was so meaningless, so immaterial that it acted as a reminder to Anton that some things should never be said in public, some things should never be said at all.

So he listened and said nothing while the other man spoke, while the boy stood mute.

The man spoke of monsters, of dark terrors turned material in the world, of greater evils abroad than the heretic Surayonnaise they'd come to war with or the unbelieving Sharai their scouts reported to the east. Anton believed him without question; Outremer was the land of miracles where the God had walked in flesh and sorrow, Surayon had been for thirty years safe harbour for magicians, he had himself seen wonders and terror at the castle of the Roq, so why not here?

But all the wickedness, all the devilry he'd seen had pivoted around Marron, had come from the boy or else followed in his shadow. And the man didn't know that, and so what he said was nonsense. He spoke of evil at the bridge, he warned of evil in the morning and never understood that the pale, silent figure at his side could be the source or the draw of more evil than he was able to imagine.

Anton let the same nonsense infest his own tongue. He

commended the man and his troop for their good work in surviving, in helping to destroy the creature they'd encountered, in returning to carry the news; he spoke not a word of blame for their failure to preserve the bridge intact, the task he'd sent them to achieve; he promised to consult with his commanders on how best to meet the challenge of the dawn in these altered circumstances, where other and more deadly enemies had arisen than those they'd come to face.

Then he dismissed the man and all his other auditors, the curious circle of his confrères and their squires, their pages and servants and other hangers-on. They moved not far off, not far enough, but they did move; that was the best that he could hope for. He daren't take Marron inside his tent, that would furnish their gossip with matter enough for days of speculation, weeks of teasing. His reputation couldn't afford it.

His reputation couldn't afford even this, a quiet talk in the open, in the firelight, in the heart of the Ransomer camp if he didn't end it by ordering Marron's immediate arrest. That would happen anyway, at his orders or otherwise; already men would be racing to carry this news to the marshal and his priestly officers, that the heretic, sorcerer, traitor Marron was returned. The boy had no chance of leaving as he had come, quietly and unchallenged; he had no chance of leaving at all, and surely must have realised that before he came.

And yet he had come, and must have had a reason, which could not be any of the reasons Anton had to be glad to see him come.

So Anton's first words to him could have been, should have been, must have been to ask why he was here; and yet they were not.

'Do you think you will be let leave this place?' he asked instead; which was almost but not quite another question altogether, *do you think I will let you leave this place?*

Marron smiled thinly, but somehow not weakly, and certainly not in submission. 'I come and go,' he said, the first words that Anton had heard from him since the world changed, and it was astonishing that his voice was even recognisable, let alone so resonant of the boy he used to be, so redolent of the summer that had been. 'Not always at my own choice, but the Ransomers do not hinder me.'

A soft hint there of a night at the Roq, slaughter and destruction, broken gates and broken minds to back up broken oaths.

Now Anton could, did, had to ask, 'Why did you come? Not to gloat, not to flaunt your powers,' *not to kill and kill again to prove them, surely not that,* 'so why?'

'Because it matters, what he just told you,' with a jerk of his head to signify the man just gone, 'because you have to listen, and you have to be ready. The people of Surayon are not your enemy, sieur; nor are the Sharai. I have been with both . . .'

'And you too are our enemy, Marron. Your words prove it, if proof were needed, but it is not. Do you imagine that I or any of us have forgotten what you did at the Roq?'

'No, sieur,' though it seemed that he at least could face it squarely, stubbornly accepting the fact of it, not flinching or turning away from the reminder. 'There was a madness that night, in me and in others. I am clear of it now,' and his hand moved to touch his arm, a healed scar where there had been a living, livid wound. Anton remembered that, he had made the wound himself. He was glad it had healed now, but couldn't read the gesture otherwise. 'You need to be free likewise,' Marron went on, 'you need to listen without judging. If you spend your days killing men of this country and men of the Sands, if you waste your strength and your steel's edge, you will die the quicker when the 'ifrit choose to meet you. You must be ready for them, and you must understand them when they come. Have your blades and arrowheads blessed by your priests, you can do that and it will work . . .'

'I cannot order such a thing done, Marron. It would have to come from the marshal; it is a matter for the brothers, not the knights.'

'You will die without it,' said bluntly, coldly, mercilessly. 'Even the best sword, even Dard would be nothing, would be a willow-wand unblessed against these creatures. Trust me, sieur . . .'

'Trust you? How?' And that was said just as bluntly, just as coldly, just as mercilessly, and it won him the silence that he'd sought, his only defence against that voice. Even the anger that he roused in response to Marron's words was entirely artificial, a cloak to cover truth. He needed not to listen, not to hear, not to be here; otherwise he was lost. And yet, where else could he be and what else do, while Marron was free and within the camp? 'Do you still carry Dard, do you still dare that, with all your history in your hand?'

'In my hand and blood; but Dard has a history of its own, sieur,' *in your hand and blood,* which he did not need to say, 'and I carry it regardless. Carry but do not use, I will not kill again. I have not, since that night.'

'Those who carry a sword should be prepared to use it.'

'So I'm told,' with a soft laugh, 'so another one keeps telling me. But for yourself, sieur, for Outremer, for all that you believe – be ready to kill 'ifrit, rather than men in the morning. See your weapons blessed, by men who can still be holy, and warn your people that there are beasts abroad. They fly, they swim, they come out of the earth; they are devils, as the Church has always taught us.'

'And so are the Surayonnaise, and so are the Sharai, as the Church has always taught us; heretics and unbelievers, greater dangers even than devils. And you are in league with all of them, Marron.'

'Not quite all, sieur. Only with the Sharai, and the Surayonnaise. And you. Esren, take me away from here.'

And Esren did, if Esren was a glimmer of gold against the night, sharper somehow than the firelight, a twisting string of brightness snared that appeared behind his shoulder a moment before he was lifted cleanly away into the darkness and out of sight, a bare two moments before a troop of brothers came running from the marshal's tents with their weapons drawn and their eyes agleam, their faces grim with the determination to face the wickedness and take the sinner, or die at their lord's command.

'Too late,' Anton murmured to their leader. 'Take me instead, I have words that must be delivered to our masters.'

Words that were nothing, ash and shadow, and what did he care? Monsters could come and drag him, drag them all to hell, and the world's loss would be less than his tonight. He touched his sword Josette and vowed that she at least should be blessed before the dawn, because he could do no other. If Marron had forsworn killing, that was all the more reason to kill, or ought to be. But he would do it dryly, with dust upon his tongue; there could be no virtue in it, where there was no hope.

16

Blood Follows the Blade

Of all the ways there were to distinguish rebel Surayon from the orthodox, the obedient states of Outremer, Elisande thought that this was prime, it spoke most clearly and most deeply to the heart and mind of her, to the memory and the soul. This was what she most missed, perhaps, when she was outwith the mountain borders: simply to stand – on her grandfather's terrace this morning, but anywhere within those borders would suffice although higher was better, highest was always best – and watch the light invade, see how the dark retreated as the stars faded first and then the lamplight at her back.

She had seen dawns in the desert, she had seen the sun rise over vast waters and distant ranges, she had seen storm-dawns and dust-dawns and dawns so gentle, so peaceful that even the birds had seemed surprised and hushed by the mystery of the moment. She'd seen a hundred, a thousand meanings of beauty in the many risings of the sun, each of them unique and each of them a wonder, but something inside her always harked back to this, always yearned to be here.

An invasion, a retreat – the words held a bitterness this morning, and had never seemed more apt. In other lands, in other seasons the sun struck upward like an erupting fire and it seemed as though the dark fled in response, after the moment of its rising. Or else light flowed into the world as though from a jug spilt below the horizon, if light could flow like milk and run upward; and then it would meet the night and tangle with it, milk and ink, and the weight and currents of the light would drive back the darkness as a salt tide drives fresh river-water back up its own channel for miles inland.

Here, not so. Here the change was slow and insidious. Daylight stole in like a thief, sneaking between the mountain-peaks and slithering down the river. The dense weave of darkness would be unpicked quietly, thread by thread until it chose to retreat – and every day it seemed indeed to be a choice, nothing forced, never a defeat – into the shelter of the valley's walls and caves where it could pool into shadow, curl like a beast inviolate and wait out the day's invasion.

Her grandfather would tell, had told his people that they could do the same, pull back into the high deep strongholds and wait, hold out, be patient, pray.

Some would do that, hide and hope, trust the wise and the strong and the powerful to work an unpredicted miracle between them. Others would fight, would have to fight; and of course the Princip depended on that resistance, he would gamble on being defied.

Herself, she could do neither. Her conscience wouldn't let her hide while her beloved country was in pain and its people were dying, while she blamed herself; no one, she had found, would let her fight. She hadn't even been allowed to go out last night with the others, on their various missions to plead for peace, for the opposing commanders in the field to raise their eyes and see the real danger. Her own djinni had refused to take her. She might have refused then to let it take any of them, except that she wasn't – quite – capable of such pettiness in such a crisis, and in any case she'd been afraid that it would disobey her and take them anyway, and then it would truly not be her djinni any longer, oath or no oath, promises or none.

She hadn't tried to have it take her to a battlefield, any battlefield this morning. She knew already the result of such a hopeless order; it was inherent in the arguments she'd been having half the night with her grandfather, with friends old and new, with commanders and servants and everyone she came face to face with.

Women could die for Surayon if they were victims, it seemed, if they were farmers in flight or innocents abroad; not if they were armed and armoured, fit and trained for fighting.

In those circumstances all they could do, all they were allowed to do by a forbidding grandfather and watchful friends and a treacherous, unreliable djinni was to stand here on the terrace and watch the infiltration of the light and wonder if this would be the last day in Surayon, the last for all of them, friends and strangers, kin and kind . . .

If all she was allowed to do was stand, at least she didn't have to do it alone, though honour required that she not show gratitude at the sound of a known footfall behind her: that she snarl, rather, to reconfirm the fuss she'd made last night.

'You don't have to make time for me, or waste the day here. I'm sure Esren would take you somewhere more interesting, if you ask it.'

'Are you? I'm not. And you can't scare me with a scowl, so don't try it.' Julianne linked arms with her, tall and cool and easy in her friendship, something distant in her gaze. Something she'd carried since last night, that Elisande had not been allowed to witness nor to hear about since, except that she knew the boy Roald had been killed. That was something to be truly offended at, perhaps, that Julianne wouldn't share what had touched her deeply; but Elisande couldn't manage any true offence, she was too busily outraged already, too noisily disgusted with her lot.

It was a mood she needed badly, urgently to maintain as a wall against other moods that were building, beckoning, threatening to overwhelm her. It was hard when her friend wouldn't cooperate, so that the best she could manage was an ongoing state of high dudgeon with her djinni.

'I'd scare Esren, if it showed itself. If it dared. It swore, it *swore* to serve me, to obey me; and the djinn don't lie, but . . .'

'Lie, perhaps not – but they do weasel, love, you taught me that yourself in the first hour of our meeting. They are subtle in their words, in a way that makes them liars beyond measure when they're dealing with us simple mortals; and they do see more than we do. If it says it serves you better by disobeying you, by serving us instead, you might try believing it instead of sulking. It did us all service last night, you're only furious because you were better kept busy here. Believe it, I wish you'd been with me instead, I do . . .'

Did she truly? Well, perhaps so, if she thought that would

have saved the boy. Not as a witness to whatever passed between her and her own boy Imber, though. That for sure she wanted to keep private.

And was entitled, and would be allowed. What could it matter, after all, on such a day? Tomorrow it might matter, if there were a tomorrow for Julianne, for Imber, for anyone. It might matter mightily to Elisande to know just exactly what her friend had said or had promised in exchange for Imber's service. Today, though, only that service had any weight at all. It was a day for battle, for alliances bought at any price; for men to be moved about the country, her country, like pieces in a game.

And for women to wait and watch and learn later what their fate would be, which brought her round full circle to her dawning mood this dawn.

Slow light, shapes out of shadow but no sunlight yet and not for a while yet. Perhaps she should not call it dawn at all when it was as deceptive and elusive as the djinn, creeping like water between rocks, insidious and secret. She used to appreciate that, to proclaim it as an image of Surayon itself, cloaked and masked but still inescapable as sun in cloud, its influence seeping throughout Outremer although the source was hidden.

No longer. The gates were down, the barbarians were riding and shadows offered no protection now. She ached for light and could not have it, could only see it like a rim of fire to the world where the sun burned on the mountains' peaks all around. She didn't want to think about fire.

She didn't want to think at all. She'd been teased all her life, that all her instincts were violent; but this was why, this was what they were for, this precise morning when she wanted to fling herself into a war precisely to stop herself thinking about its consequences.

'Elisande . . .'

'What?'

'Call the djinni.'

Call it yourself she wanted to say after last night, when it would come to her friends' calls and take them wherever they said, when it would not take her a frog's leap from her grandfather's hall although she had both begged and commanded in her exhaustion. But Julianne wouldn't take so much licence this morning, whatever she had taken last night, and Elisande wouldn't pretend to misunderstand her. So she contented herself with a surly, 'To what end?'

'To the end of taking you – or both of us, if you will have me – somewhere other than here, to do something other than stare at the creep of day while you paint it with your worst imaginings.'

'Yesterday you added your voice to the others', to have me stay exactly here while you all went off to do other things.'

'That was yesterday, and your staying was as useful as our going; how many people did you heal?'

She didn't know, she couldn't count; all she remembered was the ache of her body and the giddy maze of her mind as she poured herself into one stranger after another and still could never meet the need. 'Not enough,' she said, shrugging, 'and there will be more today. What makes you think I will be let leave, when I am so useful here?' And what was the point of healing, while the war went on wounding and wounding? She carried life in one hand, perhaps, but death in the other; and she had had enough of doing good.

'I don't believe there will be many wounded on the road today. Those who could flee have fled; the men who rode out in the dark' – the Princip among them, laying stern injunctions on his granddaughter not to follow – 'will live or die in the field, cut off from all help else. That's where we should be, if we do nothing more than tend them there.'

Which had been her own argument, more or less, which no one had listened to. She gazed up at her friend and said, 'Have you talked to your father about this?'

'No,' with a half-smile that might have meant anything. 'I am a married woman, a twice-married woman; I am no longer in his care. I might ask my husbands, either of them – but I would need to find them first.'

'We would need the djinni to take us, first. We'd never get past the men at the gates, I think they have orders to watch for me.'

'We've found a way out when we've been better guarded than this, my love. But let's try the djinni, it's so much easier.'

The day Julianne found it easy to be carried by a djinni would be a rare day indeed, and one worth celebrating. Elisande gave her a thoughtful stare, and then another shrug; she summoned the djinni, 'Esren,' with almost no expectation at all.

She was almost surprised, then, when it came. She still expected another refusal when she said, 'Esren, take us – oh, I don't know where. Take us somewhere we can be useful.'

Last night it had simply refused, the same request or one much like it. Today she felt its grip, she felt her body rise; and then, only then was she struck by another thought, an

entirely new thought, 'What about Marron, should we take
him too?'

The question was aimed at Julianne, and genuinely so; it
was the djinni that replied. 'I have told him already, it will be
better if he is here.'

Better for whom, she wondered, and for what? And could
find no answer for herself, nor any way to ask that would
bring her any answer worth the having.

Marron supposed that he was not the only one who had not
slept the night just gone. He was not even the only one who
had passed it or part of it on the palace roof. There had
been watchmen, long-sighted in starlight as he had used to
be when stars were red to him; briefly there had been the
Princip and a handful of his officers, though why they had
come to peer through and at the darkness when there were
lights and maps below, Marron couldn't guess.

Why he himself had chosen to sit, to stand, to pace cold
hours out on roof-leads when there was a warm bed and a
warm body awaiting him below – well, he could pretend not
to understand himself, but it was none too convincing a pretence. He had come from Sieur Anton; he could not go
directly to Jemel. The facts were as simple, as insurmountable
as that. And Jemel no doubt was lying waiting for him, con-
sidering the same information and misunderstanding the
result, and there was not a thing Marron could do about that.

He had watched the watchmen as they came and went, he
had watched the Princip and his lieutenants in their turn; he
had not spoken to them, nor they to him.

He gazed out at the inclosing darkness of the valley walls, up at the stars' fading and wished, yearned to have the Daughter back to show him what he could not see. At the same time he was deeply grateful to be free of it, to feel the aching misery in his bones and the hollow yearning in his belly and be able to name them weariness and hunger, nothing more. To be human again was to be false again, and there was great relief in that.

Streaks of colour in the sky, colours that were not red: dawn was coming, the sun was rising out there in the world. Not here. Here there was no sun at morning but only light, a greying that resisted colour, and today made an unwelcome end to an unwelcoming night. He'd sooner pace the stars around again, match their wheeling with his own.

He'd faced Sieur Anton, because he'd had to; he could not face Jemel. Now he stood facing cold shadow, a dawn that barely lifted the murk of night; he stared north and could see nothing, and wished fervently and without reservation to have the Daughter's eyes again, if only for a while.

If he went down to the terrace below he might see better, there was a subtlety in the air there that made distance clearer, though never so clear as the Daughter did; but one thing he had seen by starlight even before the dawn, Elisande's slight figure swathed in the darkness of a Sharai robe, watching and waiting as he was.

If he couldn't go to find Jemel, if he had spent a long night not going to find Jemel, he certainly couldn't go to Elisande.

He could have gone out, away, alone; he could have run off, not to escape his burdens but to take them with him, somewhere they could do less damage. Somewhere they could damage only him. He would have done that, surely, when he was younger – three months ago, one month. Perhaps a week, a day. Yesterday, he might have done that. Today it wasn't possible.

Besides, the djinni had told him to stay here. Others could leave, others were leaving – below him now there were voices, Elisande and Julianne: and the tall girl was saying what the short girl wanted most to hear, and she of course was arguing against herself and would lose in the end because she wanted to, and they would go out into the field together to fight or to heal or simply to learn who fought, who died, who lived besides themselves – but not he could leave, the djinni had all but said so. *Stay in the palace, if you cannot cross the worlds,* it had said.

Oh yes, he'd snarled, *stay safe while others die. Of course. Perfect employment, for a man who will not fight.*

I did not say so, it had said, unbearably calm. *If others must die in the morning, you may still die in the afternoon. If the battle is lost in your absence, be sure that death will seek you out regardless. And you would be little use in the field, if you will not fight. I will not take you there, or anywhere. You were better to remain here.*

And do what? Stupid with worry and weariness and temper, he'd heard his mouth shoot the question before his mind could stop it.

Stay out of the way of those you should not question, perhaps, the djinni had said, mockingly. *I will not give you answers; seek your own. But seek them here, if you value anything that you have found here.*

As usual, he hadn't understood it. As usual, when it mattered, there was no one he could ask for any guidance.

Instead he would and did stand and watch while the girls left, while they were lifted and carried by an unseen power on an invisible wind towards the dull glimmer of the river far below; he would and did stand and watch and make no sound when a last group of horsemen rode out to seek the war, and there was one in Sharai dress among them who didn't need to cast back his hood or turn his head for Marron to feel that jolt, that physical pain that came with a night's separation and a weight of words unspoken, impossible to speak.

And then he would and did turn his back on the brightening day and face the near emptiness of the palace, a near echo of his heart: chambers that he could not map nor guess a use for, chambers beyond chambers, beyond and below, every step he took or could take must lead him down from here. Down and away, further and further from his friends, although he would not run nor leave the palace walls without the djinni's say, and he did not think the djinni would speak to him again unless he called it, and he would not call it back from Elisande.

Jemel had passed the night as a betrayed man must, or thinks he must: alone, awake, afraid. For all the pictures his mind could draw in darkness, for all the stories he told himself against the silence, there was only the one fact that mattered, that everything turned around. It was the kernel of what was true, at the heart of all his miserable imaginings; it was the cold grit that lay swathed in the veils of the grey pearl, the stake that held the raging lion captive on its leash, the pit that was the point and purpose of the fruit.

Marron had gone to Sieur Anton, but that was not it. Jemel understood that, could even find it in himself to honour that. He still meant to kill Sieur Anton, and not for Marron's sake; that was an oath that he carried like a pebble in his mouth, unforgettable. He would delay that requital, though, until matters were otherwise resolved in Surayon. He thought that Sieur Anton would not die until he came to kill him; God would be kind, he thought, to one who had been desert-true until he'd left true desert. That had been a mistake, and Jazra had died for it. It had also led Jemel to Marron, and so to uncountable betrayals of God and his people, his tribe and every other oath that had ever mattered to him. And so to the last betrayal, this: that betrayed as he was, he still could not regret his choices or wish them all undone. If a djinni took him back to the Saren, to the spring, and Jazra was alive again and he had the chance to keep him so, to say *no, we will not go, let Hasan march with others against the Patric infidels, that is no fight of ours; what, should we die, one or the other or both together, while we are young and the days are long and the nights are longer yet? Let the old men fight their old wars, priests and imams together; we are Sharai and we fight each other, we fight for camels and gold and pride but not for God. We belong in the Sands, He set us here; why would He have us move?* – if he were given the choice to say all that and make Jazra attend him and so live, he couldn't be sure that he would do it.

Jazra but no Marron, and it was a betrayal even to think that Marron with no Jazra was a better thing, even to wonder whether it might be so. It was a betrayal, one of many, Jemel was used to thinking it quite harmless; there was no djinni would work that magic for him, it was only a story and not for telling, an inner dream of grief.

But no Jazra and no Marron either, and lying in a bed too wide and kept wakeful by the space and the silence and the chill of it: this was the other face of betrayal, and small wonder then that he had risen before the dawn to escape that bed and the constant fact that had shared it with him. Marron had come back from Sieur Anton, and had not come back to him. Jemel would have stayed with the tribes last night only to avoid this, not to have to know; but the djinni had brought him back regardless, and he had had all night to learn and to have that learning underscored by the slow, slow hours during each of which – during each minute, each waiting second of which – Marron still did not come back to him.

So he had risen into darkness, and carried the darkness with him where he went. In that dull, bitter mood, facing what seemed likely to be interminable days of equal loss and stubbornly ready to ensure it with a few sour and unequivocal words if he could only find Marron to say them to, he had found others and been offered a fight instead of an argument. Had accepted heedlessly, almost joyfully; had run to fetch weapons, more weapons than he was carrying, all the weapons that he owned or claimed; had returned to find himself being led – not without some sideways glances among his new companions, but led none the less – into a place he had never, never imagined himself encouraged or permitted or even physically able to enter.

He had broken into the imams' house in Selussin, climbed the gate and bullied the guards and shouldered open the door onto the chiefs' private council; he would not have dared, would not have dreamed of coming here despite the ever-open door and the welcome carved into the stone of the lintel, which Marron had read out to him when they passed this place before.

The men he had met readying themselves for battle were Patrics of course, Surayonnaise of course; and it seemed that the latter was the louder of their voices if they could welcome a Sharai among their number when it might be Sharai they rode against, when certainly Sharai were among the invaders hacking a brutal path through their country's broken peace.

Startled by their trust – and deeply, disturbingly unsure that he could in fact be trusted – Jemel had followed them unthinkingly along a corridor and through a doorway, beneath that inscription that he could not read; and only then, only when he was through did he stop thinking of war and grief and the grief of war, start thinking about God and faith and another face of loss.

Too late to turn and walk out, he was here now. Besides, he wanted these men to trust him, to take him with them freely to the war. This might be a test, even, conceived quickly between them while he was fetching weapons: *if he will pray with us – if the God will allow it – then he may ride with us. If not, he stays.* Or perhaps, *if not, he dies.*

Perhaps they thought their God would kill him anyway. He half thought it himself, walking stiff as a brand through the doorway of a Patric chapel; he thought he might burn as a pitch-soaked brand can burn, seemingly from the inside. Their God was fierce, Jemel knew that from Marron, who had confirmed a hundred rumours true. They did burn

children, these Patrics; they had done that at the Roq after
the attack that failed, the boys who had let down ropes for
Hasan had gone to flame and ash along with their ignorant,
innocent fellows. And Marron might blame the Ransomers
and the cold hearts of their leaders, but Jemel was free where
he was not, Jemel could blame their God.

And so fear their God, and so give that one a credit he
denied his own. It had been a long time since he'd prayed,
and a longer journey; he was heretic now in his heart, which
should go well with being a traitor in his body, if he did find
himself fighting the tribes today. He didn't mean or want to
do that, he'd still choose his own people over Marron's to
hold all this land – if for no reason else, at least the Sharai
did not burn children – but there were greater aims at stake,
and he'd fight any man who set himself in way of their pursuit.

Any man, or any God: he glared a challenge at the ceiling.
And found his eye caught by decoration, by figures painted
in red and gold and green, pictures that perhaps he could
read where the letters defeated him; and so was staring
upward to decipher their meanings as he walked, and so
walked solidly into the back of the man ahead where he was
kneeling, and would have sprawled ungainly on the tiled
floor if he hadn't been caught and held by the belt, by the
man behind.

'Easy, boy,' in a rough rasp. 'I don't care whether you give
the God your prayers, but give Him honour at least in His
own house.'

'I meant no dishonour,' hissed between his teeth as he
wrenched himself free, ready to start the day's fighting here
and now if he had to. 'I was—'

'—Staring up at the saints, I know, instead of watching where you walked. All the Catari do it, when they come in here. Tell truth, lad, I don't care if you gawp or not, and I doubt the God does either; those paintings are there to be seen, or what's the point of 'em? Just don't tread all over Markam as you go, it's disrespectful.'

To the God or to the man, Jemel wasn't clear, but it didn't after all seem worth fighting over. So long as these men's idea of respect didn't involve his kneeling as Markam was. He wouldn't do that for his own God now, far less anyone's else.

But then Markam rose, and stepped aside from the central aisle; and now that he was looking down rather than up, Jemel could see what the Patric man had been about. Not praying, or not solely praying; he had laid his weapons on the floor there before the altar, an impressive cluster of blades and only the latest in a line of such clusters.

The Princip had given orders last night, that no man go into the field without his weapons blessed. Jemel had known men who had ignored similar orders in the Sands. Dead men, mostly. He would likely know others before sunset. Hasan had been weakened by more than his wound; the sheikhs had rediscovered their own voices in his absence, and had tasted blood and smoke all yesterday. Hasan might be listened to yet, but would he be obeyed? That was no small band of sworn brothers he was leading now, it was all the tribes together, dangerously close-camped and ready to kill. They might kill Patrics, they might kill Surayonnaise, they might just kill each other; Jemel wouldn't care to be the one who told them to wait, to hold, not to kill at all. And to speak of imams, and a need to bless – the Sharai endured imams for their God's sake, but did not travel with them nor seek them out. Nor fight with them, especially not that.

Once in his life he had seen an imam employed in the Sands, seen the tribes respect him; that was at Rhabat, before Hasan led his war-party against the Roq. Then there had been a blessing of weapons indeed, but 'ifrit had been in no one's mind. It had been the only way to bring the tribes together, Jemel thought now, to make it a holy war: to tell them that they fought for God, and not for land or loot. It was a general's trick, that had perhaps saved and surely reshaped Jemel's life altogether; without a blessed arrow he couldn't have saved Julianne's and so would not have met Marron, wouldn't have been in place to save Hasan's life with that same arrow later. But the general's trick hadn't won the battle, and wouldn't win any hearts now.

Even if Hasan could find an imam, the tribes would never stand in line a second time to have their weapons touched and prayed upon. They would laugh, rather, with all the scorn of the proud Sharai. With a day's burning and looting at their backs, their robes rank with dried blood, an army or two of Patrics ahead of them and a river to fight over, more good water than any of them had seen in their lives before, what need an imam, a blessing, a warning to beware? They'd know where their blades were bound; come the battle they would rely on a strong arm and a scimitar's edge, as they always had. Jemel thought they would die in numbers, as they so often did.

Men were waiting while his thoughts ran like molten wax, wasted, useless. They had laid their weapons on the chapel floor; they looked to him to do the same. Would a Patric blessing hold, on a Sharai blade that was blessed already? He didn't know, but now would be a good time to find out and a bad, perhaps a very bad time to refuse.

He had a bow on his shoulder, too, and a quiver of arrows hung Patric-style at his back; he set them on the tiles beside the scimitar. There were extra knives in his belt, all Patric in make; he added those. And felt the weight of one more at the back, heavier than he would ever have picked out for himself. He drew it forth and added that too, managing something close to a smile at the thought of an outcast Saren boy slaying a Saren sheikh with the sheikh's own blade, after it had been blessed by a Patric priest. Perhaps he wouldn't need a killing blow, even: perhaps the merest prick would act on Bhisrat as it would on an 'ifrit, slide into flesh as if it were nothing but smoke, seek out the soul of him and send it down to hell.

Or perhaps the blade would curl and smoke like parchment in a fire, when the priest reached out to touch it. For all that Jemel knew, it might have been blessed already by an imam, as his scimitar definitely had been. Set one God's blessing against another's, in the same narrow steel – it was like setting Patric and Catari in the same narrow strip of land. Which the Gods had done, of course . . .

If there were Gods, if there could be two where each religion preached one alone. Jemel had ceased to worship, not to believe; he just wasn't sure any longer whether his belief could hold fast against the equal faith and seemingly equal miracles of the Patrics. If their priests' blessings worked as well as his imams' – and if he could respect and fear their fierce priests, where he felt little more than contempt for any imam he had met – then where was the truth of any teaching?

Here in Surayon, perhaps. It must yet be a godly land; this chapel was no disused relic of a dead faith. The paintings were fresh on the ceiling, the tiles underfoot were worn with use but still clean and uncracked, the wood that panelled the walls smelled spicy with a long generation of incense. And these men had filed in easily, familiarly, as if from regular habit. Jemel looked for another man to come, perhaps from another door; he didn't know how Patric priests dressed when they weren't armed and booted, but surely in robes as the imams did, to proclaim their difference from the common people . . .

He was doubly taken aback when no priest appeared. Rather, one of his companions stepped forward, and he not even their officer, just one of the men. He turned to face them, and spread his arms wide like a priest inviting the congregation to kneel. Jemel would not, could not, but neither did any of the men about him. Even the Sharai – who made such a virtue of their haughtiness, their refusal to stoop before their enemies or the many hardships of their lives in the Sands – even they prostrated themselves before God; but not these, apparently.

They did bow their heads, in respect rather than humility, he thought; and they responded in quiet, firm voices as the man before them prayed. Jemel couldn't follow the words. Marron had said that there was a language the Patrics used to speak only to their God; Jemel suspected that the Princip had used that old tongue to write a new religion for this land, as he had written the law.

If a man wrote his own religion, could he find a god that would adopt it? Or was there just the one God, whom any form of worship would satisfy? However Jemel phrased the question, it made as little sense as the words he heard spoken or the actions that accompanied them, the turning and bowing to east and west, to where the dark rose up at sunset and where it retreated come the dawn. It must be retreating now in the world outside this windowless chamber, with its own painted views of another world entirely. Perhaps all religions looked toward a world not real; but then, Jemel had walked in a world different from this, and had found no gods in it and little enough else.

The man who led the prayers reached down to touch and bless the blades laid out before him, but what power did he claim, to give them virtue? When he was done, Jemel retrieved his own weapons and examined them suspiciously. They were as heavy to his hand as they had been before and as sharp to his finger's touch, as bright to his eye and nothing more.

He'd distrusted the imam in Selussin, but believed in the prayers and blessings none the less; God would not punish a man for choosing a poor intermediary. Here, though, he doubted the man and the God and the prayers, all three. Where there was no tradition and no ceremony, nothing to distinguish a holy man from any other, how could there be any blessing worth more than the words that were said?

Like his fellow Sharai, he thought he would be riding into battle with nothing to rely on but the strength of his arm and the edge of his scimitar, the speed of whatever broken-down animal these men could find to carry him.

'Esren.'

Elisande said the name softly, almost sighed it on a simple exhalation, where Julianne would have expected her to scream it. She might have been summoning the djinni in her common casual manner, except that it was already there. Still there, after fetching them from the palace and bringing them, depositing them here; still hanging in the air beside Elisande's shoulder, playing the obedient servant with its usual mockery implicit. It had lingered as though it knew that if it left, it would be hailed back again – but then presumably it did know. It was a djinni, some part of its awareness should forerun it like a wisp of smoke on an unfelt breeze. Even if it were as blind as it claimed, if it lacked any true sense of the future, it must still have guessed how Elisande would react to this. It had said what it had said, it had done what it had done; it had lifted them up like hope, like a promise, and it had brought them here.

Julianne had guessed, had been certain what to expect, was flinching yet – and all in vain, as Elisande's voice made an absolute point of its calmness, its control.

'Esren, I said to bring us somewhere we could be useful.'

'You did; and so I have.'

Elisande gazed deliberately about her, and so did Julianne; it was irresistible.

They were standing on an island, rough rock and wild grasses, in the middle of the icy rushing waters that divided the valley state, the river whose path they had overflown all the way from the mountain pass to the palace. It divided the valley and divided itself about them, north and south; on either side the stream was too strong to swim, too wild to row or raft, far too broad to leap. It might have been bridged, but was not. A little way upstream there were abutments on the banks to suggest that a bridge had stood there once, and perhaps recently; it was not there now.

Simple to cross from bank to bank, of course, with the aid of an amenable djinni. If they had only had one.

Instead, they had Esren. Any minute now, a regular hissing, raging Elisande would have reminded it that it had sworn to serve and obey her; it would have replied with some portentous enigma, which by the time it was untwisted would mean only *I choose not to do so,* or else more simply *never trust a djinni.* This new patient Elisande – *diplomatic, perhaps I should say, and can she have been learning lessons from me?* – took a second glance around, just to make the point the stronger, before she said, 'I do not see what use we can be to anyone, if you abandon us here with a gulf on every side.'

'There would be little point in that,' it said, which sounded almost like agreement, 'and so I would not do it. Nor would I expect you to see what use you will be; you lack the sense.' Which might have been a common insult, or else a plain statement of fact, that she didn't have its ability to foresee what needs might come; the djinni was quite capable of either, or of turning the one into the other and so saving time and effort.

Whichever it meant, the familiar Elisande would have taken it as insult, and laughed. This one seemed to take it the other way; at any rate she nodded, and was silent. And looked about her one more time, as though she were struggling to see what was impossible for her, how events might fall out in a way that would give value to their presence here; and shrugged at last, and said, 'Very well, Esren. Leave us, if you will.'

It would and it did, although Julianne did not believe it had been waiting for permission.

In its absence, Elisande reverted. She heaved a huge groaning sigh that had nothing of patience about it, and then stooped to heave a rock up from the ground at her feet and hurl it into the swift-rushing water that encompassed them.

'I could kill it,' she said conversationally, above the splash. 'If I had the strength, the speed, the skill, whatever it takes, the *knowledge* – I could kill that spirit, and feel not a moment's guilt.'

Julianne smiled gently. 'Of course you could. And you do have what it takes. It's never said so, but I think a blessed weapon will kill a djinni as easily as an 'ifrit.'

Elisande touched the knife in her belt, in a moment's pure startlement; then she scowled and said, 'You call that easy? You want to go up against those monsters with just a dagger in your hand, blessed or not, you're welcome to it. I'll stand back and applaud.'

'Of course you will, what else? But we won't be going up against anything, 'ifrit or djinni or plain bad man, so long as we're stuck here on our own. We need them to come to us for slaughter. How can we best arrange that, do you think?'

'With Esren it's supposed to be easy, it's meant to come when I call it. And stop humouring me, or I'll wind up killing you instead.'

'What, after you showed off all that wonderful patience? Shame to spoil the effect now, don't you think?'

'Ah, maybe so. All right, you're reprieved. Not pardoned, mind. You win pardon by telling me why in hell that creature deposited us here.'

'I'd need to be a djinni myself to know that, sweet. There must be something, though – something to find, or something to wait for.'

'What do we do, then? Wait, or look?'

'Look while we're waiting, don't you think? It passes time or saves it, and either one is useful.'

Such light-hearted talk, instinctive and almost meaningless, sliding with a feather's touch over what was dark and turbulent, darker and more turbulent even than the water that scoured the sides of their small island – that talk was useful also, only that they could neither one of them keep it up. They did look around while they waited, and they lapsed into silence while they looked; and the looking couldn't do what the talking did, it couldn't even seem to buoy them up. They looked, and saw, and dark waters closed above their heads.

What they saw was a broad, flat stretch of meadow grasses, studded with boulders and meadow flowers, rising to a peak of rock at the easterly end. With a bridge to either bank, the island would surely have been given over to pasture as the banks were; its isolation had kept it wild, and beautiful in a way that those tamed acres never could be.

Beauty had no use today. There was grass, there were rocks and flowers; no matter how careful her inspection or how free her imagination, Julianne could find nothing more nor any value in that grass, those rocks, those flowers.

She looked and thought, and watched her friend; and when Elisande flung herself down on her back, full-length in the deep sweet grasses, she said, 'Secret tunnels? Hidden caves, long-lost treasures of the family?'

Elisande snorted. 'With magical properties, no doubt, that will drive all enemies back beyond our borders and ensure peace for ever? Sorry, no. We don't have legends in Surayon, only the knowledge that we found or worked out for ourselves. Some of that, most of that we've hidden from the world, but not from ourselves; we don't bury secrets. This place is called Bridge Island, because it's just downstream from the bridge. Where the bridge used to be,' her finger stabbing blindly above and behind her head, where she lay staring up at the pale sky. 'We used to invent fanciful ways to get here, when we were kids – my favourite was being carried on the wings of eagles, which is a little ironic, don't you think? – but we never tried any of them, it was only a game we played because it was impossible. And it was only impossible because there was never any point. You could graze a couple of cattle on it, but why bother, when we've got all this?' Her arms spread wide, to encompass all the broad miles of pastureland on both banks of the river. 'Land is short here, but not that short, to make it worth building a bridge to a patch of grass half the size of my grandfather's terrace.'

'So why did Esren bring us here, and why leave us?'

'Julianne, I still do not know. I have looked, and not seen; I have thought, and found no answers. Now I am waiting, as you told me to. There must be a reason. There must. Mustn't there . . . ?'

And for a moment she almost broke on the question, almost cracked her calm façade against the brutal truth of her ignorance; but did not, and Julianne wanted to applaud her for that recovery and could not, for fear of seeing her lose it all again.

At times when it is simply impossible to move, there is no need to have a reason to be still.

Marron knew this of old. So surely did Elisande's djinni, it must be ancient news to all the djinn. Why then had it troubled itself – and dealing with mortal men, fleshly creatures was truly a trouble to the spirit, it had made that abundantly clear many times – to come to him unsummoned, to tell him he should stay within the palace? It must have known that he would do exactly that, without needing to be told. If he could not stay with Sieur Anton, he could not go to Jemel; if he could not ride with Jemel, he could not go to Sieur Anton. He had nothing to do, then, but remain where he was. There was nowhere else for him to go, no one else to run to. He had seen insects trapped in spilt honey, but this was not that; honey was too warm, too fresh and sweet, too life-affirming and full of hope. He had also seen insects trapped in amber, and that was this entirely: honey-gold and honey-clear, a rank pretence at being something other than it was, while it was hard as stone and dead as stone and so too was the insect that it held.

Something must happen, he supposed, eventually. While he waited – for a Sharai raiding-party or vengeful Patrics, perhaps an onslaught of 'ifrit from the sky above the valley or the rocks below, it didn't really seem to matter – he found that he was unexpectedly hungry. Seeking a breakfast would pass a little time, at least.

The cold had numbed his fingers to all feeling, the long time standing had stiffened his knees. He stamped his feet against the tingle of sluggish blood, reminding himself that he was all too human once again, he didn't have the Daughter to cover his negligence now. As witness his hunger, sudden and urgent now that he had given a name to it.

Cramped and awkward legs were slow to hurry, down the narrow turning stair; his body was swifter, above and ahead of them. He leaned his shoulder to the wall and slid as much as stepped, swiftly felt the slide run away with him and could not catch it, could find nothing to grab hold of to catch himself and so found himself descending in a rush that was almost a fall each time his feet hit stone, only saved himself with another reckless stumble forward every time.

When there were no more steps, when there was no more curving wall to support his weight and guide his shoulder round, he was going to fall truly, entirely, there was no way to avoid that. He couldn't slow his hurtling progress, all he could do was keep moving and hope not to hit too hard when he did hit, hope not to bleed too badly or hurt too much. Even as he hurtled, there was a part of his mind that snagged against the thought, that had to be reminded that pain mattered now where bleeding did not, when for all this recent time it had been almost entirely the other way around . . .

He could not stop himself, but someone else could stop him. He came charging out of the stairwell and into the passage below, almost flying, arms whirling in search of an impossible balance even as he felt himself lose it altogether – and his lowered head plunged suddenly into something resilient just as he heard a bark, a yelp, the strangled rush of a breath forced out by violence.

So rather than sprawling full-length on the boards and matting of the passage floor, he fell in the tangle of another man's fall. An elbow caught him above the ear, just payment for the stomach-butt; otherwise he came to ground more softly than he might have done, cushioned by the other's body and the stiff embroidery of his robe.

Lying with that embroidery against his cheek, feeling the quality of it even while his eyes were still too dazed to see, Marron had a moment's time to take it in, that he had pitched over a man of rank. He had time even to wonder who it could be, when he'd thought that all the knights and lords of Surayon had ridden out to defend their country.

Below the robe below his cheek, he felt the man's chest stir and heave. Not dead, then – perhaps only winded, nothing worse than that. Winded and half-crushed beneath the weight of the idiot who had brought him down, who was still lying at his ease there on the body of this his important victim . . .

Marron scrambled up, already stammering nonsense syllables, half a dozen beginnings to an apology he couldn't begin to shape deep enough however deep he dug. Then, seeing who it was who lay like a broken poppet on the floor at his feet there, he fell abruptly and entirely mute.

'Marron.' The voice was cautious, on a breath that laboured for comfort and had not found it yet. 'Was there some reason for your, uh, urgency – something seen from the roof, that will not have been seen from the terrace?'

'No, sir.' There was nothing, he thought, that could be seen from the roof that would not have been seen from the terrace. But confession at least came easily to him, he'd been trained to it all his life, and it was good to tell a simple truth for once. 'Only I was hungry, so I went too fast on the stairs; and my legs were stiff with too long standing in the cold, so I lost balance, and—'

'—And found your landing in me. I understand you perfectly. It may be that some mystical power impelled me to walk along this corridor at precisely this moment, purely in order that I might save you a cracked head. Don't you think?'

Marron thought that this was a strange morning to be making jokes. If the man was joking. It was almost impossible to tell.

'Still,' Coren went on, 'I'm relieved to hear that you've recovered one normal human appetite, at least. It grew wearing, watching Elisande and Jemel between them take note of every mouthful they could inveigle you to eat. I don't suppose that sword you wear at your belt signifies that you've also recovered a willingness to use it?'

Marron shook his head mutely. Dard was his, a gift, and so he wore it; but what it signified was another gift that he had, a gift for killing, with or without the Daughter. He wore it as a reminder, not to use it. And lacked the words to explain, and could only hope that he would be understood without. Of all men, he thought, the King's Shadow should understand; wasn't the King the same in this at least, that he kept the Kingdom as a reminder not to rule it?

'No. I could wish that you were more surprising, but then I suppose you would be less Marron, and that might be a greater pity. It's all a pity today, this is no time for nice feelings and I hate to see a great skill wasted – but more than one person has said that it's the right choice for you, so perhaps there's a purpose to it. A warrior who will not fight, a sword that's never bloodied: it sounds like a figure from a heroic tale, or one of Rudel's ballads. I admit that my own preference would be for something more down-to-earth this morning, but perhaps you should look on that as a challenge. Find a way to surprise me, Marron – other than barrelling into me, I mean, in your pursuit of breakfast. It might be best if you attended to that first, though, for fear of causing further damage to the defences of the house. I was myself heading towards the kitchens, to see what a man might glean after a long night's plotting. Shall we go together? We could pause by my daughter's room on our way, and ask if the girls have any appetite for food.'

Among the general slipperiness of words that seemed always to mean something more than what they actually said, Marron was almost glad for the chance to seize onto a single, solid fact. Almost.

'Uh, sir, the girls . . .'

A soft thread of a sigh, anticipating unwelcome news, and, 'Yes, Marron? What of the girls, what have they done this time?'

'I don't know, sir, but – well, they're not there.'

'Ah. Again, I'm afraid you don't surprise me. Where are they?'

'I don't know,' again, and surely no surprise again. 'The djinni took them, but I don't think they knew where. I just heard them, down on the terrace . . .'

'Tell me what you heard,' crisply, no slipperiness now. 'As exactly as you can, please.'

Which he did; and then there was another sigh, which carried another wealth of meaning. 'Very well. If the djinni has taken them, no doubt it will find some way to set trouble stirring around them. Though either one of those two is capable of stirring up trouble enough on her own account, let alone the two of them together.'

'Sir, I don't believe the djinni means them any harm.'

'Do you not? Well, no. Neither do I, in fact. That does not mean that harm will not result. The djinn have their own interests, which seldom coincide with ours. Witness how that one plays with Elisande, and with the oath it swore. I could wish that my daughter were more reluctant to be played with – but I trained her to be a piece in a wider game. If it is wider than I had imagined, or if she chooses to be played by rules other than my own, I suppose I can have little to complain of. I set her loose on the world, entirely as she is; my fault, then, if she wreaks havoc where she passes. But it's hard to be philosophical after a long night and before breakfast. With me, Marron, if you please.'

'Sir, I can bring you what you want, in the solar, or—'

'—Or anywhere I can be cold and alone while I eat, as befits my station? Thank you, Marron, but no. We are soldiers and comrades today, you and I: as we were before, but perhaps more so, as there's nothing in you now to confuse us. Comrades eat together, soldiers always seek the warm; which in a great house like this must always mean the kitchen. If you don't know that lesson, learn it now.'

Marron did know it, of course he did. He was a little surprised that his companion knew it first, until he remembered that the King's Shadow had earned that title by fighting all through Outremer beside the King. Coren might have been a lordling once and become a diplomat later, but he was truly a soldier between the two. Marron had always had an eye for a good sword, and far the more so since Dard was first given to him; the broad blade that Coren wore today was no courtly ceremonial weapon, all jewels and inlay, show without strength. Rather it was a plain man's sword, the scabbard stained and the hilt rebound with wire, the form and weight of it a generation out of fashion. No smith would make such a blade today, but any smith would respect it, any soldier recognise it: if Coren had fought his way from Tallis to Ascariel, then this was the weapon he had fought with.

Clearly, he intended to fight with it again today. Only Marron wore a sword and would not use it.

Well, let them be warriors who chose to. It was easier far to be a servant – except that the King's Shadow would not allow it. Even when they came down the last stairs into the cavernous, low-arched spaces that were the cooks' domain, and found no cooks; found no women, no pages or scullions or anyone at all except for a group of men-at-arms with bandages, bruises, bloody scabs to show why they clustered round a table's end in their lord's palace rather than a fire in the field; even then, Coren would not allow Marron to fetch him bowl and spoon and beaker.

'I said, boy, we stand on equal terms today. As we did in the desert – which is what this palace and this valley will become, if the various passions of the various men out there come together this day. They will make a conflagration between them, and it will be generations before anything good grows again in Surayonnaise soil.'

'Does the King not support his own armies, then?' Marron demanded, stooping before a fireplace vast enough to roast an ox unbutchered and ladling two bowls of a boiling porridge of grains from where it hung in a cauldron above a bank of smoking turves. He drew a dipper of molten mutton-fat from a copper pan beside the fire and added a glistening aromatic stream to each bowl – there were herbs in the pot there with the fat, though he could not identify them – while Coren used the same time to fill two beakers with beer from a keg. 'Or his own priests?'

'They are the God's priests, not the King's.'

'They fight for the Kingdom. The Ransomers do.'

'They do – but few of the Ransomers are priests, and those who are were mostly soldiers first. I can't answer your questions, Marron, I'm not a djinni. The King gives his support where he deems that it is needed or desirable, or so I assume. He does not explain himself, to me or any man.'

'No, but you speak for him. I thought it was your job to explain him to other men,' *to me . . .*

A soft laugh, and, 'Would you ask me to explain what I do not myself understand? Well, yes, you might; but the King is kinder, or simply not so young. No, no, Marron. My task is to speak for him the way your mouth and tongue speak for you, no more than that. Without thought, without argument. I am more of a servant than you have ever tried to be. And a better one, I think, at least I've never run away from my master; but that's beside the point. The King is the King, Marron, and this is his Kingdom; you have simply to accept that, and not to question.'

Another day, Marron might have choked on his porridge. Without thought, without argument? This man, of all men? This morning, even a smile eluded him. Nor would he be eluded. 'You have not run from your master, but you deal with his enemies.'

'Do I?' It sounded like a genuine question, which was unfair. Marron took a breath, and spelled out his confusions.

'You are known and welcome here in Surayon, which has sealed itself off from Outremer in rebellion; and I met you in

Rhabat, where the Sharai were planning war against the Kingdom . . .'

'And where I was arguing as best I could against it. All of Outremer deals with the Sharai, Marron. And the Sharai deal with Outremer, for exactly the same reason. Trade with the left hand and battle with the right, it's an old pattern; it's old because it works. I know men who will tell you that warfare is just another form of trade. In fact, I know two girls who will tell you the same thing: one because I taught her so, the other because she's always known, by instinct, except that she believes that it's better expressed the other way around, that trade is just another form of warfare. And as for Surayon, it has never rebelled against the King; neither has he ever turned his face against it. He has always tolerated squabbles between the states.'

'This is more than a squabble, sir!'

'Is it? It's the prime of all squabbles, rather – a family of children, all with knives in their belts to snatch at in their heat. Brothers and cousins, and the land too small to satisfy – small wonder if their tempers will not hold. That's how Outremer was made; that's how we raised an army in the homelands forty years ago, from quarrelsome sons who would otherwise have been killing each other over their fathers' fiefs. The Church Fathers would say otherwise, but they stayed safe in their libraries and chapels and never marched with us, they never saw the army in the field. It's the same here. A little sunlight and a priest's blessing don't change a man's nature. He may say he does this for the glory of the God, but actually he does it for land, for territory, for borders: for somewhere he can stand and say, *this is mine, and all that is within it comes to me; strangers hold your ground, beyond my fences.*'

'The Sharai don't—'

'Marron, do you lack eyes, or is it simply common wit that's missing in you? The Sharai do, exactly. The Sharai don't farm, and they don't build walls and gated roads and guardposts; but you've travelled in the Sands, you've seen how the tribes claim and defend their territories. It's just the same. Neither is Hasan any different. He's a visionary, but all of his vision laid out only amounts to more land for the tribes to fight over. He wants a Sharai kingship, extended over the Sands and the Sanctuary Land both, but he doesn't want to rule.'

'Like the King, then?'

'Mm? Oh – not really, no. Or only a little like the King. The King rules, he just doesn't govern. And see him or not, everyone knows that he's there. Hasan doesn't want to live in Outremer, nor do any of his people. They'd be quite happy to leave it to other Catari, or to us if we were peaceable and paid our tribute duly. Then each tribe could raid the others' tribute-wagons, and they'd be entirely content.'

Marron opened his mouth to murmur that perhaps that would be better than the current dispensation, an unseen King and a cruel, frightened people. Before he could say it, though, another voice cried other news, 'Ghûl! Ghûl!'

The cry was away, above, but not far. Every eye was drawn to the doorway, to the skidding broken sounds that came ahead of the feet that made them, a man plunging recklessly, helplessly down the stairs and with no one to hold him at the foot.

And so he fell, hard on naked flags, and seemed barely to notice it; his hands like claws had hauled him up the nearest pillar before any man could reach him, so that he stood on his feet again to point, wildly behind him.

'Ghûls! In the yard, in the stables . . .'

In the stairwell too, to judge by the sounds he pointed at: hard clopping and hard, huge breathing, as though there were pack-mules coming down the steps.

The hand he pointed with should surely have had a sword in it, and did not. Marron might have offered him Dard and – almost – meant it, except that this man didn't look anything like a fighter. Like a victim rather, visibly terrified and too old to care how visible his terror was. Sparse white hair fell to his shoulders, there were spots on the skin of his face and on his trembling hand where he was still pointlessly pointing; he wore the workaday tunic of a palace servant but that it showed no signs of any work, today or any day. One of the Princip's pensioners, past use – except to make porridge, perhaps, and tend these few wounded men for a day?

'Where are the guards?' Marron murmured, standing shoulder to shoulder with Coren and stepping forward even as he registered that none of the wounded men was armed, that they were scrambling to arm themselves with kitchen-knives and cleavers.

'The guards are gone to war, Marron. The servants are gone to the mountains, those few who were left, the Princip sent them last night and he's not a man to leave an empty house protected. These few came in late and exhausted, too much hurt to travel further, or he'd have sent them too. He gave them what healing he could, but he daren't spend all his strength, or all his daughter's either. They're probably still too much hurt to fight.'

They looked it, certainly; it showed in the struggle they had to look strong, to look ready for battle against the truth of what they were and what they held, a pitiful collection of cutlery and cooking irons. Perhaps they truly believed that courage could overmaster weakness, pain, inadequate weapons and all. Marron didn't think so, though. He thought that they only wanted to die in the show of it, because die they surely would if there were ghûls on the stairs, and they surely knew it. Too weary, too hurt or too stubborn to flee further after they had fled this far, they would die here in the Princip's kitchen unless someone else could aid them. And who was there? There was Coren, who had powers as the King's Shadow that Marron couldn't guess at, but seemed rarely willing to use them. As a man he had a sword, the strength to wield it and a long lifetime's experience of battle, but the length of that lifetime must tell against him now; he was old and tired, and was no more fit to stand alone against ghûls than those other men were fit to stand beside him.

And then there was Marron. Numbed, exhausted in his turn – but young and fleet and swift to recover when there was food in his belly, with a fine sword apt for his hand and that hand well-trained for fighting. What did it matter if an oath was broken casually, for little reasons like the lives of strangers, so long as it was kept where every little thing mattered hugely? The gods or luck or bloody fate must care for Jemel and Sieur Anton, because he could not; perhaps the djinni would care for the girls, as it had taken them where he could not; Coren could surely care for himself, either with his sword or with a swift departure. That left these men, who held their lives too cheap to run. These Marron could perhaps care for, because he didn't even know their names.

Perhaps.

The more noise there was in the stairwell, the more quiet

and still they were in the kitchen. If terror was a weapon, then sound was its keenest edge. A clear, brisk rattle like hooves in a stableyard was half smothered by the wet rasping weight of oxen's breath, the muted rub of hide on stone; Marron had met ghûls before, but still found his mind leaping from shape to dreadful shape as it struggled to make sense of what it heard.

Then, at last, there was darkness moving in the shadows. Huge, ponderous figures bent below the stairs' low ceiling, squeezing through the doorway, straightening slowly in so far as ever they could stand straight.

Three, just three of them came into the kitchens. Split and shredded rags that had once made robes were clinging to rough hair and skin, to show where they had dressed and shaped themselves as women in their approach to the palace; from a distance they must have seemed like belated refugees.

The palace was a maze to Marron still; he wondered how they'd known where to come. Perhaps they could smell out living men. Or if they were slaved to the 'ifrit – as surely they must be, this attack was too bold for random ghûls – then perhaps they were guided by the stones in their tongues, driven by their masters' will. *Go there, turn here and here, go down: you will find men gathered, kill them there . . .*

Perhaps. *Kill them or die* might have been implicit, the extent of 'ifrit sight; like the djinn, they couldn't see past death's possibility. *Kill them or die*: it would do for both parties, perhaps, men and ghûls alike. Marron could see another path, though, and meant to try it.

He stepped forward, and monstrous heads turned to eye him. Whether this was the ghûls' true shape, he wasn't certain; did they, could they truly have one, who could shift their shape by will alone, or at least by will and pain? But he had seen one thus before, when it abandoned the disguise of a woman: still roughly human, though no human was ever so crudely modelled, with its gross body bowed and its brutal arms swinging below its knees, its head stretched and distorted, more horse than man if horses ever did have lions' teeth . . .

Roughly human, inhumanly rough: they carried no weapons, and needed none beyond the strength of those long, long arms and the claws that tipped them, the bite of their heavy jaws, their weight and reach and simple savagery. Marron felt more than small against them. He felt delicate as parchment, fine-drawn as an inkline, Dard like a slender nib to write their story. And he felt also that he could have written it as he chose if he had only been another man, the man he should have been, loyal to his raising and his skills. Ghûls were deadly but clumsy with it, awkward in their own bodies and slow of thought, however swift of arm. Left to themselves they would always prefer disguise and ambush to direct assault, the strike from behind and in darkness to face-to-face battle in the light. Here, Marron could have called a dance of steel and blood that would have proclaimed the triumph of man above beasts and demons, the cold and killing touch where civilisation meets barbarity. There were only three and he could kill them all, if he could only choose to do it.

Lacking that choice, lacking any, he raised the sword that he had sworn not to use again and he walked clear-sighted into a fight, crying back over his shoulder as he went.

'Lead the men away from here, Coren. You can do that, while I delay the ghûls.' The King's Shadow could walk through walls and take men and women with him, through solid rock and distance. Marron couldn't even walk between the worlds any more, and missed it badly.

He could still step from one Marron to another, though, from the confused and stubborn boy to the swordsman raised and trained. Even without the Daughter's strength and speed, he had his own share of both and the wit to use them.

'Marron, remember, kill with a single stroke; a second will only heal the harm of the first.'

'I have not forgotten.' Nor had he, any more than he had forgotten his oaths, his many oaths; any more than he had forgotten Jemel, or Sieur Anton, or himself.

He knew a hundred ways to wound a man, to drain blood and strength and yet leave him living. Few were sure in a single stroke; he couldn't afford needlework, a prick here and a prick there, when each prick undid the one before. And he didn't know the ghûlish body, how it differed from a man's, what blow might be fatal and what not. But this much he did know, that ghûls were rougher-made than men, more brutal, spirit wrapped in something closer to original clay than mortal flesh. They did bleed like men, but likely not to death, he thought. He could hew and hope, at least, where he could not hew to kill. *And if one looks to be dying, well, I can hew it again until it heals. And then again, to hurt it . . .*

It was an absurdity, a madness: to fight and mend, to mend and fight again. But it was his own madness, a nonsense of war when war was a madness in itself. He ducked neatly under the flailing club-like claw of the nearest ghûl, hesitated just a moment, and then struck hard and clean.

Dard bit, seemed indeed to leap forward in his hand in its eagerness to bite after a long fast. Bit deep, for blood and meat together: drove in beneath the swinging arm, high and rising into the massive creature's chest, so far that in a man the point must have erupted from neck or spine behind. In a man, it must have been a mortal blow. Marron gave the blade a twist to let the blood run freely, and still thought the ghûl would survive. It might be fleshly made but it was spirit still, it could shape its body to its will; anything short of a death-blow he thought it could repair, in time.

A gush of hot blood drenched his hand, as though he'd tapped a barrel. It soaked the sleeve of his robe, stinking mightily. The ghûl staggered before him, both hooked claws lifting in a way that seemed to disregard its own hurt, if it could only strike at him.

But its blood was flowing, and the one arm failed and fell back, too heavy for torn muscles and fading strength; the other had no speed to it, and Marron didn't even need to duck. He simply sidestepped watchfully and called back over his shoulder, 'Get you gone! Why do you linger?'

'Lack of confidence,' Coren said quietly at his back, 'and rightly so, it seems. You could have killed that thing, and did not.'

'Hurt, dead, what difference to you if you're not here? Muster those men together, and leave this to me.'

'Some difference to you, perhaps, if I'm not here. But, Marron, look . . .'

The ghûl he had maimed was slumped against the wall now, sliding down it, leaving a dark wet streak where its sodden mats of hair rubbed against the white plasterwork. Solitary by nature and unnaturally driven by 'ifrit, stones in their tongues to impel obedience, the others should be trampling it, he thought, struggling to be swiftest to the slaughter.

Instead the second beast was crouched above its brother and impeding the one behind, blocking its way past the long kitchen tables. Marron should have used the moment, and did not; did nothing but gape in bewilderment, then snatched for a slow understanding as the one ghûl raked a claw across the other's throat, opening a wound that could bleed only in a dribble, as there had been so much blood lost already.

Or no, not that. It bled and then it did not bleed, so swiftly closing that only a dribble escaped. And the wound that Dard had made, wide and wet, that closed also; and the creature that had been so hurt rose up strong and fresh, gazing at him with the eyes of a maddened horse set in the skull of what might have been the dream of a maddened horseman. All the world was mad, Marron thought, if it allowed a monster to remake itself in a moment, by virtue of a second wound that should have killed it dead.

'They are not stupid, Marron,' Coren said at his back, above the whispers and soft cries of the wounded men. 'They may move more slowly than you do, they may even think more slowly – but they do think, and they are as wily as any man. And they know what they are, as well as we do.'

'Well, then . . .' Could he hurt them all, so badly that they could not hurt each other? It seemed unlikely. But he was still quicker, he could worry them, distract them, draw them to himself and so do well, do something good this day and have nothing to worry him at the end of it. 'Best take those men away swiftly, Coren.'

'I'll take you first, Marron. You matter more.'

To whom – his friends, Surayon, the Kingdom? 'Not any more. The Princip took what mattered from me,' and stowed it somewhere in the palace. He had no feeling for it, no sense of where it might lie.

'You could matter as a swordsman, if you chose.'

But he had made that choice already, and didn't mean to change it. Surely he had proved that by now, if it hadn't been proved long ago?

Being a swordsman in the only way he could, he didn't glance round even to glare at the King's Shadow. Didn't speak to him either, only stood with Dard raised and ready, watching the gap between the heavy tables, the only way the ghûls could come at him, one by one. He thought he could hurt them, one by one; they could heal each other, but only one by one. That must buy time enough for Coren to open his hidden gateway and escape with what little garrison was gathered here.

But, *they are not stupid, Marron* – and he had forgotten it again, not held it close to the forefront of his mind, not given the ghûls the same respect he'd give a human foe.

Two of them laid their brute clawed hands suddenly atop those refectory tables and vaulted over on long stiff arms. Scrubbed timbers creaked under an extreme and sudden load, the force of it; one snapped, late and uselessly. The ghûls had swung themselves half across the kitchen in one simple movement. Their hooves skittered on the flags of the floor; for a brief moment they looked likely to fall, and did not.

Stood now within a long arm's reach of the wounded men with their pitiful kitchen-weapons; and ghûls have long, long arms.

Pointless for Coren to bellow, 'One stroke only – one stroke!'

Where one stroke of knife or cleaver could never kill, could barely cut tough hide; where the foe seemed barely to register the blow, even with a heavy blade buried deep in the flesh, wedged in the bone of its flailing arm; where dying seemed almost a duty, why worry whether you hurt or healed before you died, why not simply chop and chop?

They did that, those men, those doomed men. They chopped and hacked with a will, with that heedless energy born of utter despair; and – one by one as Marron had hoped to meet the ghûls, to prevent all this – they began to die.

He saw the first death, even while he was trying to watch everything that happened, everywhere. He saw the last of the ghûls – its rank hair glistening, still sodden with its own blood, that it seemed now not to miss at all – watching him, his sword, the movements of his head and hand; he saw Coren doing nothing, only standing back and watching as he was himself, that big blade wasted in an old man's hand who apparently had no strength to wield it; he still saw how the first man died under the ghûls' hand.

In a ghûl's hands, rather. One great arm swung, a claw struck and clung hold; now the other could reach out and take a more leisurely grip.

One twisted, nut-knuckled hand circled the man's upper arm, the other his neck; there seemed no effort in it, as the ghûl pulled its two hands apart.

The man had dropped his little knife, long since it seemed; now he arched his back and gave himself over entirely to screaming.

Screamed and did not stop, but was stopped rather: just as Marron was wishing the claws to grip tighter and choke back that cry, it was cut off. Not choked, not smothered; it did not dwindle, or break off into a sobbing, desperate gasp for air; it was simply gone, snapped like a string, and the room was emptier for lack of it and the man who made it.

It seemed quiet then, but not for long. The ghûls were among the men, and it seemed that there was only him to prevent a slaughter. They were too hurt, too poorly armed, unled; they needed Ransomer discipline – perhaps the first time he had missed that, or any aspect of it – and they did not have it. Coren could have, surely should have plunged forward to take command. A man who had authority over princes, and who had led in war before, how not? But Coren made no move, and Marron had a ghûl of his own yet to face. To face again, to strike again: to kill or not to kill, as his hand or mind allowed.

He meant to maim it, as he had before; its companions were too busy now to heal it. But he was prevented, forestalled. The ghûl's eyes that had been sheened with a cunning intelligence were suddenly dull, as though it had been cast into shadow. It had been shambling towards him with deadly intent; now it checked, swung its arms randomly as though it groped for what it could not see, blundered directly into a pillar broader than itself and clung to it.

Marron spared a glance for Coren, who said nothing but, 'Swiftly, swiftly now . . .'

Marron was swift, and thinking even more swiftly than his feet could run. He ran not directly towards that reckless mêlée where men ducked and rolled, stabbed and gasped and died beneath the slashing blows of two demon-creatures that they could not kill. He ran instead towards the cooking-fire, where it lay smouldering beneath its turves, still hot enough to boil porridge and render mutton-fat. On the way he slammed Dard back into its scabbard and snatched up instead a bleached and age-worn timber from the ruins of the table.

Cold ashes grated beneath his boots; no one had swept the hearth today. The pot-boys were gone, fled or dead. Julianne had borrowed one last night, and brought only his body back. She had cried for him, he remembered, when she had not for Rudel, nor for a hundred other deaths.

Marron thrust the splintered end of the plank through the blanket of turves, deep into the glowing heart of the fire beneath. Left the other end jutting out like a spear's haft and reached instead for the handle of the porridge-cauldron, where it hung from a pot-hook beneath the great manteltree.

Hot iron seared his palms. He hoisted the weight of it, cauldron and bubbling contents together, and felt it score through to the bone. It was only pain, though, and he could endure that almost with welcome, almost with contempt; what matter one more scar where he carried so many, one more hurt when he had known so much? This was a simple thing, a mindless thing, another trivial story written in his flesh.

He pivoted on his heel like a dancer, like the youths he used to watch at the fairs of his childhood as they wheeled their girls around. The cauldron spun at his arms' length, and barely a drop of the porridge spilled; wet though it was, it seemed to cling to the smooth inside surface of the pot as he whirled.

Once around, twice around while it rose higher, travelled faster, burned deeper into his hands; and then he let it go.

Felt it tear free of his flesh, and did not care. Watched it turn in the air, watched as it connected heavily with the monstrous skull of a ghûl; saw the porridge flood out before the cauldron fell, a glistening grey coat flowing down over the creature's hair and hide.

It howled even while he went on turning, stooping back to the fire and seizing hold of another scalding handle, this time the pan that held the molten mutton-fat.

Liquid enough to run down over half the ghûl's body and thick enough to cling, the porridge had made a grotesque capering fool of the creature. Half blind and terribly scalded, it danced its agony, moaned the song of it, entirely disregarding the small men who were falling back around it, gathering up their small weapons and waiting their moment to close in again.

One blow harms, the next heals – but not now. Whether it was magic or simply mystery, that was a rule for clean strikes, for individual wounds. That ghûl must have monstrous blisters swelling already beneath its monstrous hide; neither spell nor nature could count the harm it had taken now.

Or so he hoped, so he – almost – dared to expect. Let the men do their work, with whatever blades they had gleaned. No warnings this time except a hoarse cry, 'Way! Make way there . . .' as he plunged forward to hurl this second pan.

Not trusting to aim or luck a second time, he came close enough to smell the ravening ghûl, the rank rancid fur of the beast and the taint of human blood that smeared it. By contrast, the dense odour of the mutton-fat was herb-sweet: *a perfume for the stinking* he thought absurdly as he finally let the pot fly.

This time he screamed himself when the handle ripped out of his hands, taking more skin and flesh with it, but the ghûl screamed louder. Marron didn't wait to see if this one also danced.

He went back to the fire, to retrieve his plank of splintered table-wood. It was cruelly rough and heavy to his seared hands, but that was a petty cruelty, it lacked malice and intent; he lacked neither as he drew out the smoking end and whirled it around his head to make it flame.

Whirled the brand and flung it, straight and true, so that its blazing made a spear's head of light that flew clean towards the ghûl's heart.

And yes, it did know what was coming, and the noise it made was pure wordless terror. Too near to dodge, it tried to knock the brand aside. A neater creature with a quicker eye might have done that, but its own clumsiness was its betrayal. Its clawed hand met the flame, rather than the wood behind; its first tight, sharp little cry at the heat of it was lost in a soft, eruptive sound as the fire caught and gripped it, flowing up the length of its arm and so all over. Dags of hair drenched in hot oil made simple wicks; Marron had known it, and the ghûl did too.

It had never seemed so human as now, when he could see only the dark shadow of its shape at the heart of a living pyre, when its agony made an animal of it, as it would have done with any man. Marron had seen boys burn at the Roq; now he saw a ghûl burn in Surayon, and he could see little or no difference, except that this time he had set the flame himself.

A voice at his back said, 'Your sword would have been kinder.'

It was true, and he knew it; he said, 'So use yours. I have not been trained to kindness.'

And then turned round, because he'd sooner see his shame reflected than in the raw, in the raw burning flesh of the ghûl as it howled and capered like a king's fool at a feast, except that no one was laughing here; and saw that Coren had used his sword already, that the blade of it showed darkly stained in the flickering light and that the ghûl he had mazed lay slumped at the foot of its pillar now, a spreading pool at its neck-end like the stubborn shadow of a head gone missing.

Marron might have cast about to find the head itself amid all the chaos and wreckage of the kitchen, that would have filled some time, but that Coren gave him no chance; neither any relief from the club of his conscience, that beat against him in unsteady rhythm, in perfect time with the ghûl's crying.

'Oh, no,' the King's Shadow said. 'Even you have to learn to live with your choices, Marron; I won't rescue you from this one. If this is how you choose to step aside from your oath, then so be it.'

'I didn't kill them,' in a dishonest, defensive mutter.

'And yet one is dead,' with a gesture towards another bloody corpse more crudely butchered by the men around it, 'and the other is dying,' with a sudden tug on Marron's arm that pulled him out of the way of a stumbling, tottering inferno that was the ghûl aflame, and at the same time turned him round again so that he had to face it, 'and both because of what you did. Is it the fire that kills, and not you? As well use your sword and say that it is the blade that kills, and not you. Marron, I am sorry that you must lose one more thing that means so much to you. You may be the lesser for it, you will certainly be changed again and I have enjoyed knowing you as you were; but this is war, and all men lose in war. Kill that beast, and have done.'

Marron found that Dard was in his hand again, all unrealised. There was nothing now to stop him, and almost nothing to feel: only a slight hesitation which might have meant *how am I going to tell Jemel?* and which was swiftly overtaken by another thought, one that gripped his mind even as his body did its work so that in fact he barely noticed the moment when he did finally kill again.

Two rapid paces and a lunge in perfect form, like an exercise in drill, a thing that his body could easily do without his mind's attention; a wash of heat against his face that went all but unregarded, the barest hint of resistance as Dard's honed point met the dark shadow at the heart of light, hide and flesh and bone that seemed to welcome its swift intrusion, seemed almost to plunge forward in eagerness to meet it.

It was a neat kill, a sweet kill. His uncle would have applauded, and Sieur Anton also. Jemel would have been satisfied with the result. Coren said nothing, even after Marron had withdrawn his blade, had straightened and turned to face the older man.

His to speak, then, his to say his thought aloud.

'You made me do that.'

'I invited you to do that; you should not have needed the invitation. It was cruelty, to let the thing burn.'

'No. You made me do it, from before. From the moment they attacked. You stood back and did nothing, but you could have done . . .'

'I could not come to the men, to lead them out.'

'You did not try; but not that. You could have defeated the ghûls yourself, before they hurt a soul. You could have mazed them all as you did the one that came at me – and even that,' realising it as he spoke, 'you did not maze the first time, you hoped that I would find the heart to kill it. When you saw that I would not, not in my own defence,' working this out almost on his fingers, spelling his thoughts aloud as they came, 'you thought I must for the defence of others, you thought I could not bear to see hurt men dying badly; so you mazed that one that might have prevented me, but did no more than that. Men died, because you wanted to see me kill.'

'I wanted to see them saved,' the King's Shadow said softly, neutrally, 'and you were the one best placed, best skilled to save them. This is no time for delicacy, Marron, we cannot afford to have you so fine-spirited. We are at war; why do you assume that you can stand aside from all the killing, or that you will be let stand?'

'Why do you assume that I will kill for you?' Marron returned, equally softly, trying for an equal neutrality. 'Jemel is of the Sharai, and my own people – your people – turned me out.'

'Fight for us, fight for the Sharai, I do not care; fight for yourself alone, or for those you love, or for those who love you if you can distinguish between them. We will none of us fight each other today. Tomorrow, surely; but today there are monsters abroad, and we can all fight together. You *know* all of this, Marron, why are you being tiresome?'

'You told me that a young man should not get into the habit of breaking his vows; and then you forced me to it, when it was convenient to you. If I am tiresome, perhaps it is because I am tired of being used, your tool or anyone's else.'

His heart was in his mouth as he said it. He was appalled by his own daring, unless it was stupidity, or both. Daring need be neither courageous nor clever. But Coren seemed to smile faintly, certainly nodded, did not dispute the accusation.

'And yet I will use you when you are apt to the occasion. It's a wise man's habit, Marron, and an old man's necessity. Some things I can do, but many things not, or not as well. And I cannot afford, this world we have made cannot afford to have you stand idle by. We need every man who can wield a blade – and you do it with an uncommon grace and purpose. Before you were brought here, I might have hesitated long before I encouraged you to break that particular oath, or any; with the Daughter in your blood – and in your eyes, which was worse, so that you saw the world half blood already – you were too dangerous to be let loose. Almost too much so to be let live, if you could not control yourself; for certain we could not control you. Which you knew, I think, and hence that famous oath of yours. But you are yourself again, and nothing more; and you are a trained fighter and a skilled fighter, and we are needful of you. This is why you came to the Sanctuary Land, Marron, to honour your father and defend your people . . .'

And to serve the God, but Coren wisely did not mention it, which was perhaps the only wisdom that he showed in that little speech. For a man with a wise reputation, he was displaying a wonderful lack of understanding.

'I came with my friend,' Marron said, 'and then I killed him. Too many men died at my hand, or for my sake, and so I forswore killing; and now there are more dead, and these too can be laid at my door. What am I, that men should die for me? A soldier, yes, or I was once; but so were these.' And there were three dead, in order to make a killer of him. He might as well have killed them himself. It was a poor bargain reckoned in simple numbers; a monstrous fraud weighed in fighting flesh, for any one of the dead would outweigh him in muscle, in years and in experience; a monstrosity by any measure, that lives should be sacrificed simply to bring him to the point of slaughter.

He went on, 'At least they can lie in a place of honour, away from – those,' with a gesture towards the dead ghûls. 'And we can help carry them there, not leave it to their con-frères,' all of whom had been wounded even before this day began. Most had fresh hurts now, or else what had been half-healed was opened fresh again. Marron knew too well how that felt.

'There is,' a sharp look suddenly, the slightest hesitation, and 'no place, Marron. No appropriate place, in the way that you are thinking. The Princip does not favour pomp and formal rites; neither do his people. Let them see to their fallen according to their own customs, they will feel more comfortable about it.'

Marron looked the King's Shadow in the eye and called him a liar, as directly as he dared, even while his mind raced to understand. 'You fetched the Princip's son home, and a place of honour was found for him to lie. Julianne took her serving-boy to the same place, when she brought him back last night. I don't know where that is,' *I don't know where*

they lay precious things in this palace, things they want to pre-
serve out of the sight of men, 'but these soldiers will. Their
fallen friends can lie there too, with the same honour, and I
will see them so.'

Briefly, he thought that Coren would argue further; then
that he would forgo argument and strike him instead, knock
him unconscious or spirit him away in a haze of gold.

The man was all King's Shadow now, though, and no
Coren at all. He seemed to weigh all the likely consequences,
all the possible mischances, and at last shook his head in a
gesture of surrender.

'Even without, you are not in my control and never were.
Well, go your own way, lad, do what you think you must.
This is beyond me, for good or ill; I will not interfere. Be
careful, though, and think what you are doing.'

'I have been careful,' Marron said softly, 'and there is
blood on my blade, where I had sworn there would not be.
There will be no more,' *unless it is my own.*

'And that should teach me not to dice for a man's soul, is
that it?'

Marron looked deliberately towards the bodies of the
fallen men. 'Not when you dice with others' lives. You lost
the game; what did they lose, who were not playing? More
than my oath you have broken here, and you had no right.
Even the King would have no right. You might tell him
that.'

'I might. I might indeed, if I live to speak with him. It is
perhaps less likely, if you will not fight for us.'

'Enough.' Marron said it, heard himself say it. Rage
burned brightly, and at the moment, oh, he was raging. 'I
may kill again, for you or for others. You said it yourself – *if*

once, why not a dozen times more, a hundred? You also said that you would hate to see it, and you might do that also. I do not know; am I a djinni, are you? But now, let be. I will help these men with their dead, and then I will do – what I will do.' Which would involve finding Jemel, finding Sieur Anton, both of them and hopefully not together, a valley's width apart; that much, he was sure of. What more, he could not say. He was not a djinni. And the djinni had said that he should stay within the palace, but perhaps it had only meant until now, until this, so that he could kill these ghûls? Or so that the King's Shadow could manipulate him into killing these ghûls, so that he could be asked to kill again? Or—

Well. He could spend a lifetime, what was left of his lifetime trying to outguess a djinni, and likely never do it. He would do what he meant to do, and then he would leave the palace and seek out his friends, and never mind what the djinni had meant or what Coren wanted. He was not fool enough to think that he could rule himself or make his own decisions, now or soon or later; but he could have the appearance of it, he could seem to be free, and that mattered.

Out in the valley's breadth with his back to the palace and his face to the wind and riding, riding at last, no carpet but a horse beneath him and a good horse too; unsure of whom to fight or whom to kill, but certain that there would be blood on his blade before sundown; for the moment he could be glad enough to be here and not there, with these strangers and not with anyone who loved him.

The valley could give no distance, no sense of space to a

tribesman from the Sands, who had scoured all the desert from the height of the Pillar of Lives. It was trying as best it could, though, high mountain walls dropping and drawing back as they rode westerly, giving the sky more room to spread and the land beneath it; giving more room to the river too, making a wide and worrying road of water off to his right. It shimmered and danced, it was always moving and he was always glancing over as it snagged and snagged at the corner of his eye. He had seen so much water and more, much more, but that had been quite still except for what stirred within it. It had shown no movement in itself until the djinni raised it; it had always been spellcast and evil had come from it, more than one evil. All of that he understood. This running river was another matter. Its urgent strength kept him continually anxious, constantly on the watch for danger rising. An 'ifrit had lurked within it yesterday, maybe more than one, and he was ready for another, but he distrusted the river on its own account. So much water so ill-contained, so lively; he doubted its obedience, its willingness to stay within bounds. And that doubt was a good thing too, it was a blessed distraction like the horse he rode and the speed of his riding, the men about him and the certainty of war.

And the wind, the wind that was nothing like any desert wind that he knew: too cold and far too wet and heavy with the scents of strangeness. There was all the stink of yesterday's burnings there, but that was a stale smell, flattened by more water than the river and the dew could justify; and there was a sharpness that overrode it, an edge that he could not only smell but taste against his lips when he licked them. It tasted like tears, and his eyes indeed were running, but this was an alien salt that stung them.

Salt, and water: an immeasurably great mass of water, too far to see or hear but the wind brought word of it even at this distance. This was the sea, that he had heard tales of but never thought to come near, never wished to. Marron had crossed it, by his own report: a journey of weeks in a boat, a little bobbing hull of wood like a nutshell in the jaws of God . . .

Jemel shivered; he would cross the Sands on foot with a leaking waterskin, sooner than go to sea in a boat. The two vast congregations of water that he had seen, the Dead Waters and this river in Surayon, both attested to the wisdom of his fears. The one was washed through and through with alien malignity, the other was a penned demon at the head of the valley and a stretching giant here, swelling with its own potent life. And they were both insignificant, he was told, as weak as starlight next to the moon's weight and majesty, when they were considered next to the sea.

He would not see the sea this day, at least. He had that comfort. Surayon had never reached so far. Folded or open, it had never made a wall across the width of Outremer; the river splayed out, he'd been told, as the mountains fell, and a broad salt marsh lay between the valley and the coast, where sea and river mingled. Going north or south, men followed the road that hugged the hills, unless they chose the nutshell ride and took a boat to sea.

When Surayon was Folded, that road acquired a Fold of its own. Marron had told him of it, carefully not saying from whom he had heard the story. Jemel knew: silence, namelessness meant Sieur Anton.

But the road was open now, it led into Surayon like a woven thread and not directly through it like a stitch in a

hem. An army had marched up that road yesterday, one of
the armies that had come to harrow the valley. Jemel could
not reach the sea today if he had chosen to; half the fighting
men of Outremer lay between it and him.

The formal fields and their defensive, deceptive walls had
been left behind swifter than he had looked for. As the
mountains had diminished to north and south, so too had
the walls; as the valley had broadened and stretched itself, so
too had the fields. Now they rode through olive-groves and
pastures, there was sheep-dung in the turf and ought probably to have been the sheep themselves cropping in the
shade, except that war had come to Surayon and the flocks
were taken or fled.

That was the only way that he could see the war, in its
absences: no flocks of sheep or goats, no women fetching
water from the springs, no idle men or boys at play among
the trees. As he could hear it only in its silences, no voices on
the wind, no birdsong. The harsh sounds of crickets he
could hear, louder than they ought to be against the hush;
anything more clever than a cricket was gone or simply
beaten down by dread, by the taint of wet smoke encroaching.

There was nothing to be seen but the low shoulders of the
hills outflung in scarps and vales, these gentler slopes he
rode on, groves and orchards and sweet green forage.
Nothing was burning in his sight, though he stood high in
the stirrups; there was only the smell of it like a song to
destruction, a promise of what he was to find.

That smell must be riding further than he'd thought it
could on this wet and heavy wind. He was still confused by

the scale of the country, confused both ways at once. He had problems with the idea of borders in any case, of a line drawn across the land to say that this is one people and that is another. There were tribal boundaries in the Sands, of course there were, but they were as fluid as the Sands themselves, shifting in the winds or with the strengths of the tribes that held them. Permanence was different, difficult, he'd take the steady rocking of a camel's saddle any day over the steadiness of rock. And tribal lands were measured in days of riding, a week was not too long to span Saren country; here he had stood on the Princip's terrace and seen the northern border of Surayon, turned his head and seen the southern, a single valley that he could walk across in half a day and they called it a country, an independent state.

So he had squeezed his imagination, compressed his understanding until he knew that Surayon was small, the pip within the lemon. But they had been riding since the first dawn, sun-up behind the mountains and its creeping light across the sky to say so, looking for the war and had not found it. There was no surprise that he could see among the men he rode with, so he supposed that the land had not been stretched during the hours of darkness, while time had been cruelly stretching out beside him in the bed. A man of Surayon should know his own borders, penned as he'd been all his life within them. The army they rode to meet was not so near as he'd thought; its smoke had far outrun it.

That might be just as well, as they were ill-provided to face an army. Two dozen men, well-mounted but lightly armed: this was going Sharai-style and all very well for a tribal raiding-party in the Sands, but his companions were Patric and would not understand the way of it. Patrics rode in battalions and fought like chained lions, face to face until one fell. They won their victories by weight – weight of armour, weight of numbers, as they ruled the lands they governed by the weight of the stone that they cut and moved and built with – or else by simple stubbornness, outwaiting their enemies, being the last in the field at the end. They would think it shameful to strike and run as the Sharai did. It was how the Patrics had taken all this country long ago, by standing and dying and never moving on. They had pinned it down with their castles, ripped it open with their ploughshares, built a web of roads and cities all throughout. So he had heard, at least, that these lost lands had been made bad country for the Sharai way of war. But this band was fitted for nothing more. Perhaps they might come upon other Surayonnaise, before they met the army out of Ascariel; perhaps they might make a little army of their own. If so, Jemel would still not stand and hack in line, as the Patrics did. He could ride scout, stand off and use his arrows, harry the enemy's flanks, whatever came best to him at the time, how it all fell out . . .

Or none of those, if it all fell out as the wise men had been urging all night. Riding in the stink of war with weapons at belt and back, it was hard to remember that they might not fight with those they went to meet. Riding in a weary rage, it was hard to remember why he had chosen to ride with these Patric companions sooner than fight against them; it would be harder yet if they did not bring him to any kind of fighting.

There was still none to be seen as he guided his mount between twisted trees to the crest of another rise, a running rib from the southern hills. Gazing westerly, he saw land roll and roll into a far-distant haze, thicker and wetter than the shimmering heat that brought the mirage; he thought he might almost see a gleam at its heart, sunlight dazzling on immeasurable water. If Marron had been with him and no one else, if things had been utterly other than they were, he thought that one or other of them would have said the word, and they would have ridden on together until their horses were knee-deep in an ocean.

He had never seen an ocean, and still never thought to see one.

He turned his head away from what might have been the sea, and looked left to where the man Markam had ridden up beside him.

'You promised me a road, from south to north; you promised me an army, and I do not see either one.'

The smile he got in response showed no teeth, and no humour. 'Patience, hornet. You see that shale cliff, a league to the west and south of here? That marks a break in the hills, and a long vale running southerly. That's where the road lies, and that must be where the army lies; they have made a scorched hell of the vale,' and for the first time there was real passion in his voice, a pure fury, 'and have spent the night sleeping in their own creation. For now, we will ride on towards the road, which runs low behind a ridge ahead; and if we meet a scouting-party before we come to the vale's mouth, and if those scouts have yesterday's orders still in their minds, to do to all of us here what they have done to our friends and cousins in the vale there – well, perhaps we will see if a desert hornet deserves its reputation. I confess, I would welcome the chance. The Princip could have no complaint if we were attacked, and had to defend ourselves.'

Jemel thought he would be equally glad of it, for very different reasons. He had no love of this ravaged land and nothing invested in it; only a raging distress that was easier to handle if he called it simply rage, and would be easier yet if he could stop thinking at all and channel it simply from his heart into his hand.

And then he could, and did; and there was nothing, nothing at all to be glad about.

They came out of the ground, out of the harsh and sour soil that was compacted so hard around the roots of ancient trees, that had been trodden for generations by foot or hoof and disturbed only by the slow stretching of those roots beneath, soaked and baked and soaked again until it made a solid coherent mass with the rocks it covered. No grass grew there in the trees' shade, nothing grew but the trees themselves and they had to reach far down between the rocks to find anything good to feed on. Embittered by a lack of care, that soil could have nurtured nothing but the twisted olive and its black thoughts.

Nothing till now. Now the ground, that soil, those rocks all trembled beneath the gathered horses' hooves, startling beasts and riders both. Jemel had heard tell of tremors in the earth, that could rattle mountains till the land slipped from its stony core, shake buildings into their component dust, rip cracks in solid ground wide enough to swallow camels and their burdens too. He had never felt one himself and gave the stories little credence, preferring the certain knowledge of his own feet as they told him that sand might shift on the wind, shale might slip under a man's weight but what lay beneath was immovable with age and mass and endurance, all the potent majesty of rock.

His horse danced, or the ground danced beneath it; it whinnied with anxiety, and he had to bend low over its suddenly sweating neck to reassure it, when he felt most like crying out himself with shock and fear. There was a terrible wrongness to this, the same chill touch as when the sun went black in the middle of the day, and that he had seen once in his childhood.

Stooping forward with his head against the horse's ear, he could watch the earth below. He could see dust rising in little puffs and wisps, like steam forcing from under a pot-lid. He could see the hard-baked cracks in that crusty soil stir and widen, he could see great plates of earth pull free of rocks they must have bound like mortar for a century or longer; he saw a gnarled and blackened tree-root twist as though the olives themselves were coming alive within this living land, as though they would pull up their deep-delving taproots and join the march of armies. Perhaps they would, perhaps the trees would be the Princip's last defence, a long-hidden sorcery of horror.

But the trees, all this grove of trees would topple before it marched. It must do, with no binding at its roots to hold its old trunks upright. The soil seemed to upwell suddenly, all along the ridge where the horses fretted; and then it burst open, shattered, erupted into clods and dust. It broke like eggshell before the many-headed battering of innumerable serpents, all coddled as it seemed in the same deep nest. They hurled that smashed shell high, and Jemel had just a moment to see them clearly before the debris fell back in a blinding, unbreathable cloud.

Thick as his thigh they were, and black as the olives' thoughts. They flowed up and out of their dark dwelling like those thoughts made viable, twisting and glistening like the distant river as it picked itself apart like so many silverdark threads fraying into the marshland ahead.

Serpents did he name them, in that moment of their eruption? They had mouths like serpents, though their teeth were something other, unnatural needles and far too many of them, no mortal creature could eat with teeth like that. They broke out like a knot of vipers, bodies all tangled together, and they surged apart something like the river indeed, what had been one becoming many, a twisted rope in all its separate threads; but these threads were obsidian and they looked as hard as stone, as flexible as wire, as swift as a whip.

Even those needle teeth were black, and the brief glimpse he had of a gaping throat behind, ridged like a dog's. Then the choking murk descended, most of it crumbled into a bitter grit that stung the eyes, invaded nose and mouth and stifled breath.

Jemel had lived through a three-day sandstorm once, and lesser storms were commonplace in the deep of the desert. For this, he needn't even think of hood and veil; it would pass, and worse things would happen before it did.

Worse things were happening already. Horses were screaming beyond where he could see. A man's voice joined the screaming; there was no terror in that cry, nor in the horses', only pure agony, the voice of courage driven beyond extremity. Those teeth were finding out their targets in the filth; 'ifrit were feeding.

No question in his mind, but that these were 'ifrit. All but buried in all that black, he had seen hints of red like jewels aflame, eyes hidden deep where it would take a long needle to come at them. He could see them still, flashes of fire through the dust as the serpent-beasts quested for men.

Or for horses. He hadn't realised, hadn't felt it rise, only his body reacting all unaware to keep him mounted and balanced while his eyes strained and his mind raced, but his own mount had reared, its forelegs kicking wildly as though it scrabbled for a safe stand in mid-air; something worse than the lack of one made the animal topple suddenly sideways, made it crash hard to ground, made it scream.

Jemel was off already before it struck, diving and rolling. He felt more than the thick shaft of the bow beneath his back, in that tumbling roll; there was sharp rock and shifting clods of earth, but also there was something fat and hard that moved beneath his weight, reacted to it, reared up against it. He must have rolled clean across the body of an 'ifrit as it unwound itself from the tangle of its brethren, turning its hot eyes and chilly mind towards the slaughter to come.

He went on rolling downslope, letting his body's weight carry him as far as it would until he fetched up against a tree and couldn't kick himself on further.

Had to stand instead; battered and unready and half-blind, he must stumble to his feet, set his back to the tree and draw his scimitar. No hope of standing off to use his arrows in this mêlée, in this confusion of dust and bodies.

He looked upslope, squinting against the toils of dust, and saw a dark shape looming. The height of his own head it loomed and was a head itself, shining eyes and jaws agape ahead a bulk of shadow. It made a darting jab towards him, all teeth and throat like a doom awaiting, impatient for its prey.

Not he but his body ducked aside, he couldn't help it; he felt a blast of cold air above his head and the tree shake at his back as the monstrous beast slammed into it.

His eye was measuring, even as his body moved – thick as his thigh, had he thought those writhing bodies were? Thick as his chest around, rather. He couldn't see how long; too long, he thought, several times his height and this one at least would look better for being shorter.

His ducking had at least been a warrior's avoidance, not a child's fearful flinching away. He was poised and set, his scimitar drawn back and both hands now on the haft. He didn't pause, but he did pray; even as he swung, he prayed that all men's prayers might be equally effective. The grumbling and greedy Selussid priest, the Ransomers who were priests and killers both, the Surayonnaise this morning who was no kind of priest at all: they all prayed differently to different gods, and yet the lives of thousands depended on their separate blessings.

His own life was one such, here and now, and who could say whether Selussid and Surayonnaise might not have undone each other's work, the prayers of one nullifying the prayers of the other, one angry God blunting where another had made sharp . . . ? He had no way to tell, except by learning; and so he swung, and his blade met the glossy black hide of the 'ifrit.

His blade met its hide, and bit; bit and sheared through, driven by all the strength he had in arms and shoulders, all the exultant power of his body as he felt it sink deep, deep into the body of the 'ifrit. The Selussid blessing had held, or else the Surayonnaise, or both together. The serpent-beast spasmed on his blade, coiled and twisted and tried to tear it from his grasp, and could not. Jemel turned the point inside the great gashing wound and heaved like a man at a hunt, opening up a carcase with his gutting-knife. No entrails gushed out but only smoke, as though all the solid heft of the creature had coldly and instantly burned to an insubstantial ash. Its glowing eyes faded, and were dull; its hide – its carapace, perhaps, hard as shell and smooth as shell, and yet it had been as supple as snakeskin – dulled also, as though there were smoke beneath the gleam; and then it dissipated and was gone, and left him with nothing at all.

As he had been fighting, so the wind had been carrying away all the fine debris that had stung and blocked his sight. Now, granted a moment's respite, he could look around and see how much damage was being done; now he had the leisure actually to hear all the screaming.

It was an image of hell, worse than all the imams' teaching and all the tales told around a thin fire on a bitter night. Not a horse had broken free to escape the ridge, not a man remained mounted; men and beasts lay everywhere, dead and dying, broken and ripped asunder.

And yet there was hope, there were men still afoot and still fighting. Their swords were as potent as his scimitar, their companion's blessing was doing its work and so were they, cleaving brutally amid the carnage.

But even a twice-blessed blade took time and effort to slay one of these serpent-things, and there were many, many and more coming; the earth still churned, the rocks themselves were shifting with its movement, trees that had stood a thousand years were falling as new demons erupted from their roots.

Two more were coming for Jemel. He couldn't even go where he was most needed, to the heart of the battle; he must guard himself and fight his own fight for his own survival.

He set himself against the tree again and met the first serpent's hurtling charge with his blade between its teeth, felt those lethal needles rake his arm even as the fire died in its eyes, too close to his; and heaved arm and blade sideways, all the strength he had, so that the scimitar cut its way out of the first dead 'ifrit even before it had faded, and cut savagely into the second before it could strike.

That one took more killing, he took more hurts; and when he next had time to look, it was sweat that was stinging his eyes now and there were fewer men still standing, still fighting, and it seemed an inexhaustible number of the monsters to oppose them.

He stumbled over the broken ground to help them, though all the help he could offer was to draw some few of the creatures to himself, to his own slaughter. His mind had narrowed and narrowed with his eyes, his focus was so intense it was almost painful: there were 'ifrit to kill with this wondrously heavy scimitar, that grew heavier yet with every blow and yet less potent, which was strange but didn't matter, it meant only that he must strike again and yet again. And duck, too late because the creatures were moving more swiftly now, and that one had scored his shoulder; but the sharp sting of it was a spur and he'd seen horses spurred, the Patrics did that in their armour and he knew what it meant, it was to drive the horses harder and so he would be driven, another blow and another and this blade of his must be drinking the deaths of these endless 'ifrit, absorbing all the weight they lost, it was so heavy now he could barely lift it, and yet he must . . .

And did; and fought on and on, and soon there were no coherent thoughts at all but only the necessity of movement, the planting of the foot and the swinging of the arms like a peasant, like a farmer with a scythe, no art or grace but only death in his blade and death in his mind's eye, his own death looming and as many others as he could make beforehand.

For a short while he was aware of another man beside him, shoulder to shoulder; they could hew together, and guard each other against the worst. Too short a while, inadequate the guard: there was a sudden flurry of bright black bodies, he himself was sorely pressed and when he had the time to glance around his companion was gone, a sudden absence at his side that seemed the worse because Jemel had never had the chance to learn his name.

In the end, at last, too soon it came as at last it had to; there was an inexplicable trembling weakness in his arms as he raised his scimitar, he nearly lost his grip on the haft which had grown slimy with his blood, he saw the point slip low when it needed not to do that, it needed to stand high and firm and yet he could not lift it. And there was a fresh 'ifrit directly ahead of him and all he could see were the eyes of it, hot and draining, sucking, leeching the last of his strength as though it would kill him before it even touched.

He wished he had time to feel sorry; he thought that with a little time, he would remember what he had to feel sorry for, why his death must be a sadness. At the moment it eluded him.

But then the death eluded him also, strangely; he saw a sudden dark flower in one of those glowing eyes, and the glow went out before the 'ifrit crashed into him. He fell, of course, and the creature fell atop him. But those teeth that should have ravened at his throat lay still and sharp against it, only dinting by the weight of them, not cutting in the least. And then there was no weight, the thing had vanished; and instead there was a standing figure against the sky, a silhouette to block the sun, a voice; and it said, 'We came too late. I am sorry. How many are your dead?'

Why, only me, he wanted to say; but he couldn't find a voice of his own to say it with, and before he did he remembered that there had indeed been others, and perhaps they were all of them dead, and only he not. Which would be a thing to be sad about, perhaps, though not the chiefest thing, he thought.

He struggled to rise and could not until the man stooped to help him, to lift him with an easy heave of the arm as though he had himself lost half his substance in his nearness to death.

'Steady now, lad. This was a heroic battle, you've earned your pride but don't overdraw it, lean on me . . .' And then, more slowly, 'Wait – these others are of Surayon. Do the Sharai fight beside them now?'

'Against this?' Another voice, whisper-thin, without a drop of blood behind it; it was an effort even to turn his head but Jemel had to make that effort, had to see. Three men sat on the turned earth and passed a waterskin between them; all of them were bleeding, pale, close to collapse, but all were alive and seemed likely to stay so. Not alone, then; it was good not to be alone, though there was a tremendous sadness in it. 'We all fight beside each other, when we fight a thing like this. What, would you let us stand alone?'

'I did not. Those were my arrows saved you, blessed by my own priest; and be glad there were that few of you standing, that we could use the arrows. Otherwise you'd none of you be standing, we could not have come in time. But I had not realised the Sharai . . .'

His voice trailed away, in life or simply in Jemel's still-narrow mind; it did not matter. He was a man, a Patric in a black cloak over white; and Jemel knew what that meant, and he remembered something of his sadness, and the causes of it.

His scimitar was in his hand yet, he had not let it go. Now he strained to lift it, shimmering clean blade and blood-sodden haft, he struggled to point it towards this man his rescuer; and he said, 'I have been looking for a Patric man. D'Escrivey, his name is. He is a Ransomer, he wears your dress. Are you d'Escrivey? You might be. I might be seeking you . . .'

A soft, puzzled laugh, and, 'Aye, lad, you might – if I were he. I am not; my name is Karlheim, of Elessi. I served my year with the Ransomers, no more than that. Is d'Escrivey here? I have not heard. You'd do better to seek him northerly, that's where I last saw him. But you're going nowhere yet. Come on, you little infidel, put up that hero's sword and lie down with your friends there, take some water, you've lost half the blood your God has given you. Which was probably the only half you had left anyway, by the look of that scar on your throat. Steady, there, don't give me one to match it; I told you, I'm not Anton d'Escrivey. Though I'd like to know what he's done to upset the Sharai. He upset all of Outremer

long ago, but I hadn't realised his ambitions ran so much further. Perhaps you'll tell me later. For the moment I have an
army to move and I don't know the country; but I guess I'll
ask your companions about that, because I don't think you'd
be too much help there, would you? As a matter of fact, I
think you're asleep, unless you're dead already. Which would
be a shame, because I'd like to see you meet d'Escrivey. Give
me some help here, someone . . .'

Even from their island, from their utter separation on this
lowest point in all the valley princedom, the girls could still
see a great broad sweep of Surayon laid out on either bank of
the river. The swathes of open pasture, the defensive walls
and the settlements beyond the walls, Surayon-town to the
south with the Princip's palace behind it: the valley's gentle
rise on either side meant that everything was laid open to
them here, between the rushing water and the crowding
trees of the mountains' early slopes. Julianne had been
reminded of something that had taken a few minutes to pin
down; it was like a natural theatre on a massive scale, with
themselves chief players on the stage and the hushed and
expectant valley itself their audience, except that neither one
of them knew her part. That was a child's nightmare,
though, and she was a twice-married woman with a husband
on either bank; she would not dwell on failure, confusion,
fear. If they had a purpose here, they would find it out.
Elisande would; this was her country, after all, her people.
Julianne knew nothing of the land, except what she could
see; nothing of the people, except what she had seen.

Whatever lay further that she had not seen, however, she
knew that this vista spread out around her, this little view
was the heart and the soul of Surayon. Unless the Princip
was his country's soul, but she thought them much the same:
open, warm and welcoming, but with rocky heights where
she dared not tread, hidden places she could not even see,
traps and snares where she could not find her way without a
guide.

Come to think of it, that would be a good description of
Elisande also, and would have done for Rudel too. Were all
Surayonnaise so blessed, so cursed, so devious? She was
trained to watch for subtleties at court, where lives and liv-
ings, even the survival of nations could pivot on a word, a
gesture, a deeper level of meaning than the surface showed.
A whole population would be a deeper thing altogether than
a court. Her father had had her peel an onion once with her
fingers, ripping a way in and further in: soft and old and
pitted with rot on the outside, it had been stiff and white
within until her fingers suddenly found a layer that was grey
and slimy. Inside that, though, the core had still been clean
and fresh and wholesome. He'd left her to take her own
lesson from it, that even the seemingly ordinary was not as it
appeared to be and could go on changing however deep she
dug, the foul and the good lying nestled together in the
same heart and the good unsullied by the foul; she had taken
the onion to the kitchens and had watched it being fried into
her dinner. The next day, though, her father had given her a
pearl and a delicate file. She'd scraped as gently as a jewel-
doctor, as stubbornly as – well, as a curious and determined
girl looking for the lesson. Again she'd found layer within
layer, and subtle changes of colour and iridescence between

each of them. And at the heart of it, of course, a tiny piece of grit, that so much buried beauty had been founded on. By then the beauty was all destroyed, and she wondered if that were actually the lesson: not that pearls were onions, but that pearls lost their value by too close an examination, where an onion's value could not be told without it. At the end, though, there was still no onion.

Surayon might be either one, a useful onion or a beautiful pearl; she thought it would not matter, in the end. Outremer would destroy its mystery layer by layer, and justify it by that gritty heart; the Sharai would dig out whatever had value, take that and leave the rest, and never mind that it must rot abandoned.

There was smoke aplenty in the air, but that might still be from yesterday's burnings not extinguished yet. One house could smoulder for days unattended and there were dozens, maybe hundreds that had been put to the torch as the invaders passed through. And there were dozens, maybe hundreds of men Julianne could see coming and going, riding westerly or easterly alone or in small bands, some few afoot; even at the limits of her sight or the valley's turning she could identify Sharai and Patric by the dress they wore, and she could see how they kept their distances, how none of them closed for battle.

This might be news, it might be worth the telling; but when she looked around for Elisande she found her still busy, still muttering to herself head down and almost on hands and knees among the grasses.

'. . . Is this bloodwort? Yes, it is. Good for clotting, if there were enough to pack a wound, which there is not, and time enough to let it work, which there will not be. Still, pick it, save it, someone might prick their finger . . .'

Elisande had decided – decreed, rather – that as there was no other conceivable use for this fleck of land in midstream or for these two girls upon it, and as Esren had brought them here to be useful, therefore it must intend them to serve as nurses and wards for the injured. It was her one known talent, after all, to heal the sick and the hurt; and Julianne had learned by helping her, they had been sick-nurses together in the Roq and in Rhabat and in the Princip's palace yesterday. So why not here today, close to whatever action there must be? No doubt Esren would ferry the wounded across the water as they fell. If necessary, she would order it to do so. And in the meantime, she would scour every green and growing thing for any healing or nourishing effect whatsoever. This was a safe place, which might be why the djinni chose it; and she was a skilled healer, which must be why the djinni chose her; but still there was an element missing, something to force the place and the occasion, and she thought it must be some potent hidden herb that it was her task to seek out before the crisis came.

Or so she was pretending, at any rate: gazing at the ground with a fierce focus, refusing to look up or around as she picked and poked among the damp and heavy grasses, hoarding a poor harvest into the gathered belly of her skirt.

Julianne turned back to her vigil, looking for patterns in the movements of men and seeing none, living breathlessly from moment to hopeful moment until a sudden unexpected noise made her twist around sharply, and the words she might have been thinking to say unravelled themselves entirely as she went.

The noise came from Elisande – of course, there was no one and nothing else here that might have made it – and it was, startlingly, a laugh.

At least a sort of half-laugh, a choking, coughing sound of self-mockery. She had laid out all her gleanings neatly on a stretch of trampled grass, and now she was sitting back on her heels and looking at them, looking up at Julianne and back at her herbs again.

'I'm sorry, my love,' she said softly, not laughing now. 'That was pathetic.'

'Do you think so?'

'Do you not?' Her voice had an edge of challenge again, to say that Elisande was not entirely blunted. 'Look at it, an hour's labour for this . . .' Her fingers played with what she had collected, lifting and letting fall. 'Any abandoned croft could show a better crop than this, and what, I'm going to heal half an army?'

'We don't have an abandoned croft, Elisande. All we have is what you can find, because I don't know a simple from a, from a—'

'Simpleton?'

'Anyway, you may not need to heal half an army. The armies have decided not to fight.'

'Have they? Truly?' A sudden heedless scramble to her feet, scattering half of what she had worked so hard to gather; she stared, stood on tiptoe as though an extra inch would show her a deeper truth, shaded her eyes with her hand and stared again.

After a while, though, she shook her head and sank back, sank down, sank almost utterly. Briefly Julianne felt a cold fury, only that she was not certain who to be so angry with:

herself for raising such a fragile hope or Elisande for doing nothing to keep it perilously aloft, for so easily allowing it to fall.

'That's not peace,' she said, as though this were any kind of news. 'That's reconnoitring. They're sending out scouts, watching each other, waiting to strike . . .'

Shifting about like pieces on a gameboard, but Julianne left that thought unspoken. 'I didn't say peace,' she said instead, 'I said they'd decided not to fight. They're not waiting to strike, they're just waiting. Watching each other, of course, but expecting something else to happen. It's better than yesterday, love. Would they have waited even this long, if they'd met yesterday? If they'd had a chance of meeting, two armies from Outremer and the Sharai?'

No, of course they wouldn't. There'd have been no courtesies of war, and no care in the planning: only a yell of hatred, a holy curse on all unbelievers and an instant charge from either side, from both. And they'd have ridden over Surayon and hardly noticed as they trampled lives, hopes, an entire people into the bloody dust.

They might yet; they would yet, if nothing else did happen. It was strange, disturbing to find herself yearning – praying, almost – for an assault, for men to die; but it was the only way she knew to stop them killing each other. If she were a player, she'd move her pieces now to make it happen, to force it quickly. She trusted neither side in this undeclared, unconvincing truce. It needed one hothead, one holy fool, no more than that . . .

Elisande shrugged, the closest she could come to *perhaps you're right, perhaps it's too early to despair*. She gave a despairing look to the tumbled herbs that represented all her morning's work, another to the fertile but barren island on which they'd been marooned, and moaned. 'There has to be a point to this, there must be something that we're missing.'

'Must there?'

'Yes. *Yes!* It's not just that I want it, of course I do, I can't bear to sit and do nothing; but Esren said we'd be of most use here. Didn't it? Or did I dream that?'

'You know you didn't dream it, sweets. Don't work yourself into a passion.'

'Well, then. That's what it said – and the djinn know these things, Julianne, it *knew* we'd be useful if it brought us here . . .'

It knew they would be useful, but it didn't tell them how; likely both parts of that were significant. It wanted – or needed? – them to work it out for themselves. Or else to fail, perhaps that was their usefulness? Like leaving Marron at the palace, if only to stop him doing something that would make matters worse. He might stay where he was put, if he hadn't entirely lost that habit of obedience; Elisande emphatically would not. And so she was put here where she could do no harm at all, and Julianne with her to keep her from expiring in her fury . . .

Well, it was possible. As likely as anything, so far as she could judge; at least as likely as Elisande's notion, that they had some significant purpose to fulfil if they could only out-guess the djinni.

Just for form, she said, 'You could call it back, tell it to take us somewhere else . . .'

'I'm not sure it would come; and where should it take us anyway, what can we do? We did it all, last night – you with your voice, I with my hands. There is no more, if they will not let us fight. In any case, to leave would be,' a helpless gesture of her hands, 'surrender. Disaster, if the djinni has dealt straight with us. There is a purpose to this, Julianne; we can find it out; we will.'

And perhaps she would, if sheer determination were enough to draw forth answers. Privately Julianne doubted that, she'd too often seen determination defeated by simple ignorance, but she would not say so for the world.

She said nothing, then, and turned her attention back to the riders in the valley, north and south.

Of course the story changed, because it must; of course the change was for the worse, a degradation, a loss of hope. She thought it had never been otherwise, and never would. It was in the nature of humankind to hope, the nature of hope to fail, the nature of the world to decay. All life was a losing struggle against the weight of inevitable death. *God is history*, she thought suddenly, startling herself into a soft cry with the thought; she hadn't realised that she or anyone was fighting God, but the conclusion was irresistible. The djinn had foreknowledge, and even the djinn were fallible and so mortal; what else could be eternal than the sum of what had happened, the exactitude of knowledge – and how could she or anyone resist the past, or what it taught?

'What?' Elisande looked up from the depths of her silence, which had dragged her deeper and deeper down as though she sat in the bottom of a well, unreachable.

'Oh – uh, look. If there was a truce, it has been broken.' She didn't want to confess where her thinking had brought her, so far from the immediate anxiety of the day, into paths so twisted or so overhung with gloom. This was what had led her there, this was what mattered more: death had come back to Surayon, refreshed. This was what they had been waiting and watching for, what perhaps they had been set here to observe.

For some little time now, she had been watching an army emerge onto the northern flood-plain. No more scouts, no more reconnaissance – here were men in numbers, sure of their strength. Most wore black robes, though there were other colours among them; their officers had black cloaks thrown over white. They were the Ransomer army come down from the Roq, swollen by recruits en route as a river swells and swells in time of flood, between its rising and the sea.

They came down the single narrow road between the high-walled fields, a mirror to those on the opposite side of the river; they issued out in pairs abreast and spread across the grassland like a flood indeed, a slow-seeping darkness that invaded the bright green like a poison. Or like a swarm, she thought, bees to sting, locusts to consume utterly whatever they lighted on.

They could light on little here, except the earth itself to take possession of it; but that was bad enough, worse than bad. She had been guest of the Ransomers, she knew some of their intimacies at first hand and had heard tell of others. They were the last people she liked to see within these borders. Better the Sharai, who would pillage, burn the crops and houses and move on, leaving a corruptible governor behind to levy later tributes. That was slavery; but Ransomers would burn the people too. And build castles on the heights, and stay, and never trust because they never could. Their hand would always lie cold and heavy across this narrow, tender land. She tried to imagine a lifetime lived in its shadow and shuddered, and yearned to see the army of the Sharai come out of the smoke to the east there, to drive the Ransomers back. It was there, she knew, she had seen outriders come and go; she thought she could see a darker shadow building, the massing of the tribes. Under her husband Hasan, the only man who could bring them so together; and so it wasn't treachery to hope that the Sharai would be victorious over Outremer, it was loyalty to her new man and his people, and she could not be condemned for it.

Except by her father, her friends, her first husband Imber, all her old loyalties to blood and family and belief. *If they fight, we all lose,* she reminded herself fiercely, and struggled to put aside all wondering about tomorrow, how armies once encamped could be removed from Surayon again. The Sharai might not follow Hasan if he tried to lead them back to the Sands, away from war and glory; the Ransomers certainly would not follow Imber, and there was all her little influence swallowed up already. Her father had more, with the King's authority behind him, but she doubted whether Fulke would withdraw even for the King, when he had the God's will to enact and a generation of support from the fathers of the church.

Tomorrow, she would worry about that. If there were a tomorrow, for her or for any of them. At the moment, she was inclined to doubt it. She had no faith in these men, their muscles or their minds: not even in either her wise or her foolish husband, let alone in the hundreds and thousands else. Never mind their intentions, she thought that one or

another of them would fling a blade or let an arrow fly, too
soon and at the wrong target. Old enmities couldn't be put
aside so speedily. There were too many blood-debts on either
side, too heavy a burden of resentment. Each had their history, of cruelties and dispossession; each had their God, and
as she had learned – or perhaps decided – those were the
same thing, indistinguishable. What God or history
demanded could not and would not be denied.

That was her fear, and there was only one way to avoid it:
that both sides see men die, and see who killed them.

She waited, breathless and fearful, while long files of
riders unwound across the plain; she watched a patrol detach
to follow the line of the wall easterly, towards the hidden
Sharai.

She thought she knew what she had to fear. She thought
her Hasan would appear from the smoke, riding alone
with the tribes behind; she thought some high-minded
Ransomer – Marron's Sieur Anton, as like as not: there was
a man who carried his nobility in every haunted muscle of
his body, every nuance that his mind could unpick – would
go to meet him, man to man and face to face; she thought
they would speak with courtesy and respect on both sides,
and somehow there would be words said that must reluctantly, regretfully be answered with steel. She thought they
would fight, because that was the style of the day. Hope
must fail, men must be weak.

She was letting her own unhappiness colour everything in
grey, against the world's truth. Bright sunshine, a gaudy
green in the grass, only that taint of smoke to speak of
shadow: sworn enemies might meet on such a day and not
fight, or agree to fight together. It could happen. Would the

djinni have helped work to make it happen, if all would fall apart in any case?

She had no answers, to questions that couldn't be asked. What she had was fear; and actually it wasn't what she thought or what she knew that made her fearful. She thought she knew her man, and Sieur Anton and his ilk. If only Hasan could avoid Marshal Fulke, his good sense might carry the hour. What she truly feared was a fool, on either side: a man who could not see beyond his weapon's edge, some unthinking hero who would kill – from a distance, most likely with an arrow – and look for praise where he had bought disaster with a casually taken life.

She watched for it to happen, any or all of it as her mind had played it out. She watched the men ride the wall and saw that she was wrong, she'd been too subtle and too grand. No meeting of proud captains, each of whom could honour the other; that was a girl's fancy, a nursery tale, no part of war.

Instead there was simply a boiling, a sudden rush of shadow through a gateway in the wall. Men on foot, and no more than half a dozen of them against twice that many mounted: they might have the advantage of surprise, but even so it should have been a slaughter.

It was not; or not as it should have been. Men on foot should not, could not stand against horsemen; she knew that from her earliest schooling, from before she knew that she was being schooled. And yet these few in their black robes swirled around the riders and their beasts, and one by one the horses fell. Then it was black against black, Patric against Sharai, but they were too far away and their dress was too similar to tell apart from this distance. Except that she did know, she was sure that when six men were left standing, they were not a surviving half of the Ransomers. It ought not to have been possible, but—

'Sand Dancers,' Elisande said beside her.

'How can you tell? From here? Are you counting their fingers for them?' Elisande was right, and they both knew it; but she hated the knowledge and did not want it in her head, nor any of the memories that two commonplace words could carry with them.

'They killed the horses. Men of the tribes would have spared them, tried to capture them. But men of the tribes would have had better sense than to attack twice their number on horseback. Besides, those robes are black. But why are they here, and what are they fighting for?'

'Sweet, I don't know. I never have known. Theirs is another war altogether, it seems to me.'

'No, only another arm of the same, that we cannot track from here. Well, there are few of them; and here come the Ransomers for vengeance.'

Indeed, a squad of horsemen was cantering along the wall, two dozen or more with a cloaked knight prominent among them. She said, 'The Ransomers won't care about the niceties, black robes or blue. They have seen Sharai slaughter their brothers; there will be no truce.'

'Likely not. I never had much faith in it. But they can kill Dancers, and welcome so.'

'If they can kill Dancers.'

'Why not? We did. Those riders were surprised, and led by a fool. It's been how long, six hundred years that the Dancers have lived alone in the Sands? I'm sure they killed the odd braggart for reputation's sake, but reputation is all it is, Julianne. Reputation and good training, but the Ransomers also have both, and the Ransomers have been fighting for forty years. The Dancers haven't faced a real enemy in ten times that long. None of these living have risked their lives till now. They will not stand. Besides, they are Sharai; they are not stupid. Strike, and run . . .'

And so they did, back through the opening in the wall, where the horsemen could only have followed them slowly and one by one. Their leader had better sense.

'Perhaps they'll lose themselves, and starve,' Julianne muttered vindictively.

'Not they. Dancers think round corners; they'll know the secrets of those walls. Or they'll climb straight over them, as your 'ifrit did. Not your foolish boy . . .'

She meant Imber, of course, not Roald – but Julianne still felt a pang, though she hoped her face had not shown it. Roald was dead, and laid with honour with his Princip's son; let him lie. She stared into the distant haze, eyes wide enough to smart with the smoke on the wind, looking for Hasan and desperate not to see him at this most inopportune of times.

'Look,' Elisande said suddenly, startled. 'There, the Ransomers . . .'

The horsemen were milling chaotically around that narrow opening. Not trying to go in, but what, then? For a moment she thought that they were somehow knocking down the wall, to allow them safe entrance and their just revenge, if they could only flatten walls faster than the Dancers could run. But then she saw a great section topple and fall – and it fell outwards, towards the Ransomers. Whose horses were backing, wheeling, kicking and rearing, caught in a crush and close to panic, she thought, though she could not read them well from here.

It was impossible to see clearly through the massed bodies and their constant motion that took them nowhere, neither through the gap and into the field nor back and away from the wall; it was hard to see anything at all, but there was black against the green, dark and sinuous shapes gleaming in the sunlight as they came through the field's trampled crop and over the rubble of the fallen wall to vanish into the disorder of the mounted men.

Some of those were mounted no more. There were riderless horses breaking free and running fast, their discipline as broken as their harness. Others were down; she watched one fall, seeming to subside into the heaving mass like meat sucked down into a boiling pot of stew.

There were men on foot amid that desperate madness, then. If any could find space enough to stand, and keep their feet against the buffeting bodies, the raging maelstrom of noise and terror; if any could survive so long as this, survive at all against marauding 'ifrit with strength enough simply to push a strong wall over, where it lay between themselves and their prey.

'Elisande, your eyes are sharper than mine,' desert-trained, though Jemel's were better yet, the best she knew now that Marron's were his own again. 'Can you see how it goes there? They are killing each other, look . . .'

'I daresay they are,' Elisande replied in a voice so strange, so distracted that she might as well have spelled it out in syllables, *I do not care what is happening, and I am not going to look.*

Julianne turned in bewilderment; and saw what she was seeing and so understood at once, although it seemed almost an impossible thing.

Marron stood there, on their island, where he had not been a few bare moments earlier. Marron was meant to be still in the Princip's palace, far behind them; Esren had said so.

Nor was he alone. He held Jemel in his arms, but not the Jemel that Julianne could have wished for, grim-eyed and fearsome and fierce. This was Jemel hurt, atrociously hurt, unconscious; his robe was darker even than it should have been, clinging wetly to his blood-streaked body where it was not hanging in rips and shreds.

Marron lifted his eyes to gaze at both the girls. Deep crimson red they were, as though Jemel's blood had dyed them so, or else as though he wore them as a badge of war.

'Oh, Marron . . .'

Was it Elisande's voice, that despairing sigh, or was it her own? She couldn't tell.

He didn't seem to care, either way. She never had been sure how much of him was Marron and how much the Daughter, when they shared one flesh like this. He was not entirely remote, he couldn't be, or there would have been nothing but distance written on his face when he'd looked at Jemel; and yet there was little enough written there now when he looked at Elisande.

'Jemel needs your healing,' he said, as though she could not have seen that for herself.

Was it only Julianne who thought *again*? Perhaps it was. Elisande's authoritative hands guided him to lay down the insensible Sharai; they pulled away the tattered remnants of his robe; they moved rapidly, assessingly from one torn wound to another, while her voice was weak, almost whispering, chasing after what was lost already.

'How did you find him? Or us?'

'It knows,' he said, 'I could feel where he should be. I had to take him from some Patric men, but they gave me room enough, and only threw curses at me. Then I felt where you should be, and I came. Can you heal him?'

'Easier than last time,' Elisande said. 'He's not so very dead. There'll be more scars, but you won't mind that,' *you carry scars enough yourself,* her voice implied, *and not all on that tender skin of yours.* 'And I can't do it all at once; we will need those herbs, Julianne,' though her face was saying *this cannot be the reason we are here, there would be no sense in it.* 'But, Marron, I don't understand what you've done, how it helps. The djinni would have taken you to Jemel, brought you here, you didn't need . . .'

'I am not finished yet,' he said. 'Your father wanted me to fight, Julianne, he forced me to it; now I can, if I have to. If I must break one more oath, it may as well be broken beyond repair.'

'That may not be all that is broken. Grandfer might not draw it out of you again, he might not be able to . . .'

'I have not said that I would ask him to. I did not ask before; how can it matter now? See to Jemel, Elisande.' And he pulled a dagger from his belt, pricked his arm, let the Daughter flow.

Swiftly then, while his eyes were his own brown, Elisande chased him with one more question. 'Where are you going now?'

'To find Sieur Anton,' and there was none of that chill,

despairing certainty in his voice, nor in his look; only a determination so strong that yes, he would sacrifice anything, more even than he had given already if he had indeed anything more to give. 'Look after Jemel,' and this time it was a plea, or as near as he could come to it in the moment before he opened a blood-red gate and stepped through it into a golden light that folded itself around him and was gone.

Distance was not and could not be an object; he was barely aware of it as a reality. He ran not to cover ground, not to save time, but only because running was there to be done, it was here for the doing, it was his and he belonged to it as it to him. He could have run for ever; he might yet run for ever, if his running fetched him no reason to stop.

He was aware of but did not feel the heat of the world that surrounded him. He had fire in his veins that flowed to match his running, and he had a cool stillness in his mind that matched the static precision of his thoughts.

He ran over dust and rock within a wide and open bowl, under an opal sky. He was alone, if not unobserved; there was a glitter in the air about him that was more than the eternal gold, an occasional line of darkness in a shadowless land.

There was a river behind him, he remembered that, it steamed and hissed in its course, hot water on hot rocks. He had jumped from a rock in midstream and not thought twice about it, although it was a long and a perilous leap for a mortal body to attempt. His jump to the rock from the other bank had been made with a body in his arms, and he hadn't worried about that one either.

Worry seemed not to be a part of him any more, to have been cauterised or cut out, cast aside. He ran quite untroubled by his awareness of trouble in the other world, and quite aware too of that unconcern. This time around, possession had been invited and had driven deeper, with a sharper edge; he carried twin divisions within this single body, himself and another that was not him, not male, not human. In this world, it was ascendant as if by right; in the other, only by his gift.

So he, they stayed in this world for their running, until it understood and he from it understood that they had run enough in this world. Then the prick in his arm came without his ever thinking to make that happen, he didn't need to, it did the thing itself; and then it left him – but not entirely, not now, some vestige still remained, the coolness of the shadow cast – and pain flooded in to fill the vacancy, more pain than ever such a little cut deserved, and far more blood.

And it made a doorway for him, he didn't need to think about that either; and he stepped through and swiftly took it back. He had done that before, after the transition from golden rock to green island, from steam to clear air, from solitude to girls; not only the pain found relief in his being whole again, wholly filled, entirely separated. He could lose himself in what possessed him, and find a terrible comfort in the red cast of its sight, the ice and hammer of its thinking. Why be what he had been before, when he could be this strong, this safe, this simple?

This time there was a battle at a little distance, as it had known there would be. This was what he had wanted to see, or else what it had wanted him to see; despite that ruthless division in his head, he would have found it hard to say which was true, or more true. He did not try; it did not seem to matter.

There were men in the battle, and horses, and 'ifrit. He had a cold certainty in his head, an utter knowledge that Sieur Anton was among the men. He would not have been brought here else. No need for him to scan the horsemen for one who wore white beneath his cloak, although he did.

Sieur Anton was still mounted – of course, he was still mounted! – where many were not. His stallion reared and screamed, blind with terror, lashing out at man or monster indiscriminately. Not so Sieur Anton, whose blade Josette was neat, vicious, lethal. *Blessed Josette, who has said a prayer over you? Did he do so himself, in his virtue?*

Men were dying and horses too, but Sieur Anton would survive this. That was axiomatic.

Sieur Anton might survive alone. A look around showed no more men riding to his reinforcement; all that remained of the troops on the grassland were fighting now on their own account, clustered around the road that had led them down from the northern hills. There were 'ifrit there too, and broken walls, an ambush well repeated.

This one had cut the Ransomer army in two, north and south of the walled fields; the 'ifrit had severed its spine as it marched that narrow road. Or crushed it, rather: he climbed up fallen rubble to the top of the long boundary wall – his decision, or he thought so; what shared his eyes did not need them, it knew already all that he could see – and there was the proof of their power, laid out before him like a map written upon the land.

How many 'ifrit there were, he could not tell; they were enough to have struck all along the length of the road, where it was contained within those sheltering, concealing walls. The sudden collapse of so much stonework must have accounted for many of the brothers or their mounts in the first moments of the attack, the last moments of their ignorance. He could see men, horses, weapons all lying scattered in and among the heaps of rubble. Those fallen would not fight again. Some few men were heaving themselves free or trying to, hauling or dragging at stones they could barely lift; some few horses were kicking where they lay or struggling to rise, falling back with broken legs and bloody froth at their muzzles; most of the bodies were simply bodies, no hope of life in them.

Even the collapse of so long, so high a run of walls without warning could not bury an entire army. There were pockets of fighting all along the road, but this was nothing like the disciplined drill of the Ransomers in their troops, nothing like the way they had fought Hasan and his Sharai at the Roq. Disorganised, disrupted, distressed; ill-led through sheer confusion where they were led at all, where their officers or confessors had not been killed already; vulnerable, unready and afraid, the knights and brothers of the Order were fighting, yes, but they were dying too. Even where they had weapons that must have been blessed, that could pierce the shells of the 'ifrit – largely those towards the front of the march, he noted, those who had most closely followed Sieur Anton – they showed little wisdom in their use, only a desperate courage that led them to buy any damage they could achieve with their own speedy deaths.

He saw men charge hopelessly into reaching jaws, saw

them crushed and broken, hacking at the chitin that gripped
them as they died; and where their blades sliced through that
chitin, he knew they must be dying with a sense of satisfaction, as at a victory dearly bought.

But the 'ifrit could lose their jaws and still kill men. They
had taken an insect shape, as they so often did, to haunt the
nightmares perhaps of those who escaped them; fear was a
weapon as deadly as any pincer, any claw. These insects were
monstrous, though, with great plates of chitin – fit for pushing walls over – above their deep-set eyes, and vicious spurs
projecting from their shell all around. Men with swords
would find it hard to come close enough to harm, even
where their swords were blessed. Except by hurling themselves into those cruel jaws, of course – and that still left the
'ifrit with the speed and lethal sharpness of the claws that
capped its many legs, with the crushing power of its
armoured head, with its questing intelligence that sought
ever new ways to kill.

There were ghûls too, coming from the fields behind
their masters the 'ifrit. They didn't join the dozen brutal
little battles that were like knots on the string of the road;
instead they made their way along that string, long arms
reaching for the wounded. Man or horse, it made no difference; those claws could kill, and did.

He saw what was happening and knew what would come,
what must come unless help came first and swiftly.

Alone, he would have gone himself to help, and so died at
Sieur Anton's side, perhaps, or struggling to reach him. He
was not alone, and did not run to help, but ran to fetch it:
ran along the tops of the fields' walls, leaping the openings
and sometimes leaping corners to save an extra step, the

slowness of a turn. Not that he was very slow, at all. Undistracted by the slaughter close below him, undisturbed by the long falls on either side of his narrow path, he ran as though on solid ground, and left all the fighting behind him.

He ran, and came to the final wall and the trees beyond, the first thin forest of the mountains; and here he found the remainder of the Ransomer army and their new recruits, gathered in rank and waiting while Marshal Fulke paced with his officers.

Paced and prayed at a little distance from the grooms who held the horses, and cast sidelong looks along the empty road. He might be waiting for news to come back before he sent his next divisions down; he might have sent outriders to find out why there was no news, and be wondering now why he had no outriders. Certainly he knew that all was not well. Probably he was beginning to calculate the nature of the trap into which he had sent so many men, what the sorcerers of Surayon might do with a single track bounded by high walls and an army caught between them. Certainly he did not know, he was not capable of imagining the true strength of what lay ahead of him. He must have been warned of the dangers, he might even have believed the warnings – this was a cursed country, after all, of course he must expect to find cursed creatures at large within it – but he would still believe above all in his own righteousness, and the victory of the righteous.

He was an alert man, a wary man; he had paused in his pacing the moment he saw movement, a runner high on the walls. He had spoken swift words to his generals and sent them to join their divisions, not to have all the army's heads grouped together where they might be cleaved with a single blow. Other men came running at a signal, archers among them. This was no messenger of theirs for sure, this boy in a Sharai robe who was so fleet of foot, so casual of his balance on a height.

He was interested to see how near he could come before one of them knew him, and whether they would see his eyes before they saw his face; and, in either case, whether any man would shoot an arrow before he came close enough to speak to them.

Or after.

They did not, but they came close: twice close, and he might have died at either time if either man had loosed, if the arrow had flown true to heart or head, if it had been faster to strike than his hand to knock it aside. He had the speed, he could be ready for it before it left the string; but there was that distance to consider, that same curious detachment that might decide not to make the effort because he might be interested to die at such a time, when it could so much matter.

He heard the pound and suck of his own body, wetly working; he heard the thud of his feet striking ground as he leapt from the wall, and then their steady rhythm on the earth, and the earth's reply; he heard what they thought he could not possibly hear, their voices at this distance. He heard:

'Magister, it is a demon, see its eyes! The Sharai are possessed, I always said it, let me shoot . . .'

And he heard:

'No, Magister, that is not Sharai. That is the heretic squire, Marron he called himself when he was with us; he that passed himself off as a brother first and then Sieur Anton took him, but he showed himself friend to both Sharai and Surayon. His dress betrays him, and his being here; what evil else he has done, I dare not know, to make his eyes glow so. He comes as a messenger, but there is nothing he should say to you; his words are poison and deceit. His death is decreed, demanded . . .'

And in response to each, he heard:

'No, let him live for now. If he acts as messenger, I should like to know from whom, and why.'

'We have no friends in this country, Magister, to send us messages.'

'All the more reason to hear what he has to say. Quiet now, say nothing to him; this is for me alone. If he has come here to learn, better that he has only one guarded voice to learn from; wickedness is subtle, too much so for you lads. Just keep your arrows nocked and watch me, be prepared to kill him at my gesture . . .'

So they came to stand face to face, and within almost a sword's-strike distance; and if ever he could have lost his sense of distance, of being far away and untouched even when he was closest, this should have been the moment and the man to make it so. Fulke's clothes were rank with blood and smoke; his gaze was fixed, his mouth was set and grim. There was no mercy in him, for a rebellious land open to his harrowing nor for a people who had abandoned true religion in the very heart of the God's own country.

Marron had feared and hated him, when Marron was

alone. But Marron couldn't find himself, or his simple passions. He felt disinterested, unconcerned; he said, 'You are waiting for news of your men. I bring it to you. Those on the road are lost. You may yet save some of those who have reached the river, but you cannot go this way.'

'Magister, he is a demon, he lies, you must not listen to him . . . !'

'Be silent.' Fulke didn't turn his head to administer the rebuke, didn't shift his gaze; he went on staring levelly, with a slight frown and no sign of fear. 'What are you?' he asked, directly but musingly, as though it was a question he was putting to himself, to his own wide knowledge as much as to the figure now before him. 'Once, you were a boy; I remember him. Then you were traitor, renegade, apostate, and I hunted him and lost him in the hills. Now, though – now you come back with hell in your eyes, and I wonder what you are, what you have become . . . ?'

'I am wiser than I was, when I was a boy. Else I would not offer you this news. If you wish to save any of your men, Magister, you will take them to the river by another way.'

'What, have the Surayon sorcerers set a devilry to work upon the road?'

'Not the Surayonnaise, but there are demons, yes. The 'ifrit are waiting for you, and killing as you come.'

'We were told our weapons would be good against 'ifrit, if we said a blessing over them.'

'So they are, or can be. Are they good against stones? The 'ifrit have collapsed these walls atop your men, and are destroying those who survived. Weapons may score, but it takes strength and numbers to kill, and sometimes luck besides. Your men have none of these.'

'Then we will ride to their assistance.'

'Then you will die, as they are dying. The road is a trap; it would be folly to follow the dead.'

'Then perhaps we should pitch our tents here, and go no further. Any 'ifrit that ventures this far we can despatch, to protect the world beyond; meanwhile they will do our work for us, in scouring this polluted land.'

'And will you abandon your men, to share the fate of those who belong here?'

'You said my men were lost already.'

'Those on the road, I said. Those who won through to the river, some of them may be saved, and the world with them.'

'The world, I think, can save itself, with the God's guidance; but I cannot reach my men, except by that road which you tell me I may not use. Your advice is a snake that eats itself.'

'Not so. There is always more than a single road.'

'Not in this pass, and I have no time to go back and ride around the mountains, west or east.'

'You have candles, you have priests. Open the King's Eye, and lead your army through; you know the way. All hope dies else.'

Hope for whom, he did not say; perhaps he could not. Perhaps he did not care.

Jemel had known this before: the desperate sense of being trapped, caught in a body that he could not move, breathless and panicking and utterly unable to save himself.

Usually it was a dream or a half-dream as he drifted towards sleep, and he would jerk himself out of it with a cry just before he dreamed that he choked to death; and there would be comfort on waking, more than just the comfort of being awake and not choking, not trapped. There would be Jazra, or latterly there would be Marron; and being awake would be a fine thing then, and being vulnerable would be easy, no harm in the world.

Once before, it had not been a dream. Then the choking had been real, and the paralysis also; and he had felt himself fall and fall until he had entirely fallen away, into some deep deep place inside himself from where he thought he could never climb out. But Lisan had come to find him, sending her questing spirit to seek through his body and blood and bring him up again. She had mended what was torn in his throat, and he had opened eyes on a golden world and the naked body of a girl who was not his own. An imam might have thought himself in Paradise; Jemel remembered only doubt, wondering where Marron was, why not there, why her to be his shadow?

Because she could had been an answer, and acceptable. But now again he was held in that waking nightmare, his body somehow robbed from him, only an oppressive weight of flesh and bone that was a dead cage around the quick of him and would kill that too in just a little time.

He lay helpless and irredeemable, and nothing changed; he felt as though he hung on the point of death like a moth on a thorn. This would be a cruel way to spend eternity, feeling the blade in the heart and its stillness after, waiting and waiting for that stillness to reach his mind . . .

He was lucky, though, if this was luck. It did not last for

ever, it only seemed to do so; and he was neither helpless nor irredeemable, only that he could neither help nor redeem himself. He felt her come, whom he had not dared to hope for: fire against his ice.

She walked in the ways of his body, and made herself free of them. Where she went, he felt the warmth and power of her passing, and never mind if he felt it as pain. Better to have his body hurting than to have it not at all. Her trail was his path back into possession, and he followed where she led.

Followed eagerly, tirelessly, riding on the surge of pain as though it were a wave that lifted him floating and free; and felt he could do this for ever and not regret it.

And was wrong, of course, because pain is a measure of time and he was back in the blood's beat of his body again. He followed her up from the core to the skin of him, and then she left him and he tried to follow her out.

And so felt her first, warm and firmly pressed against his skin, wherever she could reach; and so defined the limits of himself, rediscovered that he had skin because that was where she ended, and so he began. And then his eyes opened, because he was still trying to be as free as she was with the world, to come and go; and he could not do it, but the closest he could come was to let the world come to him.

So his eyes opened and he saw her eyes, her face just a moment away from his. No smile, only a fierce determination, a glare that would not permit him to be weak, to die after so much effort had been expended on his behalf. It had been effort, it always was a terrible effort for her: that familiar ferocity floated like a scum atop extreme exhaustion. He could feel a tremble beneath all her skin, as though she'd physically dragged him further than her strength could bear.

He could also feel that she was naked, he could see it as she pushed herself suddenly away from him, but no matter for that. It had been so before, the last time she saved his life; it meant nothing. What he needed to know, he could not tell by looking: how it was that she had saved his life again, how he had come here, where this was and who had brought him. Even those questions lacked urgency, though. For the moment he was content to let his curiosity slip back inside himself and work there to find how badly or how deeply he was hurt, how much she had mended, how weak he was.

Lisan stirred, struggling to sit up; Julianne appeared at her side, to lift her onto her knees and ease a robe over her head. The smaller girl looked grey and ill, in need of healing on her own account. Julianne fussed with her dress briefly, then produced a flask and held it to her lips.

Lisan drank, then spluttered.

'Julianne, how did you—? I thought it was water!' She ran her hand across her face and licked it, to salvage what she could of what she'd spat or dribbled.

'I know you did,' smugly. 'I fetched it before I came to you this morning, I thought we might have need. This is all I've brought, though, so don't waste it. If you're going to cough the rest of it around, you can have water indeed. Shall I fetch some, or do you want to drink this decently, like a civilised woman in company?'

'Give me.'

Julianne gave her another drink, then brought the flask to Jemel. At that moment, his last doubts faded. Not one of their Patric wines, if she would offer it to a Sharai; only one possibility, then.

'Please . . .' he whispered, trying to haul himself upright, falling back.

'Easy, Jemel. I'll help. Here . . .'

An arm slipped under his shoulders, a quick heave and the tall girl lifted him as simply as she had Lisan. His head lolled disgracefully against her shoulder; he scowled, tried to straighten his neck and found that he could not, even so little effort was too much strain.

Julianne laughed in his ear, reading his thoughts with transparent ease. 'Don't be afraid, you'll be running around quarrelling with everyone again soon enough. It's only weariness, and weakness. You must have been in a terrible fight, there were so many wounds on you; Elisande's only healed the worst of them, all she had the strength to cope with. The rest I've patched up myself, in mortal fashion. With no proper dressings. You'll yelp when they're changed; best ask me to do that too, you won't want Marron to hear you. But at least you're not bleeding any more. You're an awful colour still, worse than she is, and she doesn't look good. You need to rest, that's all. Now stop talking so much, and drink . . .'

He would have opened his mouth, obedient as a child, impatient and greedy as a child; but it was hanging open already, a fact he only realised when she set the flask's lip against his and tipped gently.

Bitter and sweet in subtle balance, herbs and fruits: potent beyond medicine, the *jereth* coursed down his throat like a renewing draught of the desert. Gold for the Sands, green for the oases – and it was in the gold that the sweetness lay, he thought as he always had thought, and bitterness in the green. Green could be for all the wet lands beyond the borders now, and gold could be for the land of the djinn, which was nothing but gold; he'd learned so much at least, that understanding changed as the world changed, as it grew wider.

The Patrics had never understood *jereth*. They drank it for a drink, and nothing more; they had never known its meaning. Blood-dark in their glass goblets, it showed them nothing of its sources; they misunderstood its making and its uses both, the sheer burning power of the thing. Even Lisan: she wanted more, but had no true idea why she craved it so.

He felt that first mouthful lying like a liquid fire in his belly, like gold transmuted into oil, as though a lamp's fuel could contain its own flame. Let his body only absorb it, and he could shrug off this dreadful feebleness; he could draw strength from *jereth* as the Sharai had done for many, many generations. Properly taken and properly appreciated, *jereth* would drive back weariness, stiffen aching muscles and lend as much support to flagging spirits. It had saved many a life in the Sands; many a man who had lost his water and been given up as white bones walking had walked into his camp fully fleshed and lucid, thanks to the little flask he kept within his robe.

Already, simply from the taste in his mouth and the knowledge of its being in his body, Jemel could lift his head, straighten his spine, look around him. Julianne looked a little startled at the change; she would be more so shortly.

He touched his tongue to his lips, to catch what drops had slipped from the flask or from his own loose mouth before he'd swallowed. For a moment he closed his eyes, savouring, welcoming. Not to judge: this brew was not of Saren making, but that was immaterial. It had come into the world, and come to him. Besides, he was no longer Saren himself.

Words were still difficult; he should probably drink water to ease his throat. But he would have to ask for it, apparently, neither girl had thought to pass a skin. If he had to speak anyway, he might as well ask his real question.

'Where is Marron?'

Not *where am I?* or *how did I get here?* or any of the other puzzlements. He thought they could all be answered by the one, or else they did not matter.

The girls looked at each other. It was Elisande who won that exchange, or lost it; she said, 'He went north.' *Where you cannot follow him* was inherent. Neither one of them needed to glance at the raging river, or the great gulf between here and the bank. She made a point of not doing so, indeed; he had seen it already, and was starting to answer *where am I?* on his own account. On an island, clearly, surrounded by a terrible force of water. The spray of it was cool on his skin, hanging in the air like a mist that the sun could not burn off.

He looked to Julianne, who had an overrun of words where Lisan hoarded hers as close as water. He supposed that in this country, no one would hoard water; but words were treasures, meanings were gifts.

'Marron brought you to us,' she amplified, speaking hurriedly against his silence. 'You must have been in a great fight, you were horribly wounded, but I think you must have won the fight. He said he took you from some of our people, but none of your hurts were sword-wounds, so you cannot have been fighting them?'

'I was fighting 'ifrit,' he murmured, remembering. 'Many

'ifrit like serpents, or one that had made itself many; I do not know if they can do that, but they each seemed small-minded, easy to kill. It was only the numbers that defeated us. We were defeated, I think. I fought beside your people, Lisan, but they were mostly dead before yours came, Julianne. Perhaps they rescued me. I was small-minded myself by then, I could not think; only remember that there was a Patric I had to fight when I was finished with the 'ifrit, or they with me. I thought I had found him, tall and white and cloaked in black, but he said not, he said his name was Karlheim . . .'

Julianne gasped, but quite silently; he only felt it because she had her arm around his shoulders still.

It was Lisan who pressed him. 'Was he a young man, blond-headed?'

'I suppose. He wore a helmet, and all Patrics are blond to me.'

'Was he hurt?' That was Julianne, picking at the ground like a child, trying to look as though it mattered not at all.

'He seemed well. I did not kill him, at least. I thought I might die in his arms, which was very wrong.' And something else was wrong too. He was coming at it all askance, but in the end the most sidewise shuffle must bring a man to the place where he must stand. He said, 'Marron came to fetch me? I do not remember that.'

'You had swooned before he brought you here,' Elisande observed neutrally.

'Before then, I think, before he found me. How did he find me?' Jemel didn't believe in the calling power of love; he had heard of too many men and women too who lost themselves in the Sands, searching for those who were lost already.

Besides, this was Marron. There was no telling whom he would have called for, or whose calling voice he would have heard.

'He knew,' he said. 'Where you were, where we were. And so he brought you.'

Which was all the answer he needed, to all the questions that he needed to ask. Meanings were gifts and gifts could be poison, did they not know that, these girls? He'd no more asked them than he would have asked a djinni, *has Marron taken the Daughter back?* – but they'd told him regardless, and now he had that to deal with as well as another certainty. *He went north to find Sieur Anton, didn't he? Once he'd found me . . .*

'Give me more *jereth*,' he said.

'Oh, no,' Lisan objected. 'It's my turn, if either of us is to have treats.'

'Not a treat, it's needful. You don't know . . .' He would pay for it later, he would overtax his body to the breaking-point, but he had somehow to go north.

'Give it him,' came another voice, unexpected and star-tling, none of theirs.

Briefly they stared at each other, then around the tiny flat landscape of the island where nothing could hide.

Nor was it in hiding, only small and unlikely and hard to see in the bright light and the dense spray from the dashing river. Elisande found it first, but seemed to have lost her tongue with the surprise of its arrival; she simply gestured, and then glowered furiously up at where it hung like a trick of the sun in the wet air, betrayed by water-drops.

It was Julianne who spoke to it; Jemel saw no need for conversation, it had said what they should do and he thought that ought to be enough. But they were Patrics and they were girls, and so they would be elaborately cautious and take terrible risks and never know it. Even Elisande, who thought herself so wise in the ways of the desert and its peoples – even she was a child at play among scorpions, when she dabbled with the djinn.

'It is unusual to see you, Djinni Tachur, where you have not been summoned.'

'It is impossible to see me, Julianne de Rance, where I do not wish to be seen. But time presses, the river is in flood and cannot be Folded away. Give the boy what he wants; and Lisan, do you be ready to follow as he drinks. It will take you deep, so keep a thought always for your way back.'

'You mean— I have done all I can for Jemel, for anyone just now. I have no strength left . . .'

'That is true, but you need none. Enough of healing, he will endure now; but wake the *jereth* to reinforce his spirit, or he will sleep when he must needs be fighting.'

'I don't understand. He should sleep, he's exhausted and he's lost more blood than I thought a thrifty Sharai would carry with him. I don't know of any other cure but sleep.'

'Not a cure, no – but a crippled man may ride a horse, and so travel far and fast. Wake the *jereth*, Lisan. There is good cause to do it.'

'Maybe there is, but I don't know what that means. Find someone else to ride your horse, and let Jemel rest.'

'There is no one else. Follow as he drinks, you will know what to do when you see it. It takes only a touch.'

'Do it yourself, then,' but her reluctance was suddenly unconvincing, stubbornness for the sake of show, no more.

'I cannot touch him, or he dies. You know this.'

Yes, she knew – and he had had enough, more than enough of all this talking while Marron ran wild somewhere out of his sight. He snatched the flask from Julianne and upended it into his mouth.

No more than Lisan did he know what the djinni meant; no more than she was he going to ask. But he felt her hand suddenly on his chest, and that was welcome. He felt her spirit, her awareness slide in under his skin and that was oddly welcome too. She was become a familiar stranger in his body, like an imam in the Sands: alien but known, uninvited but recognised.

He felt the moment when she met the *jereth* and touched it; he felt the change. Always before – even taken properly, considered and known for what it was, all its virtues and dangers for body and mind together – it had seemed like a fire contained, sunlight held in glass. Now abruptly it was a fire released, coursing through all his body at once, a spark that became an inferno; he thought his hair should be ablaze, his ragged blood-soaked garment charring as he stared. He thought everything he looked upon should burn.

Lisan made a soft and sudden noise and fell away from him all in a rush, though that couldn't be his fault, he hadn't even been looking at her.

'What did that *do?*' she demanded, if a shocked whisper can be demanding, which in her it could.

'What did *you* do?' Julianne countered, when it became obvious that neither Jemel nor the djinni thought the question addressed to them. Jemel was barely curious enough to listen.

'I don't know. Touched the *jereth*, as the djinni said. Things look different in there, and it seemed broken, somehow. Unwhole. So I touched it as if it were damaged tissue, to start the healing; and a touch was enough. I don't have a word, for what it did. Or – yes, I do. It unFolded. Like that, like a bud opening into a flower, as big a change as that. I don't know what the flower is, what it turned into, what it does. What it's doing to Jemel . . .'

What it was doing was just what he needed; it was giving him the strength and the heart to lift his dull body, to drive it as though it were someone else's altogether. What it took to do such a thing, what it was burning to generate such heat, how much and how long he would have to pay later: these were questions that concerned him no more than they did the djinni. Flesh was a tool, and he would use it until it was entirely broken, if he had to. He wondered if this was how Marron felt, sharing his body with the Daughter. If so, it was no great surprise that he had gone back to it, that they were twinned again. In Jemel this could not last, he would burn it off like oil in a lamp, and miss it badly when it was gone and only the price of it lingered; to have been gifted this and more, and to have it always within reach, always there to call on – that would be a prize to kill for. Jemel felt not invulnerable but something close to that, powerful beyond measure. For what little time the *jereth* could keep him so, before it burned away. And to think he'd been scorning the girls and all their culture just minutes earlier, for not knowing the proper uses of *jereth* . . . He should add himself and his own people to that list of the scorned. For how many generations had they been making the liquor and trading it for common things, for cloth and gold and spices? All this time, all those long lives wasted through ignorance, when so much potency was here and needed only a healer's touch to waken it. They could have driven the Patrics into the sea long since, with an army that had drunk of this. They could do it in a day.

But not today. Today there was only him that knew, and the girls who might be guessing; today there was another fight, and there was Marron somewhere in the midst of it. Marron in pursuit of his Sieur Anton, which was a chase that Jemel would very much like to join. If they never caught the knight, that was one thing, and no bad outcome; if they did, then that was something else, and a resolution would come of it. There might be a truce declared between the Patrics and the Sharai, while they battled 'ifrit together; that was what last night had been about, and it might or might not work. Jemel had declared no truce on his own account. Last night he might have fought with the sheikh of the Saren; today he might fight with d'Escrivey. If not, he would certainly fight with both tomorrow.

He stood up, swift and sure. Both girls were staring; he thought that one at least might be looking to see the colour of his eyes. *Green and gold*, he thought, and smiled privately: gold for the fire in his bones and green for everything that grew and changed, that included him. One was sweet and the other was bitter, and both were strong; mix the two together – in a barrel, in the mouth, in him – and it should be no surprise if they came out the colour of blood. And perhaps his eyes would be red after all, to say so. Perhaps he and Marron could find each other out in the dark, by dint of how their eyes shone crimson.

He and Marron could find each other in the dark anyway, simply by reaching. He meant to keep it that way. And this was daylight, when finding Marron was harder, and more urgent.

He said, 'Esren, take me to where Marron is.'

The djinni said, 'What you have now, you should not waste. I will take you where I choose.'

'That's not what I—'

He felt the djinni's grip close around his chest, like a child's fingers locking into a fist around its toy, like a boy's grip on his knife before he's truly learned the way of it. He felt himself lifted, so that there was no ground beneath his feet; he felt so potent and so furious, he thought he might fight with the djinni first before ever he came to the men he needed to kill. He did move his hand towards his scimitar, only to find the belt slack of its weight, the scabbard empty.

Lost in his fighting before, or taken since? Taken by the Patrics or deliberately left behind by Marron, who wished so fervently that neither one of them need fight? Any of those might be the truth of it; the reality was that he was being carried to a war, and he was weaponless.

Not quite weaponless. The bow was gone too, but he still had a quiver full of arrows over his shoulder; his daggers were gone, but he still had the sheikh's knife tucked into the back of his belt. He'd meant to keep that for killing the sheikh; he might need it sooner now.

He might have used it now to unpick the intangible seams of the djinni's mortal body. He might have done that out of simple rage, except that he was not born a fool and even now, even like this he could control his temper. Angry men were careless men, and careless men were dead men in the Sands.

Besides, the djinni was carrying him high above the river; if it dropped him now, he was a dead man indeed. Dead and messy in the grass, or dead and lost, dead and sodden and drowned in the river. That was a thought to make him shudder, that a man might meet his death in too much water. Perhaps that was why the river hurried so, perhaps it was in perennial hunt for victims, for bodies it could roll and tumble down its course, for meat to feed its marshy fish . . .

Do not drop me, djinni. But it would not, or it would not have picked him up; just as he would not kill it while they flew, or it would not have picked him up. Just as wherever it was taking him, that mattered, and what he did there would matter too. Besides, unless he did the djinni's work and left it living, how could he hope to find Marron afterwards?

His eyes had always been sharp, but up here he felt truly eagle-sighted. He could see just how impossible it would be for one man afoot to find another, even in this narrow valley. He could run all the length and the width of it, he thought, both sides of the river before the *jereth*'s influence was drained; but so could Marron, and further yet. And there was the interlocking pattern of the walled fields, a bewildering maze even from above; and the broad river margins were dotted everywhere with men and horses, living and dead. And with 'ifrit, all living. And then there were the smouldering ruins of yesterday's burning, and the wooded slopes behind the walls, and the canyons and blind vales that ran up deep into the mountain ranges, where the people of Surayon had taken shelter . . . One man could hunt another for a week in this country, and never meet him. Jemel would need the djinni, it seemed that he would need to persuade the djinni; at the moment, he was persuaded that the djinni needed him.

It allowed him just a minute of that high view, perhaps to impress on him how lost he would be without its help. Then it swooped low over the grassland, low and fast, picking a weaving route between the knots of fighting men and spirits.

There were 'ifrit everywhere, so black they swallowed sunlight where they did not shrug it off like water. There were men who were organised in opposition, in defence, and men who were not; men who were effective, and men who were not. So far as Jemel could see, they were all dying anyway. Even those not doing so actively, not crushed or bleeding to death, not dangling screaming from the jaws of a demon, not dragging their mutilated bodies among their confrères and begging for a swift death, a sudden death – even those who were strong and determined, still mounted and fighting well with weapons that were fit for the work, Jemel thought that they were white bones walking, only that they hadn't realised or accepted the truth of it yet.

There were too many 'ifrit and too few men, that was all. It was a time to stand off with arrows, strike and run in the Sharai way; but these were not Sharai. Nor Surayonnaise, who were not too proud to learn from other peoples. These were Patrics, mostly Ransomers in black, the army that had come down from the north.

The djinni carried him among the fallen, where the crippled horses in their agony moved him more than the men; it skirted every scattered battle until at last it brought him to the ruins of the field-wall. No wall now, only broken stands of masonry and mounds of fallen rubble. That must have been the 'ifrit, surely, that toppled it; nothing fleshly could have done so much damage, so swiftly.

There were still 'ifrit seething out from the hidden ways behind the wreckage of the wall, but here at least they had met men who could stand against them. Unhorsed but still organised, a troop of Ransomers was holding the line with savage determination.

It was a line of dead horses they were defending, the great chargers of the Patrics hauled bodily into a rampart. It gave them an illusion of shelter, at least. That was pure Patric thinking, they always looked to build and to hold ground. Even now one of their knights was leading a sortie across the horseflesh barricade, seeking to drive back or destroy the 'ifrit between there and the rubble of the fallen wall. He would make his stand, because he knew nothing else to do. He was doing it well enough, to Jemel's inexperienced eye; while he and his companions hacked and danced and set steel edge against chitin – steel and blessed, and the blessing was the sharper edge, cutting clean and deep, the only reason they had survived this long – others had tumbled over the awkward barricade to heave and drag at yet more corpses, to keep the ground clear and build up what defence they had. If they built it higher in their minds than in reality, so much the better. Patric soldiers found the same comfort in a wall that the Sharai did in a horse and open land to ride it.

These soldiers hauled at one of their destriers, rolling it over so that Jemel could see how its belly had been ripped open, how its guts were trailing. A wall of them made a greater obstacle for the 'ifrit, if not for long. They could scramble over it fast enough; given a little longer, they could chop or chew their way through. Only meat, after all, and he'd seen them eating rock.

There were men astride the rampart with long spears, the best of the arsenal, to discourage that; those men with those spears would be the reason this troop had survived long enough to build their rampart. Jemel watched them jab and thrust at the encroaching 'ifrit, holding the wary creatures back. One came too far, too eager for blood or else simply pressed forward by its nestmates. That time the spear was driven home with a fierce cry, and sank deep into the creature's head between its bright eyes.

The fire in them faded, that iron-hard body dissolved into smoke and was gone. No exultation in the Ransomer, though, no time to celebrate what was so far short of being any kind of victory; he simply hefted his weapon and stabbed it forward again, towards the next 'ifrit.

It was that discipline, that grim resistance that had held the line, and would do so as long as the men could hold themselves, as long as their training held. Jemel guessed that would hold as long as the knight survived who led them. He was the other cause, the pivot their fate would turn around; his men were strong as a body, but they would be lost without him at their head.

No fine swordwork, no fencing down there, no neat defence and sudden thrust. It was more like axework, hew and guard, block and chop. The knight seemed to be everywhere: leading his men in a swarm against a single 'ifrit and delivering the final killer blow himself; letting them fall back while he watched their welfare, while he protected one who was injured all the way to the rampart, while he bled himself and ignored it; rallying the remainder with a cry and urging them forward again.

Jemel was so caught up in the eddying fortunes of the battle, he barely noticed when the djinni's grip loosened from his body. He was aware of stone beneath his feet, but only peripherally until he took a pace forward to see better and found his foot reaching into emptiness, clear air.

Startled, he looked down and discovered himself to be standing on a surviving remnant of the high wall, just where it broke and fell away. He glanced around, and could see no sign of the djinni.

What, was he meant to go down and find a blade, join his rampaging strength to the Ransomers' stubborn discipline? Well, perhaps – but he saw little point in it. One more man could make small difference. Especially one not born to their manner of fighting, not trained to it, not comfortable. It seemed a waste of *jereth* and of himself, not worth all the djinni's working to bring him here with this fire in his veins and his body so alive, only to have him fight as one soldier in a squad where he would inevitably be a stranger and so not trusted.

Worse, it seemed a betrayal of Marron and of all the oaths he'd sworn, to be snatched away from his pursuit for so little cause.

Still, any fight would be better than none. He sighted the ground below him in readiness to jump – and stilled abruptly as black-clad figures came slipping along the wall directly beneath him, just where he'd been about to land.

The Ransomers wore black, they wore hoods, and so did these. These were no Ransomers, though, come to support their brethren. Even looking down from the strangest of angles, Jemel knew what they were, the moment he saw them. He knew them by their dress, much like his own but for the colour, and his was dyed darker than blue by all the blood he'd lost to it; he knew them by the way they moved, desert steps even in this lush grassland, and Marron had mocked him for the same thing before now; he knew them by the curve of their scimitars that no Patric would carry, that no Patric bar Marron could fight with; he didn't need to see their hands and count their fingers.

Neither did he need to understand why they were here. They were Sand Dancers; that was enough. He felt a touch at his throat, and realised it was his own fingers' touching. There was a thick corded scar there, where Morakh had tried to kill him and only Lisan's magic had saved his life. Morakh was dead now, but it was his act also in killing Rudel that had brought all this about, letting the armies into Surayon. Dancers and 'ifrit belonged together in Jemel's mind, for all that the Dancers were his own people and had sworn their lives to goals that he had long sought himself. They should be sworn to Marron, but Morakh had tried to kill him too. More than enough . . .

He slipped over the wall's side, to climb down secretly; they were alert to the wind's breath on the grasses, they would hear if he jumped. As he went down, he let his hands and toes find out their own grips on the stone; his eyes were following the Dancers.

Following as they closed in on the men closest, where the wall of horses met the fallen wall of stones, in an angle of rubble and blood. This was where they'd reinforced the rampart; now they were lifting the bodies of their fallen brothers up, either to raise it higher with more dead flesh or else to bear them over, in hopes of burying them with honour later. Either way, when figures in black robes and hoods came to join them, seemingly to help, of course they were greeted with gratitude, as fellow Ransomers. How else?

Those men learned their mistake, but did not live to profit by the lesson. The Dancers left them lying where they had fallen, and moved on purposefully.

What their purpose was – beyond the simple killing of Patrics, always a priority for Dancers and doubly so now, when they seemed to have allied themselves with the 'ifrit – took Jemel a moment longer to determine, a moment longer than it should have done. He was distracted by a sudden doubt, a question, recognition: one of those men was not a Dancer. He was not even wearing black, only a robe as blood-dark as Jemel's own. Easy to see how it had got so stained, he joined the slaughter with a will; but his sword-work lacked a little grace in comparison, he seemed less dedicated, less given over to death. And besides, even from the back, Jemel knew him.

And was sworn to kill him, but that was almost a side-issue here. It seemed suddenly to matter not at all how the man died, so long as he did die. Jemel would not be jealous if it were another's blade that took him.

Why, how the sheikh of the Saren had joined himself with the Sand Dancers – outcasts, by tradition and his own word – were questions to be addressed later, or not at all. He was here, he was among them, he was slaying Patrics; and the path the Dancers were cutting for themselves was taking them directly towards the Ransomer knight, the man who was so clearly leading this resistance.

That man had drawn his sortie back to the rampart, to give those men rest; he had taken over one of the long spears himself and was balanced lightly on the heaped corpses, holding the resurgent 'ifrit at bay.

Never once did he look behind him, for aid or for retreat. He never thought to look behind to see if there were further trouble coming.

And so there was both, trouble and aid if Jemel could aid

him, and it must be this that the djinni had brought him here to do; so there must be a chance, at least. Unless it was simply that the djinni had a sense of humour after all. It wasn't only the one man for whom Jemel felt that shudder of recognition, and there was more than one here whom he had sworn to kill.

But that again was a matter to be settled later. He didn't look behind him either, though he did wonder again where Marron was, especially now, if he was not here.

For the moment Jemel left the sheikh's knife where it lay, tucked firmly into his belt. Lacking any weapon else, he pulled one of the arrows from the quiver that was slung across his back.

The Patrics made their arrows long, to suit their massive bows. He'd have liked to snap it shorter, but even in all the noise of the fighting, even in all the Dancers' concentration as they crept and killed their way closer to the knight, he was afraid of giving himself away with the sound of its breaking.

He gripped the arrow halfway along its shaft and stole silently along behind the last of the Dancers in their cautious file. His bare feet were noiseless on the trampled grass, he didn't breathe at all; he was even aware of the breeze and glad to have it blowing in his face, not to carry his scent ahead.

Even so the Dancer sensed him somehow, and began to turn. Wary, prepared, potentially deadly, just a moment too late: Jemel pounced at the man's first movement. It was a true pounce, an attack like a cat's, all his body fluid and grace in motion. It was a gift of the *jereth*, no talent of his own, but he rejoiced in the sense of perfect balance, the stillness at the heart even as he flung himself through the air.

An arm round the throat, tight, to choke back any cry;

legs round the waist to pull his victim off-balance and backwards, so that they fell together and the Dancer's arms flew wide and useless, no chance for him to use his bloodied scimitar.

And as they fell, already Jemel's other hand was using the arrow, thrusting it deep and deeper into the Dancer's eye, all the strength in arm and shoulder to drive it in through the socket to find out the brain, and twisting as it went.

The man made no cry, he died as silently as he had killed; and far enough behind his brothers now that they didn't hear the sound of his fall, they didn't feel his falling. Or else they did not care; men die in war, and Dancers are still men. Ignorant or unheeding, they moved on to engulf another small group of the defenders; Jemel saw none of them glance back.

Perhaps they should have done. He stooped to pick up the fallen Dancer's scimitar, and hurried after the next in line.

Properly armed and urgent, knowing now how he could use this temporary mastery from the *jereth*, he took less care to be quiet. Perhaps he wanted this one to hear and face him, to fight for life; in this at least he was no Dancer, that he found no pleasure in simple killing. It was battle, it had always been battle that made his heart sing. If the song were bitter these days, he took that as a sign that he had left his boyhood somewhere in the Sands, or at the Roq, or given it to Marron, who had lost it.

The Dancer did hear, and did twist around to meet his attack with a defence that was barely less than a blistering attack itself, that Jemel had to defend against in his turn or else be overwhelmed. He called on all his extra resources, swift and sure, and managed to stay the fury of the other's swordwork, but little more than that.

This time the Dancer next ahead did stop at the sounds of steel grating and sliding against steel, did turn to see what danger, how many threatened. There was no secrecy left for Jemel; he was determined that there should be none for the Dancers either.

Evenly matched and battling for his life – like fire and ice, he thought, hot youth and cold experience – he drew a breath and screamed. High and shrill, louder than the knight's hoarse voice yelling directions above and beyond him, around the curving of the horse-wall: loud enough to have every man's head turning that could hear.

The Patrics on the rampart heard, and turned; which had been all of his intent, to have them warned and ready. He had, he thought, just saved the life of Sieur Anton d'Escrivey, or at least given the knight the chance to save his own.

For now, he had done what he could for the common good; now he could concentrate, he could focus on keeping his own skin whole and making the Dancer bleed. If he was capable. Even with his whole body exultantly alive, preternaturally alert and swift, he was beginning to doubt it. This was like fencing with Marron, an impossible struggle against an opponent who knew his every move before he made it, and knew a wicked counter when it came.

At least he could hold his own, though, that was something. The Dancer's attacks were more circumspect now, his attitude was more wary, more respectful. In other circumstances, Jemel thought they could have fought till sundown, and all night too.

But he had no time for swordplay, simply for the vicious beauty of the thing. There were 'ifrit massing behind this horseflesh barricade, and more elsewhere; Marron was at large somewhere in the valley, he knew not where or doing what, only that it would be something foolish and dangerous and he wanted desperately to share it; this was a Sand Dancer he was fencing with, and he wanted to see him dead in the grass, a long long way from any sand to dance on.

So he let the curved blade twist in his hand, to turn and catch around the other man's. With the two locked together, he stepped forward and rammed his knee hard into the Dancer's crotch. These men trained all their lives, but they trained with steel; he'd grown up in the Saren caves, fighting with everything bar steel, because a blood-feud would mean deaths that the tribe could not afford.

The Dancer gasped, choked, wrenched his blade free but had no strength to use it; Jemel slashed with his doubled strength, saw the black robe part and the flesh beneath it, saw the blood gush out.

Saw the blood gush and stop, too soon. Saw the man still standing, when he should have been sprawled on the ground, dying or dead already; saw the wide open wound close itself again.

Saw the man smile thinly and step forward, raising his blade like an invitation, *let us fight*.

Something in Jemel nearly broke, at that moment. He was close, as close as ever he'd come to running from a challenge. Anything mortal he would fight, and gladly; anything spirit, he would try. But something that dressed itself in mortal flesh, something that bled and yet could stop the bleeding, heal the wound in moments, something that a blade could never kill . . .

He might have used the *jereth*'s gifts to his eternal shame and disgrace, by fleeing faster than a mortal body could; except that his mind was so tumbled over by the shock of it – and all the thoughts that came tumbling after: Marron and the Daughter, Elisande, a black hand whose touch could heal, images that made no picture he could understand – he only stood and gaped.

And might have died so, gaping yet, except that there was a bright flash from above, a flare of reflected light that snagged his eye; and the Dancer slumped abruptly, and fell in a huddle where he stood.

On the horse-wall behind him, a Ransomer jerked his long spear free from between the body's shoulders, and directed the point of it suspiciously towards Jemel.

He backed away, but not from the spear's point; from the body, rather, humiliated by his fear but fearful yet.

'Beware, beware of that,' he stammered. 'You cannot kill it so easily . . .'

'Can I not? Looks dead enough to me.' The spear jabbed and twisted, to make sure. The Dancer's body jerked, like a fish on a gaff; Jemel almost squealed, almost scuttled further off.

The Ransomer laughed scornfully, then sobered in a moment with a glance over his shoulder, to where 'ifrit were pressing forward.

'Quickly, boy – why should I not skewer you also? You are Sharai, as he was; and he was killing our men.'

'I am not of them,' though he had no way to prove it. 'We fought, you saw. I cried out to warn you . . .'

'You cried out because you were afraid. That's what I heard, what I saw.'

If he could have reached the man, Jemel might have killed him, in that moment before honesty reminded him that he had indeed been afraid, even if the fear came after the scream.

He stepped back, and never mind what the Ransomer thought about his courage: once out of the spear's jabbing range, he could look along the curve of the rampart and see what good – what other good, beyond that spear that had saved him – his screaming had wrought.

There were more spears at work on this side of that wet and slippery bank of bodies, and swords too. Once alerted, the Ransomers could outmatch their assailants in sheer numbers; and it seemed that where their blades cut or stabbed, the normal world applied. Jemel saw one man die, and not recover from it. Then another, and that was enough for the rest; they flickered out of sight, reappeared some distance off across the plain, beyond anything but arrow-range and these Ransomers had no arrows.

Jemel had arrows, but no bow. He was casting about in hopes of finding one when he remembered, realised, saw what he'd forgotten.

The Saren sheikh might walk and slay with Dancers now, but he was still no Dancer. He couldn't work that trick that took them walking between the worlds, winking in and out of view, here and then not here, not available for killing. He was very solidly there, facing a dozen swords alone.

He should have died then and there, and so stolen another of Jemel's oaths from him; but he cast one glance up at the sky and then turned and ran, away across the grass towards where the Dancers waited.

Several of the Ransomers started after him, but found themselves quickly called back. 'Ifrit were threatening to break through again, and keeping those penned had to be the knight's priority. Jemel still had his spearman on watch; he had also just spotted the bow that he wanted, lying with other weapons beside a line of dead men. Honour to the fallen, an armoury to him, he could throw away the Dancer's useless scimitar; but first he glanced up at his wary guard and said, 'Tell Sieur Anton d'Escrivey that he owes me for a death, and perhaps for a life too, and that I will claim for both when this is over.'

Startled, the man stared down at him, his spear jutting forward like an acknowledgement of the impotence of power against understanding. 'What do you know of Sieur Anton?'

'Enough that I mean to kill him – but not yet. Wish him joy of the 'ifrit, and much honour – and tell him my name is Jemel of the Sharai. Another day we will meet, if God allows it.'

And then, without so much as a glance along to see if the knight were watching, he turned and ran in his turn: first to that place of the dead, where he discarded the scimitar and seized the bow instead, and then away on the sheikh's trail, leaping through the grass with great strides. He could have matched Marron's speed, he thought, and his endurance too, so long as the *jereth* lasted; he could match the fleeing sheikh also, but could not catch him. They seemed to be pacing each other with no gain, except that with every step they drew closer to the distant Dancers, and if that were a gain for either one it ought to be for the man Jemel pursued.

He felt it for himself, though. He was grinning savagely as he ran, as he breathed, as he felt the pulse and fire of his blood; he would lay down some bodies on his own account, a line of honour to show the Ransomer knight, Marron, anyone. To show that spearman, if he survived to see it. Was that a scream of fear, did he think? Well, he should learn—

And then there were distant cries behind him, that were shock and fear indeed. He wondered if the 'ifrit had broken through, but did not pause to see; he kept running, and saw sudden shadows overtake him on the grass.

His eyes were dragged upward in simple startlement. He saw black shapes against the sky, and remembered 'ifrit in flight; and tried to set an arrow to his bow-string as he ran, and nearly tripped himself. Stumbled, but kept running: and saw monstrous creatures swoop low ahead of him, to snatch up the Dancers where they stood.

Not 'ifrit, these were ghûls with wings, slaves to their spirit overlords. The Dancers didn't try to run, or to resist; they looked as though they had been waiting for exactly this.

Another ghûl, lower and closer; this one swooped on the running sheikh, and took him as an eagle takes a rabbit. Jemel cried out in frustration then and did stop running at last, did nock his arrow to the string; and was bringing the bow up to aim a desperate shot when he felt a tremendous blow on his back that should have flattened him, except that great claws had curled around his body in that same moment and so he was lifted up from ground and swept away.

There were seven ghûls, and four men: two Dancers, one sheikh, and Jemel. He could still count at least, despite the bruising strike, the buffeting flight, the shock.

He could look down and see the river, the plain, the war far below him; that battle already behind him and the mountains rising ahead. After a little while, he preferred to look forward. He did not think the ghûl would drop him now, but as a means of transport it was less reassuring even than the djinni. He felt very little supported, despite the curl of claws that caged him. Besides, it stank, and groaned to itself with every effortful stroke of its wings that sent another blast of foul air down into Jemel's face.

He watched the ghûls, and the men they carried; he saw them suddenly stretch their beating wings wide and soar, rising like vultures on an uplift of air.

He felt his own ghûl do the same, and felt the change immediately. Flight was smooth and easy now, he wasn't being shaken flesh from bone. And there across the mountains was the margin of the Sands, his own country like a glimpse of blessing . . .

He ought perhaps to call the djinni, try if it would wrestle him from the ghûl and take him back. But his mind was working at last, catching up with his body: seven ghûls, and four men. At first he hadn't thought at all, he'd been as stiff and stupid as a rabbit in an eagle's claws. Then he'd assumed that he was of course a captive, a rabbit in an eagle's claws, being carried off to imprisonment or death.

There was little sense in that, though – he had no value as a prisoner, and why delay his death? – and ghûls were notoriously slow of mind, slower even than he had been, and less likely to catch up. He thought the ghûls had been sent by 'ifrit, their masters, to collect whoever survived among the Dancers and the sheikh. Death defied foresight, they wouldn't know how many. He thought they had seen men in Sharai robes, running from the Patrics; if those big horse-eyes were sharper than they looked, they might have checked for maimed hands, missing fingers.

He thought they had seized him alongside those he chased, mistaking him for just another Dancer; and now were carrying him to wherever the Dancers were being sent. Out of the valley, and into the Sands: he didn't understand it, but no matter.

He had a tight grip yet on the Patric bow, and arrows in his quiver. He knew he could trust the arrows, where the abandoned scimitar had betrayed him. These long glides gave him a chance to aim; the ghûl's tight grip held him steady.

It might of course realise what he was doing, and simply let go. If it did, he would shriek for Esren and see what befell, whether he did. But he thought the ghûl would not open its claws. Dull terror and enforced obedience, the stone in its tongue – he was sure that it had one – would keep it numbly on its course, whatever he did.

He hoped.

Without his feet on solid ground, he couldn't draw the bow as it was meant to be drawn, standing and a full arm's draw to the ear. Sharai bows were far shorter, lighter in weight, meant to be used on horse or camelback; that was his skill, and he thought he could replicate it even in a ghûl's grip, while his blood still tingled and his body felt steel-sprung, inexhaustible.

He held the bow horizontally against his locked left arm, and drew it to the chin. With his first shot, he thought his strength and eye would be good enough, he'd been shooting from the saddle all his life; he loosed at the nearest of the

Dancers and saw his arrow drift wide, far wide and fall use-lessly lost to the sand below.

One he could afford; more would come expensive. He worked another carefully out of the quiver and nocked it to the string, puzzled and thinking hard. He'd missed by so much, an unblooded boy could have done better. As an unblooded boy, he had certainly done better from his first day with a bow.

He had stood on towers and on clifftops, and felt winds when the air below was not moving at all. Up here, he thought there must be a wind indeed: wind enough to give the ghûls lift, burdened as they were with the weight of men. His movement, the Dancer's movement, he had allowed for both – but the air between, that must be moving too, and fiercely. The *jereth*'s fault, that he was unaware.

He drew the bow again and this time made allowance, an estimate – a wild guess in truth, he could do no better – for a wind he could not feel. And loosed, and saw the arrow fly; and saw it strike, hard home into the belly of the Dancer.

That man screamed, and writhed around the shaft; then something seemed to leave him quite abruptly, nothing that Jemel could see but it was not quite like a death, and the abandoned body slumped in the ghûl's talons.

The ghûl flew on, unheeding.

The other Dancer, the sheikh, both had heard the scream; they stared around, saw the man dangling, saw the arrow.

And could do nothing, they seemed not to have a voice between them to cry to the creatures that bore them, if crying would do any good. It was 'ifrit that controlled these beasts, Jemel thought, not the men they carried.

He took another arrow, and a careful aim. It was less than

a perfect shot; it struck not the Dancer, but the ghûl above. The creature bellowed, and buckled, and fell out of the sky.

Jemel watched it shrink below, and thought he saw it drop the Dancer as it fell. It was possible, he thought, that they would both survive the drop. Not likely, but possible. If so, though, they should still be separated and alone in the Sands, a long way from comfort or aid. No trouble to him, at least.

And then there was the sheikh, and Jemel would not kill that one with an arrow at a distance, though he had countless opportunities as they flew.

They flew, and as they went he used his remaining arrows to pick off the other ghûls one by one, till there were only the two left, his and the sheikh's. They paid no attention to their nestmates' sudden disappearances, slaved as they were to a distant will, a single driving urge. There was a mission here, Jemel thought, and it was the sheikh's now to perform; the ghûls were not even messengers in this, only beasts for transport.

The Sands were broken up with outcrops, ridges of black rock rising. It was hard to be sure of his ground from this unimagined angle, but he knew their direction from the sun and thought he could recognise what tribal lands lay below. He had travelled those lands once with Jazra and then again bare weeks ago, with and without Marron.

Then he saw a landmark that was unmistakable, and he knew exactly where they were and where they were heading, though not why.

The Pillar of Lives rose like a pinnacle above a ridge of rock.

From a distance it might have been a natural finger of stone upthrust, one of the many bizarre formations that God had set in the desert, or else that wind and sand together had shaped in defiance of God's original creation. Come closer, though, and it could be seen to be man's work entirely, built of countless gathered stones into a needle-shape, an arch for an eye and then a high, high tower.

Jemel knew it well, he had climbed it once and left his own contribution, his own stone at the top.

It was the top of it now that the ghûls brought them to. Brought them and left them, dropping them heedlessly onto the uneven surface and then flying on without ever touching the rock themselves.

Jemel was the swifter to recover, if only barely; he would just have had the time to fling himself onto the sheikh's back and sink the man's own dagger into his ribs.

He was curious, though; he wanted to see what the man did, why they had been brought to this of all places. The Pillar of Lives was a Sand Dancer creation, one stone for every Dancer who had ever taken the oaths and forfeited a finger in signature. It was also the place where Marron had first learned to control the Daughter, where he and Jemel had first stepped through the eye into the land of the djinn.

The sheikh got to his feet, with never a glance towards Jemel. He walked the few paces to the pillar's centre, where a few stones rose above the general level as though in a cairn. Topmost of those was the one that Jemel himself had laid there, one that he had brought back from the other world and carried up here in defiance of the Dancer Morakh and everyone else, in defiance of the world it had felt at the time; and it was that stone that the sheikh reached to lift.

He staggered, under more than the stone's weight; his face was suddenly flushed and glistening with sweat, and his breath came in brutal gasps. He lurched towards the pillar's edge – and stopped, finding Jemel suddenly between him and the drop.

'Take another,' Jemel said softly. 'You can cast down any stone else, you can dismantle the Pillar entirely and consign every man that helped to build it into hell, for all I care – but not that stone. That's mine, my oath, and it stays here until my word is broken. Put it back.'

The sheikh seemed not to understand the words, not actually to hear them; his expression didn't change, until he set down the stone quite carefully at his feet. Then the twisted pain left his features, and they fell into a neutral, assessing stare.

For a moment his eyes seemed entirely black, and Jemel couldn't suppress a shiver.

Then the sheikh drew a scimitar, and Jemel laughed.

'Those don't work,' he taunted, 'didn't you know? They cut, but it doesn't keep. Besides, you and I, we have a promise to meet. I have your knife, you have mine . . .'

The sheikh responded not at all to that, only moving forward with the wary confidence of a skilled swordsman. Better than skilled today, Jemel thought: inhumanly strong, inexhaustible, as the Dancers were.

As he was himself, today.

But he had no sword to meet and match the sheikh's blade, only a heavy knife that he found ill-balanced and unnatural in his hand. This couldn't be a fight. He tossed the knife in his hand, and then from one hand to the other, testing the weight of it and its balance in flight; then he took the blade between his fingers and cocked his arm, cocked all his body in readiness to throw.

An alert man, a watchful man can dodge a thrown knife, if he sees it thrown. Less easy from this close distance, perhaps, but the sheikh was alert, watchful, would be abnormally fast. Jemel feinted once, twice; the sheikh swayed side to side, never fully committed, eyes never leaving the hand that held the knife.

Then Jemel made his move. One more feint and he threw not the knife but himself: he rolled forward over the cobbles while the sheikh's arms were both stretched out to the sides, while his scimitar was so far out of line. Rolled inside the reach of that scimitar and came neatly to his feet like a tumbler at a fair, with the knife gripped by its haft now and the blade a bare hand's-span from its owner's chest.

A bare hand's-span, and then not so much; then nothing at all, less than nothing, buried its own length deep between his ribs.

Jemel thought he would not recover from that. He twisted the blade in the wound in any case, for satisfaction's sake; and saw more than the life-light die in the sheikh's eyes. He saw a wisp of black smoke eddy from his lips and seem to quest a moment before it dissipated into the heat of the desert day.

Jemel threw the body over the edge after he had stripped it of anything valuable, silver rings and ornaments, a buckle of gold. Then he restored his rock to its place on the cairn's height and stood staring at it for a while, wondering what was its importance here; remembering how Esren would not come near any rock fetched to this world from the other, for

fear of being trapped again as it had been in the Dead
Waters.

When he was tired of puzzling over that he gazed west
and southerly, feeling the *jereth*'s edge begin to fade now, so
that his sight was little better than it ever was. That was very
good, though, and this was a high spot, and the desert air
was clear; he would see someone coming from a distance,
from a great distance off. Whether it was a figure running or
a figure flying by a djinni's courtesy, he would see it against
the sand or against the sky, so long as he was looking. So he
would look, and so he did, and gave not a thought to leaving this place, to seeking water or shelter as any man of
sense would have done. He looked for someone to come,
and when he was tired of straining his eyes to see a dot that
was not there, he turned back to his stone again and looked
at that, and the puzzle of it.

Jemel had dropped the flask after he had drained it. Julianne
picked it up after he had left.

A last sticky dribble had accumulated in the bottom.
Julianne was curious but reluctant; Elisande insisted; the
flask was at last uptilted, and the residue dripped out onto
Julianne's waiting tongue. One precious, cherished moment
to linger over the taste of it in her mouth, and she swallowed.

Elisande was there, at her side and somehow inside her
also, both at once. She felt her like a sprite, a spirit of mischief: wicked but not malign, alien but welcome, tender and
sharp and surprising.

Then Elisande touched the *jereth* to life inside her, such a tiny drop of it there was, and it was like touching fire to the finest tissue, a flame that overswept everything at a gasp, except that it left no harm where it had passed. Rather it lingered, consuming only what was drab or weak or tired within her. She felt unexpectedly well, and better than well; she felt bright and clear, both as sparkling and as strong as the water in the river: fresh from a mountain spring, deep and full of character, understanding the darkness and breaking into light.

She felt Elisande slip outside her skin again, and could almost have gone with her, simply for the fascination of the thing. She thought she could see how it was done now, she thought she could do it herself at need. Another time, though: for now she had her own whole body to explore. She felt as though she'd barely been here before, as though she'd lived all her life in purdah and was suddenly free of the harem and all a busy city lay before her.

She became aware that Elisande was looking at her a little doubtfully, a little quizzically; she laughed, and found it unexpectedly hard to stop laughing.

'I'm sorry,' she said, chuckling still. 'This is . . . a revelation.'

Elisande shook her head. 'And all this time we've just been using it as a drink. Think how much we've wasted . . . But no one ever told us. Can we use that as excuse?'

'Sweetheart, I don't believe that anyone knew. Even the Sharai who brewed it. Jemel was – startled, wouldn't you say?'

'Mmm. Jemel had a flaskful. If it's done this to you, what in the world has it done to him?'

'And where's he gone, and what's he doing with it? I

thought that djinni of yours had taught you not to ask questions. There's no point in them – or no point in putting them to me. I can't give you answers.'

'Are you sure? Have a look, see if you can't spot him. He went north, and he's chasing after Marron.'

The suggestion was absurd. However much the valley was laid open around them like a bowl, however much the war was displayed in smudgy smoke and distant figures' manoeuvrings, it would be impossible to tell individuals at this distance, which figure was who. Hard enough, almost impossible to say that those to the north there were Ransomers, hard beset by 'ifrit . . .

Except that it wasn't impossible at all, now that she looked more carefully. Those were clearly Ransomers, the dress was unmistakable, and the way they fought. She could see that as clearly as she could see Sieur Anton, filthy with blood and work, standing high on a mound of dead horses and exhorting his troops to another greater effort, she could almost hear his voice . . .

It wasn't possible, and yet she was certain. She could see what forms the 'ifrit had taken, where they had been evil shadow-shapes before, blurred and unreadable; she could see how the men had built themselves a crude defencework of slaughtered horseflesh, which Sieur Anton bestrode with the artful balance of a natural sailor; she could see every separate man fighting for his life or his brothers' lives as they sought to keep the 'ifrit penned in. She wondered why the spirit-creatures didn't break out further down the wall, where there were no men to oppose them; and even as she wondered, she saw the wall bulge and fall at half a dozen sites at once, and a horde come forth.

Julianne gasped at the size of that army, so many, enough to swamp all the defenders she could see. Those Ransomers must be lost, surely – unless the hard work of last night could pay off even at this late hour, this desperate time. There was a movement, a line of darker blue amid the blue smoke-haze horizon to the east; it broke through and rolled in across the plain, like a ripple of shadow sliding across the still surface of a pond. Behind it came another such ripple, and then another.

Julianne stretched her new acuity of sight to another degree of impossibility, to confirm more than what she'd already guessed. Beside her, Elisande didn't need such clarity of vision to be equally certain.

'It's the tribes, Julianne. The tribes are riding.' And then, a moment later, 'Can you see him?'

It was Jemel she was supposed to be looking for, and she didn't misunderstand her friend for an instant; the question was *can you see Marron?*

And when she answered, 'Yes,' she knew that she would be equally understood. She didn't need to add *of course, Hasan is leading, where else would he be?*

'That's good,' but it wasn't, plainly it wasn't. Elisande wanted to be Jemel, invigorated and away to search for the boy they both loved. She'd had to give the best gift she had to her utmost rival; she'd had to give the last least trace of it to her friend, who would of course misuse it in searching for the wrong man entirely. The wrong men: Julianne turned and gazed southerly, searched all the southern slopes of the valley from riverspout to marshbeds, as far as she could see in every direction, far up into the trees beyond the palace, and still could not find her Imber. Jemel had suggested that he might be far to the west, beyond where the valley bent; she tried to bore her sight through the elbow of ancient rock, but even these new eyes would not oblige her there.

Even so, 'This is like standing on your grandfather's terrace,' she murmured. 'I can see whatever I want to see. How did you know?'

'Because everyone gets what they want, except me.' Then Elisande laughed at herself, and the laugh was as bitter as her words had been; and she said, 'No, but I could feel it flower inside you like it did in Jemel, only it wasn't so powerful. I'm not sure it would have been even if you'd drunk a flaskful like he did; I think perhaps it reacts to the strengths of the user, or else to what they desire. So Jemel can pretend to be Marron for as long as ever it lasts, and you – you can stand back and watch, and understand it all.'

'Is that what you think I do?'

'I know it's what you're best at. It's what your father trained you for.'

It was true. She should have been a woman high at court, scheming and manipulating behind a curtain of modesty and obedience, dancing men to her father's tune. Because it was true didn't give it any sweeter a taste. 'So what would the *jereth* have given to you, Elisande?'

'What, if I didn't have to give it all to others? I don't know, my love. Not the thing I wanted, that's for sure. Not any of the things I want, my country safe and my father living and . . .'

A wave of her hand implied a whole list. She didn't name Marron; again, she didn't need to.

'It might have given you what you most want on this island.'

'What,' ruefully, 'Marron back, and free of the Daughter? I don't think so, Julianne.'

'No, I meant an understanding why we're here, why the djinni left us here.'

'Something to do, you mean – it's you who always wants to understand it. And haven't we answered that anyway, wasn't I here to heal Jemel and wake the *jereth* in him, so that he could go and do whatever heroic thing he's doing?'

Julianne had seen him suddenly, thought she had, snared in the claws of a flying ghûl: not so heroic, more doomed to die. Her father had been taken the same way, and she had saved him; she didn't think she'd be given the chance to do so again.

Nor did she mention it to Elisande. She might have been mistaken, after all; she might have been deceived. Instead, 'I don't think so. That you could have done anywhere, Marron would have sought you out wherever. I think this place has a purpose, and so do we.'

'To sit and watch, most likely, while everything happens all around us. It's very good to watch from, you said so yourself, like Grandfer's terrace; and now you've got the eyes to see with. You'd better tell me everything.'

Elisande could see most of it for herself, but Julianne was happy to oblige; it gave her the excuse she needed to stare and stare, to watch her man at work, at war.

One of her men, at least. There was still no sign that she could see of Imber.

The great waves of tribesmen had broken up rapidly, even before they met the 'ifrit, as soon as they had seen them. Those who had raided horses yesterday – or killed their

riders in battle, and so claimed them – were faster anyway
than those still on camelback, and so outpaced them with
something like excuse; but there was nothing about the
Sharai that could make them fight in regiments. It was like
watching surf rise and shatter against a rocky shore, she
thought: all that power, all that waste and loss.

Small groups and clusters of dark-robed men swirled
around darker streams, 'ifrit where they issued forth like
stains against the green. Even the hottest heads among the
Sharai had the sense to stand off at first, to let their bowmen
shoot; even Julianne couldn't see the arrows strike and fail,
strike and fall. She could see the momentary dismay among
the riders, though, the way they checked their mounts,
glanced from side to side, watched each other watching
them. She didn't need to see, could have foreseen with her
eyes closed the necessary sequel: the spears and scimitars
lifted and the voices lifted higher, the mounts urged forward against their terror and the tribes' charge against
demonseed, against all good sense or understanding.

It was courage flung down like a banner underfoot to
ride across, a bridge into disaster; it was an idiot made of
honour. Precious few heroes would survive to show their
scars and make their boasts around the fires in years to come.
They rode in screaming, and she thought she could hear
their screams on the breeze, though it surely should have
been a storm to contain so much passion, so much fury; they
learned quickly that there were other ways to scream, and
other causes for it.

The trouble was, of course, that the Sharai travelled with
no tame imams; that they scorned imams, indeed, as much
as the imams of the Catari scorned and feared them. A holy

man might be given passage through the tribal lands, he might be made as much – or as little – welcome as law and custom and the sheikhs demanded, but he would seldom be asked to bless their endeavours and never invited to ride alongside the warriors.

So never mind all Hasan's warnings and wisdom of last night, never mind their own experience of spirits in the Sands; the Sharai had precious few weapons that were blessed and potent, and no one able to work that minor miracle for them.

They might as well have thrown stones from a distance, and charged with willow-wands for sword and spear. No matter how well-aimed the arrow, unless it struck an eye it would glance off uselessly, and they must needs be close to shoot so well from horseback. By the time they got that close, any man of the Sharai wanted his scimitar in his hand; arrows were for hunting, not for war.

So they wasted their arrows from too far off, and then they charged; and few of them came close enough even to batter at impervious shells with blades that had no cutting edge for this. They rode into a hedge of claws and jaws, of piercing and tearing, of death dressed in a dozen sharp arrays.

The lucky were shamed by their horsemanship, or by their camels' training; their mounts bolted before they came in reach of the 'ifrit, and they were carried a long way towards humiliating safety by animals that simply could not be ridden back.

Hasan, of course, was not lucky, not so lucky as to be safe. Of course he had been given a horse; and of course the sheer ferocity of his will was enough to drive it through its fear, even where he was not enough recovered to have forced it with hand and heel. Followed by his own small knot of Beni Rus, who would blood their mounts with their own blades if need be to keep the animals in line, with his progress followed by every Sharai eye on the plain, Hasan led his tribe and all the tribes against the 'ifrit invaders.

'He knows that he must,' Julianne whispered, some part of her commentary to Elisande that was as little needed as the rest, and just as useful. 'They would charge, with or without him; they would never follow him again, if he did not lead them now. So of course he must . . .'

So of course he did, knowing that many behind him would die in this charge, and knowing that he himself was better equipped to live: not so much through a better horse or better skill with rein and stirrup and blade, as through the simple fact that his blade had been blessed, long since. He had slain 'ifrit before, and ought to have had little cause to fear for his own life. Julianne feared for him, though, very greatly.

'Strike and run, that's how the Sharai fight; and if he only would . . . But he's forgotten all he ever knew, or else he's just too stubborn to live. See, his blade cuts, but one blow won't kill the creature, a monster like that, it needs hacking to pieces; and the man who rides at his back and strikes after him, useless, he might as well be a poppet with a sword of wood and silvering. And Hasan knows that; he's already turned and gone back, see, but his horse is so slow, he's having to fight it all the way; and the man's dead or he will be, there's no point in going back. But he will, he'll go back and back, and he can't guard himself for ever even with a blade that sharp. He was so sick only yesterday and he hasn't had any *jereth*, or if he had you weren't there to magic it for him . . .'

And she could hear the near-accusation in her own voice – *why weren't you there to magic it for him, why here for Jemel and not there, or why didn't you do it last night in the palace when there was all the* jereth *in the world and all the time too and you could have made a demigod of him, so strong, he could have led the world . . . ?* – and tried to choke the words back before she said them, too late to stop the feelings from showing through; and when Elisande said her name, 'Julianne,' in a dry dead voice she thought her friend only meant to quarrel with her, nothing more than that, a distraction from watching her husband die and another way to pass a dreadful time.

But she turned in any case, if only to demonstrate how utterly she was not going to quarrel; and Elisande pointed without words and without dramatics, just the gesture, nothing more.

Away to the south, from beyond the elbow where the valley turned, a party of Patrics was riding. They were approaching the river at an angle that would bring them to the bank almost opposite the girls on their island. They had scouts and outriders, they were military in their formation but certainly not Ransomers, nothing uniform in their dress and little sign of discipline in their riding; and they came at a pace that was too slow for soldiers with any real purpose in mind, somehow solemn and distraught both at once.

Among them, led by a man on foot with his head respectfully hooded, was a horse that might have seemed riderless on any other day, to other eyes than these; or it might have seemed to be simply burdened, carrying a sack of grain or a side of beef, perhaps, wrapped against the dust of its journey.

Wrapped and knotted tightly with a rope, tied firmly to the saddle of the horse; but it was too fine a horse to bear such burdens, gleaming white in the hazy light.

Elisande had recognised the horse. So too did Julianne. The two of them had spent a hot afternoon riding beside it, riding in disgrace and towards retribution, towards a marriage long ago.

Julianne, the Baroness von und zu Karlheim choked, and wheeled round; but that way there was nothing she could do but watch her other husband die, watch him give himself to death again and again, knowing that the gift would not and could not be spurned for ever. Besides, she was a married woman, twice-married and both to soldiers; she would not disgrace either the one who was somehow still miraculously living, nor the other. She should be embarrassed to have her friend see her turn to find a living man, when his comrades were bringing her the dead.

All unwittingly bringing him to her, she was sure, they could not know that she was here; nor would they have chosen to fetch him to her, if they did. More likely they were looking for help and hoped to find it, some way to cross the river to join with the Ransomers they knew to be on the northern road.

If they could see what had befallen the Ransomers, they would not be so eager. But they were coming, all innocence, they were bringing her Imber to her as Marron had brought his Jemel to Elisande. This time there was no help, no hope, neither one of them could give breath to the dead; if they could, they could not cross the river to achieve it.

That was suddenly somehow the worst of it, the greatest

outrage: that fate or freak chance was bringing her boy dead to that bank there, bare yards away, and she was here and could not cross the water to receive him.

She cried out to Esren, to carry her across; the djinni did not come. Elisande tried, sharp and demanding, still with no response.

'Elisande, you have powers that I do not, that I don't even understand. Can you not – oh, build a bridge, raise the riverbed, still the waters into ice, something?' *Surely something, or why else are you here?*

'No, my love, none of those. I'm sorry.' She didn't sound sorry, only distracted; and went on, 'Julianne, Esren lied to me. No matter how it squirms this time, it did lie when it made that oath. It swore to come to my calling; it has not. But the djinn cannot lie, that's – that's inherent, fundamental, sewn into the fabric of the world . . .'

'Then the fabric of the world has a snag in it. But Esren was desperate, when it made the oath. And mad, I think. Perhaps it still is mad. And it had been cut off from, what does it say, the world-web for so long—'

'Weft, the spirit-weft.'

'—Yes, that. It says it's crippled, it still can't see the future as other djinn do. Perhaps it couldn't foresee that it would break that oath.' Though it had seemed to guess well enough in other matters, when it wanted to. She thought the simpler explanation was the truth, that it had simply lied. And if in that, in how much else, how often?

'Something else it said,' Elisande murmured, in a tone of wonder. 'Something else, that wasn't true either . . .'

'Well, what? And what of it?'

'Never mind for now, love. Don't make me say it, I don't

want to listen to myself or I'll never believe it. Just let me
think, let me work . . .'

There was war on the north bank, that much she could see –
thanks to the *jereth*, she could see very clearly – and she
didn't want to. Every time she looked, every time she risked
a peep she thought she'd find herself a widow entire, not the
demi-widow that she was now. On the south bank, no war
that she could find; only a funeral procession and an army in
disarray, *they have lost my man, and they don't know what to
do without him.*

It was true, or it seemed to be. Some little distance behind
the advance party that bore the body, a whole parade came
trailing into view: all men, all mounted, with a great variety
of weapons, it was undoubtedly an army but it seemed
entirely purposeless, a snake without a head. It needed an
enemy to fight, and a leader to command it. Lacking both,
it seemed spiritless also, exhausted by its loss. And by whatever battle had brought him down, who had led them this
far: many of those men were freshly wounded and ill-
patched up, and there were empty saddles as well as other
bodies. They all looked weary, and wary also, though it was
the grass they watched as they rode over it, rather than the
horizon where an enemy might lurk.

Julianne wanted to cry out to them, to warn them to
beware of walls and water. She was quite pleased, quite
relieved to find that she could still care that much; though it
was a distant, detached sort of caring, nothing at all like the
passion that was driving Elisande as she stamped about the
island building little cairns of stone and gleaning tinder.

Julianne had passions of her own, but they were not

rooted like her friend's. Perhaps she lacked depth, foundation. Perhaps that was why she could love two men at once, and both of them distinctly. She might have proved as fickle as her fears, and have loved neither one of them for long; other people might have cause to be grateful that they died before she could shame them. She might be grateful herself, in years to come. Not now. Now she saw her Imber's slack cortège, and could not bear it; she turned around, and saw a miracle.

Just for a moment she saw a hint, a glimmer of gold in the air and beneath the grass, as though an image of the djinn's world had been overlaid on this one. She saw a great shadow moving to obscure the gold, a mass of black that brought her nothing but despair; she thought it was another army of the 'ifrit, coming out of that world into this.

Then the gold was gone, not so much in an instant as in a succession of instants, like a line of bubbles bursting one after another; and there indeed was a host in black, but not 'ifrit. They were mounted Ransomers, and Marshal Fulke was at their head; on his saddle-bow was a great candle of twisted wax in black and white spirals, echoed by the spiral of the smoke that twisted up from the wicks of it.

Briefly, men and horses seemed confused; then the marshal stood in his stirrups, gazed about him, started calling orders back along the column of his army. Troops broke away as he directed them, charging towards the greatest concentrations of 'ifrit – which brought them also inevitably through the greatest concentrations of the Sharai.

Julianne saw black sweep past midnight blue without a pause, apparently without a glance; she also saw the opposite, she saw black and midnight blue together in swift conversation.

The first time she saw a Ransomer spread his arms wide to encompass all the Sharai within his hearing, lift up his head and voice – that was the first time today that she wondered if she were simply dreaming all of this, all the day's disasters. Easier to believe that than this, that out of all of Outremer there was a man to be found in Ransomer dress who would call down blessings on the blades of the Sharai.

And yet there was, and more than one. She could see it happen again and again; she could see Marshal Fulke himself, still erect in his stirrups, pronouncing a general blessing on all in the field and all the weapons they bore, if only they fought 'ifrit.

It numbed her understanding of the world and the spirit-world together, even trying to imagine how that could be effective. The priests of one religion offered the blessing of their God to the blades of another God's followers, in order to give them potency against spirit-demons in inhuman earthly bodies, invulnerable bodies. She stood in a valley where sorcery was mundane, quotidian; she had seen miracles worked by holy men, and by conjurors, and by faith alone; she could not believe in these blessings. How could a Sharai give credence to the word of a Ransomer? And if they doubted even as much as she doubted, then how could the blessing possibly give an edge to their weapons?

And yet visibly, incontrovertibly it did. Those few Sharai archers with any arrows left tested them suspiciously, and saw their shafts strike 'ifrit chitin and sink in to the fletching. That was good enough. One more time the tribes attacked, in the eye-bewildering patterns of ride and counter-ride that could so baffle an enemy he might die without ever understanding which direction the blow would be coming from.

The 'ifrit seemed not to be baffled, but they died in any case. Blessed blades bit deep, to hew off threatening claws or simply thrust through the carapace to seek whatever lay inside, in lieu of heart and lights and liver. Julianne thought that was where death lay buried, and swords or spears freed it; she always had thought so, and no priest nor warrior, philosopher nor poet had ever managed to dissuade her from the opinion. Babies sometimes brought it out with them; her own mother had died that way, and Marron's too.

She saw the 'ifrit driven back through the breaches they had made in the enclosing wall. She saw men follow and fell anxious again, thinking that they would lose themselves in there where the 'ifrit would not, and so the tide of the battle could turn again.

But there were men of the Sharai, unmounted men running and climbing up onto the tops of the walls, to be both guards and guides. How they knew to do that, she couldn't tell: whether someone had warned them, or whether they had learned a humiliating lesson for themselves. Imber had learned it, but that was knowledge wasted . . .

Sharai and Ransomers both rode into the maze in pursuit of the 'ifrit, often side by side; Hasan, of course, was among the first, though Fulke remained outside, with the bulk of both the armies. Even amid those twisting walls, she thought Hasan would likely ride faster than the men above could run. He would risk losing himself entirely if his Beni Rus couldn't keep up with him, risk coming alone upon a whole nest of the 'ifrit; of course he must do that, of course he had to keep her anxious even when she couldn't see where he was or what he was doing, when she had only her imagination to feed her fears . . .

She turned south again, to confront what was no fear at all, because who could be afraid of the truth? The cortège was closer now, and the men seemed more like farmers than warriors, scanning their fields for rabbit-sign or insects. Except that no farmer had ever been so frightened even of a plague of rabbits, a locust-swarm. Something lurked, something was expected . . .

Something arrived, erupting from the ground around them like a thousand massive serpents. Their mounts must have sensed a vibration in the earth, bare moments before it burst open; half of them were rearing already or leaping sideways in a deadly absurdity, trying impossibly to lift all four hooves at once. A few trained warhorses lashed out with their forefeet, but no one it seemed had thought to bless them or the plates they were shod with; where they struck, even razor-sharp steel had no effect, though the same blow would have ripped a man's leg open and shattered the bone within.

The men reacted with an air of weary inevitability, hacking down from the saddle, hewing at the creatures as they rose. The horses were dragged down, one by one; most of the men jumped free, though a few were too slow, falling with their beasts and being either crushed or snared amid the writhing demon-snakes.

Those who could made a stand in twos and threes, back to back and using their blades like scythes, cutting swathes through the encircling creatures. Like farmers again, Julianne thought, surrounded by some wicked living crop that was tearing itself free from the soil, discovering mouths and teeth . . .

In some ways, it was more like a single crop than a nest of

snakes. There was a mindlessness to each separate head, only a general malignity overall, nothing like the common independence of 'ifrit; and yet these things shimmered blackly, had glowing red dot eyes and resisted anything except a blade that was blessed. Those blades wreaked havoc among them; the trouble, the danger was that there were simply so many, and more breaking forth at every moment.

More among the following army, too. She spared that a single reluctant glance, and saw it in chaos. A scream brought her attention swiftly back to the foreriders. One scream among many, and only a horse; she had a care for horses, but not overriding her care for men. It was only that this particular scream, she knew before she saw which horse was screaming.

Imber's horse, that carried Imber's body: it plunged and kicked, but there were snake-things swarming over its quarters now, binding its legs and fastening great sucker-jaws onto its flesh. The burden it carried was flung madly from side to side, straining the ropes that held it. At last it slipped and hung mockingly, revoltingly half-free for a moment before another sprawling lurch from the horse shook it loose altogether.

It fell to ground, into the midst of the gaping horror; now it was Julianne's turn to scream.

That caught Elisande's attention, and more than hers. There was a soft glow in the air suddenly, between herself and Imber's wrapped corpse, right on the river-bank there and still a fair way from the fighting; for a moment she was reminded of that other golden gleam she'd seen on the other bank, and she almost expected to see Marshal Fulke step out of the light and into the shadows of the world.

But it wasn't the marshal, of course, it was her father, coming as he so often had come throughout her childhood, quite without warning when she needed him the most.

Coming not quite far enough, offering her something short of what she wanted, and that was common too; but surely this time, she was no child begging for a new saddle now, surely . . .

'Father, fetch me over to that bank! I have to . . .' She couldn't say it quite, her throat was too full of sobbing, but that alone should be enough. She never wept in public, and he knew it.

'You have to do what?' He spoke as softly as ever; she heard him more clearly even than usual, despite the roar of the water between them and all the sounds of battle behind.

'Imber's horse,' she said, with a desperate gesture, 'he's dead, and it fell . . .'

'And what will you do, about either?'

She stood already full in the spray of the river, ice-cold and bitter as it was; and yet it was those few words that stilled her, colder by a distance and more bitter to receive. For a moment she could only gape; then, 'I am his *wife* . . . !'

'Perhaps. He would have said so, at any rate, and that is good enough. But even so, Julianne. Man or horse, a body is a body; there are living men and living horses to concern yourself with first.'

'They will *eat* him . . . !'

Shockingly, if shortly, her father laughed. 'No, sweetheart. They will not eat him. If he is dead, that is how they want him, no more than that. You can find him later, if you live. If any of us live. Far more useful now to help Elisande, and try to make it so.'

'Help Elisande . . . ?' She gazed around, feeling almost stupid with grief and despair, with mourning suddenly delayed. Elisande was striking fire from a flint, to catch her tinder; looking past her, Julianne saw the Princip standing on the further bank, as her father was on this. It came to her that there was no accident here, these men too had come to help Elisande. Which must surely mean that whatever she was doing really did matter . . .

'Elisande? What can I do?'

'Well, you can stand in the wind's eye for me, till I get this sodden stuff alight,' in the familiar growl that could always uplift her heart, if only by a hair and for a moment. 'Wet grass, wet air, how's a girl to make a fire . . . ?'

Julianne wasn't clear quite why she wanted to make a fire, but knew better than to ask. There were mysteries abounding here – particularly how the old men, the Princip and her father had known what Elisande was about, how they had known when and where to come, what they had been doing that they had broken off to be here and why they were needed at all, and on the wrong sides of the water – but she judged this a good time to play the incurious innocent. As well that it had become second nature to think before putting a question. The djinn gave answers, and demanded payment after; these close folk would give her nothing, she suspected, and a payment might be demanded anyway. Better to make a virtue of not wanting to know, of being not above such things but apart from them, a married woman quite unsteeped in magic; better to be content to fetch and carry at Elisande's command.

Or, indeed, to be a wind-break. Elisande could make a light from nothing in a storm, but it seemed she still needed flint and tinder like any mortal to conjure a true flame. And of course everything was damp here, in the everlasting spray from the battering waters; Julianne crouched down and pulled threads from the inner hems of the robe she wore, winning a frail smile from her friend, and, 'That's a desert habit, it's why the Sharai wear rags. Have you been in the Sands, lady?'

'Once or twice. I met my husband there . . .' *One of my husbands, the one who has the advantage now, if living is an advantage in a world where men die when you love them.*

'Well, never mind, my love. One has to meet them some-where.' She was talking for the sounds' sake, not the meaning of the words; her eyes held a different message, compassionate, distracted. It was her fingers that truly mat-tered, teasing those threads into cloudy puffs of fibre and looping them around her feathered twigs before she went to work again with flint and steel.

This time her sparks settled and caught in the fluffy stuff: a glow, a hesitant twine of smoke, a bold but tiny flame within the shield of her cupped hands. They held their breaths together, while it contended with the twig; at the first faint snap of green fibres parting, they both exhaled together, both turning their heads away from that precious flame to do it.

And caught each other's eye, and giggled together as if nobody's heart were breaking, and then fed the infant fire with shreds and shavings like two maiden aunts determined and urgent to see a precious child grow fat.

'Why do we – you – need a fire, anyway?' That question that she wasn't going to ask, had no intention of asking: it just slipped out while her guard was down, while they were just two girls together and all their attention was focused on not losing this tentative little flame, and they might as well have been away alone on a hillside somewhere and setting up camp for the night.

'I need a source, a power I can work with. Grandfer used the river, but I'm not so good with cold and wet. He used to say I had a desert soul, when he was teaching me.'

'Is that why you went to live with the Sharai?'

'Not really, no. I loved it, but he'd have sent me anyway. Ruthless, like your father. They use us, any way they choose; what's best in their judgement is the only one that counts . . . How much pain can you stand, Julianne?'

An infinitude . . . 'As much as you can load upon me.'

'Truly?'

'Truly. That and more.' *See me standing? I can stand this much. You're my friend, it's what you're for: to load me with less pain than I can stand, less than my lovers give me and less by far than I can give myself.*

'Good. Because I have made this fire, whole and strong' – it didn't look strong to Julianne, it looked shy and reluctant and liable to disappear without a word of farewell; but this was ritual as much as information, there was a rhythmic formality, almost a chant to the way that she was speaking – 'and now it has to be divided, and you must do that work. It must be carried to all the cardinal points' – north and south where the old men waited, east and west where the river ran: her hand gestured to the little cairns that she had built – 'and set to burn there with a memory of what it was before, a single point of light. I can teach it to remember, but not do that and carry.'

'How shall I carry the fire, Elisande?'

'In your hands.'

Of course, in her hands. In her cupped hands, necessarily, they had such scant fuel for it and the pieces were so small; and how could it hurt else? It was true that they had nothing else, no firepot, no shovel. Pain and sacrifice might be a part of this working, or they might not. Elisande was so focused suddenly, she seemed not to care, almost to be oblivious, only speaking about it to be sure that her work was not spoiled.

'It'll go out.' The protest was not to save herself, only that she feared to lose the fire; she'd give her hands gladly, if that was all that was asked of her. Why not? She'd given one man already, and might yet have to give the other; what was a pair of scorched hands, after that?

'No. I can keep it now, but you must hold it. It will burn where I tell it to burn, and what; I'll have it burning stone soon, and gladly. I won't let it feed on you, but the heat of it will hurt.'

She nodded. Heat did hurt. Many pretty things hurt, she thought, if you came too close, but some you had to cradle.

'Be ready now, let me just speak to it a minute . . .'

And Elisande did speak to the fire, though she didn't know the language; and she thought it brightened, whitened, stiffened under just the impact of her voice.

'Now, Julianne. Scoop with your hands right underneath, it doesn't matter if you pick up soil too, but don't leave any of the fire behind, don't let it scatter . . .'

It didn't want to scatter now, though it was made so scanty. It felt as though she picked up a bulb, something light but solid.

Light and solid and hot. Damp earth and grass was cool

only for a moment against her skin; then it began to steam beneath the smoke. Anywhere else, any time else she would just have dropped whatever it was that she carried, before her palms could blister. Here and now she set her teeth and tightened her grip and followed Elisande.

Who seemed to her to walk deliberately slowly, but perhaps that was again ritual and required, like a priest in a temple, pacing to his own blood's beat; or else it simply helped her friend to keep her mind in focus. Julianne could focus too, on something other than her searing hands. All she had to do was lift her head and look across the water, to where men were fighting for their lives, where her man had done that thing and lost, and lay neglected. That was a burning focus, and a sharper pain than any she could feel in her body. Let her flesh blister and scar; she'd wear it as a reminder, every time she reached or touched or gripped a thing, that once she'd been twice married and had lost the first and sweeter, lost her boy . . .

She'd never seen the virtue in sacrifice, never understood the priests when they told her that suffering ennobled. She thought that was a pap they sold to the poor, to anyone who truly suffered. And she still didn't feel noble, what she felt was pain, pure and meaningless, but that in itself was a virtue, a strengthening, a gift. She could do this, she could carry a thing that was too hot to carry; which being true, she could also certainly bear a thing that was too heavy and too hard to bear. Or else turn it around, look out at the seething mass of black and the men who struggled to keep their feet within it; look in vain for Imber's body and she could do that, she could endure the loss of him twice over. Which being so, she could undoubtedly endure this simple and uncomplicated pain, she could carry this fire for Elisande who so much needed her to do it.

She could, she did. To the first cairn, and let a segment of the bulb-fire fall away between her fingers when Elisande sang to it; wait and watch while it spread out across the little heap of stone and flourished, sprang to more vigorous life.

And so on to the second, thinking that she could smell her palms begin to cook, though Elisande had promised that the fire wouldn't actually consume her.

To the third, and she thought her bones were steel, and glowing, and shining through her skin; she thought her joints were locked and solid, she couldn't drop the fire now if she had chosen to, she'd have claws for hands for ever.

To the fourth, and she couldn't see the river's banks now, couldn't hear the water. Elisande had to guide her, a hand on her rigid arm to push her forward, a tug to stop. She couldn't anneal her spirit further by turning from pain to grief and back to pain again; her greedy body had seized her, wrapped her in itself and in its agony, so that she could barely remember her husbands' names and not think at all about them. That part of her which was grateful for this was very small indeed, and very deeply buried. She might hope to have it rise later, she might seek to dig it out with frantic, buckled fingers; for now, all she could do was gasp.

She had to trust that fire flowed across the fourth cairn and flourished there; she could not see, could not stand to look. She twisted in a hobbled dance, too racked to be still, too breathless to scream; all she could think was to throw herself into the river if only she could find it. Distantly, though, she felt someone grip her wrists, which would prevent her. Faintly, faintly she heard a voice, 'Oh, sweet, your poor hands! It's all done now, all over, trust me now . . .'

And there was a cooling somehow within her surely blackened, surely shrivelled flesh, a soothing from the inside out, which seemed all wrong but welcome none the less; and following close on that healing touch there was a wordless whisper in her head, a voiceless song that eased her dizzy mind, calmed her breathing, laid her down in damp sweet grass—

—And would have sung her to sleep in another moment, except that she understood herself and it that precious moment too soon for Elisande, and just in time for her. She forced her eyes to open and stared up into her friend's, bare inches away and just where she had thought to find them; said, 'Don't do that, Elisande. I don't want to sleep, I want to see.'

'Nothing to see, precious, nothing that matters. I've numbed them, and started the healing process; they need salves now, but not till they've been cleaned and it's too soon for that, even if we had the necessaries. Let them rest, don't look . . .'

'Not my hands,' she said, she explained with terrible patience. 'I can't feel my hands.' *I can't feel anything* – but that was a lie, even though she didn't say it. She only wanted it to be true. 'I want to see what you do; and I want to see what's happening.' North and south, to her Imber and her Hasan and all men else, and Elisande's precious Surayon also.

'Oh. Unh. All right, then, sit up and be good. And still don't look at your hands, keep them in your sleeves. Promise? Or I'll knot them there . . .'

She made the promise carelessly, literally not caring. What need any beauty in her hands, after today? She might have trouble naming any use for hands at all, except to hold a dagger one last time.

She might stop being so self-pitying, or so dramatic. The war was not yet lost; time to think about escaping the 'ifrit when it was clear, when it was certain that she needed to.

Elisande helped her into a sitting position, with a bare stub of rock to lean against.

'Comfortable?'

'It'll pass. So will time. You'd best get on with your show, sweetheart.'

Elisande shook her head, denying the implication, *you're wasting what's most valuable, frittering it on me.* 'I had to break a while, to let myself calm down. Nothing's more calming than a little gentle healing.'

Nothing was more exhausting by the look of her, vast eyes in a bloodless face, a tremble in her fingers where they still touched and fussed over Julianne. She was in no condition to make a major working – but there was no one else able to do it. Julianne still felt a residue of the *jereth*'s virtue inside herself, rewoken perhaps by Elisande's healing touch; she wished, she yearned to have a way to share it with her friend. Or give it her completely, that was better.

'Elisande, if there's any way you can draw strength from me to help you, it's yours, just take it.'

A smile that was almost closer to a death's-head grimace, and, 'What, after I've spent so much of myself to keep you fit for life, shall I drain you of it now? Against everything that I was ever taught, and all that I believe in? Shall I throw that all to waste, and you along with it?'

Why not, where you would throw yourself to waste? I am half wasted already. 'You must, if you need it. For all these lives . . .'

'Well, if I must, I will.'

It should have been the sort of thing one says to a fretful convalescent, but it was not. Julianne believed her implicitly. To have the chance at least to save so many lives, to save something at least of her beloved country – yes, she thought Elisande would spend herself unsparingly, and if she needed more she would spend her friend alongside. Not willingly, perhaps, but she would do it.

If she needed to. Perhaps she wouldn't. Julianne had a great respect for Elisande's endurance. That one kept going where men and lesser mortals fell and failed. Imber had fallen, Hasan might fail yet; it seemed as though only Fulke would be triumphant, and that spelled failure for all of Surayon. And still she thought that Elisande would endure. Outcast and homeless, what was indomitable in her would sustain the rest; and if nothing else, she would have Julianne at her side for company. That was predetermined. Widow and orphan, together they could chase a myth of rest over all the world, and never pine to catch it . . .

If, if, if. Even the djinn could not see that future, there was too much death in the picture to give it any semblance of the truth. For now Julianne was helpless, fuel to her friend's fire if needed and nothing more. She settled herself more comfortably against her rock, cradled her hands unfelt, unseen within the long charred sleeves of her robe, and set herself to watch.

The four cairns were flaring brightly, beacons of white

unnatural flame: a fire that fed on stone, to a girl's encouragement. Elisande walked across to the first, on the northern bank; she thrust her hands deep into the light – Julianne gasped, but why? why should Elisande spare herself, who had not stinted to use her friend? – and drew it out in strands and cables, ropes of shine that flexed and flowed and seemed to live between her fingers.

Elisande gathered them all into a hank between her hands, and flung them high and far.

For a moment they hung, and Julianne feared that they might fall back, that all her friend's strength might prove not to be enough; or else that the wind would catch and scatter them, they'd fall into the water and be dragged to loss. If light could be flung, it could be dragged also, she thought, and to its own destruction.

Those weaves, those plaits and cords of light hung and twisted, turning contrary to the wind, seeming to quest rather than drift. Then they stretched themselves across the river in a high arc, sprung and vibrant like bent sword-blades, steel under tension. White-hot steel was what they looked like, and Julianne knew how that felt in the hand, but the Princip lifted both his big hands and caught hold of those intangible cables as they came to him, as they seemed to seek him out. And knelt, and plunged them into the earth; and they held there, binding bank to bank in a fiery and impossible, an impassable bridge that would do no mortal man any good at all, she thought.

Elisande left it thus and turned to the south, to Julianne's own father. As she went by, Julianne glanced at her hands and saw no hint of burning, not so much as a reddening of the skin. It had been live fire in her own hands, a natural and wild thing; now she supposed it was something other, cool to the touch as it burned stone, something that could be gripped and moulded and spun and not burn anyone who touched it. Which would be why Julianne had had to carry it, she supposed, because Elisande needed nimble fingers for this as well as a dreadful concentration.

The same dabbling of those fingers in the fierce light, the same strands drawn out, flung up with the same force; they found the King's Shadow ready to receive them, and even ropes of light in his hands could not dispel the shadows that Julianne had always seen clinging around her father.

Now the island was poised at the centre of a double arch, like the grip of a recurved bow such as they used in Marasson; like a strung bow, it seemed almost to vibrate with possibilities.

Elisande went to the east and to the west, one after the other; and there when she had woven her glittering cables she flung them high and far again, only that this time there was no land, no waiting hand to catch them. Only the river's rush, and Julianne had been afraid of that.

No need. Again the ribbons and streamers of light stiffened and arched, and plunged down. This time, rather than rooting in the earth with a man's hands to guide them, they wove themselves into the water's turbulence, so that from her raised rock Julianne could see bright threads amid the dark river, running down and down and out of sight. She turned her head when Elisande went the other way, and saw the light flow upstream with the same ease, the same high disregard.

It felt then as though the island were no longer fixed to

the river's bed, but hung rather from these white wires, quivering with a quick anticipation. Even the rock that Julianne leaned against seemed to tremble beneath her weight. The river's noise couldn't actually be quieter, but she had to strain to hear it, as though a muffling blanket had fallen all around.

Not only the river's sound was muffled. Julianne was watching Elisande, of course, as she returned to the centre of the island; it was a snag of movement in the corner of her eye that turned her attention to the southern bank. Her father had sword in hand now and he was battling with a sudden rush of those black serpents. As he killed them they faded, like 'ifrit; but there were so many of them, and they came on and on, and how many could one man kill before they overwhelmed him . . . ?

It was a little while before she realised that he had been expecting this, waiting for it, placed there to receive it; that he was defending not his own life, but Elisande's working. Her confirmation of that lay on the north bank, where the Princip was fighting also. No question that his opponents were 'ifrit, and several of them: great scuttling creatures with burning eyes and pincers snapping at his sword-arm, trying to avoid the blade but trying more crucially to pass him by, to reach those cords of light.

Julianne turned her urgent gaze back to Elisande, willing her to hurry. That was all she could do; she had no way to help her friend, nor the old men on the banks. She still didn't understand what Elisande meant to do with all this spellcasting, but whatever it was, she should complete it soon and make it powerful, make a weapon of it, or there would be two more great names among the dead of the day, and their bodies probably doomed never to find the honourable silence of the Princip's crypt. Whatever it was, this was pivotal; the 'ifrit betrayed themselves with this sudden assault. The battle on the north bank might be as good as won – thanks to Marshal Fulke, and she hoped, she did hope to have the chance to force herself to thank him – but that on the southern bank was equally well lost, she thought. Give the 'ifrit a foothold in Outremer, and men would never prise them from it.

Something surged in the water, that was not itself water nor rock; she caught a glimpse of something long and sleek and black where the light danced against it. *Hurry, Elisande; that is us they are coming for now . . .*

Elisande threw her head up, stretched her arms out, turned slowly full circle. All her arcs and cairns, her threads and skeins of light pulsed gently, throwing strange patterns of glare across her skin as she moved, as she swayed to another pulse altogether: an alien not in rhythm with a power she could touch and use but never own, something not for human possession but gifted to her in her need, or else claimed by her in her urgent desire, or else simply Elisande massively overreaching herself, dressing herself like a child in a robe that could never be cut to her fit.

She drew both arms up, moving like a dancer, like a child to some stately, heavy music that Julianne could not hear; and her hands came together in a silent clap that would not disrupt the music, and the world was disrupted in its stead, the world changed.

Julianne's body shook in response to a thunder that made no sound, but had only impact; it felt as portentous as an earthquake, except that the ground did not shake, it was only her . . .

No, not that. The first thing Julianne did was to check on her friend, and Elisande looked more than shaken. Not dancing now, neither imperious nor overdressed: terrified, rather, terrified and helpless. Like a child again, a child who has done something terrible and important but doesn't know quite what, or what will result. She stood still, hand to mouth, staring all around her; Julianne was looking only at her, and was none the less aware of a momentous alteration in the valley. It was as though a power beyond measure had seized it at her friend's asking, no greater imperative than that; had gripped it and reshaped it, and yet done it no harm at all . . .

Had Folded it, in fact: folded and refolded it like a map refolded to hide something crucial in the crease, and she and Elisande were there in the fold of it, they could see the world as it was and the world as it appeared to be also, without themselves being anywhere within it.

Julianne ran to her friend across an island that still felt solidly rooted, in defiance of what her eyes were telling her. The two girls held tight to each other, and Elisande whispered, 'Did I, did I do that . . . ?'

'I don't think so, no.' *I think someone, something else did that, through you. Who do you think you are, girl, the God's own self, to go making or unmaking His needlework?* She'd save the rest of that for later; it didn't matter what she said now, Elisande wasn't truly listening.

Julianne wasn't truly speaking either, not speaking her heart. Her heart she thought was in her eyes, just as her friend's was: bewildered, scared, not daring to be triumphant.

What Elisande had done – or something else, some power that worked through her, Julianne emphatically did not want to believe that her little friend could make such things happen of her own will, her own words and nothing more – what had been done was to Fold the river out of the valley, as the valley itself had once been Folded out of the Kingdom.

That latter had been a fact that Julianne had lived with all the sixteen years of her life, a simple mystery that was too far away in time or miles to be frightening, just another miracle of the Sanctuary Land, as ambiguous as any that had gone before it. Even seeing it unmade, seeing Surayon unFolded had been a moment that lost its wonder, in the terror of what else was happening or would result. This, though . . .

She supposed that this was technically a lesser miracle – just a river, after all, the islands in midstream and the rushing water and the banks to either side, nothing like as all-encompassing as the valley and the hills that made it, which Elisande's grandfather had Folded and kept so for thirty years – but it felt monumentally greater, because she was here at the heart of it. She had seen it done, and the mere act of witnessing bound her into the event and the power and the arrogance of it, that the world might be swiftly and heedlessly stitched into a new shape simply to help one side or the other in a petty battle between mortal men and spirit creatures that actually belonged in another world altogether. She thought that the God of her people, the God of the Sharai, any god else should be enraged by such a meddling, such a usurpation of heavenly prerogatives.

There was no sign of temper from above, though; and just as well, when what was happening here below was so tremendous.

They couldn't stare for ever at each other, learning this new world only through flickers of reflection in the other's eyes and impressions at the corners of their own. They had to turn, to look, to see. At least they could turn together, though, arms still tightly bound around each other's bodies; that was something to cling to against the impact of the moment, that they still each had someone to cling to.

They could look east or west and still see the river where it ran, where it must run. They could see all the visible course of it and guess the rest, from lost source high in the dim purple shadow of the mountains to its far flat mingling with the sea in salty marshland. Directly north and south of them, there were the high and stony banks that contained its fierce rushing; beneath their feet was the island, and Elisande's magic could shift that no more than the urgent water could, not one finger's width along the bottom.

And yet, and yet: they could look out and see another world spread like a tapestry over this one, if tapestry could ever be so real that image might be confused for substance, threads and stitchings for flesh and sun and water.

They could see wide grassland north and south, and no river to divide it; they could see armies north and south, and no river to divide them either.

More than water parted around the island now, and ran seamlessly together again. It seemed as though the valley did the same, so that where they stood was a loop knotted out of a thread, still a part of the whole but separated from it. They could stand and watch, but from here they could not touch; they had done their deed, and there was no further task for them.

North and south, too close to watch and too far to help even before this, two men were fighting for their lives; but the Folding was done now, they needn't protect the spell-casting any longer – the girls still stood in a matrix of light, like spiders at the heart of a burning web, but those threads had been drawn tight to pull two hems of land together, and the stitching was hidden from the world around – and the Princip and the King's Shadow were fighting on the same ground suddenly, where there had been a river to divide them.

Neither man was fool enough to fight alone, where he could stand back to back with a companion. It was her own father who moved, who turned and leaped away from the rage of serpents that confronted him when the Princip cried, 'To me, Coren, to me!'

A few long bounding strides should have brought him to the river, but that they brought him first to the boundary of Elisande's Folding, where he had stood himself to catch and hold the light. Julianne couldn't tell what he was seeing, only that he couldn't see her or the river, but some kind of border surely, to say that what he crossed here was nothing natural.

It delayed him not at all. He leaped across that line, however it was that he saw it; for a moment, Julianne didn't know where he was. There was nothing so unusual in that, he was her father and the King's Shadow and in both roles he had his own gifts of disappearance, but she'd never known him vanish so precipitately. He seemed to be neither in the one world nor the other, not there where he had been nor here where she was. She half expected to see him plummet suddenly out of the sky and into the river, a bird that failed, that could not fly; except that her father neither failed nor flew, he simply went from where he was to where he wanted to be, or else where he was sent.

And there he was abruptly, seeming to step out of the air a long moment after he had stepped into it. He had been south of the river and now he was north of it, except that there was no river for him and no great stride to cover that little ground between one footfall and the next. He had been far from the embattled Princip and now he was near, near enough almost to touch, near enough certainly to help.

Julianne stole a little satisfaction from seeing him stumble as his foot touched earth. She could almost persuade herself that she had felt his stomach twist as his face twisted, more fiercely than his ankle had; she could almost for a moment believe that he had the normal complement of human organs inside his shadowy skin, that could be wrenched about and distressed as normal humans' were.

But he was her father, and he was old and tired and hurt, there was blood on his clothes and skin; and he might have gone all Shadowy and walked away from this at any time, and had not for Surayon's sake, for the Kingdom's, perhaps for the world's.

For his sake, she wished she could overstep the river as easily as he had. Failing that, she wished she could overstep it with difficulty, with great difficulty, against any test of strength or will; she wanted only to stand with him, to set her slender frame and little skill at his side to prove what help they might.

But she was simple mortal flesh, and she couldn't make that leap. No more could Elisande, but at least the two old men could help each other now. King's Shadow and Princip of Surayon, old comrades and old friends though half the Kingdom might think them irretrievably at odds: they stood shoulder to shoulder and pressed forward against the 'ifrit, stubborn determination a good substitute for the strength and speed of the young men they used to be, a better match for the strength and speed of what they faced. The 'ifrit seemed to have lost their frantic purpose; now they fought only because they were being fought, or because that was what they did, or Julianne thought so. And they died also because that was what the 'ifrit did when her father fought them, when the Princip did.

She took the time for one anxious glance back, the other side of that impossible line that she could both see and not see as though the Fold were a tuck that stretched the one world tight across the looseness of the other, but the serpent-beasts clustered there were making no attempt to cross it. Stared and twisted balefully, rather, as though they yearned to cross but could not. Or dared not, perhaps.

There were 'ifrit in the river still, trapped in the Fold with only two girls to oppose them, she could see them when the broad stillness of their backs broke the roiling of the water. And if they rose they could destroy this Folding in a moment, she and Elisande could not resist them with a bare pair of knives between the two; and she could not say where the world might go then, only that it would follow a different and a darker path.

Elisande had seen them too, of course. 'Why don't they attack?' she asked against the silence, almost petulantly, 'why didn't they attack before we did this? They must have known it would happen, and it would work against them when it did, so why didn't they try to stop us?'

'They did not and they do not because I am here, and they dare not.'

It was a thin voice, a cold voice for all that it came from the heart of the fire; and it had a body of sorts, there was a fiery spirit rising . . .

'Esren.'

'Indeed.'

The djinni it was indeed, learning it seemed from Julianne's captivity and reversing the 'ifrits' own trick, keeping them at bay by its simple presence here.

Quickly Elisande said, 'I wasn't asking you,' but that was automatic defence, and almost meaningless. Ungenerous, too; if it had truly been the djinni that had saved them to let this happen, to let them save Surayon, Julianne thought they should begrudge it nothing, that Elisande in particular should give it service, freedom, whatever it might like in return. And disguise the gift as carelessness, a heedless question demanding a price, why not? For herself she had less cause to be grateful, she was uncertain what if anything had been saved for her.

But the djinni said, 'Do I need your permission to speak?' and there was a silence that was almost palpable, a shock of stillness that could have changed the world again, and Elisande was far from generous or grateful.

'No – but that was a question, djinni, and I have answered it.'

'Nothing matters,' the djinni said, 'further than this. Here, at this point, now. Stand and look, Lisan of the Dead Waters, and see what you have done.'

She had pulled living water out of the valley, unpicked it from the tapestry, joined two battlefields into one. Beyond where her grandfather and his old friend were fighting, there were riders coming: men driving frenzied horses past the edge of terror or exhaustion, men whose mounts would carry them now into the mouth of hell, would chase death till they caught it.

Men, Ransomers, who chanted prayers as they rode; Marshal Fulke led them with his hood thrown back and his pale cropped head like a summoning in the sunlight, like a beacon, bright against black robes.

They chanted prayers against evil, and they rode down the 'ifrit and hewed from the saddle as the creatures tried to flee, too late and surely knowing so. Fulke's own blade bit deep through chitin and into whatever served as heart or life's blood to a spirit in a mortal frame. Then, as the 'ifrit's body dissipated into dust, he turned his horse towards the Princip.

His voice was still murmuring, prayers to the God who had condemned this old man and all his land for heresy. His sword was in his hand, and his face was grim. Elisande gasped; Julianne wanted to scream. Specifically, she wanted to scream at her father. *Don't let him, you're the King's Shadow, he has to listen to you. Stand in the way, if nothing else, push that stupid stubborn old man behind you . . .* Elisande had seen her father die, in one brutal moment; now her grandfather stood in the same danger and under her eye again. If necessary, Julianne would push that stupid stubborn girl behind her, not to let her see; but she wasn't sure, she didn't know Fulke's mind, she couldn't read him.

Fulke kicked his horse forward, the King's Shadow stood like a shadow and did no more than the Princip, did nothing at all.

It was a slow ride, though, not a slaying speed. One man might kill another slowly, but not on a battlefield. Fulke came up to stand his horse beside, above the Princip. How did he know him? Not by description, surely, when he hadn't been known or sighted outside Surayon for thirty years. Not by his dress of battered leather and chain, any old soldier with a life's supply of stories could boast as much; not by his noble bearing and haughty demeanour, for he had none.

However it was, Fulke did know the Princip, that was clear. And did and must still want to see him dead, that was given, it was required between those two men in this world. But the world was fractured, and darkness spilled in through the cracks; Fulke did no more, no worse than to speak.

'There are demons abroad in this country.'

'There are.' With a look that seemed somehow entirely level, although he was gazing up; with an unambiguous directness that made no compromise and allowed no doubt, that included both the 'ifrit and the Ransomers.

'Then let us be about them.'

With no more than that, Fulke rode his horse hard at the boundary and passed through it, disappearing entirely for that brief instance between north and south as he passed over the Fold. Julianne gaped, and was still gaping after he had emerged on the other bank, after he had recovered himself and his horse and begun to slash at the serpent-things that swarmed about him, after all his men had ridden after him. She had to fit all the broken pieces of her expectations into a new understanding, and it took a while. The best she could manage just then was an acceptance that the two men had not after all met in the same world, though they came from the same far country and stood on the same ground now.

Watching Fulke as he fought, though, she still thought that salvation might be an impossible stretch, as far out of reach as the river's banks were beyond her and Elisande. Wherever she looked, men were fighting; but wherever she looked there seemed to be not enough of them, never quite enough. Fulke's army might win in the north there, with the Sharai to help; but Fulke himself had left them, and had taken too many men with him and yet not enough to win the south, and it was a law of history that a force divided was a force betrayed. Those serpents in the south could surely defeat what men they had to face – and Elisande had given them a passage north, perhaps, if they could learn to cross it. She might have saved her grandfather and doomed her land, in the same moment. Perhaps Julianne should break the casting, kick down the cairns, disrupt those bonds and let the river back. Perhaps they must abandon the south of the valley, with all the dangers that implied, sooner than risk the north also . . .

Do it now and you can strand Fulke there, give him the death he deserves and the martyrdom he'd cherish, save the Surayonnaise from his later persecution . . .

Nothing could save them from the 'ifrit, though, unless Fulke could help to do it. She wished him well or well enough, she had to; and had to hope that there might after all be a God in heaven to hear the prayers that he sent skyward as he fought. Or two Gods not at war, perhaps, to give an equal hearing to the Sharai, as Surayon and the Kingdom and the Sands beyond all needed their blades, their strength alongside the Ransomers'.

And needed more, and she couldn't see any hope of finding it in all the wide valley, from her position here at the heart – until she saw movement in the shadows of the hills. She thought it was more 'ifrit, she thought they were endless, innumerable, doomed to win. She knew that simple counting decided most battles, heroes seldom had a chance.

But the shadow, the shadows, the long lines of shadow resolved themselves into people in the sunlight, a steady stream flowing down the roads and fields from the mountains and breaking out across the plain; and for a moment she didn't understand who they were. She had seen the Ransomers, the army from Ascariel, the Sharai; she had seen Sieur Anton and Marshal Fulke, her husband Hasan, she had seen the end of her husband Imber; who else was there who could come to battle willingly, leading such numbers? It had been a miracle or a series of miracles that had brought so many armies to the principality at all, it had taken high art and high diplomacy to have them all fight 'ifrit and not each other for today at least, it had still not quite been enough – and now here was one more miracle, another army when and where it was most needed.

And of course it was here, it had been here all the time. Elisande's trembling tension, her expressive silence named it and explained it. All day she had watched other people fighting over her homeland, and she had done what she could to help; now it was her own people she was watching, and there was nothing more that she could do. These were the

Surayonnaise who had been fighting Ransomers and Sharai just yesterday; more, it was also the Surayonnaise who had been fighting no one, who had retreated to their holdfasts in the hills. Someone had gone to fetch them, had blessed their weapons and brought them out in perfect time for this last blow . . .

Someone who she could see quite clearly from this vantage point they had, this inverted stage where the actors played in the auditorium all around them: someone tall and brightly blond who made her heart ache for her lost man as he rode to and fro, as he marshalled his unlikely troops and led them forward against serpent-beasts and worse.

And she watched him despite the pain of it, unless it was because of the pain, because all she could do for Imber now was hurt. She watched him as the slow time passed, as more men died and women too, because that army was not bound by religious law nor tribal custom, but the 'ifrit died too in greater numbers. She watched him and watched him and could not have said, could never later say when it was that her mind understood what she was seeing.

It was later and a lot later before she understood what else it meant, that his beloved cousin Karel must be dead in his place, must have been dead on Imber's own horse. What she knew now, all she knew now was that Imber was not dead after all, that she was not a widow in either side of her life.

She watched with more trembling intensity even than Elisande at her side, suddenly desperately fearful that he would die now under her eye, that some malign god would love the irony of that more and far more than any god ever had loved her. Not even the sudden recognition that Sherett was there too, leading a small regiment of women, not even that could distract her for longer than it took to be amazed, to stare, to turn back. When he was at bay, when his reckless youth and determined ferocity had led him too far forward of his followers, when she had to look away she'd look for Hasan to the north, and see him too fighting, killing, surviving while men and monsters died all around him; and when she'd had her dreadful fill of that she'd turn again to see how Imber lived and killed, and how he rallied these who were not his people in this that was not his land.

And she would love him, as she loved Hasan who was moulding all the tribes into an army even as she watched, who was making one people of the Sharai and making them his to do with as he would, and she knew what he would want to do and loved him none the less.

But they were two men, and each of them loved her and would not, could not brook the other. More than a river ran between them, and nothing that she could Fold away to join the two together.

They were hot with slaying, fierce in victory; she could see nothing else now, but she saw them perfectly. And had her own touch of djinnish foresight, as she saw them meeting on this field of battle, with the last of the 'ifrit slain between them and gone to nothing, leaving them bereft; and each would have a sword in his hand and a determination in his heart to claim her and to allow no claim else . . .

And she would not allow that and could not see any way to prevent it if they met, stranded as she was on an island that was inaccessible in any case and Folded out of the world where they stood and would stand against each other.

And so she waited, breathless and shaking until it was clear that they would destroy what last 'ifrit remained, that the Sharai and the Ransomers and the Surayonnaise between them all would win this day if not the next. And then, as the two men her husbands came closer and closer to her and so to each other, she finally did what she had thought of doing earlier.

She pulled herself away from Elisande and ran from one cairn to the next, and kicked them down. She scattered light and magic, let it lose itself in nothingness, brought the river back into the world so that the valley truly had two sides again, and she had a man in each.

The End of All Roads

This is the Dir'al Shahan in Ascariel, that was their greatest temple when the Ekhed governed the city. It would have been destroyed when the God gave us victory there; but the King decreed otherwise, and took it for his own. Now it is his palace, and the seat of his power.

More than that: it was his home, his shelter, his symbol. That above all, his symbol throughout the Kingdom and beyond. For many people – for the lucky ones, those who had seen it, those who had walked the streets and alleys of the golden city on its golden hill – it was what they thought of and what they saw when they thought of the King, because they had and could have no other picture for him.

It was not the building set highest on the hill, nor was it the tallest, nor the most grand in decoration. Once, yes, once all three, but that was long ago. Now it was only the oldest, and that was only by default, by destruction of what had come before. It stood on a broad platform of stone towards the summit, and was made to look small by the size of its stage, which might have contained three, four such buildings and still have left room for an army to march a quatrefoil pattern between them all. That had been the walled compound of a temple complex, dedicated to a forgotten god before the Catari came, before the Sharai had found the Sands, before the Ekhed had come north to rule until the Patrics came in turn to drive them out. Legend said that the djinn had removed the complex overnight, and left the platform bare; the imams said that too, or else they said that a tremendous storm had levelled walls and buildings, had ground the rubble to dust and swept it all away. In either case, they said it was at the will and instigation of their God, who had decreed a temple to His worship to be built there in its stead.

And so it was: high shielding walls of stone about a central court, with domes and minarets to rise above the blank faces of the walls, to be tiled and gilded to gleam in sun and starlight to declare God's glory in this holiest of cities.

That was the Dir'al Shahan as it was made, as it was meant to be. Years passed, decades, centuries. There was a palace built that stood higher on the hill, whose garden wall enclosed the peak itself, as though the Ekhed could possess the Mount and all it stood for; there were temples built whose towers rose higher, as high as their architects had dared to dream. Still the Dir'al Shahan was the glistening jewel, the Eye of God, the utmost point of the created world; when people spoke of Ascariel – as they did, everywhere in the world, in terms of hope and longing – it was the Dir'al Shahan that they meant, even where they did not name it.

And then the Patrics came from their homelands far away to claim the city, to seize it with steel and pay its price in cruelty and death. They drove the Ekhed out, slaughtered the imams and their congregations, filled the temple courts with bodies and washed the stone facings with their blood.

After the horrors of that time, once the bodies were limed in their pits and the men who had carried them down had carried water back up to scrub away the many stinks of death, the man who had led them all took the lands he had won for his Kingdom and the Dir'al Shahan for his own.

In all the years since then, he had not been seen outside the silence of its walls. In forty years the gilding had peeled and tiles had slipped, rain and sun had done their work to dull what had been glorious and no work had been done against them. There were no orders, and no one dared; where the King did not command, in his own palace no one stirred.

Desecrated by its occupation, shabby by neglect, it had become a monument to absence, of God or King depending; and it was still and nevertheless the Dir'al Shahan that people meant, when they spoke of Ascariel. They might come on pilgrimage, they might pray in all the holy places, they might fast and scourge themselves in the new-built temples to their own true God; but it was still the Dir'al Shahan that filled their dreams before they came and their eyes after, their thoughts always. Some, many thought more about the King than about the God. Even those who came and looked and went away disappointed because it did not glitter in the sunshine so brightly as it did in their imagination, even those who would rather see the building razed than restored – they all found that the one thing had turned into another thing, that they could not see those walls and domes and minarets without thinking about the man who sat within, whose reach extended as far as he could throw his Shadow, and that was far indeed.

In forty years, the King had not come out. Neither in forty years had any gone in to him, except his servants and his Shadow at his call.

Now there was a party going in, and not by invitation. The Shadow was there, and the Princip of Surayon, come to visit his old friend all unexpected. The Shadow's daughter and the Princip's granddaughter, they were there. The two sons-in-law of the Shadow, they had come this far but would not go that little step further, would not pass the doorway of the Dir'al Shahan: the one from duty and fealty and doubt, the other from piety and faith and great distaste. Imber would not cross the threshold of his King without a direct command to do so; he was sure that his wife ought not to do so either, he feared for her dreadfully and had told her so, but could not find in himself the authority to forbid her. Hasan looked at the high gate and the higher wall and could not see any palace for any King. What he saw was a great temple overrun by unbelievers and deliberately corrupted, rank in its ruin. What had been sacred could not be made secular, only profaned. He would not step through that gateway while any temporal power sat beyond, be it Patric or Catari or the Ekhed returned; nor would he have stepped through it while the imams held sway, because their God might be his God also but their worship was not. He disliked buildings, distrusted walls, resented any ceiling that closed the sky against him. Like the Ransomers, he would burn the

Dir'al Shahan sooner than he would pray there. Where Julianne prayed, whether she prayed at all was no concern of his; there was he thought advantage to having her meet and speak with the old spider in his lair. He was not in the least concerned for her safety, though her future worried him deeply. That was a dark pool, and full of shadows. His own voice was a stone dropped into it, that made ripples and showed him nothing but broken reflections that might have been his own face, might have been the Patric boy's or neither.

Like Hasan, the Ransomers looked at the palace and saw the temple, and felt the sacrilege of it like a chill in their bones in the sunlight. Not a stone of it, not a timber nor a scrap of plasterwork should have been let stand. It was the God gave the victory here, and this tribute to false worship was an abomination in His sight. None the less for that, there was a Ransomer going in. The King's Shadow had declared a truce and given safe-conduct to the Princip and to his entourage, to Hasan and to his; Marshal Fulke was prepared to lend his reluctant voice in support of that, but only so far and no further. Only this far, to this wide sweep of pavement where the palace sat like a thrown rock on a frozen pond, inappropriate and doomed. Bad enough to bring heretics and sworn enemies within the walls of the city at all; he could not countenance letting them within the walls of the palace unwatched, unguarded, armed. What protection the King might have he did not know, except that there were neither soldiers nor priests in there; and the Princip of Surayon was a witch and a warrior both, and the girl likely as bad. He was glad to have the Sharai's word not to venture through the gate, but he would not trust it. He would not set himself and his men to bar the way, against the Shadow's order; but he would have his men watch the Sharai and the Surayonnaise in their separate parties, and he himself would risk whatever wickedness the bones of the building still sustained, to guard his King against whatever wickedness the Princip and the girl might yet have planned.

He felt soiled in his triumph, he felt the God soiled in His, that it should be followed by this capitulation of honour. His only comfort – small and bare that it was, cold comfort – lay in the absence of the heretic and traitor, the apostate boy who had once worn Ransomer black. That boy was still an element in this story, camp-fire rumour placed him here, there, all over; Fulke would not be content until he had placed him squarely in a fire's heart and seen him burn. Had he been here – well, he could not have been here. Had he joined the march at any point from Surayon to here, Fulke would have burned him regardless of truce, safe-conduct or King's command. The King himself, in person, could not save that boy. There was vengeance to come against him, and Fulke held it in his heart like a treasure, but he was glad not to have spent it yet. Let the Ransomers find the boy quietly, privately, let them deal with him in their own way, within their own strong walls; no public eye, no glare of argument, only the traitor and the men he betrayed and the God to witness where they called in His debts.

No boy, but Ransomers and Sharai and Surayonnaise had made uncomfortable companions on the slow march south, and they were uncomfortable companions still; there had been no bonding along the way. Even Imber, who had drawn together the scattered forces of Surayon and led them as an army to the battle's end – even he had drawn back from them now that the fighting was done. Besides, he was in mourning for his cousin; he could no more woo his country's enemies than he could woo his wife. He had ridden with his own, the survivors from Elessi and the preacher's band of followers, those few. He had watched his wife, he had watched the Sharai that they said she was married to, that some said she had run away to marry; he had spoken to neither one in all the days of their marching, and had been ready to do so only in protest, only if he saw her speak to the Sharai.

He had ridden with his own people, and with those he had made his own. He stood with them now and was not the only one to feel glad of the great stretch of this platform, which gave such separate peoples space enough to hold themselves apart.

They stood apart, Elessans and Ransomers, Surayonnaise and Sharai: apart and exposed, the walls of the Dir'al Shahan offering all the shade there was and none of them venturing close enough to use it. To the Sharai, in the Sands the sky was shelter enough, like a tent stretched between them and God, a veil but not a barrier; they wore its midnight colour as a sign. Here, though – on levelled stone within a city walled with stone, within and above a bewildering maze of houses, stables, markets, streets all of stone, so that they wondered why they ever would have followed their sheikhs or Hasan or God Himself into this place – they felt as though even the sky had been stolen from them, ripped away. There was nothing overhead but light and glare, which might very well be the glare of God. They crouched down on their haunches and drew up the hoods of their robes, they gripped the headropes of their horses in lieu of each others' hands, under the mocking eyes of unbelievers; they stared about them and cursed their tamed cousins the Catari who had built this place as vehemently as they cursed the Patrics who had stolen it, the imams who had ever declared it holy. As long as there were camels and sheep and water in the Sands, as long as there were men and women to be grateful for that, what did God need with more?

All the groups held themselves apart, as they had ridden here, as they had fought in the valley, as they had buried their dead. The bulk of their armies they had left in the valley, camped north and south of the river, east and west of the plain, where each could see which other broke the truce. Only these few, these watchful wary few had come to Ascariel, and the Sharai, the Surayonnaise emphatically wished that they had not.

Fewer still were going further, in through the gate of the Dir'al Shahan. Those few were meeting now, solitary walkers coming together in the shadow of the wall. The King's Shadow, who knew this place of old; the Princip of Surayon who had known it also but long ago, at the Conclave that had given him his country; the two girls, and Fulke whom they did not trust. None other. There should have been one other, the girls thought, one at least, but Marron was not here. Marron, they supposed, was with Jemel; and the two boys together – together with the Daughter, which was a different thing, a greater and a worse – they might be anywhere. They hadn't been sighted since the battle. At least no one had found their bodies, but that was small reassurance, when they had a whole other world to lose themselves in and no one to send a message home.

The girls might have been angry with the boys, if they

weren't so worried. They might have been more worried still, if they weren't so nervous. The King was a mystery, he lived in closer seclusion than the strictest religious; and yet they meant to walk in on him unannounced . . .

As far as they knew, they were unannounced. He could hardly be unaware that they had come; his Shadow might have warned him days ago, that they were coming. Julianne's father was maintaining a magnificent discretion, saying nothing at all of any consequence. What that meant, even Julianne couldn't guess. Perhaps he knew that they'd be welcome within; perhaps he knew that the gates would not be opened, the walls could not be climbed.

Perhaps he knew nothing, and had simply travelled in hope and with no expectations, as they had. As they had tried to do.

Five figures, but they had walked two and two and one across the wide open stretches of the pavement, coming from different directions under a white sky and a sun of burnished copper: the old men, the girls, the Ransomer. That was how they stood before the gate, grouped but not together, not one group and not at all with one intent.

'Do we knock?' Elisande asked, deliberately savage, fiercely unfunny.

'No,' Coren said. 'We wait. When the King is ready, he admits us.'

'If he will,' from Julianne, the most doubtful, the least determined.

'He will,' and that was her father and her friend, speaking together but still not with one intent. He meant that he was sure of his ground, of his master; she that she was sure of her own purpose and the strength of it to carry her through to where she meant to be, face to face with the man she'd come to see, whether he chose to have it so or not.

'How long does he usually make you wait?'

'Julianne, I don't usually go in by the gate.' He said it with that longsuffering tone universal among fathers. She flushed, and was suddenly glad of Elisande's heat to distract notice from her own.

'You could take us in then, couldn't you? Of course you could . . .'

'. . . But of course I won't. Quite so. I'll stand with you at his gate, for as long as you choose to linger; I won't help you break into his privity.'

'I could summon my djinni, have it carry us through.'

'You could summon it, yes. Would it come?'

'I don't know,' in a sullen mutter.

'No. Well, rather than finding out and being disappointed, why not try a little quiet patience? I've never known the King be wilfully discourteous—'

'—Unless you want to count forty years of silence,' which came from the Princip, unexpectedly taking his granddaughter's part against his friend's, 'which has always seemed discourteous to me.' *Specifically to me* was how he meant it, meaning that the King's voice raised on his behalf could have eased a generation of pain and fear.

'Was I so silent?'

'On Surayon, yes. And were you so very much him?'

'If the King chose not to speak of Surayon,' Fulke hissed, as though even the full use of his voice in this company was too much taint, came too close to a contact he could not bear, 'might it not be because speaking was so unnecessary, because his subjects could see for themselves what was rancid, and smell for themselves what was corrupt?'

'When the Church Fathers could see it and smell it all the way from the homelands, you mean, and so sent you to burn it out?'

'But this is his Kingdom,' Coren said swiftly, his voice just strong enough to stand between them, 'and not yours, nor theirs, nor mine. The King makes his own choices – which is why all of us' – though his glance at Fulke corrected that, *most of us* – 'are here, to ask questions to which he if any man should have the answers. Otherwise we must ask the djinn, and that might prove unfruitful.'

Despite the doubts, despite the bickering, they did not in truth remain long at the gates of the Dir'al Shahan.

Slowly and soundlessly, those high gates drew back. Nothing mystical or potent in it: there were men at either leaf to open them. The men were gowned and hooded in the Sharai manner, which was the Ransomer manner also, although these pale yellow robes were no more Sharai in design than they were Ransomer in colour. Elisande was not the only one who tried to peer beneath the hanging rims of the hoods to see what manner of man it was that wore them; she was perhaps the only one who let her attempts be obvious, as was also her frustration when she failed.

As slow and as silent as the hinges of the great gates, another man came to lead them across the court beyond. He seemed to be a man at least, as the others did. They moved like men, though Julianne for one found herself wondering once more where the King found his servants, and how, and why they came to serve him. They might be slaves, they might be devotees; they might be lords of the Kingdom giving secret service in some undeclared bond of brotherhood. They might equally well be men of clay, animated by magic.

Had it still been a place of faith and worship, the Dir'al Shahan must have been the most striking, the most overwhelming of man's work on the earth. Within its walls it was a complex in itself, and all its complexity was a wonder that spoke more and more loudly to the glory of God. There were stairs and archways, lesser temples and rising platforms, all of a golden stone with veins that glittered under the sun; all leading the eye onward and upward to the grand consummation that it sought, the great domed temple with its spiring minarets, needle-fine and sky-piercing. If there were another such dome in the world, none there had seen or heard speak of it.

And the King sat there, or so rumour said and his Shadow had never denied it: *crouched like a toad beneath a stone* some said, or *poised like a spider at its web's heart, waiting* or simply *still as a rock, purposeless, stretching an overlong life still longer, and to what end?*

To this end, perhaps, the end that they had all pursued this far: to answer the questions of his own generation and another, to bring at least some sense of ending to a terrible adventure. The Princip's country was in ruins, many of his people were dead and the survivors were dreadfully exposed; he trusted the Ransomers' truce precisely as far as he trusted Fulke. And he believed in causes, here in the Kingdom; he believed that whatever happened had its reason and that very likely, that reason was the King's. The 'ifrit had invaded his little land, which was unheard of; they had let the Ransomers in first, and the Sharai had been there to take advantage, and he did not believe that any of this was coincidence. His son also was dead amongst his people, and he had come to ask for explanations. The Princip had all the claims of an old comrade, of a history shared, of hurts taken and gifts received; his granddaughter and her friend had the claims of youth and vulnerability, the rights of the world to come, fresh candles lit from dying flames.

So they broached the King's privity, his sanctity, his dome. His servant seemed almost to invite them, leading the way not to the great closed door but to a long arch, almost a tunnel at one side. In the blackness of its shadow, they found another door; this one stood open, and there were lights beyond.

The servant gestured them through. The King's Shadow was first, and would have entered then but that the Princip delayed him with a word.

'No, wait, Coren. I would see this man's face, before we go further.'

'Does his face matter? He serves the King; what more do you need?'

'I saw—' He was not sure what he had seen, but he thought it might have been the faintest gleam of red in the darkness beneath the hood. At any rate, 'I should like to see his face.'

'Well.' Coren raised no further objection, only seemed genuinely bemused. 'If he is content to show it to you, I am quite content that you should see it. If the King objects, no doubt he will let us know.' He turned to the man and said, 'Of your courtesy, sir? Would you lift back your hood?'

The man said nothing, but his hands did what the Shadow asked.

The girls gasped, and so did Marshal Fulke; it was he who said the name, which meant nothing to the older men.

'*Blaise . . . ?*'

His eyes were dully red, which made the girls gasp, draw back, press closer to each other.

'Blaise,' the man repeated. 'I served you once, when I was Blaise,' spoken slowly, as if the truth of this were buried deep, drowned deep in memory's well and must be grappled for in darkness, 'and called you Magister.'

'You did; nor did I release you from my service,' though Fulke's memory of it at least was fresh and bitter.

'I was released. I served you too,' the man who had been Blaise went on, turning to Julianne, 'and called you my lady.'

'You were my sergeant,' she murmured, willing him to remember it, only hoping that her voice and this little information might give him an easier path back to what had been his life. 'At Roq de Rançon, and on the way there. Do you remember?'

'I remember Roq de Rançon. I served the God there once, till my brothers drove me out. Now I serve the King. Will you go in to him?'

Julianne may not have been the only one there who thought for a moment that his red gaze fell more balefully on Fulke, when he spoke of the Ransomers; for certain she was not the only one who hoped that his current service was happier than those he had known before. That could almost seem to matter more than how his eyes were red, or why, or how it was that the King came to have such a man as servant, and in such a condition.

But then the King's Shadow strode through the brief darkness and into light, and the others followed him; and now for a while they could forget Blaise entirely if they chose to, as they had chosen before.

This place had been holy to the Patrics since their God had blessed it, choosing this of all the places of the earth to set His foot when He walked as a man. It had been holy to the Catari long before that as the seed of all creation, the first place their God had made and the source of all the rest, the last of the rough rock from which the world was moulded. Before them there had been others, other faiths – as witness the pavement where this temple stood, wide monument to a forgotten worship – and each had known something different about the Mount of Ascariel, but each had known it holy.

The Patrics who owned it now, who owned or claimed possession of all the Sanctuary Land, maintained that possession by strength of stone as much as strength of arms; they had built massively up and down the land, castles and walls and fortifications. Their architects understood power and endurance and resistance, none better. It took the Catari before them to build for beauty; and here at least, that beauty had been let live.

Fulke would not have had it so; Fulke saw the heresy in every curving line, in every gilded word he could not read. He had been offered tutors, but he would not learn the tongue: 'We have the language given us by the God; what would I need of another?' In his heart, he had been afraid. There were those who said that to understand all was to believe all; here especially, in this cradle of faith where men could run mad from a simple excess of belief, he feared to find it true. Serving a God Divided – and serving as he had, as inquisitor and judge – he knew the dangers of a divided soul. Better to be ignorant and safe, not to offer his intellect as hostage . . .

Now, in this dim and smoky lamplight after so much sun, he gazed around him, he gazed up and up and was afraid again. He could not understand the messages on the walls, but he could read beauty, he could feel its influence. More subtle perhaps than a sword, but no less powerful in time: and the King had spent years and decades here, had chosen to make his home amid the strictures of a forbidden faith, and the King could surely read them. Like Fulke, he had been a monk before ever he was a warrior; report said that he had been damnably curious even as a novice, always reading, reading, asking questions and reading more. Fulke didn't believe that any man could live among so much beauty and not be swayed, not be tempted into false-hood. This must be why the King lived in seclusion, apart from all his priests and ministers; this must be why he had so tolerated the heresies of Surayon. Fulke had not come to the Kingdom in expectation of smoking out the King himself, but he was ready for it. He'd denounce the man here in his own palace if it proved necessary, and would not fear for himself although he died for it. It was the Sanctuary Land that he feared for, if its King were turned from the true religion.

To Julianne the beauty was a tangible thing, as solid as the tiles of the floor beneath her feet, as fixed as the colours in those tiles, as calculated as the patterns in which the tiles were laid. Men had made this, and her soul rejoiced at their skill. She supposed that they had been devout, inspired; it seemed not to matter any more. There was no worship here now, no habitation for their God or any. Rather it was a man who lived here, and she didn't understand why he would want to, how he could bear to clothe himself in such a wonder or to hold himself alone beneath its majesty.

The Shadow had as many questions as the others, or more perhaps: half a lifetime of questions dammed up behind a stubborn determination not to ask, never to ask.

He at least was not overwhelmed by the place where they found themselves. Nor was the Princip at his side, though it had been many years since he was here. They'd both learned long since not to be oppressed by space, not to be uplifted by any work of man, not to be borne down by any overhanging darkness.

The dome rose above them, or closed down around them, like a sky at a human scale. Its horizon was glazed in that midnight blue that the Sharai claimed for their own colour: a gift of their God, a sign of His favour and their service. The height of it was lost in a night deeper than any that the Sharai might know, the black of shadow far beyond the touch of lamps. This was a place removed from daylight, with its high doors locked and its walls, its dome unpierced. That was another symbol, but one that turned inward here; the King showed himself how near his own grip was, how tight the shell he'd closed about himself.

To the girls, it didn't seem so small or cramped a space. There must have been room here for a thousand men to pray, more, without any of them jostling their neighbours. In the half-dark they could barely see the curve of the further wall.

Or the same wall, rather, where it curved around. Sharai
tents were long and low, black shadows that clung like
leeches to the sand, that made tunnels overground, but
Julianne had known the bright silk pavilions of the Marasson
court at play. Those were round and high, and there was
something here that reminded her of them, although they
were filled with light, so fine that the sun could still dazzle
through their fabric. She'd been in other circular chambers,
temples even; it wasn't that, or not that alone. Perhaps it was
the sense of presence, of coming under the gaze of someone
greater than herself. She'd been in many temples, and never
felt it at all; among the nobles and the Imperial family at
Marasson a girl could not escape it, not even to shelter
behind the greatness of her father. Her private giant, even he
was reduced to mortal stature where he knelt below the
Emperor's gaze.

She felt the same way here; she felt like a little girl who
might have sought the comfort of her father's hand, except
that experience had taught her to recognise those situations
where that hand could give no comfort. Which was a com-
fortless thing to know, and worse to experience. She held
Elisande's hand instead, and wondered if she could interpret
its tremble as rage held barely in check. And thought not but
was willing, eager to be proved wrong, to spare her having to
believe that her friend was as nervous as she was.

There were pillars in a wide slow circle within the wider
circle of the space. There were lamps and braziers everywhere, the air was full of smoke and shifting shadows, a
constant tugging at the corner of the eye; there were men
like Blaise who moved silently over the dense rugs underfoot,
who caught the eye more solidly but were still gone before

they had been properly seen; there was no doubt, there was never any doubt where in all this blurring beauty they must go to find the King.

To the centre, of course: to the point of balance, to the focus of the eye, to the heart of what had been so long hidden.

Here at the hub – where it was not at all hard to believe that this was stillness and all the world else spun around it, where what was hard was not to feel dizzy with that sense of being poised exactly at the point, with a long fall down on every side – there was a raised platform, a dais, what the Catari called a divan. Once, surely, there must have been an altar here; now there was an ancient chest of black wood, bound with iron where it had long since split.

On the chest, a man was sitting.

His face was on no coins, neither drawn nor described in any text. Against history's silence, legend had painted him unnaturally tall, which he was not; unnaturally broad of shoulder, which he was not; unnaturally strong and hand-some, startlingly clear of eye and voice and skin, and he was none of these. Other legends – Catari legends – had him hideous, brutal, deformed by the weights of his own cruelty. They were no more true than the Patric hagiographies. Where the man was not known but his actions were, where the power of his word abided in the absence of his voice, it was hard to be utterly certain that he was not at least a hand's span higher than his confrères and a little too wide to pass through a normal doorway, one part giant and one part wizard, sparks in his eyes and sparks in the tips of his fingers.

There might in fact have been the glimmer of stars

shifting deep within the blackness of his eyes, but no greater sign than that. He sat before them like an old man, quite nondescript, and might have been almost any man of his age; there might have been a dozen such men at market in any town on any day, and it would have been hard to tell their station, peasant or lord, if they all dressed as plainly as he did. Not one of them would have stood out among the crowd. This one could hardly stand out from himself, so modest he seemed. And yet, and yet: the girls and Fulke knew him as immediately, as coldly, as certainly as the one man who had known him long ago, the other who had known him then and since. Granted that no other man could have been sitting just here at the centre, the point, the purpose of the world – even so, this one man wore his kingship like a crown, despite the dull simplicity of his dress. If they had met him in that marketplace among a hundred, a thousand other men, they would still have recognised him on the instant; they would still have felt that sudden urge to kneel, to lower their eyes and wait for his word of greeting or dismissal.

They felt the urge, but none of them yielded to it. Even the Shadow, who knelt to the Emperor of Marasson without an apparent thought: even he stood stern and upright before his own master. His daughter was mildly surprised at it, but they had been friends first; perhaps they were friends still. Or perhaps he was more angry than he let show.

Elisande was less angry than she had claimed to be, more nervous than she would ever admit. A lifetime victim of the legend, now that she was finally where she had never expected to find herself, face to face with the King, she found herself entirely robbed of speech. She had intended to be brusque, demanding, uncharitable; instead she was silent like a child, gawping like an idiot, cruelly aware of her own mouth moving and of no sound coming out.

It was the Princip who spoke at last, and his voice was more tentative than a robust man's ought to be, as though he were feeling his way through the dark towards a long-forgotten doorway.

'Well. It is you, then.'

'Indeed. It has always been me.'

'Mmm. I did wonder, sometimes.'

'Did I give you cause?'

'No, but I wondered anyway. This seems – unlikely,' with a gesture round about, 'this eggshell. You always loved the world too much to be a monk for long.'

'And still do. I am not a prisoner here. Nor a monk,' smiling at him gently, 'whatever my reputation.' Julianne remembered her father saying that it had been the Princip in a former incarnation who had rousted the young man out of his monastery and away from his books, to teach him life and war. It had perhaps not taken too much rousting, to judge by that smile. 'I do go out into the Kingdom, in other guise than this.'

'Do you? Aye, then, so do I. Or did, while I had a son to guard my borders for me.' It was a bleak truth, bleakly said; its reminder of a life lost drew him back from memories of a life long gone, and set him plainly on his path again. 'You know why we're here. How many of my questions are you going to answer?'

'As many as you care to ask. Or dare to. Remember that questions have consequences, and nothing is more danger-ous than knowledge.'

'I have never forgotten. Even so, I have questions. I risked the journey here to ask them of you; I will risk the answers.' He was torn, manifestly torn; friendships are built on familiar deceits, and he feared to break a long, long-lost friendship on the rocks of truth. He had been lord of his land, though, more recently and for longer than he had been a friend of the King. Besides, his son was dead and his land in peril; either of those must weigh heavier in the balance than a love that had gathered dust for a generation, and the two together were insuperable.

Still he was torn, he did hesitate, he did take a long slow breath before he broke the habits of a wary lifetime to demand answers from his friend; and so he was forestalled by someone much younger and much less careful, someone whose heart and mind could match each other in their anger and distress.

'There can be no risk attached to truth. Truth is the best weapon that we have against heresy, and I am not afraid to seek it; the God will watch over me even here in the hall of His enemies.'

'I am no enemy to your God, or any.'

'You say that, and yet you live, you *live* in this place where the air is still poisoned with Catari incense, where every wall is covered with their foul verses, where every breath and glance corrupt. You say that, and yet you welcome *him*' – a gesture towards the Princip as he would give neither name nor title to one so rank, although they had fought the same enemy a week ago and travelled together ever since – 'as a friend and a subject although his every thought is blasphemous, although he led his people in rebellion against you and against the God . . .'

'Not so,' the Princip said, quite mildly. 'I never rebelled against the Kingdom. The other states rose up against me, with fire and sword – as you have done since, Marshal Fulke, slaughtering the innocent in the name of your sweet God. I closed my borders to protect me and mine, as any prince would do under such an assault. I was a loyal subject to the King then, and I am still.'

'You closed your borders with damned magic!'

'If you choose to call it that. I say with knowledge. And we have gone on learning since; and it is as well for you, for the Kingdom, for all of us that we did so, or the 'ifrit would rule in Surayon by now.'

'Can we be so sure that they do not? I hear that they can inhabit men and possess their will. If they failed in their invasion by force, why should they not invade by subtlety? That land is fit for it, where no one serves the true God truly. I saw them in Roq de Rançon, and thought they were demons there; I see no reason to change that opinion, and where better should demons find a home than in the Folded Land?'

'Folded no longer, alas; prey now to every fanatic who sees evil in doubt and wickedness in curiosity. But how did you see them at the Roq? I had not heard that they were active there, except for that one that Julianne drew through into the hermit's cave . . .'

Of course he had not heard, who would not speak to Ransomers on all the long ride here. Fulke said briefly, 'I saw them issue forth from the sealed tower. They did not stay; how could they, in a stronghold of prayer and purity? They went to seek a more suitable home and found it in Surayon, until we destroyed them.'

'From the Tower of the King's Daughter?' The Princip's eyes turned to the man who had named it so. 'When Rudel tried to lead his party out that way, he found it closed against him.'

'Indeed,' the King said. 'Closed by the 'ifrit, who must have known that he was coming and preferred to keep the Daughter in this world, and out of Surayon. They wanted it for their own man, for the Sand Dancer Morakh.'

'He was not theirs at the time, surely?'

'What does time mean, to an 'ifrit or any spirit?' the Shadow asked. 'Dangerous or otherwise, some answers are simply too elusive to be gripped; that one I have been chasing for forty years, and not come near. If they knew they would want the Daughter, they would act to keep it close and bring it closer.'

'How could they close the Tower, though?' Elisande demanded, finding her voice at last. 'I was there, we both were, Julianne and I. It was hard even to get in, harder than it should have been; and then when my— when, when Rudel tried to take us through to the land of the djinn, there was a wall there that blocked us utterly . . .'

'The two worlds do not easily or willingly share their substance,' the King said. 'The stuff of one has power in the other; it becomes dangerous out of its proper place. Lisan, you know how the djinni Esren Filash Tachur was trapped by a rock from the land of the djinn, and so held slave in the Dead Waters.'

She could do no more than nod.

'Similarly, a pebble taken from the other world and set in the tongue of a ghûl will enslave it to the will of the 'ifrit. Do that to a man, or something like it, and you will close his mouth to the world; do it to a gateway, and you close its access to the other world. Jemel did that unwittingly at the Pillar of Lives, when he brought a stone through and set it there. Which is why the 'ifrit had to go so much further, to use the gate at Roq de Rançon. They must have closed that earlier by taking a stone through from this world and setting it in the tower on the other side – or by having a ghûl do it, more likely. They would be afraid of the thing themselves, unwilling to touch it.'

Esren had refused to go near Jemel until he had crushed such a stone to powder, that he'd cut from the tongue of a ghûl. To be sure, Esren had particular reasons to fear such stones, but even so . . . The two girls exchanged glances, which said *how does he know so much?* in each direction and *because he is the King* in reply.

It was a good trick, but had barely scratched the surface of their uncertainties so far. All the little questions, they could ask them all and still be deep down in murky waters, understanding nothing. They needed some more solid rock to stand on, to lift them up above the flood; they needed to know why, what lay behind or underneath. And the Princip had fallen conspicuously silent, and was signing discreetly to them to do the same; which left Fulke free to speak unchallenged, which was either capitulation or unkindness, no telling which.

'You talk of other worlds than this,' Fulke said, 'yet I know only of Paradise and hell beyond, as the word of the God has taught us. You talk of the djinn and the 'ifrit and other creatures, where I see only demons without souls. You are the man who led the armies here, to win these lands for the God; your faith was rewarded, and the Church has supported you ever since. And yet you speak with His enemies in their own manner, and against His teachings . . .'

'The Princip of Surayon also fought, to free the Sanctuary Land from the possession of the Ekhed princes and their Catari God,' the King said mildly, gazing at Fulke with a curious interest. 'That's why I gave him the land and the title, as a reward for courage and diligence in his service.'

The Princip snorted. 'You gave me Surayon to stand as a buffer between Ascariel and Less Arvon, to keep those hothead fools from making war with each other while the Sharai raged around the borders and every Catari vassal was sharpening his mattock against the prospect of another change of overlord.'

'Well,' with a smile, 'that too. And it worked, did it not?'

'Only because you fed me to them as a bone they could both gnaw at.'

'That would always have been true, whatever I said. The Dukes of Less Arvon, the Great Duke and the Little Duke his son have both of them proved too greedy to look at a rood of land beyond their borders without wanting the profit from it; my own son the Duke here in Ascariel is too holy to believe that the God could possibly want anyone other than himself to govern. You'd have thought he'd want to be here today, would you not? But I didn't need to forbid him from coming. He's occupied already, on his knees in his new cathedral, giving thanks for a deliverance he does not understand.'

'He is on his knees and praying, giving thanks – and you are mocking him.' Fulke's voice grated at them furiously. 'You might have been wiser to have joined him. This man led an army here on a holy quest, but has been long lost to righteousness – but what of you? I hoped not to challenge my King when I came in here, I hoped only to protect him; but I will challenge you now, you give me no choice. Tell me this, straight and true – do you still serve the God I worship?'

'Serve? No. I do not serve. But then, I never did. And for that question, for this answer, I will claim a payment that is already overdue. The war is done; the Ransomers will have no further need for a Marshal Commander.'

'I do not understand you—'

Just then, just at that moment, none of them understood him, nor any part of what he had just said. The others had better hopes of it than Fulke, who was ill-made for this country and ill-trained to see what lay outside his narrow range, his strict and careful understanding of the world. The old men might have hoped to find clues from their youth together or their long experience since; the girls might have looked to sharper eyes, less trusting minds to break some hint of news before it happened.

They might all have been disappointed in themselves, but that must of necessity come later. For now, the King's voice went on speaking but none of them was listening to it; their minds were still stumbling over the sense of what he had said already, while their eyes were entirely caught up with trying to make some sense of what he was doing now, while he spoke, while his mouth did not move although his face was breaking apart.

'. . . You question whether there is truly another world than this, yet you have walked within it. When you open the King's Eye you see as I see, Magister,' and the voice was rising higher all the time and losing inflection as it rose, and yet there was still a scalding weight behind that title, 'you see two worlds contiguous, the land of men and the land of the djinn; when you walk within the open Eye, you pass from world to world and still you doubt me, because this is not what is reported within your little lore. Luckily I do not require imagination of my servants. You need not try to run to your men outside, my own man there will prevent you; nor will your Ransomers hear you if you scream . . .'

And yet Fulke did try to run, of course he did, because it was predicted that he would; and he had barely made the turn towards the door before his shoulder was seized and held. He struggled to pull free, but Blaise's arm that gripped him might as well have been cast of iron or carved from rock. This again was as it had been foretold; as if strengthened tenfold by that certainty, those fingers were as impassive to Fulke's struggles as Blaise's face was to his words.

'Blaise, man, you were my man before ever you belonged to that – that creature, remember the oaths you swore to me, to the God . . .'

By all appearances, Blaise had entirely forgotten them. But Blaise, Fulke could hold the others' eyes only for a moment, or for a series of moments, glances snatched against desire when their gaze was drawn against their will, when Fulke did scream and scream again to them and to his absent men and to his God who was not worshipped here. Through all of that, it was still the King who held their attention, because his flesh was disintegrating as they watched.

It was a slow process, or it seemed slow compared to all the deaths and the fires and the brutalities they had witnessed in Surayon, where injustice came at the speed of a blow, the leap of a flame; and yet it was too fast by years, by generations. Mortal bodies were not made to lose coherence suddenly or from within, except in the patient darkness of a crypt. What they watched here was like all the little secret changes happening between eyeblinks, the hand of time scrabbling in a frenzy. The King did not rot so much as crumble, like a corpse that had desiccated in the Sands and turned to sand itself, falling into dust as it lost any memory of itself.

It began in the eyes, where he had kept the only visible sign of his power or his strangeness, a glitter in the darkness, a hint of lights far off and busy. Now they shone and dazzled, and not only within the confines of his gaze; they shone through his skin, they danced in the spaces where his bones ought to be.

Light and shadow: it seemed that his flesh was shaped over something quite other than a skeleton. *I do not serve* he had said, and why should he, when his own body told the whole story of the God that Fulke would have him worship, when he was himself both battleground and battle?

The King had lost his bones to lights; he lost his skin, his flesh to dust. It fell away in trickles and runs, forgetful of its former shape. It seemed golden in the lamplight, and shimmered as it was swept up by the currents of light as they swirled and spun. There was no skull where his face was lost, only the patterns that dust could make in a silent, vicious wind that wound around itself, tightly and more tightly so. It ripped the King's simple garment into shreds and tatters as the fabric fell in upon itself and was snared in the rushing of that wind; it showed its own weave only in the way it drew the dust like a line, like a thread bound round and round a spinning bobbin.

It might have been Elisande who knew first what it was, if she'd been alert to an early hint; it was Julianne's father who named it.

'Djinni,' he said, which was obvious to all of them by then, except perhaps to Fulke.

It gave him no response, beyond its rising like a pillar before them. It stretched itself until it had achieved almost the height and slender grace of the pillars round about, though it still hung poised above the old chest the King had sat on and it did not try to reach into the darkness of the dome.

'Djinni Khaldor,' the Shadow said. If he were Shadow still, if he had a King to serve and chose to serve him. He named the djinni as though he recognised it; the girls recognised the name, of course, and Elisande grunted, *of course*, as though she too should have known the immediate differences between this djinni and her own, or any. 'I think you lied to me, djinni. You said "It has always been me", and that is not true. The King was once the Duc de Charelles, and the Duc was once a young man whom I knew. I will swear that he was a man of normal flesh, whatever they say of him in the wider world; and he was still so, I think, still a man until he came to be King and closed himself into this place.'

The djinni said nothing. The man who had been Shadow while the King still had a shadow to cast took a slow, angry breath and faced his betrayal squarely; said, 'I have done you service enough in the last forty years that I think you owe me some questions answered.'

'You think I lie to you, and yet you will stand and demand answers. Your thinking is as loose as your understanding; you should grip more tightly. *I* think that you have asked me questions enough for one man's lifetime, and that in only half a life.'

'I did not know then that you were a djinni.'

'You always knew that I was a djinni. What you did not know is that I was also the King. But ask your questions; I have said already that I will answer them. Only the answers may be dangerous to you, because knowledge is always chancy. I will not claim a price, except from Fulke who is paying it already.'

No one there said *let Fulke go*, or even thought it; at least one was guiltily delighted to see him held by a djinni's servant, claimed by the djinni itself.

Coren — who thought he would answer after this to no title other than his name — said, 'Where is the King my master?'

'I am the King your master.'

'Where is the man who was Duc de Charelles before he was King of Outremer?'

'I do not know.'

'It's lying,' Elisande said fiercely. 'Of course it knows, they always know. But Esren lied to me too, and they weren't supposed to do that. I thought the djinn were honest,' suddenly accusing, facing the creature where it rose, where it hovered, where it spun.

'I know you did. Why did you?'

Another day she might not have answered, she might have been wise or cunning. But another day she would not have been here in the dim light and the heavy air, watching the way it leaned against the stillness, feeling the way it leaned against the truth.

'Because I have always been told so, because it seemed to be true, because it seemed right that something made of spirit could not lie.' Men walked on the edge of darkness always, groping for a path; their only light fell behind them to show where they had been, and they called it memory or history. Or God, Julianne said; lies, said Elisande. The djinn moved in a mist, perhaps, but they stood in a pool of light that fell all ways around them. It would be unfair, it would be wrong to see so much more and not describe it truly.

'Who was it told you?'

'My father,' and she said it firmly, determinedly, almost proudly.

'And who told him and his father, who was it told the world?'

That one she had to pause, to glance at her grandfather where he stood mute and impassioned, to think about; in the end there was only one answer possible. 'The djinn,' she said, chagrined for her entire race, for their innocence and gullibility.

'The djinn indeed. Myself, indeed, I said it. Long ago now; and often since, when men gave me the opportunity.'

'What, and were you lying all the time?'

'Perhaps I was,' it said, as though that were something it too had to think about.

'Why, though? Why would you do that, great one, do you like to laugh at us little people as you lie?'

'I have laughed at humans, in my time. But perhaps I did it for some other reason; perhaps everything that I have ever

done was done to bring us here, to this place and this conversation.'

She would have asked *why?* again, but Coren broke in to
lead the djinn back to what it had said before, what Elisande
had challenged.

'And are you telling the truth now, then? I will risk that,
and ask again. Do you truly not know where the King my
friend is to be found?'

'Truly, I do not. I have watched many a human die, and
I still do not know where their spirits go when it happens.'

'Is he dead? Since when?'

'Since he died.'

'How long since?'

'Almost forty years.'

'Did you kill him?'

'Not by my touch. I came to him, and he died; that was
understood. I had foreseen it. So perhaps had he.'

Perhaps so; how could they tell, if the djinn could lie?

'What have you done with his body?'

For answer, it drifted a little away, to the further side of
the rug-strewn dais. Briefly their eyes followed it, as though
it were going to show them; then Elisande made a noise in
her throat – contempt or self-contempt, even she was uncertain – and ran forward, jumped up, pulled open the lid of
the old chest.

It would have been easily big enough to hold the new-
slain body of a man, and a bigger man than the King had
ever been. In fact what lay in there, half-curled like a child,
was something smaller than Elisande herself, the figure of a
wizened thing. She stooped and lifted it out into the light
before either of the older men could reach her.

'It's not . . .'

She genuinely thought it was not a man at all, as she lifted it. Too light, too dry, too browned and tough ever to have been human: at first she thought it was another lie, a tease, a dead man sculpted, made, a mockery. Her own father had put a poppet in a cell, and made it human-seeming; that had moved, at least, which this did not.

When she saw the skull's shape beneath the leather skin, when she saw how the thin black lips were drawn back from real teeth, she still did not think it was human, or the King. A giant monkey, dried and salted? It was still too small, too twisted surely to be a man . . .

But there was white hair clinging to the scalp of it, and no fur else. And the skull had a human shape, like no monkey that she had ever seen or heard about; and yes, it was a man, of course it was, deny it as she liked she could not change it.

Instead she knelt and laid him on the carpets; looked up at her grandfather, at the father of her friend, and said, 'Is this him?'

'Oh, yes,' the Princip said, 'it isn't lying now.'

'It might be, about how he died . . .'

'No.' Julianne had seen a man touched by the djinni, she knew what kind of death that was; and there was no visible mark on this body, only the terrible absence of its owner. Terrible and long-term: very soon after he closed the gates of the Dir'al Shahan. Outremer had been ruled by a djinni for a generation. And the djinn were supposed not to meddle in the affairs of men – but then the djinn were supposed not to lie, not to be able to, and that had proved to be as false as any lie else.

Even so, it had been the experience of men for hundreds

of years, that the djinn were not concerned with what they did or how they lived in the world. The first sign otherwise that she could think of was her own first meeting with a djinni, with this djinni. She gazed at it where it roiled in the dust of its own deception, and asked the first question of her own. 'Why are you so different? You're not like Esren, even, let alone like the djinn in the histories I've read, or the stories Jemel tells. What makes you play these games?' *Why kill a king, and spend forty years in imitation of him?*

'I am . . . incomplete,' it said, with just the faintest hesitation before the word; she reminded herself again that it was a liar and an actor, supremely skilled at both. It likely had no feeling and no doubt, only intentions; she would not be swayed.

'In what way, incomplete?'

'I have given myself away,' it said. 'Small pieces of myself, to strengthen these my servants in their tasks,' and its servants were still going about their tasks in the shadows of the great chamber, no whit disturbed. Marron might have done that too, she thought, with his red eyes and his unnatural powers, with the Daughter slowly sealing him off from the world; she was ahead of the djinni already when it said, 'And rather more of me, of my substance went long ago. It is almost its own creature now, though not a djinni, far from that. There are those of my kind who will say that I am no longer truly of the djinn; its absence diminishes me, so that I can do these things and find some amusement in them.'

And now, at last, 'Why would you want to?' from Elisande, where she knelt still above the body of the King. 'You must have known that this would happen, that you would be – reduced,' in what was almost cruel imitation, except that she could see no way to be truly cruel to something that had no true humanity, only a decaying of its proper self.

'It was necessary. The 'ifrit meant to take this world from us.'

'I thought this world was ours.'

'Lisan. We are the djinn. Do your pastures belong to the cattle, does the soil belong to the worm? You may do as you will, but we are still the djinn. The 'ifrit, though – the 'ifrit wanted this world for themselves, and they thought they could take it. We are stronger, but they are many; they thought we would not fight them. Why should we risk death, for this crude clay?'

'They thought you would not fight them,' the Princip repeated. 'They were right, weren't they?'

'Of course.'

'You used us instead, you used men to fight your spirit-battles for you.'

'We cannot meet them in our own form; and if we take solid bodies in this world as they do, we become as vulnerable as they are. Even a man can kill us, with a blessed blade. So the King lives in seclusion, and we take what precautions we can.'

'Esren isn't cautious,' Elisande said, thinking of Rhabat and the flooding of the valley, an invasion of 'ifrit blocked by one djinni and a small inland ocean.

'That djinni is unique.' *Uniquely damaged* was what it seemed to mean. 'As am I. We are both unlike our kin.'

'That unlikeness didn't stop you using my land, my people for your war.' The Princip again, in a rising anger.

'Of course not. Men are always eager to fight. The Sharai

and the Patrics would have fought each other anyway; they would both have fought in Surayon. I brought you together to let you fight for us.'

'And?'

'And what?'

'I thought you were going to go on to say that now we were all peaceful together, thanks to you.'

'That would be absurd. The Sharai and the Patrics will fight again; they will both fight the Surayonnaise.'

'But not yet,' Coren interrupted, over the Princip's grunt, 'not for a while yet. I will be sure of that much. And don't tell us who will win those fights, djinni; foreknowledge is not a human gift, because it is not a gift to humans.'

'But the 'ifrit have foreknowledge too,' Julianne objected. 'They must have known that you were leading all our armies into Surayon to face them . . .'

'Of course; but death clouds the image. They knew there would be a battle, and so did we; they hoped to win it, and so did we. They did what they could to keep your armies apart and fighting each other. If the most powerful forces in the Sanctuary Land destroyed themselves, then the 'ifrit could rule unchallenged; we would have nothing to set against them for a generation. Men fight like dogs, they hardly needed to encourage you. And then they are an army in themselves, faith is the only weapon that men have against them; and they hoped to have the Ghost Walker among their ranks, to lead the Sand Dancers and so the Sharai in a holy war. That would have been a triumph. The King's Daughter is a part of me, and they could have used it against me and mine.'

'Would the Sharai have followed Morakh? The tribes hate the Sand Dancers . . .'

'If he was the Ghost Walker,' Elisande said, 'and if he showed them they could drive the Patrics out of Outremer? Even at the cost of letting in the 'ifrit, they'd have followed him. They hate the Patrics worse than anything.'

'We were lucky, then.'

'For a while. Lucky often, I think. So many times it could have gone wrong; from that first day where you met us in the road,' and Elisande addressed the djinni again, 'and started moving us around . . .'

'It started before that,' Julianne corrected, 'when it called my father away so that I'd be alone on the road, so that I could meet you and then it could persuade us both, without a man there to interfere. Except for Blaise, I mean . . .' Her voice faltered as she remembered, as she glanced aside to see where he stood quite impassive, with the figure of Fulke silent beside him. Pain or terror had broken that one utterly, she thought, unless it was simply helplessness, that terrible weight of certainty, too much for any man to stand against . . .

'I had started long before that,' the djinni said. 'I knew what I would need, and when need it; I have been preparing this for forty years.'

'Julianne, I met your mother on a mission for the King,' her father told her suddenly, 'and it was I who brought your parents together, Elisande, and proposed the match to your grandfather here, under the suggestion of the King.'

Foreknowledge is not a gift to humans; sometimes, neither is its inverse. The girls looked at each other, and it was a shared decision that had them suddenly turning away, walking away, crossing that wide pillared space without a glance back. None of the men there sought to detain them.

The djinni presumably had known that they would go, had been entirely ready for it.

'Everything we are,' Julianne murmured as they came out into sunshine at last, in the courtyard of the Dir'al Shahan, 'everything we do. It knows *everything*. Did it make us, or did it just predict us? I can't work it out.'

'I don't think there's a distinction. What are you going to do, Julianne?'

'I don't know. I wish I could spite it somehow, but it's too late for that, the war's over.'

'And we won,' Elisande said glumly. 'But there'll be other wars, it said so. Only we'll just be fighting for ourselves next time, and I don't know if that's better or worse.'

'Worse. Definitely. I think . . . And how could we know, anyway? Maybe it's still using us, against the next time the 'ifrit want to fight. Whatever it tells us, whatever it *chooses* to tell us, it knows exactly how we're going to react anyway, so we might as well ignore it and do what we think is right for us, for Outremer, for Surayon . . .'

'Or for the Sharai? You're still married to Hasan, my love.'

'I know. And I love him, I want what's best for him and all of us.'

'And Imber?'

'Him too. I love them both.'

'Tricky. You can't stay married to them both.'

'Can't I?'

'Oh, *what?* Julianne . . .'

'Why not? My father'll love it. What better way to keep peace as long as possible between them, than to have one girl married to the lords of both armies?'

'The men won't accept it.'

'I think they will, they'll have to. It's my ultimatum: if either one wants me, they have to be prepared to share me. Neither one recognises the other marriage anyway, so that's not a problem. I can be true wife to each, just that I spend a lot of time away and travelling without them.'

'But you can't, you can't have children, not to either one of them . . .'

'No.' Traditionally children sealed an alliance, but here it was impossible. And both girls meant more than that in any case, they meant that she couldn't share either man's bed, not even once, or the whole delicate structure she was trying to build here would come crashing down. She had lied, when she said she could be a true wife; she could be a virgin wife, but nothing more. To sleep with one would be to cuckold the other, by their own laws or any. That would be political disaster, and personal catastrophe.

'Oh, Julianne . . .'

'It's all right, sweet. I can find my comforts, be a power in the shadows on both sides, it's what my father trained me for all my life.' And Hasan had his other wives, and Imber – well, Imber would suffer and endure, and be noble and honest and not take a lover because she was the one that he loved and the one that he'd married. Mostly, he would suffer; and she'd suffer to see it, and there would be nothing that either of them could do except to remind themselves that it was a small price to pay for peace, for as long as the peace should last. 'What about you, though, what will you do?'

'What, without Rudel to kick against, without my country to defend?'

'Surayon will still need defending, I think.'

'Yes, but not the same way. It'll be all negotiation and treaties now in the open, secret dealings and distrust in the shadows. We need politicians, and that's not me. And Grandfer needs to find an heir, and that's not me either; I don't want to be Principessa and urgently looking for a husband. You've got the best of them in any case. I was going to say I'd have your cast-off, but if you're not going to be casting one off, then I think I'll just come with you anyway. If you'd like to have me.'

'Elisande, I'd love it. You know that. But I won't let you waste your life on me . . .'

'Why not? Waste is my speciality.' Her voice was bleak beyond bearing, savage with self-contempt; her desperate anger needed a focus, and had found it in herself.

'I think surprising your friends is your speciality. But what will you do?'

'Look after you, sweetheart. See that your men make you happy, as best they can. Oh, it may not be for ever – though if you're planning to die a shrivelled virgin, I don't see why I shouldn't be sisterly about it. For the moment, I just can't think of anything better,' and even she wasn't sure which way she meant that. 'And when we get bored, I've always got Esren to liven us up.'

'Have you?'

'For my lifetime, it promised.'

'Elisande, I think it was lying, wasn't it?'

'Oh yes, I'm sure it was lying. It'll do what it wants to do. But as Djinni Khaldor said in there, Esren is unique. I think it gets bored too; I think it'll still come when I call it. Sometimes.'

'Just to see how it can annoy us, most likely.'

But the way she phrased that sentence was a resounding yes, a welcome and a thank you all at once. Elisande grinned and said, 'Come on, let's go and tell your husbands, see how they take the news.'

All the news, and there was a lot to tell them and a lot for them to take in; but all of it had to wait, nothing could be told or talked about for a little while yet.

There was – of course – a man waiting at the high gate, to let them out of this deceptive palace and into the gaze of all those men waiting and watching. As they emerged, Julianne was struck by a sudden thought. 'How do we tell the Ransomers that their Marshal Commander isn't coming out, that Fulke's just one of the King's servants now? They'll think we tricked him inside and killed him . . .'

'Show them the body. Let him come out and wave.'

'Will his eyes be red, do you think,' *like Marron's,* 'like Blaise's?'

'Sure to be.'

'Then they'll say he's been possessed by a demon.'

'Which is true, or true enough. So all right, let's not tell them anything. We went in all together, and we girls have come out alone; they'll think that's as it should be, except that they won't know why we were allowed to accompany the men in the first place. Leave your father to find a way to deal with the Ransomers. You've got two husbands to deal with, that's enough for any woman. I've got a djinni, and no sense of responsibility.'

There was something else that had to be dealt with first, though, something that touched them both deeply and irredeemably.

The sun glared cruelly off the white stone of the pavement, reducing men to mirage, shimmering shadows. The day's heat lay heavy in the air, dulling sounds and senses.

They saw a figure push through the gathered Sharai, and come running out into the open space between them and other groups. Distantly, they heard him cry a challenge, with a contemptuous insult for support when it brought no instant response.

They saw a man reply at last, striding from the Ransomers, sliding a black cloak from his shoulders as he went, stepping forward in vivid white.

They could not hear what passed between the two, but that was quickly done with; then it was a case of blades, a scimitar for the Sharai and a long sword for the Ransomer.

And both girls could name both men, and one at least of the swords. They scurried forward uncertainly, not knowing how to interfere, knowing only that they must; and were too late already, because another figure came chasing after the first, and he too had a sword in his hand and the girls were old friends with that one.

He used it even as he ran, he used it on himself; and then he flung his body between the two duellists and was impossibly lucky not to find himself twice skewered as he deserved – but he always had been lucky, just as he always had been desolate.

No talking this time, no mediation; all in the same movement, he seized one of the startled fighters and dragged him through a sudden raw wound in the world, a ripped red gateway to a golden land.

And the gateway closed at their backs and and there was nothing there except his blade, which he had dropped as he went through, deliberately or otherwise.

And the one left behind stood quite still for a long, long minute, as the girls did, as did the watching world; and then he stooped slowly to pick up the fallen sword, which was called Dard.